TOM SHARPE

TOM SHARPE

INDECENT EXPOSURE
THE GREAT PURSUIT
PORTERHOUSE BLUE
BLOTT ON THE LANDSCAPE

Secker & Warburg

Indecent Exposure first published in Great Britain in 1973
by Martin Secker & Warburg Limited
The Great Pursuit first published in Great Britain in 1976
by Martin Secker & Warburg Limited
Porterhouse Blue first published in Great Britain in 1974
by Martin Secker & Warburg Limited
Blott on the Landscape first published in Great Britain in 1975
by Martin Secker & Warburg.

This volume first published in Great Britain in 1986 by

The Octopus Group Limited
Michelin House
81 Fulham Road
London SW3 6RB

ISBN 0 436 45816 0

This edition distributed in 1989 in association with
Martin Secker & Warburg Ltd

Printed and bound in Great Britain by
BPCC Hazell Books Ltd
Member of BPCC Ltd
Aylesbury, Bucks, England

CONTENTS

INDECENT
EXPOSURE

CHAPTER ONE

It was Heroes Day in Piemburg and as usual the little capital of Zululand was quite unwarrantably gay. Along the streets the jacarandas bloomed unconscionably beside gardens flamboyant with azaleas while from a hundred flagpoles Britons and Boers proclaimed their mutual enmity by flying the Union Jack or the Vierkleur, those emblems of the Boer War which neither side could ever forget. In separate ceremonies across the city the two white communities commemorated ancient victories. At the Anglican Cathedral the Bishop of Piemburg reminded his unusually large congregation that their ancestors had preserved freedom from such assorted enemies as Napoleon, President Kruger, the Kaiser and Adolf Hitler. At the Verwoerd Street Dutch Reformed Church the Reverend Schlachbals urged his flock never to forget that the British had invented concentration camps and that twenty-five thousand Boer women and children had been murdered in them. In short Heroes Day provided everyone with an opportunity to forget the present and revive old hatreds. Only the Zulus were forbidden to commemorate the occasion, partly on the grounds that they had no reputable heroes to honour but for the most part because it was felt that their participation would only lead to an increase in racial tension.

To Kommandant van Heerden, Piemburg's chief of police, the whole affair was most regrettable. As one of the few Afrikaners in Piemburg to be even slightly related to a hero (his grandfather had been shot by the British after the Battle of Paardeberg for ignoring the order to cease fire) he was expected to speak on the subject of heroism at the Nationalist rally at the Voortrekker Stadium and, besides, as one of the town's leading officials, he was obliged to attend the ceremony at Settlers Park where the Sons of England were inaugurating yet another wooden bench in honour of those who had fallen in the Zulu wars some hundred years before.

In the past the Kommandant had been able to avoid all these engagements by pleading the impossibility of being in two places at the same time but since the police had recently been allocated a helicopter, this year he was denied that excuse. At intervals throughout the day the helicopter could be seen chattering across the city while the Kommandant, who disliked heights almost as much as he did public speaking, sorted through his notes in an effort to find something to say whenever he landed. Since his notes were ones he had used annually since the Congo

Crisis years before, their illegibility and general lack of relevance caused some confusion. At the Voortrekker Stadium Kommandant van Heerden's speech on heroism included the assurance that the citizens of Piemburg need have no doubt that the South African Police would leave no stone unturned to see that nothing disturbed the even tenor of their lives, while at Settlers Park his eloquence on behalf of the nuns who had been raped in the Congo, coming as it did after a passionate plea for racial harmony by a Methodist missionary, was considered not to be in the best of taste.

Finally, to round the day's business off, there was a parade of his men at the Mounted Police Barracks at which the Mayor had agreed to award a trophy for conspicuous bravery and devotion to duty.

'Interesting what you had to say about those nuns,' said the Mayor as the helicopter lifted off the ground at Settlers Park, 'I'd almost forgotten about them. Must be twelve years ago that happened.'

'I think it's just as well to remind ourselves that it could happen here,' said the Kommandant.

'I suppose so. Funny thing the ways kaffirs always seem to go for nuns. You'd think they'd like something a bit more jolly.'

'It's probably because they're virgins,' said the Kommandant.

'How very clever of you to think of that,' said the Mayor, 'my wife will be relieved to hear it.'

Below them the roofs glowed in the afternoon sun. Built in the heyday of the British Empire, the tiny metropolis still possessed an air of seedy grandeur. The City Hall, redbrick Gothic, loomed above the market square while, opposite, the Supreme Court maintained a classic formal air. Behind the railway station, Fort Rapier, once the headquarters of the British Army and now a mental hospital, stood outwardly unaltered. Patients shuffled across the great parade ground where once ten thousand men had marched and wheeled before departing for the front. The Governor's Palace had been turned into a teacher training college and students sunbathed on lawns which had once been the scene of garden parties and receptions. To Kommandant van Heerden it was all very puzzling and sad and he was just wondering why the British had abandoned their Empire so easily when the helicopter steadied itself over the Police Barracks and began to descend.

'A very fine turn-out,' said the Mayor indicating the ranks of police konstabels on the parade ground below.

'I suppose,' said the Kommandant, recalled from past splendours to the drab present. He looked down at the five hundred men drawn up in front of a saluting base. There was certainly nothing splendid about them, nor about the six Saracen armoured cars parked in a line behind them. As the helicopter bumped to the ground and its blades finally stopped turning, he helped the Mayor down and escorted him to the platform. The police band broke into a rousing march while sixty-nine guard dogs snarled and slobbered in several iron cages vacated for the occasion by the black prisoners who were normally confined in them while awaiting trial.

'After you,' said the Kommandant at the foot of the steps that led to the platform. At the top a tall thin luitenant was standing, holding the leash of a particularly large Dobermann Pinscher, whose teeth, the Mayor noted with alarm, were bared in what appeared to be an immutable snarl.

'No, after you,' said the Mayor.

'I insist. After you,' said the Kommandant.

'Listen,' said the Mayor, 'if you think I'm going to dispute these steps with that Dobermann ...'

Kommandant van Heerden smiled.

'Nothing to worry about,' he said. 'It's stuffed. That's the trophy.' He lurched on to the platform and pushed the Dobermann aside with his knee. The Mayor followed him up and was introduced to the thin luitenant.

'Luitenant Verkramp, head of the Security Branch,' said the Kommandant.

Luitenant Verkramp smiled bleakly and the Mayor sat down in the knowledge that he had just met a representative of boss, the Bureau of State Security whose reputation for torturing suspects was second to none.

'I'll just make a short speech,' said the Kommandant, 'and then you can award the trophy.' The Mayor nodded and the Kommandant went to the microphone.

'Mr Mayor, ladies and gentlemen, officers of the South African Police,' he shouted, 'we are gathered here today to pay tribute to the heroes of South African history and in particular to honour the memory of the late Konstabel Els whose recent tragic death has deprived Piemburg of one of its most outstanding policemen.'

The Kommandant's voice amplified by the loudspeaker system boomed across the parade ground and lost in the process all trace of the hesitancy he felt in mentioning the name Els. It had been Luitenant Verkramp's idea to award the stuffed Dobermann as a trophy and, glad to see the thing moved from his office, the Kommandant had agreed. Now faced with the prospect of eulogizing the dead Els, he wasn't so sure it had been a wise decision. In life Els had shot more blacks dead in the course of duty than any other policeman in South Africa and had been a constant offender against the Immorality Laws. The Kommandant looked down at his notes and ploughed on.

'A loyal comrade, a fine citizen, a devout Christian ...' To the Mayor, looking down at the faces of the konstabels before him, it was clear Konstabel Els' death had indeed been a great loss to the Piemburg constabulary. Certainly none of the faces he could see suggested those admirable characteristics which had evidently been so manifest in Konstabel Els. He was just coming to the conclusion that the average IQ must be in the region of 65 when the Kommandant finished his speech and announced that the Els Memorial Trophy had been won by Konstabel van Rooyen. The Mayor stood up and took the leash of the stuffed Dobermann from Luitenant Verkramp.

'Congratulations on winning this award,' he said when the prizewinner presented himself. 'And what did you do to be so highly honoured?'

Konstabel van Rooyen blushed and mumbled something about shooting a kaffir.

'He prevented a prisoner from escaping,' the Kommandant explained hurriedly.

'Very commendable, I'm sure,' said the Mayor and handed the leash to the konstabel. To the cheers of his fellow policemen and the applause of the public the winner of the Els Memorial Trophy staggered down the steps carrying the stuffed Dobermann as the band struck up.

'Splendid idea giving a trophy like that,' the Mayor said as they sipped tea in the refreshment tent afterwards, 'though I must say I would never have thought of a stuffed dog. Highly original.'

'It was killed by the late Konstabel Els himself,' the Kommandant said.

'He must have been a remarkable man.'

'With his bare hands,' said the Kommandant.

'Dear God,' said the Mayor.

Presently, leaving the Mayor discussing the advisability of allowing visiting Japanese businessmen to use Whites Only swimming pools with the Rev Schlachbals, the Kommandant moved away. At the entrance of the tent Luitenant Verkramp was deep in conversation with a large blonde whose turquoise dress fitted her astonishingly well. Under the pink picture hat the Kommandant recognized the features of Dr von Blimenstein, the eminent psychiatrist at Fort Rapier Mental Hospital.

'Getting free treatment?' the Kommandant asked jocularly as he edged past.

'Dr von Blimenstein has been telling me how she deals with cases of manic-depression,' said the Luitenant.

Dr von Blimenstein smiled. 'Luitenant Verkramp seems most interested in the use of electro-convulsive therapy.'

'I know,' said the Kommandant and wandered out into the open air, idly speculating on the possibility that Verkramp was attracted to the blonde psychiatrist. It seemed unlikely somehow but with Luitenant Verkramp one never knew. Kommandant van Heerden had long ago ceased trying to understand his second-in-command.

He found a seat in the shade and looked out over the city. It was there that his heart belonged, he thought, idly scratching the long scar on his chest. Since the day of his transplant operation Kommandant van Heerden had felt himself in more ways than one a new man. His appetite had improved, he was seldom tired and above all the erroneous belief that at least a portion of his anatomy could trace its ancestry back to the Norman Conquest did much to alleviate the lack of esteem he felt for the rest of himself. Having acquired the heart of an English gentleman, all that remained for him to do was acquire those outward characteristics of Englishness he found so admirable. To this end he had bought a Harris Tweed suit, a Norfolk jacket and a pair of brown brogues. At weekends he could be seen in his Norfolk jacket and brogues walking in the woods outside Piemburg, a solitary figure deep in thought or at least in those perambulations of the mind that the Kommandant imagined to be thought and which in his case revolved around ways and means of becoming an accepted member of Piemburg's English community.

He had made a start in this direction by applying for membership of the Alexandria Club, Zululand's most exclusive club, but without success. It had taken the combined efforts of the President, the Treasurer and the Secretary to convince him that being blackballed had nothing to do with the colour of his reproductive organs or the racial origins of his grandmother. In the end he had joined the Golf Club where conditions of membership were less rigorous and where he could sit in the clubhouse and listen with awe to accents whose arrogance was, he felt, authentically English. After such visits he would return home and spend the evening practising 'Jolly good show' and 'Chin up'. Now as he sat dozing in his chair he was well content with the progress he was making.

To Luitenant Verkramp the change that had come over the Kommandant since his operation suggested some sinister and secret knowledge. The advantage Verkramp had previously enjoyed by virtue of a better education and a quicker wit had quite disappeared. The Kommandant treated him with a lordly tolerance that infuriated the Luitenant, and greeted his sarcastic remarks with a benign smile. Worse still, Verkramp found the Kommandant continually interfering with his attempts to stamp out Communism, liberalism and humanism, not to mention Anglicanism and Roman Catholicism and other enemies of the South African way of life in Piemburg. When Verkramp's men raided the Masonic hall Kommandant van Heerden raised the strongest objections, and when the Security Branch arrested an archaeologist at the University of Zululand whose research suggested that there was evidence of iron workings in the Transvaal before the arrival of Van Riebeck in 1652 the Kommandant had insisted on his release. Verkramp had protested vigorously.

'There were no black bastards in South Africa before the white man came and it's treason to say there were,' he told the Kommandant.

'I know all that,' the Kommandant replied, 'but this fellow never said there were.'

'He did. He said there were iron workings.'

'Iron workings aren't people,' the Kommandant pointed out and the archaeologist, who by this time was suffering acute symptoms of anxiety, was transferred to Fort Rapier Mental Hospital. It was there that Verkramp first met Dr von Blimenstein. As she pinned the patient's arm behind his back and frogmarched him into the hospital Luitenant Verkramp gazed at her broad shoulders and heavy buttocks and knew himself to be in love. He would visit the hospital almost daily to inquire about the archaeologist's progress and would sit in the doctor's office studying the details of her face and figure before returning to the police station like a traveller from some sexual El Dorado. There he would sit for hours constructing in his mind's eye a picture of the lovely psychiatrist out of the jigsaw fragments of his numerous visits. Each trip he would bring another tiny hoard of intimate details to add to the outline he knew so well. Once it was her left arm. Another time the gentle swell of her stomach ridged by the constriction of a girdle or one large breast hard in the confines of her bra. Best of all, one summer day, the briefest glimpse of inner thigh, dimpled and white beneath a tight skirt, Ankles, knees, hands, the occasional armpit, Verkramp knew them all with an intimacy of detail that would have surprised the doctor and then again might not have.

Now as they stood in the refreshment tent Luitenant Verkramp mentioned the change that had come over the Kommandant.

'I can't understand it,' he said, offering the doctor another cream scone. 'He's taken to dressing up in fancy clothes.' Dr von Blimenstein looked at him sharply.

'What sort of fancy clothes?' she asked.

'He's got a tweed jacket with pleated pockets and a sort of belt at the back. And he's taken to wearing strange shoes.'

'Sounds fairly normal,' Dr von Blimenstein said. 'No question of perfume or an interest in women's underwear?'

Luitenant Verkramp shook his head sadly.

'But his language has changed too. He insists on talking English and he's got a picture of the Queen of England on his desk.'

'That does sound peculiar,' said the doctor.

Verkramp was encouraged.

'It doesn't seem natural for a good Afrikaner to go around saying "Absolutely spiffing, what?" does it?'

'I'd have grave doubts about the sanity of a good Englishman who went round saying that,' said the psychiatrist. 'Does he have sudden changes of mood?'

'Yes,' said Verkramp with feeling.

'Delusions of grandeur?'

'Definitely,' said Verkramp.

'Well,' said Dr von Blimenstein, 'it does look as though your Kommandant is suffering from some sort of psychic disturbance. I should keep a close watch on him.'

By the time Police Open Day was over and Dr von Blimenstein had left, Luitenant Verkramp was in a state of mild euphoria. The notion that Kommandant von Heerden was on the verge of a breakdown opened promotion prospects. Luitenant Verkamp had begun to think that shortly he would be chief of police in Piemburg.

CHAPTER TWO

Two days later Luitenant Verkramp was sitting in his office dreaming of Dr von Blimenstein when a directive arrived from the Bureau of State Security. It was marked 'For Your Eyes Only' and had accordingly been read by several konstabels before it reached him. Verkramp read the directive through avidly. It concerned breaches of the Immorality Act by members of the South African Police and was a routine memorandum sent to all Police Stations throughout South Africa.

'You are hereby instructed to investigate cases of suspected liaison between police officers and Bantu women.' Verkramp looked 'liaison' up in the dictionary and found that it meant what he had hoped. He read on and, as he read, vistas of opportunity opened before him. 'In the light of the propaganda value afforded to enemies of South Africa by press reports of court cases involving SAP officers and Bantu women, it is of national importance that ways and means be found to combat the tendency of white policemen to consort with black women. It is also in the interests of racial harmony that transracial sexual intercourse should be prevented. Where proof of such illegal sexual activity involving members of the SAP is forthcoming, no criminal proceedings should be instituted without prior notification of the Bureau of State Security.'

By the time he had finished reading the document Luitenant Verkramp was not sure whether he was supposed to prosecute offending policemen or not. What he did know was that he had been instructed to investigate 'cases of suspected liaison' and that it was 'of national importance that ways and means be found'. The notion of doing something of national importance particularly appealed to him. Luitenant Verkramp picked up the telephone and dialled Fort Rapier Mental Hospital. He had something to ask Dr von Blimenstein.

Later the same morning the two met on what had once been the parade ground for the British garrison and which now served as an exercise area for the inmates of the hospital.

'It's the ideal spot for what I have to say,' Verkramp told the doctor as they strolled among the patients. 'No one can possibly overhear us,' a remark which gave rise in the psychiatrist's bosom to the hope that he was about to propose to her. His next remark was even more promising. 'What I have to ask you concerns ... er ... sex.'

Dr von Blimenstein smiled coyly and looked down at her size nine shoes. 'Go on,' she murmured as the Luitenant's Adam's apple bobbed with embarrassment.

'Of course, it's not a subject I would normally discuss with a woman,' he muttered finally. The doctor's hopes fell. 'But since you're a psychiatrist, I thought you might be able to help.'

Dr von Blimenstein looked at him coldly. This wasn't what she wanted to hear. 'Go on,' she said reverting to her professional tone of voice. 'Out with it.'

Verkramp took the plunge.

'It's like this. A lot of policemen have anti-social tendencies. They keep doing what they shouldn't do.' He stopped hurriedly. He had begun to regret ever starting the conversation.

'And what shouldn't policemen do?' There was no mistaking the note of disapproval in her voice.

'Black women,' Verkramp blurted out. 'They shouldn't do black women, should they?'

There was really no need to wait for the answer. Dr von Blimenstein's face had gone a strange mauve colour and the veins were standing out on her neck.

'Shouldn't?' she shouted furiously. Several patients scampered away towards the main block. 'Shouldn't? Do you mean to say you've brought me out here just to tell me you've been screwing coon girls?'

Luitenant Verkramp knew that he had made a terrible mistake. The doctor's voice could be heard half a mile away.

'Not me,' yelled Verkramp desperately. 'I'm not talking about me.'

Dr von Blimenstein stared at him doubtfully. 'Not you?' she asked after a pause.

'On my honour,' Verkramp assured her. 'What I meant was that other police officers do and I thought you might have some ideas about how they can be stopped.'

'Why can't they be arrested and charged under the Immorality Act like everyone else?'

Verkramp shook his head. 'Well for one thing they are police officers which makes them rather difficult to catch and in any case it's important to avoid the scandal.' Dr von Blimenstein stared at him in disgust.

'Do you mean to tell me that this sort of thing goes on all the time?'

Verkramp nodded.

'In that case the punishment should be more severe,' said the doctor. 'Seven years and ten strokes isn't a sufficient deterrent. In my opinion any white man having sexual intercourse with a black woman should be castrated.'

'I quite agree,' said Verkramp enthusiastically. 'It would do them a lot of good.'

Dr von Blimenstein looked at him suspiciously but there was nothing to suggest irony in Verkramp's expression. He was staring at her with undisguised admiration. Encouraged by his frank agreement, the doctor continued.

'I feel so strongly about miscegenation that I would be quite prepared to carry out the operation myself. Is anything wrong?'

Luitenant Verkramp had suddenly turned very white. The idea of being castrated by the beautiful doctor corresponded so closely with his own masochistic fantasies that he felt quite overcome.

'No. Nothing,' he gasped, trying to rid himself of the vision of the doctor, masked and robed, approaching him on the operating table. 'It's just a bit hot out here.' Dr von Blimenstein took him by the arm.

'Why don't we continue our discussion at my cottage? It's cool down there and we can have some tea.' Luitenant Verkramp allowed himself to be led off the parade ground and down the hospital drive to the doctor's cottage. Like the rest of the hospital buildings, it dated from the turn of the century when it had been officers' quarters. Its stoep faced south and looked over the hills towards the coast and inside it was cool and dark. While Dr von Blimenstein made tea, Luitenant Verkramp sat in the sitting-room and wondered if he had been wise to broach the subject of sex with a woman as forceful as Dr von Blimenstein.

'Why don't you take off your jacket and make yourself comfortable?' the doctor asked when she returned with the tray. Verkramp shook his head nervously. He wasn't used to having tea with ladies who asked him to take his jacket off and besides he rather doubted if his braces would go very well with the tasteful decorations in the room.

'Oh come now,' said the doctor, 'there's no need to be formal with me. I'm not going to eat you.' Coming so shortly after the news that the doctor was an advocate of castration, the idea of being eaten by her as well was too much for Verkramp. He sat down hurriedly in a chair.

'I'm perfectly all right like this,' he said, but Dr von Blimenstein wasn't convinced.

'Do you want me to take it off for you?' she asked, getting up from her own chair with a movement that disclosed more of her legs than Luitenant Verkramp had ever seen before. 'I've had lots of practice,' she smiled at him. Verkramp could well believe it. 'In the hospital.' Feeling like a weasel fascinated by a giant rabbit, Verkramp sat hypnotized in his chair as she approached.

'Stand up,' said the doctor.

Verkramp stood up. Doctor von Blimenstein's fingers unbuttoned his jacket as he stood facing her and a moment later she was pushing his jacket back over his shoulders so that he could hardly move his arms. 'There we are,' she said softly, her face smiling gently close to his, 'that feels a lot more comfortable, doesn't it?'

Comfortable was hardly the word Luitenant Verkramp would have chosen to describe the sensation he was now experiencing. As her cool fingers began to undo his tie, Verkramp found himself swept from the safe remote world of sexual fantasy into an immediacy of satisfaction he had no means of controlling. With a volley of diminishing whimpers and an ecstatic release Luitenant Verkramp slumped against the doctor and was only prevented from falling by her strong arms. In the twilight of her hair he heard her murmur, 'There, there, my darling.' Luitenant Verkramp passed out

Twenty minutes later he was sitting rigid with remorse and embarrassment wondering what to do if she asked him if he wanted another cup of tea. To say 'No' would be to invite her to take the cup away for good while to say 'Yes' would still deprive him of the only means he had of hiding his lack of self-control. Dr von Blimenstein was telling him that a sense of guilt was always the cause of sexual problems. In Verkramp's opinion the argument didn't hold water but he was too preoccupied with the question of more tea or not to enter into the conversation with anything approaching fervour. Finally he decided that the best thing to do was to say 'Yes, please' and cross his legs at the same time and he had just come to this conclusion when Dr von Blimenstein noticed his empty cup. 'Would you care for some more tea?' she asked and reached out for his cup. Luitenant Verkramp's careful plan was wrecked before he realized it. He had expected her to come over and fetch the cup, not wait for it to be brought to her. Responding to the contradictory impulses towards modesty and good manners at the same time, he crossed his legs and stood up, in the process spilling the little bit of tea he had kept in his cup in case he should decide to say 'No' into his lap where it mingled with the previous evidence of his lack of *savoir-faire*. Luitenant Verkramp untangled his legs and looked down at himself with shame and embarrassment. The doctor was more practical. Picking the cup off the floor and prising the saucer from Verkramp's fingers, she hurried from the room and returned a moment later with a damp cloth. 'We mustn't let your uniform get stained must we?' she cooed with a motherliness which reduced most of Verkramp to a delicious limpness and quite prevented him from realizing the admission of complicity in his mishap by the 'we' and before he knew what was happening the beautiful doctor was rubbing his fly with the damp cloth.

Luitenant Verkramp's reaction was instantaneous. Once was wicked enough but twice was more than he could bear. With a contraction that bent him almost double, he jerked himself away from the doctor's tempting hands. 'No,' he squeaked, 'not again,' and leapt for cover behind the armchair.

His reaction took Dr von Blimenstein quite by surprise.

'Not what again?' she asked, still kneeling on the floor where his flight had left her.

'Not ... What? Nothing,' said Verkramp desperately struggling to distinguish some moral landmark in the confusion of his mind.

'Not? What? Nothing?' said the doctor clambering to her feet. 'What on earth do you mean?'

Verkramp turned melodramatically away and stared out of the window.

'You shouldn't have done that,' he said.

'Done what?'

'You know,' said Verkramp.

'What did I do?' the doctor insisted. Luitenant Verkramp shook his head miserably at the hills and said nothing. 'How silly you are,' the doctor went on. 'There's nothing to be ashamed of. We get quite a few involuntary emissions every day in the hospital.'

Verkramp turned on her furiously.

'That's with lunatics,' he said, disgusted by her clinical detachment. 'Sane people don't have them.' He stopped abruptly, vaguely aware of the self-accusation.

'Of course they do,' said the doctor soothingly. 'It's only natural ... between ... passionate men and women.'

Luitenant Verkramp resisted the siren tone.

'It's not natural. It's wicked.'

Dr von Blimenstein laughed softly.

'You mustn't laugh at me,' shouted Verkramp.

'And you mustn't shout at me,' said the doctor. Verkramp wilted before the tone of authority in her voice. 'Come here,' she continued. Verkramp crossed the room nervously. Doctor von Blimenstein put her hands on his shoulders. 'Look at me,' she told him. Verkramp did as he was told. 'Do you find me attractive?' Verkramp nodded dumbly. 'I'm glad,' said the doctor and taking the astonished Luitenant's head in her hands she kissed him passionately on the mouth. 'And now I'll go and rustle up something for lunch,' she said breaking away from him and before Verkramp could say anything more she was in the kitchen clattering away quite surprisingly for a woman of her size. Behind her in the kitchen doorway Luitenant Verkramp struggled with his emotions. Furious at himself, at her, and at the situation in which he found himself, he looked round for someone to blame. Sensing his dilemma Dr von Blimenstein came to his assistance.

'About the problem you mentioned,' she said, bending over seductively to get a saucepan from the cupboard under the sink, 'I think I might be able to help you after all.'

'What problem?' Verkramp asked brusquely. He'd had enough help with his problems already.

'About your men and the kaffir girls,' said the doctor.

'Oh them.' Verkramp had forgotten his original reason for coming.

'I've been thinking about it. I can see one way it might be tackled.'

'Oh really,' said Verkramp, who could think about a great many more but didn't feel up to it.

'It's really a question of psychic engineering,' the doctor continued. 'That's my term for the experiments I have been conducting here with a number of patients.'

Luitenant Verkramp perked up. He was always interested in experiments.

'I've had a number of successful cures already,' she explained, chopping a carrot up with a number of swift strokes. 'It's worked with alcoholics, transvestites and homosexuals. I can't really see any reason why it shouldn't work just as well in the case of a perversion like miscegenation.' There was no doubting Verkramp's interest now. He moved away from the kitchen doorway all attention.

'How would you go about it?' he asked eagerly.

'Well the first thing to do would be to isolate the personality factors in men with a tendency towards this sort of sexual deviation. That shouldn't be too difficult. I could work out a number of likely attributes. In fact it might be a good thing if your men were to fill in a questionnaire.'

'What? About their sex life?' Verkramp asked. He could see the sort of reception a questionnaire like that would get in the Piemburg Police Station.

'About sex and other things.'

'What other things?' Verkramp asked suspiciously.

'Oh the usual. Relations with mother. Whether the mother was the dominant figure in the home. If they were fond of their black nanny. Earliest sexual experience. Normal things like that.'

Verkramp gulped. What he had just heard sounded positively abnormal to him.

'A careful analysis of the answers should give us some lead to the sort of men who would benefit from the treatment,' Dr von Blimenstein explained.

'Do you mean to say you can tell just by answers to a questionnaire if a man wants to sleep with a kaffir?' Verkramp asked.

Dr von Blimenstein shook her head. 'Not exactly, but we'd have something to go on. After we had weeded out the likely suspects, I would interview them, in the strictest confidence, of course, and see if any were suitable for treatment.'

Verkramp was doubtful. 'I can't see anyone admitting he wanted a kaffir,' he said.

The doctor smiled. 'You would be amazed at some of the things people confess to me,' she said.

'What would you do when you'd found out?' Verkramp asked.

'First things first,' said Dr von Blimenstein, who knew the value of keeping a man in suspense. 'Let's have lunch on the stoep.' She picked up the tray and Verkramp followed her out.

By the time Luitenant Verkramp left the cottage that afternoon he had in his pocket the draft questionnaire he was to put to the men in the Piemburg Police Station but he still had no idea what form the doctor's treatment would take. All she would tell him was that she would guarantee that after a week with her no man would ever look at a black woman again. Luitenant Verkramp could well believe it.

On the other hand he had a far clearer picture of the sort of man who had transracial sexual tendencies. According to Dr von Blimenstein the signs to look for were solitariness, sudden changes of mood, pronounced feelings of sexual guilt, an unstable family background and of course an unsatisfactory sex life. As the Luitenant went through in his mind the officers and men in Piemburg one figure emerged more clearly than all the others. Luitenant Verkramp had begun to think he was about to discover the secret of the change that had come over Kommandant van Heerden.

Back in his office he read through the directive from BOSS just to make sure that he was empowered to take the action he contemplated. It was there in black and white. 'You are hereby instructed to investigate suspected cases of liaison between police officers and Bantu women.' Verkramp locked the memo away and sent for Sergeant Breitenbach.

Within the hour he had issued his instructions. 'I want him watched night and day,' he told the Security men assembled in his office. 'I want a record of everything he does, where he goes, who he meets and anything that suggests a break in his usual routine. Photograph everyone visiting his house. Put microphones in every room and tape all converstations. Tap his phone and record all his calls. Is that clear? I want the full treatment.'

Verkramp looked round the room and the men all nodded. Only Sergeant Breitenbach had any reservations.

'Isn't this a bit irregular, sir?' he asked. 'After all, the Kommandant is the commanding officer here.'

Luitenant Verkramp flushed angrily. He disliked having his orders questioned.

'I have here,' he said, brandishing the direct from BOSS, 'orders from Pretoria to carry out this investigation. Naturally,' his voice changed from authority to unction, 'I hope as I'm sure we all do that we'll be able to give Kommandant van Heerden full security clearance when we're finished but in the meantime we must carry out our orders. I need, of course, hardly remind you that the utmost secrecy must be maintained throughout this operation. All right, you may go.'

When the Security men had left, Luitenant Verkramp gave orders for the questionnaire to be xeroxed and left on his desk ready for distribution the following morning.

Next day Mrs Roussouw, whose job it was to superintend the black convicts who came from Piemburg Prison every day to do the Kommandant's housework, had her work cut out answering the front-door bell to admit a succession of Municipal Officials who seemed to think there was a damaged gas pipe under the kitchen, a mains short circuit in the living-room and a leak in the water tank in the attic.

Since the house wasn't connected to the gas and the electric stove in the kitchen functioned perfectly while there were no signs of damp on the bedroom ceiling, Mrs Roussouw did her best to deter the officials who seemed determined to carry out their duties with a degree of conscientiousness and a lack of specialized knowledge she found quite astonishing.

'Shouldn't you switch off the main supply first?' she asked the man from the Electricity Board who was laying wires in the Kommandant's bedroom.

'Suppose so,' the man said and went downstairs. When ten minutes later she found the light still on in the kitchen, Mrs Roussouw took matters into her ow<u>n</u> hands and went into the cupboard under the stairs and switched the mains off herself. There was a muffled yell from the attic where the Water Board men had been relying on a handlamp connected to a plug on the landing to help them find the non-existent leak in the cistern.

'Must be the bulb,' said one of the men and clambered down the ladder to fetch another bulb from the Kommandant's bedside light. By the time he was back in the darkness of the attic the Electricity man had assured Mrs Roussouw that there was no need to cut the mains off.

'You know your own job, I suppose,' Mrs Roussouw told him rather doubtfully.

'I can assure you it's quite safe now,' the man said. Mrs Roussouw went back under the stairs and turned the supply on again. The scream that issued from the attic where the Water Board man had his fingers in the socket of the lamp was followed by an appalling rending noise from the bedroom and the sound of falling plaster. Mrs Roussouw switched the electricity off again and went upstairs.

'Whatever will the Kommandant say when he finds what a mess you've made?' she asked the leg that hung through the hole in the ceiling. An answering groan came from the attic. 'Are you all right?' Mrs Roussouw asked anxiously. The leg wriggled vigorously.

'I told you you should have cut it off,' Mrs Roussouw told the Electricity man reprovingly. In the attic the remark provoked a string of protests and the leg jerked convulsively. The Electricity man went out onto the landing.

'What's he say?' he asked peering up the ladder into the darkness.

'He says he doesn't want it cut off,' said a voice from above.

'Just as you say,' said Mrs Roussouw and went downstairs to turn the mains on again. 'Is that better?' she asked pulling the switch down. Upstairs in the Kommandant's bedroom the leg twitched violently and was still.

'You just hang on and I'll give you a shove from below,' the Electricity man said and clambered onto the bed.

Mrs Roussouw emerged from the cupboard and went upstairs again. She was getting rather puffed with all this up and down. She had just reached the landing when there was another terrible yell from the bedroom. She hurried in and found the Electricity man lying prostrate amid the plaster on the Kommandant's bed.

'What's the matter now?' she asked. The man wiped his face and looked up at the leg reproachfully.

'It's alive,' he said finally.

'That's what you think,' said a voice from the attic.

'I'm sure I don't know what to think,' Mrs Roussouw said.

'Well I do,' the Electricity man told her, sitting up on the bed. 'I think you ought to go and cut the mains supply off again. I'm not touching that leg till you do.'

Mrs Roussouw turned wearily back to the stairs.

'This is the last time,' she told the man, 'I'm not running up and down stairs any more.'

In the end with the help of the black convicts they managed to get the unconscious Water Board official down from the attic and Mrs Roussouw was persuaded to give him the kiss of life on the couch in the Kommandant's sitting-room.

'You can get those kaffirs out of here before I do,' she told the Electricity man. 'I'm not doing any kissing with them looking on. It might give them ideas.' The Electricity man shooed the convicts out and presently the Water Board official recovered enough to be taken back to the police station.

'Bungling idiots,' Verkramp snarled when they reported back to him. 'I said bug the house, not knock it to bits.'

When Kommandant van Heerden arrived home that evening it was to find his house in considerable disorder and with most of the services cut off. He tried to make himself some tea but there was no water in the tap. It took him twenty minutes to find the stopcock and another twenty to discover a spanner that fitted it. He filled his Five Minute kettle and waited half an hour for it to boil only to learn at the end of that time that the water in it was still stone cold.

'What the hell's wrong with everything?' he wondered as he filled a saucepan and put it on the stove. Twenty minutes later he was rummaging about under the stairs trying to find the fusebox with the help of a box of matches. He had taken all the fuses out and put them back again before he realized that the main switch was off. With a sigh of relief he pulled it down to 'ON'. There was a loud bang in the fusebox and the light in the hall which had come on momentarily went out again. It took the Kommandant another half an hour to find the fuse wire and by that time he was out of matches. He gave up in disgust and went out and had dinner in a Greek café down the road.

By the time he got home again Kommandant van Heerden's temper was violent. With the help of a torch which he had bought at a garage he made his way upstairs and was appalled by the mess in his bedroom. There was a large hole in the ceiling and the bed was covered with plaster. The Kommandant sat down on the edge of the bed and shone his torch through the hole in his ceiling. Finally he turned to the phone on his bedside table and dialled the police station. He was sitting there staring out of the window wondering why it took so long for the Duty Sergeant to answer when he became aware that what looked like a shadow under the jacaranda tree across the road was smoking a cigarette. The Kommandant put the phone down and crossed to the window to take a better look. Staring into the darkness he was startled to notice another shadow under another tree. He was just wondering what two shadows were doing watching his house when the phone behind him on the bed began to squeak irately. The Kommandant picked the receiver up just in time to hear the Duty Sergeant put his down. With a curse he dialled again, changed his mind and went through to the bathroom which overlooked his back garden and opened the window. A light breeze drifted in, ruffling the curtains. The Kommandant peered out and had just decided that his back garden was free of interlopers when an azalea bush lit a cigarette. In a state of considerable alarm the Kommandant scurried back to his bedroom and dialled the police station.

'I'm being watched,' he told the Duty Sergeant when the man finally picked up the phone.

'Oh really,' said the Sergeant, who was used to nutters ringing him up in the middle of the night with stories of being spied on. 'And who is watching you?'

'I don't know,' whispered the Kommandant. 'There are two men out front and another in my back garden.'

'What are you whispering for?' the Sergeant asked.

'Because I'm being watched, of course. Why else should I whisper?' the Kommandant snarled *sotto voce*.

'I've no idea,' said the Sergeant. 'I'll just get this down. You say you're being watched by two men in the front garden and one in the back. Is that correct?'

'No,' said the Kommandant who was rapidly losing patience with the Duty Sergeant.

'But you just said –'

'I said there were two men at the front of my house and one in the back garden,' the Kommandant said, trying to control his temper.

'Two ... men ... in ... front ... of ... my ... house,' said the Sergeant writing it down slowly. 'Just getting it down,' he told the Kommandant when the latter asked what the hell he thought he was doing.

'Well, you'd better hurry up, the Kommandant shouted, losing control of himself. 'I've got a dirty great hole in the ceiling above my bed and my house has been burgled,' he went on and was rewarded for his pains by hearing the Sergeant inform somebody else at the police station that he had another nut case on the line.

'Now then, correct me if I'm wrong,' said the Sergeant before the Kommandant could reprimand him for insubordination, 'but you say there are three men watching your house, that there's a dirty great hole in your ceiling and that your house has been burgled? Is that right? You haven't left anything out?'

In his bedroom Kommandant van Heerden was on the verge of apoplexy. 'Just one thing,' he yelled into the phone, 'this is your commanding officer, Kommandant van Heerden, speaking. And I'm ordering you to send a patrol car round to my house at once.'

A sceptical silence greeted this ferocious announcement. 'Do you hear me?' shouted the Kommandant. It was clear that the Duty Sergeant didn't. He had his hand over the mouthpiece but the Kommandant could still hear him telling the konstabel on duty with him that the caller was off his head. With a slam the Kommandant replaced his receiver and wondered what to do. Finally he got to his feet and went to the window. The sinister watchers were still there. The Kommandant tiptoed to his chest of drawers and rummaged in the drawer containing his socks for his revolver. Taking it out, he made sure it was loaded and then, having decided that the hole in his ceiling made his bedroom indefensible, was tiptoeing downstairs when the phone in his bedroom began to ring. For a moment the Kommandant thought of letting it ring when the thought that it might be the Duty Sergeant ringing back to confirm his previous call sent him scurrying upstairs again. He was just in time to pick the receiver up as the ringing stopped.

Kommandant van Heerden dialled the police station.

'Have you just rung me?' he asked the Duty Sergeant.

'Depends who you are,' the Sergeant replied.

'I'm your commanding officer,' shouted the Kommandant.

The Sergeant considered the matter. 'All right,' he said finally, 'just put your phone down and we'll ring back to confirm that.'

The Kommandant looked at the receiver vindictively. 'Listen to me,' he said, 'my number is 5488. You can confirm that and I'll hold on.'

Five minutes later patrol cars from all over Piemburg were converging on Kommandant van Heerden's house and the Duty Sergeant was wondering what he was going to say to the Kommandant in the morning.

CHAPTER THREE

Luitenant Verkramp was wondering much the same thing. News of the fiasco at the Kommandant's house reached him via Sergeant Breitenbach, who had spent the evening tapping the Kommandant's telephone and who had the presence of mind to order the watching agents to leave the area before the patrol cars arrived. Unfortunately the microphones scattered about the Kommandant's house remained and Luitenant Verkramp could imagine that their presence there would hardly improve his relations with his commanding officer if they were discovered.

'I told you this whole thing was a mistake,' Sergeant Breitenbach said while Luitenant Verkramp dressed.

Verkramp didn't agree. 'What's he making such a fuss about if he hasn't got something to hide?' he asked.

'That hole in the ceiling, for one thing,' said the Sergeant. Luitenant Verkramp couldn't see it.

'Could have happened to anyone,' he said. 'Anyway he'll blame the Water Board for it.'

'I can't see them admitting responsibility for making it, all the same,' said the Sergeant.

'The more they deny it, the more he'll believe they did,' said Verkramp, who knew something about psychology. 'Anyway I'll cook up something to explain the bugs, don't worry.'

'Dismissing the Sergeant, he drove to the police station and sat up half the night concocting a memorandum to put on the Kommandant's desk in the morning.

In fact there was no need to use it. Kommandant van Heerden arrived at the police station to make someone pay for the damage to his property. He wasn't quite sure which of the public utilities to blame and Mrs Roussouw's explanation hadn't made the matter any clearer.

'Oh, you do look a sight,' she said when the Kommandant came down to breakfast after shaving in cold water.

'So does my bloody house,' said the Kommandant, dabbing his cheek with a styptic pencil.

'Language,' retorted Mrs Roussouw. Kommandant van Heerden regarded her bleakly.

'Perhaps you'd be good enough to explain what's been happening here,' he said. 'I came home last night to find the water cut off, a large hole in my bedroom ceiling and no electricity.'

'The Water Board man did that,' Mrs Roussouw explained. 'I had to give him the kiss of life to bring him round.'

The Kommandant shuddered at the thought.

'And what does that explain?' he asked.

'The hole in the ceiling, of course,' said Mrs Roussouw.

The Kommandant tried to visualize the sequence of events that had resulted from Mrs Roussouw's giving the Water Board man the kiss of life and his falling through the ceiling.

'In the attic?' he asked sceptically.

'Of course not, silly,' Mrs Roussouw said. 'He was looking for a hole in the cistern when I turned the electricity on ...'

The Kommandant was too bewildered to let her continue.

'Mrs Roussouw,' he said wearily, 'am I to understand ... oh never mind. I'll phone the Water Board when I get to the station.'

He had breakfast while Mrs Roussouw added to the confusion in his mind by explaining that the Electricity man had been responsible for the accident in the first place by leaving the current on.

'I suppose that explains the mess in here,' said the Kommandant, looking at the rubble under the sink.

'Oh, no that was the Gas man,' Mrs Roussouw said.

'But we don't use gas,' said the Kommandant.

'I know, I told him that but he said it was a leak in the mains.'

The Kommandant finished his breakfast and walked to the police station utterly perplexed. In spite of the fact that the patrol cars had been unable to find any evidence that his house had been watched, the Kommandant was certain he had been under surveillance. He even had an uneasy feeling that he was being followed to the police station but when he glanced over his shoulder at the corner there was no one in sight.

Once in his office he spent an hour on the phone haranguing the managers of the Gas, Electricity and Water Boards in an attempt to get to the bottom of the affair. It took the efforts of all three managers to convince him that their men had never been authorized to enter his house, that there was absolutely nothing the matter with his electricity or his water supply, and that there hadn't been a suspected gas leak within a mile of his house and finally that they couldn't be held responsible for the damage done to his property. The Kommandant reserved his opinion on this last point and said he would consult his lawyer. The Manager of the Water Board told him that it wasn't the business of the board to mend leaks in cisterns in any case and the Kommandant said it wasn't anybody's business to make large holes in the ceiling of his bedroom, and he certainly wasn't going to pay for the privilege of having them made.

Having raised his blood pressure to a dangerously high level in this exchange of courtesies, the Kommandant sent for the Duty Sergeant, who was dragged from his bed to explain his behaviour over the phone.

'I thought it was a hoax,' he told the Kommandant. 'It was the way you were whispering.'

The Kommandant wasn't whispering now. His voice could be heard in the cells two floors below. 'A hoax?' he yelled at the Sergeant. 'You thought it was a hoax?'

'Yes, sir, we get half a dozen every night.'

'What sort of hoaxes?' the Kommandant asked.

'People ringing up to say they're being burgled or raped or something. Mostly women.'

Kommandant van Heerden remembered when he had been a Duty Sergeant and had to agree that a lot of night calls were false alarms. He dismissed the Sergeant with a reprimand. 'Next time I call you,' he said, 'I don't want any argument. Understand?' The Sergeant understood and was about to leave the office when the Kommandant had second thoughts. 'Where the hell do you think you're going?' the Kommandant snarled. The Sergeant said that since he'd been up all night he was thinking of going back to bed. The Kommandant had other plans for him. 'I'm

putting you in charge of the investigation into the burglary at my house,'
he said. 'I want a full report on who was responsible by this afternoon.'

'Yes sir,' said the Sergeant wearily and left the office. On the stairs he
met Luitenant Verkramp, who was looking pretty jaded himself.

'He wants a full report by this afternoon on the break-in,' the Sergeant
told Verkramp. The Luitenant sighed, went back upstairs and knocked
on the Kommandant's door.

'Come in,' yelled the Kommandant. Luitenant Verkramp came in.
'What's the matter with you, Verkramp? You look as though you'd spent
the night on the tiles.'

'Just an attic of colack,' spluttered Verkramp, unnerved by the
Kommandant's percipience.

'A what?'

'An attack of colic,' said Verkramp trying to control his speech. 'Just
a slip of the foot ... er ... tongue.'

'For God's sake pull yourself together Luitenant,' the Kommandant
told him.

'Yes sir,' said Verkramp.

'What do you want to see me about?'

'It's about this business at your home, sir,' said Verkramp, 'I have
some information which may be of interest to you.'

Kommandant van Heerden sighed. He might have guessed that
Verkramp might have his grubby fingers in this particular pie. 'Well?'

Luitenant Verkramp swallowed nervously. 'We in the Security Branch,'
he began, spreading the burden of responsibility as far as possible, 'have
recently received information that an attempt was going to be made to
bug your house.' He paused to see how the Kommandant would take
the news. Kommandant van Heerden responded predictably. He sat up
in his chair and stared at Verkramp in horror.

'Good God,' he said, 'you mean ...'

'Precisely, sir,' said Verkramp. 'Acting on this information, I put your
house under twenty-four hour surveillance ...'

'You mean –'

'Exactly, sir,' Verkramp continued. 'You have probably noticed that
your house has been watched.'

'That's right,' said the Kommandant, 'I saw them there last night ...'
Verkramp nodded. 'My men, sir.'

'Across the road and in my back garden,' said the Kommandant.

'Exactly, sir,' Verkramp agreed, 'we thought they might return.'

The Kommandant was losing track of the conversation. 'Who might
return?'

'The Communist saboteurs, sir.'

'Communist saboteurs? What the hell would Communist saboteurs want to do in my house?'

'Bug it, sir,' said Verkramp. 'After the failure of their attempt yesterday I thought they might return.'

Kommandant van Heerden took a firm grip on himself.

'Are you trying to tell me that all those Gas men and Water Board officials were really Communist saboteurs ...'

'In disguise, sir. Fortunately, thanks to the efforts of my counter-agents, the attempt was foiled. One of the Communists fell through the ceiling ...'

Kommandant van Heerden leant back in his chair satisfied. He had found the person responsible for the hole in his bedroom ceiling. So that was your fault?' he said.

'Entirely,' Verkramp agreed, 'and we'll see that repairs are carried out immediately.'

The news had taken a great burden off the Kommandant's mind. On the other hand he was still puzzled.

'What I don't understand is why these Communists should want to bug my house in the first place. Who are they anyway?' he asked.

'I'm afraid I can't disclose any identities yet,' Verkramp said, and fell back on the Bureau of State Security. 'Orders from BOSS.'

'Well what the hell is the point of bugging my house?' asked the Kommandant, who knew better than to question orders from BOSS. 'I never say anything important there.'

Verkramp agreed. 'But they weren't to know that sir,' he said. 'In any case our information suggests that they were hoping to acquire material which would allow them to blackmail you.' He watched Kommandant van Heerden very closely to see how he would react. The Kommandant was appalled.

'God Almighty!' he gasped, and mopped his forehead with a handkerchief. Verkramp followed up his advantage swiftly.

'If they could get something on you, something sexual, anything a bit kinky.' He hesitated. The Kommandant was sweating profusely. 'They'd have you by the short hairs, wouldn't they?' Privately Kommandant van Heerden had to agree that they would but he wasn't admitting as much to Luitenant Verkramp. He raced through the catalogue of his nightly habits and came to the conclusion that there were several he would rather the world knew nothing about.

'The diabolical swine,' he muttered and looked at Verkramp with something approaching respect. The Luitenant wasn't such a fool after all. 'What are you going to do about it?' he asked.

'Two things,' said Verkramp. 'The first is to allay the suspicions of the Communists as far as possible by ignoring this affair at your house. Let them think we don't know what they are up to. Lay the blame on the Gas ... er ... Water Board.'

'I've done that already,' said the Kommandant.

'Good. What we have to realize is that this incident is part of a nation-wide conspiracy to undermine the morale of the South African Police. It is vital that we should do nothing premature.'

'Extraordinary,' said the Kommandant. 'Nation-wide, I had no idea there were so many Communists still at large. I thought we'd nabbed the swine years ago.'

'They spring up like dragon's teeth,' Verkramp assured him.

'I suppose they must,' said the Kommandant, who had never thought of it quite like that before. Luitenant Verkramp continued.

'After the failure of the sabotage campaign they went underground.'

'Must have done,' said the Kommandant, still obsessed with the thought of dragon's teeth.

'They've reorganized and have begun a new campaign. First to undermine our morale and secondly, when that's done, they'll start a new wave of sabotage,' Verkramp explained.

'Do you mean to tell me,' asked the Kommandant, that they are deliberately trying to obtain facts that can be used to blackmail police officers all over the country?'

'Precisely, sir,' said Verkramp. 'I have reason to believe that they are particularly interested in sexual indiscretions committed by police officers.'

The Kommandant tried to think of any sexual indiscretions he might have committed lately and rather regretfully couldn't. On the other hand he could think of thousands committed by the men under his command.

'Well,' he said finally, 'it's a good thing Konstable Els isn't with us any more. The bugger died just in time by the sound of it.'

Verkramp smiled. 'That thought had crossed my mind,' he said. Konstable Els' exploits in the field of transracial sexual intercourse were already a legend in the Piemburg Police Station.

'In any case I still don't see what you're going to do to stop this infernal campaign,' the Kommandant went on. 'If it isn't Els, there are still plenty of konstabels whose sex life could do with improvement.'

Luitenant Verkramp was delighted. 'My own view of the matter,' he said and took Dr von Blimenstein's questionnaire out of his pocket. 'I've been working on the problem with a leading member of the psychiatric profession,' he said, 'and I think we've come up with something that may serve to indicate those officers and men most vulnerable to this form of Communist infiltration.'

'Really?' said the Kommandant, who had an idea who the leading member of the psychiatric profession might be. Luitenant Verkramp handed him the questionnaire.

'With your approval, sir,' he said, 'I'd like to have these questionnaires distributed to all the men on the station. From the answers we get it should be possible to spot any likely victims of blackmail.'

Kommandant van Heerden looked at the questionnaire, which was headed innocuously enough 'Personality Research' and marked 'Strictly Confidential'. He glanced at the first few questions and found nothing to alarm him. They seemed to be concerned with profession of father, age, and the number of brothers and sisters. Before he could get any further Verkramp was explaining that he had orders from Pretoria to carry out the investigation.

'BOSS?' asked the Kommandant.

'BOSS,' said Verkramp.

'In that case, go ahead,' said the Kommandant.

'I'll leave you to fill that one in,' said Verkramp, and left the office delighted at the turn of events. He gave orders to Sergeant Breitenbach to distribute the questionnaires and telephoned Dr von Blimenstein to let her know that everything was proceeding, if not according to plan, since he hadn't had one, at least according to opportunity. Dr von Blimenstein was delighted to hear it and before Verkramp fully realized what he was doing he found that he had invited her to have dinner with him that evening. He put the phone down astonished at his good fortune. It never crossed his mind that the pack of lies about Communist blackmailers he had told the Kommandant had no reality outside his own warped imagination. His professional task was to root out enemies of the state and it followed that enemies of the state were there to be rooted out. The exact details of their activities, if any, were of little importance to him. As he had once explained in court, it was the principle of subversion that mattered, not the particulars.

If Verkramp was satisfied with the way things were going, Kommandant van Heerden, seated at his desk with the questionnaire in front of him, wasn't. The Luitenant's story was convincing enough. The Kommandant had no doubt that Communist agitators were at work in Zululand – nothing less could explain the truculence of the Zulus in the township at the recent increase in bus fares. But that saboteurs disguised as Gas men had infiltrated his own home indicated a new phase in the campaign of subversion, and a particulrly alarming one at that. The Duty Sergeant's report that the investigating team had discovered a microphone under the sink only went to prove how accurate Luitenant Verkramp's forecast had been. Ordering the Sergeant to leave the investigation to the Security Branch, the Kommandant sent a note to Verkramp which read, 'Re our discussion this morning. The presence of microphone in kitchen confirms your report. Suggest you take counteraction immediately. Van Heerden.'

With renewed confidence in the ability of his second-in-command the Kommandant decided to tackle the questionnaire Verkramp had given him. He filled in the first few questions happily enough and it was only when he had turned the page that there dawned on him the feeling that he was being led gently into a quagmire of sexual confession where every answer only dragged him deeper down.

'Did you have a black nanny?' seemed innocuous enough, and the Kommandant put 'Yes' only to find that the next question was 'Size of breasts. Large. Medium. Small.' After a moment's hesitation not unmixed with alarm he ticked 'Large', and went on to consider 'Nipple Length. Long. Medium. Short.' 'This is a bloody funny way to fight Communism,' he thought, trying to remember the length of his nanny's teats. In the end he put 'Long' and found himself faced with 'Did black nanny tickle private parts? Often. Sometimes. Infrequently?' The Kommandant looked desperately for 'Never' and couldn't find it. In the end he ticked Infrequently and turned to the next question. 'Age at First Ejaculation, Three years, four years . . . ?'

'Don't leave much to chance,' thought the Kommandant, indignantly trying to make his mind up between six years, which was quite untrue but which seemed less likely to undermine his authority than sixteen years, which was more accurate. He'd just put eight years as a compromise based on a noctural emission he'd had when he was ten when he saw that he'd walked into a trap. The next question was 'Age of First Wet Dream?' This time the list started at ten years. By the time he had rubbed out his answer to the previous question to make it consistent with a Wet Dream at eleven years, the Kommandant was in a thoroughly bad temper. He picked up the phone and called Verkramp's office. Sergeant Breitenbach answered the phone.

'Where's Verkramp?' the Kommandant demanded. The Sergeant said he was out, and could he help? The Kommandant said he doubted it. 'It's this damned questionnaire,' he told the Sergeant. 'Who's going to read it?'

'I think Dr von Blimenstein intends to,' the Sergeant said. 'She drew it up.'

'Did she?' snarled the Kommandant. 'Well you can tell Luitenant Verkramp that I have no intention of answering question twenty-five.'

'Which one is that?'

'It's the one that goes "How many times do you masterbate every day?"' said the Kommandant. 'You can tell Verkramp that I think it's an invasion of privacy to ask questions like that.'

'Yes, sir,' said Sergeant Breitenbach, studying the possible answers on the questionnaire, which ranged from five times to twenty-five times.

The Kommandant slammed down the phone and locking the questionnaire in his desk went out to lunch in a filthy temper. 'Dirty bitch, wanting to know things like that,' he thought as he stomped downstairs, and he was still grumbling to himself when he finished his lunch in the police canteen. 'I'll be up at the Golf Club if anyone wants me,' he told the Duty Sergeant and left the police station. He spent a fruitless couple of hours trying to hit a ball down the fairway before returning to the Clubhouse with the feeling that this was not one of his days.

He ordered a double brandy from the barman and took his drink out to a table on the terrace where he could sit and watch more experienced players drive off. He was sitting there absorbing the English atmosphere and trying to rid himself of the nagging conviction that the even tenor of his life was being undermined in some mysterious way when a crunch of gravel in the Clubhouse forecourt made him glance over his shoulder. A vintage Rolls-Royce had just parked and the occupants were climbing out. For a moment the Kommandant had the extraordinary sensation that he had been transported back to the 1920s. The two men who emerged from the front seat were dressed in knickerbockers and wore hats that had been out of fashion for fifty years, while their two women companions were attired in what appeared to the Kommandant to be fancy dress with cloche hats, and carried parasols. But it was less the clothes or the immaculate vintage Rolls that the voices that affected the Kommandant so profoundly. High-pitched and languidly arrogant, they seemed to reach him like some echo from the English past and with them came a rush of certitude that all was well in the world in spite of everything. The kernel of servility which was Kommandant van Heerden's innermost self and which no amount of his own authority could ever erase quivered ecstatically within him as the group passed him without so much as a glance to indicate that they were aware of his existence. It was precisely this self-absorption to the point where it transcended self and became something immutable and absolute, a Godlike self-sufficiency, that Kommandant van Heerden had always hoped to find in the English. And here it was before him in the Piemburg Golf Club in the shape of

four middle-aged men and women whose inane chatter was proof positive
that there was, in spite of wars, disasters, and imminent revolution,
nothing serious to worry about. The Kommandant particularly admired
the elegance with which the leader of the foursome, a florid man in his
fifties, clicked his fingers for the black caddie before walking over to the
first tee.

'How absolutely priceless,' shrieked one of the ladies about nothing in
particular as they followed.

'I've always said Boy was a glutton for punishment,' said the florid
man as they passed out of earshot. The Kommandant stared after them
before hurrying in to the bar to consult the barman.

'Call themselves the Dornford Yates Club,' the barman told him.
'Don't ask me why. Anyway they dress up and talk la-di-da in memory
of some firm called Bury & Co which went bust some years back. Red-
faced fellow is Colonel Heathcote-Kolkoon. He's the one they call
Bury.The plump lady is his missus. The other bloke's Major Bloxham.
Call him Boy, of all things, and he must be forty-eight if he's a day. I
don't know who the thin woman is.'

'Do they live near here?' the Kommandant asked. He didn't approve
of the barman's rather off-hand attitude to his betters but he desperately
wanted to hear more about the foursome.

'The colonel's got a place up near the Piltdown Hotel but they seem
to spend most of their time on a farm in the Underville district. It's got
a queer name like White Woman or something. I've heard they have
some pretty queer goings-on up there, too.'

The Kommandant ordered another brandy and took it out to his table
on the terrace to wait for the party to return. Presently he was joined by
the barman who stood in the doorway looking bored.

'Has the Colonel been a member here long?' the Kommandant asked.

'A couple of years,' the barman said, 'since they all came down from
Rhodesia or Kenya or somewhere. Seem to have plenty of spending
money too.'

Aware that the man was looking at him rather curiously, the
Kommandant finished his drink and strolled over to inspect the vintage
Rolls-Royce.

'1925 Silver Ghost,' said the barman who had followed him over. 'Nice
condition.'

The Kommandant grunted. He was beginning to tire of the barman's
company. He moved round the other side of the car, only to find the
barman at his elbow.

'You after them for something?' the man asked conspiratorially.

'What the hell makes you think that?' the Kommandant asked.

'Just wondered,' said the barman, and with some remark about a nod being as good as a wink which the Kommandant didn't understand, the man went back into the Clubhouse. Left to himself, the Kommandant finished his inspection of the car and was just turning away when he caught sight of something on the back seat that stopped him in his tracks. It was a book and from its back cover there stared impassively the portrait of a man. High cheek bones, slightly hooded eyelids, impeccably straight nose and a trimmed moustache, the face looked past the Kommandant into a bright and assured future. Peering through the window, Kommandant van Heerden gazed at the portrait and as he gazed knew with a certainty that passed all understanding that he was on the brink of a new phase of discovery in his search for the heart of an English gentleman. There before him on the back seat of the Rolls was portrayed with an exactitude he would never have believed possible the face of the man he wanted to be. The book was *As Other Men Are* by Dornford Yates. The Kommandant took out his notebook and wrote the title down.

By the time Colonel Heathcote-Kilkoon and his party returned to the Clubhouse, the Kommandant had left and was making his way to the Public Library in the certain knowledge that he was about to learn, from the works of Dornford Yates, the secret of that enigma which had puzzled him for so long, how to be an English gentleman.

By the time Luitenant Verkramp left the police station that evening and returned to his flat to change he was a supremely happy man. The ease with which he had allayed the Kommandant's suspicions, the results he was getting from the questionnaires, the prospects of spending the evening in the company of Dr von Blimenstein all contributed to the Luitenant's sense of well-being. Above all, the fact that the Kommandant's house was still bugged and that he would be able to lie in bed and listen to every movement the Kommandant was indiscreet enough to make in his home lent a piquancy to Verkramp's sense of achievement. Like the Kommandant, Luitenant Verkramp felt himself on the brink of a discovery that would change his whole life and transform him from merely second-in-command into a position of authority more suited to his ability. As he waited for his bath water to run, Luitenant Verkramp adjusted the receiver in his bedroom and checked the tape recorder connected to it. Before long he could make out the Kommandant shuffling about his house and opening and shutting cupboards. Satisfied that his listening device was functioning properly, Verkramp switched it off and went and had his bath. He had just finished and was climbing out when the front-door bell rang.

'Damn,' said Verkramp grabbing a towel and wondering who the hell was visiting him at this inconvenient moment. He went out into the hall trailing drops of bath water as he went, opened the door irritably and was amazed to see Dr von Blimenstein standing on the landing. 'I don't want ...' said Verkramp, reacting automatically to the sound of his doorbell at inconvenient moments before he realized who his visitor was.

'Don't you, darling?' said Dr von Blimenstein loudly and opened her musquash coat to disclose a tight-fitting dress of some extremely shiny material. 'Are you sure you don't ...'

'For hell's sake,' Verkramp said, looking wildly round. He was conscious that his neighbours were extremely respectable people and that Dr von Blimenstein, for all her education and professional standing as a psychiatrist, was not at the best of times overly worried about observing the social niceties. And now, with a bath towel round his middle and the doctor with whatever it was she had round her middle and top and bottom, was not the best of times. 'Come in quick,' he squawked. Somewhat disappointed by the reception he had given her, Dr von Blimenstein drew her coat around her and entered the flat. Verkramp hurriedly shut the door and scurried past her into the safety of his bathroom. 'I wasn't expecting you,' he shouted softly. 'I was coming up to the hospital to collect you.'

'I couldn't wait to see you,' the doctor shouted back, 'and I thought I'd give you a little surprise.'

'You did that all right,' Verkramp muttered, desperately searching for a sock that had hidden itself somewhere in the bathroom.

'I didn't quite catch that. You'll have to speak up.'

Verkramp found the sock under the washbasin. 'I said you did give me a surprise.' He hit his head on the washbasin straightening up and ended with a curse.

'You're not angry with me coming like this?' the doctor inquired. In the bathroom Verkramp sat on the edge of the bath and pulled his sock on. It was wet.

'No, of course not. Come whenever you like,' he said sourly.

'You do mean that, don't you? I mean I wouldn't like you to think I was being ... well ... intruding,' the doctor continued while Verkramp, still protesting his delight that she should visit him as often as possible, discovered that all the clothes he had carefully laid out on the lavatory seat had got wet, thanks to her precipitate arrival. By the time he emerged Luitenant Verkramp was feeling distinctly clammy, and quite unprepared for the sight that met his eyes. Doctor von Blimenstein had taken off her musquash coat and was lying provocatively on his sofa in a bright red dress which clung to her body with an intimacy of contour which astonished Verkramp and made him wonder how she had ever got into it.

'Do you like it?' the doctor inquired stretching voluptuously. Verkramp swallowed and said that he did, very much. 'It's the new wet look in stretch nylon.' Verkramp found himself staring at her breasts hypnotically and with the terrible realization that he was committed to an evening spent in public with a woman who was wearing what amounted to a semi-transparent scarlet bodystocking. Luitenant Verkramp's reputation for sober and God-fearing living was something he had always been proud of and as a devout member of the Verwoerd Street Dutch Reformed Church he was shocked by the doctor's outfit. As he drove up to the Piltdown Hotel the only consolation he could find was that the beastly garment was so tight she wouldn't be able to dance in it. Luitenant Verkramp didn't dance. He thought it was sinful.

At the Hotel the Commissionaire opened the car door and Verkramp's sense of social inadequacy, already heightened by the knowledge that his Volkswagen was parked next to a Cadillac, was increased by the man's manner.

'I want the brassière,' Verkramp said.

'The what, sir?' said the Commissionaire with his eye on Dr von Blimenstein's bosom.

'The brassière,' said Verkramp.

'You won't find one here, sir,' the Commissionaire said. Dr von Blimenstein came to the rescue.

'The brasserie,' she said.

'Oh you mean the grill room,' the Commissionaire said and, still finding it difficult to believe the evidence of his senses, directed them to the Colour Bar. Verkramp was delighted to find the lights low so that he could sit hidden from public view in a high-backed booth in a corner. Besides, Dr von Blimenstein had come to the rescue and had ordered dry martinis from the wine waiter, who had been looking superciliously at Verkramp's efforts to find something vaguely familiar in the wine list. After three martinis Verkramp was feeling decidedly better.

Dr von Blimenstein was telling him about aversion therapy.

'It's quite straightforward,' she said. 'The patient is tied to a bed while slides of his particular perversion are projected on a screen. For instance, if you're dealing with a homosexual, you show him slides of nude men.'

'Really,' said Verkramp. 'How very interesting. What do you do then?'

'At the very moment you show him the picture, you also administer an electric shock.'

Verkramp was fascinated. 'And that cures him?' he asked.

'In the end the patient shows signs of anxiety every time a slide is shown,' said the doctor.

'I can well believe it,' said Verkramp, whose own experiments with electric shock treatment had resulted in much the same anxiety on the part of his prisoners.

'The process has to be kept up for six days to be really effective,' Dr von Blimenstein continued, 'but you'd be surprised at the number of cures we have achieved by this method.'

Verkramp said he wouldn't be in the least surprised. While they ate, Dr von Blimenstein explained that a modified form of aversion therapy was what she had in mind for treating cases of miscegenation among policemen in Piemburg. Verkramp, whose mind was cloudy with gin and wine, tried to think what she meant. 'I don't quite see ...' he began.

'Nude black women,' said the doctor, smiling across her plank steak. 'Project slides of nude black women on the screen and administer an electric shock at the same time.' Verkramp looked at her with open admiration.

'Brilliant,' he said. 'Marvellous. You're a genius.' Dr von Blimenstein simpered. 'It's not my original idea,' she said modestly, 'but I suppose you could say that I have adapted it to South African needs.'

'It's a breakthrough,' said Verkramp. '*The* breakthrough one might say.'

'One likes to think so,' murmured the doctor.

'A toast,' said Verkramp raising his glass, 'I drink to your success.'

Dr von Blimenstein raised her glass. 'To our success, darling, to our success.' They drank and as they drank it seemed to Verkramp that for the first time in his life he was really happy. He was dining in a smart hotel with a lovely woman with whose help he was about to make history. No longer would the danger of South Africa becoming a country of coloureds haunt the minds of White South Africa's leaders. With Dr von Blimenstein at his side, Verkramp would set up clinics throughout the republic where white perverts could be cured of their sexual lusts for black women by aversion therapy. He leant across the table towards her entrancing breasts and took her hand.

'I love you,' he said simply.

'I love you too,' murmured the doctor, gazing back at him with an intensity almost predatory. Verkramp looked nervously round the restaurant and was relieved to find that no one was watching them.

'In a nice way, of course,' he said after a pause.

Dr von Blimenstein smiled. 'Love isn't nice, darling,' she said. 'It's dark and violent and passionate and cruel.'

'Yes ... well ...' said Verkramp who had never looked at love in this light before. 'What I meant was that love is pure. My love, that is.'

In Dr von Blimenstein's eyes a flame seemed to flicker and die down. 'Love is desire,' she said. Beneath the nylon sheath her breasts bulged onto the table, imminent with a motherly menace that Verkramp found disturbing. He shifted his narrow legs under the table and tried to think of something to say.

'I want you,' whispered the doctor, emphasizing her need by digging her crimson fingernails into the palm of Verkramp's hand. 'I want you desperately.' Luitenant Verkramp shuddered involuntarily. Beneath the table Dr von Blimenstein's ample knees closed firmly on his leg. 'I want you,' she repeated and Verkramp, who had begun to think that he was having dinner with a volcano on heat, found himself saying, 'Isn't it time we went?' before he realized the interpretation the doctor was likely to put on his sudden desire to leave the relative safety of the restaurant.

As they went out to the car, Dr von Blimenstein put her arm through Verkramp's and held him close to her. He opened the car door for her and with a wheeze of nylon the doctor slid into her seat. Verkramp, whose previous sense of social inadequacy had been quite replaced by a feeling of sexual inadequacy in the face of the doctor's open intimation of desire, climbed in hesitantly beside her.

'You don't understand,' he said, starting the car, 'I don't want to do anything that would spoil the beauty of this evening.' In the darkness Dr von Blimenstein's hand reached out and squeezed his leg.

'You mustn't feel guilty,' she murmured. Verkramp put the car into reverse with a jerk.

'I respect you too much,' he said.

Dr von Blimenstein's musquash coat heaved softly as she leant her head on his shoulder. A heavy perfume wafted across Verkramp's face. 'You're such a shy boy,' she said.

Verkramp drove out of the hotel grounds onto the Piemburg road. Far below them the lights of the city flickered and went out. It was midnight.

Verkramp drove slowly down the hill, partly because he was afraid of being booked for drunken driving but more importantly because he was terrified by the prospect that awaited him when they got back to his flat. Twice Dr von Blimenstein insisted they stop the car and twice Verkramp found himself wrapped in her arms while her lips searched for and found his own thin mouth. 'Relax, darling,' she told him as Verkramp squirmed with a feverish mixture of refusal and consent which satisifed both his own conscience and Dr von Blimenstein's belief that he was responding. 'Sex has to be learnt.' Verkramp had no need to be told.

He started the car again and drove on while Dr von Blimenstein explained that it was quite normal for a man to be afraid of sex. By the time they reached Verkramp's flat the euphoria that had followed the doctor's explanation of how she was going to cure the miscegenating policemen had quite left him. The strange mixture of animal passion and clinical objectivity with which the doctor discussed sex had aroused in the Luitenant an aversion for the subject that no electric shocks were needed to reinforce.

'Well, that was a very nice evening,' he said hopefully, parking next to the doctor's car, but Dr von Blimenstein had no intention of leaving so soon.

'You're going to ask me up for a nighcap?' she asked and, when Verkdramp hesitated, went on, 'In any case I seem to have left my handbag in your flat so I'll have to come up for a bit.'

Verkramp led the way upstairs quietly. 'I don't want to disturb the neighbours,' he explained in a whisper. In a voice that seemed calculated to wake the dead, Dr von Blimenstein said she'd be as quiet as a mouse and followed this up by trying to kiss him while he was fumbling for his key. Once inside she took off her coat and sat on the divan with a display of leg that went some way to reawakening the desire which her conversation had quenched. Her hair spilled over the cushions and she raised her arms to him. Verkramp said he'd make some coffee and went through to the kitchen. When he came back Dr von Blimenstein had turned the main light off and a reading lamp in one corner on and was fiddling with his radio. 'Just trying to get some music,' she said. Above the divan the loudspeaker crackled. Verkramp put the coffee cups down and turned to attend to the radio but Dr von Blimenstein was no longer interested in music. She stood before him with the same gentle smile Verkramp had seen on her face the day he had first met her at the hospital and before he could escape the lovely doctor had pinned him to the divan with that expertise Verkramp had once so much admired. As her lips silenced his weak protest Luitenant Verkramp lost all sense of guilt. He was helpless in her arms and there was nothing he could do.

CHAPTER FOUR

Kommandant van Heerden emerged from the Piemburg Public Library
clutching his copy of *As Other Men Are* with a sense of anticipation he
had last experienced as a boy when he swopped comics outside the cinema
on Saturday mornings. He hurried through the street, occasionally
glancing at the cover with a cartouche on the front and with the portrait
of the great author on the back. Each time he looked at the face with its
slightly hooded eyelids and brisk moustache he was filled with that sense
of social hierarchy for which his soul hankered. All the doubts about the
existence of good and evil which twenty-five years as an officer in the
South African Police had naturally inflicted on him vanished before the
assurance that radiated from that portrait. Not that Kommandant van
Heerden had ever for a moment had reason to doubt the existence of
evil. It was the lack of its opposite that he found so spiritually debilitating,
and since the Kommandant was not given to anything approaching
conceptual thought, the goodness he sought had to be seen to be believed.
Better still it had to be personified in some socially acceptable form and
here at last, breathing an arrogance that brooked no question, the face
that looked past him from the jacket of *As Other Men Are* was proof
positive that all those values like chivalry and courage, to which
Kommandant van Heerden paid so much private tribute, still existed in
the world.

Once home and ensconced in an armchair with a pot of tea made and
a cup by his side, he opened the book and began to read. 'Eve Malory
Carew tilted her sweet pretty chin,' he read, and as he read the world
of sordid crime, of murder and fraud, burglary and assault, cowardice
and deception, with which his profession brought him into daily contact,
disappeared, to be replaced by a new world in which lovely ladies and
magnificent men moved with an ease and assurance and wit towards
inevitably happy endings. As he followed the adventures of Jeremy Broke
and Captain Toby Rage, not to mention Oliver Pauncefote and Simon
Beaulieu, the Kommandant knew that he had come home. Luitenant
Verkramp, Sergeant Breitenbach and the six hundred men under his
command were happily forgotten as the hours passed and the Kommandant, his tea stone cold, read on. Occasionally he would read some
particularly moving passage aloud to savour the words more fully. At
one o'clock in the morning he glanced at his watch and was amazed that

time had passed so unnoticeably. Still, there was no need to get up early
in the morning and he had come to another stirring episode.

'The pearls that George gave me sprawl, pale and indignant by my
side,' he read aloud in what he vainly imagined was an adequate
impersonation of a female voice, 'I've taken them off. I don't want his
pearls about me; I want your arms.'

While Kommandant van Heerden was finding it a wonderful relief to
escape from the real world of sordid experience into one of pure fantasy,
Luitenant Verkramp as doing just the opposite. Now that the sexual
fantasies he had entertained about Dr von Blimenstein through many
sleepless nights seemed all too likely to be fulfilled in reality, Verkramp
found the prospect unbearable. For one thing, the attractions which an
absent and imagined Dr von Blimenstein had held had quite disappeared,
to be replaced by the awareness that she was a heavily built woman with
enormous breasts and muscular legs whose sexual needs he had no desire
whatsoever to satisfy. And for another, the walls of his apartment were
so constructed as to allow the sounds in one flat to be clearly heard in
another. To add to his worries, the doctor was drunk.

In a foolish attempt to induce in her the feminine equivalent of whisky
droop, Verkramp had plied her with Scotch from a bottle he kept for
special occasions and had been horrified not only by the doctor's capacity
for hard liquor but also by the fact that the damned stuff seemed to act
as an aphrodisiac. Deciding to try to reverse the process, he went through
to the kitchen to make some more black coffee. He had just lit the stove
when an eruption of noise from the living-room sent him scurrying back.
Dr von Blimenstein had switched on his tape recorder.

'I want an old-fashioned house with an old-fashioned fence and an
old-fashioned millionaire,' cried Eartha Kitt.

Dr von Blimenstein accompanying her was more modest in her
demands. 'I want to be loved by you, just you and nobody else but you,'
she crooned in a voice several decibels above the legal limit.

'For heaven's sake,' said Verkramp, trying to edge past her to the tape
recorder, 'you'll wake the neighbourhood.'

In the flat above, the creak of bedsprings suggested that the Verkramp's
neighbours were taking notice of the doctor's demand even if he wasn't.

'I want to be loved by you alone, boo boopy doop,' Dr von Blimenstein
continued, clasping Verkramp in her arms. In the background Miss Kitt
added to his embarrassment by announcing to the world her desire for
oil wells and Verkramp's own predilection for coloured singers.

'Whasso wrong with love, baby?' asked the doctor, managing to combine whimsy with sex in a manner Verkramp found particularly irritating.

'Yes,' he said placatorily, trying to escape from her embrace, 'If you –'

'Were the only girl in the world and I was the only boy,' bawled the doctor.

'For God's sake,' squawked Verkramp, appalled at the prospect.

'Well, you're not,' came a voice from the flat upstairs. 'You've got me to consider.'

Spurred on by this support Verkramp squeezed out of the doctor's arms and fell back on the divan.

'Give me, give me what I long for,' sang the doctor, changing her tune.

'Some fucking sleep,' yelled the man upstairs, evidently sickened by the doctor's erratic repertoire.

In the flat next door, where a lecturer in Religious Instruction lived with his wife, someone banged on the wall.

Scrambling off the divan, Verkramp hurled himself at the tape recorder.

'Let me turn that coon girl off,' he shouted. Miss Kitt was on about diamonds now.

'Leave the coon girls alone. You've turned me on,' screamed Dr von Blimenstein, tackling Verkramp by the legs and bringing him down with a crash. Squatting on top of him she pressed herself against him with an urgency that inserted the bobble of her garter belt into his mouth, and fumbled with his trouser buttons. With a revulsion that sprang from his ignorance of female anatomy, Verkramp spat the thing out only to find himself facing an even more disgusting prospect. With his horizon bounded obscenely by thighs, garter belts and those portions of the doctor which figured so largely in his fantasies but which on closer acquaintance had quite lost their charm, Verkramp fought desperately for air.

It was at this juncture that Kommandant van Heerden unwittingly chose to intervene. Enormously amplified by Verkramp's electronic equipment, the Kommandant's falsetto voice added its peculiar charm to Miss Kitt's contralto, and Dr von Blimenstein's insistent commands to Verkramp to lie still.

'Simon,' squeaked the Kommandant, oblivious of the effect he was having half a mile away, 'that last night here we buried our love alive, our glorious, blessed passion, we buried alive.'

'Whazzat?' asked Dr von Blimenstein who had ignored all Verkramp's previous entreaties in her drunken frenzy.

'Let me go,' screamed Verkramp, to whom the Kommandant's mention of burying alive seemed particularly relevant.

'Someone's being murdered in there,' squealed the Religious Instructor's wife next door.

'I must have been mad. I suppose I thought it'd die,' continued the Kommandant.

'Whazzat?' shrieked Dr von Blimenstein again, drunkenly trying to distinguish between Verkramp's frantic screams and the Kommandant's impassioned confession, a process of decoding made no less difficult by Eartha Kitt impersonating a Turk.

On the landing the man from the flat above was threatening to break the door down.

At the centre of this maelstrom of noise and movement Luitenant Verkramp stared lividly into the vermilion flounces of Dr von Blimenstein's elaborate panties and then, overcome by the hysterical fear that he was about to be castrated, took the bit between his teeth.

With a scream that could be heard half a mile away and which had the effect of stopping the Kommandant reading aloud, Dr von Blimenstein shot forward across the room, dragging the demented Verkramp inextricably entangled in her garter belt behind.

To Luitenant Verkramp the next few minutes were a foretaste of hell. Behind him the man from the flat above, by now convinced beyond doubt that he was privy to some hideous crime, hurled himself against the door. In front Dr von Blimenstein, equally convinced that she had at last aroused her lover's sexual appetite but anxious that it should express itself in a more orthodox fashion, hurled herself onto her back. As the door burst open, Verkramp peered up through the torn vermilion flounces with all the *Weltschmerz* of a decapitated Rhode Island Red. In the doorway the man from upstairs was standing dumbfounded at the spectacle.

'Now, darling, now,' screamed Dr von Blimenstein writhing ecstatically. Verkramp scrambled furiously to his feet.

'How dare you break in?' he yelled, desperately trying to convert his embarrassment into justified rage. From the floor Dr von Blimenstein intervened more effectively.

'Coitus interruptus,' she shouted, 'coitus interruptus!' Verkramp seized on the phrase, which sounded vaguely medical to him.

'She's an epileptic,' he explained as the doctor continued to twitch. 'She's from Fort Rapier.'

'Christ,' said the man, now thoroughly embarrassed himself. The Religious Instructor's wife pushed her way into the room.

'There, there,' she said to the doctor, 'It's all right. We're here.'

In the confusion Verkramp slunk away and locked himself in his bathroom. He sat there, white with humiliation and disgust, until the ambulance arrived to take the doctor back to the hospital. In the living-room Dr von Blimenstein was still shouting drunkenly about erogenous zones and the emotional hazards of interrupted coition.

When everyone had left, Verkramp emerged from the bathroom and surveyed the mess in his living-room with a jaundiced eye. The only consolation he could find for the evening's horror was the knowledge that his suspicions about the Kommandant had been confirmed. Verkramp tried to remember what that ghastly falsetto voice had said. It was something about burying someone alive. It seemed highly unlikely somehow but Luitenant Verkramp's whole evening had been calculated to induce in him the suspicion that the most respectable people were capable of the most bizarre acts. Of one thing he was absolutely certain – he never wanted to set eyes on Dr von Blimenstein again.

Kommandant van Heerden, arriving at his office next morning freshly imbued with the determination to behave like a gentleman, felt much the same. Dr von Blimenstein's questionnaire had aroused a storm of protest in the Piemburg Police Station.

'It's part of a campaign to stop the spread of Communism,' the Kommandant explained to Sergeant de Kok, who had been deputed to express the men's sense of grievance.

'What's the size of a kaffir's teats got to do with the spread of Communism?' the Sergant wanted to know. Kommandant van Heerden agreed that the connection did seem rather obscure.

'You'd better ask Luitenant Verkramp about it,' he said. 'It's his affair, not mine. As far as I'm concerned no one need answer the beastly thing. I certainly don't intend to.'

'Yes, sir. Thank you, sir,' said the Sergeant and went off to cancel Verkramp's orders.

In the afternoon the Kommandant returned to the Golf Club in the hope of catching a glimpse of the foursome who called themselves the Dornford Yates Club. He hit a few balls into the woods for the look of the thing and returned to the Clubhouse quite shortly. As he approached the stoep, he was delighted to see the vintage Rolls steal noiselessly down the drive from the main road and park overlooking the course. Mrs Heathcote-Kilkoon was driving. She was wearing a blue sweater and skirt and matching gloves. For a moment she sat in the car and then climbed out and walked round the bonnet with a wistfulness that touched the Kommandant to the quick.

'Excuse me,' she called to him, leaning on the radiator with a gesture of elegance the Kommandant had seen only in the more expensive women's magazines, 'but I wonder if you could help me.'

Kommandant van Heerden's pulse rate went up abruptly. He said he would be honoured to help her.

'I'm such a fool,' continued Mrs Heathcote-Kilkoon, 'and I know absolutely nothing about cars. I wonder if you could just have a look at it and tell me if anything's wrong.'

With a gallantry that belied his utter ignorance of motor cars in general and vintage Rolls-Royces in particular, the Kommandant fumbled with the catches of the bonnet and was presently greasily engaged in looking for anything that might indicate why the car had so fortuitously ceased to function at the top of the Golf Club drive. Behind him Mrs Heathcote-Kilkoon urged him on with an indulgent smile and the idle chatter of a fascinating woman.

'I feel so helpless when it comes to machinery,' she murmured as the Kommandant, who shared her feelings, poked his finger into a carburettor hopefully. It didn't get very far, which he judged to be a good sign. Presently, when he had inspected the fan-belt and the dip-stick, which more or less exhausted his automotive know-how, he gave up the unequal task.

'I'm so sorry,' he said, 'but I can't see anything obviously wrong.'

'Perhaps I'm just out of petrol,' smiled Mrs Heathcote-Kilkoon. Kommandant van Heerden looked at the petrol gauge and found it registered Empty.

'That's right,' he said. Mrs Heathcote-Kilkoon breathed her apologies. 'And you've been to so much trouble too,' she murmured but Kommandant van Heerden was too happy to feel that he had been to any trouble at all.

'My pleasure,' he said blushing, and was about to go and get the grease off his hands when Mrs Heathcote-Kilkoon stopped him.

'You've been so good,' she said, 'I must buy you a drink.'

The Kommandant tried to say there was no need but she wouldn't hear of it. 'I'll telephone the garage for some petrol,' she told him, 'and then I'll join you on the verandah.'

Presently the Kommandant found himself sipping a cool drink while Mrs Heathcote-Kilkoon, sucking hers through a straw, asked him about his work.

'It must be so absolutely fascinating to be a detective,' she said. 'My husband's retired you know.'

'I didn't know,' said the Kommandant.

'Of course he still dabbles in stocks and shares,' she went on, 'but it isn't the same thing, is it?'

The Kommandant said he didn't suppose it was though he wasn't quite sure as what. While Mrs Heathcote-Kilkoon chattered on the Kommandant drank in the details of her dress, the crocodile-skin shoes, the matching handbag, the discreet pearls, and marvelled at her excellence of taste. Even the way she crossed her legs had about it a demureness Kommandant van Heerden found irresistible.

'Are your people from this part of the world?' Mrs Heathcote-Kilkoon inquired presently.

'My father had a farm in the Karoo,' the Kommandant told her. 'He used to keep goats.' He was conscious that it sounded a fairly humble occupation but from what he knew of the English they held landowners in high esteem. Mrs Heathcote-Kilkoon sighed.

'How I adore the countryside,' she said. 'That's one reason why we came to Zululand. My husband retired to Umtali after the war, you know, and we loved it up there but somehow the climate affected him and we came down here. We chose Piemburg because we both adore the atmosphere. So gorgeously *fin de siècle*, don't you think?'

The Kommandant, who didn't know what *fin de siècle* meant, said that he liked Piemburg because it reminded him of the good old days.

'You're so right,' said Mrs Heathcote-Kilkoon. 'My husband and I are absolute addicts of nostalgia. If only we could put the clock back. The elegance, the charm, the gallantry of those dear dead days beyond recall.' She sighed and the Kommandant, feeling that for once in his life he had met with a kindred spirit, sighed with her. Presently when the barman reported that the garage had put the petrol in the Rolls, the Kommandant stood up.

'I mustn't keep you,' he said politely.

'It was sweet of you to help,' Mrs Heathcote-Kilkoon said and held out her gloved hand. The Kommandant took it and with a sudden impulse that sprang from page forty-nine of *As Other Men Are* pressed it to his lips. 'Your servant,' he murmured.

He was gone before Mrs Heathcote-Kilkoon could say anything and was soon driving down into Piemburg feeling strangely elated. That evening he took *Berry & Co* from the library and went home to draw fresh inspiration from its pages.

'Where've you been?' Colonel Heathcote-Kilkoon asked when his wife arrived home.

'You'll never believe it but I've been talking with a real hairyback. Not one of your slick ones but the genuine article. Absolutely out of the Ark. You'll never believe this but he actually kissed my hand when we parted.'

'How disgusting,' said the Colonel, and went off down the garden to look at his azaleas. If there was one thing he detested after white ants and cheeky kaffirs, it was Afrikaners. In the living-room Major Bloxham was reading *Country Life*.

'I suppose they can't all be swine,' he said graciously when Mrs Heathcote-Kilkoon told him about the Kommandant, 'though for the life of me I can't remember meeting one who wasn't. I knew a fellow called Botha once in Kenya. Never washed. Does your friend wash?'

Mrs Heathcote-Kilkoon snorted and went upstairs for a rest before dinner. Lying there in the still of the late afternoon listening to the gentle swirl of the lawn sprinkler, she felt a vague regret for the life she had once led. Born in Croydon, she had come from Selsdon Road via service in the Women's Auxiliary Air Force to Nairobi where her suburban background had served to earn her a commission and a husband with money. From those carefree days she had gradually descended the dark continent, swept southward on the ebb tide of Empire and acquiring with each new latitude those exquisite pretensions Kommandant van Heerden so much admired. Now she was tired. The affectations which had been so necessary in Nairobi for any sort of social life were wasted in Piemburg, whose atmosphere was by comparison wholly lower-middle-class. She was still depressed when she dressed for dinner that night.

'What's the use of going on pretending we are what we're not when no one even cares that we aren't?' she asked plaintively. Colonel Heathcote-Kilkoon looked at her with disapproval.

'Got to keep up a good front,' he barked.

'Stiff upper lip, old girl,' said Major Bloxham, whose grandmother had kept a winkle stand in Brighton. 'Can't let the side down.'

But Mrs Heathcote-Kilkoon no longer knew which side she was on. The world to which she had been born was gone and with it the social aspirations that made life bearable. The world she had made by dint of affectation was going. After scolding the Zulu waiter for serving the soup from the wrong side, Mrs Heathcote-Kilkoon rose from the table and took her coffee into the garden. There, soundlessly pacing the lawn under the lucid night sky, she thought about the Kommandant. 'There's something so real about him,' she murmured to herself. Over their port

Colonel Heathcote-Kilkoon and the Major were discussing the Battle for Normandy. There was nothing real about them. Even the port was Australian.

CHAPTER FIVE

In the following days Kommandant van Heerden, oblivious of the interest that was being focused on him both by Luitenant Verkramp and Mrs Heathcote-Kilkoon, continued his literary pilgrimage with increased fervour. Every morning, closely shadowed by the Security men detailed by Verkramp to watch him, he would visit the Piemburg Library for a fresh volume of Dornford Yates and every evening return to his bugged home to devote himself to its study. When finally he went to bed he would lie in the darkness repeating to himself his adaptation of Coué's famous formula, 'Every day and in every way, I am becoming Berrier and Berrier,' a form of auto-suggestion that had little observable effect on the Kommandant himself but drove the eavesdropping Verkramp frantic.

'What the hell does it all mean?' he asked Sergeant Breitenbach as they listened to the tape-recording of these nocturnal efforts at self-improvement.

'A berry is a sort of fruit,' said the Sergeant without much conviction.

'It's also something you do when you want to get rid of bodies,' said Verkramp, whose own taste was more funereal, 'but why the devil does he repeat it over and over again?'

'Sounds like a sort of prayer,' Sergeant Breitenbach said. 'I had an aunt who got religious mania. She used to say her prayers all the time ...' but Luitenant Verkramp didn't want to hear about Sergeant Breitenbach's aunt.

'I want a close watch kept on him all the time,' he said, 'and the moment he starts doing anything suspicious like buying a spade let me know.'

'Why don't you ask that headshrinker of yours ...' the Sergeant asked, and was startled by the vehemence of Verkramp's reply. He left the office with the distinct impression that if there was one thing Luitenant Verkramp didn't want, need or wish for, it was Dr von Blimenstein.

Left to himself Verkramp tried to concentrate his mind on the problem of Kommandant van Heerden by looking through the reports of his movements.

'Went to Library. Went to police station. Went to Golf Club. Went home.' The regularity of these innocent activities was disheartening and yet hidden within this routine there lay the secret of the Kommandant's terrible assurance and awful smile. Even the news that his house was being bugged by Communists had shaken it only momentarily and as far as Verkramp could judge the Kommandant had entirely forgotten the affair. True, he had banned Dr von Blimenstein's questionnaire but, now that Verkramp had first-hand knowledge of the doctor's sexual behaviour, he had to admit that it was a wise decision. With what amounted to, literally, hindsight Luitenant Verkramp realized that he had been on the verge of disclosing the sexual habits of every policeman in Piemburg to a woman with vested interests in the subject. He shuddered to think what use she would have put that information to and turned his attention to the question of miscegenating policemen. It was obvious that he would have to tackle that problem without outside help and after trying to remember what Dr von Blimenstein had told him about the technique he went off to the Public Library, partly to see if there were any books there on aversion therapy but also because the Library figured so frequently in Kommandant van Heerden's itinerary. An hour later, clutching a copy of *Fact & Fiction in Psychology* by H. J. Eysenck, he returned to the police station satisfied that he had got hold of the definitive work on aversion therapy but still no nearer any understanding of the change that had come over the Kommandant. His inquiries about the Kommandant's reading habits, unconvincingly prefaced by the remark that he was thinking of buying him a book for Christmas, had elicited no more than that Kommandant ven Heerden was fond of romantic novels which wasn't very helpful.

On the other hand Dr Eysenck was. By skilful use of the index Luitenant Verkramp managed to avoid having to read those portions of the book which taxed his intellectual stamina and instead concentrated on descriptions and cures effected by apomorphine and electric shock treatment. He was particularly interested in the case of the Cross Dressing Truck Driver and the case of the Corseted Engineer both of whom had come to see the error of their ways thanks in the case of the former to injections of apomorphine and of the latter to electric shocks. The treatment seemed quite simple and Verkramp had no doubt that he would be able to administer it if only he was given the opportunity. Certainly there was no difficulty about electric shock machines. Piemburg Police Station was littered with the things and Verkramp felt sure the police surgeon would be able to supply apomorphine. The main obstacle lay in the presence of Kommandant van Heerden, whose opposition to all innovations had proved such a handicap to Luitenant Verkramp in the past. 'If only the old fool would take a holiday,' Verkramp thought as he turned to the case of the Impotent Accountant only to learn to his disappointment that the man had been cured without recourse to apomorphine or electric shocks. The Case of the Prams and Handbags was much more interesting.

While Verkramp tried to forget Dr von Blimenstein by immersing himself in the study of abnormal psychology, the doctor, unaware of the fatal impact her sexuality had had on Verkramp's regard for her, tried desperately to remember the full details of their night together. All she could recall was arriving at Casualty Department of Piemburg Hospital classified according to the ambulance driver as an epileptic. When that misunderstanding had been cleared up she had been diagnosed as blind drunk and could vaguely remember having her stomach pumped out before being bundled into a taxi and sent back to Fort Rapier where her appearance had led to an unpleasant interview with the Hospital Principal the following morning. Since then she had telephoned Verkramp several times only to find that his line seemed to be permanently engaged. In the end she gave up and decided that it was unladylike to pursue him. 'He'll come back to me in due course,' she said smugly. 'He won't be able to keep away.' Every night after her bath she admired Verkramp's teeth marks in the mirror and slept with her torn vermilion panties under the pillow as proof of the Luitenant's devotion to her. 'Strong oral needs,' she thought happily, and her breasts heaved in anticipation.

Mrs Heathcote-Kilkoon was too much of a lady to have any doubts about the propriety of her acquaintance with Kommandant van Heerden. Every afternoon the vintage Rolls would steal down the drive of the golf course and Mrs Heathcote-Kilkoon would play a round of very good golf until the Kommandant arrived. Then she would save him the embarrassment of displaying his ineptness with a golf club by engaging him in conversation.

'You must think I'm absolutely frightful,' she murmured one afternoon as they sat on the verandah.

The Kommandant said he didn't think anything of the sort.

'I suppose it's because I've had so little experience of the real world,' she continued, 'that I find it so fascinating to meet a man with so much *je ne sais quoi*.'

'Oh, I don't know about that,' said the Kommandant modestly. Mrs Heathcote-Kilkoon wagged a gloved finger at him.

'And witty too,' she said though the Kommandant couldn't imagine what she was talking about. 'One somehow never expects a man in a position of responsibility to have a sense of humour and being the Kommandant of Police in a town the size of Piemburg must be an awesome responsibility. There must be nights when you simply can't get to sleep for worry.'

The Kommandant could think of several nights recently when he couldn't sleep but he wasn't prepared to admit it.

'When I go to bed,' he said, 'I go to sleep. I don't worry.' Mrs Heathcote-Kilkoon looked at him with admiration.

'How I envy you, she said, 'I suffer terribly from insomnia. I lie awake thinking about how things have changed in my lifetime and remembering the good old days in Kenya before those awful Mau-Mau came along and spoilt everything. Now look what a horrible mess the blacks have made of the country. Why they've even stopped the races at Thomson's Falls.' She sighed and the Kommandant commiserated with her.

'You should try reading in bed,' he suggested. 'Some people find that helps.'

'But what?' Mrs Heathcote-Kilkoon asked in a tone which suggested she had read everything there was to read.

'Dornford Yates,' said the Kommandant promptly and was delighted to find Mrs Heathcote-Kilkoon staring at him in astonishment. It was precisely the effect he had hoped for.

'You too?' she gasped. 'Are you a fan?'

The Kommandant nodded.

'Isn't he marvellous?' Mrs Heathcote-Kilkoon continued breathlessly, 'Isn't he absolutely brilliant? My husband and I are devoted to him. Absolutely devoted. That's one of the reasons we went to live in Umtali. Just to be near him. Just to breathe the same air he breathed and to know that we were living in the same town as the great man. It was a wonderful experience. Really wonderful.' She paused in her recital of the literary amenities of Umtali long enough for the Kommandant to say that he was surprised Dornford Yates had lived in Rhodesia. 'I've always pictured him in England,' he said, conveniently forgetting that always in this case meant a week.

'He came out during the war,' Mrs Heathcote-Kilkoon explained, 'and then went back to the house at Eaux Bonnes in the Pyrenees afterwards, the House That Berry Built you know but the French were so horrid and everything so terribly changed that he couldn't stand it and settled in Umtali till his death.'

The Kommandant said he was sorry he had died and that he would like to have known him.

'It was a great privilege,' Mrs Heathcote-Kilkoon agreed sadly. 'A very great privilege to know a man who has enriched the English language.' She paused in memory for a moment before continuing. 'How extraordinary that you should find him so wonderful. I mean I don't want to ... well ... I always thought he appealed only to the English and to find a true Afrikaner who likes him ...' she trailed off, evidently afraid of offending him. Kommandant van Heerden assured her that Dornford Yates was the sort of Englishman Afrikaners most admired.

'Really,' said Mrs Heathcote-Kilkoon, 'you do amaze me. He'd have loved to hear you say that. He had such a loathing for foreigners himself.'

'I can understand that too,' said the Kommandant. 'They're not very nice people.'

By the time they parted Mrs Heathcote-Kilkoon had said that the Kommandant must meet her husband and the Kommandant had said he would be honoured to.

'You must come and stay at White Ladies,' Mrs Heathcote-Kilkoon said as the Kommandant opened the door of the Rolls for her.

'Which white lady's?' the Kommandant inquired. Mrs Heathcote-Kilkoon reached out a gloved hand and tweaked his ear.

'Naughty,' she said delightfully, 'naughty, witty man,' and drove off leaving the Kommandant wondering what he had said to merit the charming rebuke.

'You've done what?' Colonel Heathcote-Kilkoon asked apoplectically when she told him that she had invited the Kommandant to stay. 'At White Ladies? A bloody Boer? I won't hear of it. My God, you'll be asking Indians or niggers next. I don't care what you say, I'm not having the swine in my house.'

Mrs Heathcote-Kilkoon turned to Major Bloxham. 'You explain, Boy, he'll listen to you,' and took herself to her room with a migraine.

Major Bloxham found the Colonel among his azaleas and was disheartened by his florid complexion.

'You ought to take it easy, old chap,' he said. 'Blood pressure and all that.'

'What do you expect when that damned woman tells me she's invited some blue-based baboon to come and stay at White Ladies?' the Colonel snarled, gesticulating horridly with his pruning shears.

'A bit much,' said the Major placatorily.

'A bit? It's a damned sight too much if you ask me. Not that anyone does round here. Sponging swine,' and he disappeared into a bush leaving the Major rather hurt by the ambiguity of the remark.

'Seems he's a fan of the Master,' said the Major addressing himself to a large blossom.

'Hm,' snorted the Colonel who had transferred his attentions to a rhododendron, 'I've heard that tale before. Says that to get his foot in the door and before you know what's happened the whole damned club is full of 'em.'

Major Bloxham said there was something to be said for that point of view but that the Kommandant sounded quite genuine. The Colonel disagreed.

'Used to wave a white flag and shoot our officers down,' he shouted. 'Can't trust a Boer further than you can see him.'

'But ...' said the Major trying to keep track of the Colonel's physical whereabouts while staying with his train of thought.

'But me no buts,' shouted the Colonel from a hydrangea. 'The man's a scoundrel. Got coloured blood too. All Afrikaners have a touch of the tar. A known fact. Not having a nigger in my house.' His voice distant in the shrubbery rumbled on to the insistent click of the secateurs and Major Bloxham turned back towards the house. Mrs Heathcote-Kilkoon, her migraine quite recovered, was drinking a sundowner on the stoep.

'Intransigent, my dear,' said the Major treading warily past the chihuahua that lay at her feet. 'Utterly intransigent.' Proud of his use of such a diplomatically polysyllabic communiqué the Major poured himself a double whisky. It was going to be a long hard evening.

'Cub hunting season,' said the Colonel over avocado pears at dinner. 'Look forward to that.'

'Fox in good form?' asked the Major.

'Harbinger's been keeping him in trim,' said the Colonel, 'been taking him for a ten-mile trot every morning. Good man, Harbinger, knows his job.'

'Damn fine whipper-in,' said the Major, 'Harbinger.'

At the far end of the polished mahogany table Mrs Heathcote-Kilkoon gouged her avocado resentfully.

'Harbinger's a convict,' she said presently. 'You got him from the prison at Weezen.'

'Poacher turned gamekeeper,' said the Colonel, who disliked his wife's new habit of intruding a sense of reality into his world of reassuring artifice. 'Make the best sort, you know. Good with dogs too.'

'Hounds,' said Mrs Heathcote-Kilkoon reprovingly. 'Hounds, dear, never dogs.'

Opposite her the Colonel turned a deeper shade of puce.

'After all,' continued Mrs Heathcote-Kilkoon before the Colonel could think of a suitable reply, 'if we are going to pretend we're county and that we've ridden to hounds for countless generations, we might as well do it properly.'

Colonel Heathcote-Kilkoon regarded his wife venomously. 'You forget yourself, my dear,' he said at last.

'How right you are,' Mrs Heathcote-Kilkoon answered, 'I have forgotten myself. I think we all have.' She rose from the table and left the room.

'Extraordinary behaviour,' said the Colonel. 'Can't think what's come over the woman. Used to be perfectly normal.'

'Perhaps it's the heat,' suggested the Major.

'Heat?' said the Colonel.

'The weather,' Major Bloxham explained hurriedly. 'Hot weather makes people irritable, don't you know.'

'Hot as hell in Nairobi. Never bothered her there. Can't see why it should give her the habdabs here.'

They finished their meal in silence and the Colonel took his coffee through to his study where he listened to the stockmarket report on the radio. Gold shares were up, he noted thankfully. He would ring his broker in the morning and tell him to sell West Driefontein. Then switching the radio off he went to the bookshelf and took down a copy of *Berry & Co.* and settled down to read it for the eighty-third time. Presently, unable to concentrate, he laid the book aside and went out on to the stoep where Major Bloxham was sitting in the darkness with a glass of whisky looking out at the lights of the city far below.

'What are you doing, Boy?' asked the Colonel with something akin to affection in his voice.

'Trying to remember what winkles taste like,' said the Major. 'Such a long time since I had them.'

'Prefer oysters meself,' said the Colonel. They sat together in silence for some time. In the distance some Zulus were singing.

'Bad business,' the Colonel said, breaking the silence. 'Can't have Daphne upset. Can't have this damned fellow either. Don't know what to do.'

'Don't suppose we can,' agreed the Major. 'Pity we can't put him off somehow.'

'Put him off?'

'Tell him we've got foot-and-mouth or something,' said the Major whose career was littered with dubious excuses. Colonel Heathcote-Kilkoon considered the idea and rejected it.

'Wouldn't wash,' he said finally.

'Never do. Boers,' said the Major.

'Foot-and-mouth.'

'Oh.'

There was a long pause while they stared into the night.

'Bad business,' said the Colonel in the end and went off to bed. Major Bloxham sat on thinking about shellfish.

In her room Mrs Heathcote-Kilkoon lay under one sheet unable to sleep and listened to the Zulus' singing and the occasional murmur of voices from the stoep with increasing bitterness. 'They'll humiliate him if he comes,' she thought, recalling the miseries of her youth when napkins had been serviettes and lunch dinner. It was the thought of the humiliation she would suffer by proxy as the Kommandant fumbled for the fish fork for the meat course that finally decided Mrs Heathcote-Kilkoon. She switched on the light and sat at her writing table and wrote a note on mauve deckle-edged paper to the Kommandant.

'You're going to town, Boy?' she asked the Major next morning at breakfast. 'Pop this into the police station will you?' She slid the envelope across the table to him.

'Right you are,' said Major Bloxham. He hadn't intended going to Piemburg but his position in the household demanded just this sort of sacrifice. 'Putting him off?'

'Certainly not,' Mrs Heathcote-Kilkoon said looking coldly at her husband. 'Compromising. It's the English art or so I've been led to believe. I've said we're full up and ...'

'Damned good show, my dear,' interrupted the Colonel.

'And I've asked him if he would mind putting up at the hotel instead. He can have lunch and dinner with us and I trust you'll have the decency to treat him properly if he accepts.'

'Seems a fair arrangement to me,' said the Colonel.

'Very fair,' the Major agreed.

'It's the least I can do,' said Mrs Heathcote-Kilkoon, 'in the circumstances. I've told him you'll foot the bill.'

She got up and went into the kitchen to vent her irritation on the black servants.

At Piemburg Police Station Kommandant van Heerden was busy making arrangements for his holiday. He had bought a map of the Weezen district, a trout rod and flies, a pair of stout walking boots, a deerstalker hat, a twelve-bore shotgun, some waders, and a pocket book called *Etiquette for Everyman*. Thus accoutred he felt confident that his stay with the Heathcote-Kilkoons would give him valuable experience in the art of behaving like an English gentleman.

He had even gone to the trouble of buying two pairs of pyjamas and some new socks because his old ones had mended holes in them. Having acquired the outward vestiges of Englishness, the Kommandant had practised saying 'Frightfully' and 'Absolutely' in what he hoped was an authentic accent. When it was dark he went into his garden with the trout rod and practised casting flies into a bucket of water on the lawn without ever managing to land a fly in the bucket but decapitating several dozen dahlias in the attempt.

'Practising what?' Luitenant Verkramp asked incredulously when his men reported this new activity to him.

'Fishing from a bucket,' the Security men told him.

'He's off his rocker,' Verkramp said.

'Keeps muttering to himself too. Repeats "Fascinating" and "Pleased to make your acquaintance, sir" over and over again.'

'I know that,' said Verkramp who had listened in to the Kommandant's monologue on his radio.

'Here's a list of all the things he's bought,' said another Security man. Verkramp looked down the list of waders and deerstalkers and boots, completely mystified.

'What's all this about him meeting some woman at the Golf Club?' he asked. He had never given up his original idea that the Kommandant was engaged in some sort of illicit love affair.

'Chats her up every day,' the Security men told him. 'Plump little thing with dyed hair aged about fifty-five. Drives an old Rolls.'

Verkramp gave orders to his men to find out all they could about Mrs Heathcote-Kilkoon and went back to his study of *Fact & Fiction in Psychology*. He had no sooner started than his phone rang with a message that the Kommandant wanted to see him. Verkramp put the book away and went along the passage to the Kommandant's office.

'Ah, Verkramp,' said the Kommandant, 'I'm taking a fortnight's leave as from Friday and I'm leaving you in charge here.' Luitenant Verkramp was delighted.

'Sorry to hear that, sir,' he said diplomatically. 'We'll miss you.' The Kommandant looked up unpleasantly. He didn't for one moment believe that Verkramp would miss him, particularly when he had been left in command.

'How are you getting on in the search for those Communists?' he asked.

'Communists?' said Verkramp, puzzled for a moment. 'Oh well it's a long business sir. Results take a long time.'

'They must do,' said the Kommandant feeling that he had punctured Verkramp's irritating complacency a bit. 'Well, while I'm away I expect you to concentrate on routine crime and the maintenance of law and order. I don't want to find that rapes, burglaries and murders have gone up in my absence. Understand?'

'Yes sir,' said Verkramp. The Kommandant dismissed him and Verkramp went back to his office in high spirits. The opportunity he had been waiting for had arrived at long last. He sat down at his desk and considered the manifold possibilities offered by his new authority.

'A fortnight,' he thought. 'A fortnight in which to show what I can really do.' It wasn't long but Luitenant Verkramp had no intention of wasting time. There were two things he had particularly in mind. With the Kommandant out of the way he would put into effect Plan Red Rout. Crossing to his safe he took out the folder in which all the details of the operation were kept. Months before he had drawn up the plan in secret. It was time to put it into practice. By the time Kommandant van Heerden returned from his holiday, Luitenant Verkramp was certain that he would have uncovered the network of saboteurs he was convinced was operating in Piemburg.

During the course of the morning Verkramp made a number of phone calls and in various firms throughout the city employees who didn't normally receive phone calls during working hours were called to the phone. In each case the procedure was the same.

'The mamba is striking,' said Verkramp.

'The cobra has struck,' said the secret agent. Designed as an infallible method of communicating the order to his agents to meet him at their prearranged rendezvous, it had its disadvantages.

'What was all that about?' the girl agent 745396's office asked when he put down the phone after what could hardly be called a prolonged conversation.

'Nothing,' agent 745396 replied hastily.

'You said "The cobra has struck,"' said the girl, 'I distinctly heard you. What cobra's struck? That's what I want to know.'

All over Piemburg Verkramp's system of code words aroused interest and speculation in the offices where his secret agents worked.

That afternoon Luitenant Verkramp, disguised as a motor mechanic and driving a breakdown truck, left town for the first of his appointments, and half an hour later ten miles out on the Vlockfontein road was bending over the engine of 745396's car pretending to mend a broken distributor to lend verisimilitude to his disguise while giving 745396 his instructions.

'Get yourself fired,' Verkramp told the agent.

'Done that already,' said 745396 who had taken the afternoon off without permission.

'Good,' said Verkramp wondering how the hell he was going to get the distributor together again. 'I want you to work full-time from now on.'

'Doing what?'

'Infiltrating the revolutionary movement in Zululand.'

'Where do I start?' 745396 asked.

'Start hanging about Florian's café and the Colonial Bar. Plenty of students and Commies go there. The University canteen is another place where subversives gather,' Verkramp explained.

'I know all that,' said 745396. 'Last time I went there I got chucked out on my ear.'

'The last time you went there you hadn't blown anything up,' said Verkramp. 'This time you won't just say you're a saboteur, you'll be able to prove it.'

'How?'

Verkramp led the way round to the cab of his breakdown truck and handed the agent a packet. 'Gelignite and fuses,' he explained. 'On Saturday night blow the transformer on the Durban road. Put it there at eleven and get back into town before it goes up. It's got a fifteen-minute fuse.'

745396 looked at him in astonishment. 'Jesus wept,' he said, 'you really mean it?'

'Of course I do,' snapped Verkramp, 'I've given the matter a lot of thought and it's obviously the only way to infiltrate the sabotage movement. No one's going to doubt the dedication to the Communist party of a man who's blown up a transformer.'

'I don't suppose they are,' 745396 agreed nervously. 'What happens if I get arrested?'

'You won't be,' Verkramp said.

'That's what you told me when I had to pass those messages in the men's lavatory in the Market Square,' said 745396, 'and I got nabbed for soliciting.'

'That was different. Uniformed branch got you that time.'

'Uniformed branch could get me this time,' said 745396. 'You never know.'

'I'm in charge of the uniformed branch from now on. I'm Kommandant from Friday,' Verkramp explained. 'And anyway who paid your fine?'

'You did,' 745396 admitted, 'but I got the publicity. You want to try working in an office where everyone thinks you make a habit of soliciting old men in public lavatories. It took me months to live that down and I had to move my lodgings five times.'

'We've all got to make sacrifices for a White South Africa,' said Verkramp, 'which reminds me. I want you to move your digs every few days. That's what real saboteurs do and you've got to be really convincing this time.'

'All right, so I blow the transformer. What then?'

'Do as I say. Mingle with the students and the lefties and let it be known you're a saboteur. You'll soon find the swine letting you in on their plans.'

745396 was doubtful. 'How do I prove I blew the transformer?' he asked. Verkramp considered the problem.

'You've got a point there,' he agreed, 'I suppose if you could show them some gelignite it would do the trick.'

'Fine,' said 745396 sarcastically, 'and where do I get gelly from? I don't keep the stuff handy you know.'

'The police armoury,' said Verkramp, 'I'll have a key cut and you can take some out when you need it.'

'What do I do when I've found the real saboteurs?' 745396 asked.

'Get them to blow something up and inform me before they do so that we can nab the bastards,' said Verkramp, and having arranged to drop the key of the police armoury at an arranged spot, he handed over 500 rand from Security Branch funds for expenses and left 745396 to fix the distributor he had taken to bits.

'Remember to get them to blow something up before we arrest them,' Verkramp told the agent before he left. 'It's important that we have proof of sabotage so we can hang the swine. I don't want any conspiracy trials this time. I want proof of terrorism.'

He drove off to his next rendezvous and during the course of the next two days twelve secret agents had left their jobs and had been given targets round Piemburg to destroy. Twelve keys for the police armoury had been cut and Verkramp felt confident that he was about to strike a blow for freedom and Western Civilization in Piemburg which would significantly advance his career.

Back in his office Luitenant Verkramp checked the scheme and memorized all the details carefully before burning the file on Operation Red Rout as an added precaution against a security leak. He was particularly proud of his system of secret agents whom he had recruited separately over the years and paid out of the funds allocated by BOSS for informers. Each agent used a *nom de guerre* and was known to Verkramp only by his so that there was nothing to connect him with BOSS. The method by which the agents reported back to him was similarly devious and consisted of coded messages placed in 'drops' where they were collected by Verkramp's security men. Each day of the week had a different code and a different 'drop' which ensured that Verkramp's men never met his agents, of whose existence they were only vaguely aware. The fact that the system was complex and that there were seven codes and seven drops for each agent and that there were twelve agents would have meant that there was an enormous amount of work being done had it not been for lack of Communist and subversive activity in Piemburg to be reported. In the past Verkramp had been lucky to receive more than one coded message per week, and that inevitably of no value. Now it would be different and he looked forward to an influx of information.

Having initiated Operation Red Rout, Luitenant Verkramp considered his second campaign, that against miscegenating policemen, which he had code-named White Wash. Out of deference to Dr Eysenck he had decided to try apomorphine injections as well as electric shock and sent Sergeant Breitenbach to a wholesale chemist with an order for one hundred hypodermic syringes and two gallons of apomorphine.

'Two gallons?' asked the chemist incredulously. 'Are you sure you've got this right?'

'Quite sure,' said Sergeant Breitenbach.

'And a hundred hypodermics?' asked the chemist, who still couldn't believe his ears.

'That's what I said.' insisted the Sergeant.

'I know that's what you said but it doesn't seem possible,' the chemist told him. 'What in God's name are you going to do with two gallons?'

Sergeant Breitenbach had been briefed by Verkramp.

'It's for curing alcoholics,' he said.

'Dear God,' said the chemist, 'I didn't know there was that number of alcoholics in the country.'

'It makes them sick,' the Sergeant explained.

'You can say that again,' muttered the chemist. 'With two gallons you could probably kill them all off too. Probably block the sewage system into the bargain. Anyway I can't supply it.'

'Why not?'

'Well for one thing I haven't got two gallons and wouldn't know where to get it and for another you need a doctor's prescription and I doubt if any doctor in his right mind would prescribe two gallons of apomorphine anyway.'

Sergeant Breitenbach reported his refusal to Luitenant Verkramp.

'Need a doctor's prescription,' he said.

'You can get one from the police surgeon,' Verkramp told him and the Sergeant went down to the police morgue where the surgeon was performing an autopsy on an African who had been beaten to death during questioning.

'Natural causes,' he wrote on the death certificate before attending to Sergeant Breitenbach.

'There's a limit to what I'm prepared to do, said the surgeon with a sudden display of professional ethics. 'I've got my Hippocratic oath to consider and I'm not issuing prescriptions for two gallons. A thousand cc is the most I'll do and if Verkramp wants anything more out of them he'll have to tickle their throats with a feather.'

'Is that enough?'

'At 3cc a dose you should get 330 pukes,' said the surgeon. 'Don't overdo it though. I've got my work cut out signing death certificates as it is.'

'Stingy old bastard,' said Verkramp when Sergeant Breitenbach returned from the chemist with twenty hypodermics and 1000 cc of apomorphine. 'The next thing we need is slides of kaffir girls in the raw. You can get the police photographer to take those as soon as the Kommandant leaves on Friday.'

While his deputy was making these preparations for Kommandant van Heerden's holiday, the Kommandant was adjusting himself to the change of plans occasioned by Mrs Heathcote-Kilkoon's letter. He was just passing the desk in the police station when Major Bloxham arrived.

'A letter for Kommandant van Heerden,' said the Major.

Kommandant van Heerden turned back. 'That's me,' he said. 'Pleased to make your acquantance,' and shook the Major's hand vigorously.

'Bloxham, Major,' said the Major nervously. Police stations always had this effect on him.

The Kommandant opened the mauve envelope and glanced at the letter.

'Hunting season. Always the same,' said the Major, by way of explanation, and alarmed by the suffusion of blood to the Kommandant's face. 'Damned awkward. Sorry.'

Kommandant van Heerden stuffed the letter hurriedly into his pocket.

'Yes. Well. Hm,' he said awkwardly.

'Any message?'

'No. Yes. I'll stay at the hotel,' said the Kommandant and was about to shake hands again. But Major Bloxham had already left the police station and was getting his breath back in the street. The Kommandant went upstairs to his office and read the letter again in a state of considerable agitation. It was hardly the sort of letter he had expected to receive from Mrs Heathcote-Kilkoon.

'Darling Van,' he read, 'I feel so terrible writing to you like this but I'm sure you'll understand. Aren't husbands a frightful bore? It's just that Henry's being awkward and I would so love to have you but I think it would be better for all our sakes if you stayed at the hotel. It's this wretched club thing of his and he's so stubborn and anyway I'm sure you'll be more comfortable there and you can come and eat with us. Please say you will and don't be angry, Your loving Daphne.' It was heavily scented.

Unaccustomed as he was to receiving perfumed letters on mauve deckle-edged paper from other men's wives, the Kommandant found the contents quite bewildering. What Mrs Heathcote-Kilkoon meant by calling him Darling Van and describing her husband as a dreadful bore he could only surmise, but he was hardly surprised that Henry was being awkward. Given half an inkling that his wife was writing letters like this, the Colonel had every right to be awkward and the Kommandant, recalling the Major's enigmatic remark about the hunting season being always the same, shuddered.

On the other hand the notion that he found favour in Mrs Heathcote-Kilkoon's eyes, and if the letter was anything to go by there wasn't much doubt about that, appealed to the chivalrous instincts of the Kommandant. Of course, he wouldn't be angry. Circumspect certainly but not angry. After consulting *Etiquette for Everyman* to see what it had to say about replying to amorous letters from married women and finding it of little use, the Kommandant began to draft a reply. As he couldn't decide for ten minutes whether to use Dearest, My Dear, of simply Dear the letter took some considerable time to write and in its final form read, 'dearest Daphne, Kommandant van Heerden has pleasure in accepting Colonel & Mrs Heathcote-Kilkoon's kind invitation to stay at the hotel. He also has pleasure in accepting your invitation to dinner. Yours affectionately, Van,' which the Kommandant thought was a nice blend of informal and formal and unlikely to offend anyone. He sent it up by police messenger to the Heathcote-Kilkoons' house at Piltdown. Then he turned his attention to the map and planned his route to Weezen. Lying at the foot of the Aardvark mountains the little town had something of a reputation as a health resort – had once in fact been something of a spa – but in recent years had been forgotten like Piemburg itself and replaced as a holiday centre by the skyscrapers and motels along the coast.

CHAPTER SIX

On Friday morning the Kommandant was up early and on the road to Weezen. He had packed his fishing rod and the paraphernalia he had acquired for his holiday in the boot of his car the night before and was wearing his Norfolk jacket and brown brogues. As he drove up the long hill out of Piemburg he looked down at the red tin roofs without regret. It was a long time since he had permitted himself a holiday and he was looking forward to learning at first hand how the British aristocracy really lived on their country estates. As the sun rose the Kommandant turned off the national road at Leopard's River and was presently bucketing over the corrugations of the dirt road towards the mountains. Around him the countryside varied according to the race of its occupants, being gentle undulating grassland in the white areas and, down by the Voetsak River which was part of Pondoland and therefore a black area, badly eroded scrub country where goats climbed the lower branches of the trees to gnaw at the leaves. The Kommandant practised being British by smiling at the Africans by the side of the road but got little response and after a while gave it up. At Sjambok he stopped for morning coffee which he asked for in English instead of his usual Afrikaans and was delighted when the Indian waiter diplomatically asked him if he was an overseas visitor.

He left Sjambok in high spirits and an hour later was threading the pass over Rooi Nek. At the top he stopped and got out of the car to look at the countryside which had figured recently so much in his imagination. The reality exceeded his expectations. Weezen lay on a rolling upland of gentle hills and meadows through which streams meandered to a lazy river glinting in the distance. Here and there a wood darkened a hillside or bordered the river to add a darker green to the landscape, or a grove of trees sheltered a farmhouse. In the distance the mountains rose in a great crescent above the rolling plateau and above them again a sky of impeccable blue darkened towards the meridian. To Kommandant van Heerden, emerging from the dusty dryness of the Rooi Nek pass, the countryside before him spoke of the shires of England. 'It's just like a picture on a biscuit-tin,' he murmured ecstatically, 'only more real,' before climbing back into the hot seat of his car and driving on down the curving dirt road into Weezen.

Here again his hopes were more than realized. The little town, hardly more than a village, was unspoilt. A stone-built church with a lych-gate, a colonial baronial town hall with rusting metal gargoyles, and a row of shops with an arcade looked onto a square in the centre of which Queen Victoria sat plumply staring with evident distaste over a kaffir who was lying asleep on a bench in the garden at her feet. Whatever else had changed in South Africa since her Diamond Jubilee it was clear that Weezen hadn't and the Kommandant, for whom the British Empire still retained its magic, rejoiced in the fact. 'No pot-smoking long-hairs lounging about juke boxes here,' he thought happily, stopping the car and entering a trading store which smelt of sacks and polish. He asked a tall gaunt man the way to the hotel.

'Bar or bed?' the man asked with a taciturnity the Kommandant felt was wholly authentic.

'Bed,' said the Kommandant.

'That'll be Willow Water,' the man told him. 'Half a mile on. There's a sign.'

The Kommandant went out and drove on. 'Willow Water Guest Farm,' said a sign and the Kommandant turned in down a narrow drive lined with blue gums to a low stucco building which looked less like an hotel than an abandoned pumping station of a defunct waterworks. The Kommandant stopped his car uncertainly on the mossy forecourt and looked at the building without enthusiasm. Whatever it was it wasn't what he had expected. Above the doorway he could just make out the faded inscription Weezen Spa and Philosophical Society, made pointillist by the suckers of some long-since decayed creeper. He got out and climbed the steps to the little terrace and peered through the revolving door into the interior vaguely aware that several large flies, trapped in the door, were buzzing insistently. Neither their presence nor what he could see of the foyer suggested that the place was much frequented. The Kommandant pushed through the revolving door and leaving the flies trapped on the other side stood looking around him at the white-tiled hall. Light from a glass dome in the roof illuminated what appeared to be an inquiry desk in a niche at the far end and the Kommandant crossed to it and banged the brass bell that stood there on the marble top. 'I've come to the wrong place,' he thought looking uneasily at a plaque above a doorway which said Thermal Douche No 1, and he was about to make his way back to town when a door slammed somewhere in the distance to be followed by the sound of slippers shuffling along the corridor and an elderly man appeared.

'Is this the Weezen Hotel?' the Kommandant asked.

'Don't serve drinks,' said the old man.

'I don't want a drink,' said the Kommandant, 'I'm supposed to be staying at the Weezen Hotel. A room has been booked for me by Mrs Heathcote-Kilkoon if this is the right place.'

The old man shuffled round the marble-topped desk and rooted under it for a book.

'Sign here,' he said putting the book in front of the Kommandant. 'Name, address, age, occupation and disease.' Kommandant van Heerden looked at the register with growing alarm.

'I'm sure I've come to the wrong place,' he said.

'Only hotel in Weezen you can stay in,' the old man told him. 'If you want a drink you'll have to go into town. We haven't a licence.'

The Kommandant sighed and signed the register.

'There's nothing wrong with me,' he said when he got to Disease.

'Put Obesity,' said the old man. 'Got to have something. Any next of kin?'

'I've got a second cousin in Wakkerstrom,' the Kommandant said unhappily.

'That'll do,' said the old man. 'You can have Colonic Irrigation No 6.'

'For God's sake,' said the Kommandant, 'I don't need Colonic Irrigation. There's absolutely nothing the matter with me.'

'Throat and Nose No 4 is vacant too but you don't have the same view,' said the old man shuffling off down the corridor. Reluctantly the Kommandant followed him past rooms whose enamel plaques ranged from Galvanic Therapy No 8 to Inhalation No 12. At the far end of the corridor the old man stopped outside Colonic Irrigation No 6 and unlocked the door.

'Mind the cold tap,' he said. 'It's a bit hot.'

The Kommandant followed him into the room and looked round. A white-painted bed of the sort he had last seen in hospital stood in one corner with a wardrobe whose mirror was mottled and stained. More to the point and entirely confirming the plaque on the door was a series of glazed troughs, tubs and pans which stood at the far end of the room together with a maze of brass taps and tubes whose purpose the Kommandant had no wish to explore. To add to the clinical inhospitality of the room the walls were covered in white tiles.

'Gets the sun in the morning,' said the old man. 'And the view is lovely.'

'I daresay,' said the Kommandant looking at the frosted glass windows. 'What's that smell?'

'Sulphur in the water,' the old man said. 'Want to have a look at Nose and Throat?'

'I think I'd better,' said the Kommandant. They went out into the corridor and down a side passage.

'Much better take Colonic Irrigation,' the old man told him, ushering the Kommandant into a small dark room which, while it contained less sinister eqiupment, emanated an even stronger smell of sulphur. Kommandant van Heerden shook his head.

'I'll have the first room,' he said, unable to bring himself to use words which might lead to misunderstanding. 'I'm only staying,' he explained as they went back. 'Visiting the district.'

'Well if there's anything I can do, let me know,' said the old man. 'Lunch will be in the Pump Room in half an hour,' and shuffled off leaving the Kommandant sitting on the edge of his bed surveying his room with a deep sense of disappointment. Presently he got up and went to look for someone to carry his things in. In the end he had to do it himself and arranged his bags and fishing rods as best he could to obscure the taps and tubes that so disturbed him. Then he opened the window and standing on one of the pans looked out. As the old man had said the view was lovely. Below him weedy paths led down beside what had once been a lawn to the river which was bordered, not, as the signpost had suggested, by willows, but by some trees with which the Kommandant was unfamiliar. But it was not the immediate vicinity that held his attention, not even the enormous drainpipe partially disguised as a rockery that ran, doubtless carrying tons of hideous effluent, down to the river, but the mountains. Seen from the head of Rooi Nek they had looked impressive. From Colonic Irrigation No 6 they were majestic. Their lower slopes clothed in the raiment of wattle and thorn and gum, they rose imperiously through meadows where goats munched precariously among the boulders to scree and krantz and the vacant sky.

'Must be baboons up there,' thought the Kommandant poetically and clambering down from his own eminence which was, he noted, manufactured by Fisons & Sons of Hartlepool, makers of Glazed Sanitary ware, went in search of the dining-room and lunch.

He found it in the Pump Room, a large room with a miniature marble fountain in the centre which gurgled incessantly and from which emanated the smell the Kommandant found so unusual in his room. Here, blending

with the odour of boiled cabbage from the kitchen, it was less mineral
than vegetable and the Kommandant seated himself near a window
overlooking the terrace. There were three other tables occupied in the
room which had clearly been designed to hold a hundred. Two elderly
ladies with suspiciously short hair conversed in whispers in one corner
while a man whom the Kommandant took to be a salesman sat at a
table near the fountain.

Nobody said anything to him and the Kommandant, having ordered
his lunch from the coloured waitress, tried to enter into a conversation
with the salesman.

'You come here often?' he asked above the gurgle of the fountain.

'Flatulence. They're stones,' said the young man, indicating the two
ladies in the corner.

'Really,' said the Kommandant.

'Your first time here?' asked the man.

The Kommandant nodded.

'Grows on you,' said the man. Not wishing to hear, the Kommandant
finished his meal in silence and went out into the foyer to look for the
telephone.

'You'll have to go into the village for that,' the old man told him.

'Where do the Heathcote-Kilkoons live?'

'Oh them,' said the old man with a sniff. 'Can't phone them. They're
too snooty for that. Offered a party line, they were and turned it down.
Not sharing a line with anyone they aren't. Want their privacy, they do.
And if what they say is true, they need it.' He disappeared into a room
marked Manipulation leaving the Kommandant with no alternative but
to drive to town and ask the way to the Heathcote-Kilkoons' there.

In Piemburg Kommandant van Heerden's absence had already brought
changes. Luitenant Verkramp arrived early and ensconced himself in the
Kommandant's office.

'The following men to report to me at once,' he told Sergeant
Breitenbach and handed him a list he had drawn up of ten konstabels
whose moral delinquency in the matter of miscegenation was notorious.
'And have the cells cleared on the top floor. A bed in each one and the
wall whitewashed.'

When the men presented themselves, Verkramp interviewed them one
by one.

'Konstabel van Heynigen,' he told the first man, 'you have been
sleeping with black women. Don't deny it. You have.'

Konstabel van Heynigen looked dumbfounded.

'Well, sir –' he began but Verkramp cut him short.

'Good,' he snapped, 'I'm glad you've made a clean breast of it. Now, you are going to have a course of treatment that will cure you of this disease.'

Konstabel van Heynigen had never considered raping black women as a disease. He'd always thought of it as one of the perks in an underpaid job.

'Do you agree that this treatment will benefit you?' Verkramp asked with a sternness that excluded any possibility of contradiction. 'Good. Just sign here,' and he thrust a type-written form before the astonished konstabel and pushed a ballpoint pen into his hand. Konstabel van Heynigen signed.

'Thank you. Next one,' said Verkramp.

By the end of an hour the Luitenant had treated all ten konstabels to the same swift process and had ten signed statements agreeing to aversion therapy as a cure for the disease of miscegenation.

'This is going so well,' Verkramp told Sergeant Breitenbach, 'we might as well get every man on the station to sign one.' The Sergeant gave his qualified consent.

'I think we should exclude the non-commissioned officers, don't you, sir?' he said.

Verkramp considered the matter. 'I suppose so,' he agreed grudgingly. 'We'll need someone to administer the drugs and shocks.'

While the Sergeant gave orders for all konstabels to sign the consent forms when they came on duty, Verkramp went upstairs to inspect the cells which had been cleared for treatment.

In each cell a bed had been placed facing the wall which had been whitewashed and beside the bed on a table stood a slide projector. All that was needed were the slides. Verkramp went back to his office and sent for Sergeant Breitenbach.

'Take a couple of vans out to the township and bring back a hundred coon girls,' he ordered. 'Try and pick attractive ones. Bring them back here and have the photographer photograph them in the raw.'

Sergeant Breitenbach went downstairs and drove out to Adamville, the black township outside Piemburg, to carry out what appeared on the surface to be a fairly straightforward order. In practice it turned out to be rather difficult. By the time his men had dragged a dozen young black women from their homes and locked them in the pick-up van, an angry crowd had gathered and the township was in an uproar.

'We want our women back,' yelled the crowd.

'Let us out,' screamed the girls in the van. Sergeant Breitenbach tried to explain.

'We only want to photograph them without their clothes on,' he said. 'It's to stop white policemen sleeping with Bantu women.'

As an explanation it was obviously unconvincing. The crowd evidently thought that photographing black women in the nude would have the opposite effect.

'Stop raping our women,' shouted the Africans.

'That's what we're trying to do,' said the Sergeant through a loudhailer but his words had no effect. The news that the police intended raping the girls spread like wildfire through the township. As the stones began to land round the police vans, Sergeant Breitenbach ordered his men to cock their Sten guns and gave the order to retreat.

'Typical,' said Verkramp when the Sergeant reported the incident. 'Try to help them and what do they do. Bloody riot. I tell you, kaffirs are thick. Plain stupid.'

'Do you want me to try and get some more?' the Sergeant asked.

'Of course. Ten isn't enough,' said Verkramp. 'Photograph this lot and take them back. When they see these girls haven't been raped the crowd will quieten down.'

'Yes sir,' said the Sergeant doubtfully.

He went down to the basement and supervised the police photographer who was having some difficulty getting the girls to stand still. In the end the Sergeant had to take out his revolver and threaten to shoot the girls unless they cooperated.

His second visit to the township was even less successful than the first. Wisely taking the precaution of convoying the pick-up vans with four Saracen armoured cars and several lorry loads of armed policemen, he still ran into trouble.

Addressing the incensed crowd Sergeant Breitenbach ordered the girls to be released.

'As you can see they haven't been hurt,' he shouted. Naked and bruised, the girls poured out of the vans.

'He said he'd shoot us,' one of them screamed.

In the riot that followed this announcement and the attempt to secure another ninety girls for the same treatment, the police shot four Africans dead and wounded a dozen more. Sergeant Breitenbach left the scene of carnage with twenty-five more women and a nasty cut over his left eye where he had been hit by a stone.

'Fuck the bastards,' he said as the convoy left, a comment that had unfortunate results for the twenty-five women in the vans who were

photographed and duly fucked in the police station before being released
to make their own way home. That evening Acting Kommandant
Verkramp announced to the press that four Africans had been killed in
a tribal fight in the township.

As soon as the colour transparencies were ready, Verkramp and
Sergeant Breitenbach went to the top floor where the ten konstabels were
waiting in some trepidation for the treatment to begin. The arrival of
the hypodermics and the shock machines had done nothing to improve
their morale.

'Men,' said Verkramp as they stood in the corridor, 'today you are
about to take part in an experiment which may alter the course of history.
As you know, we Whites in South Africa are threatened by millions of
blacks and if we are to survive and maintain our purity of race as God
intended we must learn not only to fight with guns and bullets but we
must fight a moral battle too. We must cleanse our hearts and minds of
impure thoughts. That is what this course of treatment is intended to do.
Now, we all have a natural aversion for kaffirs. It's part of our nature
to feel disgust for them. The course of treatment which you have
volunteered for will reinforce that feeling of disgust. That is why it is
called aversion therapy. By the end of your treatment the sight of a black
woman will make you sick and you will be conditioned to avoid all
contact with them. You won't want to sleep with them. You won't want
to touch them. You won't want to have them in your home as servants.
You won't want them washing your clothes. You won't want them in
the streets. You won't want them anywhere in South Africa . . .'

As Luitenant Verkramp's voice went higher and higher with the
catalogue of things the konstabels wouldn't want, Sergeant Breitenbach
coughed nervously. He had had a tiring day and the cut on his forehead
was throbbing painfully and he knew that one thing he didn't want was
a demented and hysterical Acting Kommandant.

'Isn't it about time we started, sir?' he said nudging Verkramp. The
Luitenant stopped.

'Yes,' he said. 'Let the experiment begin.'

The volunteers went into their cells where they were made to take off
their clothes and get into the strait-jackets which were laid out like
pyjamas on the beds. There was some trouble on this score and it required
the assistance of several non-commissioned officers to get one or two
of the larger men into them. Finally, however, the ten konstabels
were strapped down and Verkramp filled the first hypodermic with
apomorphine.

Sergeant Breitenbach watched him with growing alarm.

'The surgeon said not to overdo it,' he whispered. 'He said you could kill someone. Only 3CC.'

'You're not getting cold feet are you, Sergeant?' Verkramp asked. On the bed the volunteer regarded the needle with bulging eyes.

'I've changed my mind,' he shouted desperately.

'No, you haven't,' said Verkramp. 'We're going to do that for you.'

'Shouldn't we try it on a kaffir first?' Sergeant Breitenbach asked. 'I mean it isn't going to look very good if one of these men dies, is it?'

Verkramp thought for a moment. 'I suppose you're right,' he agreed finally. They went down to the cells on the ground floor and injected several African suspects with varying amounts of apomorphine. The results entirely confirmed Sergeant Breitenbach's worst fears. As the third black went into a coma, Verkramp looked puzzled.

'Potent stuff,' he said.

'Wouldn't it be better to stick to the electric shock machines?' the Sergeant asked.

'I suppose so,' said Verkramp sadly. He'd been looking forward to sticking needles in the volunteers. Ordering the Sergeant to send for the police surgeon to sign the death certificates, the Luitenant went back to the top floor and reassured the five vounteers who had been selected for apomorphine treatment that they needn't worry.

'You're going to have electric shocks instead,' he told them and switched on the projector. At the end of the cell a naked black woman appeared on the wall. As each volunteer had an erection, Verkramp shook his head.

'Disgusting,' he muttered attaching the terminal of the shock machine to the glans penis with a piece of surgical tape. 'Now then,' he told the Sergeant who sat beside the bed, 'every time you change the slide, give him an electric shock like this.' Verkramp wound the handle of the generator vigorously and the konstabel on the bed jerked convulsively and screamed. Verkramp examined the man's penis and was impressed. 'You can see it works,' he said and changed the slide.

Going from cell to cell, Luitenant Verkramp explained the technique and supervised the experiment. As erections followed the slides and contractions followed the shocks to be followed by more slides, more erections, more shocks and more contractions, the Luitenant's enthusiasm grew.

Sergeant Breitenbach, returning from the morgue, was less sanguine.

'You can hear them screaming in the street,' he shouted in Verkramp's ear as the corridor echoed to the shrieks of the volunteers.

'So what?' said Verkramp. 'We're making history.'

'Making a horrible din too,' said the Sergeant.

To Verkramp the screams were like music. It was as though he were conducting some great symphony in which the seasons, spring, summer, autumn and winter, were celebrated in a welter of screams and shocks and slides, erections and contractions, each of which he could summon forth or dismiss at will.

Presently he sent for a camp bed and lay down in the corridor to get some rest. 'I'm exorcizing the devil,' he thought and, dreaming of a world cleansed of sexual lust, fell asleep. When he awoke he was surprised how quiet it was. He got up and found the volunteers asleep and the Sergeants smoking in the lavatory.

'What the hell do you mean by stopping the treatment?' he shouted. 'It's got to be continuous if it's to work at all. It's called reinforcement.'

'You'll need reinforcements if you want to go on,' said one Sergeant mutinously.

'What's the matter with you?' asked Verkramp angrily.

The Sergeants looked shamefaced.

'It's a delicate matter,' Sergeant de Kok told him finally.

'What is?'

'Well we've been in there all night looking at slides of naked ladies ...'

'Coon girls not ladies,' snarled Verkramp.

'And ...' the Sergeant hesitated.

'And what?'

'We've got lover's balls,' said the Sergeant bluntly.

Luitenant Verkramp was appalled.

'Lover's balls,' he shouted. 'You've got lover's balls from looking at naked coon girls? You stand there and admit you ...' Verkramp was speechless with disgust.

'It's only natural,' said the Sergeant.

'Natural?' screamed Verkramp. 'It's downright unnatural. Where the hell is this country going to if men in your positions of authority can't control your sexual instincts? Now you listen to me. As Kommandant of this station I'm ordering you to continue the treatment. Any man refusing to do his duty will be put on the list for the next batch of volunteers.'

The Sergeants straightened their uniforms and hobbled back to the cells and a moment later the screams that were proof of their devotion to duty began again. In the morning the shift was changed and fresh non-commissioned officers took their place. Throughout the day Luitenant Verkramp went upstairs to see how they were getting on.

He had just visited one cell and was about to leave when he became aware that there was something vaguely wrong with the picture projected on the wall. He looked at it and saw it was a view of the Kruger National Park.

'Like it?' asked the Sergeant. Luitenant Verkramp stared dumbfounded at the slide. 'The next one is even better.'

The Sergeant pressed the switch and the slide changed to a close-up of a giraffe. On the bed the volunteer jerked convulsively from the electric shock. Luitenant Verkramp couldn't believe his eyes.

'Where the hell did you get those slides?' he demanded. The Sergeant looked up brightly.

'They're my holiday shots from last summer. We went to the game reserve.' He changed the slide and a herd of zebra appeared on the wall. The patient jerked with them too.

'You're supposed to be showing slides of naked black women,' Verkramp yelled, 'not fucking animals in the game reserve!'

The Sergeant was unabashed.

'I just thought they'd make a change,' he explained, 'and besides it's the first time I've had a chance to show them. We haven't got a slide projector at home.'

On the bed the patient was screaming that he couldn't stand any more.

'No more hippos, please,' he moaned. 'Dear God no more hippos. I swear I'll never touch another hippo again.'

'See what you've been and done,' said Verkramp frantically to the Sergeant. 'Do you realize what you've done? You've conditioned him to loathe animals. He won't be able to take his kids to the Zoo without becoming a nervous wreck.'

'Oh dear,' said the Sergeant, 'I am sorry. He'll have to give up fishing too in that case.'

Verkramp confiscated all the slides of the game reserve and the Durban Aquarium and told the Sergeant to show only slides of naked black women. After that he made a point of checking the slides in each cell and came across one other discrepancy. Sergeant Bischoff had included a slide of an unattractive white woman in a bathing costume among the naked blacks.

'Who the hell is this old bag?' Verkramp asked when he found the slide.

'You shouldn't have said that,' said Sergeant Bischoff looking hurt.

'Why not?' yelled Verkramp.

'That's my wife,' said the Sergeant. Verkramp could see that he had made a mistake.

'Listen,' he said, 'it's not nice to put her in with a whole lot of kaffir girls.'

'I know that,' said the Sergeant, 'I just thought it might help.'

'Help?'

'Help my marriage,' the Sergeant explained. 'She's a bit ... well, a bit flirtatious and I just thought I'd make sure one man didn't look at her again.'

Verkramp looked at the slide. 'I shouldn't have thought you need have bothered,' he said and gave orders that Mrs Bischoff wasn't to appear at a mixed gathering again.

Finally having ensured that everything was proceeding according to plan, he went down to the Kommandant's office and tried to think what else he could do to make his tenure of office a memorable one. The next step, as far as he could see, would come in the evening when his agents began work in the field.

CHAPTER SEVEN

By the time he had driven into Weezen after lunch and found it was early closing day, the Kommandant had begun to think that he was never going to find the Heathcote-Kilkoons's house. His earlier impression that time stood still in the little town was entirely reinforced by the absence of anyone in the streets in the afternoon. He wandered round looking for the Post Office only to find it shut, tried the store he had been to in the morning with equal lack of success and finally sat down in the shadow of Queen Victoria and contemplated the dusty cannas in the ornamental garden. A thin yellow dog sitting on the verandah of the store scratched itself lethargically and recalled the Kommandant to his new role. 'Mad dogs and Englishmen go out in the mid-day sun,' he thought to cheer himself up and wondered what a genuine Englishman who found himself in a strange town at this time of the day would have done. 'Gone fishing,' he imagined and with the uneasy feeling that he was being observed rather critically which resulted subliminally from the great Queen above him, he got up and drove back to the hotel.

There too the sense of inanition with which the old building was so imbued was even more marked now. The two flies were still trapped in the revolving door but they no longer buzzed. Kommandant van Heerden went down the corridor to his room and collected his rod. Then after some confusion in the revolving door, which refused to take both his rod and his basket at the same time, he was out and threading his way down the weedy paths to the river. At the foot of the enormous drainpipe he hesitated, looked to see which way the river flowed, and went upstream on the grounds that he didn't want to catch fish that had grown fat on its discharge. He had some difficulty in finding a spot which wasn't encumbered with branches and presently settled down to casting his most promising-looking fly, a large red-winged affair, onto the water. Nothing stirred beneath the surface of the river but the Kommandant was well content. He was doing what an English gentleman would do on a hot summer afternoon, and knowing how ineffectual Englishmen were in other matters he doubted if they caught anything when fishing. As time slowly passed the Kommandant's mind, somnolent in the heat, pondered gently. With something remotely akin to insight he saw himself, a plump middle-aged man standing in unfamiliar clothes on the bank of an unknown river fishing for nothing in particular. It seemed a strange thing to do yet restful and in some curious way fulfilling. Piemburg and the police station seemed very far away and insignificant. He no longer cared what happened there. He was away from it, away in the mountains, being, if not himself, at least something equivalent and he was just considering what this admiration for things English meant when a voice interrupted him.

'Oh, never fly conceals a hook!' said the voice and the Kommandant turned to find the salesman with flatulence standing watching him.

'It does as a matter of fact,' said the Kommandant who thought the remark was rather foolish.

'A quote, a quote,' said the man. 'I'm afraid I'm rather given to them. It's not a particularly sociable habit but one that arises from my profession.'

'Really,' said the Kommandant non-committally, not being sure what a quote was. He wound in his line and was disconcerted to find that his fly had disappeared.

'I see I was right after all,' said the man. 'Squamous, omnipotent and kind.'

'I beg your pardon,' said the Kommandant.

'Just another quote,' said the man. 'Perhaps I ought to introduce myself. Mulpurgo. I lecture in English at the University of Zululand.'

'Van Heerden, Kommandant South African Police, Piemburg,' said the Kommandant and was startled by the effect his announcement had on Mr Mulpurgo. He had gone quite pale and was looking decidedly alarmed.

'Is anything wrong?' asked the Kommandant.

'No,' said Mr Mulpurgo shakily. 'Nothing at all. It's just that ... well I had no idea you were ... well ... Kommandant van Heerden.'

'You've heard about me then?' the Kommandant asked.

Mr Mulpurgo nodded. It was perfectly clear that he had. The Kommandant dismantled his rod.

'I don't suppose I'll catch anything now,' he said. 'Too late.'

'Evening is the best time,' said Mr Mulpurgo looking at him curiously.

'Is it? That's interesting,' the Kommandant said as they strolled back along the river bank. 'This is my first try at fishing. Are you a keen fisherman? You seem to know a lot about it.'

'My associations are purely literary,' Mr Mulpurgo confessed, 'I'm doing my thesis on "Heaven".'

Kommandant van Heerden was astonished.

'Isn't that a very difficult subject?' he asked.

Mr Mulpurgo smiled. 'It's a poem about fish by Rupert Brooke,' he explained.

'Oh is that what it is?' said the Kommandant who, while he'd never heard of Rupert Brooke, was always interested in hearing about English literature. 'This man Brooke is an English poet?'

Mr Mulpurgo said he was.

'He died in the First World War,' he explained and the Kommandant said he was sorry to hear it, 'The thing is' continued the English lecturer, 'that I believe that while it's possible to interpret the poem quite simply as an allegory of the human condition, *la condition humaine*, if you understand me, it has also a deeper relevance in terms of the psychoalchemical process of transformation as discovered by Jung.'

The Kommandant nodded. He didn't understand a word that Mr Mulpurgo was saying but he felt privileged to hear it all the same. Encouraged by this acquiescence the lecturer warmed to his task.

'For instance the lines "One may not doubt that, somehow, good, Shall come of water and of mud" clearly indicate that the poet's intention is to introduce the concept of the philosopher's stone and its origin in the *prima materia* without in any way diverting the reader's attention from the poem's superficially humorous tone.'

They came to the enormous drain and Mr Mulpurgo helped the Kommandant with his basket. The evident alarm with which he had greeted the Kommandant's introduction had given way to nervous garrulity in the face of his friendly if uncomprehending interest.

'It's the individuation *motif* without a doubt,' he went on as they walked up the path to the hotel. ' "Paradisal grubs", "Unfading moths", "And the worm that never dies" all clearly point to that.'

'I suppose they must do,' said the Kommandant as they parted in the foyer. He went down the corridor to Colonic Irrigation No 6 feeling vaguely elated. He had spent the afternoon in an authentic English fashion, fishing and engaged in intellectual conversation. It was an auspicious start to his holiday and went some way to compensate for the disappointment he had felt on his arrival at the hotel. To celebrate the occasion he decided on a bath before dinner and spent some time searching for a bathroom before returning to his room and washing himself all over in the basin that looked most suited to that purpose and least likely to have been used for any other. As the old man had warned, the cold water was hot. The Kommandant tried the hot tap but that was just as hot and in the end he sprayed himself with warm water from a tube that was clearly too large to have been used as an enema but which left him smelling distinctly odd all the same. Then he sat on the bed and read a chapter of *Berry & Co* before going to dinner. He found it difficult to concentrate because whichever way he sat he was still faced by his stained reflection in the wardrobe mirror which made him feel that there was someone with him in the room all the time. To avoid the compulsive introspection this induced he lay back on the bed and tried to imagine what Mr Mulpurgo had been talking about. It had meant nothing at the time and even less now but the phrase 'And the worm that never dies' stuck in his mind relentlessly. It seemed unlikely somehow but remembering that worms could break in half and still go on living separate existences, he supposed it was possible that when one end was mortally ill, the other end could dissociate itself from its partner's death and go on living. Perhaps that was what was meant by terminal. It was a word he'd never understood. He'd have to ask Mr Mulpurgo, who was evidently a highly educated man.

But when he went to the Pump Room for dinner, Mr Mulpurgo wasn't there. The two ladies at the far end of the room were his only companions and since their whispered conversation was made inaudible by the gurgling of the marble fountain the Kommandant ate his dinner in what amounted to silence and watched the sky darken behind the Aardvarkberg. Tomorrow he would find the address of the Heathcote-Kilkoons and let them know he had arrived.

Seventy miles away in Piemburg the evening which had begun so uneventfully took on a new animation towards midnight. The twelve violent explosions that rocked the city within minutes of one another at eleven-thirty were so strategically placed that they confirmed entirely Luitenant Verkramp's contention that a well-organized conspiracy of sabotage and subversion existed. As the last bomb brightened the horizon, Piemburg retreated still further into that obscurity for which it was so famous. Bereft of electricity, telephones, radio mast, and with road and rail links to the outside world severed by the explosive zeal of his secret agents, the tiny metropolis' tenuous hold on the twentieth century petered out.

From the roof of the police station where he was taking the air, Verkramp found the transformation quite spectacular. One moment Piemburg had been a delicate web of street lights and neon signs, the next it had merged indistinguishably with the rolling hills of Zululand. As the distant rumble from Empire View announced that the radio tower had ceased to be such a large blot on the landscape, Verkramp left the roof and hurried down the stairs to the cells where the only people in the city who would have actively canvassed for electricity cuts were still receiving their jolts from the hand-cranked generators in the darkness. The consolation for the volunteers was the disappearance of the naked black women as the projectors went out.

In the confusion Luitenant Verkramp remained disconcertingly calm.

'It's all right,' he shouted. 'There is nothing to be alarmed about, just continue the experiment using ordinary photographs.' He went from cell to cell distributing torches which he had kept handy for just such an eventuality as this. Sergeant Breitenbach was as usual less unperturbed.

'Don't you think it's more important to investigate the cause of the power failure?' he asked. 'It sounded to me like there were a whole lot of explosions.'

'Twelve,' said Verkramp emphatically, 'I counted them.'

'Twelve bloody great explosions in the middle of the night and you aren't worried?' said the Sergeant with astonishment. Luitenant Verkramp refused to be flustered.

'I've been expecting this for some time,' he said truthfully.

'Expecting what?'

'The sabotage movement has begun again,' he said going downstairs to his office. Behind him Sergeant Breitenbach, still literally and metaphorically in the dark, tried to follow him. By the time he reached the Kommandant's office, he found Verkramp checking a list of names by the light of an emergency lamp. It crossed the Sergeant's mind that Verkramp was remarkably well prepared for the crisis that seemed to have caught the rest of the city unawares.

'I want the following people detained at once,' Verkramp told him.

'Aren't you going to check on what's been going on first?' Sergeant

Breitenbach asked. 'I mean you don't even know for sure that those explosions were made by bombs.'

Luitenant Verkramp looked up sternly.

'I've had enough experience of sabotage to know a bomb when I hear one,' he said. Sergeant Breitenbach decided not to argue. Instead he studied the list of names Verkramp had handed him and was horrified by what he saw. If Verkramp were right and the city had been disrupted by a series of bomb attacks, the consequences to public life in Piemburg would be mild by comparison with the chaos that would ensue if the men on the list were arrested. Clergymen, councillors, bank managers, lawyers, even the Mayor himself appeared to be the object of Verkramp's suspicions. Sergeant Breitenbach put the list down hurriedly. He didn't want anything to do with it.

'Don't you think you're being a bit hasty?' he asked nervously.

Luitenant Verkramp clearly didn't. 'If I am right, and I am, the city has been subjected to a premeditated campaign of sabotage. These men are all well-known –'

'You can say that again,' muttered the Sergeant.

'– opponents of the Government,' continued the Acting Kommandant. 'Many of them were Horticulturalists.'

'Horticulturalists?' asked the Sergeant who couldn't see anything wrong with being a horticulturalist. He was one himself in a small way.

'The Horticulturalists,' Verkramp explained, 'were a secret organization of wealthy farmers and businessmen who were planning to take Zululand out of the Union at the time of the Republic referendum. They were prepared to use force. Some were officers in the Piemburg Mounted Rifles and they were going to use weapons from the military arsenal.'

'But that was ten years ago,' Sergeant Brietenbach pointed out.

'Men like that don't change their opinions,' said Verkramp sententiously. 'Will you ever forgive the British for what they did to our women and children in the concentration camps?'

'No,' said the Sergeant, who hadn't had any women or children in concentration camps in the Boer war but who knew the right answer.

'Exactly,' said Verkramp. 'Well, these swine are no different and they'll never forgive us for taking Zululand out of the British Empire. They hate us. Don't you understand how the British hate us?'

'Yes,' said the Sergeant hastily. He could see that Verkramp was working himself up into a state again and he preferred to be out of the way when it came. 'You're probably right.'

'Right?' shouted Verkramp. 'I'm always right.'

'Yes,' said the Sergeant even more hastily.

'So what do they do, these Horticulturalists? Go underground for a time, then gang up with Communists and Liberalists to overthrow our glorious Afrikaner republic. These bomb attacks are the first sign that their campaign has started. Well, I'm not going to sit back and let them get away with it. I'll have those bastards in prison and squeeze the truth out of them before they can do any real harm.'

Sergeant Breitenbach waited until the seizure had run its course before demurring once again.

'Don't you think it would be safer to tell Kommandant van Heerden first? Then he can carry the can if there is a balls-up.'

Luitenant Verkramp wouldn't hear of it. 'Half the trouble in this town is due to the way the old fool treats the English,' he snapped. 'He's too bloody soft with them. Sometimes I think he prefers them to his own people.'

Sergeant Breitenbach said he didn't know about that. All he knew was that the Kommandant's grandfather had been shot by the British after the Battle of Paardeberg which was more than could be said for Verkramp's. His grandfather had sold horses to the British army and had been practically a khaki Boer but the Sergeant was too discreet to mention the fact now. Instead he picked up the list again.

'Where are we going to put them all?' he asked. 'The cells on the top floor are being used for your kaffirboetje cure and the ones in the basement are all full.'

'Take them down to the prison,' Verkramp told him, 'and see that they're kept in isolation. I don't want them cooking up any stories.'

Half an hour later the homes of thirty-six of Piemburg's most influential citizens had been raided by armed police, and angry frightened men had been hustled in their pyjamas into pick-up vans. One or two put up a desperate resistance in the mistaken belief that the Zulus had risen and had come to massacre them in their beds, a misunderstanding that arose from the total black-out into which Verkramp's agents had plunged the city. Four policemen were wounded in these battles and a local coal merchant shot his wife to save her from being raped by the black hordes before the situation was clarified.

By dawn the arrests had all been made though one or two mistakes remained to be rectified. The man torn from the arms of the lady Mayoress turned out to be not the civic dignitary himself but a neighbour he had asked to help with his election. When the Mayor was finally apprehended he was under the impression that he was being arrested for corruption in high places. 'This is disgraceful,' he shouted as he was bundled into the pick-up van. 'You have no right to pry into my private wife. I am your ewected representative,' a protest that did nothing to effect his release but went some way to explain the presence of the neighbour in his wife's bed.

In the morning after a few hours' sleep Luitenant Verkramp and Sergeant Breitenbach toured the installations which had been destroyed by the saboteurs. Once again the Acting Kommandant's grasp of the situation astonished Sergeant Breitenbach. Verkramp seemed to know exactly where to go without being told. As they surveyed the remains of the transformer on the Durban Road, the Sergeant asked him what he was going to do now.

'Nothing,' said Verkramp to his amazement. 'In a few days' time we'll be in a position to arrest the whole Communist organization in Zululand.'

'But what about all the people we arrested last night?'

'They will be interrogated and the evidence they give will help to reveal their co-conspirators,' Verkramp explained.

Sergeant Breitenbach shook his head in bewilderment.

'I hope to hell you know what you're doing,' was all he said. They drove back via the prison where Verkramp gave instructions to the teams of Security Policemen who were to conduct the interrogation round the clock.

'The usual routine,' he told them. 'Keep them standing up. No sleep. Rough them up a bit to start with. Explain they'll be tried under the Terrorist Act and have to prove their innocence. No right to a lawyer. Can be detained indefinitely and incommunicado. Any questions?'

'Any, sir?' asked one of the men.

'You heard me,' snapped Verkramp, 'I said. "Any questions?"' The men looked at him dumbly and Verkramp dismissed them and they filed off to begin their arduous duties. Luitenant Verkramp went to see Governor Schnapps to apologize for the temporary inconvenience he was causing in the prison. When he returned to the wing in which the detainees were being interrogated Luitenant Verkramp found that his orders were being obeyed to the letter.

'Who won Test Series in 1948?' shouted Sergeant Scheepers at the manager of Barclays Bank.

'I don't know,' squealed the manager who had been twice kicked in the scrotum for his failure to follow cricket.

Verkramp asked the Sergeant to come out into the corridor.

'What do you want to know that for?' he asked.

'Seems a fairly easy question,' said the Sergeant.

'I suppose it does,' said Verkramp. He went to the next cell where the Dean of Piemburg had avoided a similar fate by knowing the road distance between Johannesburg and Capetown, the age of the Prime Minister, and what the initials USA stood for.

'You said "Any questions",' the Security man explained when Verkramp demanded the reason for the quiz game.

'You dumb bastard,' Verkramp yelled, 'I said "Any questions?" not "Any questions." What do I have to do? Spell it out for you?'

'Yes sir,' said the man. Verkramp called the teams together and briefed them more explicitly.

'What we need is proof that these men have been conspiring to overthrow the government by force,' he explained, and got the Security men to write it down. 'Secondly that they have been actively inciting the blacks to rebel.' The men wrote that down too. 'Thirdly that they have been receiving money from overseas. Fourthly that they are all Communists or communist sympathizers. Is that quite clear?'

Sergeant Scheepers asked if he could tell the Mayor that one of the aldermen had said he was a cuckold.

'Of course,' Verkramp said. 'Tell him that the Alderman is prepared to give evidence to that effect. Get them started giving evidence against one another and we'll soon get to the root of this affair.'

The men went back to the cells with their list of questions and the interrogations began again. Having satisfied himself that his men were keeping to the point, Luitenant Verkramp returned to the police station to see if there were any messages from his secret agents. He was rather disappointed to find that none had arrived but he supposed it was too early to expect any concrete results.

Instead he decided to test the effectiveness of the aversion therapy on the volunteers on the top floor who were still screaming rhythmically. He sent for Sergeant Breitenbach and ordered him to bring a coon girl from the cells.

The Sergeant went away and returned with what he evidently thought was a suitable subject. She was fifty-eight if she was a day and hadn't been a beauty at half her age. Luitenant Verkramp was horrified.

'I said "Girl" not "Old bag",' he shouted. 'Take her away and get a proper girl.'

Sergeant Breitenbach went back downstairs with the old woman wondering why it was that you called a black man of seventy or eighty a boy but you couldn't call a woman of the same age a girl. It didn't seem to make sense. In the end he found a very large black girl and told her to come up with him to the top floor. Ten minutes and eight konstabels later, one of whom had a broken nose and another complained he couldn't find his testicles, they managed to get the girl up to the top floor only to find that Verkramp was still not satisfied.

'Do you really think that any sane man would find that attractive?' he asked pointing to the unconscious and battered body that the konstabels were trying to keep on its feet and off theirs. 'What I want is a nice kaffir girl that any man would find attractive.'

'Well, you go and get one then,' Sergeant Breitenbach told him. 'You just go down to the cells and tell a nice attractive black girl that the policemen on the top floor want her and see what happens.'

'The trouble with you, Sergeant,' Verkramp said as they went down for the third time, 'is that you don't understand psychology. If you want people to do things for you, you mustn't frighten them. That's particularly true with blacks. You must use persuasion.' He stopped outside a cell door. The Sergeant unlocked it and the large black girl was pitched inside. Verkramp stepped over her body and looked at the women cringing against the wall.

'Now then, there's no need to be frightened,' he told them. 'Which one of you girls would like to come upstairs to see some pictures? They are pretty pictures.' There was no great rush of volunteers. Verkramp tried again.

'No one is going to hurt you. You needn't be afraid.'

There was still no response apart from a moan from the girl on the floor. Verkramp's sickly smile faded.

'Grab the bitch,' he yelled at the konstabels and the next moment a thin black girl was being hustled upstairs.

'You see what I mean about psychology,' Luitenant Verkramp said to the Sergeant as they followed her up. Sergeant Breitenbach still had his doubts.

'I notice you didn't pick a big one,' he said.

On the top floor the girl had her clothes stripped off her by several willing konstabels whom Verkramp put down on his list for treatment and was then paraded before the volunteers in the nude. Luitenant Verkramp was delighted by their lack of positive reaction.

'Not an erection from one of them,' he said. 'That's scientific proof that the treatment works.'

Sergeant Breitenbach was, as usual, more sceptical.

'They haven't had any sleep for two days,' he said. 'If you brought Marilyn Monroe in here in the raw, I don't suppose you'd get much response.'

Verkramp looked at him disapprovingly. 'Peeping Thomas,' he said.

'I don't see what that has to do with it,' said the Sergeant. 'All I'm saying is that if you want to be really scientific you should bring a white girl up and try her on them.' Luitenant Verkramp was furious.

'What a disgusting suggestion,' he said. 'I wouldn't dream of subjecting a white girl to such a revolting ordeal.'

He gave orders for the treatment to be continued for at least another two days.

'Two more days of this and I'll be dead,' moaned one of the volunteers.

'Better dead than a black in your bed,' said Verkramp and went back to his office to draw up the plans for the mass treatment of the other five hundred and ninety men under his temporary command.

At Florian's café Verkramp's secret agents were making remarkable headway in their search for members of the sabotage movement. After years of frustration in which they had mingled in liberal circles but had been unable to find anyone remotely connected with the Communist party or prepared to admit that they approved of violence, they had suddenly met quite a number. 745396 had discovered 628461 who seemed to know something about the explosion at the telephone exchange and 628461 had gained the very definite impression that 745396 wasn't unconnected with the destruction of the transformer on the Durban Road. Likewise 885974 had bumped into 378550 at the University Canteen and was sounding him out about his part in the disappearance of the radio mast, while hinting that he could tell 378550 something about the bomb that had destroyed the railway bridge. All over Piemburg Verkramp's agents had something to report in the way of progress and busied themselves encoding messages and moving digs as instructed. By the following day the conviction that each agent held that he was onto something big grew when 745396 and 628461, who had arranged to meet at the University Canteen, found a sympathetic audience in 885974 and 378550, who had been so successful there the previous day they had decided to return. As the coalescence of conspirators continued Verkramp was kept busy trying to decode the messages. This complex process was made even more difficult because he had no idea on which day the message had been sent. 378550's message had been deposited at the foot of a tree in the park which was the correct drop for Sunday but after working at it for two hours using the code for that day Verkramp had managed to turn 'hdfpkymwrqazxtivbnkon' which was designed to be difficult to understand into 'car dog wormsel sag infrequent banal out plunge crate', which wasn't. He tried Saturday's code and got 'dahlia chrysanthemum fertilizer decorative foxglove dwarf autumn bloom shady'. Cursing himself for the limited vocabulary provided by page 33 of the

Piemburg Bulb Catalogue which he had chosen as the codebook for Saturday on account of its easy availability, Verkramp turned wearily to Friday's codebook and finally came up with the deciphered message that Agent 378550 had carried out instructions and was proceeding to new lodgings. After six hours' hard labour Verkramp felt his efforts merited something more interesting than that. He tried 885974's message and was glad to find it came out correctly first time and contained the reassuring information that the agent had made contact with several suspected saboteurs but was having difficulty in reaching the top as he was being followed.

885974's experience was not confined to him alone. In their attempts to find where the other saboteurs lived Verkramp's secret agents were trailing one another all over Piemburg or being tailed. As a result they were covering an enormous mileage every day and were too tired when they finally got home to sit down and encode the messages he expected. Then again they had to move lodgings every day on his orders and this required finding new ones so that all in all the sense of disorientation already induced by the multiple identities their work demanded became more pronounced as the days went by. By Monday 628461 wasn't sure who he was or where he lived or even what day of the week it was. He was even more uncertain where 745396 lived. Having tailed him successfully for fifteen miles up and down the sidestreets of Piemburg he wasn't altogether surprised when 745396 gave up the attempt to shake him off and returned to a lodging house on Bishoff Avenue only to find that he had left there two days before. In the end he slept on a bench in the park and 628461, who had several large blisters from all this walking, turned to go back to his digs when he became aware that someone was following him. He stepped up his limp and the footsteps behind him did the same. 628461 gave up the struggle. He no longer cared if he was followed home. 'I'll move in the morning anyway,' he decided and climbed the stairs to his room in the Lansdowne Boarding House. Behind him 378550 went back to his digs and spent the night encoding a message for Luitenant Verkramp giving the address of a suspected saboteur. Since he started it at ten-thirty on Monday and finished it at two a.m. on Tuesday Verkramp had even more difficulty than usual making out what it meant. According to Monday's codebook it read 'Suggest raid on infestation wood but pollute in the', while Tuesday's ran 'Chariot Pharoah withal Lansdowne Boarding House for Frederick Smith.' By the time Luitenant Verkramp had decided that there was no sense in 'Chariot Pharoah withal infestation wood but pollute in the' there was no point in raiding the Lansdowne Boarding House, Frederick Smith had registered at the YMCA as Piet Retief.

If Luitenant Verkramp was having difficulties in the communications field much the same could be said of both Mrs Heathcote-Kilkoon and Kommandant van Heerden.

'Are you sure he's not there?' Mrs Heathcote-Kilkoon asked the Major, whom she had sent on his daily outing to Weezen to tell the Kommandant that they were expecting him to lunch.

'Absolutely certain,' said Major Bloxham. 'I sat in the bar for nearly an hour and there was no sign of the fellow. Asked the barman if he'd seen him. Hadn't.'

'I think it's most peculiar,' said Mrs Heathcote-Kilkoon. 'His card definitely said he would stay at the hotel.'

'Damned peculiar card, if you ask me,' said the Colonel. 'Dearest Daphne, Kommandant van Heerden has pleasure –'

'I thought it was a very amusing card,' Mrs Heathcote-Kilkoon interrupted him. 'It shows what a sense of humour the Kommandant has.'

'Didn't strike me as having a sense of humour,' said the Major who had not got over his encounter with the Kommandant.

'Personally I think we should be thankful for small mercies,' said the Colonel. 'It doesn't look as if the swine is coming after all.' He went out to the yard at the back of the house where Harbinger was grooming a large black horse. 'Everything ready for tomorrow, Harbinger? Fox fit?'

'Took him for a run this morning,' said Harbinger, a thin man with eyes close together and short hair. 'He went quite quick.'

'Fine, fine,' said the Colonel. 'Well we'll get off early.' In the house Mrs Heathcote-Kilkoon was still puzzled.

'Are you sure you went to the right hotel?' she asked the Major.

'I went to the store and asked for the hotel,' the Major insisted. 'The fellow tried to sell me a bed. Seemed to think that's what I wanted.'

'It sounds most peculiar,' said Mrs Heathcote-Kilkoon.

'I said I didn't want a bed,' said the Major. 'He sent me across the road to the hotel in the end.'

'And they hadn't heard of him?'

'Didn't know anything about any Kommandant van Heerden.'

'Perhaps he'll turn up tomorrow,' said Mrs Heathcote-Kilkoon wistfully.

CHAPTER EIGHT

Unaware of the portentous events that were taking place in Piemburg, Kommandant van Heerden nevertheless spent a restless first night in his room at Weezen Spa. For one thing the strong smell of sulphur irritated his olfactory nerve and for another one of the many taps in his room insisted on dripping irregularly. The Kommandant tried to get rid of the sulphurous smell by spraying the room with the deodorant he'd brought to avoid giving bodily offence to Mrs Heathcote-Kilkoon. The resulting pot-pourri was rather nastier than the sulphur alone and in any case it made his eyes water. He got up and opened the window to let the smell out only to find that he had let a mosquito in. He shut the window again and switching on the light killed the mosquito with a slipper. He got back into bed and the tap dripped. He got out again and tightened all six taps and got back into bed. This time he was about to get to sleep when a dull rumble in the pipes suggested an air lock. There wasn't anything he could do in the way of major plumbing so he lay and listened to it while watching the moon rise mistily through the frosted glass window. In the early hours he finally slept to be awakened by a coloured maid at half-past seven bringing him a cup of tea. The Kommandant sat up and drank some tea. He had already swallowed some before he realized how horrible it tasted. For a moment the thought that he had been the victim of a poison attempt crossed his mind before he realized that the taste was due to the ubiquitous sulphur. He got out of bed and began brushing his teeth with water that tasted vile. Thoroughly fed up, he washed and dressed and went to the pump room for breakfast.

'Fruit juice,' he ordered when the waitress asked him what he wanted. He ordered a second glass when she brought the first and swilling the grapefruit round his mouth managed to eradicate some of the taste of sulphur.

'Boiled eggs or fried,' the waitress asked. The Kommandant said fried on the ground that they were less likely to be tainted. When the old man came in and asked if everything was all right, the Kommandant took the opportunity of asking him if it was possible to have some fresh water.

'Fresh?' said the old man. 'The water here is as fresh as mother nature can make it. Hot springs under here. Comes straight from the bowels of the earth.'

'I can well believe it,' said the Kommandant.

Presently he was joined by Mr Mulpurgo who sat at his usual table by the fountain.

'Good morning,' said the Kommandant cheerily and was a little hurt by the rather chilly 'Morning' he got back. The Kommandant tried again.

'How's the flatulence this morning?' he asked sympathetically.

Mr Mulpurgo ordered corn flakes, bacon and eggs, toast and marmalade before replying.

'Flatulence?'

'You said yesterday you came here for flatulence,' said the Kommandant.

'Oh,' said Mr Mulpurgo in the tone of one who didn't want to be reminded what he had said yesterday. 'Much better, thank you.'

The Kommandant refused the waitress' offer of coffee and ordered a third fruit juice.

'I've been thinking about that worm you spoke of yesterday, the one that never dies,' he said as Mr Mulpurgo attempted to get the rind off a soggy piece of bacon. 'Is it true that worms don't die?'

Mr Mulpurgo looked at him distrustfully. 'My own impression is that worms are not immune from the consequences of mortality,' he said finally, 'and that they shuffle off this mortal coil at their own equivalent of three-score years and ten.' He concentrated on his bacon and eggs and left the Kommandant to consider whether worms could shuffle off anything. He wondered what a mortal coil was. It sounded like a piece of radio equipment.

'But you mentioned one that didn't,' he said after giving the matter some thought.

'Didn't what?'

'Die.'

'I was speaking metaphorically,' Mr Mulpurgo said. 'I was talking about rebirth.' Like a reluctant Ancient Mariner prodded into action by the Kommandant's insistent curiosity Mr Mulpurgo found himself embarking on a lengthy disquisition that had been no part of his plans for the morning. He had intended working quietly in his room on his thesis. Instead an hour later he found himself strolling beside the river expounding his belief that the study of literature added a new dimension to the life of the reader. Beside him Kommandant van Heerden lumbered along occasionally recognizing a phrase which was not wholly unfamiliar but for the most part merely lost in admiration for the intellectual excellence of his companion. He had no idea what 'aesthetic awareness' or 'extended sensibilities' were though 'emotional anaemia' did suggest a lack of iron, but these were all minor problems beside the major one which was that Mr Mulpurgo for all his divagations seemed to be saying that a man could be born again through the study of literature. That at least the Kommandant discerned and the message coming from such an obviously well-informed source brought him fresh hope that he would one day achieve the transformation he so desired.

'You don't think heart transplants are any good then?' he asked when Mr Mulpurgo paused for breath. The devotee of Rupert Brooke looked at him suspiciously. Not for the first time Mr Mulpurgo had the feeling that he was having his leg pulled, but Kommandant van Heerden's face was alight with a grotesque innocence which was quite disarming.

Mr Mulpurgo chose to assume that in his own quaint way the Kommandant was reviving the arguments in favour of science put forward by C. P. Snow in his famous debate with F. R. Leavis. If he wasn't, Mr Mulpurgo couldn't imagine what he was talking about.

'Science deals only with the externals,' he said. 'What we need is to change man's nature from within.'

'I should have thought heart transplants did that very well,' said the Kommandant.

'Heart transplants don't alter man's nature in the least,' said Mr Mulpurgo who was finding the Kommandant's train of thought no less incomprehensible than the Kommandant had found his. What organ transplants had to do with extended sensibilities he couldn't begin to think. He decided to change the topic of conversation before it became too inconsequential.

'Do you know these mountains well?' he asked.

The Kommandant said he didn't personally but that his great-great-grandfather had crossed them in the Great Trek.

'Did he settle in Zululand?' Mr Mulpurgo asked.

'He was murdered there,' said the Kommandant. Mr Mulpurgo was sorry to hear it.

'By Dingaan,' continued the Kommandant. 'My great-great-grand-mother was one of the few women to survive the massacre at Blaauwkrans River. The Zulu impis swept down without warning and hacked them all to death.'

'A dreadful business,' Mr Mulpurgo murmured. His own family history was less chequered. He couldn't remember his great-great-grandmother but he felt fairly certain she hadn't been massacred by anyone.

'That's one reason we don't trust the kaffirs,' the Kommandant continued.

'There's no chance of that happening again,' Mr Mulpurgo said.

'You never can tell with kaffirs,' said the Kommandant. 'The leopard doesn't change its spots.'

Mr Mulpurgo's liberal leanings forced him to protest.

'Come now, you don't mean to say that you think today's Africans are savages,' he said mildly. 'I know some highly educated ones.'

'Blacks are savages,' insisted the Kommandant vehemently, 'and the more educated they are the more dangerous they get.'

Mr Mulpurgo sighed.

'Such a beautiful country,' he said. 'It seems such a shame that people of different races can't live amicably together in it.'

Kommandant van Heerden looked at him curiously.

'It's part of my job to see that people of different races don't live together,' he said by way of a warning. 'You take my advice and put the idea out of your mind. I wouldn't like to see a nice young fellow like you going to prison.'

Mr Mulpurgo stopped and began to hiccup. 'I wasn't suggesting,' he began but the Kommandant stopped him.

'I wasn't suggesting you were,' he said kindly. 'All of us have these ideas once in a while but it's best to forget them. If you want some black tail go up to Lourenço Marques. The Portuguese let you have it quite legally, you know. Some nice girls too, I can tell you.' Mr Mulpurgo stopped hiccuping but he still stared at the Kommandant very nervously. Life at the University of Zululand had never prepared him for an encounter such as this.

'You see,' continued the Kommandant as they resumed their walk, 'we know all about you intellectuals and your talk about education for the kaffirs and equality. Oh we keep an eye on you, you needn't worry.'

Mr Mulpurgo was not reassured. He knew perfectly well that the police kept an eye on the university. There had been too many raids to think otherwise. He began to wonder if the Kommandant had deliberately sought him out to question him. The notion brought on another attack of hiccups.

'There's only one real question in this country,' continued the Kommandant, quite unaware of the effect he was having on his companion, 'and that is who works for who. Do I work for a kaffir or does he work for me? What do you say to that?'

Mr Mulpurgo tried to say that it was a pity people couldn't work together cooperatively but he was hiccuping too much to be wholly coherent.

'Well I'm not working down some gold mine to make some black bastard rich,' said the Kommandant ignoring what he supposed was an acute attack of flatulence, 'and I'm not having a kaffir tell me to wash his car. It's dog eat dog and I'm the bigger dog. That's what you intellectuals forget.'

With this simple statement of his philosophy the Kommandant decided it was time to turn back.

'I've got to go and find where my friends live,' he said.

They walked back in silence for some time, Mr Mulpurgo mulling over the Kommandant's Spencerian view of society while the Kommandant, ignoring what he had just said about leopards and their spots, wondered if he could become an Englishman by reading books.

'How do you go about studying your poem?' he asked presently.

Mr Mulpurgo returned to the topic of his thesis with some relief.

'The main thing is to keep notes,' he explained. 'I make references and cross-references and keep them on file. For instance Brooke uses the image of smell frequently. It's there in "Lust", in "Second Best", and of course in "Dawn".'

'It's there all the time,' said the Kommandant. 'It's the water, there's sulphur in it.'

'Sulphur?' said Mr Mulpurgo absentmindedly. 'Yes, you get that in "The Last Beatitude". "And fling new sulphur on the sin incarnadined."'

'I don't know about that,' said the Kommandant uneasily, 'but they certainly put some in my tea this morning.'

By the time they reached the hotel Mr Mulpurgo had come to the conclusion that the Kommandant had no professional interest in him after all. He had recited 'Heaven' to him twice and explained what 'fish fly replete' meant and was beginning to feel that the Kommandant was quite a kind man in spite of his earlier utterances.

'I must say you have unusual interests for a policeman,' he said condescendingly as they climbed the steps to the terrace, 'I had gained quite a different impression from the newspapers.'

Kommandant van Heerden smiled darkly.

'They say a lot of lies about me in the papers,' he said. 'You mustn't believe all you hear.'

'Not as black as you're painted, eh?' said Mr Mulpurgo.

The Kommandant stopped in his tracks.

'Who said anything about me being black?' he demanded lividly.

'No one. No one,' said Mr Mupurgo appalled at his *faux pas*. 'It was purely a figure of speech.'

But Kommandant van Heerden wasn't listening. 'I'm as white as the next man,' he yelled, 'and if I hear anyone say any different I'll rip the balls off the swine. Do you hear me? I'll castrate the bugger. Don't let

me hear you saying such a thing again,' and he hurled himself through
the revolving doors with a violence that propelled the two flies quite
involuntarily into the open air. Behind him Mr Mulpurgo leant against
the balustrade and tried to stop hiccuping. When the door finally stopped
revolving he pulled himself together and went shakily down the corridor
to his room.

Having collected his keys from his room Kommandant van Heerden
went out to his car. He was still inwardly raging at the insult to his
ancestry.

'I'm as white as the next man,' he muttered pushing blindly past a
Zulu gardener who was weeding a flower-bed. He got into his car and
drove furiously into Weezen. He was still in a foul temper when he
parked in the dusty square and went up the steps into the trading store.
There were several farmers waiting to be served. The Kommandant
ignored them and spoke to the gaunt man behind the counter.

'Know where the Heathcote-Kilkoons live?' he asked.

The gaunt man ignored his question and went on attending to his
customer.

'I said do you know where the Heathcote-Kilkoons live?' the Kommandant said again.

'Heard you the first time,' the man told him, and was silent.

'Well?'

'I'm serving,' said the gaunt man. There were murmurs from the
farmers but the Kommandant was in too irritable a mood to worry.

'I asked a civil question,' he insisted.

'In an uncivil fashion,' the man told him. 'If you want answers you
wait your turn and ask decently.'

'Do you know who I am?' the Kommandant asked angrily.

'No,' said the man, 'and I don't care. I know where you are though.
On my premises and you can get the hell off them.'

The Kommandant looked wildly round. All the men in the store were
staring at him unpleasantly. He turned and lumbered out onto the
verandah. Behind him someone laughed and he thought he caught
the words 'Bloody hairy-back.' No one had called him a hairy-back
for a very long time. First a black and now a baboon. He stood for
a moment controlling himself with an effort before turning back into the
shop.

He stood in the doorway with the sunlit square behind him, a squat
silhouette. The men inside stared at him.

'My name is van Heerden,' said the Kommandant in a low and terrible
voice, 'I am Kommandant of Police in Piemburg. You will remember

me.' It was an announcement that would have caused alarm anywhere else in Zululand. Here it failed hopelessly.

'This is Little England,' said the gaunt man. 'Voetsak.'

The Kommandant turned and went. He had been told to voetsak like a dog. It was an insult he would never forget. He went blindly down the steps into the street and stood with clenched teeth squinting malevolently at the great Queen whose homely arrogance had no appeal for him now. He, Kommandant van Heerden, whose ancestors had manhandled their wagons over the Aardvark Mountains, who had fought the Zulus at Blood River, and the British at Spion Kop, had been told to voetsak like a kaffir dog by men whose kinsfolk had scuttled from India and Egypt and Kenya at the first hint of trouble.

'Stupid old bitch,' said the Kommandant to the statue and turned away to look for the post office. As he walked his rage slowly subsided to be replaced by a puzzled wonder at the arrogance of the English. 'Little England,' the gaunt man had said as if he had been proud of its being so little. To Kommandant van Heerden there was no sense in it. He stomped along the sidewalk brooding on the malfeasance of chance that had given him the power to rule without the assurance that was power's natural concomitant. In some strange way he recognized the right of the storekeeper to treat him like a dog no matter what awesome credentials he presented. 'I'm just Boeremense,' he thought with sudden self-pity and saw himself alone in an alien world unattached to any true community but outspanned temporarily among strange hostile tribes. The English had Home, that cold yet hospitable island in the North to which they could always turn. The blacks had Africa, the vast continent from which no law or rule could ever utterly remove them. But he, an Afrikaner, had only will and power and cunning between him and oblivion. No home but here. No time but now. With a fresh fear at his own inconsequence the Kommandant turned down a side street to the Post Office.

At White Ladies Mrs Heathcote-Kilkoon, idly turning the pages of a month-old *Illustrated London News* in an impractical attempt to relieve her boredom, told Major Bloxham to make her a dry Martini.

'You would think he'd let us know he wasn't coming,' she said petulantly. 'I mean it's only common courtesy to send a postcard.'

'What do you expect from a pig but a grunt?' said the Major. 'Can't make silk purses out of sows' ears.'

'I suppose you're right,' Mrs Heathcote-Kilkoon murmured, 'I see Princess Anne's been chosen Sportswoman of the Year.'

'Wonder she accepted,' said the Major. 'Seems a common sort of thing to be.'

'Oh I don't know,' said Mrs Heathcote-Kilkoon. 'They even knight jockeys these days.'

After lunch Mrs Heathcote-Kilkoon insisted on going for a drive and the Colonel who was expecting a telegram from his stockbroker drove them into Weezen and then over to the Sani Pass Hotel for tea.

The Kommandant, who had finally found their address at the Post Office, discovered the house empty when he visited it in the afternoon. He had recovered his temper though not his confidence and he was therefore not altogether surprised at the lack of welcome afforded by the empty house and the ancient Zulu butler who answered the door when he rang.

'Master gone,' the butler said and the Kommandant turned back to his car with the feeling that this was not a lucky day for him. He stood looking round at the house and garden before getting back into his car, and tried to absorb some of the amour-propre which was so evident in the atmosphere.

Well-trimmed lawns and disciplined herbaceous borders, carefully labelled rose bushes and a bush clipped to the replica of a chicken, all was ordered agreeably. Even the fruit trees in the orchard looked as though they'd been given short back and sides by a regimental barber. Against a wall a vine grew symmetrically, while the house with its stone walls and shuttered windows suggested a cosy opulence in its combination of garrison Georgian and art nouveau. On a flagstaff the Union Jack hung limply in the hot summer air and the Kommandant, forgetting his fury of the morning, was glad to see it there. It was, he supposed, because the Heathcote-Kilkoons were real Englishers not the descendants of settlers that the place was so trim and redolent of disciplined assurance. He got into his car and drove to the hotel. He spent the rest of the afternoon fishing the river with no better luck than he had had previously but recovering from the emotional upsets of the morning. Once again the strange sense of self-awareness, of seeing himself from a distance, came over him and with it came a sense of calm acceptance of himself not as he was but as he might remotely be in other, better circumstances. When the sun faded over the Aardvarks he dismantled his rod and walked back to the hotel through the swift dusk. Somewhere near him someone hiccupped but the Kommandant ignored the overture. He'd seen enough of Mr Mulpurgo for one day. He had dinner and went early to bed with a new novel by Dornford Yates. It was called *Perishable Goods*.

In Piemburg Operation White Wash was about to move into a new phase. Luitenant Verkramp had tested his ten volunteers once again in a live situation and was satisfied that the experiment had been wholly successful. Confronted with black women the volunteers had all demonstrated an entirely convincing aversion for them and Verkramp was ready to move to phase two. Sergeant Breitenbach's enthusiasm for the project was as usual less marked.

'Two hundred at a time in the drill hall?' he asked incredulously. 'Two hundred konstabels strapped to chairs and wired up in the drill hall?'

'One sergeant to operate the projector and administer the electric shocks,' Verkramp said. 'Won't be any difficulty about that.'

'There'll be a hell of a difficulty getting two hundred sane men to sit there in the first place,' said the Sergeant, 'and anyway it's impossible. Those generators aren't big enough to shock two hundred men.'

'We'll use the mains,' said Verkramp.

Sergeant Breitenbach stared at him with bulging eyes.

'You'll use what?'

'The mains,' said Verkramp. 'With a transformer of course.'

'Of course,' said the Sergeant with an insane laugh, 'a transformer off the mains. And what happens if something goes wrong?'

'Nothing is going to go wrong,' said Verkramp, but Sergeant Breitenbach wasn't listening. He was visualizing a drill hall filled with the corpses of two hundred konstabels electrocuted while being shown slides of naked black women. Quite apart from the public outcry he would almost certainly be lynched by the widows.

'I'm not having any part of this,' he said emphatically. 'You can keep it.' He turned to leave the office but the Acting Kommandant called him back.

'Sergeant Breitenbach, what we are doing is for the ultimate good of the white race in South Africa,' Verkramp said solemnly. 'Are you prepared to sacrifice the future of your country simply because you are afraid to take a risk?'

'Yes,' said Sergeant Breitenbach who couldn't see how the electrocution of two hundred policemen could possibly benefit South Africa.

Luitenant Verkramp adopted a more practical line of reasoning.

'In any case there will be fuses to prevent accidental overloading,' he said.

'15 Amp I suppose,' said the Sergeant caustically.

'Something of the sort,' said Verkramp airily. 'I'll leave the details to the police electrician.'

'More likely the mortician,' said the Sergeant, whose knowledge of power points was somewhat less limited. 'In any case you'll never get the men to submit to the ordeal. I'm not forcing any man to risk getting himself electrocuted.'

Luitenant Verkramp smiled.

'No need for force,' he said. 'They've all signed the necessary forms.'

'It's one thing to sign a form. It's another to allow someone to give you electric shocks. And what about the electricity? Where are you going to get that from? It's all been cut off since the sabotage.'

Luitenant Verkramp dialled the manager of the Electricity Board. While he waited he showed Sergeant Breitenbach the forms the men had signed. 'Read the small print at the bottom,' he told him.

'Can't without my glasses,' the Sergeant told him. Verkramp snatched the form back and read it aloud.

'I admit freely and of my own volition that I have had sexual intercourse with Bantu women and am in need of treatment,' he said before being interrupted by a horrified squawk from the telephone receiver. The manager of the Electricity Board was on the line.

'You do what?' yelled the manager, appalled at the confession he had just been privy to.

'Not me,' Verkramp tried to explain.

'I heard you quite distinctly,' the manager shouted back. 'You said "I admit freely and of my own volition that I have had sexual intercourse with Bantu women." Deny that if you can.'

'All right, I did say it ...' Verkramp began but the manager was too incensed to let him continue.

'What did I say? You can't deny it. This is an outrage. You ring me up to tell me that you sleep with kaffir girls. I've a good mind to ring the police.'

'This is the police,' said Verkramp.

'Good God, the whole world's gone mad,' shouted the manager.

'I was just reading a prisoner's confession out loud,' Verkramp explained.

'Over the phone?' asked the manager. 'And why to me of all people? I've got enough trouble on my hands without that sort of filth.'

Sergeant Breitenbach left Verkramp to sort the thing out with the Electricity Board. The tempo of events since Verkramp had taken over was so rapid the Sergeant was beginning to feel totally confused.

Much the same could be said of the state of mind of Verkramp's secret agents. Lack of sleep, the need to move their lodgings, the incessant following and being followed that was so much a part of their duties, had left them utterly exhausted and with what little hold on reality they had ever possessed badly impaired. The one sure thing they all knew was that they had been ordered to get the real saboteurs to blow something up. In Florian's café they sat round a table and worked to this end.

745396 suggested the petrol storage tanks in the railway yard as a suitable target. 628461 was in favour of the gasworks. 885974, not to be outdone, recommended the sewage disposal plant on the grounds that the ensuing epidemic would benefit the cause of world Communism, and all the others had their own favourite targets. By the time they had argued the pros and cons of each suggestion no one was clear what target had finally been selected and the air of mutual suspicion had been exacerbated by 885974 who had accused 745396 of being a police spy in the belief that this would add credibility to his own claim to be a genuine saboteur. Accusations and counter-accusations were exchanged and when the group finally left Florian's café to go their none too separate ways, each agent was determined to prove himself to the others by a demonstration of zeal for sabotage. That night Piemburg experienced a second wave of bombings.

At ten the petrol storage tanks exploded and set light to a goods train in the railway yard. At ten-thirty the gasometer exploded with a roar that blew the windows out in several neighbouring streets. As the fire brigade rushed in different directions the sewage disposal plant erupted. All over the previously darkened city fires broke out. In an attempt to prevent a further spread of the flames in the railway yard the goods train was moved down the line and in the process set fire to four tool sheds in the gardens it passed and started a grass fire which spread to a field of sugar cane. By morning Piemburg's fire-fighting force was exhausted and a dark smudge of smoke hung ominously over the city.

Sergeant Breitenbach arrived at the police station with his face covered in sticking plaster. He had been looking out of his bedroom window when the gasometer exploded. He found Verkramp desperately trying to decode several messages from his agents which he hoped would give him some lead to the new outbreak of violence. So far all he had learnt was that the petrol tanks were due to be sabotaged by a man who called himself Jack Jones who lived at the Outspan Hotel. By the time Verkramp had received and deciphered the message both the petrol tanks and Jack Jones had vanished. The manager of the Outspan hotel said he had checked out two days ago.

'What are you doing?' Sergeant Breitenbach asked as he entered the office. The Acting Kommandant stuffed the messages hurriedly into a drawer in his desk.

'Nothing,' he said nervously. 'Nothing at all.'

Sergeant Breitenbach eyed the handbook on Animal Husbandry which was the codebook for the day and wondered if Verkramp was thinking of taking up farming. In the light of the catastrophes which were taking place under his command it seemed wise of Verkramp to be thinking about retiring.

'Well?' said Verkramp, annoyed that he had been interrupted. 'What is it?'

'Isn't it about time you did something about these saboteurs? Things are getting out of hand,' said the Sergeant.

Verkramp stirred uneasily in his chair. He had the feeling that his authority was being impugned.

'I can see you got out of bed on the wrong side this morning,' he said.

'I didn't get out at all,' said the Sergeant, 'I was blown out. By the sewage disposal works.'

Verkramp smiled.

'I thought you'd cut your face shaving,' he said.

'That was the gasometer,' Sergeant Breitenbach told him. 'I was looking out the window when it blew up.'

'Through. Not out of,' said Verkramp pedantically.

'Through what?'

'Through the window. If you had been looking out the window you wouldn't have been hit by flying glass. It's really very important for a police officer to get his facts right.'

Sergeant Breitenbach pointed out that he was lucky to be still alive.

'A miss is as good as a mile,' said Verkramp.

'Half a mile,' said the Sergeant.

'Half a mile?'

'I live half a mile from the gasometer since you want the facts right,' said the Sergeant. 'What it must have been like for the people living next door to it I can't think.'

Luitenant Verkramp stood up and strode across to the window and stared out. Something about the way he was standing reminded the Sergeant of a film he had seen about a general on the eve of a battle. Verkramp had one hand behind his back and the other tucked into his tunic.

'I am about to strike a blow at the root of all this evil,' he said dramatically before turning and fixing an intense look on the Sergeant. 'Have you ever looked evil in the face?'

Sergeant Breitenbach, remembering the gasometer, said he had.

'Then you'll know what I am talking about,' said Verkramp enigmatically and sat down.

'Where do you think we should start looking?' the Sergeant asked.

'In the heart of man,' said Verkramp.

'In where?' said the Sergeant.

'In the heart of man. In his soul. In the innermost regions of his nature.'

'For saboteurs?' asked Sergeant Breitenbach.

'For evil,' said Verkramp. He handed the Sergeant a long list of names. 'I want these men to report to the Drill Hall immediately. Everything is ready. The chairs have been wired and the projector and the screen have been installed. Here is a list of the Sergeants who will administer the treatment.'

Sergeant Breitenbach stared maniacally at his commanding officer.

'You've gone mad,' he said finally. 'You must have gone out of your mind. We've got the biggest wave of bombings this country has seen, with petrol tanks and gasometers going up and radio masts coming down and all you can think about is stopping people going to bed with coons. You're fucking loony.' The Sergeant stopped, stunned by the accuracy of his last remark. Before he could draw any further conclusions from it, Luitenant Verkramp was on his feet.

'Sergeant Breitenbach,' he screamed, and the Sergeant shrank at his fury, 'are you refusing to obey an order?' A demonic hopefulness in Verkramp's tone frightened the Sergeant.

'No, sir. Not an order,' he said. The sacrosanct word recalled him to his uncritical senses. 'Law and order have to be maintained at all times.'

Luitenant Verkramp was mollified.

'Precisely,' he said. 'Well I'm the law round this town and I give the orders. My orders are that you start the treatment of aversion therapy at once. The sooner we have a truly Christian and incorruptible police force the sooner we will be able to eradicate the evil of which these bombings are merely the symptom. It's no use treating the mere manifestations of evil, Sergeant, unless we first cleanse the body politic and that, God willing, is what I intend to do. What has happened in Piemburg should be a lesson to us all. That smoke out there is a sign from Heaven of God's anger. Let us all see to it that we incur no more.'

'Yes sir. I sincerely hope so sir,' said Sergeant Brietenbach. 'Any special precautions you want taken in case we do, sir? Any guards on the remaining public installations?'

'No need, Sergeant,' said Verkramp loftily, 'I have the matter in hand.'

'Very good, sir,' said Sergeant Breitenbach and left the room to carry out his orders. Twenty minutes later he was facing near-mutiny in the drill hall as two hundred konstabels, already alarmed at the deteriorating situation in the city, refused to allow themselves to be strapped to the chairs wired to a large transformer. Quite a few had already said they would rather stand trial for sleeping with kaffir girls and take their chance of getting ten strokes with a heavy cane and do seven years' hard labour than run the risk of electrocution. Finally he telephoned Luitenant Verkramp, and explained the dilemma. Verkramp said he'd be down in five minutes.

He arrived to find the men milling about rebelliously in the Drill Hall.

'Outside,' he ordered briskly and turned to Sergeant Breitenbach. 'Assemble these men in platoons under their sergeants.'

Two hundred konstabels lined up obediently on the parade ground. Luitenant Verkramp addressed them.

'Men,' he said. 'Men of the South African Police, you have been brought here to test your steadfast loyalty to your country and your race. The enemies of South Africa have been using black women to seduce you from the path of duty. Now is your chance to prove that you are worthy of the great trust the white women of South Africa have placed in you. Your wives and mothers, your sisters and daughters look to you in this great moment of trial to prove yourself loyal fathers and husbands. The test that you have now to pass will prove that loyalty. You will singly come into the Drill Hall and be shown certain pictures. Those of you who do not respond to them will return immediately to the police station. Those of you who fail will assemble here on the parade ground to await instructions. In the meantime Sergeant Breitenbach will give the rest of you drill practice. Carry on, Sergeant.'

As the konstabels marched and countermarched up and down the hot parade ground they watched the men who were called singly disappear into the drill hall. It was quite clear that they all passed the test. None returned to the parade ground. As the last man passed through the door, Sergeant Breitenbach followed him in curious to see what had happened. In front of him the last konstabel was seized by four sergeants, had sticking plaster swiftly clapped over his mouth and was strapped to the last empty chair. Two hundred silent konstabels glared frantically at their Acting Kommandant. The lights were switched off and the projector on. On the vast screen at the end of the hall, naked as the day she was born and forty times as large, there appeared the brilliantly coloured image of a gigantic black woman. Luitenant Verkramp mounted the stage and stood in front of the screen, partially obscuring the woman's sexual organs and with an aura of pubic hairs sprouting round his head.

with a nauseating realism Verkramp opened his mouth, his face livid with projected labia.

'This is for you own good,' he said. 'By the time you leave this hall your transracial sexual tendencies will have been eradicated for ever. You will have been cleansed of the lusts of the flesh. Start the treatment.' Below him two hundred konstabels jerked in their seats with a uniformity of movement that had been noticeably lacking in their drill.

As they drove back to the police station, Sergeant Breitenbach complimented Verkramp on his cunning.

'It's all a question of psychology,' said Verkramp smugly. 'Divide and rule.'

CHAPTER NINE

At Fort Rapier Mental Hospital Dr von Blimenstein was unaware of the effect her advice about aversion therapy was having on the lives of Piemburg's policemen. She still thought about Verkramp and wondered why he hadn't contacted her but the outbreak of sabotage suggested an explanation which did something to satisfy her vanity. 'He's too busy, poor lamb,' she thought and found an outlet for her sense of disappointment by trying to cope with the influx of patients suffering from acute anxiety following the bombings. A great many were suffering from Bloodbath Phobia, and were obsessed by the belief that they were going to be chopped to pieces one morning by the black servant next door. Dr von Blimenstein was not immune to the infection, which was endemic among South African Whites, but she did her best to calm the fears of her new patients.

'Why the servant next door?' she asked a particularly disturbed woman who wouldn't even allow a black orderly into her room at the hospital to empty the chamber pot but preferred to do it herself, an action so extraordinarily menial for a white woman that it was a clear symptom of insanity.

'Because that's what my kitchen boy told me,' the woman said through her tears.

'Your kitchen boy said the servants next door would come and kill you?' Dr von Blimenstein asked patiently.

The woman struggled to control herself.

'I said to him, "Joseph, you wouldn't kill your missus, would you?" and he said, "No missus, the boy next door would kill you and I'd kill his missus for him." You see they've got it all worked out. We're going to be massacred in our beds when they bring the tea in at seven o'clock in the morning.'

'You don't think it might be wise to give up morning tea?' the doctor asked but the woman wouldn't hear of it.

'I don't think I could get through the day without my morning cup of tea,' she said. Dr von Blimenstein refrained from pointing out that there was a logical inconsistency between this assertion and her previous remarks about being cut up. Instead she wrote out her usual prescription in such cases and sent her to see the Gunnery Instructer.

'Occupational therapy,' she explained to the woman who was presently happily engaged in firing a .38 revolver into targets painted to look like black servants holding tea trays in one hand and pangas in the other.

Dr von Blimenstein's next patient suffered from Blackcock Fever which was even more frequent than Bloodbath Phobia.

'They've got such big ones,' she mumbled to the doctor when asked what the trouble was.

'Big whats?' Dr von Blimenstein asked although she could recognize the symptoms immediately.

'You know. Hoohas,' the woman muttered indistinctly.

'Hoohas?'

'Whatsits.'

'Whatsits?' said the doctor who believed that part of the cure consisted in getting the patient to express her fears openly. In front of her the woman went bright pink.

'Their wibbledy wands,' she said frantically trying to make herself understood.

'I'm afraid you'll have to make yourself clearer, my dear,' said Dr von Blimenstein, 'I've no idea what you're trying to tell me.'

The woman screwed up her courage. 'They've got long pork swords,' she said finally. Dr von Blimenstein wrote it down repeating each word. 'They ... have ... long ... pork ... swords.' She looked up. 'And what is a pork sword?' she asked brightly. The patient looked at her wildly.

'You mean to say you don't know?' she asked.

Dr von Blimenstein shook her head. 'I've no idea,' she lied.

'You're not married?' the woman asked. The doctor shook her head again. 'Well in that case I'm not telling you. You'll find out on your wedding night.' She relapsed into a stubborn silence.

'Shall we start again?' Dr von Blimenstein asked. 'A pork sword is a wibbledy wand is a whatsit is a hoo ha, is that right?'

'Oh for God's sake,' shouted the woman appalled at the catalogue of sexual euphemisms. 'I'm talking about their knobs.'

'Is a knob,' said the doctor and wrote it down. In front of her the woman squirmed with embarrassment.

'What do you want me to do? Spell it out for you?' she yelled.

'Please do,' said the doctor, 'I think we should get this matter straight.' The patient shuddered.

'Pee, Are, Eye, See, Kay, spells prick,' she screamed. She seemed to think it was the definitive term.

'You mean penis, don't you, dear?' Dr von Blimenstein asked.

'Yes,' screamed the patient hysterically, 'I mean penis, prick, pork sword, knob, the lot. What's it matter what you call it? They've all got huge ones.'

'Who have?'

'Kaffirs have. They're eighteen inches long and three inches thick and they've got foreskins like umbrellas and they –'

'Now, hold it a moment,' Dr von Blimenstein said as the woman became more hysterical. Coming on top of her previous embarrassment the suggestion was more than the woman could take.

'Hold it?' she screamed. 'Hold it?' I couldn't bear to look at it let alone hold the beastly thing.'

Dr von Blimenstein leant across the desk.

'That's not what I meant,' she said. 'You're taking this thing too far.'

'Far?' shrieked the woman. 'I'll say it's far. It's far farther than I can take it. It's instant hysterectomy. It's ...'

'You've got to try to see this –'

'I don't want to see it. That's the whole point. I'm terrified of seeing it.'

'In proportion,' shouted the doctor authoritatively.

'In proportion to what?' the woman shouted. 'In proportion to my creamy way I suppose. Well I tell you I can't take it.'

'No one is asking you to,' said the doctor. 'In the first place –'

'In the first place? In the first place? Don't tell me they'd try the second.' The patient was on her feet now.

Dr von Blimenstein left her chair and pushed the patient back into her seat.

'We mustn't let our imaginations run away with us,' she said soothingly. 'You're quite safe here with me. Now then,' she continued when the woman had calmed down, 'if we are to do any good you've got to realize that penises are merely symptoms. It's the thing behind them we've got to look for.'

The woman stared wildly round the room. 'That's not difficult,' she said. 'They're all over the place.'

Dr von Blimenstein hastened to explain. 'What I mean is the deep-seated ... Now what's the matter?' The woman had slumped to the floor. When she came round again the doctor revised her approach.

'I'm not going to say anything,' she explained, 'and I just want you to tell me what you think.'

The woman calmed down and pondered.

'They hang weights on the end to make them longer,' she said finally.

'Do they really?' said the doctor. 'That's very interesting.'

'It's not. It's disgusting.'

Dr von Blimenstein agreed that it was also disgusting.

'They walk about with half-bricks tied to the end with bits of string,' the woman continued. 'Under their trousers of course.'

'I should hope so,' said Dr von Blimenstein.

'They put butter on too to make them grow. They think butter helps.'

'I should have thought it would have made it difficult to keep the brick on,' said Dr von Blimenstein more practically. 'The string would slip off, wouldn't it?'

The patient considered the problem.

'They tie the string on first,' she said finally.

'That seems perfectly logical,' said the psychiatrist. 'Is there anything else you'd like to tell me? Your married life is quite satisfactory?'

'Well,' said the woman doubtfully, 'it could be worse if you see what I mean.' Dr von Blimenstein nodded sympathetically.

'I think we can cure your phobia,' she said making some notes. 'Now the course of treatment I'm prescribing is a little unusual at first sight but you'll soon get the hang of it. First of all what we do is this. We get you used to the idea of holding quite a small penis, a small white one and then ...'

'You get me used to doing what?' the woman asked in amazement and with a look that suggested she thought the doctor was insane.

'Holding small white penises.'

'You must be mad,' shouted the woman, 'I wouldn't dream of such a thing. I'm a respectable married woman and if you think I'm going to ...' She began to weep hysterically.

Dr von Blimenstein leant across the desk reassuringly.

'All right,' she said. 'We'll cut out the penises to begin with.'

'God Almighty,' shouted the woman, 'and I thought I needed treatment.'

Dr von Blimenstein calmed her. 'I mean we'll leave them out,' she said. 'We'll start with pencils. Have you any rooted objection to holding a pencil?'

'Of course not,' said the woman. 'Why the hell should I mind holding a pencil?'

'Or a ball-point pen?' Dr von Blimenstein watched the woman's face for any sign of hesitancy.

'Ball-points are fine with me. So are fountain pens,' said the patient.

'How about a banana?'

'You want me to hold it or eat it?' the woman inquired.

'Just hold it.'

'That's no problem.'

'A banana and two plums?'

The woman looked at her critically. 'I'll hold a fruit salad if you think it'll do me any good though what the hell you think you're getting at is beyond me.'

In the end Dr von Blimenstein began treatment by accustoming the patient to hold a vegetable marrow until it ceased to provoke any symptoms of anxiety.

While the Doctor wrestled with the psychological problems of her patients and Verkramp served his God by casting out devils, Kommandant van Heerden passed uneventful days in Weezen, fishing the river, reading the novels of Dornford Yates and wondering why, since he had called on the Heathcote-Kilkoons, they had not got in touch with him at the hotel. On the fourth day he pocketed his pride and approached Mr Mulpurgo who, being an authority on everything else, seemed the most likely person to explain the mysteries of English etiquette.

He found Mr Mulpurgo hiccuping softly to himself in an old rose arbour in the garden. The Kommandant seated himself on the bench beside the English lecturer.

'I was wondering if you could help me,' he began. Mr Mulpurgo hiccuped loudly.

'What is it?' he asked nervously. 'I'm busy.'

'If you had been invited to stay with some people in the country,' the Kommandant said, 'and you arrived at the hotel and they didn't come and visit you, what would you think?'

Mr Mulpurgo tried to figure out what the Kommandant was getting at.

'If I had been invited to stay with some people in the country,' he said, 'I don't see what I'd be doing at a hotel unless of course they owned the hotel.'

'They said the house was full.'

'Well is it?' Mr Mulpurgo inquired.

'No,' said the Kommandant, 'they're not there.' He paused. 'Well they weren't there when I went the other day.'

Mr Mulpurgo said it sounded very odd.

'Are you sure you got the dates right?' he asked.

'Oh yes. I checked them,' the Kommandant said.

'You could always phone them.'

'They're not on the phone.'

Mr Mulpurgo picked up his book again. 'You seem to be in a bit of a quandary,' he said. 'If I were you I think I'd pay them another call and if they're not there go home.'

The Kommandant nodded uncertainly. 'I suppose so,' he said. Mr Mulpurgo hiccuped again. 'Still got flatulence?' the Kommandant asked sympathetically. 'You should try holding your breath. That sometimes works.'

Mr Mulpurgo said he had already tried a number of times without results.

'I once cured a man of hiccups,' the Kommandant continued reminiscently, 'by giving him a fright. He was a car thief.'

'Really,' said Mr Mulpurgo, 'what did you do?'

'Told him he was going to be flogged.'

Mr Mulpurgo shuddered. 'How simply awful,' he said.

'He was too,' said the Kommandant. 'Got fifteen strokes ... Stopped his hiccups though.' He smiled at the thought. Beside him the English lecturer considered the terrible implications of that smile and it seemed to him, not for the first time, that he was in the presence of some elemental force for whom or which there were no questions of right or wrong, no moral feelings, no ethical considerations but simply naked power. There was something monstrous in the Kommandant's simplicity. There had been nothing even remotely metaphorical about the Kommandant's 'Dog eats dog'. It was no more than a fact of his existence. In the face of the reality of this world of brute force, Mr Mulpurgo's literary aspirations assumed a non-entity.

'I suppose you approve of flogging,' he asked knowing the answer.

'It's the only thing that really works,' said the Kommandant. 'Prison's no good. It's too comfortable. But when a man has been flogged, he doesn't forget it. It's the same with hanging.'

'Always assuming there's an after-life,' Mr Mulpurgo said. 'Otherwise I should have thought hanging was as good a way of forgetting as you could think of.'

'After-life or no after-life, a man who's been hanged doesn't commit any more crimes, I can tell you,' said the Kommandant.

'And is that all that matters to you?' Mr Mulpurgo asked. 'That he doesn't commit any more crimes?'

Kommandant van Heerden nodded.

'That's my job,' he said, 'that's what I'm paid to do.'

Mr Mulpurgo tried again.

'Doesn't life mean anything to you? The sacredness of life, its beauty and joy and innocence?'

'When I eat a lamb chop I don't think about sheep,' said the Kommandant. Mr Mulpurgo hiccuped at the imagery.

'What a terrible picture of life you have,' he said. 'There seems no hope at all.'

The Kommandant smiled. 'There's always hope, my friend,' he said patting Mr Mulpurgo's shoulder and levering himself up from the seat at the same time. 'Always hope.'

The Kommandant stumped off and presently Mr Mulpurgo rose from the arbour and walked into Weezen.

'Extraordinary number of drunks there are about these days,' Major Bloxham remarked next morning at breakfast. 'Met a fellow in bar last night. Lectures in English at the University. Can't have been more than thirty. Blind drunk and kept shouting about a purpose in liquidity of all things. Had to take him back to the hotel. Some sort of Spa.'

'Don't know what young people are coming to,' said the Colonel. 'If it isn't drink, it's drugs. Whole country's going to the dogs.' He got up and went out to the kennels to see how Harbinger was getting on.

'Spa?' asked Mrs Heathcote-Kilkoon when the Colonel had left. 'Did you say Spa, Boy?'

'Sort of run-down sort of place. Takes guests,' said the Major.

'Then that must be where the Kommandant is staying,' Mrs Heathcote-Kilkoon said. She finished her breakfast and ordered the Rolls and presently, leaving the Colonel and Major Bloxham discussing the seating at the Club dinner that evening, she drove over to Weezen. Club dinners were such boring affairs, so boring and unreal. People in Zululand lacked the chic which had made life so tolerable in Nairobi. Too *raffiné*, she thought, falling back on that small stock of French words with which she was *au fait* and which had been *de rigueur* among her friends in Kenya. That was what was such a change about the Kommandant. No one could possibly accuse him of being *raffiné*.

'There's something so earthy about him,' she murmured as she parked outside the Weezen Spa and went inside.

There was something fairly earthy about the Kommandant's room when she finally found it and knocked on the door. The Kommandant opened it in his underwear, he had been changing to go fishing, and shut it again hurriedly. By the time he opened it again properly apparelled Mrs Heathcote-Kilkoon, who had spent the interval studying the enamel plaque on the door, had drawn her own conclusions as to the origins of the smell.

'Do come in,' said the Kommandant, demonstrating once again that lack of refinement Mrs Heathcote-Kilkoon found so attractive. She entered and looked dubiously around.

'Don't let me interrupt you,' she said glancing significantly at the taps and tubes.

'No, not at all. I was just about ...'

'Quite,' said Mrs Heathcote-Kilkoon hurriedly. 'There's no need to go into the details. We all have our little ailments I daresay.'

'Ailments?' said the Kommandant.

Mrs Heathcote-Kilkoon wrinkled her nose and opened the door.

'Though to judge from the smell in here, yours are rather more serious than most.' She stepped into the corridor and the Kommandant followed her.

'It's the sulphur,' he hastened to explain.

'Nonsense,' said Mrs Heathcote-Kilkoon. 'it's lack of exercise. Well, we'll soon put that right. What you need is a good gallop before breakfast. What's your seat like?'

Kommandant van Heerden rather huffily said that as far as he knew there was nothing wrong with it.

'Well, that's something,' said Mrs Heathcote-Kilkoon.

They went out through the revolving doors and stood on the terrace where the air was fresher. Something of the acerbity went out of Mrs Heathcote-Kilkoon's manner.

'I'm so sorry you've been stranded here like this,' she said. 'It's all our fault. We looked for you at the hotel in town but I had no idea that this place existed.'

She leaned voguishly against the balustrade and contemplated the building with its stippled portico and faded legend. The Kommandant explained that he had tried to phone but that he couldn't find the number.

'Of course you couldn't, my dear,' said Mrs Heathcote-Kilkoon taking his arm and leading him down into the garden. 'We don't have one.

Henry's so secretive, you know. He plays the stock market and he can't bear the thought of anyone listening in and making a killing in kaffirs because he's heard Henry telling his broker to buy Free State Gedulds.'

'That's understandable,' said the Kommandant completely at sea.

They wandered down the path to the river and Mrs Heathcote-Kilkoon chattered away about life in Kenya and how she missed the gay times of Thomson's Falls.

'We had such a lovely place, Littlewoods Lodge, it was called after ... well never mind. Let's just say it was named after Henry's first big *coup* and of course there were acres and acres of azaleas. I think that's why Henry chose Kenya in the first place. He's absolutely mad about flowers, you know and azaleas don't do awfully well in South London.'

The Kommandant said the Colonel must have been keen on flowers to come all the way to Africa just to grow them.

'And besides there was the question of taxes,' Mrs Heathcote-Kilkoon continued, 'I mean once Henry had won the pools ... I mean when Henry came into money, it simply wasn't possible for him to live in England with that dreadful Labour government taking every penny in taxes.'

Presently, when they had walked beside the river, Mrs Heathcote-Kilkoon said she must be getting back.

'Now don't forget tonight,' she said as the Kommandant helped her into the Rolls, 'dinner's at eight. Cocktails at seven. I'll look forward to seeing you. *Au 'voir*,' and with a wave of her mauve glove she was gone.

'You've done what?' Colonel Heathcote-Kilkoon spluttered when his wife returned to say that the Kommandant was coming to dinner. 'Don't you realize it's Berry Night? We can't have some damned stranger sitting in on the Club dinner.'

'I've invited him and he's coming,' insisted Mrs Heathcote-Kilkoon. 'He's been sitting in that ghastly spa for the past week giving himself enemas out of sheer boredom simply because Boy's such an idiot he had to go and drink in the wrong bar.'

'Oh, I say,' expostulated Major Bloxham, 'that's hardly fair.'

'No, it isn't,' said Mrs Heathcote-Kilkoon, 'it isn't fair. So he's coming to dinner tonight, Club or no Club, and I expect you both to behave yourselves.'

She went up to her room and spent the afternoon dreaming of strong silent men and the musky smell of the Kommandant. Outside in the garden she could hear the click of the Colonel's secateurs as he worked off his irritation on the ornamental shrubbery. By the time Mrs Heathcote-

Kilkoon came down for tea the bush that had formerly resembled a chicken had assumed the new proportions of a parrot. So, it seemed, had the Colonel.

'Yes, my dear,' 'No, my dear,' the Colonel interjected as Mrs Heathcote-Kilkoon explained that the Kommandant would fit in perfectly well with the other members of the Club.

'After all, it's not as though he's illiterate,' she said. 'He's read the Berry books and he told me himself he was a fan of the Master.'

She left the two men and went to the kitchen to supervise the Zulu cook who among other things was desperately trying to figure out how to cook *Filet de boeuf en chemise strasbourgeoise.*

Left to themselves the two men smiled knowingly.

'Nothing like having a buffoon at a dinner,' said the Colonel. 'Should be quite fun.'

'The court jester,' said the Major. 'Get him pissed and have a lark. Might even debag the bugger.'

'That's an idea,' said the Colonel. 'Teach the swine some manners, eh?'

In his room at the Spa Kommandant van Heerden studied his book *Etiquette for Every Man* and tried to remember which fork to use for fish. At six he had another makeshift bath and sprayed himself all over with deodorant to neutralize the smell of sulphur. Then he put on the Harris Tweed suit he had had made for him at Scurfield and Todd, the English tailors in Piemburg, and which the coloured maid had pressed meticulously for him and at seven drove up to White Ladies. The gravel forecourt was crowded with cars. The Kommandant parked and went up the steps to the front door which was opened by the Zulu butler. Mrs Heathcote-Kilkoon came down the hall to receive him.

'Oh, my God,' she said by way of welcome, appalled at the Kommandant's suit – everyone else was wearing dinner jackets – and then with a greater show of *savoir-faire*, 'Well never mind. It can't be helped,' ushered the Kommandant into a room filled with smoke and talk and people.

'I can't see Henry just at the moment,' she said judiciously, steering the Kommandant to a table where Major Bloxham was dispensing drinks. 'But Boy'll make you a cocktail.'

'What's your poison, old man,' Major Bloxham asked.

The Kommandant said he'd appreciate a beer.

The Major looked askance. 'Can't have that, my dear fellow,' he said. 'Cocktails you know. The good old Twenties and all that. Have an Oom

Paul Special,' and before the Kommandant could ask what an Oom Paul Special was, the Major was busy with a shaker.

'Very tasty,' said the Kommandant sipping the drink which consisted of apple brandy, Dubonnet and, to make it Special, had an extra slug of vodka.

'Glad you like it,' said the Major. 'Knock it back and you can have a Sledge Hammer,' but before the Kommandant could experience the effects of a mixture of brandy, rum, and apple brandy on top of the Oom Paul Mrs Heathcote-Kilkoon whisked him as discreetly as the crowd would allow away to meet Henry. The Colonel regarded Kommandant van Heerden's suit with interest.

'Glad you could make it, Kommandant,' he said with an affability his wife found disturbing. 'Tell me, do Boers always wear Harris Tweed to dinner parties?'

'Now, Henry,' Mrs Heathcote-Kilkoon interjected before the Kommandant could reply, 'The Kommandant was hardly prepared for formality in the country. My husband,' she continued to the Kommandant, 'is such a stickler for . . .' The rest of the sentence was drowned by the boom of an enormous gong and as the reverberations died away the Zulu butler announced that dinner was served. It was half-past seven. Mrs Heathcote-Kilkoon hurled herself across the room and after a brief and bitter exchange of views in which she called the butler a black oaf twice, the hostess turned with a ceramic smile to the gathering. 'Just a misunderstanding about times,' she said, and with some further remark about the difficulty of getting decent servants mingled serenely with the crowd. The Kommandant, finding himself deserted, finished his Oom Paul and went over to the bar and asked for a Sledge Hammer. Then he found himself a quiet corner beside a goldfish which matched his suit and surveyed the other guests. Apart from the Colonel, whose bilious eye marked him out as a man of distinction, the other men were hardly what the Kommandant had expected. They seemed to exude an air of confident uncertainty and their conversation lacked that urbane banter he had found in the pages of *Berry & Co*. In a little group near him a small fat man was explaining how he could get a fifty per cent discount off on fridges while someone else was arguing that the only way to buy meat was wholesale. The Kommandant moved slowly round the room catching a sentence here and there about roses and the July Handicap and somebody's divorce. At the make-shift bar, Major Bloxham gave him a Third Degree.

'Appropriate, old boy, what?' he said, but before the Kommandant could drink it, the gong had reverberated again and not wishing to waste the cocktail the Kommandant poured it into the goldfish bowl before going in to dinner.

'You're to sit between La Marquise and me,' Mrs Heathcote-Kilkoon said as they stood awkwardly around the long table in the dining-room. 'That way you'll be safe,' and the Kommandant presently found himself next to what he took to be a distinctly queer man in a dinner jacket who kept calling everyone darling. He shifted his chair a little closer to Mrs Heathcote-Kilkoon, uncomfortably aware that the man was eyeing him speculatively. The Kommandant fiddled with the silver and wondered why he found the Colonel's eye on him. In a moment of silence the man on his right asked him what he did.

'Do?' said the Kommandant suspiciously. The word had too many meanings for an easy answer.

La Marquise discerned his embarrassment. 'For a living, darling, do for a living. Not me for God's sake. That I do assure you.' Round the table everyone laughed and the Kommandant added to it by saying that he was a policeman. He was about to say that he'd seen some fucking poofters in his time but ... when Mrs Heathcote-Kilkoon whispered, 'She's a woman,' in his ear. The Kommandant went from pink to pale at the thought of the gaffe he had been about to commit and took a gulp of the Australian Burgundy which it appeared the Colonel thought was almost the equal of a Chambertin '59.

By the time the coffee had been served and the port was circulating the Kommandant had quite recovered his self-confidence. He had scored twice, quite accidentally, off La Marquise, once by asking her if her husband was present, and the second time by leaning across her to reach for the salt, and jostling what there was of her well disguised bosom. On his left, flushed with wine and the Kommandant's pervasive manliness, Mrs Heathcote-Kilkoon pressed her leg discreetly against his, smiling brightly and fingering her pearls. When the Colonel rose to propose the toast to the Master, Mrs Heathcote-Kilkoon nudged him and indicated a photograph over the mantelpiece. 'That's Major Mercer,' she whispered, 'Dornford Yates.' The Kommandant nodded and studied the face that peered back disgustedly from the picture. Two fierce eyes, one slightly larger than the other; and a bristly moustache; the romantic author looked like a disgruntled sergeant major. 'I suppose that's where the word authority comes from, author,' thought the Kommandant, passing the port the wrong way. In deference to La Marquise the ladies had not withdrawn and presently the Zulu waiter brought round cigars.

'Not your Henry Clays, just Rhodesian Macanudos,' said the Colonel modestly. The Kommandant took one and lit it.

'Ever tried rolling your own?' he asked the Colonel and was surprised at the suffused look on his face.

'Certainly not,' said Colonel Heathcote-Kilkoon, already irritated by the erratic course of the port. 'Whoever heard of anyone rolling his own cigars?'

'I have,' replied the Kommandant blandly. 'My ouma had a farm in the Magaliesburg and she grew tobacco. You have to roll it on the inside of your thigh.'

'How frightfully oumanistic,' La Marquise said shrilly. When the laughter died down, the Kommandant went on.

'My ouma took snuff. We used to grind that down for her.'

The circle of flushed faces examined the man in the Harris Tweed suit whose grandmother took snuff.

'What a colourful family you have,' said the fat man who knew how to get discounts on fridges and was startled to find the Kommandant leaning across the table towards him with a look of unmistakable fury.

'If I weren't in someone else's house,' snarled the Kommandant, 'you would regret that remark.' The fat man turned pale and Mrs Heathcote-Kilkoon placed her hand restrainingly on the Kommandant's arm.

'Have I said something wrong?' the fat man asked.

'I think Mr Evans meant that your family is very interesting,' Mrs Heathcote-Kilkoon explained in a whisper to the Kommandant.

'It didn't sound like that to me,' said the Kommandant. At the end of the table Colonel Heathcote-Kilkoon, who felt that he needed to assert his authority somewhere, ordered the waiters to bring liqueurs. It was not a wise move. Major Bloxham, evidently still piqued by the failure of his Oom Paul Special and Sledge Hammer to render the Kommandant suitable for debagging, offered him some Chartreuse. As his port glass filled with the stuff, the Kommandant looked at it interestingly.

'I've never seen a green wine before,' he said finally.

'Made from green grapes, old boy,' said the Major and was delighted at the laugh he got. 'Got to drink it all in one go.' Mrs Heathcote-Kilkoon was not amused.

'How low can you get, Boy?' she asked unpleasantly as the Kommandant swallowed the glassful.

'How high can you get?' said the Major jocularly.

La Marquise added her comment. 'High? My dears,' she shrieked, 'you should sit here to find out. Absolute Gorgonzola I do assure you,' a remark which led to a misunderstanding with the waiter who brought her the cheese board. Through it all Kommandant van Heerden sat smiling happily at the warmth spreading through him. He decided to apologize to the fat man and was about to when the Major offered him another glass of Chartreuse. The Kommandant accepted graciously in spite of a sharp kick from Mrs Heathcote-Kilkoon.

'I think we should all join the Kommandant,' she said suddenly, 'we can't let him drink by himself. Boy, fill all the port glasses.'

The Major looked at her questioningly. 'All?' he asked.

'You heard me,' said Mrs Heathcote-Kilkoon, looking vindictively from the Major to her husband. 'All. I think we should all drink a toast to the South African Police in honour of our guest.'

'I'm damned if I'm going to drink a whole port glass of Chartreuse for anyone,' said the Colonel.

'Have I ever told you how Henry spent the war?' Mrs Heathcote-Kilkoon asked the table at large. Colonel Heathcote-Kilkoon turned pale and raised his glass.

'To the South African Police,' he said hurriedly.

'To the South African Police,' said Mrs Heathcote-Kilkoon with more enthusiasm, and watched carefully while the Colonel and Major Bloxham drank their glasses dry.

Happily unaware of the tension around him, the Kommandant sat and smiled. So this was how the English spent their evenings, he thought, and felt thoroughly at home.

In the silence that followed the toast and the realization of what a large glass of Chartreuse could do to the liver, Kommandant van Heerden rose to his feet.

'I should like to say how honoured I feel to be here tonight in this distinguished gathering,' he said, pausing and looking at the faces that gazed glaucously back at him. 'What I am going to say may come as something of a surprise to you.' At the end of the table Colonel Heathcote-Kilkoon shut his eyes and shuddered. If the Kommandant's speech was going to be anything like his taste in clothes and wines, he couldn't imagine what to expect. In the event he was pleasantly surprised.

'I am, as you know, an Afrikaner,' continued the Kommandant. 'Or as you British say a Boer, but I want you to know that I admire you British very much and I would like to propose a toast to the British Empire.'

It took some time for the Colonel to realize what the Kommandant had just said. He opened his eyes in amazement and was appalled to see that the Kommandant had taken a bottle of Benedictine and was filling everyone's glass.

'Now, Henry,' Mrs Heathcote-Kilkoon said when the Colonel looked imploringly at her, 'for the honour of the British Empire.'

'Dear God,' said the Colonel.

The Kommandant finished replenishing the port glasses and raised his own.

'To the British Empire,' he said and drank it down, before staring with sudden belligerence at the Colonel who had taken a sip and was wondering what to do with the rest.

'Now, Henry,' said Mrs Heathcote-Kilkoon. The Colonel finished his glass and slumped miserably in his chair.

The Kommandant sat down happily. The sense of disappointment that had so marred the early part of the evening had quite disappeared. So had La Marquise. With a brave attempt at one last 'darling' she slid, elegant to the last, beneath the table. As the full effects of Kommandant van Heerden's devotion to the British Empire began to make themselves felt, the Zulu waiter, evidently anxious to get to bed, hastened the process by producing both the cheese board and the cigars.

Colonel Heathcote-Kilkoon tried to correct him.

'Stilton and cigars don't go toge ...' he said before stumbling from the room. Behind him the party broke up. The fat man fell asleep. Major Bloxham was ill. And Mrs Heathcote-Kilkoon pressed a great deal more than her leg against the Kommandant. 'Take me ...' she said before collapsing across his lap. The Kommandant looked fondly down at her blue rinsed curls and with unusual gallantry eased her head off his flies and stood up.

'Time for bed,' he said and lifting Mrs Heathcote-Kilkoon gently from her seat carried her to her room closely followed by the Zulu butler who suspected his motives.

As he laid her on her bed Mrs Heathcote-Kilkoon smiled in her sleep. 'Not now, darling,' she murmured, evidently dreaming. 'Not now. Tomorrow.'

The Kommandant tiptoed from the room and went to thank his host for a lovely evening. There was no sign of the Colonel in the dining-room where the Dornford Yates Club lay inertly on or under the table. Only Major Bloxham showed any signs of activity and these were such as to prevent any conversation.

'Totsiens,' said the Kommandant and was rewarded for his Afrikaans farewell by a fresh eructation from the Major. As the Kommandant glanced round the room he noticed a movement from under the table. Someone was evidently trying to revive La Marquise though why this should require the removal of her trousers the Kommandant couldn't imagine. Lifting the table cloth he peered underneath. A face peered back at him. The Kommandant suddenly felt unwell. 'I've had too much,' he thought recalling what he had heard about DTs and dropping the cloth hurriedly he rushed from the room. In the darkness of the garden the click of the cicadas was joined erratically by the sound of the Colonel's secateurs but Kommandant van Heerden had no ear for them. His mind was on the two eyes that had peered back at him from beneath the table cloth – two beady eyes and a horrid face and the face was the face of Els. But Konstabel Els was dead. 'I'll be seeing pink elephants next,' he thought in horror as he got into his car and drove dangerously back to the Spa where presently he was trying to purge his system by drinking the filthy water in his room.

CHAPTER TEN

Kommandant van Heerden was not alone in suffering from the illusion that he was having hallucinations. In Piemburg Luitenant Verkramp's efforts to extirpate subversive elements in the body politic were resulting in the appearance of a new and bizarre outbreak of sabotage, this time in the streets of the city. Once again the violence had its origins in the devious nature of the Security chief's line of communication with his agents.

628461's 'drop' for Thursday was in the Bird Sanctuary. To be precise it was in a garbage can outside the Ostrich Enclosure, a convenient spot from everybody's point of view because it was a perfectly logical place to drop things into, and just the sort of place for a Security cop disguised as a hobo to get things out of. Every Thursday morning 628461 sauntered through the Bird Sanctuary, bought an ice cream from the vendor and wrapped his message in sticky silver paper and deposited it in the garbage can while ostensibly observing the habits of the ostriches. Every Thursday afternoon Security Konstabel van Rooyen, dressed authentically in rags and clutching an empty sherry bottle, arrived at the Bird Sanctuary and peered hopefully into the garbage can only to find it empty. The fact that the message had been deposited and then removed by an intermediary never occurred to anyone. 628461 didn't know that Konstabel van Rooyen hadn't collected his message and Konstabel van Rooyen had no idea that agent 628461 even existed. All he knew was that Luitenant Verkramp had told him to collect sticky pieces of ice-cream paper from the bin and there weren't any.

On the Thursday following the Kommandant's departure, 628461 coded an important message informing Verkramp that he had persuaded the other saboteurs to act in concert for once, with a view to facilitating their arrest while on a job for which they could all be hanged. He had suggested the destruction of the Hluwe Dam which supplied water for all of Piemburg and half Zululand, and, since no one could blow a dam by himself, he had urged that they all take part. Much to his surprise all eleven seconded his proposal and went home to code messages to Verkramp warning him to have his men at the dam on Friday night. It was with a sense of considerable relief that he was finally going to get some sleep that 628461 walked to the Bird Sanctuary on Thursday morning to deposit his message. It was with genuine alarm that he observed 378550 following him and with positive consternation became aware as he was buying his ice cream that 885974 was watching him from the bushes on the other side. 628461 ate his ice cream outside the hoopoe cage to avoid drawing attention to the garbage can by the Ostrich enclosure. He ate a second ice cream half an hour later staring wearily at the peacocks. Finally after an hour he bought a third Eskimo Pie and walked casually over to the Ostriches. Behind him 378550 and 885974 watched his movements with intense curiosity. So did the ostriches. 628461 finished his Eskimo Pie and dropped the silver paper in the garbage can and was just about to leave when he became aware that all his surreptitious efforts had been in vain. With an avidity that came from their having been kept waiting for an hour the ostriches rushed to the fence and poked their heads into the garbage can and one lucky bird swallowed the ice-cream wrapper. 628461 forgot himself.

'Damnation and fuck,' he said. 'They've got it. The bloody things'll eat anything.'

'Got what?' asked 378550 who thought that he was being addressed and was glad of the chance to drop his role as shadow.

628461 pulled himself together and looked at 378550 suspiciously.

'You said "They've got it",' 378550 repeated.

628461 tried to extricate himself from the situation. 'I said, "I've got it",' he explained. '"I've got it. They'll eat anything."'

378550 was still puzzled. 'I still don't see it,' he said.

'Well,' said 628461 desperately trying to explain what the omnivorousness of ostriches had to do with his devotion to the cause of world Communism, 'I was just thinking that we could get them to eat gelly and let them loose and they'd blow up all over the place.'

378550 looked at him with admiration. 'That's brilliant,' he said. 'Absolutely brilliant.'

'Of course,' 628461 told him, 'we'd have to put the explosive in something watertight first. Get them to swallow it. Fix a fuse and bingo, you've got the perfect sabotage weapon.'

885974 who didn't want to be left out of things in the bushes came over and joined them.

'French letters,' he suggested when the scheme was put to him. 'Put the gelignite in French letters and tie the ends, that'd keep it watertight.'

An hour later in Florian's café they were discussing the plan with the rest of the saboteurs. 745396 objected on the grounds that ostriches might eat anything but he doubted if even they would be foolish enough to swallow a contraceptive filled with gelignite.

'We'll try it out this afternoon,' said 628461 who felt that 745396 was somehow impugning his loyalty to Marxist Leninism and the motion was put to the vote. Only 745396 still objected and he was voted down.

While the rest of the group spent the lunch hour coding messages to Verkramp to warn him that the Hluwe Dam project was cancelled and that he might expect an onslaught of detonating ostriches. 885974 who had thought of French letters in the first place, was deputed to purchase twelve dozen of the best.

'Get Crêpe de Chine,' said 378550, who had had an unfortunate experience with another brand, 'they're guaranteed.'

885974 went into a large chemists' on Market Street and asked the young man behind the photographic counter for twelve dozen Crêpe de Chine.

'Crêpe de Chine?' asked the assistant, who was obviously new to the job. 'We don't sell Crêpe de Chine. You need a haberdashers' for that. This is a chemist shop.'

885974 who was already embarrassed by the quantity he had to ask for turned very red.

'I know that,' he muttered. 'You know what I mean. In packets of three.'

The assistant shook his head. 'They sell it in yards,' he said, 'but I'll ask if we have it,' and before 885974 could stop him had shouted across the shop to a girl who was serving some customers at the counter there.

'This gentleman wants twelve dozen Crêpe de Chine, Sally. We don't sell stuff like that do we?' he asked, and 885974 found himself the object of considerable interest to twelve middle-aged women who knew precisely what he wanted even if the assistant didn't and were amazed at the virility suggested by the number he required.

'Oh for God's sake, never mind,' he muttered and hurried from the shop. In the end he managed to get what he wanted by buying six toothbrushes and two tubes of hair cream at other chemist shops and asking for Durex Fetherlites.

'They seemed more suitable,' he explained when he met the other agents outside the Ostrich enclosure in the afternoon. With a unity of purpose noticeably absent from their previous gatherings the agents applied themselves to the business of getting an ostrich to consume high-explosive concealed in a rubber sheath.

'Better try one with sand first,' 628461 suggested, and was presently scooping each into a Durex Fetherlite, an occupation which caused some disgust to a lady who was feeding the ducks on a nearby pond. He waited until she had moved off before offering the contraceptive to the ostrich. The bird took the sheath and spat it out. 628461 got a stick and managed to retrieve the thing from the enclosure. A second attempt was equally unsuccessful and when a third try to introduce half a pound of latex-covered earth into the bird's digestive system failed, 628461 suggested coating the thing with ice cream.

'They seemed to like it this morning,' he said. He was getting sick of scrabbling through the fence for obviously well-filled condoms. Finally, after 378550 had bought two ice-creams and a chocolate bar and the sheath had been smeared with ice cream by itself and chocolate by itself and then with a mixture of the two, the proceedings were interrupted by the arrival of a Sanctuary warden fetched by the lady who had been feeding the ducks. 628461 who had just rescued the French letter from the ostriches' enclosure for the eighth time stuffed it hurriedly into his pocket.

'Are these the men you saw trying to feed the ostriches with foreign matter?' the warden asked.

'Yes, they are,' said the lady emphatically.

The warden turned to 628461.

'Were you trying to induce the bird to digest a quantity of something or other contained in the thing this lady says you were?' he asked.

'Certainly not,' said 628461 indignantly.

'You were too,' said the lady, 'I saw you.'

'I'll ask you to move along,' said the warden.

As the little group moved off 745396 pointed out how right he had been.

'I told you ostriches weren't so dumb,' he said and put 628461's back up still further. He'd just discovered that the sheath in his back pocket had burst.

'I thought you were supposed to get Crêpe de Chines,' he grumbled to 885974 and tried to empty his pocket of earth, chocolate, ice cream and ostrich droppings.

'What am I going to do with twelve dozen Frenchies?' 885974 asked.

It took 378550 to come up with a solution. 'Popcorn and honey,' he said suddenly.

'What about it?' 628461 asked.

'Coat them with popcorn and honey and I guarantee they'll swallow the things.'

At the first shop they came to 378550 bought a packet of popcorn and a pot of honey and taking a contraceptive from 885974 went back to the Bird Sanctuary to try his recipe out.

'Worked like a treat,' he reported ten minutes later. 'Swallowed the thing in one gulp.'

'What do we do when we've filled them all up and set the fuse?' 745396 asked doubtfully.

'Lay a trail of popcorn into the centre of town, of course,' 628461 told him. The group dispersed to collect their stocks of gelignite and that night at nine gathered at the Bird Sanctuary. The sense of mutual suspicion which had so informed their earlier meetings had been quite replaced by a genuine cameraderie. Verkramp's agents were beginning to enjoy themselves.

'If this works,' 628461 said, 'there's no reason why we shouldn't try the zoo.'

'I'm damned if I'm feeding contraceptives to the lions,' 745396 said.

'No need to feed them anything,' said 885974 who didn't feel like buying any more French letters. 'They'd be explosive enough on their own.'

If Verkramp's agents were cheerful, the same couldn't be said of their chief. The conviction that something had gone seriously wrong with his plans to end Communist subversion had gathered strength with the discovery by the armourer that large stocks of high-explosive and fuses were missing from the police armoury.

He reported his findings or lack of them to Luitenant Verkramp. Coming on top of a report by the police bomb-disposal squad that the detonators used in all the explosions were of a type used in the past solely by the South African Police, the armourer's news added weight to Verkramp's slow intuition that he might in some curious way have bitten off more than he could chew. It was an insight he shared with five ostriches in the Bird Sanctuary. What had seemed at the outset a marvellous opportunity to fulfil his ambitions had developed into

something from which there was no turning back. Certainly the ostriches
viewed it in that light as the secret agents discovered to their alarm when
they released the loaded birds from their enclosure. Gregarious to the
last and evidently under the impression that there was more to come in
the way of popcorn-coated contraceptives, the five ostriches strode after
the agents as the latter headed for town. By the time the mixed herd and
flock had reached the end of Market Street the agents were in a state of
near panic.

'We'd better break up,' 628461 said anxiously.

'Break up? Break up? We'll fucking disintegrate if those birds don't get
the hell out of here,' said 745396 who had never approved of the project
from the start and who seemed to have attracted the friendship of an
ostrich that weighed at least 300 lbs unloaded and which had a fifteen-
minute fuse. The next moment the agents had taken to their heels down
side roads in an effort to shake off the likely consequences of their
experiment. Undaunted, the ostriches strode relentlessly and effortlessly
behind them. At the corner of Market and Stanger Streets 745396 leapt
on to the platform of a moving bus and was appalled to see through the
back window the silhouette of his ostrich loping comfortably some yards
behind. At the traffic lights at Chapel Street it was still there. 745396
hurled himself off the bus and dashed into the Majestic Cinema which
was showing *Where Eagles Dare*.

'Show's over,' said the Commissionaire in the foyer.

'That's what you think,' said 745396 with his eye on the ostrich which
was peering inquisitively through the glass doors. 'I just want to use the
toilet.'

'Down the stairs to the left,' the Commissionaire told him and went
out to the pavement to try to move the ostrich on. 745396 went down
to the toilet and locked himself in a cubicle and waited for the explosion.
He was still there five minutes later when the Commissionaire came down
and knocked on the door.

'Is that ostrich anything to do with you?' he asked as 745396 tore
paper off the roll to prove that he was using the place for its proper
purpose.

'No,' said 745396 without conviction.

'Well, you can't leave it outside like that,' the Commissionaire told
him, 'it'll interfere with the traffic.'

'You can say that again,' said 745396.

'Say what again?' asked the Commissionaire.

'Nothing,' shouted 745396 frantically. He had reached the end of his
tether. So it appeared had the ostrich.

'One last question, do you usually –' said the Commissionaire and got no further. An extraordinary sensation of silence hit him to be followed by a wall of flame and a gigantic bang. As the front of the Majestic Cinema crumbled into the street and the lights went out agent 745396 slowly slumped on to the cracked seat of the toilet and leant against the wall. He was still there when the rescue workers found him next day, covered in plaster and quite dead.

Throughout the night rumours that Piemburg had been invaded by hordes of self-detonating ostriches spread like wildfire. So did the ostriches. A particularly tragic incident occurred at the offices of the Zululand Wild Life Preservation Society where an ostrich which had been brought in by a bird-lover exploded while being examined by the society's vet.

'I think it's got some sort of gastric disorder,' the man explained. The vet listened to the bird's crop with his stethoscope before making his diagnosis.

'Heartburn,' he said with a finality that was entirely confirmed by the detonation that followed. As the night sky erupted with bricks, mortar, and the assorted remains of both bird-lover and vet, the premises of the Wild Life Preservation Society, historically important and themselves subject to a preservation order by the Piemburg Council, disappeared for ever. Only a plume of smoke and a few large feathers, emblematic as some dissipated Prince of Wales, floated lethargically against the moon.

In his office Acting Kommandant Verkramp listened to the muffled explosions with a growing sense of despair. Whatever else was in ruins, and by the sound of it a large section of the city's shopping centre must be, his own career would shortly join in. In a frantic attempt to allay his alarming suspicions he had just searched the few messages from his secret agents only to find there confirmation that his plan if not their efforts had misfired. Agent 378550 had said that the sabotage group consisted of eleven men. Agent 885974 had said the same. So had 628461. There was a terrible congruency about the reports. In each case eleven men reported by his agent. Verkramp added one to eleven and got twelve. He had twelve agents in the field. The conclusion was inescapable and so it seemed were the consequences. Desperately searching for some way out of the mess he had got himself into, Luitenant Verkramp rose from the desk and crossed to the window. He was just in time to see a large ostrich loping purposefully down the street. With a muttered curse Verkramp opened the window and peered after the bird. 'This is the end,' he snarled and was astonished to see that at least one of his orders was obeyed. With a violent flash and a blast wave that blew out the window above him the ostrich disintegrated and Verkramp found himself sitting on the floor of his office with the inescapable conviction that his sanity was impaired.

'Impossible. It can't have been an ostrich,' he muttered, staggering back to the window. Outside the street was littered with broken glass and in a bare blackened patch in the middle of the road two feet were all that remained of the thing that had exploded. Verkramp could see that it had been an ostrich because the feet had only two toes.

In the next twenty minutes Luitenant Verkramp acted with maniacal speed. He burnt every file that could connect him with his agents, destroyed their messages and finally, ordering the police armourer to change the lock on the armoury door, left the police station in the Kommandant's black Ford. An hour later, having visited every bar in town, he had run two of his agents to earth drinking to the success of their latest experiment in sabotage in the Criterion Hotel in Verwoerd Street.

'Fuzz,' said 628461 as Verkramp entered the bar. 'Better break up.' 885974 finished his drink and went out. 628461 watched him go and was surprised to see Verkramp follow him out.

'He's making an arrest,' he thought and ordered another beer. A moment later he looked up to find Verkramp glowering down at him.

'Outside,' said Verkramp brusquely. 628461 left his bar stool and went outside and was surprised to find his fellow-saboteur sitting unguarded in the police car.

'I see you've got one of them,' 628461 said to Verkramp, and climbed in beside 885974.

'Them? Them?' Verkramp spluttered hysterically. 'He's not them. He's us.'

'Us?' said 628461, mystified.

'I'm 885974. Who are you?'

'Oh, my God,' said 628461.

Verkramp climbed into the driving seat and stared back malevolently.

'Where are the others?' he hissed.

'The others?'

'The other agents, you idiot,' Verkramp shouted. For the next two hours they searched the bars and cafés while Verkramp fulminated on the evils of sabotaging public utilities and detonating ostriches in a built-up area.

'I send you out to infiltrate the Communist movement and what do you do?' he shouted. 'Blow up half the bloody town, that's what you do. And you know where that's going to get you, don't you? On the end of the hangman's rope in Pretoria Central.'

'You might have warned us,' said 628461 reproachfully. 'You could have told us there were other agents in the field.'

Verkramp turned purple.

'Warned you?' he screamed. 'I expected you to use your common sense, not go around looking for one another.'

'Well, how the hell were we to know we were all police agents?' 885974 asked.

'I should have thought even idiots like you could tell the difference between a good Afrikaner and a Communist Jew.'

885974 thought about this.

'If it's that easy,' he said finally, clinging precariously to some sort of logic, 'I don't see how we're to blame. I mean the Communist Jews must be able to see we're good Afrikaners just by looking at us. I mean what's the point of sending out good Afrikaners to look for Communist Jews if Communist Jews can ...'

'Oh, shut up,' shouted Verkramp, who was beginning to wish that he hadn't brought up the subject in the first place.

By midnight seven other agents had been found in various parts of the city and the police car was getting rather crowded.

'What do you want us to do now?' 378550 asked as they drove round the park for the fifth time looking for the three remaining agents. Verkramp stopped the car.

'I ought to arrest you,' he snarled, 'I ought to let you stand trial for terrorism but –'

'You won't,' said 885974 who had been giving the matter some thought.

'Why won't I?' Verkramp shouted.

'Because we'll all give evidence that you ordered us to blow up the transformer and the gasometer and the –'

'I did nothing of the sort. I told you to find the Communist saboteurs,' Verkramp yelled.

'Who gave us the keys of the police armoury?' 885974 asked. 'Who supplied the explosives?'

'And what about the messages we sent you?' 628461 asked.

Verkramp stared through the windshield and contemplated a short and nasty future, at the end of which stood the hangman in Pretoria Central Prison.

'All right,' he said. 'What do you want me to do?'

'Get us past the road blocks. Get us down to Durban and give us each 500 rand,' 885974 said, 'and then forget you ever saw us.'

'What about the other three agents?' Verkramp asked.

'That's your problem,' 885974 said. 'You can find them tomorrow.'

They drove back to the police station and Verkramp collected the money and two hours later nine agents climbed out at Durban airport. Luitenant Verkramp watched them disappear into the terminal and then drove back to Piemburg. At the road block on the Durban road the sergeant waved him through for the second time and made a note of the fact that the Acting Kommandant looked drawn and ill. By four in the morning Verkramp was in bed in his flat staring into the darkness and wondering how he was going to find the other three agents. At seven he got up again and drove down to Florian's café. 885974 had advised him to look for them there. At eleven the Kommandant's car passed through the Durban Road check-point yet again and this time the Acting Kommandant had with him two men. By the time he returned eleven agents had left Piemburg for good. 745396 was in the city morgue waiting to be identified.

At Weezen Spa Kommandant van Heerden slept more soundly than his hallucination had led him to expect. He woke next morning with something of a hangover but felt better after a large breakfast in the Pump Room. In the far corner the two elderly ladies with short hair continued their endlessly whispered conversation.

Later in the morning the Kommandant walked into Weezen in the hope of bumping into Mrs Heathcote-Kilkoon who had murmured something about 'Tomorrow' as he put her to bed. He had just reached the main road and was trudging along it when a horn sounded loudly behind him and caused him to jump off the road. He looked round furiously and found Major Bloxham at the wheel of the vintage Rolls.

'Hop in,' shouted the Major. 'Just the man I'm looking for.'

The Kommandant climbed into the front seat and was glad to notice that the Major wasn't looking very well.

'To tell the truth,' said the Major when the Kommandant asked if he had recovered from the evening's entertainment, 'I'm not on top form this morning. Have to hand it to you, you Boers know how to hold your liquor. I wonder you made it back to the Spa last night.'

Kommandant van Heerden smiled at the compliment. 'It takes more than a couple of glasses to put me under the table,' he murmured modestly.

'By the way,' said the Kommandant as they drove into Weezen, 'talking of tables, is the woman in the dinner jacket all right?'

'What? La Marquise, you mean?' asked the Major. 'Funny you should mention her. As a matter of fact she's not herself or himself, difficult to tell which, you know, this morning. Said she was feeling a bit off colour.'

In his seat Kommandant van Heerden went very white. If the words 'off colour' meant anything at all in the context, and the Kommandant felt sure they did, he could well believe La Marquise was speaking the truth. There was now little doubt in his mind that he had not imagined seeing Els under the table. Removing the trousers of a drunk Lesbian was just the sort of unchivalrous act that had all the hallmarks of Konstabel Els. But Konstabel Els was dead. The Kommandant wrestled with the problem of Els resurrected until they arrived outside the Weezen Bar.

'Hair of the dog,' said the Major and went into the bar. The Kommandant followed him in.

'Gin and peppermint for me,' said Major Bloxham. 'What's yours, old boy?'

The Kommandant said he'd have the same but his mind was still elsewhere.

'Did she say what had happened?' he asked.

Major Bloxham looked at him curiously.

'You seem to have quite a thing about her,' he said finally. 'Intriguing, what?' The Kommandant looked at him sharply, and the Major continued, 'Let me see, I remember she said something rather queer at breakfast. Oh I know. She said, "I feel absolutely buggered." That's right. Seemed rather a coarse sort of thing for a woman to say.'

Beside him the Kommandant couldn't agree. If he had seen Els under the table he was pretty sure the lady was speaking no more than the simple truth. Serves the silly bitch right for dressing up in men's clothes, he thought.

'By the way Daphne sent a message,' said the Major, 'wants to know if you'll come out with the hunt tomorrow.'

The Kommandant dragged his thoughts away from the problem of Els and the transvestite Lesbian and tried to think about the hunt.

'I'd love to,' he said, 'but I'd have to borrow a gun.'

'Of course it's only a drag hunt,' continued the Major before it dawned on him that the Kommandant shot foxes. A similar dreadful misunderstanding existed in the Kommandant's mind.

'Drag hunt?' he said, looking at the Major with some disgust.

'Gun?' said Major Bloxham with equal revulsion. He looked hastily round the bar to make sure no one was listening before leaning over to the Kommandant.

'Look, old boy,' he said conspiratorially, 'a word to the wise and all that but if you'll take my advice I wouldn't go round broadcasting, well, you know what I mean.'

'Do you mean to tell me that Colonel Heathcote-Kilkoon ...' stuttered the Kommandant, trying to imagine what the Colonel looked like in drag.

'Exactly, old boy,' said the Major. 'He's terribly touchy about that sort of thing.'

'I'm not in the least surprised,' said the Kommandant.

'Just keep it under your hat,' said the Major. 'What about another drink? Your turn, I think.'

The Kommandant ordered two more gin and peppermints and by the time they had arrived had begun to think he understood Major Bloxham's role in the Heathcote-Kilkoon family. The Major's next remark confirmed it.

'Bottoms up,' he said and lifted his glass.

The Kommandant put his down on the bar and looked at him sternly.

'It's illegal,' he said, 'I suppose you realize that.'

'What is, old boy?' asked the Major.

It was the Kommandant's turn to look round the bar hastily.

'Drag hunts,' he said finally.

'Really? How extraordinary. I had no idea,' said the Major. 'I mean it's not as though anyone gets hurt or anything.'

The Kommandant shifted uneasily on his stool.

'I suppose that depends which end you're on,' he muttered.

'A bit exhausting for the poor bugger out front. I mean, running all that way but it's only twice a week,' said the Major.

Kommandant van Heerden shuddered.

'You just tell the Colonel what I've said,' he told the Major. 'Tell him it's strictly illegal.'

'Will do, old boy,' said the Major, 'though it beats me why it should be. Still you'd know about these things, being in the police and all that.'

They sat and finished their drinks in silence, each occupied with his own thoughts.

'Are you absolutely sure it's illegal, old boy,' Major Bloxham asked finally, 'I mean it's not as though it's cruel or anything. There's no actual kill.'

'I should fucking well hope not,' said the Kommandant, highly incensed.

'We just pop a kaffir out after breakfast with a bag of aniseed round his middle and an hour later we all go after him.'

'Aniseed?' the Kommandant asked. 'What's the aniseed for?'

'Gives him a bit of a scent you know,' the Major explained.

Kommandant van Heerden shuddered. Scented kaffirs being chased across country by men in their fifties dressed as women was more than he could stomach.

'What does Mrs Heathcote-Kilkoon think about it?' he asked anxiously. He couldn't see an elegant lady like her approving of drag hunting at all.

'What? Daphne? She loves it. I think she's keener than anyone else,' said the Major. 'Got a wonderful seat, you know.'

'So I've noticed,' said the Kommandant who thought the comment about Mrs Heathcote-Kilkoon's anatomy quite uncalled for. 'And what does she wear?'

Major Bloxham laughed. 'She's one of the old school. Hard as nails. Wears a topper for one thing ...'

'A topper? Do you mean she wears a top hat?' asked the Kommandant.

'Nothing less, old boy, and she doesn't spare the whip I can tell you. God help the man who refuses a fence. That woman will give him what for.'

'Charming,' said the Kommandant trying to imagine what it must be like to get what for from Mrs Heathcote-Kilkoon wearing nothing less than a top hat.

'We can give you a good mount,' said the Major.

The Kommandant anchored himself to his stool firmly.

'I daresay you can,' he said sternly, 'but I wouldn't advise you to try.'

Major Bloxham stood up.

'Got cold feet, eh?' he said nastily.

'It's not my feet I'm worried about,' said the Kommandant.

'Well, I'd better be getting back to White Ladies,' said the Major and moved towards the door. Kommandant van Heerden finished his drink and followed him out. He found the Major getting into the Rolls.

'By the way, just as a matter of interest,' the Kommandant said, 'what do you wear on these ... er ... occasions?'

Major Bloxham smiled obscenely.

'Pink, old boy, pink. What else do you think a gentleman wears?' and he let in the clutch and the Rolls moved off leaving the Kommandant filled once more with that sense of disillusionment which seemed to come whenever he put the ideal figures of his imagination to the test of reality. he stood for a moment and then wandered up into the square and stood looking up at the face of the Great Queen. For the first time he understood the look of veiled disgust he saw there. 'No wonder,' he thought, 'It can't have been much fun being Queen of a nation of pansies.' Thinking how symbolic it was that a pigeon had defecated on her bronze forehead he turned and walked slowly back to the Spa for lunch.

'Illegal?' shouted Colonel Heathcote-Kilkoon when the Major reported what the Kommandant had said. 'Hunting's illegal? Never heard such tommyrot in my life. Man's a liar. Afraid of horses I shouldn't wonder. What else did he say?'

'Admitted he shoots foxes,' said the Major.

Colonel Heathcote-Kilkoon exploded.

'Damn me, I always said the fellow was a scoundrel,' he shouted. 'And to think I've ruined my liver drinking toasts with a swine like that.'

'Don't shout, Henry dear,' Mrs Heathcote-Kilkoon said, coming in from the next room, 'I don't think my head can stand it and besides, Willy's dead.'

'Willy's dead?' asked the Colonel. 'Fit enough yesterday.'

'Go and look for yourselves,' said Mrs Heathcote-Kilkoon sadly. The two men went through to the next room.

'Good God,' said the Colonel as they looked at the goldfish bowl. 'Wonder how that happened?'

'Probably drank himself to death,' said Major Bloxham lightly. Colonel Heathcote-Kilkoon looked at him coldly.

'I don't think that's very funny,' he said and stalked out of the house. Major Bloxham wandered disconsolately onto the stoep where he found La Marquise standing staring at the view.

'And only man is vile, eh?' he said amiably. La Marquise looked at him angrily.

'Darling, you have a wonderful knack of saying the right thing at the wrong time,' she snapped, and waddled off painfully across the lawn leaving the Major wondering what had got into her.

CHAPTER ELEVEN

The sense of disillusionment which had been Kommandant van Heerden's first reaction to Major Bloxham's disclosures gave way, as he walked back to the Spa, to several new suspicions. Looking back over his recent experiences, the invitation to stay at White Ladies and his subsequent relegation to Weezen Spa, the blatant neglect he had suffered for several days after his arrival, and the overall feeling that in some indefinable way he was not welcome, the Kommandant began to feel that he had some cause for grievance. Nor was that all. The disparity which existed between the behaviour of the Heathcote-Kilkoons and that of the heroes of Dornford Yates' novels was glaring. Berry & Co didn't end up blind drunk under the table unless some French crook had drugged their champagne. Berry & Co didn't invite alcoholic Lesbians to dinner. Berry & Co didn't go riding round the country dressed ... Well, now he came to think of it, there was that story in *Jonah & Co* where Berry dressed up as a woman. But above all Berry & Co didn't consort with Konstabel Els, late or not. That was for sure.

Lying on his bed in Colonic Irrigation No 6 the Kommandant nursed his suspicions until what had begun as disillusionment turned into anger.

Nobody's going to treat me like this he thought, recalling the various insults he had had to put up with, particularly from the fat man, at the dinner. Colourful family indeed, he thought, I'll colourful you. He got up and stared at the image of himself in the mottled mirror.

'I am Kommandant van Heerden,' he said to himself and puffed out his chest in an assertion of authority and was surprised at the large surge of pride that followed this avowal of his own identity. For a moment the gap between what he was and what he would like to have been closed and he viewed the world with all the defiance of a self-made man. He was just considering the implications of this new self-satisfaction when there was a knock at the door.

'Come in,' shouted the Kommandant and was surprised to see Mrs Heathcote-Kilkoon standing in the doorway.

'Well?' said the Kommandant peremptorily and unable in so short a time to make the change from brusque authority to common courtesy the new situation clearly demanded. Mrs Heathcote-Kilkoon looked at him submissively.

'Oh darling,' she murmured. 'Oh my darling.' She stood meekly before him and looked down at her immaculate mauve gloves. 'I feel so ashamed. So terribly ashamed. To think that we've treated you so badly.'

'Yes. Well,' said the Kommandant uncertainly but still sounding as though he were interrogating a suspect.

Mrs Heathcote-Kilkoon subsided onto the bed where she sat staring at her shoes.

'It's all my fault,' she said finally, 'I should never have asked you to come.' She glanced round the horrid room to which her offer of hospitality had condemned the Kommandant and sighed. 'I should have known better than to imagine Henry would behave decently. He's got this thing about foreigners, you see.'

The Kommandant could see it. It explained for one thing the presence of La Marquise. A French Lesbian would appeal unnaturally to a transvestite Colonel.

'And then there's that wretched club of his,' Mrs Heathcote-Kilkoon continued. 'It's not so much a club as a secret society. Oh I know you think it's all terribly innocent and harmless but you don't have to live with it. You don't understand how vicious it all is. The disguise, the pretence, the shame of it all.'

'You mean it's not real?' the Kommandant asked trying to understand the full import of Mrs Heathcote-Kilkoon's outburst.

Mrs Heathcote-Kilkoon looked up at him in amazement.

'Don't tell me they fooled you too,' she said. 'Of course it's not real. Don't you see? We're none of us what we pretend to be. Henry's not a Colonel. Boy's not a Major. He's not even a boy, come to that and I'm not a lady. We're all playing parts, all terrible phonies.' She sat on the edge of the bed and her eyes filled with tears.

'What are you then?' the Kommandant demanded.

'Oh God,' moaned Mrs Heathcote-Kilkoon, 'need you ask?'

She sat there crying while the Kommandant fetched a glass of water from one of the many washbasins.

'Here, take some of this,' he said proffering the glass. 'It will do you good.'

Mrs Heathcote-Kilkoon took a sip and stared at the Kommandant frantically.

'No wonder you're constipated,' she said finally putting the glass down on the bedside table. 'What must you think of us, letting you stay in this awful place?'

The Kommandant, for whom the day seemed to have become one long confessional, thought it better not to say what he thought though he had to agree that Weezen Spa wasn't very nice.

'Tell me,' he said, 'if the Colonel isn't a Colonel, what is he?'

'I can't tell you,' said Mrs Heathcote-Kilkoon, 'I've promised never to tell anyone what he did in the war. He'd kill me if he thought I'd told you.' She looked up at him imploringly. 'Please just forget what I've said. I've done enough damage already.'

'I see,' said the Kommandant drawing his own conclusions from the Colonel's threat to kill her if she let his secret out. Whatever Henry had done during the war it was evidently hush-hush.

Mrs Heathcote-Kilkoon, judging that her tears and the admission she had just made sufficiently atoned for the discomfort of the Kommandant's accommodation, dried her eyes and stood up.

'You're so understanding,' she murmured.

'I wouldn't say that,' said the Kommandant truthfully.

Mrs Heathcote-Kilkoon went over to the mirror and began to repair the calculated ravages to her make-up.

'And now,' she said with a gaiety that surprised the Kommandant, 'I'm going to drive you over to the Sani Pass for tea. It'll do us both good to get out and you could do with a change of water.'

That afternoon was one the Kommandant would never forget. As the great car slid noiselessly over the foothills of the mountains leaving a great plume of dust to eddy over the fields and kaffir huts they passed, the Kommandant resumed something of the good nature he had so recently lost. He was sitting in a car that had once belonged to a Governor-General and in which the Prince of Wales had twice ridden during his triumphal tour of South Africa in 1925 and beside him there sat if not, evidently, a proper lady at least a woman who possessed all the apparent attributes of one. Certainly the way she handled the car excited the Kommandant's admiration and he was particularly impressed by the perfect timing she displayed in allowing the car to steal up behind a black woman with a basket on her head before squeezing the bulb of the horn and causing the woman to leap into the ditch.

'I was in the Army during the war and I learnt to drive then,' she said when the Kommandant complimented her on her skill. 'Used to drive a thirty hundredweight truck.' She laughed at the memory. 'You know everyone says the war was absolutely awful but actually I enjoyed it enormously. Never had so much fun in my life.'

Not for the first time, Kommandant van Heerden considered the strange habit of the English of finding enjoyment in the oddest places.

'What about the ... er ... Colonel? Did he have fun too?' asked the Kommandant for whom the Colonel's wartime occupation had become a matter of intense curiosity.

'What? On the Underground? I should think not,' said Mrs Heathcote-Kilkoon before realizing what she had just done. She pulled the car into the side of the road and stopped before turning to the Kommandant.

'That was a dirty trick,' she said, 'getting me to talk like that and then asking what Henry did during the war. I suppose that's a professional trick of the police. Well, it's out now,' she continued in spite of the Kommandant's protestations, 'Henry was a guard on the Underground. The Inner Circle as a matter of fact. But for God's sake promise me never to mention it.'

'Of course I won't mention it,' said the Kommandant whose respect for the Colonel had gone up enormously now that he knew he'd belonged to the inner circle of the underground.

'What about the Major? Was he in the underground too?'

Mrs Heathcote-Kilkoon laughed.

'Dear me no,' she said. 'He was some sort of barman at the Savoy. Where do you think he learnt to make those lethal concoctions of his?'

The Kommandant nodded appreciatively. He'd never thought of Major Bloxham as being a legal type but he supposed it was possible.

They drove on and had tea at the Sani Pass Hotel before returning to Weezen. It was only as they were approaching the town that the Kommandant brought up the question that had been bothering him all day.

'Do you know anyone called Els?' he asked. Mrs Heathcote-Kilkoon shook her head.

'No one,' she said.

'Are you quite sure?'

'Of course I'm sure,' she said. 'I'd hardly be likely to forget anyone with a name like Else.'

'I don't suppose you would,' said the Kommandant thinking that anyone who knew Els under any name was hardly likely to forget the brute. 'He's a thin man with little eyes and he has a flat sort of head, at the back as if someone has hit him with a blunt instrument several times.'

Mrs Heathcote-Kilkoon smiled. 'That's Harbinger to the life,' she said. 'Funny you should mention him. You're the second person to ask about him today. La Marquise said something odd about him at lunch when his name came up. She said, "I could a tale unfold." A funny sort of thing to say about Harbinger. I mean he's not exactly cultured is he?'

'No, he's not,' said the Kommandant emphatically and with a shrewd understanding of La Marquise's remark.

'Henry got him from the Weezen jail, you know. They hire out prisoners for a few cents a day and we've kept him ever since. He's our odd-job man.'

'Yes, well, I daresay he is,' said the Kommandant, 'but I'd keep an eye on him all the same. He's not the sort of fellow I'd want hanging about the place.'

'Funny you should say that,' said Mrs Heathcote-Kilkoon yet again. 'He told me once that he had been a hangman before he took to a life of crime.'

'Before?' said the Kommandant in astonishment but Mrs Heathcote-Kilkoon was too busy manoeuvring the car through the gates of Weezen Spa to hear him.

'You *will* come out with the hunt tomorrow?' she said as the Kommandant climbed out. 'I know it's an awful lot to ask after what you have had to put up with already but I would like you to come.'

The Kommandant looked at her and wondered what to say. He had enjoyed the afternoon drive and he didn't want to offend her.

'What would you like me to wear?' he asked cautiously.

'That's a point,' Mrs Heathcote-Kilkoon said. 'Look why don't you come over now and we'll see if you can get into Henry's togs.'

'Togs?' said the Kommandant wondering what obscure feminine garment a tog was.

'Riding things,' said Mrs Heathcote-Kilkoon.

'What sort of things does Henry ride in?'

'Ordinary breeches, riding breeches.'

'Ordinary ones?'

'Of course, what on earth do you think he wears? I know he's pretty odd but he doesn't ride around in the raw or anything.'

'Are you sure?' asked the Kommandant.

Mrs Heathcote-Kilkoon looked at him hard.

'Of course I'm sure,' she said. 'What on earth makes you think otherwise.'

'Nothing,' said the Kommandant, meaning to have a chat with Major Bloxham at the earliest opportunity. He climbed into the car again and Mrs Heathcote-Kilkoon drove back to White Ladies.

'There you are,' she said half an hour later as they stood in the Colonel's dressing-room. 'They fit you perfectly.'

The Kommandant looked at himself in the mirror and had to admit that the breeches looked rather splendid on him.

'You even dress the same side,' continued Mrs Heathcote-Kilkoon with a professional eye.

The Kommandant looked around the room curiously.

'Which side do you dress?' he asked and was amazed at the laughter his remark produced.

'Naughty man,' said Mrs Heathcote-Kilkoon finally, and much to the Kommandant's surprise kissed him lightly on the cheek.

In Piemburg the question of naughty men was one that was beginning to bother Luitenant Verkramp. The dispatch of his eleven remaining secret agents had not, after all, seen the end of his problems. Arriving at the police station the morning after their departure he found Sergeant Breitenbach in a state of unusual agitation.

'A fine mess you've got us into now,' he said when Verkramp asked him what was wrong.

'You mean those ostriches?' Verkramp inquired.

'No, I don't,' said the Sergeant, 'I mean the konstabels you've been giving shock treatment to. They're queer.'

'I thought those ostriches were pretty queer,' said Verkramp who still hadn't got over the sight of one blowing up almost under his nose.

'Well you haven't seen the konstabels,' Sergeant Breitenbach told him and went to the door. 'Konstabel Botha,' he shouted.

Konstabel Botha came into the office.

'There you are,' said Sergeant Breitenbach grimly. 'That's what your bloody aversion therapy's been and done. And he used to play rugby for Zululand.'

At his desk Luitenant Verkramp knew now that he was going mad. He'd felt bad enough faced with exploding ostriches but they were as nothing to the insanity he felt now confronted with the famous footballer. Konstabel Botha, hooker for Zululand, six foot four and sixteen stone, minced into the room wearing a yellow wig and with his mouth smudged hideously with lipstick.

'You lovely man,' he simpered to Verkramp, sauntering like some modish elephant about the office.

'Keep your hands off me, you bastard,' snarled the Sergeant but Luitenant Verkramp wasn't listening. The inner voices were there again and this time there was no stopping them. With his face livid and his eyes staring Verkramp collapsed screaming in his chair. He was still screaming and babbling about being God, when the ambulance arrived from Fort Rapier and he was carried downstairs struggling furiously.

Sergeant Breitenbach sat beside him in the ambulance and was there when they arrived at the hospital. Dr von Blimenstein, radiant in a white coat, was waiting.

'It's all right now. You're quite safe with me,' she said and with one swift movement had pinned Verkramp's arm between his shoulderblades and was frogmarching him into the ward.

'Poor bastard,' thought Sergeant Breitenbach gazing with alarm at her broad shoulders and heavy buttocks, 'you've got it coming to you.'

He went back to the police station and tried to think what to do. With a wave of sabotage on his hands, thirty-six irate citizens in prison and two hundred and ten queer konstabels out of a total force of five hundred, he knew he couldn't cope. Half an hour later urgent messages were going out to all police stations in the area asking them to contact Kommandant van Heerden. In the meantime, as a method of isolating the disaffected konstabels, he gave orders that they should be put through their paces on the parade ground and sent Sergeant de Kok down there to give them drill. It was not a particularly happy choice, as Sergeant Breitenbach found when he went down to see how things were going. The two hundred konstabels minced and pirouetted across the parade ground alarmingly.

'If you can't stop them marching like that, you'd better get them out of sight,' he told the Sergeant. 'It's that sort of thing gives the South African Police a bad name.'

'You've done what?' Colonel Heathcote-Kilkoon shouted when his wife told him she had invited the Kommandant to the hunt. 'A man who shoots foxes? In my breeches? By God, I'll see about that.'

'Now, Henry,' said Mrs Heathcote-Kilkoon, but the Colonel had already left the room and was hurrying to the stables where Harbinger was grooming a chestnut mare.

'How's Chaka?' he asked. As if in answer a horse in one of the stalls gave his door a resounding kick.

The Colonel peered cautiously into the darkened interior and studied an enormous black horse that stirred restlessly inside.

'Saddle him up,' said the Colonel vindictively and left Harbinger wondering how the hell he was ever going to get a saddle on the beast.

'You can't possibly ask the Kommandant to ride Chaka,' Mrs Heathcote-Kilkoon told the Colonel when he said what he had done.

'I'm not asking a man who shoots foxes to ride any of my damned horses,' said the Colonel, 'but if he chooses to he can take his chance on Chaka and good luck to him.'

A dreadful banging and the sound of curses from the direction of the stables suggested that Harbinger was not having an easy job saddling Chaka.

'Be it on your own head if the Kommandant gets killed,' said Mrs Heathcote-Kilkoon but the Colonel was unimpressed.

'Any man who shoots foxes deserves to die,' was all he said.

When Kommandant van Heerden arrived it was to find Major Bloxham resplendent in a scarlet coat standing on the steps.

'I thought you said you always wore pink,' said the Kommandant with a touch of annoyance.

'So I do, old boy, so I do. Can't you see?' He turned and went into the house followed by the Kommandant who wondered if he was colourblind. In the main room people were standing about drinking and the Kommandant was relieved to note that they were all dressed appropriately for their sex. Mrs Heathcote-Kilkoon in a long black skirt was looking quite lovely if a little pale while the Colonel's complexion matched that of his coat.

'I suppose you'll be wanting another green chartreuse,' he said, 'or perhaps yellow would suit you better this morning.'

The Kommandant said the green would suit him fine and Mrs Heathcote-Kilkoon presently drew him into a corner.

'Henry's got it into his head you go around shooting foxes,' she said, 'and he's absolutely furious. I think you ought to know he's given you the most awful horse.'

'I've never even seen a fox,' said the Kommandant with simple honesty. 'I wonder where he got that idea from.'

'Well, it doesn't much matter. He's got it and you've got Chaka. You can ride, can't you? I mean really ride.'

Kommandant van Heerden drew himself up proudly.

'Oh yes,' he said. 'I think I can ride.'

'Well I do hope you're right. Chaka's a dreadful brute. Don't for goodness sake, let him get away from you.'

The Kommandant said he certainly wouldn't and a few minutes later everyone trooped out to the yard where the hounds were waiting. So was Chaka. Massive and black, he stood some way apart from the other horses and at his head there stood the figure of a man with small eyes and a non-existent forehead.

It was difficult for Kommandant van Heerden, who in the excitement of going hunting had forgotten all about ex-Konstabel Els, to make up his mind which animal most dismayed him. Certainly the prospect of even mounting a horse as monstrous as Chaka was hardly pleasing but at least it offered a way of avoiding Els if very little, he was about to say, else. With a speed and vigour that quite took the Colonel by surprise, the Kommandant reached up and hauled himself into the saddle and from these commanding heights surveyed the throng. Below him hounds and horses milled about while the other riders mounted and then with Els on a nag vigorously blowing a horn the hunt moved off. Behind them the Kommandant urged Chaka forward tentatively. I am going foxhunting like a real Englishman, he thought as he dug his heels in a second time. It was the last coherent thought he had for some time. With a demonic lurch the great black horse shot out of the yard and into the garden. As the Kommandant desperately clung to his seat it was apparent that wherever he was going it wasn't hunting. The hounds had strung out in quite a different direction. As a rockery disappeared beneath him, as an ornamental bush looked up and disintegrated, and as the Colonel's roses shed both their labels and their petals in his wake the Kommandant was only aware that he was travelling at a great height and at a speed which seemed incredible. Ahead of him loomed the azalea bushes of which

Colonel Heathcote-Kilkoon was so proud and beyond them the open veldt. Kommandant van Heerden shut his eyes. There was not time for prayer. the next moment he was airborne.

The Kommandant's startling gallop caused mixed reactions among the huntsmen. Immaculately sidesaddled and with her top hat perched on her neat blue curls Mrs Heathcote-Kilkoon watched the Kommandant disappear over the azaleas with a combination of disgust at her husband and admiration for the Kommandant. Whatever else he might be, the Kommandant was clearly not a man to baulk at fences.

'See what you've done now,' she shouted at the Colonel who was staring at the destruction left in the wake of his retreating guest. To add to his annoyance Mrs Heathcote-Kilkoon turned her bay and galloped off in pursuit of the Kommandant churning the lawn up still more as she went.

'Got rid of the blighter,' said Major Bloxham cheerfully.

'Damned Boer,' said the Colonel. 'Shoots foxes and smashes my best roses.'

Behind them Harbinger blew his horn again happily. He'd always wanted to see what would happen if he stuffed a quid of tobacco up the great black horse's arse and now he knew.

So did Kommandant van Heerden, though he wasn't aware of the specific cause of Chaka's urgency. Still in the saddle after the first enormous jump he tried to recall what Mrs Heathcote-Kilkoon had said about not letting the horse get away from him. It seemed an uncalled-for piece of advice. If the Kommandant could have thought of any way of letting the horse get away from him without breaking his neck in the process he would have been glad to do so. As it was his only hope of survival seemed to lie in staying with the beast until it ran out of wind. With all the fortitude of a man for whom there were no alternatives, the Kommandant hunched in the saddle and watched a stone wall hurtle towards him. The wall had evidently been built with giraffes in mind. Certainly no horse could clear it. As he landed on the other side Kommandant van Heerden had the distinct impression that the animal he was riding was no horse at all but some mythical creature he'd seen portrayed so eloquently on petrol pumps. Ahead there lay open veldt and in the far distance the shadowy outlines of a wood. One thing he was determined on and that was that no horse, mythical or not, was going to career through a wood full of trees with him on its back. It was better to break one's neck on the open ground than to emerge legless on the far side of a dense wood. With a determination to end his journey

one way or another the Kommandant grasped the reins firmly and
heaved.

To Mrs Heathcote-Kilkoon, galloping desperately after him, the
Kommandant appeared in a new light. He was no longer the coarsely
attractive man of reality she had formerly seen him as but the hero of
her dreams. There was something reminiscent of a painting she had once
seen of Napoleon crossing the Alps on a prancing horse about the figure
that soared over the wall no one had been known to attempt before.
With a caution entirely justified by her longing for her new idol, Mrs
Heathcote-Kilkoon chose a gate and emerged on the other side to find
to her astonishment that both the Kommandant and Chaka had vanished.
She galloped towards the wood and was horrified to see both horse and
rider motionless on the ground. She rode up and dismounted.

When Kommandant van Heerden came to, it was to find his head
cradled in the dark lap of Mrs Heathcote-Kilkoon who was bending over
him with a look of maternal admiration on her face.

'Don't try to move,' she said. The Kommandant wiggled his toes to
see if his back was broken. His toes wiggled reassuringly. He lifted a knee
and the knee moved. His arms were all right too. There seemed to be
nothing broken. The Kommandant opened his eyes again and smiled.
Above him beneath a ring of tinted curls Mrs Heathcote-Kilkoon smiled
back and it seemed to Kommandant van Heerden that there was in that
smile a new acknowledgement of some deep bond of feeling between
them, a meeting of two hearts and minds alone on the open veldt. Mrs
Heathcote-Kilkoon read his thoughts.

'Ant-bear hole,' she said with suppressed emotion.

'Ant-bear hole?' asked the Kommandant.

'Ant-bear hole,' Mrs Heathcote-Kilkoon repeated gently.

The Kommandant tried to think what ant-bear holes had to do with
his feelings for her and apart from the rather bizarre notion that they
should get into one together couldn't think of anything. He contented
himself with murmuring 'Ant-bear hole,' with as much emotion as possible
and closed his eyes again. Beneath his head her plump thighs formed a
delightful pillow. The Kommandant sighed and nestled his head against
her stomach. A feeling of supreme happiness welled up inside him marred
only by the thought that he would have to mount that ghastly horse
again. It was a prospect that he had no intention of hastening. Mrs
Heathcote-Kilkoon dashed his hopes.

'We can't stay here,' she said. 'It's far too hot.'

The Kommandant who had begun to suspect that some large insect had begun to crawl up the inside of his breeches had to agree. Slowly he lifted his head from her lap and climbed to his feet.

'Let's go into the woods,' Mrs Heathcote-Kilkoon said. 'You need to rest and I want to make sure you haven't broken anything.'

Now that the Kommandant was up he could see what she had meant by ant-bear hole. The great black horse lay on its side, its neck broken and one foreleg deep in a hole. With a sigh of relief that he would never have to ride the beast again and that his horsemanship had been vindicated after all by the aardvark, the Kommandant allowed himself to be helped quite unnecessarily into the shade of the wood. There in an open dell shaded by the trees Mrs Heathcote-Kilkoon insisted that he lie down while she examined him for broken bones.

'You may have concussion,' she said as her experienced hands unbuttoned his jacket. In the next few moments Kommandant van Heerden began to think that she must be right. What the great English lady was doing to him must be some result of brain damage. As she stood above him and unbuckled her skirt he knew he was seeing things. I'd better just lie still until it passes over, he thought and shut his eyes.

Two miles away the hounds had picked up the scent of Fox and, with the hunt in full pursuit and Harbinger occasionally blowing his horn, were off across country.

'Wonder what happened to that damned Boer,' Major Bloxham shouted.

'I daresay he's all right,' the Colonel shouted back, 'Daphne's probably looking after him.'

Presently the hounds veered to the left and headed for a wood and ten minutes later, still mutely absorbed in their pursuit, had left the open ground and were deep in the undergrowth. The scent was stronger here and the hounds quickened their pace. Half a mile ahead Kommandant van Heerden followed suit.

He wasn't quite so mute but his absorption matched that of the pack. Above him clad only in her boots and spurs and with her top hat clinging elastically to the top of her tinted head, Mrs Heathcote-Kilkoon shouted encouragement to her new mount, occasionally lashing him on with her crop. They were so deeply engrossed in one another that they were oblivious to the crackling undergrowth that signalled the approach of the hunt. 'Jill, Jenny, Daphne, my sweet,' moaned the Kommandant unable even now to shake off the notion that he was figuring in one of Dornford Yates' novels. Mrs Heathcote-Kilkoon's imagination, sharpened by years of frustration, was more equestrian.

'Ride a cock horse to Banbury Cross to see a fine lady upon a white horse,' she shouted and was astonished to find that her invitation had been accepted.

Out of the woods raced the pack and the Kommandant who had been on the point of reaching his second climax became suddenly aware that the tongue that was licking his face was of a length and texture quite unusual in a lady of Mrs Heathcote-Kilkoon's breeding. He opened his eyes and found himself looking into the face of a large foxhound which slobbered and panted disgustingly. The Kommandant looked wildly around. The dell was filled with dogs. A tide of tails waved above him and out above them all Mrs Heathcote-Kilkoon sat impaled upon him beating around her with her riding crop.

'Down Jason. Down Snarler. Down Craven. Down van Heerden,' she yelled, her topper bobbing as vigorously as her breasts.

Kommandant van Heerden stared crazedly up at the underside of Snarler and tried to get the dog's paw out of his mouth. He had never realized before how horrible a hot dog smelt. Obedient as ever to his mistress Snarler sat – and got up promptly when the Kommandant, dreading death by suffocation, bit him. Relieved for a moment of this threat of asphyxia the Kommandant raised his head only to have it submerged a moment later by the press. The brief glimpse he had had of the outside world presented so awful a prospect that he preferred the stinking obscurity to be found under the foxhounds. Colonel Heathcote-Kilkoon and the other members of the hunt had emerged from the woods and were surveying the scene in amazement.

'Good God, Daphne, what on earth do you think you're doing?' the Kommandant heard the Colonel shout angrily.

Mrs Heathcote-Kilkoon rose to the occasion magnificently.

'What the hell do you think I'm doing?' she screamed with a display of righteous indignation the Kommandant found extraordinarily impressive but which seemed calculated to raise a question in her husband's mind the Kommandant would have preferred to remain unanswered.

'I've no idea,' shouted the Colonel who couldn't for a moment imagine what his wife was doing in the middle of a dell without her clothes. Mrs Heathcote-Kilkoon answered him. 'I'm having a shit,' she shouted with a coarseness that Kommandant van Heerden found personally humiliating but entirely apposite.

The Colonel coughed with embarrassment. 'Good God, I'm terribly sorry,' he muttered but Mrs Heathcote-Kilkoon was determined to pursue the advantage she had gained.

'And if you were gentlemen you'd turn your backs and get the hell out of here,' she screamed. Her words were immediately effective. The huntsmen turned their horses and galloped back the way they had come.

As the tide of foxhounds slowly ebbed the Kommandant found himself, naked and covered with muddy paw-marks, staring up at the lady of his and Heathcote-Kilkoon's choice. With a reluctance that did him credit she detached herself from him and stood up. Breathless with fear and a new admiration for her the Kommandant scrambled to his feet and began to look for his breeches. He knew now what British sang-froid meant.

'And I've got a stiff upper lip,' he said feeling the effects of Snarler's hindpaw.

'About the only thing stiff you have got,' said Mrs Heathcote-Kilkoon frankly.

In the bushes on the edge of the dell Harbinger giggled softly. He'd never pretended to be a gentleman and he'd always wanted to see the Colonel's wife in the nude.

CHAPTER TWELVE

As they dressed in the dell Kommandant van Heerden and Mrs Heathcote-Kilkoon were filled with post-coital depression.

'It's been so nice to meet a real man for a change,' she murmured. 'You've no idea how tiresome Henry can be.'

'I think I have,' said the Kommandant who wasn't likely to forget his recent nightmare ride. And besides the thought of meeting the Colonel again so shortly after having, as the Kommandant delicately put it, had carnal knowledge of his wife was not particularly appealing. 'I think I'll just walk back to the Spa from here,' but Mrs Heathcote-Kilkoon wouldn't hear of it.

'I'll send Boy over with the Land-Rover to pick you up,' she said. 'You're not in a fit state to walk anywhere. Certainly not after your fall and in this heat too.' Before the Kommandant could stop her, she had walked out of the wood and had mounted her horse and was riding away.

Kommandant van Heerden sat on a log and considered the romantic experience he had just undergone. 'Undergone's the word for it,' he muttered aloud and was horrified to hear the bushes part behind him and a voice say, 'Lovely bit of stuff, eh?'

The Kommandant knew that voice. He spun round and found Els grinning at him.

'What the hell are you doing here?' he asked. 'I thought you were dead.'

'Me? Dead?' said Els. 'Never.' The Kommandant began to think Els was right. There was something eternal about him like original sin. 'Been having it off with the Colonel's old woman eh?' Els continued with a familiarity the Kommandant found quite nauseating.

'What I do with my spare time is no concern of yours,' he said emphatically.

'Might be of some concern to the Colonel,' Els said cheerfully, 'I mean he might like to know —'

'Never mind what Colonel Heathcote-Kilkoon might like to know,' interrupted the Kommandant hurriedly. 'What I'd like to know is why you didn't die in Piemburg Prison with the Governor and the Chaplain.'

'That was a mistake,' said Els. 'I got muddled up with the prisoners.'

'Understandably,' said the Kommandant.

Els changed the topic.

'I'm thinking of coming back into the police,' he said. 'I'm tired of being Harbinger.'

'You're thinking of what?' said the Kommandant. He tried to raise a laugh but it didn't sound very convincing.

'I'd like to be a konstabel again.'

'You must be joking,' said the Kommandant.

'I'm not,' said Els. 'I've got my pension to think about and there's that reward money I'm owed for capturing Miss Hazelstone.'

The Kommandant considered the reward money and tried to think of an answer.

'You died intestate,' he said finally.

'I didn't, you know,' said Els. 'I died in Piemburg.'

The Kommandant sighed. He had forgotten how difficult it was to get Els to understand the simplest facts of law.

'Intestate means you died without making a will,' he explained only to find Els looking at him with interest.

'Have you made a will?' Els asked fingering his horn threateningly. He looked as though he was going to blow it.

'I don't see what that's got to do with it,' he said.

'The Colonel's got a legal right to kill you for stuffing his wife,' said Els. 'And that's what he'd do if I blew this horn and called him back.'

Kommandant van Heerden had to admit that for once Els was right. South African law reserved no penalties for husbands who shot their wives' lovers. In his career as a police officer the Kommandant had had occasion to reassure a number of men who were feeling some alarm on this account. To add to his own alarm Els raised his horn to his lips.

'All right,' said the Kommandant, 'what do you want?'

'I've told you,' said Els, 'I want my old job back.'

The Kommandant was beginning to prevaricate when the sound of a Land-Rover approaching determined the issue.

'All right, I'll see what I can do,' he said, 'though how I'm going to explain how a coloured convict is really a white konstabel, God only knows.'

'No point in spoiling the shit for a ha'p'orth of tar,' said Els making use of an expression he had picked up from Major Bloxham.

'Hear you've been having a bit of trouble, old boy,' said the Major when the Land-Rover stopped beside the body of Chaka. 'Always said that black bastard was a menace.' The Kommandant climbed in beside him and murmured his agreement but the black bastard he had in mind was not the dead horse. In the back of the truck Konstabel Els smiled happily. He was looking forward to shooting kaffirs quite legally again.

As they approached the house the Kommandant saw Colonel and Mrs Heathcote-Kilkoon standing at the top of the steps waiting for them. Once again their reactions came as a complete surprise to him. The woman with whom but an hour before he had enjoyed what could without exaggeration be called a touching intimacy now stood erect and coldly detached at the front door while her husband was exhibiting signs of evident embarrassment quite out of keeping with his role.

'Dreadfully sorry,' he muttered opening the door of the Land-Rover for the Kommandant, 'shouldn't have given you that horse in the first place.'

The Kommandant tried to think of a suitable reply to this apology.

'Ant-bear hole,' he said falling back on an expression which seemed to cover a multitude of situations.

'Quite,' said the Colonel. 'Damned nasty things. Should have been stopped.' He led the way up the steps and Mrs Heathcote-Kilkoon stepped forward to greet the Kommandant.

'So nice of you to come,' she said.

'Good of you to have me,' murmured the Kommandant blushing.

'You must try to make it more often,' said Mrs Heathcote-Kilkoon.

They went into the house where the Kommandant was greeted by La Marquise with a remark about The Flying Dutchman which he didn't particularly like.

'Don't take any notice,' Mrs Heathcote-Kilkoon said, 'I think you were wonderful. They're just jealous.'

For the next few minutes Kommandant van Heerden found himself the centre of attention. The fact that he was the first man to have cleared the high wall, albeit involuntarily, drew murmurs of admiration from everyone. Even the Colonel said he had to take off his hat to him, which considering the loss of Chaka and the state of his garden, not to mention that of his wife, the Kommandant thought was pretty generous of him. He had just explained how he had learnt to ride on his ouma's farm in Magaliesburg and had ridden for the police in Pretoria when the blow fell.

'I must say you take things pretty cool, Kommandant,' the fat man who knew how to get discounts on refrigerators said, 'coming out here and hunting when there's all this trouble in Piemburg.'

'Trouble? What trouble?' he asked.

'What? Do you mean you haven't heard?' asked the fat man. 'There's been an outbreak of sabotage. Bomb attacks all over the place. Radio mast down. Electricity cut off. Absolute chaos.'

With a curse Kommandant van Heerden dumped the glass of Cointreau he'd been drinking into the nearest receptacle.

'I'm afraid we haven't a phone,' Mrs Heathcote-Kilkoon told him as he looked wildly round the hall. 'Henry won't have one for security reasons. He's always calling his stock-broker ...'

The Kommandant was in too much of a hurry to wait and hear about Henry's stock-broker. He dashed down the steps to his car and found, as he might have expected, Els at the wheel. With the feeling that Els' presumption was somehow appropriate to the terrible news he had just received, the Kommandant climbed into the back seat. Disaster was in the air. It was certainly in the herbaceous border, where Els reversed before turning the car down the drive with a spurt of gravel that suggested he was shaking the dust of White Ladies from his feet.

From the terrace Mrs Heathcote-Kilkoon watched them leave with a feeling of sadness. 'To part is to die a little,' she murmured and went to join the Colonel who was staring morosely into a tank of tropical fish where the Kommandant's drink was already producing some unusual effects.

'So that's how poor Willy went,' said the Colonel.

As they drove into Weezen the Kommandant cursed himself for his own stupidity.

'I might have known Verkramp would foul things up,' he thought and ordered Els to stop at the local police station. The information he was given there did nothing to restore his confidence.

'They do what?' he asked in astonishment when the Sergeant in charge told him that Piemburg had been invaded by hordes of self-detonating ostriches.

'Fly in at night in their hundreds,' said the Sergeant.

'That's a damned lie for a start,' shouted the Kommandant. 'Ostriches don't fly. They can't.'

He went back to the car and told Els to drive on. Whatever ostriches could or couldn't do, one thing was sure. Something had happened in Piemburg to cut the city off from the outside world. The telephone lines had been dead for days.

As the car hurtled along the dirt road towards the head of the Rooi Nek Pass, Kommandant van Heerden had the feeling that he was leaving an idyllic world of peace and sanity and heading back into an inferno of violence at the centre of which sat the diabolical figure of Luitenant Verkramp. He was so immersed in his own thoughts that it only occurred to him once or twice to tell Els not to drive so damned dangerously.

At Sjambok the impression of imminent catastrophe was increased by the news that the road bridges had been blown outside Piemburg. At Voetsak he learnt that the Sewage Disposal plant had been destroyed. After that the Kommandant decided not to stop any more but to drive straight through to Piemburg.

An hour later as they drove down the hill from Imperial View they came to the first tangible evidence of sabotage.

A road block had been set up at the temporary bridge erected to replace the one destroyed by Verkramp's secret agents. The Kommandant got out to inspect the damage while a konstabel searched the car.

'Got to make a personal check too,' said the konstabel before the Kommandant could explain who he was and ran his hands over the Kommandant's breeches with a thoroughness that was surprising.

'Only obeying orders, sir,' said the konstabel when the Kommandant snarled that he wasn't likely to keep high explosives there. Kommandant van Heerden scrambled into the car. 'And change your shaving lotion,' he shouted. 'You stink to high heaven.'

They drove on into the city and the Kommandant was appalled to notice two konstabels walking down the pavement hand in hand.

'Stop the car,' the Kommandant told Els and got out.

'What the hell do you think you're doing?' he shouted at the two konstabels.

'We're on patrol, sir,' said the men in unison.

'What? Holding hands?' screamed the Kommandant. 'Do you want the general public to think you're fucking queers?'

The two konstabels let go of one another and the Kommandant got back into the car.

'What the hell's been going on round here?' he muttered.

In the front seat Konstabel Els smiled to himself. There had been some changes in Piemburg since he'd last been there. He was beginning to think he was going to enjoy being in the South African Police again.

By the time they arrived at the Police Station the Kommandant was in a vile temper.

'Send me the Acting Kommandant,' he shouted at the konstabel at the Duty desk and went upstairs wondering if his imagination was playing him up or there had been a suggestive leer on the man's face. The first impression that there had been a breakdown in discipline was confirmed by the state of the Kommandant's office. The windows had no glass in them and ashes from the grate had blown all over the room. The Kommandant was just staring at the mess when there was a knock and Sergeant Breitenbach entered.

'What in the name of hell has been happening round here?' the Kommandant yelled at the Sergeant who was not, he was relieved to note, exhibiting any signs of queerness.

'Well, sir –' he began but the Kommandant interrupted him.

'What do I find when I come back?' he screamed in a voice that made the Duty Konstabel wince on the floor below and several passers-by stop in the street. 'Poofters. Bombs. Exploding ostriches. Do they mean anything to you?' Sergeant Breitenbach nodded. 'I thought they fucking might. I go away on holiday and the next thing I hear is that there's an outbreak of sabotage. Road bridges being blown up. No telephones. Konstabels walking about hand in hand and now this. My own office in a shambles.'

'That was the ostriches, sir,' mumbled the Sergeant.

Kommandant van Heerden slumped into a chair and held his head. 'Dear God. It's enough to drive a man out of his mind.'

'It has, sir,' said the Sergeant miserably.

'Has what?'

'Driven a man out of his mind, sir. Luitenant Verkramp, sir.'

The name Verkramp shook the Kommandant out of his reverie.

'Verkramp!' he yelled. 'Wait till I lay my hands on the swine. I'll crucify the bastard. Where is he?'

'In Fort Rapier, sir. He's off his rocker.'

Kommandant van Heerden absorbed the information slowly.

'You mean ...'

'He's got religious mania, sir. Thinks he's God.'

The Kommandant stared at him disbelievingly. The notion that any man could think he was God when his creation was as chaotic as Verkramp's had so obviously been seemed inconceivable.

'Thinks he's God?' he mumbled. 'Verkramp?'

Sergeant Breitenbach had given the matter some thought.

'I think that's how the trouble started,' he explained. 'He wanted to show what he could do.'

'He's done that all right,' said the Kommandant limply, looking round his office.

'He's got this thing about sin, sir, and he wanted to stop policemen going to bed with black women.'

'I know all that.'

'Well he started off by giving them shock treatment and showing them photographs of naked black women and . . .'

Kommandant van Heerden stopped him.

'Don't go on,' he said, 'I don't think I can stand it.'

He got up and went over to his desk. He opened a drawer and took out a bottle of brandy he kept for emergencies and poured himself a glass. When he'd finished it he looked up.

'Now then begin at the beginning and tell me what Verkramp did.' Sergeant Breitenbach told him. At the end the Kommandant shook his head sadly.

'It didn't work then? This treatment?' he asked.

'I wouldn't say that, sir. It just didn't work the way it was meant to. I mean you'd find it difficult to get any of the konstabels who's been treated into bed with a black woman. We've tried it and they get into a frightful state.'

'You've tried to get a konstabel into bed with a black woman?' asked the Kommandant, who could see himself giving evidence at the inevitable court of inquiry and having to admit that policemen under his command had been ordered to have sexual intercourse with black women as part of their duties.

Sergeant Breitenbach nodded. 'Couldn't do it though,' he said, 'I guarantee that 'not one of those two hundred and ten men will ever go to bed with a black again.'

'Two hundred and ten?' asked the Kommandant stunned by the scale of Verkramp's activities.

'That's the number, sir. Half the force are gay,' the Sergeant told him. 'And not one of them prepared to sleep with a black woman.'

'I suppose that makes a change,' said the Kommandant looking for some relief in this recital of disasters.

'Trouble is they won't go near a white woman either. The treatment seems to have worked both ways. You should see the letters of complaint we've had from some of the men's wives.'

The Kommandant said he'd prefer not to.

'What about the exploding ostriches?' he asked. 'That have anything to do with Verkramp's religious mania?'

'Not to my knowledge,' said the Sergeant. 'That was the work of the Communist saboteurs.'

The Kommandant sighed. 'Them again,' he said wearily. 'I don't suppose you've got a lead on them, have you?'

'Well, we have made some progress, sir. We've got the description of the men who were feeding the ostriches French letters ...' He stopped. Kommandant van Heerden was staring at him wildly.

'Feeding them French letters?' he asked. 'What the hell were they doing that for?'

'The explosive was packed in contraceptives, sir. Fetherlites.'

'Fetherlights?' said the Kommandant trying to imagine what sort of ornithological offal he was on about.

'That's the brand name, sir. We've also an excellent description of a man who bought twelve dozen. Twelve women have come forward to say they remember him.'

'Twelve dozen for twelve women?' said the Kommandant. 'I should bloody well think they can remember him. I should have thought he was unforgettable.'

'They were in the shop when he tried to buy the things,' the Sergeant explained. 'Five barbers have also given us a description which tallies with that of the women.'

The Kommandant tried desperately to visualize the sort of man whose tastes were so indiscriminate. 'He can't have got far, that's for sure,' he said finally. 'Not after that lot.'

'No sir,' said Sergeant Breitenbach. 'He didn't. A man answering his description and with fingerprints that correspond with some of those on the French letters was found dead in the toilet at the Majestic Cinema.'

'I'm not in the least surprised,' said the Kommandant.

'Unfortunately we can't identify him.'

'Too emaciated I suppose,' the Kommandant suggested.

'He was killed by the bomb which went off there,' the Sergeant explained.

'Well have you made any arrests at all?'

The Sergeant nodded. 'Luitenant Verkramp ordered the arrest of thirty-six suspects as soon as the first bombings occurred.'

'Well that's something anyway,' said the Kommandant more cheerfully. 'Got any confessions out of them?'

Sergeant Breitenbach looked dubious.

'Well, the Mayor says ...' he began.

'What's the Mayor got to do with it?' asked the Kommandant with a sense of awful premonition.

'He's one of the suspects, sir,' Sergeant Breitenbach admitted awkwardly. 'Luitenant Verkramp said ...'

But Kommandant van Heerden was on his feet and white with rage.

'Don't tell me what the fucking shit says,' he screamed. 'I go away for ten days and half the town blows up, half the police force turns into raving homosexuals, half the stock of French letters is bought up by some sex maniac, Verkramp arrests the fucking Mayor. What the fuck do I care what Verkramp says. It's what he's done that's worrying me.'

The Kommandant stopped short. 'Is there anything else I ought to know?' he demanded. Sergeant Breitenbach shifted his feet nervously. 'There are thirty-five other suspects in the prison, sir. There's the Dean of Piemburg, Alderman Cecil, the manager of Barclays Bank ...'

'Oh my God, and I suppose they've all been interrogated,' squawked the Kommandant.

'Yes sir,' said Sergeant Breitenbach who knew precisely what the Kommandant meant by interrogated. 'They've been standing up for the last eight days. The Mayor's admitted he doesn't like the government but he still maintains he didn't blow up the telephone exchange. The only confession we've got that's any use is from the manager of Barclays Bank.'

'The manager of Barclays Bank?' asked the Kommandant. 'What's he done?'

'Peed in the Hluwe Dam, sir. It carries the death penalty.'

'Peeing in the Hluwe Dam carries the death penalty? I didn't know that.'

'It's in the Sabotage Act 1962. Polluting water supplies, sir,' the Sergeant said.

'Yes well,' said the Kommandant doubtfully, 'I daresay it is but all I can say is that if Verkramp thinks he can hang the manager of Barclays Bank for peeing in a dam he must be mad. I'm going up to Fort Rapier to see that bastard.'

In Fort Rapier Mental Hospital Luitenant Verkramp was still suffering from acute anxiety brought on by the wholly unexpected result of his experiment in aversion therapy and counter-terrorism. His temporary conviction that he was the Almighty had given way to a phobia about birds. Dr von Blimenstein drew her own conclusions.

'A simple case of sexual guilt together with a castration complex,' she told the nurse when Verkramp refused his dinner on the grounds that it was stuffed chicken and French lettuce.

'Take it away,' he screamed, 'I can't take any more.'

He was equally adamant about feather pillows and in fact anything vaguely reminiscent of what Dr von Blimenstein would insist on calling our feathered friends.

'No friends of mine,' said Verkramp, eyeing a pouter pigeon on the tree outside his window with alarm.

'We've got to try to get to the bottom of this thing,' said Dr von Blimenstein. Verkramp looked at her wildly.

'Don't mention that thing,' he shouted. Dr von Blimenstein took note of this fresh symptom. 'Anal complex,' she thought to herself and sent the Luitenant into panic by asking him if he had ever had any homosexual experiences.

'Yes,' said Verkramp desperately when the doctor insisted on knowing.

'Would you like to tell me about it?'

'No,' said Verkramp who still couldn't get the picture of hooker Botha in a yellow wig out of his mind. 'No. I wouldn't.'

Dr von Blimenstein persisted.

'We're never going to get anywhere unless you come to terms with your own unconscious,' she told him. 'You've got to be absolutely frank with me.'

'Yes,' said Verkramp who hadn't come to Fort Rapier to be frank with anyone.

If, during the day, Dr von Blimenstein gained the impression that sex was at the root of Verkramp's breakdown, his behaviour at night suggested another explanation. As she sat by his bedside and made notes of his ramblings, the doctor noticed a new pattern emerging. Verkramp spent much of his nights screaming about bombs and secret agents and was clearly obsessed with the number twelve. Remembering how frequently she had counted twelve explosions as the saboteurs struck she was hardly surprised that the head of Security in Piemburg should be obsessed by the number. On the other hand she gained the definite impression from Verkramp's sleep-talking that he had had twelve secret agents working for him. She decided to ask him about this new symptom in the morning.

'What does the number twelve mean to you?' she asked when she came to see him next day. Verkramp went pale and began to shake.

'I have to know,' she told him. 'It's in your own interest.'

'Shan't tell you,' said Verkramp who knew, if he knew anything, that it wasn't in his interest to tell her about the number twelve.

'Don't forget that I'm acting in a professional capacity,' said the doctor, 'and that anything you tell me remains a secret between us.'

Luitenant Verkramp was not reassured.

'Doesn't mean anything to me,' he said. 'I don't know anything about number twelve.'

'I see,' said the doctor making a note of his alarm. 'Then perhaps you'd like to tell me about the trip to Durban.'

There was no doubt now that she was close to the heart of Verkramp's neurosis. His reaction indicated that quite clearly. By the time the gibbering Luitenant had been got back into bed and given sedation, Dr von Blimenstein was satisfied that she could effect a cure. She was beginning to think that there were other advantages to be gained from her insight into his problems and the idea of marriage, never far from the doctor's mind, began to re-emerge.

'Tell me,' she said as she tucked Verkramp into bed again, 'is it true that a wife cannot be forced to give evidence against her husband?'

Verkramp said it was and, with a smile that suggested he would do well to meditate on the fact, Dr von Blimenstein left the room. When she returned an hour later, it was to find the patient ready with an explanation for his obsession with the number twelve.

'There were twelve saboteurs and they were –'

'Bullshit,' snapped the doctor, 'utter bullshit. There were twelve secret agents and they were working for you and you took them to Durban by car. Isn't that the truth?'

'Yes. No, No, it's not,' Verkramp wailed.

'Now listen to me. Balthazar Verkramp, if you go on lying I'll have you given an injection of truth drug and we'll get an accurate confession out of you before you know what's happened.'

Verkramp stared panic-stricken from the bed.

'You wouldn't,' he shrieked. 'You're not allowed to.'

Dr von Blimenstein looked round the room suggestively. It was more like a cell than a private room. 'In here,' she said, 'I can do anything I like. You're my patient and I'm your doctor and if you give any trouble I can have you in a straitjacket and there is absolutely nothing you can do about it. Now then, are you prepared to tell me about your problems and remember your secrets are safe with me. As your medical adviser no one can force me to tell them what has passed between us unless of course I was put into the witness box. Then of course I would be under oath.'

The doctor paused before continuing, 'You did say that a wife couldn't
be forced to give evidence against her husband, didn't you?'

To Verkramp the alternatives he was now facing were if anything
more shocking than exploding ostriches and camp konstabels. He lay in
bed and wondered what to do. If he refused to admit that he was
responsible for all the bombings and violence in the city, the doctor
would use the truth drug to get it out of him and he would have forfeited
her good-will into the bargain. If he admitted it openly, he would escape
the legal consequences of his zeal only to be led to the altar. There
seemed to be little choice. He swallowed nervously, stared round the
room for the last uncommitted time and asked for a glass of water.

'Will you marry me?' He said finally.

Dr von Blimenstein smiled sweetly.

'Of course, I will, darling. Of course I will,' and a moment later
Verkramp was in her arms and the doctor's mouth was pressed closely
over his lips. Verkramp shut his eyes and considered a lifetime of Dr von
Blimenstein. It was, he supposed, preferable to being hanged.

When Kommandant van Heerden arrived at Fort-Rapier to see the
Luitenant it was not surprising that he found his way strewn with
extraordinary obstacles. In the first place he found the clerk in the
Inquiry Desk at Admissions decidedly unhelpful. The fact that the clerk
was a catatonic schizophrenic chosen by Dr von Blimenstein for his
general immobility to help out at a time of acute staff shortage led to a
sharp rise in the Kommandant's blood pressure.

'I demand to see Luitenant Verkramp,' he shouted at the motionless
catatonic and was about to resort to violence when a tall man with an
exceedingly pale face interrupted.

'I think he's in Ward C,' the man told him. The Kommandant thanked
him and went to Ward C only to find it was filled with manic-depressive
women. He returned to Admissions and after another one-sided altercation
with the catatonic clerk was told by the tall thin man who happened to
be passing through again that Verkramp was definitely in Ward H. The
Kommandant went to Ward H and while unable to diagnose what the
patients there were suffering from was grateful to note that Verkramp
wasn't. He went back to Admissions in a foul temper and met the thin
tall man in the corridor.

'Not there?' the man inquired. 'Then he's certainly in Ward E.'

'Make up your mind,' shouted the Kommandant angrily. 'First you
say he's in Ward C, then in Ward H and now Ward E.'

'Interesting point you've just raised,' said the man.

'What point?' asked the Kommandant.

'About making up your mind,' said the man. 'It presupposes in the first place that there is a distinction between the mind and the brain. Now if you had said "Make up your brain" the implications would have been quite different.'

'Listen,' said the Kommandant, 'I've come here to see Luitenant Verkramp not swop logic with you.' He went off down the corridor again in search of Ward E only to learn that it was in the Bantu section which made it unlikely Verkramp was in it whatever he was suffering from. The Kommandant went back to Admissions swearing to murder the tall man if he could find him. Instead he found himself confronted by Dr von Blimenstein who pointed out acidly that he was in a hospital and not in a police station and would he kindly behave accordingly. Somewhat subdued by this evidence of authority the Kommandant followed her into her office.

'Now then, what is it you want?' she asked seating herself behind her desk and eyeing him coldly.

'I want to visit Luitenant Verkramp,' said the Kommandant.

'Are you parent, relative or guardian?' asked the doctor.

'I'm a police officer investigating a crime,' said the Kommandant.

'Then you have a warrant? I should like to see it.'

The Kommandant said he hadn't a warrant. 'I am Kommandant of Police in Piemburg and Verkramp is under my command. I don't need a warrant to visit him wherever he is.'

Dr von Blimenstein smiled patronizingly.

'You obviously don't understand hospital rules,' she said. 'We have to be very careful who visits our patients. We can't have them being disturbed by casual acquaintances or by being asked questions about their work. After all, Balthazar's problems largely stem from overwork and I'm afraid I hold you responsible.'

The Kommandant was so astonished by hearing Verkramp called Balthazar that he couldn't think of a suitable reply.

'Now, if you could let me have some idea of the sort of questions you wish to put to him, I might be able to assist you,' continued the doctor, conscious of the advantage she had already gained.

The Kommandant could think of a great many questions he would like to put to the Luitenant but he thought it wiser not to mention them now. He explained that he simply wanted to find out if Verkramp could shed any light on the recent series of bombings.

'I see,' Dr von Blimenstein said. 'Now if I understand you rightly, you are quite satisfied with the way the Luitenant handled the situation in your absence?'

Kommandant van Heerden decided that a policy of appeasement was the only one likely to persuade the doctor to allow him to interview Verkramp.

'Yes,' he said, 'Luitenant Verkramp did everything he could to put a stop to the trouble.'

'Good,' said Dr von Blimenstein encouragingly, 'I'm glad to hear you say that. You see it's important that the patient shouldn't be made to feel in any way guilty. Balthazar's problems are largely the result of a long-standing sense of guilt and inadequacy. We don't want to intensify those feelings now, do we?'

'No,' said the Kommandant who could well believe that Verkramp's problem had to do with guilt.

'I take it then, that you are absolutely satisfied with his work and feel that he has handled the situation with skill and an exceptional degree of conscientiousness. Is that correct?'

'Definitely,' said the Kommandant, 'he couldn't have done better if he had tried.'

'In that case I think it is quite all right for you to see him,' Dr von Blimenstein said and switched off the portable tape recorder on her desk. She got up and went down the passage followed by the Kommandant who was beginning to feel that he had in some subtle way been outmanoeuvred. After climbing several flights of stairs they came to yet another corridor. 'If you'll just wait here,' said the doctor, 'I'll go and tell him that you want to see him,' and leaving the Kommandant in a small waiting-room she went off to Verkramp's private room.

'We've got a visitor,' she announced gaily as Verkramp cringed in his bed.

'Who is it?' he asked weakly.

'Just an old friend,' she said. 'He just wants to ask you a few questions. Kommandant van Heerden.'

Verkramp assumed a new and dreadful pallor.

'Now there's no need to worry,' Dr von Blimenstein said, sitting down on the edge of the bed and taking his hand. 'You don't have to answer any questions unless you want to.'

'Well, I don't,' said Verkramp emphatically.

'Then you shan't,' she said, extracting a bottle from her pocket and a lump of sugar.

'What's that?' Verkramp asked nervously.

'Something to help you not to answer any questions, my darling,' said the doctor and popped the lump of sugar into his mouth. Verkramp chewed it up and lay back.

Ten minutes later the Kommandant who was trying to keep his temper at the long wait by reading a magazine about motor cars was horrified by the sound of screams coming from the corridor. It sounded as though one of the patients was enduring the torments of hell.

Dr von Blimenstein came into the room. 'He's ready to see you now,' she said, 'but I want to warn you that he's to be handled gently. This is one of his good days and we don't want to upset him do we?'

'No,' said the Kommandant trying to make himself heard above the demented shrieks. The doctor unlocked a door and the Kommandant peered very nervously inside. What he saw sent him hurriedly back into the corridor.

'No need to be alarmed,' said the doctor and pushed him into the room. 'Just put your questions to him gently and don't excite him.' She locked the door behind him and the Kommandant found himself alone in a small room with a screaming scurrying creature that had when the Kommandant could catch a glimpse of its face some of the features of Luitenant Verkramp. The thin nose, the fierce eyes and the angular shape were those of the Kommandant's second-in-command but there the resemblance ended. Verkramp didn't scream like that, in fact the Kommandant couldn't think what did. Verkramp didn't slobber like that, Verkramp didn't scurry sideways like that, and above all Verkramp didn't cling to the window bars like that.

As the Kommandant pressed himself terrified into a corner by the door he knew that he had made a wasted trip. Whatever else the day had taught him, one thing was quite sure: Luitenant Verkramp's insanity was unquestionable.

'Ugh, ugh, snow man balloon fill up baboon,' shrieked Verkramp and hurled himself from the window bars and disappeared under the bed still shrieking only to reappear precipitously scrabbling for the Kommandant's legs. The Kommandant kicked him off and Verkramp shot across the room and up the window bars. 'Let me out of here,' yelled the Kommandant and found himself beating on the door with dementia that almost equalled that of Verkramp. An eye regarded him bleakly through the spy hole in the door.

'You're quite sure you've asked him all the questions you want to?' Dr von Blimenstein asked.

'Yes, yes,' shouted the Kommandant desperately.

'And there's no question of Balthazar being held responsible for what has happened?'

'Responsible?' screamed the Kommandant. 'Of course he's not responsible.' It seemed a totally unnecessary question to ask.

Dr von Blimenstein unlocked the door and the Kommandant staggered into the corridor. Behind him Verkramp was still gibbering from the window, his eyes alight with an intensity the Kommandant had no doubt was a sign of incurable insanity.

'One of his good days,' said the doctor, locking the door and leading the way back to her office.

'What did you say was the matter with him?' the Kommandant asked wondering what Verkramp's bad days were like.

'Mild depression brought on by overwork.'

'Good heavens,' said the Kommandant, 'I wouldn't have thought that was mild.'

'Ah but then you've had no experience of mental illness,' said the doctor. 'You judge these things from a lay position.'

'I wouldn't say that,' said the Kommandant. 'Do you think he'll ever recover?'

'Positive,' said the doctor. 'He'll be as right as rain in a few days time.'

Kommandant van Heerden deferred to her professional opinion and with a politeness that sprang from the conviction that she had a hopeless case on her hands thanked her for her help.

'If there's anything I can do at any time,' she told him, 'don't hesitate to call on me.'

With a silent prayer that he would never have to, the Kommandant left the hospital. In his room Luitenant Verkramp continued his trip. It was the first time he'd taken LSD.

CHAPTER THIRTEEN

If Kommandant van Heerden's visit to Fort Rapier Mental Hospital had given him a new and terrible insight into the irrational depths of the human psyche, his next appointment did nothing to remove the impression that everyone in Piemburg had changed for the worse in his absence. Certainly the thirty-six men who stumbled from their cells to receive the Kommandant's profound apologies and expressions of regret were no longer the upstanding and prominent public figures of a fortnight before. The Mayor, whom the Kommandant had decided to see first, couldn't reciprocate the process. His eyes were swollen and black as a result, the Security Sergeant told the Kommandant, of the suspect's having banged himself against the door knob of his cell. Since the cells weren't equipped with door knobs it didn't seem a likely explanation. The rest of the Mayor wasn't in much better shape. He had been kept standing for eight days with a bag over his head and hadn't been allowed to perform his private functions let along his public ones in the manner to which his office entitled him. As a result he was distinctly soiled and suffering from the delusion that he was presiding at a Mayoral banquet.

'This has been a most unfortunate incident,' the Kommandant began, holding a handkerchief to his nose.

'I'm privileged to be here today in this august assembly,' mumbled the Mayor.

'I would like to proffer my...' said the Kommandant.

'Most sincere congratulations on...' the Mayor interrupted.

'For this unwarranted action,' said the Kommandant.

'It is not all of us who have the honour...'

'In keeping you under lock and key.'

'Serve the public to the best...'

'Won't happen again.'

'Look forward to...'

'Oh bugger me,' said the Kommandant who had lost track of the conversation. In the end, after being helped by three warders to sign a statement he couldn't even see, let alone read, to say that he had no complaints to make about the way he had been treated and thanking the police for their protection, the Mayor was carried out to a waiting ambulance and allowed to go home.

Several of the other detainees were less amenable to reason and one or two hardboured the illusion that the Kommandant was merely a new and more sinister interrogator.

'I know what you want me to say,' the manager of Barclays Bank declared when he saw the Kommandant. 'All right I'll admit it. I am a member of the Anglican Church and a Communist.'

The Kommandant looked at the manager in some confusion. The manager's face was badly bruised and his ankles terribly swollen from standing so long.

'Are you really?' said the Kommandant doubtfully.

'No,' said the manager encouraged by this dubious note. 'I'm not. I hardly every go to Church. Only when my wife insists and she's a Baptist.'

'I see,' said the Kommandant, 'but you are a Communist.'

'Oh my God,' wailed the manager, 'would I be a bank manager if I was a Communist?'

The Kommandant pushed the form indemnifying the police across the desk. 'I don't give a stuff what you are so long as you sign this form,' he said irritably. 'If you refuse I'm going to charge you with sabotage.'

'Sabotage,' croaked the manager in terror, 'but I haven't committed sabotage.'

'By your own admission you've peed in the Hluwe Dam and that constitutes sabotage in terms of the General Laws Amendment Act of 1962.'

'Peeing in a dam?'

'Polluting the public water supply. Carries the death penalty.' The manager signed the form and was helped out.

By the time the Kommandant had dealt to his own satisfaction with the detainees, it was already late at night and he was still faced with the intractable problem of the wave of bombings. True there had been no explosions since the ostriches had destroyed themselves and so many public buildings but public confidence would only be restored when the saboteurs were caught. The Kommandant left the prison and told Els to drive him back to the police station.

As he mounted the steps and passed the Duty desk where a konstabel was soliciting a man who had come in to complain that his car had been stolen, the Kommandant realized the enormity of the task before him. With a demoralized force of policemen he had to defend the city against saboteurs so well organized that they used police high-explosive for their bombings and who, apart from one dead man in the toilet of the Majestic Theatre, were wholly unidentifiable. It was a task that would have defeated a lesser man and Kommandant van Heerden had no illusions. He was a lesser man.

He ordered a mixed grill from a Greek café and sent for Sergeant Breitenbach.

'These secret agents that Verkramp was always talking about,' he said, 'do you know anything about them?'

'I think you'll find he lost touch with them,' said the Sergeant.

'Not the only thing he's lost touch with, I can tell you,' said the Kommandant with feeling. Sergeant's terrible antics were still fresh in his memory. 'Does anyone else know who they are?'

'No, sir.'

'There must be records,' said the Kommandant.

'Burnt, sir.'

'Burnt? Who burnt them?'

'Verkramp did when he went mad, sir.'

'What, the whole bloody lot?'

Sergeant Breitenbach nodded. 'He had a file called Operation Red

Rout. I never saw what was in it but I know he burnt it the night the ostriches went off. They affected him badly, sir, those ostriches. He was a changed man after one exploded in the street out there.'

'Yes, well, that doesn't help us very much,' said the Kommandant, as he finished his mixed grill and wiped his mouth. 'You know,' he continued leaning back in his chair, 'there's been something puzzling me for a long time and that is, why did the Communists bug my house? Verkramp seemed to think they wanted to get something on me. Didn't seem likely. I don't do anything.'

'No sir,' said the Sergeant. He looked round the room rather nervously. 'Do you think Luitenant Verkramp will ever recover, sir?' he asked.

Kommandant van Heerden had no doubts on that score.

'Not a celluloid rat's chance in hell,' he said cheerfully. Sergeant Breitenbach looked relieved.

'In that case, I think you ought to know that those microphones weren't placed there by Communists, sir.' He paused to allow the implications of the remark to sink in.

'You mean...' said the Kommandant turning an alarming colour.

'Verkramp, sir,' said the Sergeant hurriedly.

'You mean that bastard bugged my house?' yelled the Kommandant. Sergeant Breitenbach nodded dumbly, and waited for the Kommandant's outburst to exhaust itself.

'He said he had orders from BOSS to do it, sir,' he said when the Kommandant calmed down a little.

'BOSS?' said the Kommandant. 'Orders from BOSS.' A new note of alarm in his voice.

'That's what he said, sir. I don't think he did though,' Sergeant Breitenbach told him.

'I see,' said the Kommandant trying to think why the Bureau of State Security should be so interested in his private life. The idea was not reassuring. People who interested BOSS frequently fell out of tenth-storey windows in Security Headquarters in Johannesburg.

'I think it was all part of his insanity, sir,' the Sergeant continued, 'part of his purity campaign.'

The Kommandant looked at him weakly.

'Dear God,' he said. 'Are you trying to tell me that all Verkramp's talk about Communist agents was simply an excuse to find out if I was having an affair?'

'Yes, sir,' said Sergeant Breitenbach desperately determined not to say whom the Kommandant was thought to be having an affair with.

'Well all I can say is that Verkramp's lucky to be in an insane asylum. If he weren't I'd have the bastard reduced to the ranks.'

'Yes sir,' said the Sergeant. 'No explosions tonight.' He was anxious to change the topic of conversation away from the Kommandant's private life. Kommandant van Heerden looked out through his glassless windows and sighed.

'None last night. None the night before. None since Verkramp went into the loony bin. Odd that, isn't it?' he said.

'Very odd sir.'

'All the attacks coincided with Verkramp's being in charge,' continued the Kommandant. 'All the high-explosive came from the police armoury. Very odd indeed.'

'Are you thinking what I'm thinking?' asked the Sergeant.

Kommandant van Heerden looked at him intently.

'I'm not thinking about what I'm thinking and I'd advise you to do the same,' he said. 'It doesn't bear thinking about.' He relapsed into silence and considered the appalling prospect revealed by Sergeant Breitenbach's information. If there had been no Communist agents involved in the bugging of his house ... He stopped himself following that train of thought. And what was boss's interest in the business? Again it seemed a dangerous line to follow.

'Well, all I know is that we've got to produce those saboteurs in court and have them convicted or my job isn't going to be safe. There's going to be a public outcry about this and someone's got to stand on the scaffold.' He got up wearily. 'I'm going to bed,' he said, 'I've had enough for one day.'

'Just one more thing, sir, that I think you ought to consider,' said the Sergeant. 'I've been doing some calculations about the bombings.' He put a piece of paper in front of the Kommandant. 'If you look here you'll see that there were twelve explosions on each of the nights in question. Right?' Kommandant van Heerden nodded. 'The day before you left on holiday. Luitenant Verkramp ordered twelve new keys cut for the police armoury.' He paused and the Kommandant sat down again and held his head.

'Go on,' he said finally. 'Let's get it over.'

'Well, sir,' continued the Sergeant, 'I've been checking the men who picked up the messages from the secret agents and it begins to look as if there were twelve agents too.'

'Are you trying to tell me that Verkramp organized these attacks himself?' the Kommandant asked and knew that it was an unnecessary question. It was obvious what Sergeant Breitenbach thought.

'It begins to look like it, sir,' he said.

'But what the hell for? It doesn't make fucking sense,' shouted the Kommandant frantically.

'I think he was mad all the time, sir,' said the Sergeant.

'Mad?' shouted the Kommandant. 'Mad? He wasn't just mad. He was fucking insane.'

By the time Kommandant van Heerden got to bed that night he was almost insane himself. The extraordinary events of the day had taken their toll. As he passed a fitful night tossing and turning in his bed, images of exploding ostriches and homosexual policemen mingled disturbingly with Mrs Heathcote-Kilkoon clad in nothing but a top hat and boots riding an enormous black horse over a landscape pitted with bomb craters while Els smiled demonically in the background.

In Fort Rapier Mental Hospital the author of most of the Kommandant's misfortunes spent a pretty unpleasant night himself. True it wasn't as bad as the trip he'd been on during the day but it was bad enough to convince Dr von Blimenstein that she might have misjudged the strength of the dose she had given him.

Only Konstabel Els slept well. Ensconced in Verkramp's flat which he was ostensibly guarding, he had found the Luitenant's stock of girlie magazines and having leafed through them had gone to sleep dreaming about Konstabel Botha whose yellow wig Els thought most fetching. Once or twice he twitched in his sleep like a dog dreaming of a hunt. In the morning he got up and drove round to the Kommandant's house where muttered curses from the kitchen suggested that the Kommandant was not finding the editorial in the *Zululand Chronicle* much to his taste.

'I knew it, I knew it,' he shouted brandishing the offending article which accused the police of incompetence, the torture of innocent people and a general inability to maintain law and order. 'They'll be demanding a Court of Inquiry next. What the hell is this country coming to? How the hell do they expect me to maintain law and order when half my men are fucking fairies?'

Mrs Roussouw was shocked. 'Language,' she said tartly. 'Walls have ears.'

'And that's another thing,' snapped the Kommandant, 'do you realize I've been living in what amounts to an auditorium for the past month? This place has more bugs...'

But Mrs Roussouw had heard enough. 'I won't have you say that,' she said. Outside the window Konstabel Els grinned to himself and listened to the ensuing argument with a deepening sense of pleasure. By the time Kommandant van Heerden left the house Mrs Roussouw had been persuaded to stay on as housekeeper but only after the Kommandant had been forced to apologize for his criticism of her work.

At the police station another group of irate women were waiting for the Kommandant when he arrived.

'Deputation of policemen's wives, sir,' said Sergeant Breitenbach when the Kommandant had negotiated the stairs where the women were gathered.

'What the hell do they want?' the Kommandant demanded.

'It's to do with their husbands being queer,' the Sergeant explained. 'They've come to demand redress.'

'Redress?' squawked the Kommandant. 'Redress? How the hell can I redress them?'

'I don't think you quite understand,' said the Sergeant, 'they want you to do something about their husbands.'

'Oh, all right. Show them in,' said the Kommandant wearily. Sergeant Breitenbach left the room and presently the Kommandant found himself confronted by twelve large and clearly frustrated women.

'We've come here to register an official complaint,' said the largest lady who was evidently the spokesman for the group.

'Quite,' said the Kommandant, 'I quite understand.'

'I don't think you do,' said the woman. The Kommandant looked at her and thought that he did.

'I gather that this matter concerns your husbands,' he said.

'Exactly,' said the large woman. 'Our husbands have been subject to experiments which have deprived them of their manhood.'

The Kommandant wrote the complaint down on a piece of paper.

'I see,' he said, 'and what do you expect me to do about it?'

The large woman looked at him distastefully.

'We want this matter straightened out without delay,' she said. The Kommandant sat back and stared at her.

'Straightened out?'

'Yes,' said the large lady emphatically.

The Kommandant tried to think what to do. He decided to try flattery.

'I think the remedy is in your own hands,' he said with a suggestive smile. It was clearly the wrong thing to have said.

'How disgusting,' shouted the woman, 'how utterly revolting.'

Kommandant van Heerden turned bright red.

'No please,' he said, 'please ladies ...' but there was no holding the women.

'It'll be carrots and candles next,' shouted one woman.

'Ladies, you misunderstand me,' said the Kommandant desperately trying to calm them down. 'All I meant was that if you'll only get together ...'

Kommandant van Heerden turned bright red.

'No please,' he said, 'please ladies ...' but there was no holding the women.

'It'll be carrots and candles next,' shouted one woman.

'Ladies, you misunderstand me,' said the Kommandant desperately trying to calm them down. 'All I meant was that if you'll only get together ...'

In the pandemonium that ensued Kommandant van Heerden could be heard saying that he was sure that if they took a firm stand and all pulled together ...

'For God's sake take a grip on yourselves,' he yelled as the women stood round his desk shouting. Sergeant Breitenbach entered the room and with the help of two heterosexual konstabels restored order.

In the end a distinctly dishevelled Kommandant told the ladies that he would do what he could.

'You may rest assured that I shall bend over backwards to see that your husbands return to their conjugal duties,' he said and the women filed out of the office. On the stairs Konstabel Els asked several of them if he could be of any assistance and made three appointments for the evening. When they had all left the Kommandant asked Sergeant Breitenbach to have photographs of nude men taken.

'We'll have to do the thing in reverse,' he said.

'Black men or white men, sir?'

'Both,' said the Kommandant, 'we don't want any more cock-ups.'

'Don't you think we ought to get the advice of a proper psychiatrist?' the Sergeant inquired.

Kommandant van Heerden considered the matter.

'Where do you think Verkramp got the idea from in the first place?' he asked.

'He had been reading a book by a professor called Ice Ink.'

'Sounds a funny sort of name for a professor,' said the Kommandant.

'Sounds a funny sort of professor,' said the Sergeant, 'and I still think we ought to get a proper psychiatrist to help.'

'I suppose so,' the Kommandant agreed doubtfully. The only psychiatrist he knew was Dr von Blimenstein and he was wary of asking her for assistance.

By the end of the morning he had revised his opinion. A deputation of Piemburg's businessmen had been to see him with a view to forming a group of vigilantes to assist the police in their so far fruitless efforts to

protect life and property from the terrorists and the Kommandant had
received several summonses from lawyers alleging that their clients,
namely the Mayor and thirty-five other prominent citizens, had been
illegally detained and tortured. To cap it all he had received a telephone
call from the Commissioner of Police in Zululand demanding the
immediate apprehension of the men responsible for the sabotage attacks.

'I hold you personally responsible, van Heerden,' shouted the Commissioner who had been looking for an excuse to demote the Kommandant
for years. 'Understand that. Personally responsible for what has occurred.
Either we have some action or I'll be asking for you resignation.
Understand?'

The Kommandant understood and put down the receiver with the
look of a very large rat in a very tight corner.

In the next half hour the consequences of the Commissioner's threat
began to make themselves felt.

'I don't care who they are,' shouted the Kommandant at Sergeant
Breitenbach, 'I want every group of eleven men arrested on sight.'

'What, even the Mayor and the Aldermen?' asked the Sergeant.

'No,' screamed the Kommandant. 'Not the Mayor and the Aldermen
but every other suspicious group.'

As usual Sergeant Breitenbach equivocated.

'I think that would be asking for trouble, sir,' he pointed out.

'Trouble?' yelled the Kommandant. 'What do you think we've got
already? It's my neck that's on the block and if you think I'm going to
give that fucking Commissioner the opportunity to lop it off you've got
another think coming.'

'It's BOSS I'm thinking about, sir,' said the Sergeant.

'BOSS?'

'Luitenant Verkramp's agents were presumably men from the Bureau
of State Security in Pretoria, sir. If we arrested them I don't think BOSS
would appreciate it.'

The Kommandant looked frantically at him.

'Well what the hell do you want me to do?' he asked with a growing
sense of hysteria. 'The Commissioner tells me to arrest the men who did
the bombings. You tell me that I'll have BOSS up in arms if I do. What
the fuck can I do?'

Sergeant Breitenbach had no idea. In the end the Kommandant
countermanded his orders to arrest all groups of eleven men and dismissing
the Sergeant sat at his desk confronted with a problem that seemed
insoluble.

Ten minutes later he had arrived at a solution and he was about to

send Els down to the cells to collect eleven black prisoners who were
going to blow themselves up in a stolen car filled with police gelignite as
proof that the South African Police in general and Kommandant van
Heerden in particular could act with speed and efficiency against
Communist saboteurs when it occurred to him that the scheme had a
flaw. The men seen feeding the ostriches had all been white. With a curse
the Kommandant returned to the problem.

'Verkramp must be insane,' he muttered for the umpteenth time and
was just considering the nature of the Luitenant's insanity when he came
up with a brilliant solution.

Picking up the phone, the Kommandant rang Dr von Blimenstein and
made an appointment to see her after lunch.

'You want me to do what?' Dr von Blimenstein asked when the
Kommandant made his suggestion to her. She moved to switch the tape
recorder on but the Kommandant reached over and unplugged it.

'You don't seem to understand,' said the Kommandant with a grim
determination to get the doctor to see reason. 'You can either co-operate
with me or I'll have Verkramp out of here and charge him with wilful
destruction of public property and sabotage and he'll stand trial.'

'But you can't possibly expect me to ...' said the doctor moving
towards the door. With a sudden swiftness she jerked it open only to find
herself face to face with Konstabel Els. She closed the door hurriedly and
came back into the room.

'This is outrageous,' she protested. Kommandant van Heerden smiled
horridly.

'You can't arrest my Balthazar,' continued the doctor trying to
maintain some fortitude in the face of that smile. 'Why only yesterday
you told me that he had handled the whole affair very skilfully and with
an exceptional degree of conscientiousness.'

'Skilfully?' bawled the Kommandant. 'Skilfully? I'll tell you how skilful
that bastard has been. Your fucking Balthazar has been responsible for
the biggest outbreak of sabotage this country has ever seen. Why,
compared with him the guerrillas on the Zambesi are playing soldiers.
He's been personally responsible for the destruction of four road bridges,
two railway lines, a transformer, the telephone exchange, four petrol
storage tanks, one gasometer, five thousand acres of sugar cane and a
radio mast and you have the nerve to tell me he's been skilful.'

Dr von Blimenstein slumped into her chair and stared at him.

'You've got no proof,' she whimpered finally. 'And besides he's not
well.'

Kommandant van Heerden leant across the desk and leered into her face. 'Well?' he asked. 'Well? By the time the hangman's through with him he'll look a bloody sight worse, believe me.'

Dr von Blimenstein did believe him. She shut her eyes and shook her head to rid herself of the Kommandant's leer and the dreadful vision of her fiancé on the gallows. Satisfied that he had made his point the Kommandant relaxed.

'After all it's only doing what the poor fellows tried to do themselves and failed,' he explained. 'It's not as though we're asking them to go against their own natural inclinations.'

Dr von Blimenstein opened her eyes and looked at him imploringly.

'But Balthazar and I are engaged to get married,' she said.

It was Kommandant van Heerden's turn to be shocked. The idea of the bosomy doctor married to the apelike creature he had seen scampering about his cell the day before took his breath away. He began to understand the look of abject terror he had seen in Verkramp's eyes.

'Congratulations,' he muttered. 'In that case there's all the more reason for you to do what I'm suggesting.'

Dr von Blimenstein nodded miserably, 'I suppose so,' she said.

'Now then, let's get down to details,' said the Kommandant. 'You will arrange to have eleven patients with a record of suicide attempts placed in an isolation ward. You will then use your perversion therapy to indoctrinate them with Marxist-Leninist ideas ...'

'But that's impossible,' said the doctor, 'you can't use aversion therapy to give people ideas. You can only cure them of habits.'

'That's what you think,' the Kommandant told her. 'You want to come and look what ideas your Balthazar has managed to give my konstabels. He hasn't cured them of any habits, I can tell you.'

Dr von Blimenstein tried another tack. 'But I don't know anything about Marxist-Leninism,' she said.

'That's a pity,' said the Kommandant and tried to think of someone who did. The only person he knew was serving a twenty-five year sentence in Piemburg Prison.

'Never mind about that,' he said finally, 'I'll arrange for someone to come here who does.'

'And then what are you going to do?' the doctor asked.

Kommandant van Heerden smiled. 'I think you can safely leave the rest to me,' he said and got up. As he left the office he turned and thanked the doctor for her cooperation.

'Remember it's all for the good of Balthazar,' he said and followed by Konstabel Els went out to his car. In her office Dr von Blimenstein considered the terrible task the Kommandant had given her. 'I suppose it's only another form of euthanasia,' she thought and began to draw up a list of suitably suicidal patients. Dr von Blimenstein had always agreed with the form of mental treatment meted out in the Third Reich.

The same could hardly be said of the man in Piemburg Prison who was the next person the Kommandant visited. Sentenced to twenty-five years for his part in the Rivonia conspiracy, about which he had in fact known nothing, Aaron Geisenheimer had spent six years in solitary confinement consoling himself with the thought that a revolution was about to take place which would bring him if not into his own at least out of someone else's – that thought and the Bible, which, thanks to the religious policy of the prison authorities, was the only book the lapsed Jew was allowed to read. Since Aaron Geisenheimer had spent his youth in an obsessive study of the works of Marx, Engels and Lenin and since too he came of a long line of rabbinical scholars, it was hardly surprising that after six years of more or less enforced acquaintanceship with the Holy Writ he was now a mine of scriptural information. He was also no fool, as the prison chaplain knew to his cost. The Chaplain would emerge from Isolation Cell Two after an hour of Christian counselling with Geisenheimer in some doubt as to the divinity of Christ and with a tendency to think of *Das Kapital* as coming somewhere between Chronicles 1 and the Song of Solomon. To make matters worse, Aaron Geisenheimer supplemented his daily ration of thirty minutes in the exercise yard by attending every possible service in the prison chapel where his critical presence forced the Chaplain to raise the intellectual standards of his sermons to the point where they were totally unintelligible to the rest of the congregation while still open to considerable criticism from the Marxist. In the light of the Chaplain's complaints the Governor of the Prison was delighted to hear that Kommandant van Heerden was considering having Geisenheimer transferred to Fort Rapier.

'Do what you like with the bastard,' Governor Schnapps told the Kommandant, 'I'll be glad to get him off my hands. He's even got some of my warders wearing Maoist badges.'

The Kommandant thanked him and went down to Isolation Cell Two where the prisoner was deep in Amos.

'It says here "Therefore the prudent shall keep silence in that time; for it is an evil time,"' Geisenheimer told him when the Kommandant asked if he had any complaints.

Kommandant van Heerden looked round the cell. 'A bit short of space in here,' he said. 'Not room to swing a cat.'

'Yes, there is that to be said for it,' said Geisenheimer.

'Like to move to more spacious accommodation?' the Kommandant inquired.

'*Timeo Danaos et dona ferentis,*' said Geisenheimer.

'Don't you talk Kitchen Kaffir to me,' the Kommandant yelled. 'I asked you if you would like bigger accommodation.'

'No,' said Geisenheimer.

'Why the hell not?' asked the Kommandant.

'It says here "As if a man did flee from a lion, and a bear met him; or went into the house, and leaned his hand on the wall, and a serpent bit him." It seems a sensible point of view.'

Kommandant van Heerden didn't want to take issue with Amos but he was still puzzled.

'Must get a bit lonely here at times,' he said.

Geisenheimer shrugged.

'I believe it's a characteristic of solitary confinement,' he said philosophically.

The Kommandant went back to Governor Schnapps and told him that there was no doubt in his mind that Geisenheimer was out of his. That afternoon the Marxist was transferred to a ward in Fort Rapier Mental Hospital where he found eleven other beds and the complete works of Marx and Lenin kindly supplied by the confiscated books department of the Piemburg Police Station. As the Kommandant delivered them to Dr von Blimenstein he was reminded of the aversion therapy for the homosexual konstabels.

'One other thing,' he said when the doctor explained that she had eleven suitable suicides lined up, 'I'd be glad if you'd drop by the Drill Hall this afternoon. I want some advice about getting some queers back to normal.'

CHAPTER FOURTEEN

As the Kommandant drove down to the Drill Hall where Sergeant Breitenbach had assembled two hundred and ten protesting konstabels, he felt pleased with the way things were turning out. Certainly there were still difficulties ahead but at least a start had been made in getting things back to normal. It would take a day or two to get the suicides ready for their arrest and the Kommandant still hadn't made up his mind exactly how to go about it. Studying the back of Konstabel Els' head once again he found consolation in its shape and colour. What human ingenuity and design could not accomplish in the way of destroying inconvenient evidence, Konstabel Els through chance and unthinking malice could, and the Kommandant had frequently cherished the hope that Els would include himself in the process. It seemed unlikely somehow. Chance, it appeared, favoured the Konstabel. It certainly didn't favour those with whom he came into contact and the Kommandant had little doubt that Els would bungle the arrest of the eleven patients to an extent that would eliminate any subsequent attempts to prove them innocent.

By the time they reached the Drill Hall Kommandant van Heerden was in a more cheerful frame of mind. The same could not be said for the two hundred and ten konstabels who were objecting to the idea of undergoing aversion therapy for the second time.

'You've no idea what we might come out as this time, sweetie,' one of them told Sergeant Breitenbach, 'I mean you simply don't know, do you?'

Sergeant Breitenbach had to admit that in the light of what had happened previously he didn't.

'You couldn't be worse than you are,' he said with feeling.

'I don't know,' simpered the konstabel, 'we might be absolute animals.'

'It's a chance I'm prepared to take,' said the Sergeant.

'And what about us, dear? What about us? I mean it's not much fun not knowing what you're going to be from one moment to the next, is it? It's upsetting, that's what it is.'

'What about all the gear we've bought, too?' said another konstabel. 'Cost a small fortune. Bras and panties and all. They won't take it back you know.'

Sergeant Breitenbach shuddered and was just wondering how he was ever going to get them into the hall when the Kommandant arrived and relieved him of the responsibility.

'I'll appeal to their patriotism,' he said looking with evident distaste at Konstabel Botha's wig. He collected a loudhailer and addressed the queers.

'Men,' he shouted. His voice, resonant with doubt, boomed out over the parade ground and into the city. 'Men of the South African Police, I realize that the experience you have lately undergone is not one that you wish to repeat. I can only say that it is in the interest of the country as a whole that I have ordered this new treatment which will turn you back into the fine upstanding body of men you once were. This time a trained psychiatrist will supervise the treatment and there will be no balls-up.' Loud laughter interrupted the Kommandant at this point and a particularly oafish konstabel who appeared to be wearing false eyelashes winked suggestively at him. Kommandant van Heerden, already exhausted by the swift turn of events, lost his cool.

'Listen, you shower of filth,' he screamed voicing his true opinions with an amplification that could be heard two miles away, 'I've seen some arse-bandits in my time but nothing to equal you. A more disgusting lot of gobblers and moffies it's never been my misfortune to meet. By the time I've finished with you I'll have you back to fucking normal.' He singled out the Konstabel with the false eyelashes for personal abuse and was just telling him that he'd never look another sphincter in the face without coming over all queer when Dr von Blimenstein arrived and restored order. As the doctor walked slowly but significantly towards them, the konstabels fell silent and eyed her large frame with respect.

'If you don't mind, Kommandant,' she said as the Kommandant's blood pressure fluttered down to something approaching normal, 'I think I'll try a different approach.' Kommandant van Heerden handed her the loudhailer and a moment later her dulcet tones were echoing across the parade ground.

'Boys,' said the doctor using a more appropriate epithet, 'I want you all to think of me,' she paused seductively, 'as a friend, not as someone to be afraid of.' A tremor of nervous excitation ran down the ranks. The prospect of being a friend of someone so redolent of frustrated sex, whatever its gender, obviously appealed to the konstabels. As Dr von Blimenstein continued her talk the Kommandant turned away satisfied that everything was under control now that the doctor's magnetic hermaphroditism was exerting its influence over the queers. He found Sergeant Breitenbach in the drill hall checking the transformer.

'What a horrible woman,' said the Sergeant. Dr von Blimenstein was telling the konstabels about the pleasures they could expect from heterosexual intercourse.

'The future Mrs Verkramp,' said the Kommandant lugubriously. 'He's proposed to her.' He left the Sergeant mulling over this fresh proof of Verkramp's insanity to deal with another problem. A deputation of ministers from the Dutch Reformed Church had arrived to add their objections to those of the konstabels.

The Kommandant shepherded them into an office at the back of the hall and waited until Dr von Blimenstein had got her patients seated before discussing the problem with the black-coated ministers.

'You have no right to tamper with man's nature,' the Rev Schlachbals said when the doctor arrived. 'God has made us what we are and you are interfering with his work.'

'God didn't make all these men poofters,' said the doctor, her language confirming the minister's opinion that she was the instrument of the devil. 'Man did and man must put the mistake right.'

Kommandant van Heerden nodded in agreement. He thought she had put the case very well. The Rev Schlachbals clearly didn't.

'If man can turn decent young Christians into homosexuals by scientific means,' he insisted, 'the next step will be to turn blacks into whites and then where will we be? The whole of Western Civilization and Christianity in South Africa is at stake.'

Kommandant van Heerden nodded again. It was obvious that the minister had a point. Dr von Blimenstein didn't think so.

'You clearly misunderstand the nature of behavioural psychology,' she explained. 'All we are doing is rectifying mistakes that have been made. We are not altering essential characteristics.'

'You're not trying to tell me that these young men are essentially, er ... homosexual,' said the dominie. 'You're impugning the moral foundations of our entire community.'

Dr von Blimenstein refused to admit it.

'What absolute nonsense,' she said. 'All I'm saying is that aversion therapy can exert a degree of moral pressure which nothing else can match.'

Kommandant van Heerden, who had been giving some thought to the matter of turning blacks into whites by electric shocks, butted in to point out that if that were the case thousands of blacks would already be white.

'We're always giving them electric shocks,' he said. 'It's part of our normal interrogation procedure.'

The Rev Schlachbals wasn't impressed. 'That's quite different, punishment is good for the soul,' he said. 'What the doctor is doing is tampering with God's work.'

'Are you trying to tell me that God ordained that these konstabels should remain fairies?' the Kommandant asked.

'Certainly not,' said the minister, 'all I'm saying is that she has no right to use scientific means to change them. That can only be accomplished by moral effort on our part. What is needed is prayer. I shall go in to the hall and kneel down ...'

'You do that,' said the Kommandant, 'and I won't be held responsible for what happens.'

'... and pray for the forgiveness of sins,' continued the minister.

In the end it was agreed that the two approaches to the problem should be tried at the same time. Dr von Blimenstein would proceed with the aversion therapy while the Rev Schlachbals conducted a religious service in the hope of effecting a spiritual conversion. The joint effort was entirely successful, though it took the Rev Schlachbals some time to accommodate himself to the prospect of leading the congregation in 'Rock of Ages Cleft for Me' to the accompaniment of slides depicting nude males of both races projected twice lifesize above his head. To begin with the congregation's singing was pretty ragged too but Dr von Blimenstein soon picked up the beat and pressed the shock button most emphatically whenever a particularly high note was called for. Strapped to their chairs, the two hundred and ten konstabels gave vent to their feelings with a fervour the minister found most rewarding.

'It's a long time since I've known a congregation to be so enthusiastic,' he told the Rev Diederichs, who took over from him after three hours.

'God works in a mysterious way,' said the Rev Diederichs.

In Fort Rapier Aaron Geisenheimer was having much the same thought though in his case it was not so much God as the process of history whose ways were so mysterious. The arrival of eleven patients whose intelligence was proclaimed by the fact that the political situation in South Africa had prompted them all to attempt suicide without being foolish enough to succeed gave the eminent Marxist food for thought. So did the attitude of the hospital authorities, who put no obstacle in the way of his lecturing them on the intricacies of dialectical materialism but seemed anxious that he should. Mulling over this extraordinary change in his fortune he came to the conclusion that the police were anxious to obtain fresh evidence for a new trial though why they should want to increase a life sentence any further he could not imagine. Whatever their motives he decided to afford them no opportunity and resolutely refrained from discussing Communism with his new companions. Instead, to give vent to his need for conversation which had been compulsive enough before his confinement and hadn't been improved by six years in solitary, he instructed the eleven men in Biblical history to such good effect that within a week he had rid them all of their suicidal tendencies and had turned them into convinced Christians.

'Goddammit,' snarled the Kommandant inconsequentially when Dr von Blimenstein told him that Geisenheimer wasn't cooperating. 'You'd think the bastard would be only too glad to poison their minds with Marxism. We can't have twelve ardent Christians in the dock.'

'Oh, I don't know,' said the doctor, 'after all you did have the Dean of Johannesburg.'

'That was different,' the Kommandant told her, 'he was a Communist.' He tried to think of some way round the problem. 'Can't you hypnotize the swine or something?'

Dr von Blimenstein could not see what good that would do.

'Tell them to wake up Communists,' said the Kommandant. 'You can do anything with hypnotism. I once saw a hypnotist turn a man into a plank and sit on him.'

Dr von Blimenstein said it was different with ideas.

'You can't make people do things that they wouldn't want to do in their ordinary life. You can't make them act against their own moral sense.'

'I don't suppose that bloke wanted to be a plank,' said the Kommandant, 'not in ordinary life anyway, and as for moral sense I should have thought your suicides have a great deal in common with Communists. All the Communists I've met have wanted to give the vote to the blacks and if that isn't suicidal, tell me what is.'

He left her with the warning that something had to be done quickly. 'Pretoria will be sending down a team of investigators shortly and then we'll all be in the shit,' he said.

Later the same day he had the same trouble with the Rev Schlachbals this time over the introduction of nude women into the treatment for the queers.

'That doctor wants to bring girls up here from the strip clubs in Durban and parade them up and down in front of the boys,' the Rev Schlachbals complained. 'She says she wants to test their reactions. I won't stand for it.'

'It seems a good idea to me,' said the Kommandant.

The Rev Schlachbals looked at him disapprovingly.

'That is as maybe,' he said, 'but it's too much for me. I've stood for men but naked ladies are another matter.'

'Have it your own way,' said the Kommandant. The Rev Schlachbals blushed.

'I don't mean what you mean,' he said and walked out.

The Kommandant gave Dr von Blimenstein permission to go ahead with the test and later in the day several blowsy girls from Durban went through their routine in front of the konstabels while Sergeant Breitenbach went along the rows with a swagger stick making sure that everyone responded properly.

'All present and erect, sir,' he said when he had finished.

Kommandant van Heerden thanked the doctor for her assistance and accompanied her to her car.

'It's been no trouble,' said the doctor, 'I found the whole experience most valuable. It's not every woman can say she's had such a stimulating effect on two hundred and ten men at the same time.'

'Two hundred and eleven, doctor,' said the Kommandant with unusual gallantry and left the doctor with the impression that she had made a conquest. He had just caught sight of Els who was apparently about to rape one of the chorus girls.

'Amazing woman,' said Sergeant Breitenbach, 'I don't envy Verkramp's chances with her.'

'That's one marriage that wasn't made in heaven,' said the Kommandant.

At White Ladies Mrs Heathcote-Kilkoon had come to much the same conclusion about her own marriage to the Colonel. Ever since her brief taste of happiness in the dell, her thoughts had turned again and again to the Kommandant. So had the Colonel's.

'Damned man comes here, ruins my best roses, flogs an expensive horse to death, pollutes a tank of tropical fish, poisons poor Willy and finally goes off with a damned good whipper-in,' he said irritably.

'I had rather a soft spot for Harbinger,' said La Marquise tenderly.

For the most part though, the Kommandant's visit was forgotten and the brief glimpse of fearful reality his presence had given to the members of the Dornford Yates Club lent a new and frenetic gaiety to their efforts to evoke the past. They drove over to Swaziland to gamble at the casino at Piggs Peak in memory of Berry's great coup at San Sebastian in *Jonah & Co* where he had won four thousand nine hundred and ninety-five pounds. Colonel Heathcote-Kilkoon lost forty before giving up and driving home through a thunderstorm trying to maintain an insouciance he didn't feel. They went racing but again without luck. The Colonel made a point of backing only black horses in memory of Chaka.

'Blue-based baboon,' he said in a voice that carried his unique blend of Inner Circle County across the heads of the crowd. 'That damned jockey was pulling.'

'We should organize our own races, Berry,' said the fat man. 'There was a car race in *Jonah & Co*.'

'By Jove, I do believe he's right,' said La Marquise who was doubling as Piers, Duke of Padua.

'The cars were called Ping and Pong,' Major Bloxham said. 'And the race was from Angoulême to Pau. It was two hundred and twenty miles.'

Next day the dusty roads of Zululand saw the great race from Weezen to Dagga and back and by nightfall the Colonel, as Berry, had made good his losses of the previous days. Admittedly Weezen was hardly

Angoulême and Dagga's resemblance to Pau was limited to a view of distant mountains but the Club made good these deficiencies in their own imaginations and by driving with a wholly authentic disregard for other road users. Even Berry & Co could hardly have complained and among other trophies the Colonel collected two goats and a guinea fowl. In the back seat of the Rolls Mrs Heathcote-Kilkoon did her best to be Daphne but her heart wasn't in it. Much the same could be said for the Duke of Padua, who insisted that the fat man stop at Sjambok while she bought an inflatable ring. That night Mrs Heathcote-Kilkoon told the Colonel she was going down to Piemburg next morning.

'Another perm, eh?' said the Colonel. 'Well don't overdo things. It's Berry Puts Off His Manhood night tomorrow.'

'Yes dear,' said Mrs Heathcote-Kilkoon.

The next day she was up early and on her way to Piemburg. As the great car slid down the Rooi Nek, Mrs Heathcote-Kilkoon felt free and strangely youthful. Chin in air, eyebrows raised, lids lowered, the faintest of smiles hovering about her small red mouth, she leaned back with an indescribable air of easy efficiency which was most attractive. Only the parted lips at all betrayed her eagerness ...'

She was still in a playful mood when she was shown into the Kommandant's office by Sergeant Breitenbach.

'My darling,' she said as soon as the door was shut, and skipped across the room a vision of elegance in mauve silk.

'For God's sake,' spluttered the Kommandant, unwinding her arms from his neck.

'I had to come, I couldn't wait,' said Mrs Heathcote-Kilkoon.

Kommandant van Heerden looked frantically round his office. Something about shitting on one's own doorstep was on the tip of his tongue but he managed not to say it. Instead he asked after the Colonel.

Mrs Heathcote-Kilkoon reclined in a chair. 'He's absolutely furious with you,' she said. Kommandant van Heerden went pale.

'You can't blame him, can you?' she continued. 'I mean, think how you'd feel in his position.'

The Kommandant didn't have to think how he'd feel. He knew.

'What's he going to do?' he asked anxiously, the vision of the cuckold Colonel shooting him looming large in his mind. 'Has he got a gun?'

Mrs Heathcote-Kilkoon leant back and laughed. 'Has he got a gun? My dear, he's got an arsenal,' she said. 'Haven't you seen his armoury?'

The Kommandant sat down hurriedly and got up almost at once. Coming on top of the terrible position Verkramp had put him in, this new threat not only to his position but to his life was the last straw. Mrs Heathcote-Kilkoon sensed his feelings.

'I shouldn't have come,' she said taking the words out of the Kommandant's mouth. 'But I simply had to tell you . . .'

'As if I hadn't got enough fucking trouble on my hands without this,' snarled the Kommandant, his instinct for survival sweeping away what few pretensions he had previously maintained in her company. Mrs Heathcote-Kilkoon adjusted her language to his mood.

'Doesn't Doodoo love his mummy any more?' she cooed.

'Of course he does,' he snapped, taking refuge in the third person from the threat of extinction doodoos brought to mind. He was about to say that he had enough on his fucking plate without jealous husbands when there was a knock on the door and Sergeant Breitenbach entered.

'Urgent telegram for Verkramp, sir,' he said. 'From BOSS. I thought you'd want to see it.' The Kommandant snatched the message from him and stared at it.

'INSTANT EXPLANATION SAB STROKE SUBV PIEMBURG STOP URGENT CARR STROKE INTERRO COMBLIBS STOP DETAIL ACTION STOP SAB STROKE SUBV BOSS TEAM FOLLOWING,' he read and stared at the Sergeant uncomprehendingly. 'What the hell does it mean?' he asked.

Sergeant Breitenbach glanced meaningfully at Mrs Heathcote-Kilkoon.

'Never mind her,' shouted the Kommandant, 'tell me what the thing means.'

Sergeant Breitenbach looked at the telegram.

'Instant explication sabotage subversion Piemburg stop Urgent arrest interrogation Communists and Liberals stop Detail action taken stop Sabotage subversion team from Bureau of State Security following.'

'Oh my God,' moaned the Kommandant for whom the news that a team of investigators from BOSS was on its way came as the final death knell. 'Now what do we do?'

In her chair Mrs Heathcote-Kilkoon sat listening with a sense of being at the heart of the action, where decisions of far-reaching moment were made and real men made up real minds to do real things. It was a strangely exhilarating experience. The gulf between fantasy and fact which years of reading Dornford Yates and playing Daphne to the Colonel's Berry across the dark continent had created in her mind suddenly closed. This was it, whatever it was, and Mrs Heathcote-Kilkoon, so long excluded from It, wanted to be part of It.

'If only I could help you,' she said melodramatically as the door closed behind Sergeant Breitenbach, who had just admitted he couldn't.

'How?' said the Kommandant who wanted to be left alone to think of someone he could arrest before the BOSS team arrived.

'I could be your glamorous spy,' she said.

'We're not short of glamorous spies,' said the Kommandant shortly, 'what we need are suspects.'

'What sort of suspects?'

'Eleven bloody lunatics who know how to use high explosive and hate Afrikanerdom enough to want to put the clock back a thousand years,' said the Kommandant morosely, and surprised to see Mrs Heathcote-Kilkoon tilt back her lovely head and laugh.

'What's the matter now?' he asked feeling pretty hysterical himself.

'Oh how frightfully funny,' Mrs Heathcote-Kilkoon shrieked. 'How absolutely priceless. Do you realize what you've just said?'

'No,' said the Kommandant as the tinted curls tossed delightfully.

'Don't you see? The Club. Eleven lunatics. Boy, Berry, Jonah ... Oh it's too gorgeous.'

Kommandant van Heerden sat down at his desk, the light of understanding glazing his bloodshot eyes. As Mrs Heathcote-Kilkoon's laughter amazed Sergeant Breitenbach in the next room and awoke in Konstabel Els memories of other days and other places, Kommandant van Heerden knew that his troubles were over.

'Two birds with one stone,' he muttered and pressed the bell for Sergeant Breitenbach.

Twenty minutes later Mrs Heathcote-Kilkoon, somewhat astonished by her rapid dismissal from the Kommandant's office but still chortling over her joke, was at the hairdresser's.

'I think I'll have a black rinse for a change,' she told the assistant with an intuitive sense of occasion.

CHAPTER FIFTEEN

In the Drill Hall, so recently the scene of sexual conversion, Kommandant van Heerden briefed his men.

'The saboteurs are based on a house called White Ladies near Weezen,' he told the assembled officers. 'They are led by an ex-Colonel in the British secret service, one of their top men who served in the inner circle of the underground during the war. His second-in-command is a Major Bloxham and the sabotage group has used as its cover a club organized ostensibly for literary purposes. They are in possession of a considerable quantity of arms and ammunition and I anticipate fierce resistance when we surround the house.'

'How do we know they are the men we are after?' Sergeant Scheepers of the Security Branch asked.

'I realize this may come as something of a surprise to you, Sergeant,' the Kommandant answered with a smile. 'But we of the uniformed police also have our agents in the field. You Security Branch fellows aren't the only ones to work undercover.' He paused to let this information sink in. 'For the past year Konstabel Els has been working in the Weezen area at considerable risk to himself and disguised as a convict.' Standing to one side of the Kommandant Konstabel Els blushed modestly. 'Thanks to his efforts we were able to infiltrate the Communist organization. Furthermore,' he added before anyone could point out that Konstabel Els was hardly a reliable witness, 'over the past two weeks I have investigated the matter personally and on the spot. I have confirmed Konstabel Els' findings and can vouch for the fact that these people are all avowed enemies of the Republic, maintain unquestioning loyalty to Britain and are utterly ruthless. An attempt was made to kill me while out riding.'

'Is there any other evidence that these men are responsible for the sabotage attacks in Piemburg?' Sergeant Breitenbach asked.

The Kommandant nodded. 'A very good question, Sergeant,' he said. 'In the first place Konstabel Els will go into the witness box and give evidence that he frequently heard the Colonel and his associates discussing the need for a change of government in South Africa. Secondly Els will swear that on the nights the attacks took place the group left the house early and didn't get to bed until dawn. Thirdly and most significantly, a member of the group has turned State's witness and will give evidence that these allegations are all correct. Does that satisfy you, Sergeant?'

'It all seems rather circumstantial, sir,' said Sergeant Breitenbach doubtfully. 'I mean is there any hard evidence?'

'Yes,' said the Kommandant emphatically and rummaging in his pocket he produced a small object. 'Have any of you seen one of these?' he asked. It was clear that everyone in the room had seen a police detonator. 'Good,' continued the Kommandant. 'Well, this was found in the stables at White Ladies.'

'By Konstabel Els?' Sergeant Breitenbach inquired.

'By me,' said the Kommandant, and made a mental note to send Els ahead with a police van filled to the roof with gelignite, fuses, detonators and contraceptives to ensure that enough hard evidence to satisfy Sergeant Breitenbach was there when the rest of the force arrived. In the meantime he explained the layout of the house and garden and ordered a full force of Saracen armoured cars, two hundred policemen armed with Sterling machine guns, German guard dogs and Dobermann Pinschers to be deployed.

'Remember we are dealing with professional killers,' he said finally. 'These fellows aren't amateurs.'

By the time Mrs Heathcote-Kilkoon emerged suitably washed, set and permed from the hairdressers she was just in time to see the convoy led by five Saracen armoured cars grinding through the main street. She stood for a moment gazing at the policemen crowding the lorries and admiration for the Kommandant's obvious efficiency swelled in her breast. As the last lorry containing German guard dogs disappeared round the corner she turned and walked back to the police station to tell him once again how much she had missed him, an opinion confirmed by the Sergeant at the Duty desk.

'But where has he gone?' she asked plaintively.

'Sorry, ma'am,' said the Sergeant, 'I'm not allowed to tell you.'

'But isn't there any way I can find out?'

'Well if you follow that convoy, I daresay you'll find him,' said the Sergeant and Mrs Heathcote-Kilkoon went out into the street disappointed and rather hungry. To console herself she went into Lorna's Causerie in Dirk's Arcade and had a pot of tea and some cup cakes.

I'll try again later, she thought. He can't have gone far. But when an hour later she went round to the police station again it was to learn that the Kommandant wouldn't be returning until the following day.

'How extraordinary, you'd think he would have told me,' she said

exuding an aura of middle-class charm that had subdued stronger men
than the Duty Sergeant.

'This mustn't go any further,' he told her confidingly, 'but they've
gone up to Weezen.'

'On manoeuvres?' asked Mrs Heathcote-Kilkoon hopefully.

'To get those saboteurs,' said the Sergeant.

'In Weezen?'

'That's right,' the Sergeant said, 'but don't tell anyone I told you.'

Mrs Heathcote-Kilkoon said she certainly wouldn't and went out into
the street astonished by this new turn of events. She was half-way back
to the Rolls when the full realization of what she had done dawned on
her.

'Oh my God,' she wailed and ran the rest of the way to the Rolls only
to find that she'd left the keys somewhere. She searched her bag but the
keys weren't there. In a state of utter distraction she ran back to the
hairdresser's and came out five minutes later empty-handed. As she stood
in the street despairingly a taxi drew up.

Mrs Heathcote-Kilkoon jumped in. 'To Weezen and fast,' she said.
The driver turned round and shook his head.

'That's seventy miles,' he said. 'Can't do it.'

'I'll pay you double fare,' Mrs Heathcote-Kilkoon said frantically and
opened her bag. 'That'll pay you for the return journey.'

'All right,' said the driver.

'For God's sake hurry,' she told him, 'it's a matter of life and death.'

The taxi moved off and was soon bucketing over the corrugations on
the road into the mountains. Far ahead forked lightning on the horizon
heralded the approach of a storm.

As the lightning flickered around him and the hailstones rattled on the
roof of his van Konstabel Els switched on the windshield wipers and
peered into the gloom. Driving with his usual disregard for other traffic
on the road, his own life and that of anyone living within half a mile of
the van should it explode, Els was looking forward to the evening's
entertainment. It would compensate him for the tone of voice Colonel
Heathcote-Kilkoon had used to address him in the past. 'I'll Harbinger
him,' Els thought with relish. By the time he reached Weezen night had
fallen. Els drove on and turned up the drive to White Ladies. With a
show of bravado occasioned by his knowledge of the drinking habits of
the household he drove the van into the yard at the back of the house
and switched off the engine. A black face peered into the van. It was
Fox.

'Harbinger,' he said. 'You've come back.'

'Yes,' said Els, 'I've come back.'

Konstabel Els climbed out of the van and went round to the back and opened the doors. Then he turned back and called, 'Fox, you kaffir, come here.' But there was no answer. Responding to the same instinct for self-preservation which marked his namesake he was off across the garden and into the trees and putting as much ground as he could between him and the man in the uniform of the South African Police whom he knew by the name of Harbinger. Fox knew death when he saw it.

Inside the house Colonel Heathcote-Kilkoon and his guests were less discerning.

'Wonder what's happened to Daphne,' the Colonel thought as he dressed for the party. 'Typical of her to be late tonight.' He peered into the mirror, and was mollified. A frock of pale pink georgette, with long bell-shaped sleeves and a black velvet girdle knotted at one side, fitted him seemingly like a glove. A large Leghorn hat, its black velvet streamers fastened beneath his chin, heavily weighted with a full-blown rose over one eye, threatened to hide his rebellious mop of hair. White silk stockings and a pair of ordinary pumps completed his attire. A miniature apron, bearing the stencilled legend 'An English Rose' upon its muslin, left no doubt about his identity.

'Berry to the life,' he murmured and consulted *Jonah & Co* Chapter XI to see if there was anything he had left out. Then picking up his bead bag he went downstairs where the others had gathered waiting for revels to begin.

'I'm an Incroyable,' Major Bloxham told La Marquise who had come as Sycamore Tight.

'Absolutely, darling,' she shrieked shrilly.

Colonel Heathcote-Kilkoon's entrance as Berry as An English Rose was greeted with rapturous applause. The Colonel waited for the laughter to die down before addressing his guests.

'As you all know,' he said, 'every year we celebrate our annual meeting with a final re-enactment of one of the great episodes in the life of Berry & Co. Tonight it is Chapter XI of *Jonah & Co*, Berry Puts Off His Manhood. I'm glad to see there has been such a good turn-out this year.'

After a few more words about the necessity of keeping the flag flying in foreign parts which La Marquise took as a compliment, the Colonel told Major Bloxham to switch the record player on and presently was dancing a Tango with him.

'These step-ins of Daphne's are damned tight,' he said as they went into a reverse turn.

'So's La Marquise,' said the Major.

In the darkness outside the window Konstabel Els watched the proceedings with interest. 'I always wondered why he was so keen on roses,' he thought, eyeing the Colonel with new appreciation.

He went back to the van and began to carry the evidence of the Colonel's attempt to overthrow the government of South Africa into the harness room. By the time he had packed several hundred pounds of gelignite on to shelves that had previously held nothing more incriminating than saddle soap he had begun to regret letting Fox escape. Finally when the last carton of Durex Fetherlites had been safely installed, Els lit a cigarette and sat back in the darkness to consider what other measures to take.

'Party seems to be going with a bang,' he heard the fat man tell Major Bloxham from the terrace where the two men were urinating intermittently on to a bed of begonias. Els took the hint and stubbed his cigarette out but the remark had given him a new idea. He crept out of the harness room and presently was carrying buckets of kerosene from the fuel store across the yard and pouring them into the Colonel's wine cellar where they splashed unnoticed over the Australian burgundy. To add to the inflammatory mixture Els then fetched several bundles of gelignite and tossed them into the cellar. Finally, to prevent anyone leaving the house without giving some indication where they had gone, he poured a solution of aniseed on the doormats before climbing into the van and driving down to the main gate to wait for the police convoy. When there was no sign of it after ten minutes, Els decided to go back and see how the party was getting on.

'Got to kill time,' he muttered as he strolled up through the orchard. Ahead of him White Ladies, brilliantly illuminated for the occasion, exuded an atmosphere of discreet abandon. The Tango had been replaced by the Black Bottom and the Colonel was sitting this one out with La Marquise while Major Bloxham and the fat man were debating what to put into a cocktail called a Monkey Gland. With a fine disregard for the Colonel's herbaceous border Els groped his way round the house and found a window which gave him an excellent view of the proceedings and he was studying An English Rose with an appreciative eye when La Marquise looked up and spotted him.

In the second armoured car Kommandant van Heerden was having second thoughts about giving Els three hundred pounds of gelignite to plant. He was the only person to know the layout and besides I'd have heard it if it had gone off, he thought and consoled himself with the realization that it might not be such a bad thing if Els did bungle the part he had been given to play. No arrests, no trouble with confessions and no Els, and he once again wondered if he had been wise to listen to Mrs Heathcote-Kilkoon. All in all, he decided, he had very little choice in the matter. If she was foolish enough to let her husband know that he had been cuckolded and the Colonel threatened to shoot a member of the South African Police and a senior member at that, he had only himself to blame for what followed. The Kommandant couldn't remember if Mrs Heathcote-Kilkoon had actually said that her husband had threatened to shoot him but in any case the suspicion that he might was enough. More to the point was the appeal the Colonel would make to the Bureau of State Security. If there was one sort of suspect BOSS really liked after Jewish millionaires whose parents had emigrated from Petrograd, it was Englishmen of the old school with links with the Anglican Church. The Colonel's outspoken contempt for Afrikaners would silence any suspicion that he might be entirely innocent while his wartime experience in the underground and his training in explosives made him precisely the sort of man BOSS had been looking for over the years. The Kommandant remembered the Union Jack flying in front of White Ladies. In the eyes of BOSS that alone would damn the Colonel and his Club as traitors.

Finally, to salve what little remained of his conscience, the Kommandant recalled the fate of his grandfather who had been shot after the Battle of Paardeburg by the British.

Tit for tat, he thought and ordered the driver to stop at the police station in Weezen. There he insisted on seeing the Sergeant in charge.

'Colonel Heathcote-Kilkoon a communist?' asked the Sergeant who finally made his appearance in a pair of pyjamas. 'There must be some mistake.'

'Our information is that he's a saboteur trained by British intelligence,' said the Kommandant. 'Have you checked his wartime career in your security reports?'

'What sec ...' the Sergeant began before realizing his mistake. 'No.'

'I always keep a file copy in case Security HQ lose the one I send them,' said the Kommandant. 'Amazing how many times they have mislaid things I've sent them.' He looked round the police station approvingly. 'Like the way things are done here, Sergeant. About time you had some promotion. The main thing is to keep copies of your security reports.'

He went outside and the Sergeant was amazed at the size of the task force required to arrest Colonel Heathcote-Kilkoon. As if to provide final proof that the Colonel was indeed the Communist saboteur trained by British intelligence, a sudden burst of firing came from the direction of White Ladies. Kommandant van Heerden dived into the Saracen and the Sergeant returned to his office and sat down at his typewriter to draft a report on the Colonel. It was much easier than he had expected, thanks to the forgetfulness of the Kommandant, who had left a specimen of his own report on the desk.

As the convoy moved off again the Sergeant typed out his suspicions. They were dated six months earlier.

'Better late than never,' he thought as he typed.

His view of things was shared by Mrs Heathcote-Kilkoon's taxi driver.

'There's ice on the road,' he told her when she asked him to step on it.

'Nonsense,' said Mrs Heathcote-Kilkoon. 'it's a hot night.'

'There's been a hailstorm, lady and if it isn't ice it's a thin coating of mud and as slippery as hell,' and to prove his point put the car into a slight skid on the next corner.

'You don't want to end up over a cliff,' he went on, righting the car, 'that wouldn't do you no good at all.'

In the back seat Mrs Heathcote-Kilkoon couldn't imagine that anything was going to do her much good. What had started out with less than the emotional force involved in her monthly choice of hairstyle had turned into a paroxysm of uncertainty. Melodramatic mock confessions were one thing. They added spice to the boredom of existence. But armoured cars and convoys of policemen armed with rifles and accompanied by snarling guard dogs were something else again. 'One can have too much of a good thing,' she thought recalling the logistics of her lover's concern. They argued a quite disproportionate devotion, not to mention a terrifying lack of sense of humour.

'I was only joking,' she murmured and was not consoled by the taxi driver's next remark.

'Looks like the army's been through here,' he said as the car slewed through the mud churned up by the convoy. 'Shouldn't be surprised if it wasn't tanks.'

'I should,' said Mrs Heathcote-Kilkoon more correctly and stared apprehensively into the darkness.

In the living-room at White Ladies her husband was doing the same and with even greater apprehension. La Marquise's sudden scream at the sight of the face at the window had provided An English Rose with an opportunity for a display of chivalry calculated to restore the Colonel's confidence in his rightful sex which La Marquise's interest had somewhat undermined.

'I'll deal with the swine,' he shouted and dashed into his study with all the speed his wife's step-ins allowed, to emerge a moment later with a sporting rifle. 'Only one way to deal with intruders,' he said and fired into the garden.

To Konstabel Els flitting across the lawn the accuracy of the shot came as something of a surprise. Aimed at a neatly trimmed bush some twenty yards to his right which to the Colonel's alcoholic eye had the look of an intruder, the bullet ricochetted off a rockery and sang unpleasantly past Konstabel Els' head. Els took cover in a sunken garden and unfastened his holster. Outlined against the light in a window he could see the Colonel peering out. Els took careful aim over the Colonel's shoulder and fired and was delighted by the consternation his deliberate near miss caused in the house. As the lights went out and the Colonel shouted orders to keep down, Els crawled away and was presently well hidden in a clump of azaleas, where he could keep an eye on the back door. The Battle of White Ladies had begun.

'God Almighty,' yelled An English Rose as a third bullet, this time from a different part of the garden, ruffled the night air and shattered a vase on the mantelpiece, 'it's a bloody uprising. The natives have risen.' With a vindictiveness that came from the realization that the kaffirs were using more sophisticated weapons than assegais and knobkerries he prepared to defend his corner of Western Civilization against the tide of barbarism he had always expected. Behind him the members of the Dornford Yates Club, sobered by the prospect of an imminent bloodbath, stumbled into the study where Major Bloxham was handing out rifles and ammunition. With a military authority he had never before exercised the Colonel deployed his forces.

'Boy, take the front room. Toby, the kitchen,' he ordered. 'The rest of you spread out in the library and breakfast-room and keep firing.'

'What shall I do?' asked La Marquise.

'Pass the ammunition and keep your powder dry,' shouted the Colonel bitterly. La Marquise crawled into the study and began to undress. If the black hordes were coming, there was no point in maintaining the fiction that she was a man.

'There's no such thing as a fate worse than death,' she muttered in the darkness.

'What's that?' whispered Major Bloxham.

'I said all cats are grey when the candles are out,' said La Marquise.

'You can say that again,' said the Major busily trying to rid himself of his Incroyable costume.

In the azalea bushes Konstabel Els lay and listened to the hail of gunfire issuing from the house. It was going to be a good night. He had no doubt about that now.

In the second armoured car Kommandant van Heerden was less sanguine. The knowledge that he was moving into an area where Konstabel Els was involved in a private war brought back memories of previous holocausts initiated by Els.

'The stupid bastard will probably shoot his own side,' he thought when Sergeant Breitenbach came to ask for orders.

'Open fire at long range,' he told the Sergeant, 'I don't want anyone getting too close.' Presently two hundred policemen had disembarked from the lorries and had crawled into the bushes that marked the boundary of White Ladies and were adding their concentrated fire to that of Els and the Dornford Yates Club.

'Why not send in the armoured cars?' Sergeant Breitenbach asked.

'Certainly not,' said the Kommandant, appalled at the idea that he should be driven into close proximity to Konstabel Els and three hundred pounds of gelignite, not to mention the obviously irate Colonel and whatever weapons he had in his arsenal. 'We'll wear them down first and then move in.'

'Wear them down's about right,' said the Sergeant as the police fire cut a swathe through the ornamental hedges of the Colonel's garden. In the background the hounds of the Dornford Yates pack were giving tongue and lending a new sense of urgency to the snarls of the police dogs in the rear lorries.

Inside the house the realization that they were surrounded and that the black hordes were armed with the very latest in automatic weapons had slowly dawned on most of the defenders. La Marquise was no longer interested. Deserting her post she crawled upstairs to put on some clean underwear in anticipation of her approaching ordeal when she was hit by a burst of machine-gun fire. She was the first casualty of the battle.

In the kitchen the Zulu butler, with greater presence of mind, left the house and made his way to a telephone box on the outskirts of Weezen and dialled the operator.

'Get me the police station,' he told her. The operator wasn't to be told.

'Don't you speak to me like that, kaffir,' she shouted. 'You ask nicely.'

'Yes, missus,' said the butler relapsing into the required tone of servility. 'Ambulance please, missus.'

'Black or white ambulance?' the operator inquired.

The butler considered the question.

'White ambulance, missus,' he said finally.

'It's not for you, is it?' the girl inquired. 'Kaffirs can't ride in white ambulances. They have to be fumigated afterwards.'

'Not for me, missus,' the butler told her. 'For white boss.'

'What address?'

'White Ladies,' said the butler.

'Which white lady's?'

'White Ladies House,' said the butler as a fresh outburst of firing lent urgency to his request.

'I know that, kaffir,' screamed the operator. 'I know white ladies live in houses. I know she doesn't live in a mud hut like you. What I want to know is which white lady's.'

'Mrs Heathcote-Kilkoon,' said the butler.

'Why didn't you say so in the first place?' shouted the operator. The butler put down the receiver and went out into the inhospitable night where his white masters were killing one another with a ferocity he found incomprehensible.

'No point in getting caught in the middle,' he thought and began to walk carefully into Weezen. Occasionally a stray bullet whirred overhead. The butler kept his head down. In the main street he was stopped by a policeman and asked for his pass.

'You're under arrest,' said the konstabel when the butler admitted he hadn't got a pass with him. 'Can't have savages wandering about in the middle of the night without passes.'

'Yes, baas,' said the butler and climbed into the paddywagon.

To Konstabel Els the arrival of the police convoy was a mixed blessing. The fact that he was in some sort of no-man's-land between two opposing forces each defending Western Civilization was something of a hazard. As the Colonel's erratic fire swept through the leaves above him and was answered by the burst of machine-gun fire in his rear, Els began to think the time had come to make his presence felt. He crawled through the azaleas until he reached the corner of the house and then made a wild dash into the yard and was about to light a match to ignite the kerosene he had poured into the wine cellar when it occurred to him that he was endangering both the evidence he had planted so carefully in the harness

room and his own life. He fetched a hose and took it into the harness
room and presently was playing a sprinkler over the gelignite. He was
so busy at his work that he was unaware of the figure that flitted heavily
across the yard and into the darkness by the kennels. Assured that he
had taken every sensible precaution Els shut the door of the harness room
and slipped back across the yard.

This ought to flush the buggers out, he thought, striking a match and
dropping it into the kerosene before dashing for cover. A moment later
a sheet of flame lit the night sky and an explosion erupted in the basement
of White Ladies. With considerable satisfaction Konstabel Els peered out
of the azaleas and studies his handiwork while behind him the police
ceased their fire. There was indeed no need to continue. Apart from the
occasional report of an exploding bottle of Australian burgundy buried
under tons of rubble the occupants of White Ladies had ended their
resistance. Berry Puts Off His Manhood night had ended.

Colonel Heathcote-Kilkoon alone did not stop to watch his house burn.
He was too busy stumbling across open ground in search of cover. As he
went he cursed his wife for her absence. 'Wouldn't have happened if
she'd been here,' he gasped, a tribute less to her power of personality
than to the constriction of her pantie girdle which was playing havoc
with his innards. Spurred on by shouts that greeted the conflagration of
his home and by the need to apprise those of his neighbours who had
not been woken by the sound of battle that the natives had risen, An
English Rose blundered into a wood and wrestled with his girdle.

'Got to get it off before I burst,' he muttered, only to decide ten
minutes later that there was no question of bursting in spite of his vain
efforts to get it off. In the end he decided that sleep might deflate him
and crawling into the cover of a bush lay still.

From the turret of his armoured car Kommandant van Heerden surveyed
what remained of White Ladies with a mixture of satisfaction and regret.

'No doubt about their being the saboteurs now, Sergeant?' he asked
Sergeant Breitenbach.

'None at all,' said the Sergeant. 'There's enough gelignite in the stables
to blow up half Piemburg.'

Kommandant van Heerden disappeared hurriedly into the armoured
car. His muffled voice could be heard urging the driver to get the hell
out. Sergeant Breitenbach went round to the back door.

'It's all right,' he told the Kommandant, 'it won't go off. Someone's
been playing a hose on it.'

'You sure?' asked the Kommandant. Sergeant Breitenbach said he wouldn't be standing there if he wasn't and the Kommandant finally emerged and stared at the smouldering building. 'Better get the fire brigade here,' he said. 'We don't want any more explosions and I want a body count as soon as possible.'

'How many suspects do you expect?' asked the Sergeant.

'Eleven will do,' said the Kommandant and clambered back into the Saracen to get some sleep.

At the entrance to what had once been her home Mrs Heathcote-Kilkoon's taxi was stopped by a Sergeant and several konstabels armed with machine-guns.

'Sorry, lady,' the Sergeant said, 'but orders is orders and no one is allowed in.'

'But I live here, officer,' said Mrs Heathcote-Kilkoon dredging a seductive smile from the depths of her despair.

'Not any more you don't,' said the Sergeant. 'This is one house you won't be living in again.'

In the back of the taxi Mrs Heathcote-Kilkoon clutched her coat to her and shivered. To add to her troubles the taxi-driver insisted on being paid before he drove her any further.

'How can I pay?' she pleaded. 'All I ever had is in there,' and she pointed to the smudge of smoke that darkened the night sky over the azaleas.

'You said you'd pay me double fare when we got here,' the driver insisted, 'I didn't come all this way for nothing.'

'But I've nothing to give you,' Mrs Heathcote-Kilkoon said wearily.

'We'll see about that,' said the driver and turned the car in the road. Half a mile further on he pulled into the side and climbed into the back seat.

'I suppose it's only fare,' Mrs Heathcote-Kilkoon murmured as his coarse hands fumbled with her panties.

CHAPTER SIXTEEN

It was characteristic of Konstabel Els that his feelings as he watched the end of White Ladies were less ambiguous than those of the Kommandant. If he felt any regret, it was that his efforts of fire-raising had been so completely successful. He had at least hoped that the flames would have driven some survivors of the Dornford Yates Club out into the open where they could be shot down at leisure like men or more correctly as men dressed as women. Els particularly regretted the failure of his late employer to put in an appearance. He had been looking forward to despatching An English Rose with a degree of lingering incivility he felt the Colonel merited.

Long before the ashes were cool, Konstabel Els was busy in the ruins counting the bodies and making sure that no one had been overlooked. By the time he had finished he had managed to recover the melted remains of Mrs Heathcote-Kilkoon's jewels and was beginning to think that something else was missing.

Stumbling around in the ashes he counted the bodies again.

'There's only eleven here,' he told Sergeant Breitenbach, who was watching him with some revulsion.

'Who cares?' asked the Sergenat rhetorically.

'I do,' said Els. 'There ought to be thirteen.' He did some mental arithmetic. 'Still wrong,' he said finally. 'There's still one missing.'

'How many servants?' asked the Sergeant.

'I'm not counting kaffirs,' said Els, 'I'm talking about people.'

'Which one is it?'

'Looks like the Colonel,' said Els bitterly. 'Shifty bastard. Typical of him to get away.'

Sergeant Breitenbach said he thought it was very sensible but he went over the armoured car and knocked on the door.

'What is it now?' the Kommandant asked sleepily.

'Els says the Colonel got away,' said the Sergeant and was amazed at the rapidity with which Kommandant van Heerden responded.

'Get the dogs,' he yelled frantically, 'get the dogs. We've got to find the swine.' As Sergeant Breitenbach gave orders for the Dobermann Pinschers to be released, Konstabel Els went off to the kennels and presently the gravel forecourt was filled with snarling police dogs and slobbering foxhounds, each pack busily disputing the right of the other to be there. In the middle of the seething mass Kommandant van Heerden, appalled at the knowledge that Mrs Heathcote-Kilkoon's irate husband was still at large and doubtless imbued with a new sense of grievance, tried to avoid getting bitten.

'Down Jason, down Snarler,' he yelled vainly trying to repeat the magic formula that had worked so well in the dell. Here it was less successful. Busy about their private business the hounds snapped and snarled at one another in an ever-increasing vortex of confusion and the Kommandant was just beginning to think he was going to be bitten to death when Els rode up on his nag leading Mrs Heathcote-Kilkoon's bay. The Kommandant climbed into the saddle thankfully and looked around.

'I suppose you could say I was MFHDP,' he said proudly. Els blew his horn and the hunt moved off through the gate and across the field.

'What's DP stand for?' Els asked as they followed.

The Kommandant looked at him irritably. 'Police dogs, of course,' he said and spurring the bay galloped after the hounds who had picked up the scent of The English Rose. Compounded of Chanel No 5 and aniseed, it was unmistakable. Even the Dobermann Pinschers loping ominously behind the fox hounds could pick it up. In the light of the early dawn they quickened their pace.

So did Colonel Heathcote-Kilkoon, whose sleep had not deflated him sufficiently to escape from the intractable embrace of his wife's corsets. Stumbling about the thicket in an attempt to rid himself of the beastly things, the Colonel heard the sound of Els' horn and read its message rightly. As the first foxhounds breasted the horizon a mile away the Colonel broke cover and headed for the river. As he ran he scattered the less obdurate accessories of An English Rose. The frock of pale pink georgette, the bell-shaped sleeves, the Leghorn hat and the miniature apron fluttered behind him on the veldt, pathetic remnants of an Imperial dream. At the river bank the Colonel hesitated before diving in. 'Got to lose the scent,' he thought as he surfaced and allowed the current to carry him downstream.

'He's given us the slip,' Els shouted as the hounds milled round the discarded garments.

'I can see that,' said the Kommandant studying the torn fragments of pink with considerable distaste. 'Are you sure it's not Major Bloxham?' he asked. 'He said he always wore pink.'

But Els was already down by the river with the foxhounds and sniffing the air. 'He's gone thataway,' he said finally pointing downstream and blowing his horn set off along the river bank. Kommandant van Heerden followed slowly.

The sun had risen and with it there came to the Kommandant a sudden sense of regret. There was no need to hurry now. Els was on the trail and had scented blood and from long experience the Kommandant knew he would never give up. Besides there was no doubt now that he was safe from BOSS. Verkramp's errors of judgement had been buried in the wreckage of White Ladies and no one would question the Kommandant's efficient handling of the matter now that he had eleven corpses and three

hundred pounds of gelignite to prove it. He felt safe at last and with his
sense of security there returned the desire to do the gentlemanly thing.
Certainly chasing elderly colonels dressed as women across the countryside
wasn't a gentlemanly occupation. There was something vaguely sordid
about it. With one last glance at the tailless haunches of the Dobermanns
gliding menacingly among the willows, the Kommandant turned his bay
and rode slowly back to the house. On the way he met Sergeant
Breitenbach in an armoured car and with a rejuvenated sense of chivalry
pointed in quite the wrong direction. 'They've gone thataway,' he shouted
and watched the Sergeant disappear over the hillside. Far down the river
Els sounded his horn and the Kommandant thought he heard the cry,
'Gone to earth.' It was followed by the sound of yelping.

In the back of the taxi Mrs Heathcote-Kilkoon had spent her night
watching the night sky turn crimson over the taxi-driver's shoulder and
had responded with a degree of agitation that lent weight to his conviction
that she was actively enjoying what he was doing. As the reflected glow
ebbed from the sky Mrs Heathcote-Kilkoon's writhing ebbed with it and
the taxi-driver fell asleep. As she detached herself from him and climbed
out of the car, it occurred to her to search his pockets for money but she
discarded the thought. There was more to be gained in the house. When
the armoured cars drove out of the yard in pursuit of her husband, Mrs
Heathcote-Kilkoon adjusted her dress and then scrambled through the
hedge and walked up to the house. A mound of blackened rubble, it had
little to remind her of the past. In any case Mrs Heathcote-Kilkoon was
more concerned with the future. She hadn't left the suburbs of South
London for the dangers and discomforts of life in Africa for nothing. She
climbed the steps which had been the scene of so many welcomes and
which still retained something of their old warmth and surveyed the
ruins. Then stepping adroitly between her old friends she made her way
to her bedroom and began to dig in the ashes.

As the sound of the horn reached him Colonel Heathcote-Kilkoon
scrambled out of the river and disappeared into the trees. He stumbled
through the undergrowth and five minutes later found himself at the foot
of a cliff. He could go no further. Behind him the yelps of the hounds
grew more insistent on the far side of the river. The Colonel listened
breathlessly for a moment and then turned and searched for somewhere
to hide. He found it in an overhang of rock. Crawling inside he found
himself in some sort of cave, dark and deep and with a narrow entrance.
If only I could block it up, he thought and the next moment, with a

presence of mind that had come rather late in life, he was out in the sunlight and struggling with a thorn bush which resolutely defied his efforts to pull it up by the roots. Below him the sound of the pack seemed closer and spurred on by this indication of danger, the Colonel hauled the bush out of the ground, a feat which had it not been for his wife's corsets would certainly have ruptured him. He crawled back into the hole and dragged the thorn bush behind him. That ought to keep them out, he thought grimly, crouching in the darkness oblivious to the paintings of other hunts that glimmered from the walls of the cave.

On the river bank Konstabel Els and the hounds sniffed the air. There was nothing to indicate which way their quarry had gone. Els wondered what he would have done had he been in the Colonel's shoes and came to the conclusion that he would have headed into the thick bush on the far side of the river. Urging his nag forward, Els waded into the water and with the hounds swarming around him crossed over. A few minutes later the leading hounds had picked up the trail and were following a line through the trees. Els pushed on after them and came out into the open to find the pack giving tongue round a thorn bush which appeared to be growing in the most unlikely fashion from inside a cave. Els dismounted and considered the situation while the Dobermann Pinschers snarled and the foxhounds greeted their old master with a friendliness that was not reciprocated. With reckless disregard for life and limb Els waded into the pack and peered into the thorn bush. A moment later his 'Gone to earth' echoed from the cliff face.

In his burrow Colonel Heathcote-Kilkoon recognized the call and the voice had something familiar about it. Hope surged in his breast. If Harbinger was outside, he was safe. He started to push the thorn bush forward to crawl out but was instantly dissuaded by three Dobermanns who threw themselves into the gap with bared teeth. The Colonel hauled the thorn bush back and tried shouting but his words were drowned by the noise of the pack.

Outside Konstabel Els sat on a rock and lit a cigarette. He was in no hurry. Can't shoot him, he thought recalling the MFH's adamant veto on the shooting of foxes; what I need is a terrier. Els began to cast about for a suitable substitute. Presently he was scrambling among the rocks on one side of the cliff. It was hot work and the sun was up and it took Els half an hour to find what he was looking for. In the end he grabbed a large snake that was sunning itself on a ledge and holding it by the tail made his way back to the earth. The dogs backed away and Els dropped the snake into the thorn bush with a snigger and watched it slither into the darkness. A moment later a convulsive shudder shook the thorn bush to be followed by a scream as the corseted Colonel erupted from his burrow and hurtled across the scree and into the trees. 'Gone away,' yelled Els and watched with a smile as the hounds surged after him. Silly bugger, he thought, he ought to know grass snakes are harmless. Screams and snarls from the bushes marked the end of the hunt and Els pushed his way among the dogs and took out his knife.

To Kommandant van Heerden jogging back to White Ladies the sight that greeted him was full of poignancy he would never forget. It put him in mind of the heroines in the books of the author whose portrait had once adorned the wall of the dining-room. True, Mrs Heathcote-Kilkoon was no slender girl and the magic that clung to her was wholly black, but these discrepancies were as nothing to the vision of tragic grief she presented. The Kommandant left the horse at the gate and crossed the gravel to her side. Only then did Mrs Heathcote-Kilkoon raise her tinted head.

'It's buried ...' she began, tears ravaging her lovely features. Kommandant van Heerden looked down at the corpse beside her feet and shook his head.

'Not Berry, Daphne. Boy,' he murmured. But Mrs Heathcote-Kilkoon was obviously too far gone in grief to hear.

'My precious treasure ...' she shrieked and threw herself down to scrabble in the ashes. The Kommandant knelt beside her and shook his head again sadly.

'They've gone for good, my darling,' he whispered and was astonished at the fresh paroxysm of grief that racked her body. Cursing himself for the lack of tact that had made him use an endearment at a time like this, he took her hand in his.

'They've gone to a better world,' he said gazing into her deep grey eyes. Mrs Heathcote-Kilkoon thrust him away imperiously.

'You're lying,' she cried, 'they can't have. They're all I've got,' and disregarding her delicate hands she dug into the rubble. Beside her, overcome by emotion, the Kommandant knelt and watched.

He was still maintaining his steadfast vigil when Els rode up on his nag waving something.

'I've got it. I've got it,' he shouted triumphantly and dismounted. Kommandant van Heerden regarded him bleakly through eyes dimmed with tears and motioned him away. But Els lacked the Kommandant's sense of occasion. He ran up the steps into the ruins eagerly and waved something in the Kommandant's face.

'Look at that. Isn't it a fine one?' he shouted. Kommandant van Heerden shut his eyes in horror.

'For God's sake, Els, there's a time and a place ...' he shouted dementedly but Els was already daubing his cheeks and forehead.

'You're blooded,' he shouted, 'you're blooded.'

The Kommandant rose frantically to his feet.

'You swine,' he screamed, 'You filthy swine.'

'I thought you'd like the brush,' Els said in a puzzled tone of voice. It was obvious that he was cut to the quick by the Kommandant's rejection of his offering. So it appeared was Mrs Heathcote-Kilkoon. As the Kommandant turned to make his apologies for Konstabel Els' appalling lapse of taste, the Colonel's widow struggled to her feet.

'It's mine, you thief,' she screamed and lunged at Els furiously. 'You had no right to take it, I want it back,' a claim whose justice the Kommandant had to admit while deploring the fact that Mrs Heathcote-Kilkoon should want to make it.

'Give it to her,' he shouted at Els, 'it's hers by right,' but before Els could proffer his ghastly souvenir, Mrs Heathcote-Kilkoon, evidently intent on more practical reparation for the loss of her conjugal rights, had hurled herself on the konstabel and was tearing at his trousers.

'Dear God,' bawled the Kommandant as Els fell back into the ashes.

'Help,' screamed Els evidently imbued with the same suspicion as to her intentions.

'It's mine,' shrieked Mrs Heathcote-Kilkoon, clawing at Els' pants. Kommandant van Heerden shut his eyes and tried to shut out too the screams from Els.

'That it should come to this,' he thought and was trying to reconcile this new evidence of feminine fury with that gentle image of Mrs Heathcote-Kilkoon he had nurtured in the past when with a shriek of triumph the Colonel's widow got to her feet. The Kommandant opened his eyes and stared at the strange object in her hand. It was not, he was thankful to note, what he had expected. Mrs Heathcote-Kilkoon's hand held a dark lump of metal in whose misshapen surface there gleamed here and there large brilliant stones. Twisted and melted though they were, the Kommandant could still recognize traces of Mrs Heathcote-Kilkoon's bijouterie. Clutching the great ingot to her breast she looked once more the woman he had known.

'My darlings,' she shrieked, her voice radiant with frenetic gaiety, 'my precious darlings.'

The Kommandant turned sternly to Els who was still lying prone and shaken by his recent experience.

'How many times have I told you not to nick things?' he demanded. Els smiled weakly and got to his feet.

'I was only looking after them,' he said by way of explanation.

The Kommandant turned away and followed Mrs Heathcote-Kilkoon down the steps.

'Have you a car?' he asked solicitously. Mrs Heathcote-Kilkoon shook her head.

'Then I'll send for a taxi,' said the Kommandant.

A fresh pallor blanched Mrs Heathcote-Kilkoon's face.

'You've got to be joking,' she muttered before collapsing in a dead faint in his arms.

'Poor thing,' thought the Kommandant, 'it's all been too much for her.' He picked her up and carried her gently over to a Saracen. As he lowered her to the floor he noticed that she still clutched the nugget in her limp hand.

'The British bulldog,' he thought and closed the door.

When the police convoy finally left White Ladies Mrs Heathcote-Kilkoon had revived sufficiently to sit up. She was still obviously stunned by the change in her fortunes and the Kommandant tactfully didn't bring the subject up. Instead he busied himself with some paperwork and ran over in his mind things he had still to do.

He had left Sergeant Breitenbach with a small body of men to guard the scene of the crime and had arranged for photographs of the cache of high-explosives and detonators in the harness room to be supplied to the press. He would write up a full report on the affair for the Commissioner of Police and forward a copy to BOSS and he would announce to the press that another revolutionary conspiracy to overthrow the Republic had been nipped in the bud. He might even hold a press conference. In the end he decided not to on the grounds that journalists were a breed of men who didn't make the job of the police in South Africa any easier and he saw no reason why they should rely on him for their information. He had, in any case, more important matters to worry about than public opinion.

There was for instance the problem of the Colonel's widow and, while he had every sympathy for her in her present plight, the Kommandant was alive to the possibility that the distressing action he had been forced to take might well have ended the good feeling she had once felt for him. As the convoy approached Piemburg the Kommandant inquired as to her plans.

'Plans?' asked Mrs Heathcote-Kilkoon roused from her silent reverie. 'I have no plans.'

'You have friends in Umtali,' said the Kommandant hopefully. 'They would surely put you up.'

Mrs Heathcote-Kilkoon nodded. 'I suppose so,' she said.

'Better than a police cell,' said the Kommandant and explained that he ought to hold her as a witness. 'Of course if you give me your word not to leave the country ...' he added.

That evening the Rolls stopped at the Customs Post at Beit Bridge.

'Anything to declare?' asked the Rhodesian Customs officer.

'Yes,' said Mrs Heathcote-Kilkoon with feeling. 'It's good to be back with one's own kith and kin.'

'Yes, ma'am,' said Customs Officer Van der Merwe and waved her through. As she drove through the night Mrs Heathcote-Kilkoon began to sing to keep herself awake.

'Rule Britannia, Britannia rules the waves, Britons never never will be slaves,' she shrieked happily as the car knocked an African cyclist into the ditch. Mrs Heathcote-Kilkoon was too tired to stop. 'Teach him to drive without lights,' she thought and put her foot on the accelerator. In the glove compartment a fortune in gold and diamonds rolled unevenly about.

In the week that followed the Kommandant was kept to busy to worry about Mrs Heathcote-Kilkoon's disappearance. The team of Security men who came down from Pretoria to report on the affair were sent up to Weezen to investigate.

'Try the storekeeper,' the Kommandant suggested. 'Very helpful fellow.' The Security men tried the storekeeper and were infuriated by his refusal to speak Afrikaans.

'I've seen enough coppers,' he told them, 'to last me a lifetime. I've ordered one off the premises already and I'm ordering you. This is Little England and you can get the hell out.'

By the time they returned to Pretoria they could find nothing to criticize in the Kommandant's handling of the affair. The fact that the victims of police action were found on examination to be wearing women's clothes in the case of the men and a jockstrap in the case of La Marquise added weight to the Kommandant's claim that the safety of the Republic had been threatened. Even in the Cabinet the Kommandant's handling of the affair received a friendly reception.

'Nothing like the threat of terrorism to keep the electorate on our side,' said the Minister of Justice, 'We could do with an incident like this before every election.'

At Fort Rapier Luitenant Verkramp viewed the outcome of the affair in a different light. Now that the immediate cause of his insanity had been removed, Verkramp had regained sufficient rationality to regard his proposal to Dr von Blimenstein as a temporary aberration.

'I must have been mad,' he told the doctor when she reminded him of their engagement.

Dr von Blimenstein looked at him reproachfully.

'After all I've done for you,' she said finally.

'Done for me is about right,' said Verkramp.

'I'd planned such a lovely honeymoon too,' the doctor complained.

'Well I'm not going,' said Verkramp, 'I've had enough trips to last me a lifetime.'

'Is that your last word?' asked the doctor.

'Yes,' said Verkramp.

Dr von Blimenstein left the room and ordered the nurse to put Verkramp under restraint. Ten minutes later Verkramp was in a straitjacket and Dr von Blimenstein was closeted with the Hospital Chaplain.

That afternoon Kommandant van Heerden, visiting Fort Rapier to inquire about Aaron Geisenheimer, found Dr von Blimenstein dressed, rather ostentatiously, he thought, in a picture hat and a shark-skin suit.

'Going somewhere?' he asked. In the rush of events he had forgotten about Verkramp's impending marriage.

'We're honeymooning in Muizenberg,' said the doctor.

Kommandant van Heerden sat down suddenly in a chair.

'And Verkramp's quite well?' he asked.

In the light of the Kommandant's gallantry at their last meeting Dr von Blimenstein overlooked the imputation.

'A touch of last-minute nerves,' she said, 'but I think it'll go off without a hitch.' She hesitated before continuing, 'I know it's a lot to ask but I wonder if you would be best man?'

Kommandant van Heerden tried to think what to say. The thought that he would be in any way instrumental in joining the author of so many of his misfortunes to a woman as totally unloveable as Dr von Blimenstein had its appealing side. The thought of the doctor as Mrs Verkramp had nothing to recommend it.

'I suppose Verkramp has given up all idea of returning to his post?' he inquired hopefully. Dr von Blimenstein was pleased to reassure him.

'You've nothing to worry about,' she said. 'Balthazar will be on duty just as soon as we get the honeymoon over.'

'I see,' said the Kommandant, rising. 'In that case I think I had better see him now.'

'He's in Hypnotherapy,' said the doctor as the Kommandant went out into the corridor. 'Tell him I won't be long.'

The Kommandant went down the passage and asked a nurse the way. At Hypnotherapy the nurse opened the door and smiled.

'Here's your best man,' she said and ushered the Kommandant into the ward where Verkramp was sitting up in bed surrounded by an inferno of chrysanthemums.

'You too?' Verkramp groaned as the Kommandant entered and sat down on a chair by the bed.

'Just popped in to see if there was anything you needed,' said the Kommandant. 'I had no idea you were getting married.'

'I'm not getting married,' said Verkramp, 'I'm being married.'

'I see they've given you a clean straitjacket for the occasion,' said the Kommandant anxious to keep off controversial topics.

'Won't be needing that in a minute,' said the nurse. 'Will we?' She picked up a hypodermic and pulling back the bedclothes rolled Verkramp on to his stomach.

'I don't want . . .' shouted Verkramp but the nurse had already plunged the needle into his backside. By the time she withdrew it the Kommandant was feeling distinctly agitated while Verkramp had relapsed into an unusual torpor.

'There we are,' said the nurse propping him up again and unfastening his straitjacket. 'No need for this horrid old thing now, is there?'

'I do,' said Verkramp.

The nurse smiled at the Kommandant and left the room.

'Listen,' said the Kommandant, appalled at what he had just witnessed, 'is it true that you don't want to marry this woman?'

'I do,' said Verkramp. The Kommandant, who had been on the brink of assuring him that there was no need for him to go through with the marriage looked nonplussed.

'But I thought you said you didn't,' he said.

'I do,' said Verkramp.

'There's still a chance to change your mind,' said the Kommandant.

'I do,' said Verkramp.

'Well I'm damned,' muttered the Kommandant. 'You certainly change your mind quickly.'

'I do,' said Verkramp. At that moment the nurse returned with the ring.

'Does he often go into this "I do" routine?' the Kommandant asked as he slipped the ring into his pocket.

'It's a new treatment that Dr von Blimenstein has developed,' the nurse told him. 'It's called CIRS.'

'I should think it must be,' said the Kommandant.

'Chemically Induced Repetitive Syndrome,' the nurse explained.

'I do,' said Verkramp.

'Good God,' said the Kommandant suddenly realizing the full implications of the treatment. If Dr von Blimenstein could get Verkramp unwillingly to the altar by chemically induced hypnosis and get him saying 'I do' all the way there, she could do anything. Kommandant van Heerden visualized the outcome. Hundreds of innocent and respectable citizens could be induced to confess to sabotage, membership of the Communist party, training in guerrilla warfare and any crime you cared to name. Worse still, Dr von Blimenstein was not the sort of woman to hesitate when it came to advancing her husband's career by such dubious methods. The Kommandant was just considering this new threat to his position as Chief of Police when the bride arrived with the hospital Chaplain and a bevy of patients who had been raked in as bridesmaids. A tape recorder struck up the wedding march and the Kommandant slipping the ring into Verkramp's hand left the room. He had no intention of being best man at a wedding that marked the end of his own career. He went out on to the parade ground and wandered miserably among the inmates cursing the irony of fate that had saved him from the consequences of Verkramp's deliberate attempts to oust him only to destroy him now. It would have been better to have let Verkramp take the rap for the activities of his secret agents than to have allowed him to marry Dr von Blimenstein. The Kommandant was just wondering if there was anything he could do even at this late hour when he became aware of a disturbance outside Hypnotherapy. Dr von Blimenstein was being escorted, weeping, from the makeshift chapel.

Kommandant van Heerden hurried across.

'Something go wrong?' he asked eagerly.

'He said "I do",' the nurse explained. Dr von Blimenstein wept uncontrollably.

'But I thought he was supposed to,' said the Kommandant.

'Not when the Chaplain asked if anyone present knew of any reason why these two should not be joined in holy wedlock,' the nurse explained. A broad smile broke across the Kommandant's face.

'Oh well,' he said cheerfully, 'Verkramp seemed to know his own mind after all,' and slapping the disconsolate doctor on the back with 'You can't win them all', he went into the ward to congratulate the ex-bridegroom.

With Konstabel Els, his problem was rather different. The telephone call from the taxidermist at the Piemburg Museum verged on the hysterical.

'He wanted me to stuff it,' the taxidermist told the Duty Sergeant.

'What's wrong with stuffing a fox's brush?' asked the Sergeant who couldn't see what all the fuss was about.

'But I keep telling you it wasn't a fox's brush. It was a phallus,' screamed the taxidermist.

'A false what?' the Sergeant asked.

'Not a false anything. A real phallus.'

'You're not making much sense, you know,' said the Sergeant.

The taxidermist took a deep breath and tried again. In the end the Sergeant put him through to the Kommandant who knew exactly what the man was talking about.

'No need to worry,' he said soothingly, 'I'll take the matter in hand at once.'

The taxidermist looked at the phone with disgust.

'You do that small thing,' he said and put the receiver down thankfully. Kommandant van Heerden sent for Els.

'I thought we'd seen the last of that beastly thing,' he said. Els looked downcast.

'I wanted to keep it as a souvenir,' he explained, 'I was thinking of having it mounted.'

'Mounted?' shouted the Kommandant. 'You must be out of your mind. Why can't you give it a rest?'

Els said he would try.

'You'll do more than that,' the Kommandant told him. 'If I catch you flashing the thing again, I'll book you.'

'What with?' Els asked.

'Indecent Exposure,' snarled the Kommandant. Els went away to get rid of his trophy.

As the weeks passed and Piemburg resumed its slow routine the memory of exploding ostriches and the outbreak of sabotage passed into the safe hands of local legend. Kommandant van Heerden was well content to see it go. Looking back over the events of those days he found himself wondering at the great difference between life and literature. It doesn't do to read to much, he thought, recalling the fate that literary endeavours had held in store for Colonel Heathcote-Kilkoon and the members of the Dornford Yates Club. Instead the Kommandant chose to carry on the traditions of the English gentleman in practice. He added the foxhounds of the Colonel's pack to the police kennels where they struck up friendly relations with the Dobermann Pinschers and he put Konstabel Els in charge of them. Els, it seemed, had a way with dogs. The Kommandant acquired a horse and ordered a crimson hunting coat from the tailors and twice a week he could be seen riding to hounds in Chaste Valley with Els on a nag and a convict running for his life with a bag of aniseed tied round his middle. Sometimes he even invited Dr von Blimenstein, who was quite fond of riding. It seemed the least he could do for the poor woman now that Verkramp had jilted her and in any case he felt it was wise to keep on the right side of her.

All in all he was well content. Whatever had happened, the Values of Western Civilization were still safe in Piemburg and as MFHDP Kommandant van Heerden maintained those traditions which went with the heart of an English gentleman.

THE GREAT
PURSUIT

CHAPTER ONE

When anyone asked Frensic why he took snuff he replied that it was because by rights he should have lived in the eighteenth century. It was, he said, the century best suited to his temperament and way of life, the age of reason, of style, of improvement and expansion and those other characteristics he so manifestly possessed. That he didn't, and happened to know that the eighteenth century hadn't either, only heightened his pleasure at his own affectation and the amazement of his audience and, by way of paradox, justified his claim to be spiritually at home with Sterne, Swift, Smollett, Richardson, Fielding and other giants of the rudimentary novel whose craft Frensic so much admired. Since he was a literary agent who despised nearly all the novels he handled so successfully, Frensic's private eighteenth century was that of Grub Street and Gin Lane and he paid homage to it by affecting an eccentricity and cynicism which earned him a useful reputation and armoured him against the literary pretensions of unsaleable authors. In short he bathed only occasionally, wore woollen vests throughout the summer, ate a great deal more than was good for him, drank port before lunch and took snuff in large quantities so that anyone wishing to deal with him had to prove their hardiness by running the gauntlet of these deplorable habits. He also arrived early for work, read every manuscript that was submitted to him, promptly returned those he couldn't sell and just as promptly sold the others and in general conducted his business with surprising efficiency. Publishers took Frensic's opinions seriously. When Frensic said a book would sell, it sold. He had a nose for a bestseller, an infallible nose.

It was, he liked to think, something he had inherited from his father, a successful wine-merchant whose own nose for a palatable claret at a popular price had paid for that expensive education which, together with Frensic's more metaphysical nose, gave him the edge over his competitors. Not that the connection between a good education and his success as a connoisseur of commercially rewarding literature was direct. He had arrived at his talent circuitously and if his admiration for the eighteenth century, while real, nevertheless concealed an inversion, it was by exactly the same process that he had arrived at his success as a literary agent.

At twenty-one he had come down from Oxford with a second-class degree in English and the ambition to write a great novel. After a year behind the counter of his father's wine shop in Greenwich and at his desk in a room in Blackheath the 'great' had been abandoned. Three more years as an advertising copywriter and the author of a rejected novel about life behind the counter of a wine shop in Greenwich had completed the demolition of his literary ambitions. At twenty-four Frensic hadn't needed his nose to tell him he would never be a novelist. The two dozen literary agents who had refused to handle his work had said so already. On the other hand his experience of them had revealed a profession entirely to his taste. Literary agents, it was obvious, lived interesting, comfortable and thoroughly civilized lives. If they didn't write novels, they met novelists, and Frensic was still idealistic enough to imagine that this was a privilege; they spent their days reading books; they were their own masters, and if his own experience was anything to go by they showed an encouraging lack of literary perspicacity. In addition they seemed to spend a great deal of time eating and drinking and going to parties, and Frensic, whose appearance tended to limit his sensual pleasures to putting things into himself rather than into other people, was something of a gourmet. He had found his vocation.

At twenty-five he opened an office in King Street next to Covent Garden and sufficiently close to Curtis Brown, the largest literary agency in London, to occasion some profitable postal confusion, and advertised his services in the *New Statesman*, whose readers seemed more prone to pursue those literary ambitions he had so recently relinquished. Having done that he sat down and waited for the manuscripts to arrive. He had to wait a long time and he was beginning to wonder just how long his father could be persuaded to pay the rent when the postman delivered two parcels. The first contained a novel by Miss Celia Thwaite of The Old Pumping Station, Bishop's Stortford and a letter explaining that *Love's Lustre* was Miss Thwaite's first book. Reading it with increasing nausea, Frensic had no reason to doubt her word. The thing was a hodgepodge of romantic drivel and historical inaccuracy and dealt at length with the unconsummated love of a young squire for the wife of an absent-bodied crusader whose obsession with his wife's chastity seemed to reflect an almost pathological fetishism on the part of Miss Thwaite herself. Frensic wrote a polite note explaining that *Love's Lustre* was not a commercial proposition and posted the manuscript back to Bishop's Stortford.

The contents of the second package seemed at first sight to be more promising. Again it was a first novel, this time called *Search for a Lost Childhood* by a Mr P. Piper who gave as his address the Seaview Boarding House, Folkestone. Frensic read the novel and found it perceptive and deeply moving. Mr Piper's childhood had not been a happy one but he wrote discerningly about his unsympathetic parents and his own troubled adolescence in East Finchley. Frensic promptly sent the book to Jonathan Cape and informed Mr Piper that he foresaw an immediate sale followed by critical acclaim. He was wrong. Cape rejected the book. Bodley Head rejected it. Collins rejected it. Every publisher in London rejected it with comments that ranged from the polite to the derisory. Frensic conveyed their opinions in diluted form to Piper and entered into a correspondence with him about ways of improving it to meet the publishers' requirements.

He was just recovering from this blow to his acumen when he received another. A paragraph in *The Bookseller* announced that Miss Celia Thwaite's first novel, *Love's Lustre*, had been sold to Collins for fifty thousand pounds, to an American publisher for a quarter of a million dollars, and that she stood a good chance of winning The Georgette Heyer Memorial Prize for Romantic Fiction. Frensic read the paragraph incredulously and underwent a literary conversion. If publishers were prepared to pay such enormous sums for a book which Frensic's educated taste had told him was romantic trash, then everything he had learnt from F. R. Leavis and more directly from his own supervisor at Oxford, Dr Sydney Louth, about the modern novel was entirely false in the world of commercial publishing; worse still it constituted a deadly threat to his own career as a literary agent. From that moment of revelation Frensic's outlook changed. He did not discard his educated standards. He stood them on their head. Any novel that so much as approximated to the criteria laid down by Leavis in *The Great Tradition* and more vehemently by Miss Sydney Louth in her work, *The Moral Novel*, he rejected out of hand as totally unsuitable for publication while those books they would have dismissed as beneath contempt he pushed for all he was worth. By virtue of this remarkable reversal Frensic prospered. By the time he was thirty he had established an enviable reputation among publishers as an agent who recommended only those books that would sell. A novel from Frensic could be relied upon to need no alterations and little editing. It would be exactly eighty thousand words long or, in the case of historical romance where the readers were more voracious, one hundred and fifty thousand. It would start with a bang, continue with more bangs and end happily with an even bigger bang. In short, it would contain all those ingredients that public taste most appreciated.

But if the novels Frensic submitted to publishers needed few changes, those that arrived on his desk from aspiring authors seldom passed his scrutiny without fundamental alteration. Having discovered the ingredients of popular success in *Love's Lustre*, Frensic applied them to every book he handled so that they emerged from the process of rewriting like literary plum puddings or blended wines and incorporated sex, violence, thrills, romance and mystery, with the occasional dollop of significance to give them cultural respectability. Frensic was very keen on cultural respectability. It ensured reviews in the better papers and gave readers the illusion that they were participating in a pilgrimage to a shrine of meaning. What the meaning was remained, necessarily, unclear. It came under the general heading of meaningfulness but without it a section of the public who despised mere escapism would have been lost to Frensic's authors. He therefore always insisted on significance, and while on the whole he lumped it with insight and sensibility as being in any large measure as lethal to a book's chances as a pint of strychnine in a clear soup, in homeopathic doses it had a tonic effect on sales.

So did Sonia Futtle, whom Frensic chose as a partner to handle foreign publishers. She had previously worked for a New York agency and being an American her contacts with US publishers were invaluable. And the American market was extremely profitable. Sales were larger, the percentage from authors' royalties greater, and the incentives offered by Book Clubs enormous. Appropriately for one who was to expand their business in this direction, Sonia Futtle had already expanded personally in most others and was of distinctly unmarriageable proportions. It was this as much as anything that had persuaded Frensic to change the agency's name to Frensic & Futtle and to link his impersonal fortune with hers. Besides, she was an enthusiast for books which dealt with interpersonal relations and Frensic had developed an allergy to interpersonal relationships. He concentrated on less demanding books, thrillers, detective stories, sex when unromantic, historical novels when unsexual, campus novels, science fiction and violence. Sonia Futtle handled romantic sex, historical romance, liberation books whether of women or negroes, adolescent traumas, interpersonal relationships and animals. She was particularly good with animals, and Frensic, who had once almost lost a finger to the heroine of *Otters to Tea*, was happy to leave this side of the business to her. Given the chance he would have relinquished Piper too. But Piper stuck to Frensic as the only agent ever to have offered him the slightest encouragement and Frensic, whose success was in inverse proportion to Piper's failure, reconciled himself to the knowledge that he could never abandon Piper and that Piper would never abandon his confounded *Search for a Lost Childhood*.

Each year he arrived in London with a fresh version of his novel and Frensic took him out to lunch and explained what was wrong with it while Piper argued that a great novel must deal with real people in real situations and could never conform to Frensic's blatantly commercial formula. And each year they would part amicably, Frensic to wonder at the man's incredible perseverance and Piper to start work in a different boarding-house in a different seaside town on a different search for the same lost childhood. And so year after year the novel was partially transformed and the style altered to suit Piper's latest model. For this Frensic had no one to blame but himself. Early in their acquaintance he had rashly recommended Miss Louth's essays in *The Moral Novel* to Piper as something he ought to study and, while Frensic had come to regard her appreciations of the great novelists of the past as pernicious to anyone trying to write a novel today, Piper had adopted her standards as his own. Thanks to Miss Louth he had produced a Lawrence version of *Search for a Lost Childhood*, then a Henry James; James had been superseded by Conrad, then by George Eliot; there had been a Dickens version and even a Thomas Wolfe; and one awful summer a Faulkner. But through them all there stalked the figure of Piper's father, his miserable mother and the self-consciously pubescent Piper himself. Derivation followed derivation but the insights remained implacably trite and the action non-existent. Frensic despaired but remained loyal. To Sonia Futtle his attitude was incomprehensible.

'What do you do it for?' she asked. 'He's never going to make it and those lunches cost a fortune.'

'He is my *memento mori*,' said Frensic cryptically, conscious that the death Piper served to remind him of was his own, the aspiring young novelist he himself had once been and on the betrayal of whose literary ideals the success of Frensic & Futtle depended.

But if Piper occupied one day in his year, a day of atonement, for the rest Frensic pursued his career more profitably. Blessed with an excellent appetite, an impervious liver and an inexpensive source of fine wines from his father's cellars, he was able to entertain lavishly. In the world of publishing this was an immense advantage. While other agents wobbled home from those dinners over which books are conceived, publicized or bought, Frensic went portly on eating, drinking and advocating his novels *ad nauseam* and boasting of his 'finds'. Among the latter was James Jamesforth, a writer whose novels were of such unmitigated success that he was compelled for tax purposes to wander the world like some alcoholic fugitive from fame.

It was thanks to Jamesforth's itinerantly drunken progress from one tax haven to the next that Frensic found himself in the witness box in the High Court of Justice, Queen's Bench Division in the libel case of Mrs Desdemona Humberson *versus* James Jamesforth, author of *Fingers of Hell*, and Pulteney Press, publishers of the said novel. Frensic was in the witness box for two hours and by the time he stepped down he was a shaken man.

CHAPTER TWO

'Fifteen *thousand* pounds plus costs,' said Sonia Futtle next morning, 'for inadvertent libel? I don't believe it.'

'It's in the paper,' said Frensic handing her *The Times*. 'Next to the bit about the drunken lorry driver who killed two children and got fined a hundred and fifty pounds. Mind you he did lose his licence for three months too.'

'But that's insane. A hundred and fifty pounds for killing two children and fifteen thousand for libelling a woman James didn't even know existed.'

'On a zebra crossing,' said Frensic bitterly. 'Don't forget the zebra crossing.'

'Mad. Stark staring raving mad,' said Sonia. 'You English are out of your minds legally.'

'So's Jamesforth,' said Frensic, 'and you can forget him as one of our authors. He doesn't want to know us.'

'But we didn't do anything. We aren't supposed to check his proofs out. Pulteneys should have done that. They'd have spotted the libel.'

'Like hell they would. How does anyone spot a woman called Desdemona Humberson living in the wilds of Somerset who grows lupins and belongs to the Women's Institute? She's too improbable for words.'

'She's also done very nicely for herself. Fifteen grand for being called a nymphomaniac. It's worth it. I mean if someone called me a raving nymphomaniac I'd be only too glad to accept fifteen –'

'Doubtless,' said Frensic, forestalling a discussion of this highly unlikely eventuality. 'And for fifteen thousand I'd have hired a drunken lorry driver and had her erased on a zebra crossing. Split the difference with the driver and we would have still been to the good. And while I was about it I would have had Mr Galbanum slaughtered too. He should have had more sense than to advise Pulteneys and Jamesforth to fight the case.'

'Well it was innocent libel,' said Sonia. 'James didn't mean to malign the woman.'

'Oh quite. The fact remains that he did and under the Defamation Act of 1952 designed to protect authors and publishers from actions of this sort, innocent libel demands that they show they took reasonable care –'

'Reasonable care? What does that mean?'

'According to than senile old judge it means going to Somerset House and checking to see if anyone called Desdemona was born in 1928 and married a man called Humberson in 1951. Then you go throughout the Lupin Growers' Association Handbook looking for Humbersons and if they're not there you have a whack at the Women's Institute and finally the telephone directory for Somerset. Well, they didn't do all that so they got lumbered for fifteen thousand and we've got the reputation of handling authors who libel innocent women. Send your novels to Frensic & Futtle and get sued. We are the pariahs of the publishing world.'

'It can't be as bad as all that. After all, it's the first time it's happened and everyone knows that James is a souse who can't remember where he's been or who he's done.'

'Can't they just. Pulteney's can. Hubert rang up last night to say that we needn't send them any more novels. Once *that* word gets round we are going to have what is euphemistically called a cash flow problem.'

'We're certainly going to have to find someone to replace James,' said Sonia. 'Bestsellers like that don't grow on trees.'

'Nor lupins,' said Frensic and retired to his office.

All in all it was a bad day. The phone rang almost incessantly. Authors demanded to know if they were likely to end up in the High Court of Justice, Queen's Bench Division, because they had used the names of people they were at school with, and publishers turned down novels they would previously have accepted. Frensic sat and took snuff and tried to remain civil. By five o'clock he was finding it increasingly difficult and when the Literary Editor of the *Sunday Graphic* phoned to ask if Frensic would contribute an article on the iniquities of the British libel laws he was downright rude.

'What do you want me to do?' he shouted. 'Stick my head in a bloody noose and get hauled up for contempt of court? For all I know that blithering idiot Jamesforth is going to appeal against the verdict.'

'On the grounds that you inserted the passage which libelled Mrs Humberson?' the editor asked. 'After all it was suggested by the defence counsel –'

'By God, I'll have you for slander,' shouted Frensic. 'Galbanum had the gall to say that in court where he's protected but if you repeat that in public I'll institute proceedings myself.'

'You'd have a hard time,' said the editor. 'Jamesforth wouldn't make a good witness. He swears you advised him to jack Mrs Humberson up sexwise and when he wouldn't you altered the proofs.'

'That's a downright lie,' yelled Frensic. 'Anyone would think I wrote my authors' novels for them!'

'As a matter of fact a great many people do believe just that,' said the editor. Frensic hurled imprecations and went home with a headache.

If Wednesday was bad, Thursday was no better. Collins rejected William Lonroy's fifth novel *Seventh Heaven* as being too explicit sexually. Triad Press turned down Mary Gold's *Final Fling* for the opposite reason and Cassells even refused *Sammy The Squirrel* on the grounds that it was preoccupied with individual acquisition and lacked community concern. Cape rejected this, Secker rejected that. There were no acceptances. Finally there was a moment of high drama when an elderly clergyman whose autobiography Frensic had repeatedly refused to handle, explaining each time there wasn't a large reading public for a book that dealt exclusively with parish life in South Croydon, smashed a vase with his umbrella and only consented to leave with his manuscript when Sonia threatened to call the police. By lunchtime Frensic was bordering on hysteria.

'I can't stand it,' he whimpered. The phone rang and Frensic shied. 'If it's for me, tell them I'm not in. I'm having a breakdown. Tell them –'

It was for him. Sonia put her hand over the mouthpiece.

'It's Margot Joseph. She says she's dried up and doesn't think she can finish –'

Frensic fled to the safety of his own office and took his phone off the hook.

'For the rest of the day I'm not in,' he told Sonia when she came through a few minutes later. 'I shall sit here and think.'

'In that case you can read this,' said Sonia and put a parcel on his desk. 'It came this morning. I haven't had time to open it.'

'It's probably a bomb,' said Frensic gloomily and undid the string. But the package contained nothing more threatening than a neatly typed manuscript and an envelope addressed to Mr F. A. Frensic. Frensic glanced at the manuscript and noted with satisfaction that its pages were pristine and its corners unthumbed, a healthy sign which indicated that he was the first recipient and that it hadn't gone the rounds of other agents. Then he looked at the title-page. It said simply PAUSE O MEN FOR THE VIRGIN, A Novel. There was no author's name and no return address. Odd. Frensic opened the envelope and read the letter inside. It was brief and impersonal and mystifying.

Cadwalladine & Dimkins
Solicitors
596 St Andrew's Street
Oxford

> *Dear Sir,*
> *All communications concerning the possible sale, publication and copyright of the*

enclosed manuscript should be addressed to this office marked for the Personal Attention of P. Cadwalladine. The author, who wishes to remain strictly anonymous, leaves the matter of terms of sale and choice of a suitable nom de plume *and related matters entirely in your hands.*
Yours faithfully,
Percy Cadwalladine.

Frensic read the letter through several times before turning his attention to the manuscript. It was a very odd letter. An author who wished to remain strictly anonymous? Left everything concerning sale and choice of *nom de plume* and related matters entirely in his hands? Considering that all the authors he had ever dealt with were notoriously egotistical and interfering there was a lot to be said for one who was so self-effacing. Positively endearing, in fact. With the silent wish that Mr Jamesforth had left everything in his hands Frensic turned the title page of *Pause O Men for the Virgin* and began to read.

He was still reading an hour later, his snuff box open on the desk and his waistcoat and the creases of his trousers powdered with snuff. Frensic reached unthinkingly for the box and took another large pinch and wiped his nose with his third handkerchief. In the next office the phone rang. People climbed the stairs and knocked on Sonia's door. Traffic rumbled outside in the street. Frensic was oblivious to these extraneous sounds. He turned another page and read on.

It was half past six when Sonia Futtle finished for the day and prepared to leave. The door of Frensic's office was shut and she hadn't heard him go. She opened it and peered inside. Frensic was sitting at his desk staring fixedly through the window over the dark roofs of Covent Garden with a slight smile on his face. It was an attitude she recognized, the posture of triumphant discovery.

'I don't believe it,' she said standing in the doorway.

'Read it,' said Frensic. 'Don't believe me. Read it for yourself.' His hand flicked dismissively towards the manuscript.

'A good one?'

'A bestseller.'

'Are you sure?'

'Positive.'

'And of course it's a novel?'

'One hopes so,' said Frensic, 'fervently.'

'A dirty book,' said Sonia, who recognized the symptoms.

'Dirty,' said Frensic, 'is hardly adequate. The mind that penned – if

minds can pen – this odyssey of lust is of a prurience indescribable.' He got
up and handed her the manuscript.

'I will value your opinion,' he said with the air of a man who had regained
his authority.

But if it was a jaunty Frensic who went home to his flat in Hampstead that
night, it was a wary one who came back next morning and wrote a note on
Sonia's scratch pad. 'Will discuss the novel with you over lunch. Not to be
disturbed.' He went into his office and shut the door.

For the rest of the morning there was little to indicate that Frensic had
anything more important on his mind than a vague interest in the antics of
the pigeons on the roof opposite. He sat at his desk staring out of the window,
occasionally reaching for the phone or jotting something on a piece of paper.
For the most part he just sat. But external appearances were misleading.
Frensic's mind was on the move, journeying across the internal landscape
which he knew so well and in which each publishing house in London was
a halt for bargaining, a crossroads where commercial advantages were
exchanged, favours given and little debts repaid. And Frensic's route was
a devious one. It was not enough to sell a book. Any fool could do that,
given the right book. The important thing was to place it in precisely the
right spot so that the consequences of its sale would have maximum
effect and ramify out to advance his reputation and promote some future
advantage. And not his alone but that of his authors. Time entered into
these calculations, time and his intuitive assessment of books that had yet
to be written, books by established authors which he knew would be
unsuccessful and books by new writers whose success would be jeopardized
by their lack of reputation. Frensic juggled with intangibles. It was his
profession and he was good at it.

Sometimes he sold books for small advances to small firms when the very
same book offered to one of the big publishing houses would have earned
its author a large advance. On these occasions the present was sacrificed to
the future in the knowledge that help given now would be repaid by the
publications of some novel that would never sell more than five hundred
copies but which Frensic, for reasons of his own, wished to see in print. Only
Frensic knew his own intentions, just as only Frensic knew the identities of
those well-reputed novelists who actually earned their living by writing
detective stories or soft porn under pseudonyms. It was all a mystery and
even Frensic, whose head was filled with abstruse equations involving
personalities and tastes, who bought what and why, and all the details of
the debts he owed or was owed, knew that he was not privy to every corner
of the mystery. There was always luck and of late Frensic's luck had changed.

When that happened it paid to walk warily. This morning Frensic walked very warily indeed.

He phoned several friends in the legal profession and assured himself that Cadwalladine & Dimkins, Solicitors, were an old, well-established and highly reputable firm who handled work of the most respectable kind. Only then did he phone Oxford and ask to speak to Mr Cadwalladine about the novel he had sent him. Mr Cadwalladine sounded old-fashioned. No, he was sorry to say, Mr Frensic could not meet the author. His instructions were that absolute anonymity was essential and all matters would have to be referred to Mr Cadwalladine personally. Of course the book was pure fiction. Yes, Mr Frensic could include an extra clause in any contract exonerating the publishers from the financial consequences of a libel action. In any case he had always assumed such a clause to be part of contracts between publishers and authors. Frensic said they were but that he had to be absolutely certain when dealing with an anonymous author. Mr Cadwalladine said he quite understood.

Frensic put the phone down with a new feeling of confidence, and returned less warily to his interior landscape where imaginary negotiations took place. There he retraced his route, stopped at several eminent publishing houses for consideration, and travelled on. What *Pause O Men for the Virgin* needed was a publisher with an excellent reputation to give it the imprimatur of respectability. Frensic narrowed them down and finally made up his mind. It would be a gamble but it would be a gamble that was worth taking. He would have to have Sonia Futtle's opinion first.

She gave it to him over lunch in a little Italian restaurant where Frensic entertained his less important authors.

'A weird book,' she said.

'Quite,' said Frensic.

'But it's got something. Compassionate,' said Sonia, warming to her task.

'I agree.'

'Deeply insightful.'

'Definitely.'

'Good story line.'

'Excellent.'

'Significant,' said Sonia.

Frensic sighed. It was the word he had been waiting for. 'You really think that?'

'I do. I mean it. I think it's really got something. It's good. I really do.'

'Well,' said Frensic doubtfully, 'I may be an anachronism but . . .'

'You're role-playing again. Be serious.'

'My dear,' said Frensic, 'I am being serious. If you say that stuff is significant I am delighted. It's what I thought you'd say. It means it will appeal to those intellectual flagellants who can't enjoy a book unless it hurts. That I happen to know that, from a genuinely literary standpoint, it is an abomination is perhaps beside the point but I am entitled to protect my instincts.'

'Instincts? No man had fewer.'

'Literary instincts,' said Frensic. 'And they tell me that this is a bad, pretentious book and that it will sell. It combines a filthy story with an even filthier style.'

'I didn't see anything wrong with the style,' said Sonia.

'Of course you didn't. You're an American and Americans aren't burdened by our classical inheritance. You can't see that there is a world of difference between Dreiser and Mencken or Tom Wolfe and Bellow. That's your prerogative. I find such lack of discrimination invaluable and most reassuring. If you accept sentences endlessly convoluted, spattered with commas and tied into knots with parentheses, unrelated verbs and qualifications of qualifications, and which, to parody, have, if they are to be at all comprehended, to be read at least four times with the aid of a dictionary, who am I to quarrel with you? Your fellow-countrymen, whose rage for self-improvement I have never appreciated, are going to love this book.'

'They may not go such a ball on the story line. I mean it's been done before you know. *Harold and Maude*.'

'But never in such exquisitively nauseating detail,' said Frensic and sipped his wine. 'And not with Lawrentian overtones. Besides that's our trump. Seventeen loves eighty. The liberation of the senile. What could be more significant than that? By the way when is Hutchmeyer due in London?'

'Hutchmeyer? You've got to be kidding,' said Sonia. Frensic held up a piece of ravioli in protest.

'Don't use that expression. I am not a goat.'

'And Hutchmeyer's not the Olympia Press. He's strictly middle-brow. He wouldn't touch this book.'

'He would if we baited the trap right,' said Frensic.

'Trap?' said Sonia suspiciously. 'What trap?'

'I was thinking of a very distinguished London publisher to take the book first,' said Frensic, 'and then you sell the American rights to Hutchmeyer.'

'Who?'

'Corkadales,' said Frensic.

Sonia shook her head. 'Corkadales are far too old and stodgy.'

'Precisely,' said Frensic. 'They are prestigious. They are also broke.'

'They should have dropped half their list years ago,' said Sonia.

'They should have dropped Sir Clarence years ago. You read his obituary?' But Sonia hadn't.

'Most entertaining. And instructive. Tributes galore to his services to Literature, by which they meant he had subsidized more unread poets and novelists than any other publisher in London. The result: they are now broke.'

'In which case they can hardly afford to buy *Pause O Men for the Virgin.*'

'They can hardly afford not to,' said Frensic. 'I had a word with Geoffrey Corkadale at the funeral. He is not following in his father's footsteps. Corkadales are about to emerge from the eighteenth century. Geoffrey is looking for a bestseller. Corkadales will take *Pause* and we will take Hutchmeyer.'

'You think Hutchmeyer is going to be impressed?' said Sonia. 'What the hell have Corkadales got to offer?'

'Distinction,' said Frensic, 'a most distinguished past. The mantelpiece against which Shelley leant, the chair Mrs Gaskell was pregnant in, the carpet Tennyson was sick on. The incunabula of, if not *The Great Tradition*, at least a very important strand of literary history. By accepting this novel for free Corkadales will confer cultural sanctity on it.'

'And you think the author will be satisfied with that? You don't think he'll want money too?'

'He'll get the money from Hutchmeyer. We're going to sting Mr Hutchmeyer for a fortune. Anyhow, this author is unique.'

'I got that from the book,' said Sonia. 'How else is he unique?'

'He doesn't have a name, for one thing,' said Frensic and explained his instructions from Mr Cadwalladine. 'Which leaves us with an entirely free hand,' he said when he finished.

'And the little matter of a pseudonym,' said Sonia. 'I suppose we could kill two birds with one stone and say it was by Peter Piper. That way he'd see his name on the cover of a novel.'

'True,' said Frensic sadly, 'I'm afraid poor Piper is never going to make it any other way.'

'Besides, it would save the expense of his annual lunch and you wouldn't have to go through yet another version of his *Search for a Lost Childhood.* By the way, who is the model this year?'

'Thomas Mann,' said Frensic. 'One dreads the thought of sentences two pages long. You really think it would put an end to his illusions of literary grandeur?'

'Who knows?' said Sonia. 'The very fact of seeing his name on the cover of a novel and being taken for the author ...'

'It's the only way he's ever going to get into print, I'll stake my reputation on that,' said Frensic.

'So we'll be doing him a favour.'

That afternoon Frensic took the manuscript to Corkadales. On the front under the title Sonia had added 'by Peter Piper'. Frensic spoke long and persuasively to Geoffrey Corkadale and left the office that night well pleased with himself.

A week later the editorial board of Corkadales considered *Pause O Men for the Virgin* in the presence of that past upon which the vestige of their reputation depended. Portraits of dead authors lined the panelled walls of the editorial room. Shelley was not there, nor Mrs Gaskell, but there were lesser notables to take their place. Ranged in glass-covered bookshelves there were first editions, and in some exhibition cases relics of the trade. Quills, Waverley pens, pocket-knives, an inkbottle Trollope was said to have left in a train, a sandbox used by Southey, and even a scrap of blotting paper which, held up to a mirror, revealed that Henry James had once inexplicably written 'darling'.

In the centre of this museum the Literary Director, Mr Wilberforce, and the Senior Editor, Mr Tate, sat at an oval walnut table observing the weekly rite. They sipped Madeira and nibbled seedcake and looked disapprovingly at the manuscript before them and then at Geoffrey Corkadale. It was difficult to tell which they disliked most. Certainly Geoffrey's suede suit and floral shirt did not fit the atmosphere. Sir Clarence would not have approved. Mr Wilberforce helped himself to some more Madeira and shook his head.

'I cannot agree,' he said. 'I find it wholly incomprehensible that we should even consider lending our name, our great name, to the publication of this ... thing.'

'You didn't like the book?' said Geoffrey.

'Like it? I could hardly bring myself to finish it.'

'Well, we can't hope to please everyone.'

'But we've never touched a book like this before. We have our reputation to consider.'

'Not to mention our overdraft,' said Geoffrey. 'And to be brutally frank, we have to choose between our reputation and bankruptcy.'

'But does it have to be this awful book?' said Mr Tate. 'I mean have you read it?'

Geoffrey nodded. 'As a matter of fact I have. I know that my father didn't make a habit of reading anything later than Meredith but ...'

'Your poor father,' said Mr Wilberforce with feeling, 'must be turning in his grave at the very thought –'

'Where, with any luck, he will shortly be joined by the so-called heroine of this disgusting novel,' said Mr Tate.

Geoffrey rearranged a stray lock of hair. 'Considering that papa was cremated I shouldn't have thought that this turning of her joining him would be very easy,' he murmured. Mr Wilberforce and Mr Tate looked grim. Geoffrey adjusted his smile. 'Your objection then I take it is based on the fact that the romance in this novel is between a seventeen-year-old boy and an eighty-year-old woman?' he said.

'Yes,' said Mr Wilberforce more loudly than was his wont, 'it is. Though how you can bring yourself to use the word "romance" ...'

'The relationship then. The term doesn't matter.'

'It's not the term I'm worried about,' said Mr Tate. 'It's not even the relationship. If it simply stuck to that it wouldn't be so bad. It's the bits in between that get me. I had no idea ... oh well never mind. The whole thing is so awful.'

'It's the bits in between,' said Geoffrey, 'that will sell the book.'

Mr Wilberforce shook his head. 'Personally I'm inclined to think we would run the risk, the gravest risk of being prosecuted for obscenity,' he said, 'and in my view quite rightly.'

'I agree,' said Mr Tate. 'I mean, take the episode where they use the rocking horse and the douche –'

'For God's sake,' squawked Mr Wilberforce. 'It was bad enough having to read it. Do we have to hold a post-mortem?'

'The term is applicable,' said Mr Tate. 'Even the title ...'

'All right,' said Geoffrey, 'I grant you that it's a bit tasteless but –'

'Tasteless? What about the part where he –'

'Don't, Tate, don't, there's a good fellow,' said Mr Wilberforce feebly.

'As I was saying,' continued Geoffrey, 'I'm prepared to admit that that sort of thing isn't everyone's cup of tea ... oh for goodness sake, Wilberforce ... well anyway I can think of half a dozen books like it ...'

'I can't, thank God,' said Mr Tate.

'... which in their time were considered objectionable but –'

'Name me one,' shouted Mr Wilberforce. 'Just name me one to equal this!' His hand shook at the manuscript.

'*Lady Chatterley*,' said Geoffrey.

'Pah,' said Mr Tate. 'By comparison *Chatterley* was pure as the driven snow.'

'Anyway *Chatterley*'s banned,' said Mr Wilberforce.

Geoffrey Corkadale heaved a sigh. 'Oh God,' he muttered, 'someone tell him that the Georgians aren't around any longer.'

'More's the pity,' said Mr Tate. 'We did rather well with some of them. The rot set in with *The Well of Loneliness*.'

'And there's another filthy book,' said Mr Wilberforce, 'but we didn't publish it.'

'The rot set in,' Geoffrey interrupted, 'when Uncle Cuthbert took it into his woolly head to pulp Wilkie's *Ballroom Dancing Made Perfect* and published Fashoda's *Guide to the Edible Fungi* in its place.'

'Fashoda was a bad choice,' Mr Tate agreed. 'I remember the coroner was most uncomplimentary.'

'Let's get back to our present position,' said Geoffrey, 'which from a financial point of view is just as deadly. Now Frensic has offered us this novel and in my view we ought to accept it.'

'We've never had dealings with Frensic before,' said Mr Tate. 'They tell me he drives a hard bargain. How much is he demanding this time?'

'A purely nominal sum.'

'A nominal sum? Frensic? That doesn't sound like him. He usually asks the earth. There must be a snag.'

'The damned book's the snag. Any fool can see that,' said Mr Wilberforce.

'Frensic has wider views,' said Geoffrey. 'He foresees a Transatlantic purchase.'

There was an audible sigh from the two old men.

'Ah,' said Mr Tate, 'an American sale. That could make a considerable difference.'

'Exactly,' said Geoffrey, 'and Frensic is convinced that the book has merits the Americans might well appreciate. After all it's not all sex and there are passages with Lawrentian overtones, not to mention references to many important literary figures. The Bloomsbury Group for instance, Virginia Woolf and Middleton Murry. And then there's the philosophy.'

Mr Tate nodded. 'True. True,' he said. 'It's the sort of pot of message Americans might fall for but I don't see what good that is going to do us.'

'Ten per cent of the American royalties,' said Geoffrey. 'That's what good it's going to do us.'

'The author agrees to this?'

'Mr Frensic seems to think so and if the book makes the bestseller lists in the States it will consequently sell wildly over here.'

'If,' said Mr Tate. 'A very big if. Who has he in mind as the American publisher?'

'Hutchmeyer.'

'Ah,' said Mr Tate, 'one begins to see his drift.'

'Hutchmeyer,' said Mr Wilberforce, 'is a rogue and a thief.'

'He is also one of the most successful promoters in American publishing,' said Geoffrey. 'If he decides to buy a book it will sell. And he pays enormous advances.'

Mr Tate nodded. 'I must say I have never understood the working of the American market but it's true they often pay enormous advances and Hutchmeyer is flamboyant. Frensic could well be right. It's a chance I suppose.'

'Our only chance,' said Geoffrey. 'The alternative is to put the firm up for auction.'

Mr Wilberforce poured some more Madeira. 'It seems a terrible come-down,' he said. 'To think that we should have sunk to this . . . this pseudo-intellectual pornography.'

'If it keeps us financially solvent . . .' said Mr Tate. 'Who is this man Piper anyway?'

'A pervert,' said Mr Wilberforce firmly.

'Frensic tells me he's a young man who has been writing for some time,' said Geoffrey. 'This is his first novel.'

'And hopefully his last,' said Mr Wilberforce. 'Still I suppose it could have been worse. Who was that dreadful creature who had herself castrated and then wrote a book advertising the fact?'

'I should have thought that was an impossibility,' said Geoffrey. 'Castrated herself. Now himself I –'

'You're probably thinking of *In Cold Blood* by someone called McCullers,' said Mr Tate. 'Never did read the book myself but people tell me it was foul.'

'Then we are all agreed,' said Geoffrey to change the subject from one so close to the bone. Mr Tate and Mr Wilberforce nodded sadly.

Frensic greeted their decision without overt enthusiasm.

'We can't be sure of Hutchmeyer yet,' he told Geoffrey over lunch at Wheelers. 'There must be no leaks to the press. If this gets out Hutchmeyer won't bite. I suggest we simply refer to it as *Pause*.'

'It's appropriate,' said Geoffrey. 'It will take at least three months to get the proofs done.'

'That will give us time to work on Hutchmeyer.'

'And you really think there's a chance he will buy?'

'Every chance,' said Frensic. 'Miss Futtle exercises enormous charms for him.'

'Extraordinary,' said Geoffrey with a shudder. 'Still, having read *Pause* there's obviously no accounting for tastes.'

'Sonia is also an excellent saleswoman,' said Frensic. 'She makes a point of asking for very large advances and that always impresses Americans. It shows we have faith in the book.'

'And this fellow Piper agrees to our ten per cent cut?'

Frensic nodded. He had spoken to Mr Cadwalladine. 'The author has left all the terms of the negotiations and sale entirely in my hands,' he said truthfully. And there the matter rested until Hutchmeyer flew into London with his entourage in the first week of February.

CHAPTER THREE

It was said of Hutchmeyer that he was the most illiterate publisher in the world and that having started life as a fight promoter he had brought his pugilistic gifts to the book trade and had once gone eight rounds with Mailer. It was also said that he never read the books he bought and that the only words he could read were those on cheques and dollar bills. It was said that he owned half the Amazon forest and that when he looked at a tree all he could see was a dustjacket. A great many things were said about Hutchmeyer, most of them unpleasant, and, while each contained an element of truth, added together they amounted to so many inconsistencies that behind them Hutchmeyer could guard the secret of his success. That at least no one doubted. Hutchmeyer was immensely successful. A legend in his own lifetime, he haunted the insomniac thoughts of publishers who had turned down *Love Story* when it was going for a song, had spurned Frederick Forsyth and ignored Ian Fleming and now lay awake cursing their own stupidity. Hutchmeyer himself slept soundly. For a sick man, remarkably soundly. And Hutchmeyer was always sick. If Frensic's success lay in outeating and outdrinking his competitors, Hutchmeyer's was due to his hypochondria. When he hadn't an ulcer or gallstones, he was subject to some intestinal complaint that necessitated a régime of abstinence. Publishers and agents coming to his table found themselves obliged to plough their way through six courses, each richer and more alarmingly indigestible than the last, while Hutchmeyer toyed with a piece of boiled fish, a biscuit and a glass of mineral water. From these culinary encounters Hutchmeyer rose a thinner and richer man while his guests staggered home wondering what the hell had hit them. Nor were they allowed time to recover. Hutchmeyer's peripatetic schedule – London today, New York tomorrow, Los Angeles the day after – had a dual purpose. It provided him with an excuse to insist on speed and avoided prolonged negotiations, and it kept his sales staff on their toes. More than one contract had been signed by an author in the throes of so awful a hangover that he could hardly put pen to paper, let alone read the small print. And the small print in Hutchmeyer's contracts was exceedingly small. Understandably so, since it contained clauses that invalidated almost everything set out in bold type. To add to the hazards of doing business with Hutchmeyer, most of them legal, there was his manner. Hutchmeyer was gross, partly by nature and partly as a reaction to the literary aestheticism he was exposed to. It was one of the qualities he appreciated about Sonia Futtle. No one had ever called her aesthetic.

'You're like a daughter to me,' he said hugging her when she arrived at his suite in the Hilton. 'What's my baby got for me this time?'

'One humdinger,' said Sonia disengaging herself and climbing on to the bicycle exerciser that accompanied Hutchmeyer everywhere. Hutchmeyer selected the lowest chair in the room.

'You don't say. A novel?'

Sonia cycled busily and nodded.

'What's it called?' asked Hutchmeyer for whom first things came first.

'*Pause O Men for the Virgin.*'

'*Pause O Men for the* what?'

'*Virgin,*' said Sonia and cycled more vigorously than ever.

Hutchmeyer glimpsed a thigh. 'Virgin? You mean you've got a religious novel that's hot?'

'Hot as Hades.'

'Sounds good, a time like this. It fits with the Jesus freaks and Superstar and Zen and how to mend automobiles. And it's women's year so we got The Virgin.'

Sonia stopped peddling. 'Now don't get carried away, Hutch. It's not that kind of virgin.'

'It's not?'

'No way.'

'So there's different kinds of virgin. Sounds interesting. Tell me.' And Sonia Futtle, seated on the bicycle machine, told him while her legs moved up and down with a delicious lethargy that lulled his critical faculties. Hutchmeyer made only token resistance. 'Forget it,' he said when she had finished. 'You can deepsix that crap. Eighty years old and still fucking. That I don't need.'

Sonia climbed off the exerciser and stood in front of him. 'Don't be a dumbcluck, Hutch. Now you listen to me. You're not going to throw this one out. Over my dead body. This book's got class.'

Hutchmeyer smiled happily. This was Fuller Brush talking. The sales pitch. No soft sell. 'Convince me.'

'Right,' said Sonia. 'Who reads? Don't answer. I'll tell you. The kids. Fifteen to twenty-one. They read. They got the time. They got the education. Literary rate peak is sixteen to twenty. Right?'

'Right,' said Hutchmeyer.

'Right, so we've got a seventeen-year-old boy in the book with an identity crisis.'

'Identity crisises is out. That stuff went the way of all Freud.'

'Sure, but this is different. This boy isn't sick or something.'

'You kidding? Fucking his own grandmother isn't sick?'

'She isn't his grandmother. She's a woman a –'

'Listen baby, I'll tell you something. She's eighty, she's no goddam woman no more. I should know. My wife, Baby, is fifty-eight and she's drybones. What the beauty surgeons have left of her. That woman has had more taken out of her than you'd believe possible. She's got silicon boobs and degreased thighs. She's had four new maidenheads to my knowledge and her face lifted so often I've lost count.'

'And why?' said Sonia. 'Because she wants to stay all woman.'

'All woman she ain't. More spare parts than woman.'

'But she reads. Am I right?'

'Reads? She reads more books than I sell in a month.'

'And that's my point. The young read and the old read. You can kiss the in-betweens goodbye.'

'You tell Baby she's old and you can kiss yourself goodbye. She have your fanny for a dishcloth. I mean it.'

'What I'm saying is that you've got literacy peak sixteen to twenty, then a gap and another LP sixty on out. Tell me I'm lying.'

Hutchmeyer shrugged. 'So you're right.'

'And what's this book about?' said Sonia. 'It's –'

'Some crazy kid shacked up with Grandma Moses. It's been done some place else. Tell me something new. Besides, it's dirty.'

'You're wrong, Hutch, you're so wrong. It's a love story, no shit. They mean something to one another. He needs her and she needs him.'

'Me, I need neither of them.'

'They give one another what they lack alone. He gets maturity, experience, wisdom, the fruit of a lifetime ...'

'Fruit? Fruit? Jesus, you want me to throw up or something?'

'... and she gets youth, vitality, life,' Sonia continued. 'It's great. I mean it. A deep, meaningful book. It's liberationist. It's existentialist. It's ... Remember what *The French Lieutenant's Woman* did? Swept America. And *Pause* is what America's been waiting for. Seventeen loves eighty. Loves, Hutch, L.O.V.E.S. So every senior citizen is going to buy it to find out what they've been missing and the students will go for the philosophomore message. Pitch it right and we can scoop the pool. We get the culture buffs with significance, the weirdos with the porn and the marshmallows with romance. This is the book for the whole family. It could sell by the –'

Hutchmeyer got up and paced the room. 'You know, I think maybe you've got something there,' he said. 'I ask myself "Would Baby buy this story?" and I have to say yes. And what that woman falls for the whole world buys. What price?'

'Two million dollars.'

'Two million . . . You've got to be kidding.' Hutchmeyer gaped.

Sonia climbed back on to the bicycle machine. 'Two million. I kid you not.'

'Go jump, baby, go jump. Two million? For a novel? No way.'

'Two million or I go flash my gams at Milenberg.'

'That cheapskate? He couldn't raise two million. You can hawk your pussy all the way to Avenue of the Americas it won't do you no good.'

'American rights, paperback, film, TV, serialization, book clubs . . .'

Hutchmeyer yawned. 'Tell me something new. They're mine already.'

'Not on this book they're not.'

'So Milenberg buys. You get no price and I buy him. What's in it for me?'

'Fame,' said Sonia simply. 'Just fame. With this book you're up there with the all-time greats. *Gone With The Wind*, *Forever Amber*, *Valley of The Dolls*, *Dr Zhivago*, *Airport*, *The Carpetbaggers*. You'd make the *Reader's Digest Almanac*.'

'The *Reader's Digest Almanac*?' said Hutchmeyer in an awed voice. 'You really think I could make that?'

'Think? I know. This is a prestige book about life's potentialities. No kitsch. Message like Mary Baker Eddy. A symphony of words. Look who's bought it in London. No fly-by-night firm.'

'Who?' said Hutchmeyer suspiciously.

'Corkadales.'

'Corkadales bought it? The oldest publishing –'

'Not the oldest. Murrays are older,' said Sonia.

'So, old. How much?'

'Fifty thousand pounds,' said Sonia glibly.

Hutchmeyer stared at her. 'Corkadales paid fifty thousand pounds for this book? Fifty grand?'

'Fifty grand. First time off. No hassle.'

'I heard they were in trouble,' said Hutchmeyer. 'Some Arab bought them?'

'No Arab. It's a family firm. So Geoffrey Corkadale paid fifty grand. He knows this book is going to get them out of hock. You think they'd risk that sort of money if they were going to fold?'

'Shit,' said Hutchmeyer, 'somebody's got to have faith in this fucking book . . . but two million! No one's ever paid two million for a novel. Robbins a million but . . .'

'That's the whole point, Hutch. You think I ask two million for nothing? Am I so dumb? It's the two million makes the book. You pay two million and people know, they've got to read the book to find out what you paid for. *You* know that. You're in a class on your own. Way out in front. And then with the film . . .'

'I'd want a cut of the film. No single-figure percentage. Fifty-fifty.'

'Done,' said Sonia. 'You've got yourself a deal. Fifty-fifty on the film it is.'

'The author . . . this Piper guy, I'd want him too,' said Hutchmeyer.

'Want him?' said Sonia, sobering. 'Want him for what?'

'To market the product. He's going to be out there up front where the public can see him. The guy who fucks the geriatrics. Public appearances across the States, signings, TV talk shows, interviews, the whole razzamat-taz. We'll build him up like he's a genius.'

'I don't think he's going to like that,' said Sonia nervously, 'he's shy and reserved.'

'Shy? He washes his jock in public and he's shy?' said Hutchmeyer. 'For two million he'll chew asses if I tell him.'

'I doubt if he'd agree –'

'Agree he will or there's no deal,' said Hutchmeyer. 'I'm throwing my weight behind his book, he has to too. That's final.'

'OK, if that's the way you want it,' said Sonia.

'That's the way I want it,' said Hutchmeyer. 'Like the way I want you . . .'

Sonia made her escape and hurried back to Lanyard Lane with the contract.

She found Frensic looking decidedly edgy. 'Home and dry,' she said, dancing heavily round the room.

'Marvellous,' said Frensic. 'You are brilliant.'

Sonia stopped cavorting. 'With a proviso.'

'Proviso? What proviso?'

'First the good news. He loves the book. He's just wild about it.'

Frensic regarded her cautiously. 'Isn't he being a bit premature? He hasn't had a chance to read the bloody thing yet.'

'I told him about it . . . a synopsis and he loved it. He sees it as filling a much-needed gap.'

'A much-needed gap?'

'The generation gap. He feels –'

'Spare me his feelings,' said Frensic. 'A man who can talk about filling much-needed gaps is deficient in ordinary human emotions.'

'He thinks *Pause* will do for youth and age what *Lolita* did for . . .'

'Parental responsibility?' suggested Frensic.

'For the middle-aged man,' said Sonia.

'For God's sake, if this is the good news can leprosy be far behind.'

Sonia sank into a chair and smiled. 'Wait till you hear the price.'

Frensic waited. 'Well?'

'Two million.'

'Two million?' said Frensic trying to keep the quaver out of his voice. 'Pounds or dollars?'

Sonia looked at him reproachfully. 'Frenzy, you are a bastard, an ungrateful bastard. I pull off –'

'My dear, I was merely trying to ascertain the likely extent of the horrors you are about to reveal to me. You spoke of a proviso. Now if your friend from the Mafia had been prepared to pay two million pounds for this verbal hogwash I would have known the time had come to pack up and leave town. What does the swine want?'

'One, he wants to see the Corkadales contract.'

'That's all right. There's nothing wrong with it.'

'Just that it doesn't mention the sum of fifty thousand pounds Corkadales have paid for *Pause*,' said Sonia. 'Otherwise it's just dandy.'

Frensic gaped at her. 'Fifty thousand pounds? They didn't pay –'

'Hutchmeyer needed impressing so I said . . .'

'He needs his head read. Corkadales haven't fifty thousand pennies to rub together, let alone pounds.'

'Right. Which he knew. So I told him Geoffrey had staked his personal fortune. Now you know why he wants to see the contract?'

Frensic rubbed his forehead and thought. 'I suppose we could always draw up a new contract and get Geoffrey to sign it *pro tem* and tear it up when Hutchmeyer's seen it,' he said at last. 'Geoffrey won't like it but with his cut of two million . . . What's the next problem?'

Sonia hesitated. 'This one you won't like. He insists, but insists, that the author goes to the States for a promotional tour. Senior-citizens-I-have-loved sort of stuff on TV and signings.'

Frensic took out his handkerchief and wiped his face. 'Insists?' he spluttered. 'He can't insist. We've got an author who won't even sign his name to a contract, let alone appear in public, some madman with agoraphobia or its equivalent and Hutchmeyer wants him to parade round America appearing on TV?'

'Insists, Frenzy, insists. Not wants. Either the author goes or the deal is off.'

'Then it's off,' said Frensic. 'The man won't go. You heard what Cadwalladine said. Total anonymity.'

'Not even for two million?'

Frensic shook his head. 'I told Cadwalladine we were going to ask for a large sum and he said money didn't count.'

'But two million isn't money. It's a fortune.'

'I know it is, but . . .'

'Try Cadwalladine again,' said Sonia and handed him the phone. Frensic tried again. At length. Mr Cadwalladine was emphatic. Two million dollars was a fortune but his instructions were that his client's anonymity meant more to him than mere . . .

It was a dispiriting conversation for Frensic.

'What did I tell you,' he said when he had finished. 'We're dealing with some sort of lunatic. Two lunatics. Hutchmeyer being the other.'

'So we're just going to sit back and watch twenty per cent of two million dollars disappear down the plughole and do nothing about it?' said Sonia. Frensic stared miserably across the roofs of Covent Garden and sighed. Twenty per cent of two million came to four hundred thousand dollars, over two hundred thousand pounds. That would have been their commission on the sale. And thanks to James Jamesforth's libel action they had just lost two more valuable authors.

'There must be some way of fixing this,' he muttered. 'Hutchmeyer doesn't know who the author is any more than we do.'

'He does too,' said Sonia. 'It's Peter Piper. His name's on the title-page.'

Frensic looked at her with new appreciation. 'Peter Piper,' he murmured, 'now there's a thought.'

They closed the office for the night and went down to the pub across the road for a drink.

'Now if there were some way we could persuade Piper to act as under-study . . .' said Frensic after a large whisky.

'And after all it would be one way of getting his name into print,' said Sonia. 'If the book sells . . .'

'Oh it will sell all right. With Hutchmeyer anything sells.'

'Well then, Piper would have got his foot in the publishing door and perhaps we could get someone to ghost *Search* for him.'

Frensic shook his head. 'He'd never stand for that. Piper has principles I'm afraid. On the other hand if Geoffrey could be persuaded to agree to publish *Search for a Lost Childhood* as part of the present contract ... I'm seeing him tonight. He's holding one of his little suppers. Yes I think we may be on to something. Piper would do almost anything to get into print and a trip to the States with all expenses paid ... I think we'll drink to that.'

'Anything is worth trying,' said Sonia. And that night before setting out for Corkadales Frensic returned to the office and drew up two new contracts. One by which Corkadales agreed to pay fifty thousand for *Pause O Men for the Virgin* and the second guaranteeing the publication of Mr Piper's subsequent novel, *Search for a Lost Childhood*. The advance on it was five hundred pounds.

'After all, it's worth the gamble,' said Frensic as he and Sonia locked the office again, 'and I'm prepared to put up five hundred of our money if Geoffrey won't play ball on the advance to Piper. The main thing is to get a copperbottomed guarantee that they will publish *Search*.'

'Geoffrey has ten per cent of two million at stake too,' said Sonia as they separated. 'I should have thought that would be a persuasive argument.'

'I shall do my level best,' said Frensic as he hailed a taxi.

Geoffrey Corkadale's little suppers were what Frensic in a bitchy moment had once called badinageries. One stood around with a drink, later with a plate of cold buffet, and spoke lightly and allusively of books, plays and personalities, few of which one had read, seen or known but which served to provide a catalyst for those epicene encounters which were the real purpose of Geoffrey's little suppers. On the whole Frensic tended to avoid them as frivolous and a little dangerous. They were too androgynous for comfort and besides he disliked running the risk of being discovered talking glibly on a subject he knew absolutely nothing about. He had done that too often as an undergraduate to relish the prospect of continuing it into later life. And the very fact that there were never any women of marriageable propensity, they were either too old or unidentifiable – Frensic had once made a pass at an eminent theatre critic with horrifying consequences – tended to put him off. He preferred parties where there was just the faintest chance that he would meet someone who would make him a wife and at Geoffrey's gatherings the expression was taken literally. And so Frensic usually avoided them and confined his sex life to occasional desultory affairs with women sufficiently in their prime not to resent his lack of passion or charm, and to passionate feelings for young women on tube trains, which feelings he was incapable of expressing between Hampstead and Leicester Square. But this evening he came with a purpose, only to find that the rooms were crowded. Frensic poured himself a drink and mingled in the hope of cornering Geoffrey. It took some time. Geoffrey's elevation to the head of Corkadales lent him an appeal he had previously lacked and Frensic found himself subjected to a scrutiny of his opinion of *The Prancing Nigger* by a poet from Tobago who confessed that he found Firbank both divine and offensive. Frensic said those were his feelings too but that Firbank had been remarkably seminal, and it was only after an hour and by the unintentional stratagem of locking himself in the bathroom that he managed to corner Geoffrey.

'My dear, you are too unkind,' said Geoffrey when Frensic, after hammering on the door, finally freed himself with the help of a jar of skin cleanser. 'You should know we never lock the boys' room. It's so unspontaneous. The chance encounter . . .'

'This isn't a chance encounter,' said Frensic, dragging Geoffrey in and shutting the door again. 'I want a word with you. It's important.'

'Just don't lock it again . . . oh my God! Sven is obsessively jealous. He goes absolutely berserk. It's his Viking blood.'

'Never mind that,' said Frensic, 'we've had Hutchmeyer's offer. It's substantial.'

'Oh God, business,' said Geoffrey, subsiding on to the lavatory seat. 'How substantial?'

'Two million dollars,' said Frensic.

Geoffrey clutched at the toilet roll for support. 'Two million dollars?' he said weakly. 'You really mean two *million* dollars? You're not pulling my leg?'

'Absolute fact,' said Frensic.

'But that's magnificent! How wonderful. You darling –'

Frensic pushed him roughly back on the seat. 'There's a snag. Two snags, to be precise.'

'Snags? Why must there always be snags? As if life wasn't complicated enough without snags.'

'We had to impress him with the amount you paid for the book,' said Frensic.

'But I hardly paid anything. In fact . . .'

'Exactly, but we have to tell him you paid fifty thousand pounds in advance and he wants to see the contract.'

'Fifty thousand pounds? My dear chap, we couldn't –'

'Quite,' said Frensic, 'you don't have to explain your financial situation to me. You're in . . . you've got a cash-flow problem.'

'To put it mildly,' said Geoffrey, twisting a strand of toilet paper between his fingers.

'Which Hutchmeyer is aware of, which is why he wants to see the contract.'

'But what good is that going to do. The contract says . . .'

'I have here,' said Frensic fishing in his pocket, 'another contract which will do some good and reassure Hutchmeyer. It says you agree to pay fifty thousand . . .'

'Hang on a moment,' said Geoffrey, getting to his feet, 'if you think I'm going to sign a contract that says I'm going to pay you fifty thousand quid you're labouring under a misapprehension. I may not be a financial wizard but I can see this one coming.'

'All right,' said Frensic huffily and folded the contract, 'if that's the way you feel about it bang goes the deal.'

'What deal? You've already signed the contract for us to publish the novel.'

'Not your deal. Hutchmeyer's. And with it goes your ten per cent of two million dollars. Now if you want . . .'

Geoffrey sat down again. 'You really mean it, don't you?' he said at last.

'Every word,' said Frensic.

'And you really promise that Hutchmeyer has agreed to pay this incredible sum?'

'My word,' said Frensic with as much dignity as the bathroom allowed, 'is my bond.'

Geoffrey looked at him sceptically. 'If what James Jamesforth says is . . . All right. I'm sorry. It's just that this has come as a terrible shock. What do you want me to do?'

'Just sign this contract and I'll write out a personal IOU for fifty thousand pounds. That ought to be a guarantee . . .'

They were interrupted by someone hammering on the door. 'Come out of there,' shouted a Scandinavian voice, 'I know what you're doing!'

'Oh Christ, Sven,' said Geoffrey and struggled with the lock. 'Calm yourself, dearest,' he called, 'we were just discussing business.'

Behind him Frensic prudently armed himself with a lavatory brush.

'Business,' yelled the Swede, 'I know your business . . .'

The door sprang open and Sven glared wild-eyed into the bathroom.

'What is he doing with that brush?'

'Now, Sven dear, do be reasonable,' said Geoffrey. But Sven hovered between tears and violence.

'How could you, Geoffrey, how could you?'

'He didn't,' said Frensic vehemently.

The Swede looked him up and down. 'And with such a horrid baggy little man too.'

It was Frensic's turn to look wild-eyed. 'Baggy I may be,' he shouted, 'but horrid I am not.'

There was a moment's scuffle and Geoffrey urged the sobbing Sven down the passage. Frensic put his weapon back in its holder and sat on the edge of the bath. By the time Geoffrey returned he had devised new tactics.

'Where were we?' asked Geoffrey.

'Your *petit ami* was calling me a horrid baggy little man,' said Frensic.

'My dear, I'm so sorry but really you can count yourself lucky. Last week he actually struck someone and all the poor man had come to do was mend the bidet.'

'Now about this contract. I'm prepared to make a further concession,' said Frensic. 'You can have Piper's second book, *Search for a Lost Childhood* for a thousand pounds advance . . .'

'His *next* novel? You mean he's working on another?'

'Almost finished it,' said Frensic, 'much better than *Pause*. Now you can have it for practically nothing just so long as you sign this contract for Hutchmeyer.'

'Oh all right,' said Geoffrey, 'I'll just have to trust you.'

'If you don't get it back within the week to tear up you can go to Hutchmeyer and tell him it's a fraud,' said Frensic. 'That's your guarantee.'

And so in the bathroom of Geoffrey Corkadale's house the two contracts were signed. Frensic staggered home exhausted and next morning Sonia showed Hutchmeyer the Corkadale contract. The deal was on.

CHAPTER FOUR

In the Gleneagle Guest House in Exforth Peter Piper's nib described neat black circles and loops on the forty-fifth page of his notebook. Next door Mrs Oakley's vacuum cleaner roared back and forth making it difficult for Piper to concentrate on this his eighth version of his autobiographical novel. The fact that his new attempt was modelled on *The Magic Mountain* did not help. Thomas Mann's tendency to build complex sentences and to elaborate his ironic perceptions with a multitude of exact details did not transfer at all easily to a description of family life in Finchley in 1953 but Piper persisted with the task. It was, he knew, the hallmark of genius to persist and he knew just as certainly that he had genius. Unrecognized genius to be sure but one day, thanks to his capacity for taking infinite pains, the world would acclaim it. And so, in spite of the vacuum cleaner and the cold wind blowing from the sea through the cracks in the window, he wrote.

Around him on the table were the tools of his trade. A notebook in which he put down ideas and phrases which might come in handy, a diary in which he recorded his deepest insights into the nature of existence and a list of each day's activities, a tray of fountain pens and a bottle of partially evaporated black ink. The latter was Piper's own invention. Since he was writing for posterity it was essential that what he wrote should last indefinitely and without fading. For a while he had imitated Kipling in the use of Indian ink but it tended to clog his pen and to dry before he could even write one word. The accidental discovery that a bottle of Waterman's Midnight Black left open in a dry room acquired a density surpassing Indian ink while still remaining sufficiently fluid to enable him to write an entire sentence without recourse to his handkerchief had led to his use of evaporated ink. It gleamed on the page with a patina that gave substance to his words, and to ensure that his work had infinite longevity he bought leatherbound ledgers, normally used by old-fashioned firms of accountants or solicitors, and ignoring their various vertical lines, wrote his novels in them. By the time he had filled a ledger it was in its own way a work of art. Piper's handwriting was small and extremely regular and flowed for page after page with hardly a break. Since there was very little conversation in any of his novels, and that only of the meaningful and significant kind requiring long sentences, there were very few pages with broken lines or unfilled spaces. And Piper kept his ledgers. One day, perhaps when he was dead, certainly when his genius was recognized, scholars would trace the course of his development through these encrusted pages. Posterity was not to be ignored.

On the other hand the vacuum cleaner next door and the various intrusions of landladies and cleaners had to be ignored. Piper refused to allow his mornings to be interrupted. It was then that he wrote. After lunch he took a walk along whatever promenade he happened to be living opposite at the time. After tea he wrote again and after supper he read, first what he had written during the day and second from the novel that was serving as his present model. Since he read rather more quickly than he wrote he knew *Hard Times*, *Nostromo*, *The Portrait of a Lady*, *Middlemarch* and *The Magic Mountain* almost off by heart. With *Sons and Lovers* he was word-perfect. By thus confining his reading to only the greatest masters of fiction he ensured that lesser novelists would not exercise a malign influence on his own work.

Besides these few masterpieces he drew inspiration from *The Moral Novel*. It lay on his bedside table and before turning out the light he would read a page or two and mull Miss Louth's adjurations over in his mind. She was particularly keen on 'the placing of characters within an emotional framework, a context as it were of mature and interrelated susceptibilities, which corresponds to the reality of the experience of the novelist in his own time and thus enhances the reality of his fictional creations'. Since Piper's own experience had been limited to eighteen years of family life in Finchley, the death of his parents in a car crash, and ten years of boarding-houses, he found it difficult in his work to provide a context of mature and interrelated susceptibilities. But he did his best and subjected the unsatisfactory marriage of the late Mr and Mrs Piper to the minutest examination in order to imbue them with the maturity and insightfulness Miss Louth demanded. They emerged from his emotional exhumation with feelings they had never felt and insights they had never had. In real life Mr Piper had been a competent plumber. In *Search* he was an insightful one with tuberculosis and a great number of startlingly ambiguous feelings towards his wife. Mrs Piper came out, if anything, rather worse. Modelled on Frau Chauchat out of Isabel Archer she was given to philosophical disquisitions, to slamming doors, to displaying bare shoulders and to private sexual feelings for her son and the man next door which would have horrified her. For her husband she had only contempt mixed with disgust. And finally there was Piper himself, a prodigy of fourteen burdened by a degree of self-knowledge and an insight into his parents' true feelings for one another that would, had he in fact possessed them, have made his presence in the house utterly unbearable. Fortunately for the sanity of the late Mr and Mrs Piper and for the safety of Piper himself, he had at fourteen been a singularly dull child and with none of the perceptions he subsequently claimed for himself. What few feelings he had were concentrated on the person of his English mistress at school, a Miss Pears, who, in an unguarded moment, had complimented little Peter on a short story he had in fact copied almost verbatim from an old copy of *Horizon* he had found in a school cupboard. From this early derived promise Piper had gained his literary ambitions – and from the fatigue of a tanker driver who, four years later, had fallen asleep at the wheel of his lorry, crossed a main road at sixty miles an hour and obliterated Mr and Mrs Piper who were doing thirty on their way to visit friends in Amersham, he had acquired the wherewithal to pursue them. At eighteen he had inherited the house in Finchley, a substantial sum from the insurance company, and his parents' savings. Piper had sold the house, had banked all his capital and, to provide himself with a pecuniary motive to write, had lived off the capital ever since. After ten years and several million unsold words he was practically penniless.

He was therefore delighted to receive a telegram from London which said

URGENT SEE YOU RE SALE OF NOVEL ETC ONE THOUSAND POUNDS ADVANCE
PLEASE PHONE IMMEDIATELY FRENSIC.

Piper phoned immediately and caught the midday train in a state of wild
anticipation. His moment of recognition had arrived at last.

In London Frensic and Sonia were also in a state of anticipation, less wild
and with sombre overtones.

'What happens if he refuses?' asked Sonia as Frensic paced his office.

'God alone knows,' said Frensic. 'You heard what Cadwalladine said,
"Do what you please but in no way involve my client." So it's Piper or bust.'

'At least I managed to squeeze another twenty-five thousand dollars out
of Hutchmeyer for the tour, plus expenses,' said Sonia. 'I should have
thought that was a sufficient inducement.'

Frensic had doubts. 'With anyone else,' he said, 'but Piper has principles.
For God's sake don't leave a copy of the proofs of *Pause* around where he
can see what he's supposed to have written.'

'He's bound to read the book sometime.'

'Yes, but I want him signed up for the tour first and with some of
Hutchmeyer's money in his pocket. He won't find it so easy to back out
then.'

'And you really think the Corkadales' offer to publish *Search For a Lost
Childhood* will grab him?'

'Our trump card,' said Frensic. 'What you've got to realize is that with
Piper we are treating a subspecies of lunacy known as *dementia novella* or
bibliomania. The symptoms are a wholly irrational urge to get into print.
Well, I'm getting Piper into print. I've even got him one thousand pounds
which is incredible considering the garbled rubbish he writes. He's being
paid twenty-five thousand dollars to make the tour. Now all we've got to
do is play our cards right and he'll go. The Corkadales' contract is our ace.
I mean, the man would murder his own mother to get *Search* published.'

'I thought you said his parents were dead,' said Sonia.

'They are,' said Frensic. 'To the best of my knowledge the poor fellow
has no living relatives. I wouldn't be at all surprised if we aren't his nearest
and dearest.'

'It's amazing what twenty per cent commission on two million dollars
will do to some people,' said Sonia. 'I've never thought of you in the role of
a foster-father.'

It was amazing what the prospect of having his novel published had done
to Piper's morale. He arrived in Lanyard Lane wearing the blue suit he
kept for formal visits to London and an expression of smug self-satisfaction

that alarmed Frensic. He preferred his authors subdued and a little depressed.

'I'd like you to meet Miss Futtle, my partner,' he said when Piper entered. 'She deals with the American side of the business.'

'Charmed,' said Piper bowing slightly, a habit he had derived from Hans Castorp.

'I just adored your book,' said Sonia, 'I think it's marvellous.'

'You did?' said Piper.

'So insightful,' said Sonia, 'so deeply significant.'

In the background Frensic stirred uncomfortably. He would have chosen less brazen tactics and Sonia's accent, borrowed, he suspected, from Georgia in 1861, disturbed him. On the other hand it seemed to affect Piper favourably. He was blushing.

'Very kind of you to say so,' he murmured.

Frensic asserted himself. 'Now, as to the matter of Corkadales' contract to publish *Search*,' he began and looked at his watch. 'Why don't we go down and discuss the whole thing over a drink?'

They went downstairs to the pub across the road and while Frensic bought drinks Sonia continued her assault.

'Corkadales are one of the oldest publishing houses in London. They are terribly prestigious but I just think we've got to do everything to see your work reaches a wide audience.'

'The thing is,' said Frensic, returning with two single gin and tonics for himself and Sonia and a double for Piper, 'that you need exposure. Corkadales will do for a start but their sales record is none too good.'

'It isn't?' said Piper who had never thought of such mundane things as sales.

'They're naturally old-fashioned and if they do take *Search* – and that's still not entirely certain – are they going to be the best people to push it? That's the question.'

'But I thought you said they'd agreed to buy?' said Piper uncomfortably.

'They've made an offer, a good offer, but are we going to accept it?' said Frensic. 'That's what we have to discuss.'

'Yes,' said Piper. 'Yes, we are.'

Frensic looked questioningly at Sonia. 'The US market?' he asked.

Sonia shook her head.

'If we're going to sell to a US publisher we need someone bigger than Corkadales over here first. Someone with get-up-and-go who's going to promote the book in a big way.'

'My feelings exactly,' said Frensic. 'Corkadales have the prestige but they could kill it stone dead.'

'But ...' began Piper, by now thoroughly disturbed.

'Getting a first novel off the ground in the States isn't easy,' said Sonia. 'And with a new British author it's like ...'

'Trying to sell fireworks in hell?' suggested Frensic, doing his best to avoid Eskimos and ice cream.

'The words from my mouth,' said Sonia. 'They don't want to know.'

'They don't?' said Piper.

Frensic bought another round of drinks. When he returned Sonia was into tactics.

'A British author in the States needs a gimmick. Thrillers are easy. Historical romance better still. Now if *Search* were about Regency beaux, or better still Mary Queen of Scots, we'd have no problem. That sort of stuff they lap up but *Search* is a deeply insight –'

'What about *Pause O Men for the Virgin*?' said Frensic. 'Now there's a book that is going to take America by storm.'

'Absolutely,' said Sonia. 'Or would have done if the author could go to promote it.'

They relapsed into gloomy silence.

'Why can't he go?' asked Piper.

'Too ill,' said Sonia.

'Too reserved and shy,' said Frensic. 'I mean he insists on using a *nom de plume*.'

'A *nom de plume*?' said Piper amazed that an author didn't want his name on the cover of his book.

'It's tragic really,' said Sonia. 'He's having to throw away two million dollars because he can't go.'

'Two million dollars?' said Piper.

'And all because he's got osteo-arthritis and the American publisher insists on his making a promotional tour and he can't do it.'

'But that's terrible,' said Piper.

Frensic and Sonia nodded more gloomily than before.

'And he's got a wife and six children,' said Sonia. Frensic started. The wife and six children weren't in the script.

'How awful,' said Piper.

'And with terminal osteo-arthritis he'll never write another book.' Frensic started again. That wasn't in the script either. But Sonia ploughed on. 'And maybe with that two million dollars he could have taken a new course of drugs ...'

Frensic hurried away for some more drinks. This was really laying it on with a trowel.

'Now if we could only get someone to take his place,' said Sonia looking deeply and significantly into Piper's eyes. 'The fact that he is prepared to use a *nom de plume* and the American publisher doesn't know . . .' She left the implications to be absorbed.

'Why can't you tell the American publisher the truth?' he asked.

Frensic, returning this time with two singles and a triple for Piper, intervened. 'Because Hutchmeyer is one of those bastards who would take advantage of the author and drop his price,' he said.

'Who's Hutchmeyer?' asked Piper.

Frensic looked at Sonia. 'You tell him.'

'He just happens to be about the biggest publisher in the States. He sells more books than all the publishers in London and if he buys you you're made.'

'And if he doesn't it's touch and go,' said Frensic.

Sonia took up the running. 'If we could get Hutchmeyer to buy *Search* your problems would be over. You'd have guaranteed sales and enough money to go on writing for ever.'

Piper considered this glorious prospect and sipped his triple gin. This was the ecstasy he had been waiting so many years for, the knowledge that at last he was going to see *Search* in print and if Hutchmeyer could be persuaded to buy it . . . ah bliss! An idea grew in his befuddled mind. Sonia saw it dawning and jogged it along.

'If there was only some way of bringing you and Hutchmeyer together,' she said. 'I mean, supposing he thought you had written *Pause* . . .'

But Piper was there already. 'Then he'd buy *Search*,' he said and was smitten by immediate doubts. 'But wouldn't the author of the other book mind?'

'Mind?' said Frensic. 'My dear fellow, you would be doing him a favour. He's never going to write another book and if Hutchmeyer refuses to go ahead with the deal . . .'

'And all you would have to do is go and take his place on the promotional tour,' said Sonia. 'It's as simple as that.'

Frensic put in his oar. 'And you would be paid twenty-five thousand dollars and all expenses into the bargain.'

'It would be marvellous publicity,' said Sonia. 'Just the sort of break you need.'

Piper absolutely agreed. It *was* just the sort of break he needed. 'But wouldn't it be illegal? Me going around pretending I'd written a book I hadn't?' he asked.

'You'd naturally have the real author's permission. In writing. There would be nothing illegal about it. Hutchmeyer wouldn't have to know, but then he doesn't read the books he buys and he's simply a businessman in books. All he wants is an author to go round signing books and putting in an appearance. In addition to which he has taken an option on the author's second novel.'

'But I thought you said the author couldn't write a second book?' said Piper.

'Exactly,' said Frensic, 'so Hutchmeyer's second book from the same author would be *Search for a Lost Childhood*.'

'You'd be in and made,' said Sonia. 'With Hutchmeyer behind you, you couldn't go wrong.'

They went round the corner to the Italian restaurant and continued the discussion. There was still something bothering Piper. 'But if Corkadales want to buy *Search* isn't that going to make things difficult. They know the author of this other book.'

Frensic shook his head. 'Not a chance. You see we handled his work for him and he can't come to London so it's all between the three of us. No one else will ever know.'

Piper smiled down into his spaghetti. It was all so simple. He was on the brink of recognition. He looked up into Sonia's face. 'Oh well. All's fair in love and war,' he said, and Sonia smiled back. She raised her glass. 'I'll drink to that,' she murmured.

'To the making of an author,' said Frensic.

They drank. Later that night in Frensic's flat in Hampstead Piper signed two contracts. The first sold *Search for a Lost Childhood* to Corkadales for the advance sum of one thousand pounds. The second stated that as the author of *Pause O Men for the Virgin* he agreed to make a promotional tour of the United States.

'On one condition,' he said as Frensic opened a bottle of champagne to celebrate the occasion.

'What's that?' said Frensic.

'That Miss Futtle comes with me,' said Piper. There was a bang as the chapagne cork hit the ceiling. On the sofa Sonia laughed gaily. 'I second that motion,' she said.

Frensic carried it. Later he carried a very drunk Piper through to his spare room and put him to bed.

Piper smiled happily in his sleep.

CHAPTER FIVE

Piper awoke next morning and lay in bed with a feeling of elation. He was going to be published. He was going to America. He was in love. Suddenly everything he had dreamt of had come true in the most miraculous fashion. Piper had no qualms. He got up and washed and looked at himself in the bathroom mirror with a new appreciation of his previously unrecognized gifts. The fact that his sudden good fortune was derived from the misfortune of an author with terminal arthritis no longer disturbed him. His genius deserved a break and this was it. Besides, the long years of frustration had anaesthetized those moral principles which so informed his novels. A chance reading of Benvenuto Cellini's Autobiography helped too. 'One's duty is to one's art,' Piper told his reflection in the bathroom mirror as he shaved, adding that there was a tide in the affairs of men which taken at its flood led on to fortune. Finally there was Sonia Futtle.

Piper's dedication to his art had left him little time for real feelings for real people and that little time he had devoted to avoiding the predatory advances of several of his landladies or to worshipping at a distance attractive young women who stayed at the boarding-houses he frequented. And those girls he had taken out had proved, on acquaintance, to be uninterested in literature. Piper had reserved himself for the great love affair, one that would equal in intensity the affairs he had read about in great novels, a meeting of literary minds. In Sonia Futtle he felt he had found a woman who truly appreciated what he had to offer and one with whom he could enter into a genuine relationship. If anything more was needed to convince him that he need have no hesitation in going to America to promote someone else's work it was the knowledge that Sonia was going with him. Piper finished shaving and went out into the kitchen to find a note from Frensic saying he had gone to the office and telling Piper to make himself at home. Piper made himself at home. He had breakfast and then, taking his diary and bottle of evaporated ink through to Frensic's study, settled down at the desk to write his radiant perceptions of Sonia Futtle in his diary.

But if Piper was radiant, Frensic wasn't. 'This thing could blow up in our faces,' he told Sonia when she arrived. 'We got the poor sod drunk and he signed the contract but what happens if he changes his mind?'

'No way,' said Sonia. 'We make a down-payment on the tour and you take him round to Corkadales this afternoon and get him to sign for *Search*. That way we sew him up good and tight.'

'Methinks I hear the voice of Hutchmeyer speaking,' said Frensic. 'Sew him up good and tight. Tight being the operative word. Good I have doubts about.'

'It's for his own,' said Sonia. 'Name me some other way he's ever going to see *Search* in print.'

Frensic nodded his agreement. 'Geoffrey is going to have a fit when he sees what he's agreed to publish. *The Magic Mountain* in East Finchley. The mind boggles. You should have read Piper's version of *Nostromo*, likewise set in East Finchley.'

'I'll wait for the reviews,' said Sonia. 'In the meantime we'll have made a cool quarter of a million. Pounds, Frenzy, not dollars. Think of that.'

'I have thought of that,' said Frensic. 'I have also thought what will happen if this thing goes wrong. We'll be out of business.'

'It isn't going to go wrong. I've been on the phone to Eleanor Beazley of the "Books To Be Read" programme. She owes me a favour. She's agreed to squeeze Piper into next week's –'

'No,' said Frensic. 'Definitely not. I won't have you rushing Piper –'

'Listen, baby,' said Sonia, 'we've got to strike while the iron's hot. We get Piper on the box saying he wrote *Pause* and he ain't going to back out nohow.'

Frensic regarded her with distaste. 'He ain't going to back out nohow? Charming. We're really getting into Mafia-land now. And kindly don't "baby" me. If there is one expression I abominate it's being called "baby". And as for putting the poor demented Piper on the box, have you thought what effect this is going to have on Cadwalladine and his anonymous client?'

'Cadwalladine has agreed to the substitution in principle,' said Sonia. 'What's he got to complain about?'

'There is a difference between "in principle" and "in practice",' said Frensic. 'What he actually said was that he would consult his client.'

'And has he let you know?'

'Not yet,' said Frensic, 'and in some ways I rather hope he turns the idea down. At least it would put an end once and for all to the internecine strife between my greed and my scruples.'

But even that relief was denied him. Half an hour later a telegram was delivered. CLIENT AGREES TO SUBSTITUTION STOP ANONYMITY OVERRIDING CONSIDERATION CADWALLADINE.

'So we're in the clear,' said Sonia. 'I'll confirm Piper for Wednesday and see if the *Guardian* will run a feature on him. You get on to Geoffrey and arrange for Piper to exchange contracts for *Search* this afternoon.'

'That could lead to misunderstandings,' said Frensic. 'Geoffrey happens to think Piper wrote *Pause* and since Piper hasn't read *Pause*, let alone written the thing ...'

'So you take him out to lunch and liquor him up and ...'

'Have you ever considered,' asked Frensic, 'going into the kidnapping business?'

In the event there was no need to liquor Piper up. He arrived in a state of euphoria and installed himself in Sonia's office where he sat gazing at her meaningfully while she telephoned the literary editors of several daily papers to arrange prepublication interviews with the author of the world's most expensively purchased novel, *Pause O Men for the Virgin*. In the next office Frensic coped with the ordinary business of the day. He phoned Geoffrey Corkadale and made an appointment for Piper in the afternoon, he listened abstractedly to the whining of two authors who were having difficulties with their plots, did his best to assure them that it would all come right in the end and tried to ignore the intimations of his own instincts which were telling him that with the signing up of Piper the firm of Frensic & Futtle had bitten off more than they could chew. Finally when Piper went downstairs to the washroom Frensic managed to have a word with Sonia.

'What gives?' he asked, a lapse into transatlantic brevity that indicated his disturbed state of mind.

'The *Guardian* have agreed to interview him tomorrow and the *Telegraph* say they'll let me –'

'With Piper. Whence the fixed smile and the goggle eyes?'

Sonia smiled. 'Has it ever occurred to you that he might find me attractive?'

'No,' said Frensic. 'No it hasn't.'

Sonia's smile faded. 'Get lost,' she said.

Frensic got lost and considered this new and quite incomprehensible development. It was one of the fixed stars in his firmament of opinions that no one in his right mind could find Sonia Futtle attractive apart from Hutchmeyer, and Hutchmeyer had evidently perverse tastes both in books and in women. That Piper should be in love with her, and at such short notice, intruded a new dimension into the situation – which in his opinion was sufficiently crowded already. Frensic sat down behind his desk and wondered what advantages could be gained from Piper's infatuation.

'At least it gets me off the hook,' he muttered finally and went next door again. But Piper was back in his chair gazing with adoring eyes at Sonia. Frensic retreated and phoned her.

'From now on, he's your pigeon,' he told her. 'You dine, wine him and anything else that pleases you. The man's besotted.'

'Jealousy will get you nowhere,' said Sonia smiling at Piper.

'Right,' said Frensic, 'I want no part of this corruption of the innocent.'

'Squeamish?' said Sonia.

'Extremely,' said Frensic and put down the phone.

'Who was that?' asked Piper.

'Oh just an editor at Heinemann. He's got a crush on me.'

'Hm,' said Piper disgruntedly.

And so while Frensic lunched at his club, a thing he did only when his ego, vanity or virility (such as it was) had taken a bashing in the real world, Sonia swept the besotted Piper off to Wheelers and fed him on dry Martinis, Rhine wine, salmon cutlets and her own brand of expansive charm. By the time they emerged into the street he had told her in so many words that he considered her the first woman in his life to have possessed both the physical and mental attractions which made for a real relationship and one who moreover understood the true nature of the creative literary act. Sonia Futtle was not used to such ardent confessions. The few advances she had had in the past had been expressed less fluently and had largely consisted of inquiries as to whether she would or wouldn't and Piper's technique, borrowed almost entirely from Hans Castorp in *The Magic Mountain* with a bit of Lawrence thrown in for good measure, came as a pleasant surprise. There was an old-fashioned quality about him, she decided, which made a nice change. Besides, Piper, for all his literary ambitions, was personable and not without an angular charm and Sonia could accommodate any amount of angular charm. It was a flushed and flattered Sonia who stood on the pavement and hailed a taxi to take them to Corkadales.

'Just don't shoot your mouth off too much,' she said as they drove across London. 'Geoffrey Corkadale's a fag and he'll do the talking. He'll probably say a whole lot of complimentary things about *Pause O Men for the Virgin* and you just nod.'

Piper nodded. The world was a gay, gay place in which anything was possible and everything permissible. As an accepted author it became him to be modest. In the event he excelled himself at Corkadales. Inspired by the sight of Trollope's inkpot in the glass case he launched into an explanation of his own writing techniques with particular reference to the use of evaporated ink, exchanged contracts for *Search*, and accepted Geoffrey's praise of *Pause* as a first-rate novel with a suitably ironical smile.

'Extraordinary to think he could have written that filthy book,' Geoffrey whispered to Sonia as they were leaving. 'I had expected some long-haired hippie and my dear, this one is out of the Ark.'

'Just shows you can never tell,' said Sonia. 'Anyway you're going to get a lot of excellent publicity for *Pause*. I've got him on the "Books To Be Read" programme.'

'How very clever you are,' said Geoffrey. 'I'm delighted. And the American deal is definitely on?'

'Definitely,' said Sonia.

They took another taxi and drove back towards Lanyard Lane.

'You were marvellous,' she told Piper. 'Just stick to talking about your pens and ink and how you write your books and refuse to discuss their content and we'll have no trouble.'

'Nobody seems to discuss books anyway,' said Piper. 'I thought the conversation would be quite different. More literary.'

He got out in Charing Cross Road and spent the rest of the afternoon browsing in Foyle's while Sonia went back to the office and reassured Frensic.

'No problems,' she said. 'He had Geoffrey fooled.'

'That's hardly surprising,' said Frensic, 'Geoffrey is a fool. Wait till Eleanor Beazley starts asking him about his portrayal of the sexual psyche of an eighty-year-old woman. That's when the fat's going to be in the fire.'

'She won't. I've told her he never discusses his past work. She's to stick to biographical details and how he works. He's really convincing when he gets on to pens and ink. Did you know he uses evaporated ink and writes in leatherbound ledgers? Isn't that quaint?'

'I'm only surprised he doesn't use a quill,' said Frensic. 'It's in keeping.'

'It's good copy. The *Guardian* interview with Jim Fossie is tomorrow morning and the *Telegraph* wants him for the colour supplements in the afternoon. I tell you this bandwagon is beginning to roll.'

That night, as Frensic made his way back to his flat with Piper, it was clear that the bandwagon had indeed begun to roll. The newsstands announced BRITISH NOVELIST MAKES TWO MILLION IN BIGGEST DEAL EVER.

'Oh what a tangled web we weave when first we practise to deceive,' murmured Frensic and bought a paper. Beside him Piper nursed the large green hardback copy of Thomas Mann's *Doctor Faustus* which he had bought at Foyle's. He was thinking of utilizing its symphonic approach in his third novel.

CHAPTER SIX

Next morning the bandwagon began to roll in earnest. After a night spent dreaming of Sonia and preparing himself for the ordeal, Piper arrived at the office to discuss his life, literary opinions and methods of work with Jim Fossie of the *Guardian*. Frensic and Sonia hovered anxiously in the background to ensure discretion but there was no need. Whatever Piper's limitations as a writer of novels, as a putative novelist he played his role expertly. He spoke of Literature in the abstract, referred scathingly to one or two eminent contemporary novelists, but for the most part concentrated on the use of evaporated ink and the limitations of the modern fountain pen as an aid to literary creation.

'I believe in craftmanship,' he said, 'the old-fashioned virtues of clarity and legibility.' He told a story about Palmerston's insistence on fine writing by the clerks in the Foreign Office and dismissed the ball-pen with contempt. So obsessive was his concern with calligraphy that Mr Fossie had ended the interview before he realized that no mention had been made of the novel he had come to discuss.

'He's certainly different from any other author I've ever met,' he told Sonia as she saw him out. 'All that stuff about Kipling's notepaper, for God's sake!'

'What do you expect from genius?' said Sonia. 'Some spiel about how brilliant his novel is?'

'And how brilliant is this genius's novel?'

'Two-million-dollars worth. That's the reality value.'

'Some reality,' said Mr Fossie with more percipience than he knew.

Even Frensic, who had anticipated disaster, was impressed. 'If he keeps that up we'll be all right,' he said.

'We're going to be fine,' said Sonia.

After lunch the *Daily Telegraph* photographer insisted, thanks to a chance remark by Piper that he had once lived near the scene of the explosion in *The Secret Agent* in Greenwich Park, on taking his photographs as it were on location.

'It adds dramatic interest,' he said evidently supposing the explosion to have been a real one. They went down on the riverboat from Charing Cross, Piper explaining to the interviewer, Miss Pamela Wildgrove, that Conrad had been a major influence on his work. Miss Wildgrove made a note of the fact. Piper said Dickens had also been an influence. Miss

Wildgrove made a note of that fact too. By the time they reached
Greenwich her notebook was crammed with influences but Piper's own
work had hardly been mentioned.

'I understand *Pause O Men for the Virgin* deals with the love affair
between a seventeen-year-old boy and ...' Miss Wildgrove began but
Sonia intervened.

'Mr Piper doesn't wish to discuss the content of his novel,' she said
hurriedly. 'We're keeping the book under wraps.'

'But surely he's prepared to say ...'

'Let's just say it is a work of major importance and opens new ground
in the area of age differentials,' said Sonia and hurried Piper away to be
photographed incongruously on the deck of the *Cutty Sark*, in the grounds
of the Maritime Museum and by the Observatory. Miss Wildgrove
followed disconsolately.

'On the way back stick to ink and your ledgers,' Sonia told Piper and
Piper followed her advice with a distinctly nautical flavour while Sonia
shepherded her charge back to the office.

'You did very well,' she told him.

'Yes, but hadn't I better read this book I'm supposed to have written?
I mean, I don't even know what it's about.'

'You can do that on the boat going over to the States.'

'Boat?' said Piper.

'Much nicer than flying,' said Sonia. 'Hutchmeyer is arranging some
big reception for you in New York and it will draw bigger crowds at the
dockside. Anyway we've done the interviews and the TV programme
isn't till next Wednesday. You can go back to Exforth and pack. Get
back here Tuesday afternoon and I'll brief you for the programme. We're
leaving from Southampton Thursday.'

'You're wonderful,' said Piper fervently, 'I want you to know that.'
He left the office and caught the evening train to Exeter. Sonia sat on
in her office and thought wistfully about him. Nobody had ever told her
she was wonderful before.

Certainly Frensic didn't next morning. He arrived at the office in a
towering rage carrying a copy of the *Guardian*.

'I thought you told me all he was going to talk about was inks and
pens,' he shouted at the startled Sonia.

'That's right. He was quite fascinating.'

'Well then kindly explain all this about Graham Greene being a
second-rate hack,' Frensic yelled and thrust the article under her nose.
'That's right. Hack. Graham Greene. A hack. The man's insane!'

Sonia read the article and had to admit that it was a bit extreme.

'Still, it's good publicity,' she said. 'Statements like that will get his name before the public.'

'Get his name before the courts more like,' said Frensic. 'And what about this bit about *The French Lieutenant's Woman* ... Piper hasn't even written one single publishable word and here he is castigating half a dozen eminent novelists. Look what he says about Waugh. Quote "... a very limited imagination and an overrated style ..." unquote. Waugh just happens to have been one of the finest stylists of the century. And "limited imagination" coming from a blithering idiot who hasn't got any imagination at all. I tell you Pandora's box will be a tea-party by comparison with Piper on the loose.'

'He's entitled to his opinions,' said Sonia.

'He isn't entitled to have opinions like these,' said Frensic. 'God knows what Cadwalladine's client will say when he reads what he's supposed to have said, and I shouldn't think Geoffrey Corkadale is too pleased to know he's got an author on his list who thinks Graham Greene is a second-rate hack.' He went into his office and sat miserably wondering what new storm was going to break. His nose was playing all hell with him.

But the storm when it did break came from an unexpected direction. From Piper himself. He returned to the Gleneagle Guest House in Exforth madly in love with Sonia, life, his own newly established reputation as a novelist and his future happiness to find a parcel waiting for him. It contained the proofs of *Pause O Men for the Virgin* and a letter from Geoffrey Corkadale asking him if he would mind correcting them as soon as possible. Piper took the parcel up to his room and settled down to read. He started at nine o'clock that night. By midnight he was wide awake and halfway through. By two o'clock he had finished and had begun a letter to Geoffrey Corkadale stating very precisely what he thought of *Pause O Men for the Virgin* as a novel, as pornography, as an attack on established values both sexual and human. It was a long letter. By six o'clock he had posted it. Only then did he go to bed, exhausted by his own fluent disgust and harbouring feelings for Miss Futtle that were the exact reverse of those he had held for her nine hours earlier. Even then he couldn't sleep but lay awake for several hours before finally dozing off. He woke again after lunch and went for a haggard walk along the beach in a state bordering on the suicidal. He had been tricked, conned, deceived by a woman he had loved and trusted. She had deliberately bribed him into accepting the authorship of a vile, nauseating, pornographic ... He ran out of adjectives. He would never forgive her. After contemplating the ocean bleakly for an hour he returned to the boarding-house, his mind made up. He composed a terse telegram stating that he had no intention of going through with the charade and had no wish to see Miss Futtle ever again. That done he confided his darkest thoughts to his diary, had supper and went to bed.

The following morning the storm broke in London. Frensic arrived in a good mood. Piper's absence from his flat had relieved him of the obligation to play host to a man whose conversation had consisted of the need for a serious approach to fiction and Sonia Futtle's attractions as a woman. Neither topic had been at all to Frensic's taste and Piper's habit at breakfast of reading aloud passages from *Doctor Faustus* to illustrate what he meant by symbolic counterpoint as a literary device had driven Frensic from his own home even earlier than was his custom. With Piper in Exfort he had been spared that particular ordeal but on his arrival at the office he was confronted with fresh horrors. He found Sonia, whitefaced and almost tearful, clutching a telegram, and had been about to ask her what the matter was when the phone rang. Frensic answered it. It was Geoffrey Corkadale. 'I suppose this is your idea of a joke,' he said angrily.

'What is?' said Frensic thinking of the *Guardian* article about Grahame Greene.

'This bloody letter,' shouted Geoffrey.

'What letter?'

'This letter from Piper. I suppose you think it's funny to get him to write abusive filth about his own beastly book.'

It was Frensic's turn to shout. 'What about his book?' he yelled.

'What do you mean "What about it"? You know damned well what I mean.'

'I've no idea,' said Frensic.

'He says here he considers it one of the most repulsive pieces of writing it's ever been his misfortune to have to read –'

'Shit,' said Frensic frantically wondering how Piper had got hold of a copy of *Pause*.

'Yes, that too,' said Geoffrey. 'Now where does he say that? Here we are. "If you imagine even momentarily that for motives of commercial cupidity I am prepared to prostitute my albeit so far unknown but not I think unconsiderable talent by assuming even remotely and as it were by proxy responsibility for what in my view and that of any right-minded person can only be described as the pornographic outpourings of verbal excreta ..." There! I knew it was embedded somewhere. Now what do you say to that?'

Frensic stared venomously at Sonia and tried to think of something to say. 'I don't know,' he muttered. 'It sounds odd. How did he get the blasted book?'

'What do you mean "How did he get the book"?' yelled Geoffrey. 'He wrote the thing, didn't he?'

'Yes, I suppose so,' said Frensic edging towards the safety of admitting he didn't know who had written it and that he had been hoodwinked by Piper. It didn't seem a very safe position to adopt.

'What do you mean "You suppose so"? I send him proofs of his own book to correct and I get this abusive letter back. Anyone would think he'd never read the damned thing before. Is the man mad or something?'

'Yes,' said Frensic for whom the suggestion came as a Godsend, 'the strain of the past few weeks ... nervous breakdown. Very highly strung you know. He gets into these states.'

Geoffrey Corkadale's fury abated a little. 'I can't say I'm at all surprised,' he admitted. 'Anyone who can go to bed with an eighty-year-old woman must have something mentally wrong with him. What do you want me to do with these proofs?'

'Send them round to me and I'll see he corrects them,' said Frensic. 'And in future I suggest you deal with Piper through me here. I think I understand him.'

'I'm glad someone does,' said Geoffrey. 'I don't want any more letters like this one.'

Frensic put the phone down and turned on Sonia. 'Right,' he yelled, 'I knew it. I just knew it would happen. You heard what he said?'

Sonia nodded sadly. 'It was our mistake,' she said. 'We should have told them to send the proofs here.'

'Never mind the bloody proofs,' snarled Frensic, 'our mistake was coming up with Piper in the first place. Why Piper? The world is full of normal, sane, financially motivated, healthily commercial authors who would be glad to stick their name to any old trash, and you had to come up with Piper.'

'There's no need to go on about it,' said Sonia. 'Look what he's said in this telegram.'

Frensic looked and slumped into a chair. ' "Yours ineluctably Piper"? In a telegram? I wouldn't have believed it ... Well at least he's put us out of our misery though how the hell we're going to explain to Geoffrey that the Hutchmeyer deal is off ...'

'It isn't off,' said Sonia.

'But Piper says –'

'Screw what he says. He's going to the States if I have to carry him. We've paid him good money, we've sold his lousy book and he's under obligation to go. He's not going to back out on that contract now. I'm going down to Exforth to talk with him.'

'Leave well alone,' said Frensic, 'that's my advice. That young man can –' but the phone rang and by the time he had spent ten minutes discussing the new ending of *Final Fling* with Miss Gold, Sonia had left.

'Hell hath no fury ...' he muttered, and returned to his own office.

Piper took his afternoon walk along the promenade like some late migrating bird whose biological clock had let it down. It was summer and he should have gone inland to cheaper climes but the atmosphere of Exforth held him. The little resort was nicely Edwardian and rather prim and served in its old-fashioned way to help bridge the gap between Davos and East Finchley. Thomas Mann, he felt, would have appreciated Exforth with its botanical gardens, its clock golf, its pier and tessellated toilets, its bandstand and its rows of balustraded boarding-houses staring south towards France. There were even some palm trees in the little park that separated the Gleneagle Guest House from the promenade. Piper strolled beneath them and climbed the steps in time for tea.

Instead he found Sonia Futtle waiting for him in the hall. She had driven down at high speed from London, had rehearsed her tactics on the way and a brief encounter with Mrs Oakley on the question of coffee for non-residents had whetted her temper. Besides, Piper had rejected her not only as an agent but as a woman, and as a woman she wasn't to be trifled with.

'Now you just listen to me,' she said in decibels that made it certain that everyone in the guest-house would. 'You can't get out of this so easily. You accepted money and you –'

'For God's sake,' spluttered Piper, 'don't shout like that. What will people think?'

It was a stupid question. In the lounge the residents were staring. It was clear what they thought.

'That you're a man no woman can trust,' bawled Sonia pursuing her advantage, 'that you break your word, that you ...'

But Piper was in flight. As he went down the steps and into the street Sonia followed in full cry.

'You deliberately deceived me. You took advantage of my inexperience to make me believe –'

Piper plunged wildly across the road into the park. 'I deceived you?' he counter-attacked under the palms. 'You told me that book was –'

'No I didn't. I said it was a bestseller. I never said it was good.'

'Good? It's disgusting. It's pure pornography. It debases ...'

'Pornography? You've got to be kidding. So you haven't read anything later than Hemingway you've got this idea any book deals with sex is pornographic.'

'No I don't,' protested Piper, 'what I meant was it undermines the foundations of English literature ...'

'Don't give me that crap. You took advantage of Frenzy's faith in you as a writer. Ten years he's been trying to get you published and now when we finally come up with this deal you throw it back at us.'

'That's not true. I didn't know the book was that bad. I've got my reputation to think of and if my name is on –'

'Your reputation? What about our reputation?' said Sonia as they skirmished past a bus queue on the front. 'You ever thought what you're doing to that?'

Piper shook his head.

'So where's your reputation? As what?'

'As a writer,' said Piper.

Sonia appealed to the bus queue. 'Whoever heard of you?'

Clearly no one had. Piper fled down on to the beach.

'And what is more no one ever will,' shouted Sonia. 'You think Corkadales are going to publish *Search* now? Think again. They'll take you through the courts and break you moneywise and then they'll blacklist you.'

'Blacklist me?' said Piper.

'The blacklist of authors who are never to be published.'

'Corkadales aren't the only publishers,' said Piper now thoroughly confused.

'If you're on the blacklist no one will publish you,' said Sonia inventively. 'You'll be finished. As a writer *finito*.'

Piper stared out at the sea and thought about being *finito* as a writer. It was a terrible prospect.

'You really think ...' he began but Sonia had already changed her tactics.

'You told me you loved me,' she sobbed sinking on to the sand close to a middle-aged couple. 'You said we would ...'

'Oh Lord,' said Piper, 'don't go on like that. Not here.'

But Sonia went on, there and elsewhere, combining a public display of private anguish with the threat of legal action if Piper didn't fulfil his part of the bargain and the promise of fame as a writer of genius if he did. Gradually his resolve weakened. The blacklist had hit him hard.

'I suppose I could always write under another name,' he said as they stood at the end of the pier. But Sonia shook her head.

'Darling, you're so naïve,' she said. 'Don't you see that what you write is instantly recognizable. You can't escape your own uniqueness, your own original brilliance ...'

'I suppose not,' said Piper modestly, 'I suppose that's true.'

'Of course it's true. You're not some hack turning books out to order. You're you, Peter Piper. Frenzy has always said there's only one you.'

'He has?' said Piper.

'He's spent more time on you than any other author we handle. He's had faith in you and this is your big opportunity, the chance to break through into fame ...'

'With someone else's awful book,' Piper pointed out.

'So it's someone else's, it might have had to be your own. Like Faulkner with *Sanctuary* and the rape with the corncob.'

'You mean Faulkner didn't write that?' said Piper aghast.

'I mean he did. He had to so he'd get noticed and have the breakthrough. Nobody'd bought him before *Sanctuary* and afterwards he was famous. With *Pause* you don't have to do that. You keep your artistic integrity intact.'

'I hadn't thought of it like that,' said Piper.

'And later when you're known as a great novelist you can write your autobiography and set the world straight about *Pause*,' said Sonia.

'So I can,' said Piper.

'Then you'll come?'

'Yes. Yes, I will.'

'Oh, darling.'

They kissed on the end of the pier and the tide, rising gently under the moon, lapped below their feet.

CHAPTER SEVEN

Two days later a triumphant if exhausted Sonia walked into the office to announce that she had persuaded Piper to change his mind.

'Brought him back with you?' said Frensic incredulously. 'After that telegram? Good Lord, you must have positively Circean charms for the poor brute. How on earth did you do it?'

'Made a scene and quoted Faulkner,' said Sonia simply.

Frensic was appalled. 'Not Faulkner again. We had him last summer. Even Mann's easier to move to East Finchley. Every time I see a pylon now I ...'

'This was *Sanctuary*.'

Frensic sighed. 'That's better I suppose. Still the thoughts of Mrs Piper ending up in some brothel in Memphis-cum-Golders Green ... And you mean to say he's prepared to go on with the tour? That's incredible.'

'You forget I'm a salesperson,' said Sonia. 'I could sell sunlamps in the Sahara.'

'I believe you. After that letter he wrote Geoffrey I thought we were done for. And he is quite reconciled to being the author of what he chose to call the most repulsive piece of writing it had ever been his misfortune to have to read?'

'He sees it as a necessary step on the road to recognition,' said Sonia. 'I managed to persuade him it was his duty to suppress his own critical awareness in order to achieve –'

'Critical awareness my foot,' said Frensic, 'he hasn't got any. Just so long as I don't have to put him up again.'

'He's staying with me,' said Sonia, 'and don't smirk. I just want him where I can reach him.'

Frensic stopped smirking. 'And what is the next event on the agenda?'

'The "Books To Be Read" programme. It will help get him ready for the TV appearances in the States.'

'Quite so,' said Frensic. 'Added to which it has the advantage of getting him committed to the authorship of *Pause* with what is termed the maximum exposure. One can hardly see him backing out after that.'

'Frenzy dear,' said Sonia, 'you are a born worrier. It's going to work out all right.'

'I just hope you're right,' said Frensic, 'but I shall be relieved when you leave for the States. There's many a slip 'twixt cup and lip, and –'

'Not this cup and these lips,' said Sonia smugly, 'no way. Piper will go on the box ...'

'Like a lamb to the slaughter?' suggested Frensic.

It was an apt simile and one that had already occurred to Piper who had begun to have qualms.

'Not that I doubt my love for Sonia,' he confided to his diary which, now that he had moved into Sonia's flat, had taken the place of *Search* as his main mode of self-expression. 'But it is surely arguable that my honesty as an artist is at stake whatever Sonia may say about Villon.'

And in any case Villon's end didn't commend itself to Piper. To calm his conscience he turned once again to the Faulkner interview in *Writers at Work*. Mr Faulkner's view on the artist was most reassuring. 'He is completely amoral,' Piper read, 'in that he will rob, borrow, beg or steal from anybody and everybody to get the work done.' Piper read right through the interview and came to the conclusion that perhaps he had been wrong to abandon his Yoknapatawpha version of *Search* in favour of *The Magic Mountain*. Frensic had disapproved on the grounds that the prose had seemed a bit clotted for the story of adolescence. But then Frensic was so commercial. It had come as a considerable surprise to Piper to learn that Frensic had so much faith in him. He had begun to suspect that Frensic was merely fobbing him off with his annual lunches but Sonia had reassured him. Dear Sonia. She was such a comfort. Piper made an ecstatic note of the fact in his diary and then turned on the television set. It was time he decided what sort of image he wanted to present on the 'Books To Be Read' programme. Sonia said image was very important and with his usual gift for derivation Piper finally adopted Herbert Herbison as his model. Sonia came home that night to find him muttering alliterative clichés to his reflection in her dressing-table mirror.

'You've just got to be yourself,' she told him. 'It's no use trying to copy other people.'

'Myself?' said Piper.

'Natural. Like you are with me.'

'You think it will be all right like that?'

'Darling, it will be fine. I've had a word with Eleanor Beazley and she'll go easy on you. You can tell her all about your work methods and pens and things.'

'Just so long as she doesn't ask me why I wrote that bloody book,' said Piper gloomily.

'You'll be great,' said Sonia confidently. She was still insisting that everything would be just fine when three days later at Shepherd's Bush Piper was led away to be made up for the interview.

For once she was wrong. Even Geoffrey Corkadale, whose authors seldom achieved a circulation sufficient to warrant their appearance on 'Books To Be Read' and who therefore tended to ignore the programme, could see that Piper was, to put it mildly, not himself. He said as much to Frensic who had invited him over for the evening in case the need should arise for a fresh explanation as to who had actually written *Pause O Men for the Virgin*.

'Come to think of it, I don't suppose he is,' said Frensic staring nervously at the image on the screen. Certainly Piper had a stricken look about him as he sat opposite Eleanor Beazley and the title faded.

'Tonight I have in the studio with me Mr Peter Piper,' said Miss Beazley addressing the camera, 'the author of a first novel, *Pause O Men for the Virgin*, which will shortly be published by Corkadales, price £3.95, and which has been bought for the unheard-of sum of ...' (there was a loud thump as Piper kicked the microphone) 'by an American publisher.'

'Unheard-of is about right,' said Frensic. We could have done with that bit of publicity.'

Miss Beazley did her best to make good the erasure. She turned to Piper. 'Two million dollars is a very large sum to be paid for a first novel,' she said, 'it must have come as a great shock to you to find yourself ...'

There was another thump as Piper crossed his legs. This time he managed to kick the microphone and spill a glass of water on the table at the same time.

'I'm sorry,' he shouted. Miss Beazley continued to smile expectantly as water dribbled down her leg. 'Yes, it was a great shock.'

'No,' said Piper.

'I wish to God he'd stop twitching like that,' said Geoffrey. 'Anyone would think he'd got St Vitus's dance.'

Miss Beazley smiled solicitously. 'I wonder if you'd care to tell us something about how you came to write the book in the first place?' she asked.

Piper gazed stricken into a million homes. 'I didn't ...' he began, before jerking his leg forward galvanically and knocking the microphone on to the floor. Frensic shut his eyes. Muffled voices came from the set. When he looked again Miss Beazley's insistent smile filled the screen.

'*Pause O Men* is a most unusual book,' she was saying. 'It's a love story about a young man who falls in love with a woman much older than himself. Was this something you had had in mind for a long time? I mean was it a theme that had occupied your attention?'

The face of Piper appeared again. Beads of perspiration were visible on his forehead and his mouth was working uncontrollably. 'Yes,' he bawled finally.

'Christ, I don't think I can stand much more of this,' said Geoffrey. 'The poor fellow looks as though he's going to burst.'

'And did it take you long to write it?' asked Miss Beazley.

Again Piper struggled for words, looking desperately round the studio as he did so. Finally he took a sip of water and said 'Yes.'

Frensic mopped his brow with a handkerchief.

'To change the subject,' said the indefatigable Miss Beazley whose smile had a positively demented gaiety about it now, 'I understand that your working methods are very much your own. You were telling me earlier that you always write in long-hand?'

'Yes,' said Piper.

'And you grind your own ink?'

Piper ground his teeth and nodded.

'This was an idea you got from Kipling?'

'Yes. *Something Of Myself.* It's in there,' said Piper.

'At least he's warming up,' said Geoffrey only to have his hopes blighted by Miss Beazley's ignorance of Kipling's autobiography.

'Something of yourself is in your novel?' she asked hopefully. Piper glared at her. It was obvious he disliked the question.

'The ink,' he said, 'it's in *Something Of Myself.*'

Miss Beazley's smile took on a bemused look. 'Is it? The ink?'

'He used to grind it himself,' said Piper, 'or rather he got a boy to grind it for him.'

'A boy? How very interesting,' said Miss Beazley searching for some way out of the maze. Piper refused to help.

'It's blacker if you grind your own Indian ink.'

'I suppose it must be. And you find that using a very black Indian ink helps you to write?'

'No,' said Piper, 'it gums up the nib. I tried diluting it with ordinary ink but it still wouldn't work. It got in the ducts and blocked them up.' He stopped suddenly and stared at Miss Beazley.

'Ducts? It blocks the ducts?' she said, evidently supposing Piper to be referring to some strange conduit of inspiration. 'You mean you found your ...' she groped for a less old-fashioned alternative but gave up the struggle to remain contemporary, 'you found your muse wouldn't ...'

'Daemon,' said Piper abruptly, still in the role of Kipling.

Miss Beazley took the insult in her stride. 'You were talking about ink,' she said.

'I said it blocked the ducts of the fountain pen. I couldn't write more than one word at a time.'

'That's hardly surprising,' said Geoffrey. 'It would be bloody odd if he could.'

It was evidently a thought that had occurred to Piper too. 'I mean I had to keep stopping and wiping the nib all the time,' he explained. 'So what I do now is I ...' He stopped. 'It sounds silly.'

'It sounds insane,' said Geoffrey but Miss Beazley would have none of it.

'Go on,' she said encouragingly.

'Well, what I do now is I get a bottle of Midnight Black and let it dry out a bit and then when it's sort of gooey if you see what I mean I dip my nib in and ...' Piper faltered to a stop.

'How very interesting,' said Miss Beazley.

'Well at least he's said something even if it wasn't very edifying,' said Geoffrey. Beside him Frensic stared at the set forlornly. He could see now that he should never have allowed himself to be persuaded to agree to the scheme. It was bound to end in disaster. So was the programme. Miss Beazley tried to get back to the book.

'When I read your novel,' she said, 'I was struck by your understanding of the need for a mature woman's sexuality to find expression physically. Would I be wrong to suppose that there is an autobiographical element in your writing?'

Piper goggled at her vindictively. That he should be supposed to have written *Pause O Men for the* beastly *Virgin* was bad enough, to be taken for the main protagonist in the drama of perversion was more than he could bear. Frensic felt for him and cringed in his chair.

'What did you say?' yelled Piper reverting to his earlier explosive mode of expression. This time he combined it with fluency. 'Do you really think I approve of the filthy book?'

'Well naturally I thought ...' Miss Beazley began but Piper swept her objections aside.

'The whole thing's disgusting. A boy and an eighty-year-old woman. It debases the very foundations of English literature. It's a vile monstrous degenerate book and it should never have been published and if you think –'

But viewers of the 'Book To Be Read' programme were never to hear what Piper supposed Miss Beazley to have thought. A figure interposed itself between the camera and the couple in the chairs, a large figure and clearly a very disturbed one that shouted 'Cut! Cut!' and waved his hands horribly in the air.

'God Almighty,' gasped Geoffrey, 'what the hell's going on?'

Frensic said nothing. He shut his eyes to avoid the sight of Sonia Futtle hurling herself about the studio in a frantic attempt to prevent Piper's terrible confession from reaching its enormous audience. There was an even more startling crackle from the TV set. Frensic opened his eyes again in time to catch a glimpse of the microphone in mid-air and then in the silence that followed watched the ensuing chaos. In the understandable belief that a lunatic had somehow got into the studio and was about to attack her, Miss Beazley shot out of her chair and dived for the door. Piper stared wildly round while Sonia, catching her foot in a cable, crashed forward across the glass-topped table and sprawled revealingly on the floor. For a moment she lay there kicking and then the screen went blank and a sign appeared. It said OWING TO CIRCUMSTANCES BEYOND OUR CONTROL TRANSMISSION HAS BEEN TEMPORARILY SUSPENDED. Frensic regarded it balefully. It seemed gratuitous. That circumstances were now beyond anyone's control was perfectly obvious. Thanks to Piper's high-mindedness and Sonia Futtle's ghastly intervention his career as a literary agent was done for. The morning papers would be filled with the exposé of The Author Who Wasn't. Hutchmeyer would cancel the contract and almost certainly sue for damages. The possibilities were endless and all of them awful. Frensic turned to find Geoffrey looking at him curiously.

'That *was* Miss Futtle, wasn't it?' he said.

Frensic nodded dumbly.

'What on earth was she doing hurling herself about like that for? I've never seen anything so extraordinary in my life. A bloody author starts lambasting his own novel. What did he say it was? A vile monstrous degenerate book debasing the very foundations of English literature. And the next thing you know is his own agent behaving like a gargantuan banshee, yelling "Cut!" and hurling mikes about the place. Something out of a nightmare.'

Frensic sought frantically for an explanation. 'I suppose you could call it a happening,' he muttered.

'A happening?'

'You know, a sort of random, inconsequential occurrence,' said Frensic lamely.

'A random ... inconsequential ... ?' said Geoffrey. 'If you think there aren't going to be any consequences ...'

Frensic tried not to think of them. 'It certainly made it a very memorable interview,' he said.

Geoffrey goggled at him. 'Memorable? I should think it will go down in history.' He stopped and regarded Frensic open-mouthed. 'A happening? You said a happening. Good Lord, you mean to say you put them up to it?'

'I what?' said Frensic.

'Put them up to it. You deliberately stage-managed that shambles. You got Piper to say all those extraordinary things about his own novel and then Miss Futtle bursts in and goes berserk and you've pulled the biggest publicity stunt ...'

Frensic considered this explanation and found it better than the truth.

'I suppose it was rather good publicity,' he said modestly. 'I mean most of those interviews are rather tame.'

Geoffrey helped himself to some more whisky. 'Well I must take my hat off to you,' he said. 'I wouldn't have had the nerve to dream up a thing like that. Mind you, that Eleanor Beazley has had it coming to her for years.'

Frensic began to relax. If only he could get hold of Sonia before she was arrested or whatever they did to people who burst into TV studios and disrupted programmes, and before Piper could do any more damage with his literary highmindedness, he might be able to save something from the catastrophe.

In the event there was no need. Sonia and Piper had already left the studio in a hurry followed by Eleanor Beazley's shrill voice uttering threats and imprecations and the programme producer's still shriller promise to take legal action. They fled down the corridor and into a lift and shut the door.

'What did you mean by –' Piper began as they descended.

'Drop dead,' said Sonia. 'If it hadn't been for me you'd have landed us all in it up to the eyeballs, shooting your mouth off like that.'

'Well, she said –'

'The hell with what she said,' shouted Sonia, 'it was what *you* were saying that got to me. Looks great, an author telling half a million viewers that his own novel stinks.'

'But it isn't my own novel,' said Piper.

'Oh yes it is. It is now. Wait till you see tomorrow's papers. They're going to have headlines to make you famous. AUTHOR SLAMS OWN NOVEL ON TV. You may not have written *Pause* but you're going to have a hard time proving it.'

'Oh God,' said Piper. 'What are we to do?'

'Get the hell out of here fast,' said Sonia as the lift doors opened. They crossed the foyer and went out to the car. Sonia drove and twenty minutes later they were back at her flat.

'Now pack,' she said. 'We're moving out of here before the press get on to us.'

Piper packed, his mind racing with conflicting emotions. He was saddled with the authorship of a dreadful book, there was no backing out, he was committed to a promotional tour of the States and he was in love with Sonia. When he had finished he made one last attempt at resistance.

'Look, I really don't think I can go on with this,' he said as Sonia lugged her suitcase to the door. 'I mean my nerves can't stand it.'

'You think mine are any better – and what about Frenzy? A shock like that could have killed him. He's got a heart condition.'

'A heart condition?' said Piper. 'I had no idea.'

Nor had Frensic when she phoned him from a call box an hour later.

'I have a what?' he said. 'You wake me in the middle of the night to tell me I've got a heart condition?'

'It was the only way to stop him backing out. That Beazley woman blew his mind.'

'The whole programme blew mine,' said Frensic, 'and to make matters worse I had Geoffrey gibbering beside me all the time too. It's fine experience for a reputable publisher to watch one of his authors describe his own book as a vile degenerate thing. It does something to the soul. And to cap it all Geoffrey thought I'd put you up to rushing on like that screaming "Cut".'

'Put me up to it?' said Sonia. 'I had to do that to stop –'

'*I* know all that but *he* didn't. He thinks it's some sort of publicity stunt.'

'But that's great,' said Sonia. 'Gets us off the hook.'

'Get us on it if you ask me,' said Frensic grimly. 'Anyway where are you? Why the call box?'

'We're going down to Southampton,' said Sonia. 'Now, before he changes his mind again. There's a spare berth on the *QE2* and she's sailing tomorrow. I'm not taking any more chances. We're sailing with her if I have to bribe my way on board. And if that doesn't work I'm going to keep him holed up in a hotel where the press can't get at him until we have him word-perfect on what he's to say about *Pause*.'

'Word-perfect? You make him sound like a performing parrot –'

But Sonia had rung off and was back in the car driving down the road to Southampton.

The next morning a bemused and weary Piper walked unsteadily up the gangway and down to his cabin. Sonia stopped at the Purser's Office. She had a telegram to send to Hutchmeyer.

CHAPTER EIGHT

In New York MacMordie, Hutchmeyer's Senior Executive Assistant, brought him the telegram.

'So they're coming early,' said Hutchmeyer. 'Makes no difference. Just got to get this ball moving a bit quicker is all. Now then, MacMordie, I want you to organize the biggest demonstration you can. And I mean the biggest. You got any angles?'

'With a book like that the only angle I've got is Senior citizens mobbing him like he's the Beatles.'

'Senior Citizens don't mob the Beatles.'

'Okay, so he's Valentino come to life. Whoever. Some great star of the twenties.'

Hutchmeyer nodded. 'That's more like it,' he said. 'The nostalgia angle. But that's not enough. Senior Citizens you don't get much impact.'

'Absolutely none,' said MacMordie. 'Now if this guy Piper was a gay liberationist Jew-baiter with a nigger boyfriend from Cuba called O'Hara I could really call up some muscle. But with a product that screws old women ...'

'MacMordie, how often have I got to tell you what the product is and what the action is are two separate things? There doesn't have to be any connection. You've got to get coverage any way you can.'

'Yes but with a British author nobody's ever heard of and a first-timer who wants to know?'

'I do,' said Hutchmeyer. 'I do and I want a hundred million TV viewers to know too. And I mean know. This guy Piper has to be famous this time next week and I don't care how. You can do what you like just so long as when he steps ashore it's like Lindbergh's flown the Atlantic first time. So you get yourself a pussy posse and every pressure group and lobby you can find and see he gets charisma.'

'Charisma?' said MacMordie doubtfully. 'With the picture we've got of him for the cover you want charisma too? He looks sick or something.'

'So he's sick! Who cares what he looks like? All that matters is he becomes the spinster's prayer overnight. Get Women's Lib involved, and that's a good idea of yours about the fags.'

'We get a lot of little old ladies and the Ms brigade and the gays down on the docks could be we'd have a riot on our hands.'

'That's right,' said Hutchmeyer, 'a riot. Throw the lot at him. A cop gets hurt is good. And some old lady has a coronary, that's good too. She gets pushed in the drink is better still. By the time we've finished with his image this Piper's going to be like he was pied.'

'Pied?' said MacMordie.

'With rats for Chrissake.'

'Rats? You want rats too?'

Hutchmeyer looked at him dolefully. 'Sometimes, MacMordie, I think you've just got to be goddam illiterate,' he snarled. 'Anyone would think you'd never heard of Edgar Allan Poe. And another thing. When Piper's finished stirring the shit publicitywise down here I want him put on the plane up to Maine. Baby wants to meet him.'

'Mrs Hutchmeyer wants to meet this jerk?' said MacMordie.

Hutchmeyer nodded helplessly. 'Right. Like she was crazy for me to get her that guy who wrote about cracking his whip all the time. What the fuck was his name?'

'Portnoy,' said MacMordie. 'We couldn't get him. He wouldn't come.'

'Was that surprising? It was a wonder he could walk after what he'd done to himself. That stuff saps you.'

'We didn't publish him either,' said MacMordie.

'Well there's that too,' Hutchmeyer agreed, 'but we publish this Piper and if Baby wants him she's going to have him. You know something, MacMordie, you'd think at her age and all the operations she's had and being on a diet and all she'd have laid off a bit. I mean can you do it twice a day every goddam day of the year? Well, me neither. But that woman is insatiable. She's going to eat this cuntlapper Piper alive.'

MacMordie made a note to book the company plane for Piper.

'Could be there won't be so much of him to eat by the time the reception committee down here is finished with him,' he said morosely. 'The way you want it things could get rough.'

'The rougher the better. By the time my fucking wife is through with him he's going to know just how rough things can get. You know what that woman's been into now?'

'No,' said MacMordie.

'Bears,' said Hutchmeyer.

'Bears?' said MacMordie. 'You don't mean it. Isn't that a little dangerous? I'd have to be fucking desperate to even think of bears. I knew a woman once who had this German Shepherd but –'

'Not that way,' shouted Hutchmeyer, 'Jesus, MacMordie, we're talking about my wife, not some crazy bitch dog lover. Have some respect please.'

'But you said she was into bears and I thought –'

'The trouble with you, MacMordie, is you don't think. So she's into bears. Doesn't mean the bears are into her for Chrissake. Whoever heard of a woman into anything sexual? It isn't possible.'

'I don't know. I knew a woman once with this –'

'You want to know something, MacMordie, you know some fucking horrible women no kidding. You should get yourself a decent wife.'

'I got a decent wife. I don't go messing no longer. I just don't have the energy.'

'Should eat Wheatgerm and Vitamin E like I do. Helps get it up better than anything. What were we talking about?'

'Bears,' said MacMordie avidly.

'Baby's got this thing about ecology and wildlife. Been reading about animals being human and all. Some guy called Morris wrote a book ...'

'I read that too,' said MacMordie.

'Not that Morris. This Morris worked in a zoo and had a naked ape and writes this book about it. Must have shaved the fucking thing. So Baby reads it and the next thing you know she has bought a lot of bears and things and let them loose round the house. Place is thick with bears and the neighbours start complaining just when I'm applying to join the Yacht Club. I tell you, that woman give me a pain in the ass all the problems she manages to come up with.'

MacMordie looked puzzled. 'If this Morris guy went in for apes how come Mrs Hutchmeyer is into bears?' he asked.

'Whoever heard of a fucking naked ape in the Maine woods? It's impossible. The thing would freeze to death first snowfall and it's got to be natural.'

'Isn't natural having bears in your backyard. Not any place I know.'

'First thing I said to Baby. I said you want an ape it's okay with me but bears is into another ballgame. Know what she said? She said she'd had a naked fucking ape round the house forty years and bears needed protecting. Protecting? Three hundred fifty pounds they weigh and they need protection? Anyone round the place needs protection it's got to be me.'

'What did you do then?' asked MacMordie.

'Got myself a machine-gun and told her the first bear I saw coming into the house I'd blow its fucking head off. So the bears got the message and took to the woods and now it's all fine up there.'

It was all fine at sea too. Piper woke the next morning to find himself in a floating hotel but since his adult life had been spent moving from one boarding-house to another, each with a view of the English Channel, there was nothing very surprising about his new circumstances. True, the luxury he was now enjoying was better than the amenities offered by the Gleneagle Guest House in Exforth, but surroundings meant little to Piper. The main thing in his life was his writing and he continued his routine on the ship. In the morning he wrote at a table in his cabin and after lunch lay with Sonia on the sundeck discussing life, literature and *Pause O Men for the Virgin* in a haze of happiness.

'For the first time in my life I am truly happy,' he confided to his diary and that band of future scholars who would one day study his private life. 'My relationship with Sonia has added a new dimension to my existence and extended my understanding of what it means to be mature. Whether this can be called love only time will tell but is it not enough to know that we interrelate so personally? I can only find it in myself to regret that we have been brought together by so humanly debasing a book as *POMFTV*. But as Thomas Mann would have said with that symbolic irony which is the hallmark of his work "Every cloud has a silver lining", and one can only agree with him. Would that it were otherwise!!! Sonia insists on my re-reading the book so that I can imitate who wrote it. I find this very difficult, both the assumption that I am the author and the need to read what can only influence my own work for the worse. Still, I am persevering with the task and *Search for a Lost Childhood* is coming along as well as can be expected given the exigencies of my present predicament.'

There was a great deal more in the same vein. In the evening Piper insisted on reading what he had written of *Search* aloud to Sonia when she would have preferred to be dancing or playing roulette. Piper disapproved of such frivolities. They were not part of those experiences which made up the significant relationships upon which great literature was founded.

'But shouldn't there be more action?' said Sonia one evening when he had finished reading his day's work. 'I mean nothing ever seems to happen. It's all description and what people think.'

'In the contemplative novel thought is action,' said Piper quoting verbatim from *The Moral Novel*. 'Only the immature mind finds satisfaction in action as an external activity. What we think and feel determines what we are and it is in the essential areness of the human character that the great dramas of life are enacted.'

'Ourness?' said Sonia hopefully.

'Areness,' said Piper. 'Are with an A.'

'Oh.'

'It means essential being. Like *Dasein*.'

'Don't you mean "design"?' said Sonia.

'No,' said Piper, who had once read several sentences from Heidegger, '*Dasein*'s got an A too.'

'You could have fooled me,' said Sonia. 'Still, if you say so.'

'And the novel if it is to justify itself as a mode of intercommunicative art must deal solely with experienced reality. The self-indulgent use of the imagination beyond the parameter of our personal experience demonstrates a superficiality which can only result in the unrealization of our individual potentialities.'

'Isn't that a bit limiting?' said Sonia. 'I mean if all you can write about is what has happened to you you've got to end up describing getting up in the morning and having breakfast and going to work ...'

'Well, that's important too,' said Piper, whose morning's writing had consisted of a description of getting up and having breakfast and going to school. 'The novelist invests these events with his own intrinsic interpretation.'

'But maybe people don't want to read about that sort of thing. They want romance and sex and excitement. They want the unexpected. That's what sells.'

'It may sell,' said Piper, 'but does it matter?'

'It matters if you want to go on writing. You've got to earn your bread. Now *Pause* sells ...'

'I can't imagine why,' said Piper. 'I read that chapter you told me to and honestly it's disgusting.'

'So reality isn't all that nice,' said Sonia, wishing that Piper wasn't quite so highminded. 'We live in a crazy world. There are hijackings and killings and violence all over and *Pause* isn't into that. It's about two people who need one another.'

'People like that shouldn't need one another,' said Piper, 'it's unnatural.'

'It's unnatural going to the moon and people still do it. And there are rockets with nuclear warheads pointing at one another ready to blow the world apart and just about everywhere you look there's something unnatural going on.'

'Not in *Search*,' said Piper.

'So what's that got to do with reality?'

'Reality,' said Piper reverting to *The Moral Novel*, 'has to do with the realness of things in an extra-ephemeral context. It is the re-establishment in the human consciousness of traditional values ...'

While Piper quoted on, Sonia sighed and wished that he would establish traditional values like ask her to marry him or even just climb into bed with her one night and make love in a good old-fashioned way. But here again Piper had principles. In bed at night his activities remained firmly literary. He read several pages of *Doctor Faustus* and then turned to *The Moral Novel* as to a breviary. Then he switched off the light and resisted Sonia's charms by falling fast asleep.

Sonia lay awake and wondered if he was queer or she unattractive, came to the conclusion that she was closeted with some kind of dedicated nut and, hopefully, a genius and decided to postpone any discussion of Piper's sexual proclivities to a later date. After all, the main thing was to keep him cool and collected through the publicity tour and if chastity was what Piper wanted, chastity was what he was going to get.

In fact it was Piper himself who raised the issue one afternoon as they lay on the sundeck. He had been thinking about what Sonia had said about his lack of experience and the need for a writer to have it. In Piper's mind experience was equated with observation. He sat up and decided to observe and was just in time to pay close attention to a middle-aged woman climbing out of the swimming bath. Her thighs, he noted, were dimpled. Piper reached for his ledger of Phrases and wrote down 'Legs indented with the fingerprints of ardent time,' and then as an alternative, 'the hallmarks of past passion.'

'What are?' said Sonia looking over his shoulder.

'The dimples on that woman's legs,' Piper explained, 'the one that's just sitting down.'

Sonia examined the woman critically.

'They turn you on?'

'Certainly not,' said Piper, 'I was merely making a note of the fact. It could come in useful for a book. You said I needed more experience and I'm getting it.'

'That's a hell of a way to get experience,' said Sonia, 'voyeurizing ancient broads.'

'I wasn't voyeurizing anything. I was merely observing. There was nothing sexual about it.'

'I should have known,' said Sonia and lay back in her chair.

'Known what?'

'That there was nothing sexual about it. There never is with you.'

Piper sat and thought about the remark. There was a touch of bitterness about it that disturbed him. Sex. Sex and Sonia. Sex with Sonia. Sex and love. Sex with love and sex without love. Sex in general. A most perplexing subject and one that had for sixteen years upset the even tenor of his days and had produced a wealth of fantasies at variance with his literary principles. The great novels did not deal with sex. They confined themselves to love, and Piper had tried to do the same. He was reserving himself for that great love affair which would unite sex and love in an all-embracing and wholly rewarding totality of passion and sensibility in which the women of his fantasies, those mirages of arms, legs, breasts and buttocks, each particular item serving as the stimulus for a different dream, would merge into the perfect wife. With her because his feelings were on the highest plane he would be perfectly justified in doing the lowest possible things. The gulf that divided the beast in Piper from the angel in his truly beloved would be bridged by the fine flame of their passion, or some such. The great novels said so. Unfortunately they didn't explain how. Beyond love merged with passion there stretched something: Piper wasn't sure what. Presumably happiness. Anyway marriage would absolve him from the interruptions of his fantasies in which a predatory and beastly Piper prowled the dark streets in search of innocent victims and had his way with them which, considering that Piper had never had his way with anyone and lacked any knowledge of female anatomy, would have landed him either in hospital or in the police courts.

And now in Sonia he seemed to have found a woman who appreciated him and should by rights have been the perfect woman. But there were snags. Piper's perfect woman, culled from the great novels, was a creature who combined purity with deep desires. Piper had no objection to deep desires provided they remained deep. Sonia's didn't. Even Piper could tell that. She emanated a readiness for sex which made things very awkward. For one thing it deprived him of his right to be predatory. You couldn't very well be beastly if the angel you were supposed to be beastly to was being even beastlier than you were. Beastliness was relative. Moreover it required a passivity that Sonia's kisses proved she lacked. Locked occasionally in her arms, Piper felt himself at the mercy of an enormously powerful woman and even Piper with his lack of imagination could not see himself being predatory with her. It was all extremely difficult and Piper, sitting on the sundeck watching the ship's wake widening towards the horizon, was struck once again by the contradiction between Life and Art. To relieve his feelings he opened his ledger and wrote, 'A mature relationship demands the sacrifice of the Ideal in the interests of experience and one must come to terms with the Real.'

That night Piper armed himself to come to terms with the Real. He had two large vodkas before dinner, a bottle of Nuits St Georges, which seemed to be appropriately named for the encounter, during the meal, following this with a Benedictine with his coffee and finally went down in the elevator breathing alcohol endearments over Sonia.

'Look, you don't have to,' she said as he fondled her on the way down. Piper remained determined.

'Darling, we're two mature people,' he mumbled and walked unsteadily to the cabin. Sonia went inside and switched on the light. Piper switched it off again.

'I love you,' he said.

'Look, you don't have to appease your conscience,' said Sonia. 'And anyhow ...'

Piper breathed heavily and seized her with dedicated passion. The next moment they were on the bed.

'Your breasts, your hair, your lips ...'

'My period,' said Sonia.

'Your period,' murmured Piper. 'Your skin, your ...'

'Period,' said Sonia.

Piper stopped. 'What do you mean, your period?' he asked vaguely aware that something was amiss.

'My period period,' said Sonia. 'Get it?'

Piper had got it. With a bound the author by proxy of *Pause O Men for the Virgin* was off the bed and into the bathroom. There were more contradictions between Life and Art than he had ever dreamt of. Like physiological ones.

In the big house overlooking Freshman's Bay in Maine, Baby Hutchmeyer, *née* Sugg, Miss Penobscot 1935, lay languorously on her great waterbed and thought about Piper. Beside her was a copy of *Pause* and a glass of Scotch and Vitamin C. She had read the book three times now, and with each reading she had felt increasingly that here at last was a young author who truly appreciated what an older woman had to offer. Not that Baby was, in most aspects older. At forty, read fifty-eight, she still had the body of an accident-prone eighteen-year-old and the face of an embalmed twenty-five. In short she had what it takes, the It in question having been taken by Hutchmeyer in the first ten years of their married life and left for the last thirty. What Hutchmeyer had to give by way of attention and bovine passion he bestowed on secretaries, stenographers and the occasional stripper in Las Vegas, Paris or Tokyo. In return for Baby's complaisancy he gave her money, indulged her enthusiasms whether artistic, social, metaphysical or ecocultural, and boasted in public about their happy marriage. Baby made do with bronzed young interior decorators and had the house and herself redone more times than was strictly necessary. She frequented hospitals that specialized in cosmetic surgery and Hutchmeyer, arriving home from one of his peripatetic passions, had once failed to recognize her. It was then that the matter of divorce first came up.

'So I don't grab you,' said Baby, 'well you don't grab me either. The last time you had it up was the fall of fifty-five and you were drunk then.'

'I must have been,' said Hutchmeyer and immediately regretted it. Baby pulled the rug from under.

'I've been looking into your affairs,' she said.

'So I have affairs. A man in my position's got to prove his virility. You think I'm going to get financial backing when I need it if I'm too old to screw.'

'You're not too old to screw,' said Baby, 'and I'm not talking about those affairs. I'm talking financial affairs. Now you want a divorce it's all right with me. We split fifty-fifty and the price is twenty million bucks.'

'Are you crazy?' yelled Hutchmeyer. 'No way!'

'Then no divorce. I've done an audit on your books and those are the affairs I'm talking of. Now if you want the Internal Revenue boys and the FBI and the courts to know you've been evading taxes and accepting bribes and handling laundered money for organized crime ...'

Hutchmeyer didn't. 'You go your way I'll go mine,' he said bitterly.

'And just remember,' said Baby, 'that if anything happens to me like I die suddenly and like unnaturally I've stashed photocopies of all your little misdemeanours with my lawyers and in a bank vault too ...'

Hutchmeyer hadn't forgotten it. He had an extra seat belt installed in Baby's Lincoln and saw to it she didn't take any risks. The interior decorators returned and so did actors, painters and anyone else Baby fancied. Even MacMordie got dragged one night into the act and was promptly docked a thousand dollars from his salary for what Hutchmeyer lividly called fringe benefits. MacMordie didn't see it that way and had protested to Baby. Hutchmeyer reimbursed him two thousand and apologized.

But for all these side-effects Baby remained unsatisfied. When she wasn't able to find someone or something interesting to do, she read. At first Hutchmeyer had welcomed the move into literacy as an indication that Baby was either growing up or dying down. As usual he was wrong. The strain of self-improvement that had manifested itself in her numerous cosmetic operations combined now with intellectual aspirations to form a fearful hybrid. From being a simple if scarred broad Baby graduated to a well-read woman. The first intimation Hutchmeyer had of this development came when he returned from the Frankfurt Book Fair to find her into *The Idiot*.

'You find it what?' he said when she told him she found it fascinating and relevant. 'Relevant to what?'

'To the spiritual crisis in contemporary society,' said Baby. 'To us.'

'*The Idiot*'s relevant to us?' said Hutchmeyer, scandalized. 'A guy thinks he's Napoleon and icepicks some old dame and that's relevant to us? That is all I need right now. A hole in the head.'

'You've got one. That's *Crime and Punishment*, Dummkopf. For a publisher you know but nothing.'

'I know how to sell books. I don't have to read the goddam things,' said Hutchmeyer. 'Books is for people who don't get satisfaction in doing things. Like vicarious.'

'They teach you things,' said Baby.

'Like what? Having apoplectic fits?' said Hutchmeyer who had finally got his bearings on *The Idiot*.

'Epileptic. A sign of genius. Like Mohammed had them.'

'So now I've got an encyclopedia for a wife,' said Hutchmeyer, 'and with Arabs. What are you going to do? Turn this house into a literary Mecca or something?' And leaving Baby with the germ of this idea he had flown hurriedly to Tokyo and the physical pleasures of a woman who couldn't speak English let alone read it. He came back to find Baby had been into Dostoyevsky and out the other side. She was devouring books with as little discrimination as her bears were now devouring blueberry patches. She hit Ayn Road with as much fervour as Tolstoy, swept amazingly through Dos Passos, lathered in Lawrence, saunaed in Strindberg and then birched herself with Céline. The list was endless and Hutchmeyer found himself married to a biblionut. To make matters worse Baby got into authors. Hutchmeyer loathed authors. They talked about their books and Hutchmeyer under threat from Baby found himself forced to be relatively polite and apparently interested. Even Baby found them disappointing but since the presence of even one novelist in the house sent Hutchmeyer's blood pressure soaring she was generous in her invitations and continued to live in hopes of finding one who lived in the flesh up to his words on paper. And with Peter Piper and *Pause O Men for the Virgin* she felt sure that here at last was a man and his book without discrepancy. She lay on the waterbed and savoured her expectations. It was such a romantic novel. In a significant sort of way. And different.

Hutchmeyer came through from the bathroom wearing a quite unnecessary truss.

'That thing suits you,' said Baby studying the contraption dispassionately. 'You should wear it more often. It gives you dignity.'

Hutchmeyer glared at her.

'No, I mean it,' Baby continued. 'Like it gives you a supportive role.'

'With you to support I need it,' said Hutchmeyer.

'Well, if you've got a hernia you should have it operated on.'

'Seeing what they've done with you I don't need no operations,' Hutchmeyer said. He glanced at *Pause* and went through to his room.

'You still like that book?' he called out presently.

'First good book you've published in years,' said Baby. 'It's beautiful. An idyll.'

'A what?'

'An idyll. You want me to tell you what an idyll is?'

'No,' said Hutchmeyer, 'I can guess.' He climbed into bed and thought about it. An idyll? Well if she said an idyll, an idyll was what it would be to a million other women. Baby was infallible. Still, an idyll?

CHAPTER NINE

There was nothing idyllic about the scene that greeted Piper when the ship berthed in New York. Even the fabulous view of the skyline and the Statue of Liberty, which Sonia had promised would send him, didn't. A heavy mist hung over the river and the great buildings only emerged from it as they moved slowly past the Battery and inched into the berth. By that time Piper's attention had been drawn from the view of Manhattan to a large number of people with visibly different backgrounds and opinions who were gathered on the roadway outside the Customs shed.

'Boy, Hutch has really done you proud,' said Sonia as they went down the gangway. There were shouts from the street and a glimpse of banners some of which said ambiguously, 'Welcome To Gay City', and others even more ominously, 'Go Home, Peipmann'.

'Who on earth is Peipmann?' Piper asked.

'Don't ask me,' said Sonia.

'Peipmann?' said the Customs Officer not bothering to open their bags. 'I wouldn't know. There's a million hags and fags out there waiting for him. Some are for lynching him and others for worse. Have a nice trip.'

Sonia hustled Piper away with their luggage through a barrier to where MacMordie was waiting with a crowd of reporters. 'Pleased to make your acquaintance, Mr Piper,' he said. 'Now if you'll just step this way.'

Piper stepped this way and was immediately surrounded by cameramen and reporters who shouted incomprehensible questions.

'Just say "No comment",' shouted MacMordie as Piper tried to explain that he had never been to Russia. 'That way nobody gets the wrong idea.'

'It's a bit late for that, isn't it?' said Sonia. 'Who the hell told these goons he was in the KGB?'

MacMordie grinned with complicity and the swarm with Piper at its centre moved out into the entrance hall. A squad of cops fought their way through the newsmen and escorted Piper into an elevator. Sonia and MacMordie went down the stairs.

'What in the name of hell gives?' asked Sonia.

'Mr Hutchmeyer's orders,' said MacMordie. 'A riot he asks for, a riot he gets.'

'But you didn't have to say that about him being a hit man for Idi Amin,' said Sonia bitterly. 'Jesus wept!'

At street level it was clear that MacMordie had said a great many other things about Piper, all of them conflicting. A contingent of Survivors of Siberia surged round the entrance chanting, 'Solzhenitsyn Yes. Piperovsky No.' Behind them a band of Arabs for Palestine, acting on the assumption that Piper was an Israeli Minister travelling incognito on an arms-buying mission, battled with Zionists whom MacMordie had alerted to the arrival of Piparfat of the Black September Movement. Farther back a small group of older Jews carried banners denouncing Piepmann but were heavily outnumbered by squads of Irishmen whose information was that O'Piper was a leading member of the IRA.

'Cops are all Irish,' MacMordie explained to Sonia. 'Best to have them on our side.'

'And which goddam side is that?' said Sonia but at that moment the elevator doors opened and an ashen-faced Piper was hustled into public view by his police escort. As the crowd outside surged forward the reporters continued their indefatigable quest for the truth.

'Mr Piper, would you mind just telling us who and what the hell you are?' one of them shouted above the din. But Piper was speechless. His eyes started out of his head and his face was grey.

'Is it true that you personally shot ... ?'

'Can we take it that your government isn't negotiating the purchase of Minutemen rockets?'

'How many people are still in mental ...'

'I know one who soon will be if you don't do something fast,' said Sonia thrusting MacMordie forward. MacMordie launched himself into a fray.

'Mr Piper has nothing to say,' he yelled gratuitously before being hurled to one side by a cop who had just been hit by a bottle of

Seven-Up thrown by an Anti-Apartheid protestor for whom Van Piper was a White South African racist. Sonia Futtle shoved past him.

'Mr Piper is a famous British novelist,' she bawled but the time had passed for such unequivocal statements. More missiles rained against the wall of the building, banners disintegrated and were used as weapons, and Piper was dragged back into the hall.

'I haven't shot anyone,' he squawked. 'I've never been to Poland.' But no one heard him. There was a crackle of walkie-talkies and an urgent plea for police reinforcements. Outside the Survivors of Siberia had succumbed to the Gay Liberationists who were fighting for their own. A number of middle-aged dragsters broke through the police cordon and swooped on Piper.

'No, I'm nothing of the kind,' he yelled as they tried to rescue him from the cops. 'I'm simply a normal ...' Sonia grabbed a pole which had once held a sign saying 'Golden Oldies Love You', and fended off the falsies of one of Piper's captors.

'Oh no he's not,' she shrieked, 'he's mine!' and dewigged another. Then flailing about her she drove the Gay Liberationists out of the lobby. Behind her Piper and the cops cowered while MacMordie shouted encouragement. In the medley outside Arabs For Palestine and Zionists For Israel momentarily united and completed the demolition of Gay Liberation before joining battle again. By that time Sonia had dragged Piper into the elevator. MacMordie joined them and pressed the button. For the next twenty minutes they went up and down while the struggle for Piparfat, O'Piper and Peipmann raged on outside.

'You've really screwed things up now,' Sonia told MacMordie. 'It takes me all my time to get the poor guy over here and you have to arrange Custer's Last Stand for a welcome.'

In the corner the poor guy was sitting on the floor. MacMordie ignored him. 'The product needed exposure and it's sure getting it. This will hit prime time TV. I wouldn't wonder there aren't news flashes going out now.'

'Great,' said Sonia, 'and what have you got laid on for us next? The *Hindenburg* disaster?'

'So this is going to hit the headlines ...' MacMordie began but there was a low moan from the corner. Something had already hit Piper. His hand was bleeding. Sonia knelt beside him.

'What happened, honey?' she asked. Piper pointed wanly at a frisbee on which were painted the words Gulag Go. The frisbee was edged with razor blades. Sonia turned on MacMordie.

'I suppose that was your idea too,' she yelled. 'Frisbees with razor blades. You could guillotine someone with a thing like that.'

'Me? I didn't have a thing –' MacMordie began but Sonia had stopped the elevator.

'Ambulance! Ambulance,' she shouted, but it was an hour before the police managed to get Piper out of the building. By that time Hutchmeyer's instructions had been carried out. So had a large number of protestors who had been rushed to hospital. The streets were littered with broken glass, smashed banners and tear-gas canisters. As Piper was helped into the ambulance his eyes were streaming tears. He sat nursing his injured hand and the conviction that he had come to a mad-house.

'What did I do wrong?' he asked Sonia pathetically.

'Nothing. Nothing at all.'

'You were great, just great,' said MacMordie appreciatively and studied Piper's wound. 'Pity there's not more blood.'

'What more do you want?' snarled Sonia. 'Two pounds of flesh? Haven't you got enough already?'

'Blood,' said MacMordie. 'Colour TV you can tell the difference from ketchup. This has got to be authentic.' He turned to the nurse. 'You got any whole blood?'

'Whole blood? For a scratch like that you want whole blood?' she said.

'Listen,' said MacMordie, 'this guy's a haemophiliac. You going to let him bleed to death?'

'I am not a haemophiliac,' protested Piper but the siren drowned his voice.

'He needs a transfusion,' shouted MacMordie. 'Give me that blood.'

'Are you out of your fucking mind?' screamed Sonia as MacMordie grappled with the nurse. 'Hasn't he been through enough without you wanting to give him a blood transfusion?'

'I don't want a transfusion,' squeaked Piper frantically. 'I don't need one.'

'Yes but the TV cameras do,' said MacMordie. 'In Technicolor.'

'I will not give the patient ...' said the nurse but MacMordie had grabbed the bottle and was wrestling with the cap.

'You don't even know his blood group,' the nurse yelled as the cap came off.

'No need to,' said MacMordie and emptied most of the bottle over Piper's head.

'Now look what you've done,' bawled Sonia. Piper had passed out.

'Okay, so we resuscitate him,' said MacMordie. 'This is going to make Kildare look like nothing,' and he clamped the oxygen mask over Piper's face. By the time Piper was lifted out of the ambulance on a stretcher he looked like death itself. Under the mask and the blood his face had turned purple. In the excitement nobody had thought to turn the oxygen on.

'Is he still alive?' asked a reporter who had followed the ambulance.

'Who knows?' said MacMordie enthusiastically. Piper was carried into Casualty while a bloodstained Sonia tried to calm the nurse who was having hysterics.

'It was too terrible. Never in my whole life have I known such a thing and in my ambulance too,' she screamed at the TV cameras and reporters before being led away after her patient. As the crimson stretcher with Piper's body was lifted on to a trolley and wheeled away, MacMordie wiped his hands with satisfaction. Around him the TV cameras buzzed. The product had got exposure. Mr Hutchmeyer would be pleased.

Mr Hutchmeyer was. He watched the riot on TV with evident satisfaction and all the fervour of a fight enthusiast.

'That's my boy,' he yelled as a young Zionist flattened an innocent Japanese passenger off the ship with a placard saying 'Remember Lod'. A cop tried to intervene and was promptly felled by something in drag. The picture joggled violently as the cameraman was hit from behind. When it finally steadied it was focused on an elderly woman lying bleeding on the ground.

'Great,' said Hutchmeyer, 'MacMordie's done a great job. That boy's got a real talent for action.'

'That's what you think,' said Baby, who knew better.

'What the hell do you mean by that?' said Hutchmeyer, momentarily diverted. Baby shrugged.

'I just don't like violence is all.'

'Violence? So life is violent. Competitive. That's the way the cookie crumbles.'

Baby studied the screen. 'There's two more cookies just crumbled now,' she said.

'Human nature,' said Hutchmeyer, 'I didn't invent human nature.'

'Just exploit it.'

'Make a living.'

'Make a killing if you ask me,' said Baby. 'That woman's not going to make it.'

'Shit,' said Hutchmeyer.

'Took the word out of my mouth,' said Baby. Hutchmeyer concentrated on the screen and tried to ignore Baby. A police posse with Piper came out of Customs.

'That's him,' said Hutchmeyer. 'The motherfucker looks like he's pissing himself.'

Baby looked and sighed. The haunted Piper was just as she had hoped, young, male, pale, sensitive and intensely vulnerable. Like Keats at Waterloo she thought.

'Who's the fatso with MacMordie?' she asked as Sonia kneed a Ukrainian who had just spat on her dress.

'That's my girl,' shouted Hutchmeyer enthusiastically. Baby looked at him incredulously.

'You've got to be joking. One bounce with that female Russian shotput and you'd bust your truss.'

'Never mind my goddam truss,' said Hutchmeyer, 'I'm just telling you that that baby there is the greatest little saleswoman in the world.'

'Great she may be,' said Baby, 'little she ain't. That Muscovite doubled up with lover's balls knows that. What's her name?'

'Sonia Futtle,' said Hutchmeyer dreamily.

'I could have guessed,' said Baby, 'she's just futtled an Irishman now. He'll never ride again.'

'Jesus,' said Hutchmeyer and retreated to his study to avoid the disillusionment of Baby's commentary. He put a call through to New York office for a computer forecast on predicted sales of *Pause O Men for the Virgin* in the light of this great new publicity. Then he got through to Production and ordered another half million copies. Finally a call to Hollywood and a demand for another five per cent in TV serial takings. And all the time his mind was busy with wanton thoughts of Sonia Futtle and some natural way of killing what remained of Miss Penobscot 1935 so that he wouldn't have to part with twenty million dollars to get a divorce. Maybe MacMordie could come up with something. Like fucking her to death. That would be natural. And this Piper guy had a hard-on for old women. Could be there was something there.

In the emergency theatre at the Roosevelt Hospital doctors and surgeons struggled to save Piper's life. The fact that appearances led them to suppose he had bled to death from a head wound while his symptoms were those of suffocation made their task more complicated than it might otherwise have been. The hysterical nurse was no help at all.

'He said he was a bleeder,' she told the chief surgeon who could see that already. 'He said he had to have a transfusion. I didn't want to do it and he said he didn't want one and she told him not to and he got at the blood bank and then he passed out and then they put him on resuscitation and –'

'Put her on sedation,' shouted the surgeon as the nurse was dragged out still screaming. On the operating table Piper was bald. In a desperate attempt to find the site of the wound his hair had been clipped.

'So where the fuck's the haemorrhage?' said the surgeon, shining a light down Piper's left ear in the hope of finding some source for this terrible loss of blood. By the time Piper revived they were none the wiser. The scratch on his hand had been cleansed and covered with a Band-Aid and through a needle in his right wrist he was getting the transfusion he had dreaded. Finally they cut off the supply and Piper got off the table.

'You've had a lucky escape,' said the surgeon. 'I don't know what you're suffering from but you want to take it easy for a while. Maybe the Mayo could come up with an answer. We sure as hell can't.'

Piper wobbled out into the corridor bald as a coot. Sonia burst into tears.

'Oh my God what have they done to you, my darling?' she wailed. MacMordie studied Piper's bald head thoughtfully.

'That doesn't look so good,' he said finally and went into the theatre. 'We've got ourselves a problem,' he told the surgeon.

'No need to tell me. Diagnostically I wouldn't know.'

'Yeah,' said MacMordie, 'it's like that. Now what he needs is bandages round his head. I mean he's famous and there's all those TV guys out there and he's going to come out looking like Kojak and he's an author. That isn't going to improve his image.'

'His image is your problem,' said the surgeon, 'mine just happens to be his illness.'

'You cut his hair all off,' said MacMordie. 'Now how about a whole heap of bandages? Like right across his face and all. This guy needs his anonymity till his hair grows back.'

'No way,' said the surgeon, true to his medical principles.

'A thousand dollars,' said MacMordie and went to fetch Piper. He came reluctantly and clutching Sonia's arm pathetically. By the time he emerged and went outside with Sonia on one side and a nurse on the other only two frightened eyes and his nostrils were visible.

'Mr Piper has nothing to say,' said MacMordie quite unnecessarily. Several million viewers could see that. Piper's bandaged face had no mouth. For them he could have been the invisible man. The cameras zoomed in for close-ups and MacMordie spoke.

'Mr Piper has authorized me to say that he had no idea his great novel

Pause O Men for the Virgin would arouse the degree of public controversy that has marked the start of his lecture tour of this country ...'

'His what?' demanded a reporter.

'Mr Piper is Britain's greatest novelist. His novel *Pause O Men for the Virgin* published by Hutchmeyer Press and available at seven dollars ninety –'

'You mean his novel caused all this?' said an interviewer.

MacMordie nodded. '*Pause O Men for the Virgin* is the most controversial novel of this century. Read it and see what has caused this terrible sacrifice on Mr Piper's part ...'

Beside him Piper swayed groggily and had to be helped down the steps to the waiting car.

'Where are you taking him to now?'

'He's being flown to a private clinic for diagnostic treatment,' said MacMordie and the car moved off. In the back seat Piper whimpered through his bandages.

'What's that, darling?' Sonia asked. But Piper's mumble was incomprehensible.

'What was all that about a diagnostic treatment,' Sonia asked MacMordie. 'He doesn't need –'

'Just to throw the press and media off the trail. Mr Hutchmeyer wants you to stay with him at his residence in Maine. We're going to the airport. Mr Hutchmeyer's private plane is waiting.'

'I'll have something to say to Mr Goddam Hutchmeyer when I see him,' said Sonia. 'It's a wonder you didn't get us all killed.'

MacMordie turned in his seat. 'Listen,' he said, 'you try promoting a foreign writer. He's got to have a gimmick like he's won the Nobel Prize or been tortured in the Lubianka or something. Charisma. Now what's this Piper got? Nothing. So we build him up. We have ourselves a little riot, a bit of blood and all and overnight he's charismatic. And with those bandages he's going to be in every home tonight on TV. Sell a million copies on that face alone.'

They drove to the airport and Sonia and Piper climbed aboard *Imprint One*. Only when they had taken off did Sonia remove the bandages from Piper's face.

'We'll have to leave the rest on till your hair starts to grow again,' she said. Piper nodded his bandaged head.

From Maine Hutchmeyer phoned his congratulations to MacMordie. 'That scene outside the hospital was the greatest,' he said. 'That's going to blow a million viewers' minds. Why we've made a martyr out of him.

Like a sacrificial lamb on the altar of great literature. I tell you, MacMordie, for this you get a bonus.'

'It was nothing,' said MacMordie modestly.

'How did he take it?' asked Hutchmeyer.

'Well he seemed a little confused is all,' said MacMordie. 'He'll get over it.'

'All authors have confused minds,' said Hutchmeyer, 'it's natural with them.'

CHAPTER TEN

And Piper spent the flight in a confused state of mind. He still wasn't sure what had hit him or why and his mixed reception as O'Piper, Piparfat, Peipmann, Piperovsky *et al* added to the problems already confronting him as the suppositious author of *Pause*. And in any case as a putative genius Piper had assumed so many different identities that past personae compounded those of the present. So did shock, MacMordie's bloodbath, suffocation, resuscitation, and the fact that he was wearing a turban of bandages over an unscathed scalp. He stared out of the window and wondered what Conrad or Lawrence or George Eliot would have done in his position. Apart from the certainty that they wouldn't have been in it, he could think of nothing. And Sonia was no great help. Her mind seemed set on making the financial most from his ordeal.

'Either way we've got him over a barrel,' she said as the plane began to descend over Bangor. 'You're too sick to go through with this tour.'

'I absolutely agree,' said Piper.

Sonia crushed his hopes. 'He won't wear that one,' she said. 'With Hutchmeyer it's the contract counts. You could be on an intravenous drip and you'd still have to make appearances. So we sting him for compensation. Like another twenty-five thousand dollars.'

'I think I would rather go home,' said Piper.

'The way I'm going to play it you'll go home with fifty grand.'

Piper raised objections. 'But won't Mr Hutchmeyer be very cross?'

'Cross? He'll blow his top.'

Piper considered the prospect of Mr Hutchmeyer blowing his top and disliked it. It added yet another awful ingredient to a situation that was already sufficiently alarming. By the time the plane landed he was in a state of acute anxiety and it took all Sonia's coaxing to get him down the steps and into the waiting car. Presently they were speeding through pine forests towards the man whom Frensic in an unguarded moment had spoken of as the Al Capone of the publishing world.

'Now you leave all the talking to me,' said Sonia, 'and just remember that you're a shy introverted author. Modesty is the line to take.'

The car turned down a drive towards a house that had proclaimed itself by the gate as 'The Hutchmeyer Residence'.

'No one can call that modest,' said Piper staring out at the house. It stood in fifty acres of park and garden, birch and pine, an ornate shingle-style monument to the romantic eclecticism of the late nineteenth century as embodied in wood by Peabody and Stearns, Architects. Sprouting towers, dormer windows, turrets with dovecotes, piazzas with oval windows cut in their latticework, convoluted chimneys and angled balconies, the Residence was awe-inspiring. They drove under a porte-cochère into a courtyard already crammed with cars and got out. A moment later the enormous front door opened and a large red-faced man bounded down the steps.

'Sonia baby,' he bawled and hugged her to his Hawaiian shirt, 'and this must be Mr Piper.' He crunched Piper's hand and stared fiercely into his face. 'This is a great honour, Mr Piper, a very great honour to have you with us,' still holding Piper's hand he propelled him up the steps and through the door. Inside, the house was as remarkable as the exterior. A vast hall incorporated a thirteenth-century fireplace, a Renaissance staircase, a minstrels' gallery, an excruciatingly ferocious portrait of Hutchmeyer in the pose of J. P. Morgan as photographed by Steichner, and underfoot a mosaic floor depicting a great many stages in the manufacture of paper. Piper stepped cautiously across falling trees, a log jam and a vat of boiling wood pulp and up several more steps at the top of which stood a woman of breathtaking shape.

'Baby,' said Hutchmeyer, 'I want you to meet Mr Peter Piper. Mr Piper, my wife, Baby.'

'Dear Mr Piper,' murmured Baby huskily, taking his hand and smiling as far as the surgeons had permitted, 'I've been just dying to meet you. I think your novel is just the loveliest book I've been privileged to read.'

Piper gazed into the limpid azure contact lenses of Miss Penobscot 1935 and simpered. 'You're too kind,' he murmured. Baby tucked his hand under her arm and together they went into the piazza lounge.

'Does he always wear a turban?' Hutchmeyer asked Sonia as they followed.

'Only when he gets hit with a frisbee,' said Sonia coldly.

'Only when he gets hit with a frisbee,' bawled Hutchmeyer roaring with laughter. 'You hear that, Baby. Mr Piper only wears a turban when he gets hit with a frisbee. Isn't that the greatest?'

'Edged with razor blades, Hutch. With goddam razor blades!' said Sonia.

'Yeah, well that's different of course,' said Hutchmeyer deflating. 'With razor blades is different.'

Inside the piazza lounge stood a hundred people. They clutched glasses and were talking at the tops of their voices.

'Folks,' bawled Hutchmeyer and stilled the din, 'I want you all to meet Mr Peter Piper, the greatest novelist to come out of England since Frederick Forsyth.'

Piper smiled inanely and shook his head with unaffected modesty. He was not the greatest novelist to come out of England. Not yet. His greatness lay in the future and it was on the point of his tongue to state this clearly when the crowd closed round him eager to make his acquaintance. Baby had chosen her guests with care. Against their geriatric backdrop her own reconstituted charms would stand out all the more alluringly. Cataracts and fallen arches abounded. So did bosoms, as opposed to breasts, dentures, girdles, surgical stockings and the protuberant tracery of varicose veins. And strung round every puckered neck and blotchy wrist were jewels, an armoury of pearls and diamomds and gold that hung and wobbled and glistened to detract the eye from the lost battle with time.

'Oh, Mr Piper, I just want to say how much pleasure ...'

'I can't tell you how much it means to me to ...'

'I think it's fascinating to meet a real ...'

'If you would just sign my copy ...'

'You've done so much to bring people together ...'

With Baby on his arm Piper was swallowed up in the adulating crowd.

'Boy, he's really going over big,' said Hutchmeyer, 'and this is Maine. What's he going to do to the cities?'

'I hate to think,' said Sonia watching anxiously as Piper's turban bobbed among the hairdos.

'Wow them. Zap them. We'll sell two million copies if this is anything to indicate. I got a computer forecast after the welcome he got in New York and –'

'Welcome? You call that riot a welcome?' said Sonia bitterly. 'You could have got us killed.'

'Great copy,' said Hutchmeyer, 'I'm going to give MacMordie a bonus. That boy's got talent. And while we're on the subject let me say I've got a proposition to make to you.'

'I've heard your propositions, Hutch, and the answer is still no.'
'Sure but this is different.' He steered Sonia over to the bar.

By the time he had signed fifty copies of *Pause O Men for the Virgin* and
drunk, unthinkably, four Martinis, Piper's earlier apprehensions had
entirely vanished. The enthusiasm with which he was being greeted had
the merit that it didn't require him to say anything. He was bombarded
from all sides by compliments and opinions. They seemed to come in two
sizes. The thin women were intense, the ones with obesity problems
cooed. No one expected Piper to contribute more than the favour of his
smile. Only one woman broached the subject of his novel and Baby
immediately intervened.

'Knock you up, Chloe?' she said. 'Now why should Mr Piper want to
do that? He's got a very tight schedule to meet.'

'So not everyone's had the benefit of a pussy lift,' said Chloe with a
hideous wink at Piper. 'Now the way I read it Mr Piper's book is about
going into the natural in a big way ...'

But Baby dragged Piper away before he could hear what Chloe had
to say about going into the natural in a big way.

'What's a pussy lift?' he asked.

'That Chloe's just a cat,' said Baby, leaving Piper under the happy
illusion that pussy lifts were things cats went up and down in. By the
time the party broke up Piper was exhausted.

'I've put you in the Boudoir bedroom,' said Baby as she and Sonia
escorted him up the Renaissance staircase. 'It's got a wonderful view of
the bay.'

Piper went into the Boudoir bedroom and looked around. Originally
designed to combine convenience with medieval simplicity, it had been
refurbished by Baby with an eye to the supposedly sensual. A heart-
shaped bed stood on a carpet of intermingled rainbows which competed
for radiance with a furbelowed stool and an Art Deco dressing-table. To
complete the ensemble a large and evidently demented Spanish gipsy
supported a tasselled lampshade on a bedside table while a black glass
chest of drawers gleamed darkly against the Wedgwood blue walls. Piper
sat down on the bed and looked up at the great timber rafters. There
was a solid craftsmanship about them that contrasted with the ephemeral
brilliance of the furnishings. He undressed and brushed his teeth and
climbed into bed. Five minutes later he was asleep.

An hour later he was wide awake again. There were voices coming
through the wall behind his quilted bedhead. For a moment Piper
wondered where on earth he was. The voices soon told him. The

Hutchmeyers' bedroom was evidently next to his and their bathroom had a connecting door. During the next half an hour Piper learnt to his disgust that Hutchmeyer wore a truss, that Baby objected to his use of the wash-basin as a urinal, that Hutchmeyer didn't give a damn what she objected to, that Baby's late and unlamented mother, Mrs Sugg, would have done the world a service by having an abortion before Baby was born, and finally that on one traumatic occasion Baby had washed down a sleeping pill with Dentaclene from a glass containing Hutchmeyer's false teeth so would he kindly not leave the things in the medicine cabinet. From these distressing domestic details the conversation veered to personalities. Hutchmeyer thought Sonia mighty attractive. Baby didn't. All Sonia Futtle had got were her hooks into a cute little innocent. It took Piper a moment or two to recognize himself in this description and he was just wondering if he liked being called little and cute when Hutchmeyer riposed by saying he was an asslicking motherfucking Limey who just happened to have written a book that would sell. Piper most definitely didn't like that. He sat up in bed fumbled with the anatomy of the Spanish gipsy and switched the light on. But the Hutchmeyers had warred themselves to sleep.

Piper got out of bed and waded across the carpet to the window. Outside in the darkness he could just make out the shapes of a yacht and a large cruiser lying out at the end of a long narrow jetty. Beyond them across the bay a mountain was silhouetted against the starry sky and the lights of a small town shone faintly. Water slapped on the rocky beach below the house and in any other circumstances Piper would have felt the need to muse on the beauties of nature and their possible use in some future novel. Hutchmeyer's opinion of him had driven such thoughts from his mind. He got out his diary and committed to paper his observations that Hutchmeyer was the epitome of everything that was vulgar, debased, stupid and crassly commercial about modern America and that Baby Hutchmeyer was a woman of sensitivity and beauty, and deserved something better than to be married to a coarse brute. Then he got back into bed, read a chapter of *The Moral Novel* to restore his faith in human nature, and fell asleep.

Breakfast next morning proved a further ordeal. Sonia wasn't up and Hutchmeyer was in his friendliest mood.

'What I like about you is you give your readers a good fuck fantasy,' he told Piper who was trying to make up his mind which breakfast cereal to try.

'Wheatgerm is great for Vitamin E,' said Baby.

'That's for potency,' said Hutchmeyer. 'Piper's potent already, eh Piper? What he needs is roughage.'

'I'm sure he'll get all he needs of roughage from you,' said Baby. Piper poured himself a plateful of Wheatgerm.

'Now like I was saying,' Hutchmeyer continued, 'what readers want is –'

'I'm sure Mr Piper knows already what readers want,' said Baby, 'he doesn't have to hear it over breakfast.'

Hutchmeyer ignored her. 'A guy comes home from work what's he to do? Has himself a beer and watches TV, eats and goes to bed too tired to lay his wife so he reads a book –'

'If he's that tired why does he need to read a book?' asked Baby.

'He's too damned tired to sleep. Needs something to send him off. So he picks up a book and has fantasies he's not in the Bronx but in ... where did you set your book?'

'East Finchley,' said Piper, having trouble with a mouthful of Wheatgerm.

'Devon,' said Baby, 'the book is set in Devon.'

'Devon?' said Hutchmeyer. 'He says it's set in East Finchley, he ought to know for Chrissake. He wrote the goddam thing.'

'It's set in Devon and Oxford,' said Baby stubbornly. 'She has this big house and he –'

'Devon's right,' said Piper, 'I was thinking of my second book.'

Hutchmeyer glowered. 'Yeah, well, wherever. So this guy in the Bronx has fantasies he's in Devon with this old broad who's crazy about him and before he knows it he's asleep.'

'That's a great recommendation,' said Baby, 'and I don't think Mr Piper writes his books with insomniacs in the Bronx in mind. He portrays a developing relationship ...'

'Sure, sure he does but –'

'The hesitations and uncertainties of a young man whose feelings and emotional responses deviate from the socially accepted norms of his socio-sexual age grouping.'

'Right,' said Hutchmeyer, 'no question about it. He's a deviant and –'

'He is not a deviant,' said Baby, 'he is a very gifted adolescent with an identity problem and Gwendolen ...'

While Piper munched his Wheatgerm the battle about his intentions in writing *Pause* raged on. Since Piper hadn't written the book and Hutchmeyer hadn't read it, Baby came out on top. Hutchmeyer retreated to his study and Piper found himself alone with a woman who, for quite the wrong reasons, shared his own opinion that he was a great writer. And cute. Piper had reservations about being called cute by a woman whose own attractions were sufficiently at odds with one another to be disturbing. In the dim light of the party the night before he had supposed her to be thirty-five. Now he was less sure. Beneath her blouse her bra-less breasts pointed to the early twenties. Her hands didn't. Finally there was her face. It had a masklike quality, a lack of anything remotely individual, irregular or out of harmony with the faces of the two-dimensional women he had seen staring so fixedly from the pages of women's magazines like *Vogue*. Taut, impersonal and characterless it held a strange fascination for him, while her limpid azure eyes ... Piper found himself thinking of Yeats's *Sailing to Byzantium* and the artifice of jewelled birds that sang. To steady himself he read the label on the Wheatgerm jar and found that he had just consumed 740 milligrammes of phosphorus, 550 of potassium, together with vast quantities of other essential minerals and every Vitamin B under the sun.

'It seems to have a lot of Vitamin B,' he said, avoiding the allure of those eyes.

'The Bs give you energy,' murmured Baby.

'And As?' asked Piper.

'Vitamin A smooths the mucous membranes,' said Baby and once again Piper was dimly conscious that beneath this dietetic commentary there lurked an undertow of dangerous suggestion. He looked up from the Wheatgerm label and was held once more by that masklike face and limpid azure eyes.

CHAPTER ELEVEN

Sonia Futtle rose late. Never an early riser, she had slept more heavily than usual. The strain of the previous day had taken its toll. She came downstairs to find the house empty apart from Hutchmeyer who was growling into the telephone in his study. She made herself some coffee and interrupted him.

'Have you seen Peter?' she asked.

'Baby's taken him some place. They'll be back,' said Hutchmeyer. 'Now about that proposition I put to you ...'

'No way. F & F is a good agency. We're doing well. So what would I want to change?'

'It's a Vice-Presidency I'm offering you,' said Hutchmeyer, 'and the offer stays open.'

'The only offer I'm interested in right now,' said Sonia, 'is the one you're going to make my client for all the physical injury and mental suffering and public ridicule he sustained as a result of yesterday's riot you organized at the docks.'

'Physical injury? Mental suffering?' shouted Hutchmeyer incredulously. 'That was the greatest publicity in the world and you want me to make an offer?'

Sonia nodded. 'Compensation. In the region of twenty-five thousand.'

'Twenty-five ... Are you crazy? Two million I give him for that book and you want to take me for another twenty-five grand?'

'I do,' said Sonia. 'There is nothing in the contract that says my client has to be subjected to violence, assault and the attentions of lethal frisbees. Now you organized that caper –'

'Go jump,' said Hutchmeyer.

'In that case I shall advise Mr Piper to cancel the tour.'

'You do that,' shouted Hutchmeyer, 'and I'll sue for non-fulfilment of contract. I'll take him to the cleaners. I'll goddam ...'

'Pay up,' said Sonia taking a seat and crossing her legs provocatively.

'Jesus,' said Hutchmeyer admiringly, 'I'll say this for you, you've got nerve.'

'Not all I got,' said Sonia, exposing a bit more, 'I've got Piper's second novel too.'

'And I have the option on it.'

'If he finishes it, Hutch, if he finishes it. You keep this sort of pressure up on him he's likely to Scott Fitzgerald on you. He's sensitive and –'

'I heard all that already. From Baby. Shy, sensitive, my ass. The sort of stuff he writes he ain't sensitive. Got a hide like a fucking armadillo.'

'Which, since you haven't read it ...' said Sonia.

'I don't have to read it. MacMordie read it and he said it made him almost fetch up and MacMordie don't fetch up easy.'

They wrangled on until lunch, happily embroiled in threat and counter-threat and the financial game of poker which was their real expertise. Not that Hutchmeyer paid up. Sonia had never expected him to, but at least it took his mind off Piper.

The same could not be said for Baby. Their walk along the shore to the studio after breakfast had confirmed her impression that at long last she had met a writer of genius. Piper had talked incessantly about literature and for the most part with an incomprehensibility that Baby found so impressive that she returned to the house feeling that she had undergone a cultural experience of the most profound kind. Piper's impressions were rather different, an amalgam of pleasure at having such an attentive and interested audience and wonder that so perceptive a woman could find the book he was supposed to have written anything less than disgusting. He went up to his room and was about to get out his diary when Sonia entered.

'I hope you've been discreet,' she said. 'That Baby's a ghoul.'

'A ghoul?' said Piper. 'She's a deeply sensitive ...'

'A ghoul in gold lamé pants. So what's she been doing with you all morning?'

'We went for a walk and she told me about her interest in conservation.'

'Well she didn't have to. You've only got to look at her to see she's done a great job. Like on her face.'

'She's very keen on health foods,' said Piper.

'And sandblasting,' said Sonia. 'Next time she smiles take a look at the back of her head.'

'At the back of her head? What on earth for?'

'To see how far the skin stretches. If that woman laughed she'd scalp herself.'

'Well all I can say is that she's a lot better than Hutchmeyer,' said Piper, who hadn't forgotten what he had been called the night before.

'Hutch I can handle,' said Sonia, 'no problems there. I've got him eating out of my hand so don't foul things up by making goo-goo eyes at his wife and blowing your top about things literary.'

'I am not making goo-goo eyes at Mrs Hutchmeyer,' said Piper indignantly, 'I wouldn't dream of such a thing.'

'Well she's making them at you,' said Sonia. 'And another thing, keep that turban on. It suits you.'

'It may suit me, but it's very uncomfortable.'

'It will be a lot more uncomfortable if Hutch finds out you didn't get hit with a frisbee,' said Sonia.

They went down to lunch. Thanks to a call for Hutchmeyer from Hollywood which kept him out of the room for most of the meal it was a lot easier than breakfast. He came in as they were having coffee and looked at Piper suspiciously.

'You heard of a book called *Harold and Maude*?' he asked.

'No,' said Piper.

'Why?' said Sonia.

Hutchmeyer looked at her balefully. 'Why? I'll tell you why,' he said. 'Because *Harold and Maude* just happens to be about an eighteen-year-old

who falls in love with an eighty and they've already made the movie.
That's why. And I want to know how come no one told me I was buying
a novel that had already been written by someone else and –'

'Are you suggesting that Piper's guilty of plagiarism?' said Sonia.
'Because if you are let me –'

'Plagiarism?' yelled Hutchmeyer. 'What plagiarism? I'm saying he stole
the goddam story and I've been had for a sucker by some two-bit –'

Hutchmeyer had turned purple and Baby intervened. 'If you're going
to stand there and insult Mr Piper,' she said, 'I am not going to sit here
and listen to you. Come along, Mr Piper. You and I will leave these
two –'

'Stop,' bawled Hutchmeyer, 'I've paid two million dollars and I want
to know what Mr Piper has to say about it. Like ...'

'I assure you I have never read *Harold and Maude*,' said Piper, 'I've
never even heard of it.'

'I can vouch for that,' said Sonia. 'Besides, it's quite different. It's not
the same at all ...'

'Come, Mr Piper,' said Baby and shepherded him out of the room.
Behind them Hutchmeyer and Sonia could be heard shouting. Piper
staggered across the piazza lounge and sank ashen-faced into a chair.

'I knew it would go wrong,' he muttered.

Baby looked at him curiously. 'What would go wrong, honey?' she
asked. Piper shook his head despondently. 'You didn't copy that book,
did you?'

'No,' said Piper, 'I've never even heard of it.'

'Then you've got nothing to worry about. Miss Futtle will sort it out
with him. They're two of a kind. Now why don't you go and have a
rest?'

Piper went dolefully upstairs with her and into his room. Baby went
into her bedroom thoughtfully and shut the door. Her intuition was
working overtime. She sat on the bed and thought about his words, 'I
knew it would go wrong.' Peculiar. What would go wrong? One thing
at least was clear in her mind. He had never heard of *Harold and Maude*.
That was sincerity speaking. And Baby Hutchmeyer had lived with
insincerity long enough to recognize the truth when she heard it. She
waited a while and then went along the passage and quietly opened the
door of Piper's room. He was sitting with his back to her at the table by
the window. At his elbow was a bottle of ink and in front of him a large
leatherbound book. He was writing. Baby watched for a minute and then
very gently shut the door and went back to the great waterbed inspired.
She had just seen true genius at work. Like Balzac. Downstairs there was

the rumble of Hutchmeyer and Sonia Futtle in battle. Baby lay back and stared into space, filled with a terrible sense of her own inutility. In the next room a solitary writer strove to convey to her and millions like her the significance of everything he thought and felt, to create a world enhanced by his imagination which would move into the future a thing of beauty and a joy forever. Downstairs those two word-merchants haggled and fought and ultimately marketed his work. And she did nothing. She was a barren creature without use or purpose, self-indulgent and insignificant. She turned her face to a Tretchikoff and presently fell asleep.

She woke an hour later to the sound of voices from the next room. They were faint and indistinct. Sonia and Piper talking. She lay and listened but could distinguish nothing. Then she heard Piper's door shut and their voices in the passage. She got off the bed and crossed to the bathroom and unbolted the door. A moment later she was in Piper's room. The leatherbound book was still there on the table. Baby crossed the room and sat down. When she got up half an hour later Baby Hutchmeyer was a different woman. She went back through the bathroom, locked the door again and sat before her mirror filled with a terrible intention.

Hutchmeyer's intentions were pretty terrible too. After his row with Sonia he had retreated to his study to blast hell out of MacMordie for not telling him about *Harold and Maude* but it was Saturday and MacMordie wasn't available for blasting. Hutchmeyer called his home number and got no reply. He sat back fuming and wondering about Piper. There was something wrong with the guy, something he couldn't put his finger on, something that didn't fit in with his idea of an author who had written about screwing old women, something weird. Hutchmeyer's suspicions were aroused. He'd known a lot of authors and none of them had been like Piper. No way. They had talked about their work all the time. But this Piper ... He'd love to have a talk with him, get him alone and give him a drink or two to loosen him up. But when he came out of his study it was to find Piper screened by women. Baby was down with a fresh dressing of warpaint and Sonia presented him with a book.

'What's that?' said Hutchmeyer recoiling.

'*Harold and Maude*,' said Sonia. 'Peter and I bought it in Bellsworth for you. You can read it and see for yourself –'

Baby laughed shrilly. 'This I must see. Him readng.'

'Shut up,' said Hutchmeyer. He poured a large highball and handed it to Piper. 'Have a highball, Piper.'

'I won't if you don't mind,' said Piper. 'Not tonight.'

'First goddam writer I ever met who doesn't drink,' said Hutchmeyer.

'First real writer you ever met period,' said Baby. 'You think Tolstoy drank?'

'Jesus,' said Hutchmeyer, 'how should I know?'

'That's a lovely yacht out there,' said Sonia to change the subject. 'I didn't know you were a sailing man, Hutch.'

'He isn't,' said Baby before Hutchmeyer could point out that his boat was the finest ocean racer money could buy and that he'd take on any man who said it wasn't. 'It's part of the props. Like the house and the neighbours and —'

'Shut up,' said Hutchmeyer.

Piper left the room and went up to the Boudoir bedroom to confide some more dark thoughts about Hutchmeyer to his diary. When he came down to dinner Hutchmeyer's face was more flushed than usual and his belligerence index was up several points. He had particularly disliked listening to an exposé of his married life by Baby who had, woman-to-woman, discussed with Sonia the symbolic implications of truss-wearing by middle-aged husbands and its relevance to the male menopause. And for once his 'Shut up' hadn't worked. Baby hadn't shut up, she had opened out with further intimate details of his habits so that Hutchmeyer was in the process of telling her to go drown herself when Piper entered the room. Piper wasn't in a mood to put up with Hutchmeyer's lack of chivalry. His years as a bachelor and student of the great novels had infected him with a reverence for Womanhood and very firm views on husbands' attitudes to wives and these didn't include telling them to go drown themselves. Besides, Hutchmeyer's blatant commercialism and his credo that what readers wanted was a good fuck-fantasy had occupied his mind all day. In Piper's opinion what readers wanted was to have their sensibilities extended and fuck-fantasies didn't come into the category of things that extended sensibilities. He went in to dinner determined to make the point. The opportunity occurred early on when Sonia, to change the subject, mentioned *Valley of The Dolls*. Hutchmeyer, glad to escape from the distressing revelations about his private life, said it was a great book.

'I absolutely disagree with you,' said Piper. 'It panders to the public taste for the pornographic.'

Hutchmeyer choked on a piece of cold lobster. 'It does what?' he said when he had recovered.

'It panders to the public taste for pornography,' said Piper, who hadn't read the book but had seen the cover.

'It does, does it?' said Hutchmeyer.

'Yes.'

'And what's wrong with pandering to public taste?'

'It's debasing,' said Piper.

'Debasing?' said Hutchmeyer, eyeing him with mounting fury.

'Absolutely.'

'And what sort of books do you think the public are going to read if you don't give them what they want?'

'Well I think ...' Piper began before being silenced by a kick under the table from Sonia.

'I think Mr Piper thinks –' said Baby.

'Never mind what you think he thinks,' snarled Hutchmeyer, 'I want to hear what Piper thinks he thinks.' He looked expectantly at Piper.

'I think it is wrong to expose readers to books that are lacking in intellectual content,' said Piper, 'and which are deliberately designed to inflame their imaginations with sexual fantasies that –'

'Inflame their sexual fantasies?' yelled Hutchmeyer, interrupting this quotation from *The Moral Novel*. 'You sit there and tell me you don't hold with books that inflame their readers' sexual fantasies when you've written the filthiest book since *Last Exit*?'

Piper steeled himself. 'Yes, as a matter of fact I do. And as another matter of fact I ...'

But Sonia had heard enough. With sudden presence of mind she reached for the salt and knocked the waterjug sideways into Piper's lap.

'You ever hear anything like that?' said Hutchmeyer as Baby left the room to fetch a cloth and Piper went upstairs to put on a fresh pair of trousers 'The guy has the nerve to tell me I got no right to publish ...'

'Don't listen to him,' said Sonia, 'he's not himself. He's upset. It was that riot yesterday. The blow he got on the head. It's affected him.'

'Affected him? I'll say it has and I'm going to affect the little asshole too. Telling me I'm a goddam pornographer. Why I'll show him ...'

'Why don't you show me your yacht?' said Sonia putting her arms round his neck, a move designed at one and the same time to prevent Hutchmeyer from leaping out of his chair to pursue the retreating Piper and to indicate a new willingness on her part to listen to propositions of all kinds. 'Why don't you and me go out and take a cosy little sail around the bay?'

Hutchmeyer succumbed to the soothing influence. 'Who the hell does he think he is anyhow?' he asked with unconscious acumen. Sonia didn't answer. She clung to his arm and smiled seductively. They went out on to the terrace and down the path to the jetty.

Behind them from the piazza lounge Baby watched them thoughtfully. She knew now that in Piper she had found the man she had been waiting for, an author of real merit and one who, without a drink inside him, could stand up to Hutchmeyer and tell him to his face what he thought of him and his books. One too who appreciated her as a sensitive, intelligent and perceptive woman. She had learnt that from Piper's diary. Piper had expressed himself freely on the subject, just as he had given vent to his opinion that Hutchmeyer was a coarse, crass, stupid and commercially motivated moron. On the other hand there had been several references to *Pause* in the diary that had puzzled her and particularly his statement that it was a disgusting book. It seemed a strangely objective criticism for a novelist to make about his own work and while she didn't agree with him it raised him still further in her estimation. It showed he was never satisfied. He was a truly dedicated writer. And so, standing in the piazza lounge staring through limpid azure contact lenses at the yacht moving slowly away from the jetty, Baby Hutchmeyer was herself filled with a sense of dedication, a maternal dediction amounting to euphoria. The days of useless inactivity were over. From now on she would stand between Piper and the harsh insensitivity of Hutchmeyer and the world. She was happy.

Upstairs Piper was anything but. The first flush of his courage in challenging Hutchmeyer had ebbed away leaving him with the horrible feeling that he was in desperate trouble. He took his wet trousers off and sat on the bed wondering what on earth to do. He should never have left the Gleneagle Guest House in Exforth. He should never have listened to Frensic and Sonia. He should never have come to America. He should never have betrayed his literary principles. As the sunset faded Piper got up and was just looking for another pair of trousers when there was a knock at the door and Baby entered.

'You were wonderful,' she said, 'really wonderful.'

'Kind of you to say so,' said Piper interposing the fur-belowed stool between his trouserless self and Mrs Hutchmeyer and conscious that if anything more was needed to infuriate Mr Hutchmeyer it was to find the two of them in this compromising situation.

'And I want you to know I appreciate what you have written about me,' continued Baby.

'Written about you?' said Piper groping in the cupboard.

'In your diary,' said Baby. 'I know I shouldn't have ...'

'What?' squawked Piper from the depths of the cupboard. He found a pair of trousers and struggled into them.

'I just couldn't help it,' said Baby. 'It was lying open on the table and ...'

'Then you know,' said Piper emerging from the cupboard.

'Yes,' said Baby.

'Christ,' said Piper and slumped on to the stool. 'Are you going to tell him?'

Baby shook her head. 'It's between us two.'

Piper considered this and found it only faintly reassuring. 'It's been a terrible strain,' he said finally. 'I mean not being able to talk to anyone about it. Apart from Sonia of course but she's no help.'

'I don't suppose she is,' said Baby who didn't for one moment suppose that Miss Futtle appreciated being told what a deeply sensitive, intelligent and perceptive person another woman was.

'Well she wouldn't be,' said Piper, 'I mean it was her idea in the first place.'

'It was?' said Baby.

'She said it would work out all right but I knew I would never be able to keep up the pretence,' continued Piper.

'I think that does you great credit,' said Baby trying desperately to imagine what Miss Futtle had had in mind in persuading Piper to pretend that he ... There was something very screwy about all this. 'Look, why don't we go downstairs and have a drink and you can tell me all about it.'

'I've got to talk to someone,' said Piper, 'but won't they be down there?'

'They've gone out on the yacht. We've got all the privacy in the world.'

They went downstairs to a little corner room with a balcony which hung out over rocks and the water lapping the beach.

'It's my hidey hole,' said Baby indicating the rows of books lining the walls. 'Where I can be myself.' She poured two drinks while Piper looked miserably at the titles. They were as confusing as his own situation and seemed to argue an eclecticism he found surprising. Maupassant leant against Hailey who in turn propped up Tolkien, and Piper, whose self was founded upon a few great writers, couldn't imagine how anyone could be themselves in these surroundings. Besides, there were a large number of detective stories and thrillers and Piper held very strong views on such trite works.

'Now tell me all about it,' said Baby soothingly and settled herself on a sofa. Piper sipped his drink and tried to think where to begin.

'Well you see I've been waiting for ten years now,' he said finally, 'and ...'

Dusk deepened into night outside as Piper told his story. Beside him Baby sat enthralled. This was better than books. This was life, life not as she had known it but as she had always wanted it to be. Exciting and mysterious and filled with strange, extraordinary hazards which excited her imagination. She refilled their glasses and Piper, intoxicated by her sympathy, spoke on more fluently than he had ever written. He told the story of his life as an unrecognized genius alone in a garret, in any number of garrets looking out on to the windswept sea, struggling through months and years to express with pen and ink and those exquisite curlicues she had so admired in his notebooks the meaning of life and its deepest significance.

Baby gazed into his face and invested it all with a new romance. Peasoup fogs returned to London. Gas lamps gleamed on the seafronts as Piper took his nightly stroll along the promenade. Baby drew copiously on her fund of half-remembered novels to add these details. Finally there were villains, tawdry rogues out of Dickens, Fagins of the literary world in the form of Frensic & Futtle of Lanyard Lane who lured the genius from his garret with the false promise of recognition. Lanyard Lane! The very name evoked for Baby a legendary London. And Covent Garden. But best of all there was Piper standing alone on a sea wall with the waves breaking below him staring fixedly out across the English Channel, the wind blowing through his hair. And here in front of her was the man himself with his peaked anxious face and tortured eyes, the living embodiment of undiscovered genius as she had visualized it in Keats and Shelley and all those other poets who had died so young. And between him and the harsh relentless reality of Hutchmeyer and Frensic and Futtle there was only Baby herself. For the first time she felt needed. Without her he would be hounded and persecuted and driven to ... Baby prophesied suicide or madness and certainly a haunted, hunted future, with Piper prey to the commercial rapacity of all those forces which had conspired to compromise him. Baby's imagination raced on into melodrama.

'We can't let it happen,' she said impetuously as Piper ran out of self-pity. He looked at her sorrowfully.

'What can I do?' he asked.

'You've got to get away,' said Baby and turned to the door on to the balcony and flung it open. Piper looked dubiously out into the night. The wind had risen and nature, imitating art or Piper's modicum of art, was hurling waves against the rocks below the house. The gusts caught at the curtains and threw them flapping into the room. Baby stood between them gazing out across the bay. Her mind was inflamed with images from novels. The night escape. The sea lashing at a small boat. A great house blazing in the darkness and two lovers locked in one another's arms. She saw herself in new guises, no longer the disregarded wife of a rich publisher, a creature of habits and surgical artifice, but the heroine of some great novel: *Rebecca, Jane Eyre, Gone With The Wind*. She turned back into the room and Piper was astonished at the intensity of her expression. Her eyes gleamed and her mouth was firm with purpose. 'We will go together,' she said and reached out her hand.

Piper took it cautiously. 'Together?' he said. 'You mean ...'

'Together,' said Baby. 'You and I. Tonight.' And holding Piper's hand she led the way out into the piazza lounge.

CHAPTER TWELVE

In the middle of the bay Hutchmeyer wrestled with the helm. His evening had not been a success. It was bad enough to be insulted by one of his own authors, a unique experience for which nothing in twenty-five years in the book trade had prepared him; it was even worse to be out in a yacht in the tail end of a typhoon on a pitch-dark night with a crew that consisted of one cheerfully drunk woman who insisted on enjoying herself.

'This is great,' she shouted as the yacht heaved and a wave broke over the deck, 'England here we come.'

'Oh no we don't,' said Hutchmeyer and put the helm over in order to avoid the possibility that they were heading out into the Atlantic. He stared out into the darkness and then down at the binnacle. At that moment *Romain du Roy* took a terrible turn, water flushed along the rail and into the cockpit. Hutchmeyer clung to the wheel and cursed. Beside him in the darkness Sonia squealed, whether from fear or excitement Hutchmeyer neither knew nor cared. He was wrestling with nautical problems beyond his meagre knowledge. In the dim recesses of his memory he seemed to remember that you shouldn't have sails up in a storm. You rode storms out.

'Hold this,' he yelled to Sonia and waded below into the cabin to find a knife. Another wave broke over the cockpit and into his face as he emerged.

'What are you doing with that thing?' Sonia asked. Hutchmeyer brandished the knife and clung to the rail.

'I'm going to make goddam certain we don't hit land,' he shouted as the yacht scudded forward alarmingly. He crawled along the deck and hacked at every rope he could find. Presently he was writhing in canvas. By the time he had untangled himself they were no longer scudding. The yacht wallowed.

'You shouldn't have done that,' said Sonia, 'I was getting a real high out of that zoom.'

'Well, I wasn't,' said Hutchmeyer, peering into the night. It was impossible to tell where they were. A black sky hung overhead and the lights along both shores seemed to have gone out. Or they had. Out to sea.

'Christ,' said Hutchmeyer dismally. Beside him Sonia played with the wheel happily. There was something exhilarating about being out in a storm on a dark night that appealed to her sense of adventure. It awoke her combative instincts. Something tangible to pit herself against. And besides, Hutchmeyer's despondency was reassuring. At least she had taken his mind off Piper – and off her too. A storm at sea was no scene for seduction. And Hutchmeyer's efforts in that direction had been heavy-handed. Sonia had sought refuge in Scotch. Now as they rose and fell with each successive wave she was cheerfully drunk.

'We'll just have to sit the storm out,' said Hutchmeyer presently but Sonia demanded action.

'Start the motor,' she said.

'What the hell for? We don't know where we are. We could run aground.'

'I want the wind in my hair and the spume in my face,' yelled Sonia.

'Spume?' said Hutchmeyer hoarsely.

'And a man at the helm with his hand on the tiller . . .'

'You got a man at the helm,' said Hutchmeyer taking it from her.

The yacht lurched into the wind and waves sucked at the dragging mainsail. Sonia laughed. 'A real man, a he-man, a seaman. A man with salt in his veins and a sail in his heart. Someone to stir the blood.'

'Stir the blood,' muttered Hutchmeyer. 'You'll get all the blood-stirring you want if we hit a rock. I should never have listened to you. Coming out on a night like this.'

'You should have listened to the weather report,' said Sonia, 'that's what you should have listened to. All I said was . . .'

'I know what you said. You said, "Let's take a sail round the bay." That's what you said.'

'So we're having a little sail. The challenge of the elements. I think it's just wonderful.'

Hutchmeyer didn't. Wet, cold and bedraggled he clutched the wheel and searched the darkness for some sign of the shoreline. It was nowhere to be seen.

'Challenge of the elements my ass,' he thought bitterly, and wondered why it was that women had so little sense of reality.

It was a thought that would have found an echo in Piper's heart. Baby had changed. From being the deeply perceptive intelligent woman he had described in his diary she had become a quite extraordinarily urgent creature hell-bent on getting him out of the house in the middle of a most unsuitably stormy night. To make matters worse she seemed determined to come with him, a course of action calculated in Piper's opinion to put his already strained relations with Mr Hutchmeyer to a test which even flight was hardly likely to mitigate. He made the point to Baby as she led the way through the piazza lounge and into the great hall.

'I mean we can't just walk out together in the middle of the night,' he protested standing on a mosaic vat of boiling wood pulp. Hutchmeyer glowered down from his portrait on the wall.

'Why not?' said Baby, whose sense of the melodramatic seemed to be heightened in these grandiose surroundings. Piper tried to think of a persuasive answer and could only come up with the rather obvious one that Hutchmeyer wouldn't like it. Baby laughed luridly.

'Let him lump it,' she said and before Piper could point out that Hutchmeyer's lumping it was going to be personally disadvantageous and that in any case he would prefer the dangers involved in pulling the wool over Hutchmeyer's eyes as to the authorship of *Pause* to the more terrible ones of running off with his wife, Baby had clutched his hand again and was leading him up the Renaissance staircase.

'Pack your things as quickly as you can,' she said in a whisper as they stood outside the door of the Boudoir bedroom.

'Yes but ...' Piper began whispering involuntarily himself. But Baby had gone. Piper went into his room and switched on the light. His suitcase lay uninvitingly against the wall. Piper shut the door and wondered what on earth to do now. The woman must be demented to think that he was going to ... Piper staggered across the room to the window trying to rid himself of the notion that all this was really happening to him. There was an awful hallucinatory quality about the experience which fitted in with everything that had taken place since he had stepped ashore in New York. Everyone was stark staring mad. What was more they acted out their madness without a moment's hesitation. 'Shoot you as soon as look at you' was the expression that sprang to mind. It certainly sprang to mind five minutes later when Piper, his case still unpacked, opened the door of the Boudoir bedroom and poked his head outside. Baby was coming down the corridor with a large revolver in her hand. Piper shrank back into his room.

'You'd better pack this,' she said.

'Pack it?' said Piper still glowering at the thing.

'Just in case,' said Baby. 'You never know.'

Piper did. He sidled round the bed and shook his head. 'You've got to understand ...' he began but Baby had dived into the drawers of the dressing-table and was piling his underclothes on the bed.

'Don't waste time talking. Get this suitcase,' she said. 'The wind's dying down. They could be back at any moment now.'

Piper looked longingly at the window. If only they would come back now before it was too late. 'I really do think we ought to reconsider this,' he said. Baby stopped emptying the drawers and turned to him. Her taut face was alight with unventured dreams. She was every heroine she had ever read, every woman who had gone off happily to Siberia or followed her man across the Sherman-devastated South. She was more, at once the inspiration and protectress of this unhappy youth. This was her one chance of realization and she was not going to let it escape her. Behind was Hutchmeyer, the years of servitude to boredom and artifice, of surgical restoration and constructed enthusiasms; in front Piper, the knowledge that she was needed, a new life filled with meaning and significance in the service of this young genius. And now at this moment of supreme sacrifice, the culmination of so many years of expectation, he was hesitating. Baby's eyes filled with tears and she raised her arms in supplication.

'Don't you understand what this means?' she asked. Piper gaped at her. He understood only too well what it meant. He was alone in an enormous house with the demented wife of America's richest and most powerful publisher and she was proposing that they should run away together. And if he didn't she would almost certainly tell Hutchmeyer the true story of *Pause* or invent some equally frightful tale about how he had tried to seduce her. And finally there was the gun. It lay on the bed where she had dropped it. Piper glanced at the thing and as he did so Baby took a step forward, the tears that had gathered in her eyes ran down her cheeks and carried with them a contact lens. She fumbled for it on the counterpane and encountered the gun. Piper hesitated no longer. He grabbed the suitcase and plumped it on the bed and the next moment was packing it hastily with his shirts and pants. He didn't stop until everything was in, his ledgers and pens and his bottle of Waterman's Midnight Black. Finally he sat on it and fastened the catches. Only then did he turn towards her. Baby was still groping on the bed.

'I can't find it,' she said, 'I can't find it.'

'Leave it, we don't need a thing like that,' said Piper anxious to avoid any further acquaintance with firearms.

'I must have it,' said Baby, 'I can't get along without it.'

Piper humped the suitcase off the bed and Baby found the contact lens. And the gun. Clutching the one while trying to reinsert the other she followed Piper into the corridor. 'Take your bag down and come back for mine,' she told him and went into her own bedroom. Piper went downstairs, encountered the glowering portrait of Hutchmeyer and came back again. Baby was standing by the great waterbed wearing a mink. Beside her were six large travel bags.

'Look,' said Piper, 'are you sure you really want ...'

'Yes, oh yes,' said Baby. 'It's what I've always dreamt of doing. Leaving all this ... this falsehood and starting afresh.'

'But don't you think ...' Piper began again but Baby was not thinking. With a grand final gesture she picked up the gun and fired it repeatedly into the waterbed. Little spurts of water leapt into the air and the room echoed deafeningly with the shots.

'That's symbolic,' she cried and tossed the gun across the room. But Piper didn't hear her. Grabbing three travel bags in each hand he staggered out of the bedroom and dragged them along the corridor, his ears ringing with the sound of gunfire. He knew now that she was definitely out of her mind and the sight of the expiring waterbed had been another awful reminder of his own mortality. By the time he reached the bottom of the stairs he was panting and puffing. Baby followed him, a wraith in mink.

'Now what?' he asked.

'We'll take the cruiser,' she said.

'The cruiser?'

Baby nodded, her imagination once more inflamed with images from novels. The night flight across the water was essential.

'But won't they ...' Piper began.

'That way they'll never know where we've gone,' said Baby. 'We'll land down the coast and buy a car.'

'Buy a car?' said Piper. 'But I haven't any money.'

'I have,' said Baby and with Piper lugging the travel bags behind her they went through the lounge and down the path to the jetty. The wind had fallen but still the water was choppy and slapped against the wooden piles and the rocks so that drifts of spray sprang up wetly against Piper's face.

'Put the bags aboard,' said Baby, 'I've got to go back for something.'

Piper hesitated for a moment and stared with mixed feelings out across the bay. He wasn't sure whether he wanted Sonia and Hutchmeyer to heave in sight now or not. But there was no sign of them. In the end he dropped the bags down into the cruiser and waited. Baby returned with a briefcase.

'My alimony,' she explained, 'from the safe.' Clutching her mink to her, she clambered down into the cruiser and went to the controls. Piper followed her unsteadily.

'Low on fuel,' she said. 'We'll need some more.' Presently Piper was trudging back and forth between the cruiser and the fuel store at the far side of the courtyard behind the house. It was dark and occasionally he stumbled.

'Isn't that enough?' he asked after the fifth journey as he handed the cans down to Baby in the cruiser.

'We can't afford to make mistakes,' she replied. 'You wouldn't want us to run out of gas in the middle of the bay.'

Piper set off for the store again. There was no doubt in his mind that he had already made a terrible mistake. He should have listened to Sonia. She had said the woman was a ghoul and she was right. A demented ghoul. And what on earth was he doing in the middle of the night filling a cruiser with cans of petrol? It wasn't an activity even vaguely related with being a novelist. Thomas Mann wouldn't have been found dead doing it. Nor would D. H. Lawrence. Conrad might have, just. Even then it was highly unlikely. Piper consulted *Lord Jim* and found nothing reassuring in it, nothing to justify this insane activity. Yes, insane was the word. Standing in the fuel store with two more cans Piper hesitated. There wasn't a single novelist of any merit who would have done what he was doing. They would all have refused to be party to such a scheme. Which was all very well, but then none of them had been in the awful predicament he was in. True, D. H. Lawrence had run off with Mr Somebody-or-other's wife, Frieda, but presumably of his own accord and because he was in love with the woman. Piper was most certainly not in love with Baby and he wasn't doing this of his own accord. Definitely not. Having consulted these precedents Piper tried to think how to live up to them. After all, he hadn't spent the last ten years of his life being the great novelist for nothing. He would take a moral stand. Which was rather easier said than done. Baby Hutchmeyer wasn't the sort of woman who would understand taking a moral stand. Besides there wasn't time to explain. The best thing to do would be to stay where he was and not go down to the boat again. That would put her in a spot when Hutchmeyer and Sonia got back. She'd have her work cut out explaining what she was doing on board the cruiser with her bags packed and ten five-gallon cans of gasolene stashed around the cabin. At least she wouldn't be able to argue that he had forced her to elope with him – if elope was the right word for running away with another man's wife. Not if he wasn't there. On the other hand there was his suitcase on board too. He would have to get that off. But how? Well of course if he didn't go back down there she would come looking for him and in that case ... Piper peered out of the store and seeing that the courtyard was clear, stole across it to the front door and into the house. Presently he was looking out from behind the lattice of the piazza lounge at the boat. Around him the great wooden house creaked. Piper looked at his watch. It was one o'clock. Where had Sonia and Hutchmeyer got to? They should have been back hours ago.

On board the cruiser Baby was having the same thought about Piper. What was keeping him? She had started the engine and checked the fuel gauge and was ready to go now and he was holding everything up. After ten minutes she became genuinely alarmed.

And with each succeeding minute her alarm grew. The sea was calm now and if he didn't come soon ...

'Genius is so unpredictable,' she muttered finally and climbed back on to the jetty. She went round the house and across the yard to the fuel store and switched on the light. Empty. Two jerry-cans standing in the middle of the floor were mute testimony to Piper's change of heart. Baby went to the door.

'Peter,' she called, her thin voice dying in the night air. Thrice she called and thrice there was no reply.

'Oh heartless boy!' she cried and this time it seemed there was an answer. It came faintly from the house in the form of a crash and a muffled shout. Piper had tripped over an ornamental vase. Baby headed across the court and up the steps to the door. Once inside she called again. In vain. Standing in the centre of the great hall Baby looked up at the portrait of her detested husband and it seemed to her overwrought imagination that a smile played about those gross arrogant lips. He had won again. He would always win and she would always remain the plaything of his idle hours.

'Never!' she shouted in answer to the clichés that fluttered hysterically about her mind and to the portrait's unspoken scorn. She hadn't come this far to be deprived of her right to freedom and romance and significance by a pusillanimous literary genius. She would do something, something symbolic that would stand as a testimony to her independence. From the ashes of the past she would arise anew like some wild phoenix from the ... Flames? Ashes? The symbolism drew her on. It would be an act from which there could be no going back. She would burn her boats. Baby, urged on by heroines of several hundred novels, flew back across the courtyard, opened a jerry-can and a moment later was trailing gasolene back to the house. She sloshed it up the steps, over the threshold, across the manifold activities of the mosaic floor, up more steps into the piazza lounge and across the carpet to the study. Then with the reckless abandon that so became her in her new role she seized a table lighter from the desk and lit it. A sheet of flame engulfed the room, scurried into the lounge, hurtled across the hall and out into the night. Then and only then did Baby turn and open the door to the terrace.

Meanwhile Piper, after his brief contretemps with the ornamental vase, was busy on the cruiser. He had heard her call and had seized his opportunity to retrieve his suitcase. He ran down the path to the jetty and clambered aboard. Above him the huge house loomed dark with derived menace. Its towers and turrets, culled from Ruskin and Morris and distilled into shingle through the architectural extravagance of Peabody and Stearns, merged with the lowering sky. Only behind the lattice of the piazza were there lights and these were dim. So was the interior of the cruiser. Piper fumbled about among the travel bags and jerry-cans for his suitcase. Where the hell had it got to? He found it finally under the mink coat and was just disentangling it when he was stopped by a sudden roar from the house and the flicker of flames. Dropping the coat he stumbled to the cabin door and looked out dumbfounded.

The Hutchmeyer Residence was ablaze. Flames shot up across the windows of Hutchmeyer's study. More flames danced behind the latticework. There was a crash of breaking glass as windows shattered in the heat and almost simultaneously from behind the house a mushroom of flame billowed up into the sky followed by the most appalling explosion. Piper gaped, transfixed by the enormity of what was happening. And as he gaped a slim figure detached itself from the shadows of the house and ran across the terrace towards him. It was Baby. The bloody woman must have ... but Piper had no time to follow this obvious train of thought to its conclusion. As Baby ran towards him another train appeared round the side of the house, a train of flames that danced and skipped, held for a moment and then flickered on along the trail of gasolene Piper had left from the fuel store. Piper watched it coming and then, with a presence of mind that was wholly his own and owed nothing to *The Moral Novel*, he clambered onto the jetty and wrestled with the ropes that held the cruiser.

'We've got to get away before that fire ...' he yelled to Baby as she rushed along the jetty towards him. Baby looked over her shoulder at the fuse.

'Oh my God,' she shrieked. The dancing flames were scurrying closer. She leapt down into the boat and into the cabin.

'It's too late,' shouted Piper. The flames were licking along the jetty now. They would reach the boat with its cargo of gas and then ... Piper dropped the line and ran. In the cabin of the cruiser, Baby struggled to find her alimony, grabbed the mink, dropped it again, and finally found the case she was looking for. She turned back towards the door but the flames had reached the end of the jetty and as she looked they leapt the gap. There was no hope. Baby turned to the controls, put the throttle full on, and as the cruiser surged forward, she scrambled out of the cabin and, still clutching the briefcase, dived over the side. Behind her the cruiser gathered speed. Flames flickered somewhere inside to mark its progress and then seemed to die down. Finally it disappeared into the darkness of the bay, the roar of its motor drowned by the much more powerful roar of the blazing house. Baby swam ashore and stumbled up the rocky beach. Piper was standing on the lawn staring in horror at the house. The flames had reached the upper storeys now, they glowed behind windows briefly, there was the crash of breaking glass as more windows splintered and then great gusts of flame shot out to lick up the sides of the shingle. Within minutes the entire façade was ablaze. Baby stood beside Piper proudly.

'There goes my past,' she murmured. Piper turned to look at her. Her hair straggled down her head and her face was naked of its pancake mask. Only her eyes seemed real and in the reflected glow Piper could see that they shone with a demented joy.

'You're out of your tiny mind,' he said with uncharacterisic frankness. Baby's fingers tightened on his arm.

'I did it all for you,' she said. 'You understand that, don't you? We have to plunge into the future unfettered by the past. We have to commit ourselves irrevocably by some free act and make an existential choice.'

'Existential choice?' shrieked Piper. The flames had reached the decorative dovecotes now and the heat was intense. 'You call setting fire to your own house an existential choice? That's not an existential choice, that's a bloody crime, that is.'

Baby smiled happily at him. 'You must read Genet, darling,' she murmured and still gripping his arm pulled him away across the lawn towards the trees. In the distance there came the wail of sirens. Piper hurried. They had just reached the edge of the forest when the night air was split by another series of explosions. Far out across the bay the cruiser had exploded. Twice. And silhouetted against the second ball of flame Piper seemed to glimpse the mast of a yacht.

'Oh my God,' he muttered.

'Oh my darling,' murmured Baby in response and turned her face to his.

CHAPTER THIRTEEN

Hutchmeyer was in a foul temper. He had been insulted by an author, he had proved himself an inept yachtsman, had lost his sails, and finally his virility had been put in doubt by Sonia Futtle's refusal to take his overtures seriously.

'O come on now, Hutch baby,' she had said, 'put it away. This is no time to be proving your manhood. Okay, so you're a man and I'm a woman. I heard you. And I don't doubt you. I really don't. You've got to believe me, I don't. Now you just put your clothes back on again and ...'

'They're wet,' said Hutchmeyer. 'They're soaking wet. You want me to catch my death of pneumonia or something?'

Sonia shook her head. 'Let's just get on back to the house and you can be nice and dry in no time at all.'

'Yeah, well you just tell me how I'm going to get us back home with the mainsail in the water. So all we do is go round in circles. That's what we do. Aw come on, honey ...'

But Sonia wouldn't. She went up on deck and looked across the water. In the cabin doorway Hutchmeyer, pinkly naked and shivering, made one last plea. 'You're all woman,' he said, 'you know that. All woman. I got a real respect for you. I mean we've got ...'

'A wife,' said Sonia bluntly, 'that's what you've got. And I've got a fiancé.'

'You've got a what?' said Hutchmeyer.

'You heard me. A fiancé. Name of Peter Piper.'

'That little –' but Hutchmeyer got no further. His attention had been drawn to the shoreline. He could see it now quite clearly. By the light of a blazing house.

'Look at that,' said Sonia, 'somebody's having one hell of a house-warming.'

Hutchmeyer grabbed the binoculars and peered through them. 'What do you mean "somebody"?' he yelled a moment later. 'That's no somebody. That's my house!'

'That was your house,' said Sonia practically, before the full implications of the blaze dawned on her, 'oh my God!'

'You're damn right,' Hutchmeyer snarled and hurled himself at the starter. The marine engine turned over and the yacht began to move. Hutchmeyer wrestled with the wheel and tried to maintain course for the holocaust that had been his home. Over the port gunwale the mainsail acted as a trawl and the *Romain du Roy* veered to the left. Naked and panting, Hutchmeyer fought to compensate but it was no good.

'I'll have to ditch the sail,' he shouted and at that moment a dark shape appeared silhouetted against the blaze. It was the cruiser. Travelling at speed towards them she too had begun to burn. 'My God, the bastard's going to ram us,' he yelled but the next moment the cruiser proved him wrong. She exploded. First the jerry-cans in the cabin blew up and portions of the cruiser cavorted into the air; second what remained of the hull careered towards them and the main fuel tanks blew. A ball of flame ballooned out and from it there appeared a dark oblong lump which arced through the air and fell with a terrible crash through the foredeck of the yacht. The *Romain de Roy* lifted her stern out of the water, slumped back and began to settle. Sonia, clinging to the rail, stared around her. The hull of the cruiser was sinking with a hissing noise. Hutchmeyer had disappeared and a second later Sonia was in the water as the yacht keeled over, tilted and sank. Sonia swam away from the wreckage. Fifty yards away the sea was alight with flaming fuel from the cruiser and by this eerie light she saw Hutchmeyer in the water behind her. He was clinging to a piece of wood.

'Are you okay?' she called.

Hutchmeyer whimpered. It was obvious that he was not okay. Sonia swam over to him and trod water.

'Help, help,' squawked Hutchmeyer.

'Take it easy,' said Sonia, 'just don't panic. You can swim, can't you?'

Hutchmeyer's eyes goggled in his head. 'Swim? What do you mean "swim"? Of course I can swim. What do you think I'm doing?'

'So you're okay,' said Sonia. 'Now all we got to do is swim ashore ...'

But Hutchmeyer was gurgling again. 'Swim ashore? I can't swim that far. I'll drown. I'll never make it. I'll ...'

Sonia left him and headed towards the floating wreckage. Maybe she

could find a lifejacket. Instead she found a number of empty jerry-cans.
She swam back with one to Hutchmeyer.

'Hang on to this,' she told him. Hutchmeyer exchanged his piece of
wood for the can and clung to it. Sonia swam off again and collected
two more jerry-cans. She also found a piece of rope. Tying the cans
together she looped the rope round Hutchmeyer's waist and knotted it.

'That way you can't drown,' she said. 'Now you just stay right here
and everything is going to be just fine.'

Hutchmeyer, balancing on his raft of cans, stared at her maniacally.
'Fine?' he shrieked. 'Fine? My house is being burnt, some crazy swine
tries to murder me with a fireboat, my beautiful yacht is sunk underneath
me and everything is just fine?'

But Sonia was already out of earshot, swimming for the shore with a
steady sidestroke that would not tire her. All her thoughts were centred
on Piper. He had been in the house when she left and now all that was
left of the house ... She turned over and looked across the water. The
house still bulked large upon the horizon, a yellow, ruddy mass from
which sparks flew continually upwards, and as she watched a great flame
leapt up. The roof had evidently collapsed. Sonia turned on her side and
swam on. She had to get back to find out what had happened. Perhaps
poor darling Peter had had another of his accidents. She prepared herself
for the worst while taking refuge in the maternal excuse that he was
accident-prone before recognizing that Piper's accidents had not after all
been of his making. It had been MacMordie who had arranged the riot
on their arrival in New York. She could hardly blame Piper for that. If
anyone was to blame it had been ...

Sonia shut out the thought of her own culpability by wondering about
the boat that had careered out of the darkness at them and exploded.
Hutchmeyer had said someone had tried to murder him. It seemed an
extraordinary notion but then again it was extraordinary that his house
had caught fire. Put these two events together and it argued an organized
and premeditated action. In that case Piper was not responsible. Nothing
he had ever done had been organized and premeditated. He was plain
accident-prone. With this reassuring thought Sonia reached the beach
and clambered ashore. For several minutes she lay on the ground to get
her strength back and as she lay there another dreadful possibility crossed
her mind. If Hutchmeyer had been right and someone had really tried
to murder him it was all too likely that finding Piper and Baby alone in
the house they had first ... Sonia staggered to her feet and set off through
the trees towards the fire. She had to find out what had happened. And

supposing it had been an accident there was still the chance that the shock of being present when the great house ignited had caused Piper to blurt out to someone that he wasn't the real author of *Pause*. In which case the fat would really be in the fire. If the fat wasn't already. It was the first question she put to a fireman she found dousing a blazing bush in the garden.

'Well if there was he's roasted to a cinder,' he said. 'Some crazy guy loosed off a whole lot of shots when we got here but the roof fell in and he hasn't fired since.'

'Shots?' said Sonia. 'You did say shots?'

'With a machine-gun,' said the fireman, 'from the basement. But like I said the roof fell in and he hasn't fired no more.'

Sonia looked at the glowing mass. Heat waves gusted into her face. Someone firing a machine-gun from the basement? It didn't make sense. Nothing made sense. Unless of course you accepted Hutchmeyer's theory that someone had deliberately set out to murder him.

'And you're quite sure nobody escaped?' she asked.

The fireman shook his head.

'Nobody,' he said. 'We were the first truck to get here and apart from the shooting there hasn't anything come out of there. And the guy who did the shooting just has to be a goner.'

So was Sonia. For a moment she tried to steady herself and then she collapsed. The firemen hoisted her over his shoulder and carried her ' an ambulance. Half an hour later Sonia Futtle was fast asleep in hospital. She had been heavily sedated.

Hutchmeyer on the other hand was wide awake. He sat naked except for the jerry-cans in the back of the Coastguard launch that had rescued him and tried to explain what he had been doing in the middle of the bay at two o'clock in the morning. The Coastguard didn't appear to believe him.

'Okay, Mr Hutchmeyer, so you weren't on board your cruiser when she bombed out ...'

'My cruiser?' yelled Hutchmeyer. 'That wasn't my cruiser. I was on board my yacht.'

The Coastguard regarded him sceptically and pointed to a piece of wreckage on the deck. Hutchmeyer stared at it. The words *Folio Three* were clearly visible, painted on the wood.

'*Folio Three*'s my boat,' he muttered.

'Thought it just might be,' said the Coastguard. 'Still if you say you weren't on her ...'

'On her? On her? Whoever was on that boat is barbecued duck by now. Do I look like I was ...'

Nobody said anything and presently the launch bumped into the shore below what remained of the Hutchmeyer Residence and Hutchmeyer was helped ashore, wrapped in a blanket. In single file they made their way through the woods to the drive where a dozen police cars, fire trucks and ambulances were gathered.

'Found Mr Hutchmeyer floating out there with these,' the Coastguard told the Police Chief and indicated the jerry-cans. 'Thought you might be interested.'

Police Chief Greensleeves looked at Hutchmeyer, at the jerry-cans, and back again. He was obviously very interested.

'And this,' said the Coastguard and produced the piece of wood with *Folio Three* written on it.

Police Chief Greensleeves studied the name. '*Folio Three* eh? Mean anything to you, Mr Hutchmeyer?'

Huddled in the blanket Hutchmeyer was staring at the glowing ruins of his house.

'I said, does *Folio Three* mean anything to you, Mr Hutchmeyer?' the Police Chief repeated and followed Hutchmeyer's gaze speculatively.

'Of course it does,' said Hutchmeyer, 'it's my cruiser.'

'Mind telling us what you were going out on your cruiser this time of the night?'

'I wasn't on my cruiser. I was on my yacht.'

'*Folio Three* is a cruiser,' said the Coastguard officiously.

'I know it's a cruiser,' said Hutchmeyer. 'What I'm saying is that I wasn't on it when the explosion occurred.'

'Which explosion, Mr Hutchmeyer?' said Greensleeves.

'What do you mean "which explosion"? How many explosions have there been tonight?'

Police Chief Greensleeves looked back at the house. 'That's a good question,' he said, 'a very good question. It's a question I keep asking myself. Like how come nobody calls the Fire Department to say the house is burning until it's too late. And when we get there how come somebody is so anxious we don't put the fire out they open up with a heavy machine-gun from the basement and blast all hell out of a fire truck.'

'Somebody opened fire from the basement?' said Hutchmeyer incredulously.

'That's what I said. With a goddam machine-gun, heavy calibre.'

Hutchmeyer looked unhappily at the ground. 'Well I can explain that,' he began and stopped.

'You can explain it? I'd be glad to hear your explanation, Mr Hutchmeyer.'

'I keep a machine-gun in the romper room.'

'You keep a heavy-calibre machine-gun in the romper room? Like to tell me why you keep a machine-gun in the romper room?'

Hutchmeyer swallowed unhappily. He didn't like to at all. 'For protection,' he muttered finally.

'For protection? Against what?'

'Bears,' said Hutchmeyer.

'Bears, Mr Hutchmeyer? Did I hear you say "bears"?'

Hutchmeyer looked round desperately and tried to think of a reasonable answer. In the end he told the truth. 'You see one time my wife was into bears and I . . .' he tailed off miserably.

Police Chief Greensleeves studied him with even keener interest. 'Mrs Hutchmeyer was into bears? Did I hear you say Mrs Hutchmeyer was into bears?'

But Hutchmeyer had had enough. 'Don't keep asking me if that's what you heard,' he shouted. 'If I say Mrs Hutchmeyer was into bears she was into goddam bears. Ask the neighbours. They'll tell you.'

'We sure will,' said Chief Greensleeves. 'So you go out and buy yourself some artillery? To shoot bears?'

'I didn't shoot bears. I just had the gun in case I had to.'

'And I suppose you didn't shoot up fire trucks either?'

'Of course I didn't. Why the hell should I want to do a thing like that?'

'I wouldn't know, Mr Hutchmeyer, any more than I'd know what you were doing in the middle of the bay in the raw with a heap of empty gas-cans tied round you and your house is on fire and nobody has called the Fire Department.'

'Nobody called . . . You mean my wife didn't call . . .' Hutchmeyer gaped at Greensleeves.

'Your wife? You mean you didn't have your wife with you out in the bay on board your cruiser?'

'Certainly not,' said Hutchmeyer. 'I've told you already I wasn't on my cruiser. My cruiser tried to ram me on my yacht and blew up and . . .'

'So where's Mrs Hutchmeyer?'

Hutchmeyer looked around desperately. 'I've no idea,' he said.

'Okay, take him down the station,' said the Police Chief, 'we'll go into this thing more thoroughly down there.' Hutchmeyer was bundled into the back of the police car and presently they were on their way into

Bellsworth. By the time they reached the station Hutchmeyer was in an advanced state of shock.

So was Piper. The fire, the exploding cruiser, the arrival of the fire engines and police cars with their wailing sirens and finally the rapid machine-gun fire from the romper room had all served to undermine what little power of self-assertion he had ever possessed. As the firemen ran for cover and the police dropped to the ground he allowed himself to be led away through the woods by Baby. They hurried along a path and came out in the garden of another large house. People were standing outside the front door gazing at the smoke and flames roaring into the air over the trees. Baby hesitated a moment and then, taking advantage of the cover of some bushes, dragged Piper along below the house and into the woods on the other side.

'Where are we going?' Piper asked after another half mile. 'I mean we can't just walk away like this as if nothing had happened.'

'You want to go back?' hissed Baby.

Piper said he didn't.

'Right, so we've got to get some mileage,' said Baby. They went on and passed three more houses. After two miles Piper protested again.

'They're bound to wonder what's become of us,' he said.

'Let them wonder,' said Baby.

'I don't see that's going to do us any good,' said Piper. 'They are going to find out you deliberately set fire to the house and then there's the cruiser. It's got all my things on it.'

'It had all your things on it. Right now they're not on it any more. They're either at the bottom of the bay or they're floating around alongside my mink. When they find them you know what they're going to think?'

'No,' said Piper.

Baby giggled. 'They're going to think we went with them.'

'Went with them?'

'Like we're dead,' said Baby with another sinister giggle. Piper didn't see anything to laugh about. Death even by proxy wasn't a joke and besides he had lost his passport. It had been in the suitcase with his precious ledgers.

'Right, so they'll know you're dead,' said Baby when he pointed this out to her. 'Like I said, we have to make a break with the past. So we've made it. Completely. We're *free*. We can go anywhere and do anything. We've broken the fetters of circumstance.'

'You may see it that way,' said Piper, 'I can't say I do. As far as I'm concerned the fetters of circumstance happen to be a lot stronger than they ever were before all this happened.'

'Oh you're just a pessimist,' said Baby. 'I mean you've got to look on the bright side.'

Piper did. Even the bay was lit up by the conflagration and a number of boats had gathered offshore to watch the blaze.

'And just how do you think you're going to explain all this?' he said, forgetting for the moment that he was free and that there was no going back. Baby turned on him violently.

'Who's to explain to?' she demanded. 'We're dead. Get it, dead. We don't exist in the world where that happened. That's past history. It hasn't got anything to do with us. We belong to the future.'

'Well someone's going to have to explain,' said Piper, 'I mean you can't just go round burning houses down and exploding boats and hope that people aren't going to ask questions. And what happens when they don't find our bodies at the bottom of the bay?'

'They'll think we floated out to sea or the sharks got us or something. That's not our problem what they think. We've got our new lives to live.'

'Fat chance there's going to be of that,' said Piper, not to be consoled. But Baby was undismayed. Grasping Piper's hand she led the way on through the woods.

'Dual destiny, here we come,' she said gaily. Behind her Piper groaned. Dual destiny with this demented woman was the last thing he wanted. Presently they came out of the woods again. In front of them stood another large house. Its windows were dark and there was no sign of life.

'We'll hole up here until the heat's off,' said Baby using a vernacular that Piper had previously only heard in B-movies.

'What about the people who live here?' he asked. 'Aren't they going to mind if we just move in?'

'They won't know. This is the Van der Hoogens' house and they're away on a world tour. We'll be safe as houses.'

Piper groaned again. In the light of what had just happened at the Hutchmeyer house the saying seemed singularly inappropriate. They crossed the grass and went round a gravel path to the side door.

'They always leave the key in the glasshouse,' said Baby. 'You just stay here and I'll go get it.' She went off and Piper stood uncertainly by the door. Now if ever was his chance to escape. But he didn't take it. He had lived too long in the shadow of other authors' identities to be able now to act on his own behalf. By the time Baby returned he was shaking. A reaction to his predicament had set in. He wobbled into the house after her. Baby locked the door behind them.

*

In Hampstead Frensic got up early. It was Sunday, the day before
publication, and the reviews of *Pause O Men for the Virgin* should be in
the papers. He walked up the hill to the newsagent and bought them all,
even the *News of The World* which didn't review books but would be
consoling reading if the reviews were bad in the others or, worse still,
non-existent. Then, savouring his self-restraint, he strolled back to his
flat without glancing at them on the way and put the kettle on for
breakfast. He would have toast and marmalade and go through the
papers as he ate. He was just making coffee when the telephone rang. It
was Geoffrey Corkadale.

'You've seen the reviews?' he asked excitedly. Frensic said he hadn't.

'I've only just got up,' he said, piqued that Geoffrey had robbed him
of the pleasure of reading the evidently excellent coverage. 'I gather from
your tone that they're good.'

'Good? They're raves, absolute raves. Listed to what Frieda Gormley
has to say in *The Times*, "The first serious novel to attempt the
disentanglement of the social complicity surrounding the sexual taboo
that has for so long separated youth from age. Of its kind *Pause O Men
for the Virgin* is a masterpiece." '

'Gormless bitch,' muttered Frensic.

'Isn't that splendid?' said Geoffrey.

'It's senseless,' said Frensic. 'If *Pause* is the first novel to attempt the
disentanglement of complicity, and Lord alone knows how anyone does
that, it can't be "of its kind". It hasn't got any kind. The bloody book
is unique.'

'That's in the *Observer*,' said Geoffrey not to be discouraged, 'Sheila
Shelmerdine says, "*Pause O Men* blah blah blah moves us by the very
intensity of its literary merits while at the same time demonstrating a
compassionate concern for the elderly and the socially isolated. This
unique novel attempts to unfathom those aspects of life which for too
long have been ignored by those whose business it is to advance the
frontiers of social sensibility. A lovely book and one that deserves the
widest readership." What do you think of that?'

'Frankly,' said Frensic, 'I regard it as unmitigated tosh but I'm
delighted that Miss Shelmerdine has said it all the same. I always said
it would be a money-spinner.'

'You did, you most certainly did,' said Geoffrey, 'I have to hand it to
you, you've been absolutely right.'

'Well we'll have to see about that,' said Frensic before Geoffrey could
become too effusive. 'Reviews aren't everything. People have yet to buy
the book. Still, it augurs well for American sales. Is there anything else?'

'There's a rather nasty piece by Octavian Dorr.'

'Oh good,' said Frensic. 'He's usually to the point and I like his style.'

'I don't,' said Geoffrey. 'He's far too personal for my taste and he should stick to the book. That's what he's paid for. Instead he has made some rather odious comparisons. Still I suppose he has given us some quotable quotes for the jacket of Piper's next book and that's the main thing.'

'Quite,' said Frensic and turned with relish to Octavian Dorr's column in the *Sunday Telegraph*, 'I just hope we do as well with the weeklies.'

He put the phone down, made some toast and settled down with Octavian Dorr whose piece was headed 'Permissive Senility'. It began, 'It is appropriate that the publishers of *Pause O Men for the Virgin* by Peter Piper should have printed their first book during the reign of Catherine The Great. To so-called heroine of this their latest has many of the less attractive characteristics of that Empress of Russia. In particular a fondness amounting to sexual mania for the favours of young men and partiality for indiscretion that was, to say the least, regrettable. The same can be said for the publishers, Corkadales ...'

Frensic could see exactly why Geoffrey had hated the review. Frensic found it entirely to his taste. It was long and strident and while it castigated the author, the publisher and the public whose appetite for perverse eroticism made the sale of such novels profitable, and then went on to blame society in general for the decline in literary values, it nevertheless drew attention to the book. Mr Dorr might deplore perverse eroticism but he also helped to sell it. Frensic finished the review with a sigh of relief and turned to the others. Their praise, the presumptuous pap of progressive opinion, earnest, humourless and sickeningly well-meaning, had given *Pause* the imprimatur of respectability Frensic had hoped for. The novel was being taken seriously and if the weeklies followed suit there was nothing to worry about.

'Significance is all,' Frensic murmured and helped his nose to snuff. 'Prime the pump with meaningful hogwash.'

He settled back in his chair and wondered if there was anything he could do to ensure that *Pause* got the maximum publicity. Some nice big sensational story for the daily papers ...

CHAPTER FOURTEEN

In the event Frensic had no need to worry. Five hours to the west the sensational story of Piper's death at sea was beginning to break. So was Hutchmeyer. He sat in the police chief's office and stared at the chief and told his story for the tenth time to an incredulous audience. It was empty gasolene cans that were fouling things up for him.

'Like I've told you, Miss Futtle tied them to me to keep me afloat while she went to get help.'

'She went to get help, Mr Hutchmeyer? You let a little lady go and get help ...'

'She wasn't little,' said Hutchmeyer, 'she's goddam large.'

Chief Greensleeves shook his head sorrowfully at this lack of chivalry. 'So you were out in the middle of the bay with this Miss Futtle. What was Mrs Hutchmeyer doing all this time?'

'How the hell would I know? Setting fire to my hou ...' Hutchmeyer stopped himself.

'That's mighty interesting,' said Greensleeves. 'So you're telling us Mrs Hutchmeyer is an arsonist.'

'No I'm not,' shouted Hutchmeyer, 'all I know is –' He was interrupted by a lieutenant who came in with a suitcase and several articles of clothing, all sodden.

'Coastguards found these out in the wreckage,' he said and held a coat up for inspection. Hutchmeyer stared at it in horror.

'That's Baby's,' he said. 'Mink. Cost a fortune.'

'And this?' asked the lieutenant indicating the suitcase.

Hutchmeyer shrugged. The lieutenant opened the case and removed a passport.

Greensleeves took it from him. 'British,' he said. 'British passport in the name of Piper, Peter Piper. The name mean anything to you?'

Hutchmeyer nodded. 'He's an author.'

'Friend of yours?'

'One of my authors. I wouldn't call him a friend.'

'Friend of Mrs Hutchmeyer maybe?' Hutchmeyer ground his teeth.

'Didn't hear that, Mr Hutchmeyer. Did you say something?'

'No,' said Hutchmeyer.

Chief Greensleeves scratched his head thoughtfully. 'Seems like we've got ourselves another little problem here,' he said finally. 'Your cruiser blows out of the water like she's been dynamited and when we go look see what do we find? A mink coat that's Mrs Hutchmeyer's and a bag that belongs to a Mr Piper who just happens to be her friend. You think there's any connection?'

'What do you mean "any connection"?' said Hutchmeyer.

'Like they was on that cruiser when she blew?'

'How the hell would I know where they were? All I know is that whoever was on that cruiser tried to kill me.'

'Interesting you say that,' said Chief Greensleeves, 'very interesting.'

'I don't see anything interesting about it.'

'Couldn't be the other way round, could it?'

'Could what be the other way round?' said Hutchmeyer.

'That you killed them?'

'I did what?' shouted Hutchmeyer and let go his blanket. 'Are you accusing me of –'

'Just asking questions, Mr Hutchmeyer. There's no need for you getting excited.'

But Hutchmeyer was out of his chair. 'My house burns down, my cruiser blows up, my yacht's sunk under me, I'm in the water drowning some hours and you sit there and suggest I killed my ... why you fat bastard I'll have my lawyers sue you for everything you've got. I'll –'

'Sit down and shut up,' bawled Greensleeves. 'Now you just listen to me. Fat bastard I may be but no New York mobster's going to tell me. We know all about you, Mr Hutchmeyer. We don't just sit on our asses and watch you move in and buy up good real estate with money that could be laundered for the Mafia and we don't know about it. This isn't Hicksville and it isn't New York. This is Maine and you don't carry any weight round here. And we don't like your sort moving in and buying us up. We may be a poor state but we ain't dumb. Now, are you going to tell us what really happened with your wife and her fancy friend or are we going to have to drag the bay and sift the ashes of your house till we find them?'

Hutchmeyer slumped nakedly back into his chair, appalled at the glimpse he had just been given of his social standing in Frenchman's Bay. Like Piper, he knew now that he should never have come to Maine. He was more than ever convinced of his mistake when the lieutenant came in with Baby's travel bags and pocket book.

'There's a whole lot of money in the bag,' he told Greensleeves. The Chief pawed through it and extracted a wad of wet notes. 'Seems like Mrs Hutchmeyer was going some place with a lot of dollars when she died,' he said. 'So now we've really got ourselves a problem. Mrs

Hutchmeyer on that cruiser with her friend, Mr Piper. Both got baggage
with them and money. And then "Bam" their cruiser explodes just like
that. I reckon we're going to have to send divers down to see if they can
find the bodies.'

'Have to start quick,' said the lieutenant. 'The way the tide's running
they could be out to sea by now.'

'So we start now,' said Greensleeves and went out into the lobby where
some reporters were waiting.

'Got any theory?' they asked.

Greensleeves shook his head. 'We got two people missing presumed
drowned. Mrs Baby Hutchmeyer and a Mr Piper. He's a British author.
That's all for now.'

'What about this Miss Futtle?' said the lieutenant. 'She's missing too.'

'And what about the house being burnt down?'

'We're waiting for a report on that,' said Greensleeves.

'But you do suspect deliberate arson?'

Greensleeves shrugged. 'You put all these things together and work
out what I suspect,' he said and pressed on. Five minutes later the wires
were buzzing with the news that Peter Piper, the famous author, was
dead in bizarre circumstances.

In the Van der Hoogen mansion the victims of the tragedy listened to
the news of their deaths on a transistor in the gloom of a bedroom on
the top floor. Part of the gloom resulted from the shutters on the windows
and part, from Piper's point of view, from the prospect that his death
opened up before him. It was bad enough being an author by proxy,
but being a corpse by proxy was awful beyond belief. Baby on the other
hand greeted the news gaily.

'We've made it,' she said. 'They're not even going to come looking for
us. You heard what they said. With the tide running the skindivers aren't
expecting to find the bodies.'

Piper looked miserably round the bedroom. 'It's all very well you
talking,' he said. 'What you don't seem to understand is that I don't
have an identity. I've lost my passport and all my work. How on earth
am I going to get back to England? I can't go to the Embassy and ask
for another passport. And the moment I appear in public I'm going to
be arrested for arson and boat-burning and attempted murder. You've
landed us in a ghastly mess.'

'I've freed you from the past. You can be anyone you want to be now.'

'All I want to be is myself,' said Piper.

Baby looked at him dubiously. 'From what you told me last night you weren't yourself before,' she said, 'I mean what sort of self were you being the author of a book you didn't write?'

'At least I knew what I wasn't. Now I don't even know that.'

'You're not a dead body. That's one good thing.'

'I might just as well be,' said Piper looking lugubriously at the sheeted forms of the furniture as if they were so many shrouds cloaking those different authors he had so happily aspired to be. The dim light filtering through the shuttered windows added to the impression that he was sitting in a tomb, the sepulchre of his literary ambitions. A sense of profound melancholy settled on him and with it the imagery of *The Flying Dutchman* doomed to wander the seas until such day ... but for Piper there would be no release. He had been party to a crime, a whole number of crimes, and even if he went to the police now they wouldn't believe him. Why should they? Was it likely that a rich woman like Baby would burn down her own home and blow up an expensive cruiser and sink her husband's yacht? And even if she admitted that she was to blame for the whole thing, there would still be a trial and Hutchmeyer's lawyers would want to know why his suitcase had been on the boat. And finally the fact that he hadn't written *Pause* would come out and then everyone would suspect ... not even suspect, they would be certain he was a fraud and after the Hutchmeyer money. And Baby had stolen a quarter of a million dollars from the safe in Hutchmeyer's study. Piper shook his head hopelessly and looked up to find her watching him with interest.

'No way, baby,' she said evidently reading his mind. 'It's dual destiny for us now. You try anything and I'll turn myself in and say you forced me.'

But Piper was past trying anything. 'What are we going to do now?' he asked. 'I mean we can't just sit here in someone else's house for ever.'

'Two days, maybe three,' said Baby, 'then we'll move on.'

'How? Just how are we going to move on?'

'Simple,' said Baby, 'I'll call for a cab and we'll take a flight from Bangor. No problems. They won't be looking for us on dry land ...'

She was interrupted by a crunch on the drive. Piper went to the shutters and looked down. A police car had stopped outside.

'The cops,' Piper whispered. 'You said they wouldn't be looking for us.'

Baby joined him at the window. A bell chimed eerily two floors below. 'They're merely checking the Van der Hoogens to ask if they heard anything suspicious last night,' she said. 'They'll go away again.' Piper stared down at the two policemen. All he had to do now was to call out and ... but Baby's fingers tightened on his arm and Piper made no

sound. Presently after wandering round outside the house the two cops
got back into their car and drove away.

'What did I tell you?' said Baby, 'no problems. I'll go down to the
kitchen and get us something to eat.'

Left to himself Piper paced the dim room and wondered why he hadn't
called out to those two policemen. The simple, obvious reasons no longer
sufficed. If he had called out it would have been some proof that he'd
had nothing to do with the fire ... at least an indication of innocence.
But he had made no move. Why not? He had had a chance to escape
from this mess and he hadn't taken it. Not through fear only but more
alarmingly out of a willingness, almost a desire, to remain alone in this
empty house with an extraordinary woman. What sort of terrible
complicity was it that had prevented him? Baby was mad. He had no
doubt in his mind about that and yet she exercised a weird fascination
for him. He had never met anyone in his life before like her. She was
oblivious of the ordinary conventions that ordered other people's lives
and she could look calmly down at the police and say 'They will go away
again' as if they were simply neighbours paying a social call. And they
had. And he had done what she had expected and would go on doing
it, even to the point of being anyone he wanted in this circumscribed
freedom she had created round him by her actions. Anyone he wanted?
He could only think of other authors but none had been in his predicament,
and without a model to guide him Piper was thrown back on his own
limited resources. And on Baby's. He would become what she wanted.
That was the truth of the matter. Piper glimpsed the attraction she held
for him. She knew what he was. She had said so last night before
everything had started to go wrong. She had said he was a literary genius
and she had meant it. For the first time he had met someone who knew
what he really was and having found her he couldn't let her go. Exhausted
by this frightening realization Piper lay down on the bed and closed his
eyes and when Baby came upstairs with a tray she found him fast asleep.
She looked at him fondly and then putting the tray down, took a sheet
from a chair and covered him with it. Under the shroud Piper slept on.

In the police station Hutchmeyer would have done the same if they had
let him. Instead, still naked beneath the blanket, he was subjected to
interminable questions about his relations with his wife and with Miss
Futtle and what Piper meant to Mrs Hutchmeyer and finally why he
had chosen a particularly stormy night to go sailing in the bay.

'You usually go sailing without checking the weather?'

'Look I told you we just went out for a sail. We weren't figuring on going places, we just got up ...'

'From the dinner table and said, "Let's just you and me ..."'

'Miss Futtle suggested it,' said Hutchmeyer.

'Oh she did, did she? And what did Mrs Hutchmeyer have to say about you going sailing with another woman?'

'Miss Futtle isn't another woman. Not that sort of other woman. She's a literary agent. We do business together.'

'Naked on a yacht in the middle of a mini-hurricane you do business together? What sort of business?'

'We weren't doing business on the yacht. It was a social occasion.'

'Kind of thought it was. I mean naked and all.'

'I wasn't naked to begin with. I just got wet so I took my clothes off.'

'You just got wet so you took your clothes off? Are you sure that was the only reason you were naked?'

'Of course I'm sure. Look, no sooner had we got out there than the wind blew up ...'

'And the house blew up. And your cruiser blew up. And Mrs Hutchmeyer blew up and this Mr Piper ...' Hutchmeyer blew up.

'Okay, Mr Hutchmeyer, if that's the way you want it,' said Greensleeves as Hutchmeyer was pinned back into his chair. 'Now we're really going to get tough.'

He was interrupted by a sergeant who whispered in his ear. Greensleeves sighed. 'You're sure?'

'That's what she says. Been up at the hospital all day.'

Greensleeves went out and looked at Sonia. 'Miss Futtle? You say you're Miss Futtle?'

Sonia nodded. 'Yes,' she said. The police chief could see that Hutchmeyer had been telling the truth after all. Miss Futtle was not a little lady, not by a long way.

'Okay, we'll take your statement in here,' he said and took her into another office. For two hours Sonia made her statement. When Greensleeves came out he had an entirely new theory. Miss Futtle had been most cooperative.

'Right,' he said to Hutchmeyer, 'now we'd like you to tell us just what happened down in New York when Piper arrived. We understand you arranged a kind of riot for him.'

Hutchmeyer looked wildly round. 'Now wait a minute. That was just a publicity stunt. I mean ...'

'And what I mean,' said Greensleeves, 'is that you set this Mr Piper up for a target for every crazy pressure group going. Arabs, Jews, Gays, the IRA, the blacks, old women, you name it, you let them loose on the guy and you call that a publicity stunt?'

Hutchmeyer tried to think. 'Are you telling me that one of those groups did this thing?' he asked.

'I'm not telling you anything, Mr Hutchmeyer. I'm asking.'

'Asking what?'

'Asking you if you think it was so goddam clever setting Mr Piper up for a target when the poor guy hadn't done anything worse than write a book for you? Doesn't seem you did yourself or him a favour the way things have worked out, does it?'

'I didn't think anything like this ...'

Greensleeves leant forward. 'Now I'm just telling you something for your own good, Mr Hutchmeyer. You're going to get the hell out of here and not come back. Not if you know what's good for you. And next time you dream up a publicity stunt for one of your authors you'd better get him a goddam bodyguard first.'

Hutchmeyer staggered out of the office.

'I need some clothes,' he said.

'Well you're not going to get any back at your house. It's all burnt down.'

On a bench Sonia Futtle was weeping.

'What's the matter with her?' said Hutchmeyer.

'She's all broken up with this Piper's dying,' said Greensleeves, 'and it kind of surprises me you aren't grief-stricken about the late Mrs Hutchmeyer.'

'I am,' said Hutchmeyer, 'I just don't show my feelings is all.'

'So I noticed,' said Greensleeves. 'Well you'd better go comfort your alibi. We'll send out some clothes.'

Hutchmeyer crossed to the bench in his blanket. 'I'm sorry ...' he began but Sonia was on her feet.

'Sorry?' she shrieked, 'you murdered my darling Peter and now you say you're sorry?'

'Murdered him?' said Hutchmeyer. 'All I did was ...'

Greensleeves left them to it and sent out for some clothes. 'We can forget this case,' he told the lieutenant, 'this is Federal stuff. Terrorists in Maine. I mean who the hell would believe it?'

'You don't think it was the Mafia then?'

'What's the matter who it was? We aren't going to get anywhere to solving it is all I know. The FBI can handle this case. I know when I'm out of my depth.'

In the end Hutchmeyer, dressed in a dark suit that didn't fit him properly, and the still inconsolable Sonia were driven to the airport and took the company plane to New York.

They landed to find that MacMordie had laid on the media. Hutchmeyer lumbered down the steps and made a statement.

'Gentlemen,' he said brokenly, 'this has been a double tragedy for me. I have lost the most wonderful, warm-hearted little wife a man ever had. Forty years of happy marriage lie ...' He broke off to blow his nose. 'It's just terrible. I can't express the full depths of my feelings.'

'Peter Piper was a young novelist of unsurpassed brilliance. His passing has been a great blow to the world of letters.' He paraded his handkerchief again and was prompted by MacMordie.

'Say something about his novel,' he whispered.

Hutchmeyer stopped sniffing and said something about *Pause O Men for the Virgin* published by Hutchmeyer Press price seven dollars ninety and available at all ... Behind him Sonia wept audibly and had to be escorted to the waiting car. She was still weeping when they drove off.

'A terrible tragedy,' said Hutchmeyer, still under the influence of his own oratory, 'really terrible.'

He was interrupted by Sonia who was pummelling MacMordie.

'Murderer,' she screamed, 'it was all your fault. You told all those crazy terrorists he was in the KGB and the IRA and a homosexual and now look what's happened!'

'What the hell's going on?' yelled MacMordie, 'I didn't do ...'

'The fucking cops up in Maine think it was the Symbionese Liberation Army or The Minutemen or someone,' said Hutchmeyer, 'so now we've got another problem.'

'I can see that,' said MacMordie as Sonia blacked his eye. Finally, refusing Hutchmeyer's offer of hospitality, she insisted on being driven to the Gramercy Park Hotel.

'Don't worry,' said Hutchmeyer as she got out, 'I'm going to see that Baby and Piper go to their Maker with all the trimmings. Flowers, a cortège, a bronze casket ...'

'Two,' said MacMordie, 'I mean they wouldn't fit ...'

Sonia turned on them. 'They're dead,' she screamed. 'Dead. Doesn't that mean anything to you? Haven't you any consciences? They were real people, real living people and now they're dead and all you can talk about is funerals and caskets and –'

'Well we've got to recover the bodies first,' said MacMordie practically, 'I mean there's no use talking about caskets, we don't have no bodies.'

'Why don't you just shut your mouth?' Hutchmeyer told him, but Sonia had fled into the hotel.

They drove on in silence.

For a while Hutchmeyer had considered firing MacMordie but he changed his mind. After all he had never liked the great wooden house in Maine and with Baby dead ...

'It was a terrible experience,' he said, 'a terrible loss.'

'It must have been,' said MacMordie, 'all that loveliness gone to waste.'

'It was a showhouse, part of the American heritage. People used to come up from Boston just to look at it.'

'I was thinking of Mrs Hutchmeyer,' said MacMordie. Hutchmeyer looked at him nastily.

'I might have expected that from you, MacMordie. At a time like this you have to think about sex.'

'I wasn't thinking sex,' said MacMordie, 'she was a remarkable woman characterwise.'

'You can say that again,' said Hutchmeyer. 'I want her memory embalmed in books. She was a great book-lover you know. I want a leather-bound edition of *Pause O Men for the Virgin* printed with gold letters. We'll call it the Baby Hutchmeyer Memorial Edition.'

'I'll see to it,' said MacMordie.

And so while Hutchmeyer resumed his role as publisher Sonia Futtle lay weeping on her bed in the Gramercy Park. She was consumed by guilt and grief. The one man who had ever loved her was dead and it was all her fault. She looked at the telephone and thought of calling Frensic but it would be the middle of the night in England. Instead she sent a telegram. PETER PRESUMED DEAD DROWNED MRS HUTCHMEYER DITTO POLICE INVESTIGATING CRIME WILL CALL WHEN CAN SONIA.

CHAPTER FIFTEEN

Frensic arrived in Lanyard Lane next morning in fine fettle. The world was a splendid place, the sun was shining, the people would shortly be in the shops buying *Pause* and best of all Hutchmeyer's cheque for two million dollars was nestling happily in the F & F bank account. It had arrived the previous week and all that needed to be done now was to subtract four hundred thousand dollars' commission and transfer the remainder to Mr Cadwalladine and his strange client. Frensic would see to it this morning. He collected his mail from the box and stumped upstairs to his office. There he seated himself at his desk, took his first pinch of Bureau for the day and went through the letters in front of him. It was near the bottom of the pile that he came upon the telegram.

'Telegrams, really!' he muttered to himself in criticism of the extravagant hurry of an insistent author and opened it. A moment later Frensic's rosy view of the world had disintegrated, to be replaced by fragmentary and terrible images that rose from the cryptic words on the form. Piper dead? Presumed drowned? Mrs Hutchmeyer ditto? Each staccato message became a question in his mind as he tried to cope with the information. It was a minute before Frensic could realize the full import of the thing and even then he doubted and took refuge in disbelief. Piper couldn't be dead. In Frensic's comfortable little world death was something your authors wrote about. It was unreal and remote, a fabrication, not something that happened. But there, in these few words unadorned by punctuation marks and typed on crooked strips of paper, death intruded. Piper was dead. So was Mrs Hutchmeyer but Frensic accorded her no interest. She wasn't his responsibility. Piper was. Frensic had persuaded him to go to his death. And POLICE INVESTIGATING CRIME robbed him of even the consolation that there had been an accident. Crime and death suggested murder and to be confronted with Piper's murder added to Frensic's sense of horror. He sagged in his chair ashen with shock.

It was some time before he could bring himself to read the telegram again. But it still said the same thing. Piper dead. Frensic wiped his face with his handkerchief and tried to imagine what had happened. This time PRESUMED DROWNED held his attention. If Piper was dead why was there the presumption that he had drowned? Surely they knew how he had died. And why couldn't Sonia call? WILL CALL WHEN CAN added a new dimension of mystery to the message. Where could she be if she couldn't phone straightaway? Frensic visualized her lying hurt in a hospital but if that was the case she would have said so. He reached for the phone to put a call through to Hutchmeyer Press before realizing that New York was five hours behind London time and there would be no one in the office yet. He would have to wait until two o'clock. He sat staring at the telegram and tried to think practically. If the police were investigating the crime it was almost certain they would follow their inquiries into Piper's past. Frensic foresaw them discovering that Piper hadn't in fact written *Pause*. From that it would follow that ... my God, Hutchmeyer would get to know and there'd be the devil to pay. Or, more precisely, Hutchmeyer. The man would demand the return of his two million dollars. He might even sue for breach of contract or fraud. Thank God the money was still in the bank. Frensic sighed with relief.

To take his mind off the dreadful possibilities inherent in the telegram he went through to Sonia's office and looked in the filing cabinet for the letter from Mr Cadwalladine authorizing Piper to represent the author on the American tour. He took it out and studied it carefully before putting it back. At least he was covered there. If there was any trouble with Hutchmeyer Mr Cadwalladine and his client were party to the deception. And if the two million had to be refunded they would be in no position to grumble. By concentrating on these eventualities Frensic held at bay his sense of guilt and transferred it to the anonymous author. Piper's death was his fault. If the wretched man had not hidden behind a *nom de plume* Piper would still be alive. As the morning wore on and he sat unable to work at anything else Frensic's feeling of grievance grew. He had been fond of Piper in an odd sort of way. And now he was dead. Frensic sat miserably at his desk looking out over the roofs of Covent Garden and mourned Piper's passing. The poor fellow had been one of nature's victims, or rather one of literature's victims. Pathetic. A man who couldn't write to save his life ...

The phrase brought Frensic up with a start. It was too apt. Piper was dead and he had never really lived. His existence had been one long battle to get into print and he had failed. What was it that drove men like him to try to write, what fixation with the printed word held them at their desks year after year? All over the world there were thousands of other Pipers sitting at this very moment in front of blank pages which they would presently fill with words that no one would ever read but which in their naïve conceit they considered to have some deep significance. The thought added to Frensic's melancholy. It was all his fault. He should have had the courage and good sense to tell Piper that he would never be a novelist. Instead he had encouraged him. If he had told him Piper would still be alive, he might even have found his true vocation as a bank clerk or plumber, have married and settled down – whatever that meant. Anyway, he wouldn't have spent those forlorn years in forlorn guest-houses in forlorn seaside resorts living by proxy the lives of Conrad and Lawrence and Henry James, the shadowy ghost of those dead authors he had revered. Even Piper's death had been by way of being a proxy one as the author of a novel he hadn't written. And somewhere the man who should have died was living undisturbed.

Frensic reached for the phone. The bastard wasn't going to go on living undisturbed. Mr Cadwalladine could relay a message to him. He dialled Oxford.

'I'm afraid I've got some rather bad news for you,' he said when Mr Cadwalladine came on the line.

'Bad news? I don't understand,' said Mr Cadwalladine.

'It concerns the young man who went to America as the supposed author of that novel you sent me,' said Frensic.

Mr Cadwalladine coughed uncomfortably. 'Has he ... er ... done something indiscreet?' he asked.

'You could put it like that,' said Frensic. 'The fact of the matter is that we are likely to have some problems with the police.' Mr Cadwalladine made more uncomfortable noises which Frensic relished. 'Yes, the police,' he continued. 'They may be making inquiries shortly.'

'Inquiries?' said Mr Cadwalladine, now definitely alarmed. 'What sort of inquiries?'

'I can't be too certain at the moment but I thought I had better let you and your client know that he is dead,' said Frensic.

'Dead?' croaked Mr Cadwalladine.

'Dead,' said Frensic.

'Good Lord. How very unfortunate.'

'Quite,' said Frensic. 'Though from Piper's point of view "unfortunate" seems rather too mild a word, particularly as he appears to have been murdered.'

This time there was no mistaking Mr Cadwalladine's alarm. 'Murdered?' he gasped, 'You did say "murdered"?'

'That's exactly what I said. Murdered.'

'Good God,' said Mr Cadwalladine. 'How very dreadful.'

Frensic said nothing and allowed Mr Cadwalladine to dwell on the dreadfulness of it all.

'I don't quite know what to say,' Mr Cadwalladine muttered finally.

Frensic pressed home his advantage. 'In that case if you will just give me the name and address of your client I will convey the news to him myself.'

Mr Cadwalladine made negative noises. 'There's no need for that. I shall let him know.'

'As you wish,' said Frensic. 'And while you're about it you had also better let him know that he will have to wait for his American advance.'

'Wait for his American advance? You're surely not suggesting ...'

'I am not suggesting anything. I am merely drawing your attention to the fact that Mr Hutchmeyer was not privy to the substitution of Mr Piper for your anonymous client and, that being the case, if the police should unearth our little deception in the course of their inquiries ... you take my point?'

Mr Cadwalladine did. 'You think Mr ... er ... Hutchmeyer might ... er ... demand restitution?'

'Or sue,' said Frensic bluntly, 'in which case it would be as well to be in a position to refund the entire sum at once.'

'Oh definitely,' said Mr Cadwalladine for whom the prospect of being sued evidently held very few attractions. 'I leave the matter entirely in your hands.'

Frensic ended the conversation with a sigh. Now that he had passed some of the responsibility on to Mr Cadwalladine and his damned client he felt a little better. He took a pinch of snuff and was savouring it when the phone rang. It was Sonia Futtle calling from New York. She sounded extremely distressed.

'Oh Frenzy, I'm sorry,' she said, 'it's all my fault. If it hadn't been for me this would never have happened.'

'What do you mean your fault?' said Frensic. 'You don't mean you ...'

'I should never have brought him over here. He was so happy ...' she broke off and there was the sound of sobs.

Frensic gulped. 'For God's sake tell me what's happened,' he said.

'The police think it was murder,' said Sonia and sobbed again.

'I gathered that from your telegram. But I still don't know what happened. I mean how did he die?'

'Nobody knows,' said Sonia, 'that's what's so awful. They're dragging the bay and going through the ashes of the house and ...'

'The ashes of the house?' said Frensic, trying desperately to square a burnt house with Piper's presumed death by drowning.

'You see Hutch and I went out in his yacht and a storm blew up and then the house caught fire and someone fired at the firemen and Hutch's cruiser tried to ram us and exploded and we were nearly killed and ...'

It was a confused and disjointed account and Frensic, sitting with the phone pressed hard to his ear, tried in vain to form a coherent picture of what had occurred. In the end he was left with a series of chaotic images, an insane jigsaw puzzle in which, though the pieces all fitted, the final picture made no sense at all. A huge wooden house blazing into the night sky. Someone inside this inferno fending off firemen with a heavy machine-gun. Bears. Hutchmeyer and Sonia on a yacht in a hurricane. Cruisers hurtling across the bay and finally, most bizarre of all, Piper being blown to Kingdom Come in the company of Mrs Hutchmeyer wearing a mink coat. It was like a glimpse of hell.

'Have they no idea who did it?' he asked.

'Only some terrorist group,' said Sonia. Frensic swallowed.

'Terrorist group? Why should a terrorist group want to kill poor Piper?'

'Well because of all the publicity he got in that riot in New York,' said Sonia. 'You see when we landed ...'

She told the story of their arrival and Frensic listened in horror. 'You mean Hutchmeyer deliberately provoked a riot? The man's mad.'

'He wanted to get maximum publicity,' Sonia explained.

'Well he's certainly succeeded,' said Frensic.

But Sonia was sobbing again. 'You're just callous,' she wept. 'You don't seem to see what this means ...'

'I do,' said Frensic, 'it means the police are going to start looking into Piper's background and ...'

'That we're to blame,' cried Sonia, 'we sent him over and we are the ones –'

'Now hold it,' said Frensic, 'if I'd known Hutchmeyer was going to rent a riot for his welcome I would never have consented to his going. And as for terrorists ...'

'The police aren't absolutely certain it was terrorists. They thought at first that Hutchmeyer had murdered him.'

'That's more like it,' said Frensic. 'From what you've told me it's nothing more than the truth. He's an accessory before the fact. If he hadn't ...'

'And then they seemed to think the Mafia could be involved.'

Frensic swallowed again. This was even worse. 'The Mafia? What would the Mafia want to kill Piper for? The poor little sod hadn't ...'

'Not Piper. Hutchmeyer.'

'You mean the Mafia were trying to kill Hutchmeyer?' said Frensic wistfully.

'I don't know what I mean,' said Sonia, 'I'm telling you what I heard the police say and they mentioned that Hutchmeyer had had dealings with organized crime.'

'If the Mafia wanted to kill Hutchmeyer why did they pick on Piper?'

'Because Hutch and I were out on the yacht and Peter and Baby ...'

'What baby?' said Frensic desperately incorporating this new and grisly ingredient into an already cluttered crimescape.

'Baby Hutchmeyer.'

'Baby Hutchmeyer? I didn't know the swine had any ...'

'Not that sort of baby. Mrs Hutchmeyer. She was called Baby.'

'Good God,' said Frensic.

'There's no need to be so heartless. You sound as if you didn't care.'

'Care?' said Frensic. 'Of course I care. This is absolutely frightful. And you say the Mafia ...'

'No I didn't. I said that's what the police said. They thought it was some sort of attempt to intimidate Hutchmeyer.'

'And has it?' asked Frensic trying to extract a morsel of comfort from the situation.

'No,' said Sonia, 'he's out for blood. He says he's going to sue them.'

Frensic was horrified. 'Sue them? What do you mean "sue them"? You can't sue the Mafia and anyway ...'

'Not them. The police.'

'Hutchmeyer's going to sue the police?' said Frensic now totally out of his depth.

'Well first off they accused him of doing it. They held him for hours and grilled him. They didn't believe his story that he was out on the yacht with me. And then the gas-cans didn't help.'

'Gas-can? What gas-can?'

'The ones I tied round his waist.'

'You tied gas-cans round Hutchmeyer's waist?' said Frensic.

'I had to. To stop him from drowning.'

Frensic considered the logic of this remark and found it wanting. 'I should have thought ...' he began before deciding there was nothing to be gained by regretting that Hutchmeyer hadn't been left to drown. It would have saved a lot of trouble.

'What are you going to do now?' he asked finally.

'I don't know,' said Sonia, 'I've got to wait around. The police are still making inquiries and I've lost all my clothes ... and oh Frenzy it's all so horrible.' She broke down again and wept. Frensic tried to think of something to cheer her up.

'You'll be interested to hear that the reviews in the Sunday papers were all good,' he said but Sonia's grief was not assuaged.

'How can you talk about reviews at a time like this?' she said. 'You just don't care at all.'

'My dear I do. I most certainly do,' said Frensic, 'it's a tragedy for all of us. I've just been speaking to Mr Cadwalladine and explaining that in the light of what has happened his client will have to wait for his money.'

'Money? Money? Is that all you think about, money? My darling Peter is dead and ...'

Frensic listened to a diatribe against himself, Hutchmeyer and someone called MacMordie, all of whom in Sonia's opinion thought only about money. 'I understand your feelings,' he said when she paused for breath, 'but money does come into this business and if Hutchmeyer finds out that Piper wasn't the author of *Pause* ...'

But the phone had gone dead. Frensic looked at it reproachfully and replaced the receiver. All he could hope now was that Sonia kept her wits about her and that the police didn't carry their investigations too far into Piper's past history.

In New York Hutchmeyer's feelings were just the reverse. In his opinion the police were a bunch of half-wits who couldn't investigate anything properly. He had already been in touch with his lawyers only to be advised that there was no chance of suing Chief Greensleeves for wrongful arrest because he hadn't been arrested.

'That bastard held me for hours with nothing on but a blanket,' Hutchmeyer protested. 'They grilled me under hot lamps and you tell me I've got no comeback. There ought to be a law protecting innocent citizens against this kind of victimization.'

'Now if you could show they'd roughed you up a bit we could maybe do something but as it is ...'

Having failed to get satisfaction from his own lawyers Hutchmeyer turned his attention to the insurance company and got even less comfort there. Mr Synstrom of the Claims Department visited him and expressed doubts.

'What do you mean you don't necessarily go along with the police theory that some crazy terrorists did this thing?' Hutchmeyer demanded.

Mr Synstrom's eyes glinted behind silver-rimmed spectacles. 'Three and a half million dollars is a lot of money,' he said.

'Of course it is,' said Hutchmeyer, 'and I've been paying my premiums and that's a lot of money too. So what are you telling me?'

Mr Synstrom consulted his briefcase. 'The Coastguard recovered six suitcases belonging to Mrs Hutchmeyer. That's one. They contained all her jewellery and her best clothing. That's two. Three is that Mr Piper's suitcase was on board that boat and we've checked it contained all his clothes too.'

'So what?' said Hutchmeyer.

'So if this is a political murder it seems peculiar that the terrorists made them pack their bags first and loaded them aboard the cruiser and then set fire to the boat and arsoned the house. That doesn't fit the profile of terrorist acts of crime. It looks like something else again.'

Hutchmeyer glared at him. 'If you're suggesting I blew myself up in my own yacht and bumped off my wife and most promising author ...'

'I'm not suggesting anything,' Mr Synstrom said, 'all I'm saying is that we've got to go into this thing a lot deeper.'

'Yeah, well you do that,' said Hutchmeyer, 'and when you've finished I want my money.'

'Don't worry,' said Mr Synstrom, 'we'll get to the bottom of this thing. With three and a half million at stake we've incentive.'

He got up and made for the door. 'Oh and by the way it may interest you to know that whoever arsoned your house knew exactly where everything was. Like the fuel store. This could have been an inside job.'

He left Hutchmeyer with the uncomfortable notion that if the cops were morons, Mr Synstrom and his investigators weren't. An inside job? Hutchmeyer thought about the words. And all Baby's jewellery on board. Maybe ... just supposing she *had* been going to run off with that jerk Piper? Hutchmeyer permitted himself the luxury of a smile. If that was the case the bitch had got what was coming to her. Just so long as those incriminating documents she had deposited with her lawyers didn't suddenly turn up. That wasn't such a pleasant prospect. Why couldn't Baby have gone some simpler way, like a coronary?

CHAPTER SIXTEEN

In Maine the Van der Hoogens' mansion was shuttered and shrouded and empty. As Baby had promised their departure had passed unnoticed. Leaving Piper alone in the dim twilight of the house she had simply walked into Bellsworth and bought a car, a secondhand estate.

'We'll ditch it in New York and buy something different,' she said as they drove south. 'We don't want to leave any trail behind us.'

Piper, lying on the floor in the back, did not share her confidence. 'That's all very well,' he grumbled, 'but they're still going to be looking for us when they don't find our bodies out in the bay. I mean it stands to reason.'

But Baby drove un unperturbed. 'They'll reckon we were washed out to sea by the tide,' she said. 'That's what would have happened if we had really drowned. Besides I heard in Bellsworth they picked up your passport and my jewels in the bags they found. They've got to believe we're dead. A woman like me doesn't part with pearls and diamonds until the good Lord sends for her.'

Piper lay on the floor and found some sense in this argument. Certainly Frensic & Futtle would believe he was dead and without his passport and his ledgers ... 'Did they find my notebooks too?' he asked.

'Didn't mention them but if they got your passport, and they did, it's even money your notebooks were with them.'

'I don't know what I'm going to do without my notebooks,' said Piper, 'they contained my life's work.'

He lay back and watched the tops of the trees flashing past and the blue sky beyond, and thought about his life's work. He would never finish *Search for a Lost Childhood* now. He would never be recognized as a literary genius. All his hopes had been destroyed in the blaze and its aftermath. He would go through what remained of his existence on earth posthumously famous as the author of *Pause O Men for the Virgin*. It was an intolerable thought and provoked in him a growing determination to put the record straight. There had to be some way of issuing a disclaimer. But disclaimers from beyond the grave were not easy to fabricate. He could hardly write to *The Times Literary Supplement* pointing out that he hadn't in fact written *Pause* but that its authorship had been foisted on him by Frensic & Futtle for their own dubious ends. Letters signed 'the late Peter Piper' ... No, that was definitely out. On the other hand it was insufferable to go down in literary history as a pornographer. Piper wrestled with the problem and finally fell asleep.

When he woke they had crossed the state line and were in Vermont. That night they booked into a small hotel on the shores of Lake Champlain as Mr and Mrs Castorp. Baby signed the register while Piper carried two empty suitcases purloined from the Van der Hoogen mansion into the cabin.

'We'll have to buy some clothes and things tomorrow,' said Baby. But Piper was not concerned with such material details. He stood at the window staring out and tried to adjust himself to the extraordinary notion that to all intents and purposes he was married to this crazy woman.

'You realize we are never going to be able to separate,' he said at last.

'I don't see why not,' said Baby from the depths of the shower.

'Well for one simple reason I haven't got an identity and can't get a job,' said Piper, 'and for another you've got all the money and if either of us gets picked up by the police we'll go to prison for the rest of our lives.'

'You worry too much,' said Baby. 'This is the land of opportunity. We'll go some place nobody will think of looking and begin all over again.

'Such as where?'

Baby emerged from the shower. 'Like the South. The Deep South,' she said. 'That's one place Hutchmeyer is never going to come. He's got this thing about the Ku Klux Klan. South of the Mason-Dixon he's never been.'

'And what the hell am I going to do in the Deep South?' asked Piper.

'You could always try your hand at writing Southern novels. Hutch may not go South but he certainly publishes a lot of novels about it. They usually have this man with a whip and a girl cringing on the cover. Surefire bestsellers.'

'Sounds just my sort of book,' said Piper grimly and took a shower himself.

'You could always write it under a pseudonym.'

'Thanks to you I'd bloody well have to.'

As night fell outside the cabin Piper crawled into bed and lay thinking about the future. In the twin bed beside him Baby sighed.

'It's great to be with a man who doesn't pee in the washbasin,' she murmured. Piper resisted the invitation without difficulty.

The next morning they moved on again, following back roads and driving slowly and always south. And always Piper's mind nagged away at the problem of how to resume his interrupted career.

In Scranton, where Baby traded the estate for a new Ford, Piper took the opportunity to buy two new ledgers, a bottle of Higgins Ink and an Esterbrook pen.

'If I can't do anything else I can at least keep a diary,' he explained to Baby.

'A diary? You don't even look at the landscape and we eat in McDonalds so what's to put in a diary?'

'I was thinking of writing it retrospectively. As a form of vindication. I would –'

'Vindication? And how can you write a diary retrospectively?'

'Well I'd start with how I was approached by Frensic to come to the States and then work my way forward day by day with the voyage across and everything. That way it would look authentic.'

Baby slowed the car and pulled into a rest area. 'Let's just get this straight. You write the diary backwards ...'

'Yes, I think it was April the 10th Frensic sent me the telegram ...'

'Go on. You start 10 April and then what?'

'Well then I'd write how I didn't want to do it and how they persuaded me and promised to get *Search* published and everything.'

'And where would you finish?'

'Finish?' said Piper. 'I wasn't thinking of finishing. I'd just go on and ...'

'So what about the fire and all?' said Baby.

'Well I would put that in too. I'd have to.'

'And how it started by accident, I suppose?'

'Well, no. I wouldn't say that. I mean it didn't did it?'

Baby looked at him and shook her head. 'So you'd put in how I started it and sent the cruiser out to blow up Hutchmeyer and the Futtle? Is that it?'

'I suppose so,' said Piper. 'I mean that's what did happen and ...'

'And that's what you call vindication. Well you can forget it. No way. You want to vindicate yourself that's fine with me but you don't implicate me at the same time. Duel destiny I said and duel destiny I meant.'

'It's all very well for you to talk,' said Piper morosely, 'you're not lumbered with the reputation of having written that filthy novel and I am ...'

'I'm just lumbered with a genius is all,' said Baby and started the car again. Piper sat slumped in his seat and sulked.

'The only thing I know how to do is write,' he grumbled, 'and you won't let me.'

'I didn't say that,' said Baby, 'I just said no retrospective diaries. Dead men tell no tales. Not in diaries they don't and anyhow I don't see why you feel so strongly about *Pause*. I thought it was a great book.'

'You would,' said Piper.

'The thing that really puzzles me is who did write it. I mean they had to have some real good reason for staying under cover.'

'You've only got to read the beastly book to see that,' said Piper. 'All that sex for one thing. And now everyone's going to think I did it.'

'And if you had written the book you would have cut out all the sex?' said Baby.

'Of course. That would be the first thing and then ...'

'Without the sex the book wouldn't have sold. That much I do know about the book trade.'

'So much the better,' said Piper. 'It debases human values. That is what that book does.'

'In that case you should rewrite it the way you think it ought to have been written ...' and amazed at this sudden inspiration she lapsed into thoughtful silence.

Twenty miles farther on they entered a small town. Baby parked the car and went into a supermarket. When she returned she was holding a copy of *Pause O Men for the Virgin*.

'They're selling like wild-fire,' she said and handed him the book.

Piper looked at his photograph on the back cover. It had been taken

in those halcyon days in London when he had been in love with Sonia
and the inane face that smiled up at him seemed to be that of a stranger.
'What am I supposed to do with this?' he asked. Baby smiled.

'Write it.'

'Write it?' said Piper. 'But it's already been –'

'Not the way you would have written it, and you're the author.'

'I'm bloody well not.'

'Honey, somewhere out there in the great wide world there is a man
who wrote that book. Now he knows it, and Frensic knows it and that
Futtle bitch knows it and you and I know it. That's the lot. Hutch
doesn't.'

'Thank God,' said Piper.

'Right. And if that's the way you feel, just imagine the way Frensic &
Futtle must be feeling now. Two million Hutch paid for that novel.
That's a lot of money.'

'It's a ludicrous sum,' said Piper. 'Did you know that Conrad only
got –'

'No and I'm not interested. Right now what interests me is what
happens when you rewrite this novel in your own beautiful handwriting
and Frensic gets the manuscript.'

'Frensic gets . . .' Piper began but Baby silenced him.

'Your manuscript,' she said, 'from beyond the grave.'

'My manuscript from beyond the grave? He'll do his nut.'

'Right first time, and we follow that up with a demand for the advance
and full royalties,' said Baby.

'Well, then he'll know I'm still alive,' Piper protested. 'He'll go straight
to the police and . . .'

'He does that he's going to have a lot of explaining to do to Hutch
and everyone. Hutch will set his legal hound-dogs on him. Yes sir, we've
got Messrs Frensic & Futtle right where we want them.'

'You are mad,' said Piper, 'stark staring mad. If you seriously think
I'm going to rewrite this awful . . .'

'You were the one who wanted to retrieve your reputation,' said Baby
as they drove out of town. 'And this is the only way you can.'

'I wish I could see how.'

'I'll show you,' said Baby. 'Leave it to momma.'

That evening in another motel room Piper opened his ledger, arranged
his pen and ink as methodically as they had once been arranged in the
Gleneagle Guest House and with a copy of *Pause* propped up in front of
him began to write. At the top of the page he wrote 'Chapter One', and

underneath, 'The house stood on a knoll. Surrounded by three elms, a beech and a deodar whose horizontal branches gave it the air ...'

Behind him Baby relaxed on a bed with a contented smile. 'Don't make too many alterations this draft,' she said. 'We've got to make it look really authentic.'

Piper stopped writing. 'I thought the whole point of the exercise was to retrieve my lost reputation by rewriting the thing ...'

'You can do that with the second draft,' said Baby. 'This one is to light a fire under Frensic & Futtle. So stay with the text.'

Piper picked up his pen again and stayed with the text. He made several alterations per page and then crossed them out and added the originals from the book. Occasionally Baby got up and looked over his shoulder and was satisfied.

'This is really going to blow Frensic's mind,' she said but Piper hardly heard her. He had resumed his old existence and with it his identity. And so he wrote on obsessively, lost once more in a world of someone else's imagining and as he wrote he foresaw the alterations he would make in the second draft, the draft that would save his reputation. He was still copying at midnight when Baby had gone to bed. Finally at one, tired but vaguely satisfied, Piper brushed his teeth and climbed into bed too. In the morning he would start again.

But in the morning they were on the road again and it was not until late afternoon that Baby pulled into a Howard Johnson's in Beanville, South Carolina, and Piper was able to start work again.

While Piper started his life again as a peripatetic and derivative novelist Sonia Futtle mourned his passing with a passion that did her credit and disconcerted Hutchmeyer.

'What do you mean she won't attend the funeral?' he yelled at MacMordie when he was told that Miss Futtle sent her regrets but was not prepared to take part in a farce simply to promote the sales of *Pause*.

'She says without bodies in the coffins ...' MacMordie began before being silenced by an apoplectic Hutchmeyer. 'Where the fuck does she think I'm going to get the bodies from? The cops can't get them. The insurance investigators can't get them. The fucking coastguard divers can't get them. And I'm supposed to go find the things? By this time they're way out in the Atlantic some place or the sharks have got them.'

'But I thought you said they were weighted down like with concrete,' said MacMordie, 'and if they are ...'

'Never mind what I said, MacMordie. What I'm saying now is we've got to think positive about Baby and Piper.'

'Isn't that a bit difficult? Them being dead and missing and all. I mean ...'

'And I mean we've got a promotional set-up here that can put *Pause* right up the charts.'

'The computer says sales are good already.'

'Good? Good's not enough. They've got to be terrific. Now the way I see it we've got an opportunity for building this Piper guy up with a reputation like ... Who was that bastard got himself knocked off in a car smash?'

'Well there's been so many it's a little difficult to ...'

'In Hollywood. Famous guy.'

'James Dean,' said MacMordie.

'Not him. A writer. Wrote a great book about insects.'

'Insects?' said MacMordie. 'You mean like ants. I read a great book about ants once ...'

'Not ants for Chrissake. Things with long legs like grasshoppers. Eat every goddam thing for miles.'

'Oh, locusts. *The Day of the Locust*. A great movie. They had this one scene where there's a guy jumping up and down on this little kid and –'

'I don't want to know about that movie, MacMordie. Who wrote the book?'

'West,' said MacMordie, 'Nathanael West. Only his real name was Weinstein.'

'So who cares what his real name was? Nobody's ever heard of him and he gets himself killed in a pile-up and suddenly he's famous. With Piper we've got it even better. I mean we've got mystery. Maybe mobsters. House burning, boats exploding, the guy's in love with old women and suddenly it's all happening to him.'

'Past tense,' said MacMordie.

'Damn right, and that's what I want on him. His past. A full run-down on him, where he lived, what he did, the women he loved ...'

'Like Miss Futtle?' said MacMordie tactlessly.

'No,' yelled Hutchmeyer, 'not like Miss Futtle. She won't even come to the poor guy's funeral. Other women. With what he put in that book there've got to be other women.'

'With what he put in that book they'll have maybe died by now. I mean the heroine was eighty and he was seventeen. This Piper was twenty-eight, thirty so it's got to have been eleven years ago which would put her up in the nineties and around that age they tend to forget things.'

'Jesus, do I have to tell you everything? Fabricate, MacMordie, fabricate. Call London and speak to Frensic and get the press cuttings. There's bound to be something there we can use.'

MacMordie left the room and put through the call to London. He returned twenty minutes later with the news that Frensic was being uncooperative.

'He says he doesn't know anything,' he told a glowering Hutchmeyer. 'Seems this Piper just sent in the book, Frensic read it, sent it to Corkadales, they liked it and bought and that's about the sum total. No background. Nothing.'

'There's got to be something. He was born some place, wasn't he? And his mother ...'

'No relatives. Parents dead in a car smash. I mean it's like he never had an existence.'

'Shit,' said Hutchmeyer.

Which was more or less the word that sprang to Frensic's mind as he put the phone down after MacMordie's call. It was bad enough losing an author who hadn't written a book without having demands for background material on his life. The next thing would be the press, some damned woman reporter hot on the trail of Piper's tragic childhood. Frensic went into Sonia's office and hunted through the filing cabinet for Piper's correspondence. It was, as he expected, voluminous. Frensic took the file back to his desk and sat there wondering what to do with the thing. His first inclination to burn it was dissipated by the realization that if Piper had written scores of letters to him from almost as many different boarding-houses over the years, he had replied as often. The copies of Frensic's replies were there in the file. The originals were presumably still in safe keeping somewhere. With an aunt? Or some ghastly boarding-house keeper? Frensic sat and sweated. He had told MacMordie that Piper had no relatives, but what if it turned out that he had an entire lineage of avaricious aunts, uncles and cousins anxious to cash in on royalties? And what about a will? Knowing Piper as well as he did, Frensic thought it unlikely he had made one. In which case the matter of his legacy might well end up in the courts and then ... Frensic foresaw appalling consequences. On the one hand the anonymous author demanding his advance, and on the other ... And in the middle the firm of Frensic & Futtle being dragged through the mud, exposed as the perpetrators of fraud, sued by Hutchmeyer, sued by Piper's relatives, forced to pay enormous damages and vast legal costs and finally bankrupted. And all because some demented client of Cadwalladine had insisted on preserving his anonymity.

Having reached this ghastly conclusion Frensic took the file back to
the cabinet, re-labelled it Mr Smith as a mild precaution against intruding
eyes and tried to think of some defence. The only one seemed to be that
he had merely acted on the instructions of Mr Cadwalladine and since
Cadwalladine & Dimkins were eminently respectable solicitors they would
be as anxious to avoid a legal scandal as he was. And so presumably
would the genuine author. It was small consolation. Let Hutchmeyer get
a whiff of the impersonation and all hell would be let loose. And finally
there was Sonia, who, if her attitude on the phone had been anything
to go by, was in a highly emotional state and likely to say something
rash. Frensic reached for the phone and dialled International to put
through a call to the Gramercy Park Hotel. It was time Sonia Futtle
came back to England. When he got through it was to learn that Miss
Futtle had already left, and should, according to the desk clerk, be in
mid-Atlantic.

' "Is" and "above",' corrected Frensic before realizing that there was
something to be said for American usage.

That afternoon Sonia landed at Heathrow and took a taxi straight to
Lanyard Lane. She found Frensic in a mood of apparently deep mourning.

'I blame myself,' he said, forestalling her lament, 'I should never have
allowed poor Piper to have jeopardized his career by going over in the
first place. Our only consolation must be that his name as a novelist has
been made. It is doubtful if he would ever have written a better book
had he lived.'

'But he didn't write this one,' said Sonia.

Frensic nodded. 'I know. I know,' he murmured, 'but at least it
established his reputation. He would have appreciated the irony. He was
a great admirer of Thomas Mann you know. Our best memorial to him
must be silence.'

Having thus pre-empted Sonia's recriminations Frensic allowed her to
work off her feelings by telling the story of the night of the tragedy and
Hutchmeyer's subsequent reaction. At the end he was none the wiser.

'It all seems most peculiar,' he said when she had finished. 'One can
only suppose that whoever did it made a terrible mistake and got the
wrong person. Now if Hutchmeyer had been murdered ...'

'I would have been murdered too,' said Sonia through her tears.

'We must be grateful for small mercies,' said Frensic.

Next morning Sonia Futtle resumed her duties in the office. A fresh batch
of animal stories had come in during her absence and while Frensic
congratulated himself on his tactics and sat at his desk silently praying

that there would be no further repercussions Sonia busied herself with *Bernie the Beaver*. It needed a bit of rewriting but the story had promise.

CHAPTER SEVENTEEN

In a cabin in the Smoky Mountains Piper held the same opinion about *Pause*. He sat out on the stoop and looked down at the lake where Baby was swimming and had to admit that his first impression of the novel had been wrong. He had been misled by the passages of explicit sex. But now that he had copied it out word for word he could see that the essential structure of the story was sound. In fact there were large sections of the book which dealt meaningfully with matters of great significance. Subtract the age difference between Gwendolen and Anthony, the narrator, and eradicate the pornography and *Pause O Men for the Virgin* had the makings of great literature. It examined in considerable depth the meaning of life, the writer's role in contemporary society, the anonymity of the individual in the urban collective and the need to return to the values of earlier, more civilized times. It was particularly good on the miseries of adolescence and the satisfaction to be found in the craftsmanship of furniture-making. 'Gwendolen ran her fingers along the gnarled and knotted oak with a sensual touch that belied her years. "The hardiness of time has tamed the wildness of the wood," she said. "You will carve against the grain and give form to what has been formless and insensate."' Piper nodded approvingly. Passages like that had genuine merit and better still they served as an inspiration to him. He too would cut against the grain of this novel and give form to it, so that in the revised version the grossness of the bestseller would be eliminated, and the sexual addenda which defiled the very essence of the book would be removed and it would stand as a monument to his literary gifts. Posthumously perhaps, but at least his reputation would be retrieved. In years to come critics would compare the two versions and deduce from his deletions that in its earlier uncommercial form the original intentions of the author had been of the highest literary quality and that the novel had subsequently been altered to meet the demands of Frensic and Hutchmeyer and their perverse view of public taste. The blame for the bestseller would lie with them and he would be exonerated. More, he would be acclaimed. He closed the ledger and stood up as Baby came out of the water and walked up the beach to the cabin.

'Finished?' she asked. Piper nodded.

'I shall start the second version tomorrow,' he said.

'While you're doing that I'll take the first down into Ashville and get it copied. The sooner Frensic gets it the sooner we're going to light a fire under him.'

'I wish you wouldn't use that expression,' said Piper, 'lighting fires. And anyway where are you going to mail it from? They could trace us from the postmark.'

'We shan't be here from the day after tomorrow. We rented the cabin for a week. I'll drive down to Charlotte and catch a flight to New York and mail it there. I'll be back tomorrow night and we move on the day after.'

'I wish we didn't have to move all the time,' said Piper, 'I like it here. There's been nobody to bother us and I've had time to write. Why can't we just stay on?'

'Because this isn't the Deep South,' said Baby, 'and when I said Deep I meant it. There are places down Alabama, Mississippi, that just nobody has ever heard of and I want to see them.'

'And from what I've read about Mississippi they aren't partial to strangers,' said Piper, 'they are going to ask questions.'

'You've read too many Faulkners,' said Baby, 'and where we're going a quarter of a million dollars buys a lot of answers.'

She went inside and changed. After lunch Piper swam in the lake and walked along the shore, his mind filled with possible changes he was going to make in *Pause Two*. Already he had decided to change the title. He would call it *Work in Regress*. There was a touch of *Finnegans Wake* about it which appealed to his sense of the literary. And after all Joyce had worked and reworked his novels over and over again with no thought for their commercial worth. And in exile from his native land. For a moment Piper saw himself following in Joyce's footsteps, incognito and endlessly revising the same book, with the difference that he could never emerge from obscurity into fame in his own lifetime. Unless of course his work was of such an indisputable genius that the little matter of the fire and the burning boats and even his apparent death would become part of the mystique of a great author. Yes, greatness would absolve him. Piper turned and hurried back along the shore to the cabin. He would start work at once on *Work in Regress*. But when he got back he found that Baby had already taken the car and his first manuscript and driven into Ashville. There was a note for him on the table. It said simply, 'Gone today. Here tomorrow. Stay with it. Baby.'

Piper stayed with it. He spent the afternoon with a pen going through *Pause* changing all references to age. Gwendolen lost fifty-five years and became twenty-five and Anthony gained ten which made him twenty-seven. And in between times Piper scored out all those references to peculiar sexual activities which had ensured the book's popular appeal. He did this with particular vigour and by the time he had finished was filled with a sense of righteousness which he conveyed to his notebook of Ideas. 'The commercialization of sex as a thing to be bought and sold is at the root of the present debasement of civilization. In my writing I have striven to eradicate the Thingness of sex and to encapsulate the essential relationship of humanity.' Finally he made himself supper and went to bed.

In the morning he was up early and at his table on the stoop. In front of him the first page of his new ledger lay blank and empty waiting for his imprint. He dipped his pen in the ink-bottle and began to write. 'The house stood on a knoll. Surrounded by three elms, a beech and a ...' Piper stopped. He wasn't sure what a deodar was and he had no dictionary to help him. He changed it to 'oak' and stopped again. Did oak have horizontal branches? Presumably some oaks did. Details like that didn't matter. The essential thing was to get down to an analysis of the relationship between Gwendolen and the narrator. Great books didn't bother with trees. They were about people, what people felt about people and what they thought about them. Insight was what really mattered and trees didn't contribute to insight. The deodar might just as well stay where it was. He crossed out 'oak' and put 'deodar' above it. He continued the description for half a page and then hit another problem. How could the narrator, Anthony, be on holiday from school when he was now twenty-seven. Unless of course he was a schoolmaster in which case he would have to teach something and that meant knowing about it. Piper tried to remember his own schooldays and a model on which to base Anthony, but the masters at his school had been nondescript men and had left little impression on him. There was only Miss Pears and she had been a mistress.

Piper put down his pen and thought about Miss Pears. Now if she had been a man ... or if she were Gwendolen and he was Anthony ... and if instead of being twenty-seven Anthony had been fourteen ... or better still if his parents had lived in a house on a knoll surrounded by three elms, a beech and a ... Piper stood up and paced the stoop, his mind alive with new inspiration. It had suddenly come to him that from the raw material of *Pause O Men for the Virgin* it might be possible to distil the essence of *Search for a Lost Childhood*. Or if not distil, at least amalgamate the two. There would have to be considerable alterations. After all tuberculotic plumbers didn't live on knolls. On the other hand his father hadn't actually had tuberculosis. He had got it from Lawrence and Thomas Mann. And a love affair between a schoolboy and his teacher was a very natural occurrence, provided of course that it didn't become physical. Yes, that was it. He would write *Work in Regress* as *Search*. He sat down at the table and picked up his pen and began to copy. There was no need now to worry about changing the main shape of the story. The deodar and the house on the knoll and all the descriptions of houses and places could remain the same. The new ingredient would be the addition of his troubled adolescence and the presence of his tormented parents. And Miss Pears as Gwendolen, his mentor, adviser and teacher with whom he would develop a significant relationship, meaningfully sexual and without sex.

And so once more the words formed indelibly black upon the page with all the old elegance of shape that had so satisfied him in the past. Below him the lake shone in the summer sunlight and a breeze ruffled the trees around the cabin, but Piper was oblivious to his surroundings. He had picked up the thread of his existence where it had broken in the Gleneagle Guest House in Exforth and was back into *Search*.

When Baby returned that evening from her flight to New York with the copy of his first manuscript now safely mailed to Frensic & Futtle, Lanyard Lane, London, she found Piper his old self. The trauma of the fire and their flight had been forgotten.

'You see, what I am doing is combining my own novel with *Pause*,' he explained as she poured herself a drink. 'Instead of Gwendolen being ...'

'Tell me about it in the morning,' said Baby. 'Right now I've had a tiring day and tomorrow we've got to be on the road again.'

'I see you've bought another car,' said Piper looking out at a red Pontiac.

'Air-conditioned and with South Carolina plates. Anyone thinks they're going to come looking for us, they're going to have a hard time. I didn't even trade in this time. Sold the Ford in Beanville and took a Greyhound to Charlotte and bought this in Ashville on the way back. We'll change again farther south. We're covering our tracks.'

'Not by sending copies of *Pause* to Frensic, we aren't,' said Piper, 'I mean he's bound to know I haven't died.'

'That reminds me. I sent him a telegram in your name.'

'You did what?' squawked Piper.

'Sent him a telegram.'

'Saying what?'

'Just, quote Transfer advance royalties care of First National Bank of New York account number 478776 love Piper unquote.'

'But I haven't got an account ...'

'You have now, honey. I opened one for you and made the first deposit. One thousand dollars. Now when Frensic gets that birthday greeting –'

'Birthday greeting? You send a telegram demanding money and you call that a birthday greeting?'

'Had to delay it somehow till he'd had time to read the original of *Pause*,' said Baby, 'so I said he had a birthday on the 19th and they're holding it over.'

'Christ,' said Piper, 'some damned birthday greeting. I suppose you realize he's got a heart condition? I mean shocks like this could kill him.'

'Makes two of you,' said Baby. 'He's effectively killed you ...'

'He did nothing of the sort. You were the one to sign my death certificate and end my career as a novelist.'

Baby finished her drink and sighed. 'There's gratitude for you. Your career as a novelist is just about to begin.'

'Posthumously,' said Piper bitterly.

'Well, better late than never,' said Baby, and took herself off to bed.

The next morning the red Pontiac left the cabin and wound up the curving mountain road in the direction of Tennessee.

'We'll go west as far as Memphis,' said Baby, 'and ditch the car there and double back by Greyhound to Chattanooga. I've always wanted to see the Choo Choo.'

Piper said nothing. He had just realized how he had met Miss Pears/Gwendolen. It had been one summer holiday when his parents had taken him down to Exforth and instead of sitting on the beach with them he had gone to the public library and there ... The house no longer stood on a knoll. It was at the top of the hill by the cliffs and its windows stared out to sea. Perhaps that wasn't such a good idea. Not in the second version. No, he would leave it where it was and concentrate on relationships. In that way there would be more consistency between *Pause* and *Work in Regress*, more authenticity. But in the third revision he would work on the setting and the house would stand on the cliffs above Exforth. And with each succeeding draft he would approximate a little more closely to that great novel on which he had been working for ten years. Piper smiled to himself at this realization. As the author of *Pause O Men for the Virgin* he had been given the fame he had always sought, had had fame forced upon him, and now by slow, persistent rewriting of that book he would reproduce the literary masterpiece that had been his life's work. And there was absolutely nothing Frensic could do about it.

That night they slept in separate motels in Memphis and next morning met at the bus depot and took the Greyhound to Nashville. The red Pontiac had gone. Piper didn't even bother to inquire how Baby had disposed of it. He had more important things on his mind. What, for instance, would happen if Frensic produced the real original manuscript of *Pause* and admitted that he had sent Piper to America as the substitute author?

'Two million dollars,' said Baby succinctly when he put this possibility to her.

'I don't see what they have to do with it,' said Piper.

'That's the price of the risk he took playing people poker with Hutch. You stake two million on a bluff you've got to have good reasons.'

'I can't imagine what they are.'

Baby smiled. 'Like who the real writer is. And don't give me that crap about a guy with six children and terminal arthritis. There's no such thing.'

'There isn't?' said Piper.

'No way. So we've got Frensic willing to risk his reputation as a literary agent for a percentage of two million and an author who goes along with him to preserve his precious anonymity from disclosure. That adds up to one hell of a weird set of circumstances. And Hutch hears what's going on he's going to murder them.'

'If Hutchmeyer hears what we've been doing he isn't going to be exactly pleased,' said Piper gloomily.

'Yes but we aren't there and Frensic is. In Lanyard Lane and by now he's got to be sweating.'

And Frensic was. The arrival of a large packet mailed in New York and addressed Personal, Frederick Frensic, had excited his curiosity only mildly. Arriving early at the office he had taken it upstairs with him and had opened several letters before turning his attention to the package. But from that moment onwards he had sat petrified staring at its contents. In front of him lay, neatly Xeroxed, sheet after sheet of Piper's unmistakable handwriting and just as equally unmistakably the original manuscript of *Pause O Men for the Virgin*. Which was impossible. Piper hadn't written the bloody book. He couldn't have. It was out of the question. And anyway why should anyone send him Xeroxed copies of a manuscript? The manuscript. Frensic rummaged through the pages and noted the corrections. The damned thing *was* the manuscript of *Pause*. And it was in Piper's handwriting. Frensic got up from his desk and went through to the filing cabinet and brought back the file now marked Mr Smith and compared the handwriting of Piper's letters with that of the manuscript. No doubt about it. He even reached for a magnifying glass and studied the letters through it. Identical. Christ. What the hell was going on? Frensic felt most peculiar. Some sort of waking nightmare had taken hold of him. Piper had written *Pause*? The obstacles in the way of such a supposition were insuperable. The little bugger couldn't have written anything and if he had ... even if he quite miraculously had, what about Mr Cadwalladine and his anonymous client? Why should Piper have sent him the typed copy of the book through a solicitor in Oxford? And anyway the sod was dead. Or was he? No, he was definitely dead, drowned, murdered ... Sonia's grief had been too real for disbelief. Piper was dead. Which brought him full circle to the question, who had sent this post-mortem manuscript? From New York? Frensic looked at the postmark. New York. And why Xeroxed? There had to be a reason. Frensic grabbed the package and rummaged inside it in the hope that it might contain some clue like a covering letter. But the package was empty. He turned to the outside. The address was typed. Frensic turned the packet over in search of a return address but there was nothing there. He turned back to the pages and read several more. There could be no doubting the authenticity of the writing. The corrections on every page were conclusive. They had been there in exactly the same form in every annual copy of *Search for a Lost Childhood*, a sentence scratched neatly out and a new one written in above. Worst of all, there were even the spelling mistakes. Piper had always spelt necessary with two cs and parallel with two rs, and here they were once again as final proof that the little maniac had actually penned the book which had gone to print with his name on the title-page. But the decision to use his name hadn't been Piper's. He had only been consulted when the book had already been sold ...

Frensic's thoughts spiralled. He tried to remember who had suggested Piper. Was it Sonia, or had he himself ...? He couldn't recall and Sonia wasn't there to help him. She had gone down to Somerset to interview the author of *Bernie the* blasted *Beaver* and to ask for amendments in his opus. Beavers, even voluble beavers, didn't say 'Jesus wept' and 'Bloody hell', not if they wanted to get into print as children's bestsellers. Frensic did, several times, as he stared at the pages in front of him. Pulling himself together with an effort, he reached for the phone. This time Mr Cadwalladine was going to come clean about his client. But the telephone beat Frensic to it. It rang. Frensic cursed and picked up the receiver.

'Frensic & Futtle, Literary Agents ...' he began before being stopped by the operator.

'Is that Mr Frensic, Mr Frederick Frensic?'

'Yes,' said Frensic irritably. He had never liked his Christian name.

'I have a birthday greeting for you,' said the operator.

'For me?' said Frensic. 'But it isn't my birthday.'

But already a taped voice was crooning 'Happy Birthday To You, Happy Birthday, Dear Frederick, Happy Birthday To You.'

Frensic held the receiver away from his ear. 'I tell you it isn't my bloody birthday,' he shouted at the recording. The operator came back on the line.

'The greetings telegram reads TRANSFER ADVANCE ROYALTIES CARE OF FIRST NATIONAL BANK OF NEW YORK ACCOUNT NUMBER FOUR SEVEN EIGHT SEVEN SEVEN SIX LOVE PIPER. I will repeat that. TRANSFER ...' Frensic sat and listened. He was beginning to shake.

'Would you like that account number repeated once again?' asked the operator.

'No,' said Frensic. 'Yes.' He grabbed a pencil with an unsteady hand and wrote the message down.

'Thank you,' he said without thinking as he finished.

'You're welcome,' said the operator. The line went dead.

'Like hell I am,' said Frensic and put the phone down. He stared for a moment at the word 'Piper' and then groped his way across the room to the cubicle in which Sonia made coffee and washed the cups. There was a bottle of brandy there, kept for emergency resuscitation of rejected authors. 'Rejected?' Frensic muttered as he filled a tumbler. 'More like resurrected.' He drank half the tumbler and went back to his desk feeling little better. The nightmare quality of the manuscript had doubled now with the telegram but it was no longer incomprehensible. He was being blackmailed. 'Transfer advance royalties ...' Frensic suddenly felt faint. He got out of his chair and lay down on the floor and shut his eyes.

After twenty minutes he got to his feet. Mr Cadwalladine was going to learn that it didn't pay to tangle with Frensic & Futtle. There was no point in phoning the wretched man again. Stronger measures were needed now. He would have the bastard squealing the name of his client and there would be an end to all this talk of professional confidentiality. The situation was desperate and desperate remedies were called for. Frensic went downstairs and out into the street. Half an hour later, armed with a parcel that contained sandals, dark glasses, a lightweight tropical suit and a Panama hat, he returned to the office. All that was needed now was an ambulance-chasing libel lawyer. Frensic spent the rest of the morning going through *Pause* for a suitable identity and then phoned Ridley, Coverup, Makeweight and Jones, Solicitors of Ponsett House.

Their reputation as shysters in cases of libel was second to none. Mr Makeweight would see Professor Facit at four.

At five to four, Frensic, armed with a copy of *Pause O Men for the Virgin* and peering dimly through his tinted glasses, sat in the waiting-room and looked down at his sandals. He was rather proud of them. If anything distinguished him from Frensic, the literary agent, it was, he felt, those awful sandals.

'Mr Makeweight will see you now,' said the receptionist. Frensic got up and went down the passage to the door marked Mr Makeweight and entered. An air of respectable legal fustiness clung to the room. It didn't to Mr Makeweight. Small, dark and effusive, he was rather too quick for the furnishings. Frensic shook hands and sat down. Mr Makeweight regarded him expectantly. 'I understand you are concerned with a passage in a novel,' he said.

Frensic put the copy of *Pause* on the desk.

'Well, I am rather,' he said hesitantly. 'You see ... well it's been drawn to my attention by some of my colleagues who read novels − I am not a novel-reader myself you understand − but they have pointed out ... well I'm sure it must be a coincidence ... and they have certainly found it very funny that ...'

'That a character in this novel resembles you in certain ways?' said Mr Makeweight, cutting through Frensic's hesitations.

'Well I wouldn't like to say that he resembles me ... I mean the crimes he commits ...'

'Crimes?' said Mr Makeweight, taking the bait. 'A character resembling you commits crimes? In this novel?'

'It's the name you see. Facit,' said Frensic leaning forward to open *Pause* at the page he had marked. 'If you read the passage in question you will see what I mean.'

Mr Makeweight read three pages and looked up with a concern that masked his delight. 'Dear me,' he said, 'I do see what you mean. These are exceedingly serious allegations.'

'Well they are, aren't they?' said Frensic pathetically. 'And my appointment as Professor of Moral Sciences at Wabash has yet to be confirmed and, quite frankly, if it were thought for one moment ...'

'I take your point,' said Mr Makeweight. 'Your career would be put in jeopardy.'

'Ruined,' said Frensic.

Mr Makeweight selected a cigar happily. 'And I suppose we can take it that you have never ... that these allegations are quite without foundation. You have never for instance seduced one of your male students?'

'Mr Makeweight,' said Frensic indignantly.

'Quite so. And you have never had intercourse with a fourteen-year-old girl after dosing her lemonade with a barbiturate?'

'Certainly not. The very idea revolts me. And besides I'm not sure I would know how to.'

Mr Makeweight regarded him critically. 'No, I daresay you wouldn't,' he said finally. 'And there is no truth in the accusation that you habitually fail students who reject your sexual overtures?'

'I don't make sexual overtures to students, Mr Makeweight. As a matter of fact I am neither on the examining board nor do I give tutorials. I am not part of the University. I am over here on a sabbatical and engaged in private research.'

'I see,' said Mr Makeweight, and made a note on his pad.

'And what makes it so much more embarrassing,' said Frensic, 'is that at one time I did have lodgings in De Frytville Avenue.'

Mr Makeweight made a note of that too. 'Extraordinary,' he said, 'quite extraordinary. The resemblance would seem to be almost exact. I think, Professor Facit, in fact I do more, I know that ... provided of course that you haven't committed any of these unnatural acts ... I take it you have never kept a Pekinese ... no. Well as I say, provided you haven't and indeed even if you have, I can tell you now that you have grounds for taking action against the author and publishers of this disgraceful novel. I should estimate the damages to be in the region of ... well to tell the truth I shouldn't be at all surprised if they don't constitute a record in the history of libel actions.'

'Oh dear,' said Frensic, feigning a mixture of anxiety and avarice, 'I was rather hoping it might be possible to avoid a court case. The publicity, you understand.'

Mr Makeweight quite understood. 'We'll just have to see how the publishers respond,' he said. 'Corkadales aren't a wealthy firm of course but they'll be insured against libel.'

'I hope that doesn't mean the author won't have to ...'

'Oh he'll pay all right, Professor Facit. Over the years. The insurance company will see to that. A more deliberate case of malicious libel I have never come across.'

'Someone told me that the author, Mr Piper, has made a fortune out of the book in America,' said Frensic.

'In that case I think he will have to part with it,' said Mr Makeweight.

'And if you could expedite the matter I would be most grateful. My appointment at Wabash ...'

Mr Makeweight assured him that he would put the matter in hand at once and Frensic, having given his address as the Randolph Hotel, Oxford, left the office well pleased. Mr Cadwalladine was about to get the shock of his life.

So was Geoffrey Corkadale. Frensic had only just returned to Lanyard Lane and was divesting himself of the disgusting sandals and the tropical suit when the phone rang. Geoffrey was in a state bordering on hysteria. Frensic held the phone away from his ear and listened to a torrent of abuse.

'My dear Geoffrey,' he said when the publisher ran out of epithets. 'What have I done to deserve this outburst?'

'Done?' yelled Corkadale. 'Done? You've done for this firm for one thing. You and that damnable Piper ...'

'*De Mortuis nil nisi* ...' Frensic began.

'And what about the bloody living?' screamed Geoffrey. 'And don't tell me he didn't speak ill of this Professor Facit knowing full well that the swine was alive because ...'

'What swine?' said Frensic.

'Professor Facit. The man in the book who did those awful things ...'

'Wasn't he the character with satyriasis who ...'

'Was?' bawled Geoffrey. 'Was? The bloody maniac is.'

'Is what?' said Frensic.

'Is! Is! The man's alive and he's filing a libel action against us.'

'Dear me. How very unfortunate.'

'Unfortunate? It's catastrophic. He's gone to Ridley, Coverup, Makeweight and ...'

'Oh no,' said Frensic, 'but they're absolute rogues.'

'Rogues? They're bloodsuckers. Leeches. They'd get blood out of a stone and with all this filth in the book about Professor Facit they've got a watertight case. They're dunning us for millions. We're finished. We'll never ...'

'The man you want to speak to is a Mr Cadwalladine,' said Frensic. 'He acted for Piper. I'll give you his telephone number.'

'What good is that going to do? It's deliberate libel ...'

But Frensic was already dictating Mr Cadwalladine's telephone number and with apologies because he had a client in the room next door he put the phone down on Geoffrey's ravings. Then he changed out of the tropical suit, phoned the Randolph and booked a room in the name of

Professor Facit and waited. Mr Cadwalladine was bound to call and
when he did Frensic was going to be ready and waiting. In the meantime
he sought further inspiration by studying Piper's telegram. 'Transfer
advance royalties care of account number 478776.' And the little bastard
was supposed to be dead. What in God's name was going on? And what
on earth was he going to tell Sonia? And where did Hutchmeyer fit into
all this? According to Sonia the police had grilled him for hours and
Hutchmeyer had come out of the experience a shaken man, and had
even threatened to sue the police. That didn't sound like the action of a
man who ... Frensic put the notion of Hutchmeyer kidnapping Piper
and demanding his money back by proxy as too improbable for words.
If Hutchmeyer had known that Piper hadn't written *Pause* he would have
sued. But Piper apparently had written *Pause*. The proof was there in
front of him in the copy of the manuscript. Well he would have to screw
the truth out of Cadwalladine and with Mr Makeweight in the wings
demanding enormous damages, Mr Cadbloodywalladine was going to
have to come clean.

He did. 'I don't know who the author of this awful book is,' he
admitted in faltering tones when he rang up half an hour later.

'You don't know?' said Frensic, faltering incredulously himself. 'You
must know. You sent me the book in the first place. You gave me the
authorization to send Piper to the States. If you didn't know you had no
right ...' Mr Cadwalladine made negative noises. 'But I've got a letter
here from you saying ...'

'I know you have,' said Mr Cadwalladine faintly. 'The author gave
his consent and ...'

'But you've just said you don't know who the bloody author is,' shouted
Frensic, 'and now you tell me he gave his consent. His written consent?'

'Yes,' said Mr Cadwalladine.

'In that case you've got to know who he is.'

'But I don't,' said Mr Cadwalladine. 'You see I've always dealt with
him through Lloyds Bank.'

Frensic's mind boggled. 'Lloyds Bank?' he muttered. 'You did say
Lloyds Bank?'

'Yes. Care of the manager. It's such a very respectable bank and I
never for one moment supposed ...'

He left the sentence unfinished. There was no need to end it. Frensic
was already ahead of him. 'So what you're saying is that whoever wrote
this bloody novel sent the thing to you by way of Lloyds Bank in Oxford
and that whenever you've wanted to correspond with him you've had to
do so through the bank. Is that right?'

'Precisely,' said Mr Cadwalladine, 'and now that this frightful libel case has come up I think I know why. It puts me in a dreadful situation. My reputation ...'

'Stuff your reputation,' shouted Frensic, 'what about mine? I've been acting in good faith on behalf of a client who doesn't exist and on your instructions and now we've got a murder on our hands and ...'

'This terrible libel action,' said Mr Cadwalladine. 'Mr Corkadale told me that the damages are bound to amount to something astronomical.'

But Frensic wasn't listening. If Mr Cadwalladine's client had to correspond with him through Lloyds Bank the bastard must have something to hide. Unless of course it was Piper. Frensic groped for a clue. 'When the novel first came to you there must have been a covering letter.'

'The manuscript came from a typing agency,' said Mr Cadwalladine. 'The covering letter was sent a few days earlier via Lloyds Bank.'

'With a signature?' said Frensic.

'The signature of the bank manager,' said Mr Cadwalladine.

'That's all I need,' said Frensic. 'What is his name?'

Mr Cadwalladine hesitated. 'I don't think ...' he began but Frensic lost patience.

'Damn your scruples, man,' he snarled, 'the name of the bank manager and quick.'

'The late Mr Bygraves,' said Mr Cadwalladine sadly.

'The what?'

'The late Mr Bygraves. He died of a heart attack climbing Snowdon at Easter.'

Frensic slumped in his chair. 'He had a heart attack climbing Snowdon,' he muttered.

'So you see, I don't think he's going to be able to help us very much,' continued Mr Cadwalladine, 'and anyway banks are very reticent about disclosing the names of their clients. You have to have a warrant, you know.'

Frensic did know. It was one of the few things about banks he had previously admired. But there was something else that Mr Cadwalladine had said earlier ... something about a typing agency. 'You said the manuscript came from a typing agency,' he said. 'Have you any idea which one?'

'No. But I daresay I could find out if you'll give me time.' Frensic sat holding the receiver while Mr Cadwalladine found out. 'It's the Cynthia Bogden Typing Service,' he told Frensic at long last. He sounded distinctly subdued.

'Now we're getting somewhere,' said Frensic. 'Ring her up and ask where ...'

'I'd rather not,' said Mr Cadwalladine.

'You'd rather not? Here we are in the middle of a libel action which is probably going to cost you your reputation and ...'

'It's not that,' interrupted Mr Cadwalladine. 'You see, I handled the divorce case ...'

'Well that's all right ...'

'I was acting for her ex-husband,' said Mr Cadwalladine. 'I don't think she'd appreciate my ...'

'Oh all right, I'll do it,' said Frensic. 'Give me her number.' He wrote it down, replaced the receiver and dialled again.

'The Cynthia Bogden Typing Service,' said a voice, coyly professional.

'I'm trying to trace the owner of a manuscript that was typed by your agency ...' Frensic began but the voice cut him short.

'We do not divulge the names of our clients,' it said.

'But I'm only asking because a friend of mine ...'

'Under no circumstances are we prepared to confide confidential information of the sort ...'

'Perhaps if I spoke to Mrs Bodgen,' said Frensic.

'You are,' said the voice and rang off. Frensic sat at his desk and cursed.

'Confidential information my foot,' he said and slammed the phone down. He sat thinking dark thoughts about Mrs Bogden for a while and then called Mr Cadwalladine again.

'This Bogden woman,' he said, 'how old is she?'

'Around forty-five,' said Mr Cadwalladine, 'why do you ask?'

'Never mind,' said Frensic.

That evening, having left a note on Sonia Futtle's desk saying that urgent business would keep him out of town for a day or two, Frensic travelled by train to Oxford. He was wearing a lightweight tropical suit, dark glasses and a Panama hat. The sandals were in his dustbin at home. He carried with him in a suitcase the Xeroxed manuscript of *Pause*, a letter written by Piper and a pair of striped pyjamas. Dressed in the last he climbed into bed at eleven in the Randolph Hotel. His room had been booked for Professor Facit.

CHAPTER EIGHTEEN

In Chattanooga Baby had fulfilled her ambition. She had seen the Choo Choo. Installed in Pullman Car Number Nine, she lay on the brass bedstead and stared out of the window at the illuminated fountain playing across the tracks. Above the main building of the station tube lighting emblazoned the night sky with the words Hilton Choo Choo and below, in what had once been the waiting-room, dinner was being served. Beside the restaurant there was a crafts shop and in front of them both stood huge locomotives of a bygone era, their cow-catchers freshly painted and their smokestacks gleaming as if in anticipation of some great journey. In fact they were going nowhere. Their fireboxes were cold and empty and their pistons would never move again. Only in the imagination of those who stayed the night in the ornate and divided Pullman cars, now motel bedrooms, was it still possible to entertain the illusion that they would presently pull out of the station and begin the long haul north or west. The place was part museum, part fantasy and wholly commercial. At the entrance to the car park uniformed guards sat in a small cabin watching the television screen on which each platform and each dark corner of the station was displayed for the protection of the guests. Outside the perimeter of the station Chattanooga spread dark and seedy with boarded hotel windows and derelict buildings, a victim of the shopping precincts beyond the ring of suburbs.

But Baby wasn't thinking about Chattanooga or even the Choo Choo. They had joined the illusions of her retarded youth. Age had caught up with her and she felt tired and empty of hope. All the romance of life had gone. Piper had seen to that. Travelling day after day with a self-confessed genius whose thoughts were centred on literary immortality to the exclusion of all else had given Baby a new insight into the monotony of Piper's mind. By comparison Hutchmeyer's obsession with money and power and wheeling and dealing now seemed positively healthy. Piper evinced no interest in the country-side nor the towns they passed through and the fact that they were now in, or at least on the frontier of, the Deep South and that wild country of Baby's soft-corn imagination appeared to mean nothing to him. He had hardly glanced at the locomotives drawn up in the station and seemed only surprised that they weren't travelling anywhere on them. Once that had been impressed on him he had retreated to

his stateroom and had started work again on his second version of
Pause.

'For a great novelist you've just got to be the least observant,' Baby
said when they met in the restaurant for dinner. 'I mean don't you ever
look around and wonder what it's all about.'

Piper looked around. 'Seems an odd place to put a restaurant,' he
said. 'Still, it's nice and cool.'

'That just happens to be the air-conditioning,' said Baby irritably.

'Oh, is that what it is,' said Piper. 'I wondered.'

'He wondered. And what about all the people who have sat right here
waiting to take the train north to New York and Detroit and Chicago
to make their fortunes instead of scratching a living from a patch of dirt?
Doesn't that mean anything to you?'

'There don't seem many of them about,' said Piper looking idly at a
woman with an obesity problem and tartan shorts, 'and anyway I thought
you said the trains weren't running any more.'

'Oh my God,' said Baby, 'I sometimes wonder what century you're
living in. And I suppose it doesn't mean a thing to you that there was a
battle here in the Civil War?'

'No,' said Piper. 'Battles don't figure in great literature.'

'They don't? What about *Gone With The Wind* and *War and Peace*? I
suppose they aren't great literature.'

'Not English literature,' said Piper. 'What matters in English literature
is the relationships people have with one another.'

Baby dug into her steak. 'And people don't relate to one another in
battles? Is that it?'

Piper nodded.

'So when one guy kills another that's not relating in a way that
matters?'

'Only transitorily,' said Piper.

'And when Sherman's troops go looting and burning and raping their
way from Atlanta to the sea and leave behind them homeless families
and burning mansions that isn't altering relationships either so you don't
write about it?'

'The best novelists wouldn't,' said Piper. 'It didn't happen to them
and therefore they couldn't.'

'Couldn't what?'

'Write about it.'

'Are you telling me a writer can only write what has really happened
to him? Is that what you're saying?' said Baby with a new edge to her
voice.

'Yes,' said Piper, 'you see it would be outside the range of his experience and therefore ...'

He spoke at length from *The Moral Novel* while Baby slowly chewed her way through her steak and thought dark thoughts about Piper's theory.

'In that case you're going to need a lot more experience is all I can say.'

Piper pricked up his ears. 'Now wait a minute,' he said, 'if you think I want to be involved in any more house-burning and boat-exploding and that sort of thing –'

'I wasn't thinking of that sort of experience. I mean things like burning houses don't count do they? It's relationships that matter. What you need is experience in relating.'

Piper ate uneasily. The conversation had taken a distasteful turn. They finished their meal in silence. Afterwards Piper returned to his stateroom and wrote five hundred more words about his tortured adolescence and his feeling for Gwendolen/Miss Pears. Finally he turned out the electric oil lamp that hung above his brass bedstead and undressed. In the next compartment Baby readied herself for Piper's first lesson in relationships. She put on a very little nightdress and a great deal of perfume and opened the door to Piper's stateroom.

'For God's sake,' squawked Piper as she climbed into bed with him.

'This is where it all begins, baby,' said Baby, 'relationshipwise.'

'No, it doesn't,' said Piper. 'It's –'

Baby's hand closed over his mouth and her voice whispered in his ear.

'And don't think you're going to get out of here. They've got TV cameras on every platform and you go hobbling out there in the raw the guards are going to want to know what's been going on.'

'But I'm not in the raw,' said Piper as Baby's hand left his mouth.

'You soon will be, honey,' Baby whispered as her hands deftly untied his pyjamas.

'Please,' said Piper plaintively.

'I aim to, honey, I aim to,' said Baby. She lifted her nightdress and her great breasts dug into Piper's chest. For the next two hours the brass bedstead heaved and creaked as Baby Hutchmeyer, *née* Sugg, Miss Penobscot 1935, put all the expertise of her years to work on Piper. And in spite of himself and his invocation of the precepts in *The Moral Novel*, Piper was for the first time lost to the world of letters and moved by an inchoate passion. He writhed beneath her, he pounded on top, his mouth sucked at her silicon breasts and slithered across the minute scars on her stomach. All the time Baby's fingers caressed and dug and scratched and squeezed until Piper's back was torn and his buttocks marked by the curve of her nails and all the time Baby stared into the dimness of the stateroom dispassionately and wondered at her own boredom. 'Youth must have its fling,' she thought to herself as Piper hurled himself into her yet again. But she was no longer young, and flinging without feeling was not her scene. There was more to life than fucking. Much more, and she was going to find it.

In Oxford Frensic was up and about and finding it when Baby returned to her own compartment and left Piper sleeping exhaustedly next door. Frensic had got up early and had breakfasted before eight. By half-past he had found the Cynthia Bogden Typing Service in Fenet Street. With what he hoped was the expectant look of an American tourist he haunted the church opposite and sat in one of the pews staring back through the open door at the entrance to the Bogden Bureau. If he knew anything about middle-aged women who were divorced and ran their own businesses, Miss Bogden would be the first to arrive in the morning and the last to leave at night. By quarter past nine Frensic certainly hoped so. The trail of women he had seen entering the office were not at all to his taste but at least the first to arrive had been the most presentable. She had been a large woman but Frensic's brief glimpse had told him that her legs were good and that if Mr Cadwalladine had been right about her being forty-five she didn't look it. Frensic left the church and pondered his next step. There was no point in going into the Agency and asking Miss Bogden point blank who had sent her *Pause*. Her tone the previous day had indicated that more subtle tactics were necessary.

Frensic made his next move. He found a flower shop and went inside. Twenty minutes later two dozen red roses were delivered to the Bogden Typing Service with a note which said simply, 'To Miss Bogden from an Admirer.' Frensic had thought of adding 'ardent' but had decided against it. Two dozen expensive red roses argued an ardency by themselves. Miss Bogden or more properly Mrs Bogden, and the reversion indicated a romantic direction to that lady's thoughts, would supply the adjective. Frensic wandered round Oxford, had coffee in the Ship and lunch back at the Randolph. Then, gauging that enough time had elapsed for Miss Bogden to have digested the implications of the roses, he went to Professor Facit's room and phoned the Agency. As before, Miss Bogden answered. Frensic took a deep breath, swallowed and presently heard himself asking with an agony of unaffected coyness if she would do him the honour and privilege of having dinner with him at the Elizabeth. There was a sibilant pause before Miss Bogden replied.

'Do I know you?' she asked archly. Frensic squirmed.

'An admirer,' he murmured.

'Oo,' said Miss Bogden. There was another pause while she observed the proprieties of hesitation.

'Roses,' said Frensic garrottedly.

'Are you quite sure? I mean it's rather unusual ...'

Frensic silently agreed that it was. 'It's just that ...' he began and then took the plunge. 'I haven't had the nerve before and ...' The garrotte tightened.

Miss Bogden on the other hand breathed sympathy. 'Better late than never,' she said softly.

'That's what I thought,' said Frensic who didn't.

'And you did say the Elizabeth?'

'Yes,' said Frensic, 'shall we say eight in the bar?'

'How will I know you?'

'I know you,' said Frensic and giggled involuntarily. Miss Bodgen took it as a compliment.

'You haven't told me your name.'

Frensic hesitated. He couldn't use his own and Facit was in *Pause*. It had to be someone else. 'Corkadale,' he muttered finally, 'Geoffrey Corkadale.'

'Not *the* Geoffrey Corkadale?' said Miss Bogden.

'Yes,' stammered Frensic hoping to hell that Geoffrey's epicene reputation hadn't reached her ears. It hadn't. Miss Bogden cooed.

'Well in that case ...' She left the rest unsaid.

'Till eight,' said Frensic.

'Till eight,' echoed Miss Bogden. Frensic put the phone down and sat limply on the bed.

Then he lay down and had a long nap. He woke at four and went downstairs. There was one last thing to do. He didn't know Miss Bogden and there must be no mistake. He made his way to Fenet Street and stationed himself in the church. He was there at five-thirty when the trail of awful women came out of the office. Frensic sighed with relief. None of them was carrying a bunch of red roses. Finally the large woman appeared and locked the door. She clutched roses to her ample bosom and hurried off down the street. Frensic emerged from the church and watched her go. Miss Bogden was definitely well preserved. From her permed head to her pink shoes by way of a turquoise costume there was a tastelessness about the woman that was almost inspired. Frensic went back to the hotel and had a stiff gin. Then he had another, took a bath and rehearsed various approaches that seemed likely to elicit from Miss Bogden the name of the author of *Pause*.

On the other side of Oxford, Cynthia Bogden prepared herself for the evening with the same thoroughness with which she did everything. It had been some years since her divorce and to be asked to dine at the Elizabeth by a publisher augured well. So did the roses, carefully arranged in a vase, and the nervousness of her admirer. There had been nothing brash about the voice on the telephone. It had been an educated voice and Corkadales were most respectable publishers. And in any case Cynthia Bogden was in need of admirers. She selected her most seductive costume, sprayed herself in various places with various aerosols, fixed her face and set out prepared to be wined, dined and, not to put too fine a point on it, fucked. She entered the foyer of the Elizabeth exuding an uncertain hauteur and was somewhat startled when a short baggy man sidled up to her and took her hand.

'Miss Bogden,' he murmured, 'your fond admirer.'

Miss Bogden looked down at her fond admirer dubiously. She was still looking down at him half an hour later and three pink gins later as they made their way to the table Frensic had reserved in the farthest corner of the restaurant. He held her chair for her and then, conscious that perhaps he hadn't come as far up to her expectations as he might have done, threw himself into the part of fond admirer with a desperate gallantry and inventiveness that surprised them both.

'I first glimpsed you a year ago when I was up for a conference,' he told her having ordered the wine waiter to bring them a bottle of not too dry champagne, 'I saw you in the street and followed you to your office.'

'You should have introduced yourself,' said Miss Bogden.

Frensic blushed convincingly. 'I was too shy,' he murmured, 'and besides I thought you were ...'

'Married?' said Miss Bogden helpfully.

'Exactly,' said Frensic, 'or shall we say attached. A woman as ... er ... beautiful ... er ...'

It was Miss Bogden's turn to blush. Frensic plunged on. 'I was overcome. Your charm, your air of quiet reserve, your ... how shall I put it ...' There was no need to put it. While Frensic burrowed into an avocado pear, Cynthia Bogden savoured a shrimp. Baggy this little man might be but he was clearly a gentleman and a man of the world. Champagne at twelve pounds a bottle was sufficient indication of his honourable intentions. When Frensic ordered a second, Miss Bogden protested feebly.

'Special occasion,' said Frensic wondering if he wasn't overdoing things a bit, 'and besides we have something to celebrate.'

'We do?'

'Our meeting for one thing,' said Frensic, 'and the success of a mutual venture.'

'Mutual venture?' said Miss Bogden, her thoughts veering sharply to the altar.

'Something we both had a hand in,' continued Frensic, 'I mean we don't usually publish that sort of book but I must say it's been a great success.'

Miss Bogden's thoughts turned away from the altar. Frensic helped himself to more champagne. 'We're a very traditional publishing house,' he said, 'but *Pause O Men for the Virgin* is what the public demands these days'

'It was rather awful, wasn't it?' said Miss Bogden, 'I typed it myself you know.'

'Really?' said Frensic.

'Well I didn't like my girls having to do it and the author was so peculiar about it.'

'Was he?'

'I had to phone up ever so often,' said Miss Bogden. 'But you don't want to hear about that.'

Frensic did but Miss Bogden was adamant. 'We mustn't spoil our first evening talking shop,' she said and in spite of more champagne and a large Cointreau all Frensic's attempts to steer the conversation back to the subject failed. Miss Bogden wanted to hear about Corkadales. The name seemed to appeal to her.

'Why don't you come back to my place?' she asked as they walked beside the river after dinner. 'For a nightcap.'

'That's frightfully kind of you,' said Frensic prepared to pursue his quarry to the bitter end. 'Are you sure I wouldn't be imposing on you?'

'I'd like that,' said Miss Bogden with a giggle and took his arm, 'to be imposed on by you.' She steered him to the car-park and a light blue MG. Frensic gaped at the car. It did not accord with his notion of what a forty-five-year-old head of a typing bureau should drive and besides he was unused to bucket seats. Frensic squeezed in and was forced to allow Miss Bogden to fasten his safety belt. Then they drove rather faster than he liked along the Banbury Road and into a hinterland of semi-detached houses. Miss Bogden lived at 33 Viewpark Avenue, a mixture of pebbledash and Tudor. She pulled up in front of the garage. Frensic fumbled for the catch of his safety belt but Cynthia Bogden was there before him and leaning expectantly. Frensic nerved himself for the inevitable and took her in his arms. It was a long kiss and a passionate one, made even less enjoyable for Frensic by the presence of the gear lever in his right kidney. By the time they had finished and climbed out of the car he was having third and fourth thoughts about the whole enterprise. But there was too much at stake to falter now. Frensic followed her into the house. Miss Bogden switched on the hall light.

'Would you like a drinkie?' she asked.

'No,' said Frensic with a fervour that came largely from the conviction that she would offer him cooking sherry. Miss Bogden took his refusal as a compliment and once more they grappled, this time in the company of a hat stand. Then taking his hand she led the way upstairs.

'The you-know-what's in there,' she said helpfully. Frensic staggered into the bathroom and shut the door. He spent several minutes staring at his reflection in the mirror and wondering why it was that only the most predatory women found him attractive and wishing to hell they didn't and then, having promised himself that he would never again be rude about Geoffrey Corkadale's preferences, he came out and went into the bedroom. Cynthia Bogden's bedroom was pink. The curtains were pink, the carpet pink, the padded and quilted bedhead pink and the lampshade beside it pink. And finally there was a pink Frensic wrestling with the intricacies of Cynthia Bodgen's pink underwear while muttering pinkish endearments in her pink ear.

An hour later Frensic was no longer pink. Against the pink sheets he was puce and having palpitations to boot. His efforts to get into her good books among other less savoury things had done something to his circulatory system and Miss Bogden's sexual skills, nurtured in a justifiably broken marriage and gleaned, Frensic suspected, from some frightful manual on how to make sex an adventure, had led him to contortions which would have defied the imaginations of his most sexually obsessed authors. As he lay panting, alternatively thanking God it was all over and wondering if he was going to have a coronary, Cynthia bent her permed head over him.

'Satisfied?' she asked. Frensic stared at her and nodded frantically. Any other answer would have invited suicide.

'And now we'll have a little drinkie,' she said and skipping to Frensic's amazement lightly off the bed she went downstairs and returned with a bottle of whisky. She sat down on the edge of the bed and poured two tots.

'To us,' she said. Frensic drank deeply and held out his glass for more. Cynthia smiled and handed him the bottle.

In New York Hutchmeyer was having problems too. They were of a different sort to Frensic's but since they involved three and a half million dollars the effect was much the same.

'What do you mean they aren't prepared to pay?' he yelled at MacMordie who had reported that the insurance company were holding back on compensation. 'They got to pay. I mean why should I insure my property if they aren't going to pay when it's arsonized?'

'I don't know,' said MacMordie, 'I'm just telling you what Mr Synstrom said.'

'Get me Synstrom,' yelled Hutchmeyer. MacMordie got Synstrom. He came up to Hutchmeyer's office and sat blandly regarding the great publisher through steel-rimmed glasses.

'Now I don't know what you're trying to get at –' Hutchmeyer began.

'The truth,' said Mr Synstrom. 'Just the plain truth.'

'That's okay by me,' said Hutchmeyer, 'just so long as you pay up when you've got it.'

'The thing is, Mr Hutchmeyer, we know how that fire started.'

'How?'

'Someone deliberately lit the house with a can of gasolene. And that someone was your wife . . .'

'You know that?'

'Mr Hutchmeyer, we've got analysts who can figure out the nail varnish your wife was wearing when she opened that safe and took out that quarter of a million dollars you had stashed there.'

Hutchmeyer eyed him suspiciously. 'You can?' he said.

'Sure. And we know too she loaded that cruiser of yours with fifty gallons of gasolene. She and that Piper. He carried the cans down and we've got their prints.'

'What the hell would she do that for?'

'We thought you might have the answer to that one,' said Mr Synstrom.

'Me? I was out in the middle of the goddam bay. How should I know what was going on back at my house?'

'We wouldn't know that, Mr Hutchmeyer. Just seems a kind of coincidence you go sailing with Miss Futtle in a storm and your wife is setting out to burn your house down and fake her own death.'

Hutchmeyer paled. 'Fake her own death? Did you say . . .'

Mr Synstrom nodded. 'We call it the Stonehouse syndrome in the trade,' he said. 'It happens every once in a while someone wants the world to think they're dead so they disappear and leave their nearest and dearest to claim the insurance. Now you've put in a claim for three and a half million dollars and we've got no proof your wife isn't alive some place.'

Hutchmeyer stared miserably at him. He was considering the awful possibility that Baby was still around and with her she was carrying all that evidence of his tax evasions, bribes and illegal dealings that could send him to prison. By comparison the forfeiture of three and a half million dollars was peanuts.

'I just can't believe she'd do a thing like that,' he said finally. 'I mean we had a happy marriage. No problems. I gave her everything she asked for ...'

'Like young men?' said Mr Synstrom.

'No, not like young men,' shouted Hutchmeyer, and felt his pulse.

'Now this Piper writer was a young man,' said Mr Synstrom, 'and from what we've heard Mrs Hutchmeyer had a taste for ...'

'Are you accusing my wife of ... My God, I'll ...'

'We're not accusing anyone of anything, Mr Hutchmeyer. Like I've said we're trying to get at the truth.'

'And are you telling me that my wife, my own dear little Baby, filled that cruiser with gasolene and deliberately tried to murder me by aiming it at my yacht in the middle of –'

'That's exactly what I'm saying. Mind you, that could have been an accident,' said Mr Synstrom, 'the cruiser blowing up where she did.'

'Yeah, well from where I was standing it didn't look like an accident. You can believe it didn't,' said Hutchmeyer. 'You want to have a cruiser come out of the night straight for you before you go round making allegations like you've just done.'

Mr Synstrom got to his feet. 'So you still want us to continue with our investigations?' he said.

Hutchmeyer hesitated. If Baby was still alive the last thing he wanted was investigations. 'I just don't believe my Baby would have done a thing like that is all,' he said.

Mr Synstrom sat down again. 'If she did and we can prove it I'm afraid Mrs Hutchmeyer would stand trial. Arson, attempted murder, defrauding an insurance company. And then there's Mr Piper. He's an accessory. Bestselling author, I hear. I guess he could always get a job in the prison library. Make a sensational trial too. Now if you don't want all of that ...'

Hutchmeyer didn't want any of that. Sensational trials with Baby in the box pleading that ... Oh no! Definitely not. And *Pause* was selling by the hundred thousand, had passed the million mark and with the movie of the book in production the computer was overheating with the stupendous forecasts. Sensational trials were out.

'What's the alternative?' he asked.

Mr Synstrom leant forward. 'We could come to an arrangement,' he said.

'We could,' Hutchmeyer agreed, 'but that still leaves the cops ...'

Mr Synstrom shook his head. 'They're sitting around waiting to see what we come up with. Now the way I see it ...'

By the time he had finished Hutchmeyer saw it that way too. The insurance company would announce that the claim had been met in full and in return Hutchmeyer would write a disclaimer. Hutchmeyer did. Three and a half million dollars was worth every cent for keeping Baby 'dead'.

'What happens if you're right and she turns up out of the blue?' Hutchmeyer asked as Synstrom got up to leave.

'Then you've really got problems,' he said. 'That's what I'd say.'

He left and Hutchmeyer sat back and considered those problems. The only consolation he could find was that if Baby was still alive she had problems too. Like coming back to life and going to prison. She wasn't fool enough to do that. Which left Hutchmeyer free to go his own way. He could even marry again. His thoughts turned to Sonia Futtle. Now there was a *real* woman.

CHAPTER NINETEEN

Two thousand miles to the south Baby's problems had taken on a new dimension. Her attempt to give Piper the experience he needed relationshipwise had succeeded too well and where before he had thrown himself into *Work in Regress* he now insisted on throwing himself into her as well. The years of his celibacy were over and Piper was making up for them in a hurry. As he lay each night kissing her reinforced breasts and gripping her degreased thighs Piper experienced an ecstasy he could never have found with another woman. Baby's artificiality was entirely to his taste. Lacking so many original parts she had none of those natural physiological disadvantages he had found in Sonia. She had, as it were, been expurgated and Piper, himself in the process of expurgating *Pause*, derived enormous satisfaction from the fact that with Baby he could act out the role he had been assigned as a narrator in the book and with a woman who if she was much older than him didn't look it. And Baby's response added to his pleasure. She combined lack of fervour with sexual expertise so that he didn't feel threatened by her passion. She was simply there to be enjoyed and didn't interfere with his writing by demanding his constant attention. Finally her intimate knowledge of the novel meant that she could respond word-perfect to his cues. When he murmured, 'Darling, we're being so heuristically creative,' at the penultimate moment of ecstasy, Baby, feeling nothing, could reply, 'Constating, my baby,' in unison with her prototype the ancient Gwendolen on page 185, and thus maintain quite literally the fiction that was the essential core of Piper's being.

But if Baby met Piper's requirements as the ideal lover the reverse was not true. Baby found it unflattering to know that she was merely a stand-in for a figment of his imagination and not even his own imagination but that of the real author of *Pause*. Knowing this, Piper's ardour took on an almost ghoulish quality so that Baby, staring over his shoulder at the ceiling, had the horrid feeling that she might just as well not have been present. At such moments she saw herself as something that had coalesced from the pages of *Pause*, a phantom of the opus which was Piper's pretentious name for what he was now doing in *Work in Regress* and intended to continue in another version. Her future seemed destined to be the recipient of his derived feelings, a sexual artefact compiled from words upon pages to be ejaculated into and then set aside while he put pen to paper. Even the routine of their days had altered. Piper insisted on writing each morning and driving through the heat of the day and stopping early at a motel so that he could read to her what he had written that morning and then relate.

'Can't you just say "fuck" once in a while?' Baby asked one evening at a motel in Tuscaloosa. 'I mean that's what we're doing so why not name it right?'

But Piper wouldn't. The word wasn't in *Pause* and 'relating' was an approved term in *The Moral Novel*.

'What I feel for you ...' he began but Baby stopped him.

'So I read the original. I don't need to see the movie.'

'As I was saying,' said Piper, 'what I feel for you is ...'

'Zero,' said Baby, 'absolute zero. You've got more feelings towards that inkbottle you're always sticking your pen in than you have towards me.'

'Well, I like that ...' said Piper.

'I don't,' said Baby and there was a new note of desperation in her voice. For a moment she thought of leaving Piper there in the motel and going off on her own. But the moment passed. She was tied by the irrevocable act of the fire and her disappearance to this literary mongol whose notion of great writing was to step backwards in time in futile imitation of novelists long dead. Worst of all, she saw in Piper's obsession with past glories a mirror-image of herself. For forty years she too had waged a war with time and had by surgical recession maintained the outward appearance of the foolish beauty who had been Miss Penobscot 1935. They had so much in common and Piper served to remind her of her own stupidity. All that was gone now, the longing to be young again and the sense of knowing she was still sexually attractive. Only death remained and the certainty that when she died there would be no call for the embalmer. She had seen to that in advance.

She had seen to more than that. She had already died by fire, by water, by the bizarre circumstances of her own romantic madness. Which gave her something more in common with Piper. They were both nonentities moving in a limbo of monotonous motels, he with his ledgers and her body but she with nothing more than a sense of meaninglessness and a desperate futility. That night while Piper related, Baby, inanimate beneath him, made up her mind. They would leave the beaten track of motels and drive down dirt roads into the hinterland of the Deep South. What happened to them there would be beyond her choosing.

What was happening to Frensic was definitely beyond his choosing. He sat at the Formica-topped table in Cynthia Bogden's kitchen and tried to eat his cornflakes and forget what had occurred towards dawn. Driven frantic by Cynthia's omnivorous sexuality he had proposed to the woman. It had seemed in his whisky-sodden state the only defence against a fatal coronary and a means of getting her to tell him who had sent her *Pause*. But Miss Bogden had been too overwhelmed to discuss minor matters of that sort in the middle of the night. In the end Frensic had snatched a few hours sleep and had been woken by a radiant Cynthia with a cup of tea. Frensic had staggered through to the bathroom and had shaved with someone else's razor and had come down to breakfast determined to force the issue. But Miss Bogden's thoughts were confined to their wedding day.

'Shall we have a church wedding?' she asked as Piper toyed biliously with a boiled egg.

'What? Oh. Yes.'

'I've always wanted a church wedding.'

'So have I,' said Frensic with as much enthusiasm as if she had suggested a crematorium. He savaged the egg and decided on the direct approach. 'By the way did you ever meet the author of *Pause O Men for the Virgin?*'

Miss Bogden dragged her thoughts away from aisles, altars and Mendelssohn. 'No,' she said, 'the manuscript came by post.'

'By post?' said Frensic, dropping his spoon. 'Isn't that rather unusual?'

'You're not eating your egg,' said Miss Bogden. Frensic took a spoonful of egg into his dry mouth.

'Where did it come from?'

'Lloyds Bank,' said Miss Bogden and poured herself another cup of tea. 'Another cup for you?'

Frensic nodded. He needed something to wash the egg down with. 'Lloyds Bank?' he said finally. 'But there must have been words you couldn't read. What did you do then?'

'Oh I just rang up and asked.'

'You phoned? You mean you phoned Lloyds Bank and they'd ...'

'Oh you are silly, Geoffrey,' said Miss Bogden, 'I didn't phone Lloyds Bank. I had this other number.'

'What other number?'

'The one I had to ring, silly,' said Miss Bogden and looked at her watch. 'Oh look at the time. It's almost nine. You've made me late, you naughty boy.' And she rushed out of the kitchen. When she returned she was dressed for the day. 'You can call a taxi when you're ready,' she said, 'and we'll meet at the office.' She kissed Frensic passionately on his egg-filled mouth and went out.

Frensic got to his feet and spat the egg into the sink and turned the tap on. Then he took a pinch of snuff, helped himself to some more tea and tried to think. A phone number she had to ring? The whole business became more extraordinary the further he delved into it. And for once delved was the right word. In looking for the source of *Pause* he had dug himself ... Frensic shuddered. Dug was the right word too. In the plural it was exact. He went through to the lavatory and sat there miserably for ten minutes trying to concentrate on his next move. A phone number? An author who insisted on making corrections by telephone? There was an insanity about all this that made his own actions over the past few days look positively rational. And there was absolutely nothing rational about proposing to Miss Cynthia Bogden. Frensic finished his business in the lavatory and came out. On a small table in the hall stood a telephone. Frensic crossed to it and looked through Miss Bogden's private list of numbers but there was nothing there to indicate the author. Frensic returned to the kitchen, made himself a cup of instant coffee, took some more snuff and finally telephoned for a taxi.

It came at ten and at half-past Frensic shuffled into the Typing Agency. Miss Bogden was waiting for him. So were twelve awful women sitting at typewriters.

'Girls,' Miss Bogden called euphemistically as Frensic peered anxiously into the office, 'I want you all to meet my fiancé, Mr Geoffrey Corkadale.'

The women all rose from the seats and gaggled congratulations on Frensic while Miss Bogden suppurated happiness.

'And now the ring,' she said when the congratulations died down. She led the way out of the office and Frensic followed. The bloody woman would want a ring. Just so long as it wasn't too expensive. It was.

'I think I like the solitaire,' she told the jeweller in the Broad. Frensic flinched at the price and was about to put his entire scheme in jeopardy when he was struck by a brilliant thought. After all, what was five hundred pounds when his entire future was at stake?

'Oughtn't we to have it engraved?' he said as Cynthia put it on her finger and admired its brilliance.

'What with?' she cooed.

Frensic simpered. 'Something secret,' he whispered, 'something we two alone will understand. A *code d'amour*.'

'Oh you are awful,' said Miss Bogden. 'Fancy thinking of something like that.' Frensic glanced at the jeweller uncomfortably and applied his lips to the perm again.

'A code of love,' he explained.

'A code of love?' echoed Miss Bogden. 'What sort of code?'

'A number,' said Frensic, and paused. 'Some number that only we would know had brought us together.'

'You mean ... ?'

'Exactly,' said Frensic forestalling any alternatives, 'after all, you typed the book and I published it.'

'Couldn't we just have Till Death Do Us Part?'

'Too much like the TV series,' said Frensic who had very much earlier intentions. He was saved by the jeweller.

'You'd never get that inside the ring. Not Till Death Do Us Part. Too many letters.'

'But you could do numbers?' said Frensic.

'Depends how many.'

Frensic looked inquiringly at Miss Bogden. 'Five,' she said after a moment's hesitation.

'Five,' said Frensic. 'Five teeny weeny little numbers that are our code of love, our own, our very own itsy bitsy secret.' It was his last desperate act of heroism. Miss Bogden succumbed. For a moment she had ... but no, a man who could in the presence of an austere jeweller By Appointment to Her Majesty talk openly about five teeny weeny itsy bitsy numbers that were their code of love, such a man was above suspicion.

'Two oh three five seven,' she simpered.

'Two oh three five seven,' said Frensic loudly. 'You're quite sure? We don't want to make any mistakes.'

'Of course I'm sure,' said Miss Bogden, 'I'm not in the habit of making mistakes.'

'Right,' said Frensic plucking the ring from her finger and handing it to the jeweller, 'stick them on the inside of the thing. I'll be back to collect it this afternoon,' and taking Miss Bogden firmly by the arm he steered her towards the door.

'Excuse me, sir,' said the jeweller, 'but if you don't mind ...'

'Mind what?' said Frensic.

'I would prefer it if you paid now sir. With engraving, you understand, we have to ...'

Frensic understood all too well. He released Miss Bogden and sidled back to the counter.

'Er ... well ...' he began but Miss Bogden was still between him and the door. This was no time for half-measures. Frensic took out his cheque book.

'I'll be with you in a moment, dear,' he called. 'You just go over the road and look at dresses.'

Cynthia Bogden obeyed her instincts and stayed where she was.

'You do have a cheque card, sir?' said the jeweller.

Frensic looked at him gratefully. 'As a matter of fact, I don't. Not on me.'

'Then I'm afraid it will have to be cash, sir.'

'Cash?' said Frensic. 'In that case ...'

'We'll go to the bank,' said Miss Bogden firmly. They went to the bank in the High Street. Miss Bogden seated herself while Frensic conferred at the counter.

'Five hundred pounds?' said the teller. 'We'll have to have proof of identity and telephone your own branch.'

Frensic glanced at Miss Bogden and lowered his voice. 'Frensic,' he said nervously, 'Frederick Frensic, Glass Walk, Hampstead but my business account is with the branch in Covent Garden.'

'We'll call you when we have confirmation,' said the teller.

Frensic blanched. 'I'd be grateful if you didn't ...' he began.

'Didn't what?'

'Never mind,' said Frensic and went back to Miss Bogden. He had to get her out of the bank before that blasted teller started hollering for Mr Frensic.

'This is going to take some time, darling. Why don't you toddle back to . . .'

'But I've taken the day off and I thought . . .'

'Taken the day off?' said Frensic. If this sort of stress went on much longer it would take years off. 'But . . .'

'But what?' said Miss Bogden.

'But I'm supposed to be meeting an author for lunch. Professor Dubrowitz. From Warsaw. He's only over for the day and . . .' He hustled her out of the bank promising to come to the office just as soon as he could. Then with a sigh of relief he went back and collected five hundred pounds.

'Now for the nearest telephone,' he said to himself as he pocketed the money and descended the steps. Cynthia Bogden was still there.

'But . . .' Frensic began and gave up. With Miss Bogden there were no buts.

'I thought we'd just go and get the ring first,' she said taking his arm, 'then you can go and have lunch with your boring old professor.'

They went back to the jewellers and Frensic paid £500. Only then did Miss Bogden allow him to escape.

'Call me as soon as you've finished,' she said pecking his cheek. Frensic promised to and hurried off to the main post office. In a foul temper he dialled 23507.

'The Bombay Duck Restaurant,' said an Indian who was unlikely to have written *Pause*. Frensic slammed the phone down and tried another combination of the digits in the ring. This time he got MacLoughlin's Fish Emporium. Then he ran out of change. He went across to the main counter and handed over a five-pound note for a 6½p stamp and returned with a pocketful of coins. The phone booth was occupied. Frensic stood beside it looking belligerent while an apparently subnormal youth plighted his acned troth to a girl who giggled audibly. Frensic spent the time trying to remember the exact number and by the time the youth had finished he had got it. Frensic went in and dialled 20357. There was a long pause and the sound of the ringing tone before anyone answered. Frensic plunged a coin into the machine.

'Yes,' said a thin querulous voice, 'who is it?'

Frensic hesitated a moment and then coarsened his voice. 'This is the General Post Office, telephone faults department,' he said. 'We are trying to trace a crossed connection in a junction box. If you would just give me your name and address.'

'A fault?' said the voice. 'We haven't had any faults.'

'You soon will have. There's a burst water main and we need your name and address.'

'But I thought you said you had a crossed connection?' said the voice peevishly. 'Now you say there's a water main ...'

'Madam,' said Frensic officiously, 'the burst water main is affecting the junction box and we need your help to locate it. Now if you will be so good as to give me your name and address ...' There was a long pause during which Frensic gnawed a nail.

'Oh well if you must,' said the voice at long last, 'the name is Dr Louth and the address is 44 Cowpasture Gardens ... Hello, are you there?'

But Frensic was miles away in a world of terrible conjecture. Without another word he replaced the receiver and staggered out into the street.

In Lanyard Lane Sonia sat at her typewriter and stared at the calendar. She had returned from Somerset, satisfied that Bernie the Beaver would use less forceful language in future, to find two messages for her. The first was from Frensic saying that he would be out of town on business for a few days and would she mind coping. That was queer enough. Frensic usually left fuller explanations and a telephone number where she could call him in case of emergencies. The second message was even more peculiar and in the shape of a long telegram from Hutchmeyer: POLICE ESTABLISHED DEATHS PIPER AND BABY ACCIDENTAL NO RESPONSIBILITY TERRORISTS RUNNING AWAY WITH EACH OTHER CRAZY ABOUT YOU ARRIVING THURSDAY ALL MY LOVE HUTCHMEYER.

Sonia studied the message and found it at first incomprehensible. Deaths accidental? No responsibility terrorists running away with each other? What on earth did it mean? For a moment she hesitated and then dialled International and was put through to New York and Hutchmeyer Press. She got MacMordie.

'He's in Brasilia right now,' he said.

'What's all this business about Piper's death being accidental?' she asked.

'That's the theory the police have come up with,' said MacMordie, 'like they were eloping some place with all that fuel on board when she blew.'

'Eloping? Piper and that bitch eloping? In the middle of the night with a cabin cruiser? Somebody's out of their mind.'

'I wouldn't know,' said MacMordie, 'all I'm saying is what the cops and the insurance company have come up with. And that Piper had this big thing for old women. I mean take his book. It shows.'

'Like hell it does,' said Sonia before recalling that MacMordie didn't know Piper hadn't written it.

'If you don't believe me, call the cops in Maine or the insurers. They'll tell you.'

Sonia called the insurers. They were more likely to come up with the truth. They had money at stake. She was put through to Mr Synstrom.

'And you really believe he was running off with Mrs Hutchmeyer and it was all an accident?' she said when he had given his version of the event. 'I mean you're not having me on?'

'This is the Claims Department,' said Mr Synstrom firmly. 'We don't have people on. It's not our line of business.'

'Well it sounds crazy to me,' said Sonia, 'she was old enough to be his mother.'

'If you want further delineation of the circumstances surrounding the accident I suggest you speak to the Maine State police,' said Mr Synstrom and ended the conversation.

Sonia sat stunned by this new development. That Piper had preferred that awful old hag ... From being in love with his memory one minute she was out of it the next. Piper had betrayed her and with the knowledge there came a new sense of bitterness and reality. In life, now that she came to think about it, he had been a bit dreary and her love had been less for him as a man than for his aptitude as a husband. Given the chance she could have made something of him. Even before his death she had made him famous as an author and had he lived they would have gone on to greater things. It was not for nothing that Brahms was her favourite composer. There would have been little Pipers' each to be helped towards a suitable career by a woman who was at the same time a mother and a literary agent. That dream had ended. Piper had died with a surgically preserved bitch in a mink coat.

Sonia looked at the telegram again. It had a new message for her now. Piper was not the only man ever to have found her attractive. There was still Hutchmeyer, a widowed Hutchmeyer whose wife had stolen her darling from her. There was a fine irony in the thought that by her action, Baby had made it possible for Hutchmeyer to marry again. And marry her he would. It was marriage or nothing. There would be no messing.

Sonia reached for a sheet of paper and put it in the typewriter. Frenzy would have to be told. Poor old Frenzy, she would miss him but wedlock called and she must respond. She would explain her reasons and then leave. It seemed the best thing to do. There would be no recriminations

and in a way she was sacrificing herself for him. But where on earth had
he got to, and why?

CHAPTER TWENTY

Frensic was in Blackwell's bookshop. Half hidden among the stacks of
English literary criticism he stood with a copy of *The Great Pursuit* in his
hand and *Pause* propped up on the shelf in front of him. *The Great Pursuit*
was Dr Sydney Louth's latest, a collection of essays dedicated to F. R.
Leavis and a monument to a lifetime's execration of the shallow, the
obscene, the immature and the non-significant in English literature.
Generations of undergraduates had sat mesmerized by the turgid
inelegance of her style while she denounced the modern novel, the
contemporary world and the values of a sick and dying civilization.
Frensic had been among those undergraduates and had imbibed the
truisms on which Dr Louth's reputation as a scholar and a critic had
been founded. She had praised the obviously great and cursed the rest
and for that simple formula she was known as a great scholar. And all
this in language which was the antithesis of the stylistic brilliance of the
writers she praised. But it was her anathema which had stuck in Frensic's
mind, those bitter graceless curses she had heaped on other critics and
those who disagreed with her. By her denunciations she had implanted
the inhibitions which had spoilt Frensic and so many others like him who
had wanted to write. To appease her he had adopted the grotesque
syntax of her lectures and essays. By their style Louthians were instantly
recognizable. And by their sterility.

For three decades her influence on English literature had been
malignant. And all her imprecations on the present had been hallowed
by the great past which had she been a living influence at the time would
never have existed. Like some religious fanatic she had consecrated the
already sacred and had bred an intellectual intolerance that denied a
living to the less than best. There were only saints in Dr Louth's calendar,
saints and devils who failed the test of greatness. Hardy, Forster,
Galsworthy, Moore and Meredith, even Peacock, consigned to outer
darkness and oblivion because they did not measure up to Conrad or
Henry James. And what about poor Trollope and Thackeray? More
devils. The less than best. And Fielding ... The list was endless. And for
the present generation the only hope of salvation was to genuflect to her
opinions and learn by rote the answers to her literary catechism. And

this arid bitch had written *Pause O Men for the Virgin*. Frensic inverted
the title and found it wholly appropriate. Dr Louth had given birth to
nothing. The stillborn opinions in *The Moral Novel* and now *The Great
Pursuit* would moulder and decompose upon the shelves a few more years
and be forgotten. And she had known it and had written *Pause* to seek
an anonymous immortality. The clues were there to be seen. Frensic
wondered how he could have missed them. On page 269 of *Pause*: 'And
so inexorably their livingness became lovingness, a rhythmic lovingness
that placed them within a new dimension of feeling so that the really
real became an ...' Frensic shut the book before he came to 'apprehended
totality'. How many times in his youth had he heard her use those fearful
words? And used them himself in his essays for her. That 'placed' too
was proof enough but followed by so many meaningless abstractions and
a 'really real' it was conclusive. He thrust both books under his arm and
went to the counter to pay for them. There were no doubts left, and
everything was explained, the obsessive precautions to preserve the
author's anonymity, the readiness to allow Piper to act as substitute ...
But now Piper was claiming to have written *Pause*.

Frensic walked more slowly across the Parks deep in thought. Two
authors for the same book? And Piper had been a devotee of Dr Louth.
The Moral Novel was his scripture. In which case he could well have ...
No. Miss Bogden had not been lying. Frensic increased his pace and
strode beside the river towards Cowpasture Gardens. Dr Louth was going
to learn that she had made a bad mistake in sending her manuscript to
one of her former pupils. Because that was what it was all about. In her
conceit she had chosen Frensic out of a hundred other agents. The irony
of her gesture would have appealed to her. She had never had much
time for him. 'A mediocre mind' she had once written at the end of one
of his essays. Frensic had never forgiven her. He was going to get his
revenge.

He left the Parks and entered Cowpasture Gardens. Dr Louth's house
stood at the far end, a large Victorian mansion with an air of deliberate
desuetude as if the inhabitants were too committed intellectually to notice
overgrown borders and untended lawns. And there had been, Frensic
recalled, cats.

There were still cats. Two sat on a window-ledge and watched as
Frensic walked to the front door and rang the bell. He stood waiting and
looked around. If anything the garden had regressed still further towards
the pastoral which Dr Louth had so extolled in literature. And the
Monkey Puzzle tree stood there as unclimbable as ever. How often had
he looked out of the window at that Monkey Puzzle tree while Dr Louth

intoned the need for a mature moral purpose in all art. Frensic was about
to fall into a nostalgic reverie when the door opened and Miss Christian
peered out at him uncertainly.

'If you're from the telephone people ...' she began but Frensic shook
his head.

'My name is ...' he hesitated as he tried to recall a favoured pupil.
'Bartlett. I was a student of hers in 1955.'

Miss Christian pursed her lips. 'She's isn't seeing anyone,' she said.

Frensic smiled. 'I just wanted to pay my respects. I've always regarded
her as the greatest influence in my development. Seminal you know.'

Miss Christian savoured 'seminal'. It was the password. 'In 1955?'

'The year she published *The Intuitive Felicity*,' said Frensic to bring out
the bouquet of that vintage.

'So it was. It seems so long ago now,' said Miss Christian and opened
the door wider. Frensic stepped into the dark hall where the stained-
glass windows on the stairs added to the air of sanctity. Two more cats
sat on chairs.

'What did you say your name was?' said Miss Christian.

'Bartlett,' said Frensic. (Bartlett had got a First.)

'Ah, yes, Bartlett,' said Miss Christian. 'I'll just go and ask her if she
will see you.'

She went away down a threadworn passage to the study. Frensic stood
and gritted his teeth against the odour of cats and the almost palpable
atmosphere of intellectual high-mindness and moral intensity. On the
whole he preferred the cats.

Miss Christian shuffled back. 'She will see you,' she said. 'She seldom
sees visitors now but she will see you. You know the way.'

Frensic nodded. He knew the way. He went down the length of worn
carpet and opened the door.

Inside the study it was 1955. In twenty years nothing had changed.
Dr Sydney Louth sat in an armchair tilted on the lip of an ashtray and
a cup of cold half-finished tea on the table at her elbow. She did not
look up as Frensic entered. That was an old habit, too, the mark of an
inner concentration so profound that to disturb it was the highest
privilege. A red ballpen wriggled illegibly in the margin of the essay.
Frensic took his seat opposite her and waited. There were advantages to
be gained from her arrogance. He laid the copy of *Pause*, still in its
Blackwell's wrapping, on his knees and studied the bowed head and busy
hand. It was all exactly as he had remembered it. Then the hand stopped
writing, dropped the ballpen and reached for the cigarette.

'Bartlett, dear Bartlett,' she said and looked up. She stared at him dimly and Frensic stared back. He had been wrong. Things had changed. The face he looked at was not the face he remembered. Then it had been smooth and slightly plump. Now it was swollen and corrugated. A plexus of dropsical wrinkles bagged under the eyes and scored her cheeks, and from the lip of this reticulated mask there hung the cigarette. Only the expression in the eyes remained the same, dimmer but burning with the certainty of her own rightness.

The conviction faded as Frensic watched. 'I thought ...' she began and looked at him more closely, 'Miss Christian precisely said ...'

'Frensic. You were my supervisor in 1955,' said Frensic.

'Frensic?' The eyes filled with conjecture now. 'But you said Bartlett ...'

'A little deceit,' said Frensic, 'to guarantee this interview. I'm a literary agent now. Frensic & Futtle. You won't have heard of us.'

But Dr Louth had. The eyes flickered. 'No. I'm afraid I haven't.'

Frensic hesitated and chose a circuitous approach. 'And since ... well ... since you were my supervisor I was wondering, well, if you would consider ... I mean it would be a great favour to ask ...' Frensic paraded deference.

'What do you want?' said Dr Louth.

Frensic unwrapped the packet on his lap. 'You see we have a novel and if you would write a piece ...'

'A novel?' The eyes behind the wrinkles glinted at the wrapping paper. 'What novel?'

'This,' said Frensic, and passed her *Pause O Men for the Virgin*. For a moment Dr Louth stared at the book and the cigarette slouched on her lip. Then she cringed in her chair.

'That?' she whispered. The cigarette dropped from her lip and smouldered on the essay on her lap. 'That?'

Frensic nodded and leaning forward removed the cigarette and put the book down. 'It seemed your sort of book,' he said.

'My sort of book?'

Frensic sat back in his chair. The centre of power had passed to him. 'Since you wrote it,' he said, 'I thought it only fair ...'

'How did you know?' She was staring at him with a new intensity. There was no high moral purpose in that intensity now. Only fear and hatred. Frensic basked in it. He crossed his legs and looked out at the Monkey Puzzle tree. He had climbed it.

'Mainly through the style,' he said, 'and to be perfectly frank, by critical analysis. You used the same words too often in your books and I placed them. You taught me that, you see.'

There was a long pause while Dr Louth lit another cigarette. 'And you expect me to review it?' she said at last.

'Not really,' said Frensic, 'it's unethical for an author to review her own work. I just wanted to discuss how best we could announce the news to the world.'

'What news?'

'That Dr Sydney Louth, the eminent critic, had written both *Pause* and *The Great Pursuit*. I thought an article in *The Times Literary Supplement* would do to start the controversy raging. After all, it's not every day that a scholar produces a bestseller, particularly the sort of book she has spent her life denouncing as obscene ...'

'I forbid it,' Dr Louth gasped. 'As my agent ...'

'As your agent it is my business to see that the book sells. And I can assure you that the literary scandal the announcement will provoke in circles where your name has previously been revered ...'

'No,' said Dr Louth, 'that must never happen.'

'You're thinking of your reputation?' inquired Frensic gently. Dr Louth did not reply.

'You should have thought of that before. As it is you have placed me in a very awkward situation. I have a reputation to maintain too.'

'Your reputation? What sort of reputation is that?' She spat the words at him.

Frensic leant forward. 'An immaculate one,' he snarled, 'beyond your comprehension.'

Dr Louth tried to smile. 'Grub Street,' she muttered.

'Yes, Grub Street,' said Frensic, 'and proud of it. Where people write without hypocrisy for money.'

'Lucre, filthy lucre.'

Frensic grinned. 'And what did you write for?'

The mask looked at him venomously. 'To prove that I could,' she said, 'that I could write the sort of trash that sells. They thought I couldn't. A sterile critic, impotent, an academic. I proved them wrong.' Her voice rose.

Frensic shrugged. 'Hardly,' he said. 'Your name is not upon the title-page. Until it is no one will ever know.'

'No one must ever know.'

'But I intend to tell them,' said Frensic. 'It will make fascinating reading. The anonymous author, Lloyds Bank, the Typing Service, Mr Cadwalladine, Corkadales, your American publisher ...'

'You mustn't,' she whimpered, 'no one must ever know. I tell you I forbid it.'

'It's no longer in your hands,' said Frensic, 'it's in mine and I will not sully them with your hypocrisy. Besides I have another client.'

'Another client?'

'The scapegoat Piper who went to America for you. He has a reputation, too, you know.'

Dr Louth sniggered. 'Like yours, immaculate I suppose.'

'In conception, yes,' said Frensic.

'But which he was prepared to put in jeopardy for money.'

'If you like. He wanted to write and he needed the money. You, I take it, don't. You mentioned lucre, filthy lucre. I am prepared to bargain.'

'Blackmail,' snapped Dr Louth and stubbed out her cigarette.

Frensic looked at her with a new disgust. 'For a moral coward who hides behind a *nom de plume* your language is imprecise. Had you come to me in the first place I would not have engaged Piper but since you chose anonymity at the expense of honesty I am now in the position of having to choose between two authors.'

'Two? Why two?'

'Because Piper claims he wrote the book.'

'Let him claim. He accepted the onus, let him bear it.'

'He also claims the money.'

Dr Louth glared at the smouldering fire. 'He has been paid,' she said finally. 'What more does he want?'

'Everything,' said Frensic.

'And you're prepared to let him have it?'

'Yes,' said Frensic. 'My reputation is at stake too. If there's a scandal I will suffer.'

'A scandal,' Dr Louth shook her head. 'There must be no scandal.'

'But there will be,' said Frensic. 'You see, Piper is dead.'

Dr Louth shivered suddenly. 'Dead? But you said just now ...'

'There is the estate to be wound up. It will go to court and with two million dollars ... Need I say more?'

Dr Louth shook her head. 'What do you want me to do?' she asked.

Frensic relaxed. The crisis was over. He had broken the bitch. 'Write a letter to me denying that you ever wrote the book. Now.'

'Will that suffice?'

'To begin with,' said Frensic. Dr Louth got up and crossed to her desk. For a minute or two she sat there writing. When she had finished she handed Frensic the letter. He read it through and was satisfied.

'And now the manuscript,' he said, 'the original manuscript in your own handwriting and any copies you may have made.'

'No,' she said, 'I will destroy it.'

'We will destroy it,' said Frensic, 'before I leave.'

Dr Louth turned back to the desk and unlocked a drawer and took out a box. She crossed to her chair by the fire and sat down. Then she opened the box and took the pages out. Frensic glanced at the top one. It began 'The house stood on a knoll. Surrounded by three elms, a beech and a deodor whose horizontal branches ...' He was looking at the original of *Pause*. A moment later the page was on fire and blazing up into the chimney. Frensic sat and watched as one by one the pages flared up, crinkled to black so that the words upon them stood out like white lace, broke and caught in the draught and were swept up the chimney. And as they blazed Frensic seemed to catch out of the corner of his eye the gleam of tears in the runnels of Dr Louth's cheeks. For a moment he faltered. The woman was cremating her own work. Trash she had called it and yet she was crying over it now. He would never understand writers and the contradictory impulses that were the source of their invention.

As the last page disappeared he got up. She was still huddled over the grate. For a second time Frensic was tempted to ask her why she had written the book. To prove her critics wrong. That wasn't the answer. There was more to it than that, the sex, the ardent love affair ... He would never learn from her. He left the room quietly and went down the passage to the front door. Outside the air was filled with small black flakes falling from the chimney and near the gate a young cat jumped up clawing at a fragment which danced in the breeze.

Frensic took a deep breath of fresh air and hurried down the road. He had his things to collect from the hotel and then a train to catch to London.

Somewhere south of Tuscaloosa Baby dropped the road map out of the window of the car. It fluttered behind them in the dust and was gone. As usual Piper noticed nothing. His mind was intent on *Work In Regress*. He had reached page 178 and the book was going well. In another fortnight of hard work he would have finished it. And then he would start the third revision, the one in which not only the characters were changed but the setting of every scene. He had decided to call it *Postscript to a Childhood* as a precursor to his final, commercially unadulterated novel *Search for a Lost Childhood* which was to be considered in retrospect as the very first draft of *Pause* by those same critics who had acclaimed that obnoxious novel. In this way his reputation would have been rescued from the oblivion of facile success and scholars would be able to trace the insidious influence of Frensic's commercial recommendations upon his original talent. Piper smiled to himself at his own ingenuity. And after all there could be other yet-to-be-discovered novels. He would go on writing 'posthumously' and every few years another novel would turn up on Frensic's desk to be released to the world. There was nothing Frensic could do about it. Baby was right. By deceiving Hutchmeyer Frensic & Futtle had made themselves vulnerable. Frensic would have to do what he was told. Piper closed his eyes and lay back in his seat contentedly. Half an hour later he opened them again and sat up. The car, a Ford that Baby had bought in Rossville, was lurching on a bad road surface. Piper looked out and saw they were driving along a road built on an embankment. On either side tall trees stood in dark water.

'Where are we?' he asked.

'I've no idea,' said Baby.

'No idea? You've got to know where we are heading.'

'Into the sticks is all I know. And when we get some place we'll find out.'

Piper looked down at the dark water beneath the trees. The forest had a sinister quality to it that he didn't like. Always before they had travelled along homely, cheerful roads with only the occasional stretch of kudzu vine crawling across trees and banks to suggest wild natural growth. But this was different. There were no billboards, no houses, no gas stations, none of those amenities which had signified civilization. This was a wilderness.

'And what happens if when we do get some place there isn't a motel?' he asked.

'Then we'll have to make do with what there is,' said Baby, 'I told you we were coming to the Deep South and this is where it's at.'

'Where what's at?' said Piper staring down at the black water and thinking of alligators.

'That's what I've come to find out,' said Baby enigmatically and braked the car to a standstill at a crossroads. Piper peered through the windshield at a sign. Its faded letters said BIBLIOPOLIS 15 MILES.

'Looked like your kind of town,' said Baby and turned the car on to the side road. Presently the dark water forest thinned and they came out into an open landscape with lush meadows hazy with heat where cattle grazed in long grass and clumps of trees stood apart. There was something almost English about this scenery, an English parkland gone to seed, luxuriant yet immanent with half-remembered possibilities. Everywhere the distance faded into haze blurring the horizon. Piper, looking across the meadows, felt easier in his mind. There was a sense of domesticity here that was reassuring. Occasionally they passed a wooden shack part-hidden by vegetation and seemingly unoccupied. And finally there was Bibliopolis itself, a small town, almost a hamlet, with a river running sluggishly beside an abandoned quay. Baby drove down to the riverside and stopped. There was no bridge. On the far side an ancient ropy ferry provided the only means of crossing.

'Okay, go ring the bell,' said Baby. Piper got out and rang a bell that hung from a post.

'Harder,' said Baby as Piper pulled on the rope. Presently a man appeared on the far shore and the ferry began to move across.

'You wanting something?' said the man when the ferry grounded.

'We're looking for somewhere to stay,' said Baby. The man peered at the licence plate on the Ford and seemed reassured. It read Georgia.

'There ain't no motel in Bibliopolis,' said the man. 'You'd best go back to Selma.'

'There must be somewhere,' said Baby as the man still hesitated.

'Mrs Mathervitie's Tourist Home,' said the man and stepped aside. Baby drove on to the ferry and got out.

'Is this the Alabama river?' she asked. The man shook his head.

'The Ptomaine River, ma'am,' he said and pulled on the rope.

'And that?' asked Baby, pointing to a large dilapidated mansion that was evidently ante-bellum.

'That's Pellagra. Nobody lives there now. They all died off.'

Piper sat in the car and stared gloomily at the sluggish river. The trees along its bank were veiled with Spanish moss like widows' weeds and the dilapidated mansion below the town put him in mind of Miss Havisham. But Baby, when she got back into the car and drove off the ferry, was clearly elated by the atmosphere.

'I told you this was where it's at,' she said triumphantly. 'And now for Mrs Mathervitie's Tourist Home.'

They drove down a tree-lined street and stopped outside a house. A signboard said Welcome. Mrs Mathervitie was less effusive. Sitting in the shadow of a porch she watched them get out of the car.

'You folks looking for some place?' she asked, her glasses glinting in the sunset.

'Mrs Mathervitie's Tourist Home,' said Baby.

'Selling or staying? Cos if it's cosmetics I ain't in the market.'

'Staying,' said Baby.

Mrs Mathervitie studied them critically with the air of a connoisseur of irregular relationships.

'I only got singles,' she said and spat into the hub of a sun flower, 'no doubles.'

'Praise be the Lord,' said Baby involuntarily.

'Amen,' said Mrs Mathervitie.

They went into the house and down a passage.

'This is yourn,' said Mrs Mathervitie to Piper and opened a door. The room looked out on to a patch of corn. On the wall there was an oleograph of Christ scourging the moneylenders from the Temple and a cardboard sign that decreed NO BROWNBAGGING. Piper looked at it dubiously. It seemed a thoroughly unnecessary injunction.

'Well?' said Mrs Mathervitie.

'Very nice,' said Piper who had spotted a row of books on a shelf. He looked at them and found they were all Bibles.

'Good Lord,' he muttered.

'Amen,' said Mrs Mathervitie and went off with Baby down the passage leaving Piper to consider the sinister implications of NO BROWNBAGGING. By the time they returned he was no nearer a solution to the riddle.

'The Reverend and I are happy to accept your hospitality,' said Baby. 'Aren't we, Reverend?'

'What?' said Piper. Mrs Mathervitie was looking at him with new interest.

'I was just telling Mrs Mathervitie how interested you are in American religion,' said Baby. Piper swallowed and tried to think what to say. 'Yes,' seemed the safest.

There was an extremely awkward silence broken finally by Mrs Mathervitie's business sense.

'Ten dollars a day. Seven with prayers. Providence is extra.'

'Yes, well I suppose it would be,' said Piper.

'Meaning?' said Mrs Mathervitie.

'That the good Lord will provide,' interjected Baby before Piper's slight hysteria could manifest itself again.

'Amen,' said Mrs Mathervitie. 'Well which is it to be? With prayers or without?'

'With,' said Baby.

'Fourteen dollars,' said Mrs Mathervitie, 'in advance.'

'Pay now and pray later?' said Piper hopefully.

Mrs Mathervitie's eyes gleamed coldly. 'For a preacher ...' she began but Baby intervened. 'The Reverend means we should pray without ceasing.'

'Amen,' said Mrs Mathervitie and knelt on the linoleum.

Baby followed her example. Piper looked down at them in astonishment.

'Dear God,' he muttered.

'Amen,' said Mrs Mathervitie and Baby in unison.

'Say the good words, Reverend,' said Baby.

'For Christ's sake,' said Piper for inspiration. He didn't know any prayers and as for good words ... On the floor Mrs Mathervitie twitched dangerously. Piper found the good words. They came from *The Moral Novel*.

'It is our duty not to enjoy but to appreciate,' he intoned, 'Not to be entertained but to be edified, not to read that we may escape the responsibilities of life but that, through reading, we may more properly understand what it is that we are and do and that born anew in the vicarious experience of others we may extend our awareness and our sensibilities and so enriched by how we read we may be better human beings.'

'Amen,' said Mrs Mathervitie fervently.

'Amen,' said Baby.

'Amen,' said Piper and sat down on the bed. Mrs Mathervitie got to her feet.

'I thank you for those good words, Reverend,' she said and left the room.

'What the hell was all that about?' said Piper when her footsteps had faded. Baby stood up and raised a finger to her lips.

'No cussing. No brownbagging.'

'And that's another thing ...' Piper began but Mrs Mathervitie's footsteps came down the passage again.

'Conventicle's at eight,' she said poking her head round the door. 'Doesn't do to be late.'

Piper regarded her biliously. 'Conventicle?'

'Conventicle of the Seventh Day Church of The Servants of God,' said Mrs Mathervitie. 'You said you wanted prayers.'

'The Reverend and I will be right with you,' said Baby. Mrs Mathervitie removed her head. Baby took Piper's arm and pushed him towards the door.

'Good God, you've really landed us –'

'Amen,' said Baby as they went out into the passage. Mrs Mathervitie was waiting on the porch.

The Church is in the town square,' she said as they climbed into the Ford and presently they were driving down the darkened street where the Spanish moss looked even more sinister to Piper. By the time they stopped outside a small wooden church in the square he was in a state of panic.

'They won't want me to pray again, will they?' he whispered to Baby as they climbed the steps to the church. From inside there came the sound of a hymn.

'We're late,' said Mrs Mathervitie and hurried them down the aisle. The church was crowded but a row of seats at the very front was empty. A moment later Piper found himself clutching a hymnbook and singing an extraordinary hymn called 'Telephoning To Glory'.

When the hymn ended there was a scuffling of feet and the congregation knelt and the preacher launched into prayer.

'Oh Lord we is all sinners,' he declared.

'Oh Lord we is all sinners,' bawled Mrs Mathervitie and the rest of the congregation.

'Oh Lord we is all sinners waiting to be saved,' continued the preacher.

'Waiting to be saved. Waiting to be saved.'

'From the fires of hell and the snares of Satan.'

'From the fires of hell and the snares of Satan.'

Beside Piper Mrs Mathervitie had begun to quiver. 'Hallelujah,' she cried.

When the prayer ended a large black woman who was standing beside the piano began 'Washed In The Blood Of The Lamb' and from there it was but a short step to 'Jericho' and finally a hymn which went 'Servants of the Lord we Pledge our Faith in Thee' with a chorus of 'Faith, Faith, Faith in The Lord, Faith in Jesus is Mightier than the Sword'. Much to his own amazement Piper sang as loudly as anyone and the enthusiasm began to get to him. By this time Mrs Mathervitie was stomping her foot while several other women were clapping their hands. They sang the hymn twice and then went straight into another about Eve and The Apple. As the reverberations died away the preacher raised his hands.

'Brothers and sisters ...' he began, only to be interrupted.

'Bring on the serpents,' shouted someone at the back.

The preacher lowered his hands. 'Serpents night's Saturday,' he said. 'You know that.'

But the cry 'Bring on the serpents,' was taken up and the large black lady struck up 'Faith in The Lord and the Snakes won't Bite, Them's has Faith is Saved all Right.'

'Snakes?' said Piper to Mrs Mathervitie, 'I thought you said this was Servants of The Lord.'

'Snakes is Saturday,' said Mrs Mathervitie looking decidedly alarmed herself. 'I only come Thursdays. I don't hold with serpentizing.'

'Serpentizing?' said Piper suddenly alive to what was about to happen, 'Jesus Wept.' Beside him Baby was already weeping but Piper was too

concerned for his own safety to bother about her. A sack was brought
down the aisle by a tall gaunt man. It was a large sack, a large sack
which writhed. So did Piper. A moment later he had shot out of his seat
and was heading for the door only to find his way blocked by a number
of other people who evidently shared his lack of enthusiasm for being
confined in a small church with a sackful of poisonous snakes. A hand
shoved him aside and Piper fell back into his seat again. 'Let's get the
hell out of here,' he shouted to Baby but she was looking with rapt
attention at the pianist, a small thin man who was thumping away on
the keys with a fervour that was possibly due to what looked like a small
boa constrictor which had twined itself round his neck. Behind the piano
the large black lady was using two rattlesnakes as maracas and singing
'Bibliopolis we Hold Thee Dear, Snakes Infest us we don't Fear' – which
certainly didn't apply to Piper. He was about to make another dash for
the door when something slithered across his feet. It was Mrs Mathervitie.
Piper sat petrified and moaned. Beside him Baby was moaning too. There
was a strange seraphic look on her face. At that moment the man with
the sack lifted from it a snake with red and yellow bands across its body.

'The Coral,' someone hissed. The strains of 'Bibliopolis we Hold Thee
Dear' faded abruptly. In the silence that followed Baby got to her feet
and moved hypnotically forward. By the dim light of the candles she
looked majestic and beautiful. She took the snake from the man and held
it aloft and her arm became a caduceus, she tore her blouse to the waist
and exposed two voluptuously pointed breasts. There was another gasp
of horror. Naked breasts were out in Bibliopolis. On the other hand the
coral snake was in. As Baby lowered her arm the outraged snake sank
its fangs into six inches of plastic silicon. For ten seconds it writhed there
before Baby detached it and offered it the other breast. But the coral had
had enough. So had Piper. With a groan he joined Mrs Mathervitie on
the floor. Baby, triumphantly topless, tossed the coral into the sack and
turned to the pianist.

'Launch into the deep, brother,' she cried.

And once again the little church reverberated to the strains of
'Bibliopolis we Hold Thee Dear, Snakes Infest us we don't Fear.'

CHAPTER TWENTY-ONE

In his Hampstead flat Frensic lay in his morning bath and twiddled the hot tap with his big toe to maintain an even temperature. A good night's sleep had helped to undo the ravages of Cynthia Bogden's passion and he was in no hurry to go to the office. He had things to think about. It was all very well congratulating himself for his subtlety in unearthing the genuine author of *Pause* and forcing her to renounce all rights in the book but there were still problems to be faced. The first of these concerned the continuing existence of Piper and his inordinate claim to be paid for a novel he hadn't written. On the face of it this seemed a minor problem. Frensic could now go ahead and deposit the two million dollars less his own and Corkadales' commissions in account number 478776 in the First National Bank of New York. This seemed at first sight the sensible thing to do. Pay Piper and be rid of the rogue. On the other hand it was succumbing to blackmail and blackmailers tended to renew their demands. Give in once and he would have to give in again and again and in any case transferring the money to New York would necessitate explaining to Sonia that Piper wasn't dead. One whiff of that and she'd be off after him like a scalded cat. Perhaps he might be able to fudge the issue and tell her that Mr Cadwalladine's client had given instructions for the royalties to be paid in this way.

But beyond all these technical problems there lay the suspicion that Piper hadn't come up with this conspiracy to defraud on his own initiative. Ten years of the recurrent *Search for a Lost Childhood* was proof enough that Piper lacked any imagination at all and whoever had dreamt this devious plot up had a remarkably powerful imagination. Frensic's suspicions centred on Mrs Baby Hutchmeyer. If Piper, who was supposed to have died with her, was still alive there was every reason to believe that Baby Hutchmeyer had survived with him. Frensic tried to analyse the psychology of Hutchmeyer's wife. To have endured forty years of marriage to that monster argued either masochism or resilience beyond the ordinary. And then to burn an enormous house to the ground, blow up a cruiser and sink a yacht, all of them belonging to her husband and all in a matter of twenty minutes ... Clearly the woman was insane and couldn't be relied upon. At any moment she might resurrect herself and drag from his temporary grave the wretched Piper. What would follow this momentous event blew Frensic's mind. Hutchmeyer would go litigiously berserk and sue everyone in sight. Piper would be dragged through the courts and the entire story of his substitution for the real author would be announced to the world. Frensic got out of the bath and dried himself to ward off the spectre of Piper in the witness box.

And as he dressed the problem became more and more complicated. Even if Baby Hutchmeyer didn't decide to go in for self-exhumation there was every chance that she would be discovered by some nosey reporter who might at this very moment be hungrily tracking her down. What the hell would happen if Piper told the truth? Frensic tried to foresee the outcome of his revelations, and was just making himself some coffee when he remembered the manuscript. The manuscript in Piper's handwriting. Or at least the copy. That was the way out. He could always deny Piper's allegation that he hadn't written *Pause* and produce that manuscript copy as proof. And even if the psychotic Baby backed Piper up, nobody would believe her. Frensic sighed with relief. He had found a way out of the dilemma. After breakfast he walked up the hill to the tube station and caught a train in a thoroughly good mood. He was a clever fellow and it would take more than the benighted Piper and Baby Hutchmeyer to put one across him.

He arrived at Lanyard Lane to find the office locked. That was odd. Sonia Futtle should have been back from Bernie the Beaver the previous day. Frensic unlocked the door and went in. No sign of Sonia. He crossed to his desk and there lying neatly separated from the rest of the mail was an envelope. It was addressed in Sonia's handwriting to him. Frensic sat down and opened it. Inside was a long letter which began 'Dearest Frenzy' and ended, 'Your loving Sonia.' In between these endearments Sonia explained with a wealth of nauseating sentimentality and self-deception how Hutchmeyer had asked her to marry him and why she had accepted. Frensic was flabbergasted. And only a week before the girl had been crying her eyes out over Piper. Frensic took out his snuff box and red spotted handkerchief and thanked God he was still a bachelor. The ways and wiles of women were quite beyond him.

They were quite beyond Geoffrey Corkadale too. He was still in a state of nervous agitation over the threatened libel suit of Professor Facit versus the author, publisher and printer of *Pause O Men for the Virgin* when he received a telephone call from Miss Bogden.

'I did what?' he asked with a mixture of total incredulity and disgust. 'And stop calling me darling. I don't know you from a bar of soap.'

'But Geoffrey sweetheart,' said Miss Bogden, 'you were so passionate, so manly ...'

'I was not!' shouted Geoffrey. 'You've got the wrong number. You can't say these things.'

Miss Bogden could and did. In detail. Geoffrey Corkadale curdled.

'Stop,' he yelled, 'I don't know what the hell has been going on but if you think for one moment that I spent the night before last in your beastly arms ... dear God ... you must be out of your bloody mind.'

'And I suppose you didn't ask me to marry you,' screamed Miss Bogden, 'and buy me an engagement ring and ...'

Geoffrey slammed the phone down to shut out this appalling catalogue. The situation was sufficiently desperate on the legal front without demented women claiming he had asked them to marry him. Then, to forestall any resumption of Miss Bogden's accusations, he left the office and made his way to his solicitors to discuss a possible defence in the libel action.

They were singularly unhelpful. 'It isn't as if the defamation of Professor Facit was accidental,' they told him. 'This man Piper evidently set out with deliberate malice to ruin the reputation of the Professor. There can be no other explanation. In our opinion the author is entirely culpable.'

'He also happens to be dead,' said Geoffrey.

'In that case it rather looks as though you are going to have to bear the entire costs of this action and, frankly, we would advise you to settle.'

Geoffrey Corkadale left the solicitors' office in despair. It was all that bloody man Frensic's fault. He should have known better than to have dealt with a literary agent who had already been involved in one disastrous libel action. Frensic was libel-prone. There was no other way of looking at it. Geoffrey took a cab to Lanyard Lane. He was going to tell Frensic what he thought of him. He found Frensic in an unusually affable mood.

'Mr dear Geoffrey, how very nice to see you,' he said.

'I haven't come to exchange compliments,' said Geoffrey, 'I've come to tell you that you've landed me in the most appalling mess and ...'

Frensic raised a hand.

'You mean Professor Facit? Oh I shouldn't worry too much ...'

'Worry too much? I've got every right to worry and as for too much, with bankruptcy staring me in the face just how much is too much?'

'I've been making some private inquiries,' said Frensic, 'in Oxford.'

'You have?' said Geoffrey. 'You don't mean to say he actually did do all those frightful things? That ghastly Pekinese for instance?'

'I mean,' said Frensic pontifically, 'that no one in Oxford has ever heard of a Professor Facit. I've checked with the Lodging House Syndicate and the university library and they had no records of any Professor Facit ever having applied for a ticket to use the library. And as for his statement that he once lived in De Frytville Avenue, it's quite untrue.'

'Good Lord,' said Geoffrey, 'if nobody up there has ever heard of him ...'

'It rather looks as if Messrs Ridley, Coverup, Makeweight and Jones have just tried to ambulance-chase once too often and are hoist with their own petard.'

'My dear fellow, this calls for a celebration,' said Geoffrey. 'And you mean to say you went up there and found all this out ...'

But Frensic was modesty itself. 'You see, I knew Piper pretty well. After all he had been sending me stuff for years,' he said as they went downstairs, 'and he wasn't the sort of fellow to set out to libel someone deliberately.'

'But I thought you told me that *Pause* was his first book,' said Geoffrey.

Frensic regretted his indiscretion. 'His first *real* book,' he said. 'The rest was just ... well, a bit derivative. Not the sort of stuff I could ever have sold.'

They strolled across to Wheeler's for lunch. 'Talking of Oxford,' said Geoffrey when they had ordered, 'I had the most extraordinary phone call this morning from some lunatic woman called Bogden.'

'Really?' said Frensic, spilling dry Martini down his shirt front. 'What did she want?'

'She claimed I'd asked her to marry me. It was absolutely awful.'

'It must have been,' said Frensic, finishing his drink and ordering another kind. 'Mind you, some women will go to any lengths ...'

'From what I could gather I was the one to have gone to any lengths. Said I'd bought her an engagement ring.'

'I hope you told her to go to hell,' said Frensic, 'and talking of marriages I've got some news too. Sonia Futtle is going to marry Hutchmeyer.'

'Marry Hutchmeyer?' said Geoffrey. 'But the man's only just lost his wife. You'd think he'd have the decency to wait a bit before sticking his head in the noose again.'

'An apt metaphor,' said Frensic with a smile, and raised his glass.

His worries were over. He had just realized that in marrying Hutchmeyer Sonia had acted more wisely than she knew. She had effectively spiked the enemy's guns. A bigamous Hutchmeyer was no threat, and besides, a man who could find Sonia physically attractive must be besotted and a besotted Hutch would never believe his new wife had once been party to a conspiracy to deceive him. All that remained was to implicate Piper financially. After an excellent lunch Frensic walked back to Lanyard Lane and thence to the bank. There he subtracted Corkadales' ten per cent and his own commission and despatched one million four hundred thousand dollars to account number 478776 in the First National Bank of New York. He had honoured his side of the contract. Frensic went home by taxi. He was a rich and happy man.

So was Hutchmeyer. Sonia's whirlwind acceptance of his whirlwind proposal had taken him by surprise. The thighs that had over the years so entranced him were his at last. Her ample body was entirely to his taste. It bore no scars, none of the surgical modifications that in Baby's case had served to remind him of his faithlessness and the artificiality of their relationship. With Sonia he could be himself. There was no need to assert himself by peeing in the washbasin every night or to prove his virility by badgering strange girls in Rome and Paris and Las Vegas. He could relapse into domestic happiness with a woman who had energy enough for both of them. They were married in Cannes and that night as Hutchmeyer lay supine between those hustling thighs he gazed up at her breasts and knew that this was for real. Sonia smiled down at his contented face and was contented herself. She was a married woman at long last.

And married to a rich man. The next night Hutchmeyer celebrated by losing forty grand at Monte Carlo and then, in memory of the good fortune that had brought them together, chartered a vast yacht with an experienced skipper and a competent crew. They cruised in the Aegean. They explored the ruins of ancient Greece and, more profitably, a deal involving supertankers which were going cheap. And finally they flew back to New York for the première of the film, *Pause.*

There in the darkness, garlanded with diamonds, Sonia finally broke down and wept. Beside her Hutchmeyer understood. It was a deeply moving movie with fashionable radicals playing Gwendolen and Anthony and combined *Lost Horizon, Sunset Boulevard* and *Deep Throat* with *Tom Jones.* Under MacMordie's financial tutelage the critics raved. And all the time the profits from the novel poured in. The movie boosted sales and there was even talk of a Broadway musical with Maria Callas in the leading role. To keep sales moving ever upwards Hutchmeyer consulted the computer and ordered a new cover for the book with the result that people who had bought the book before found themselves buying it yet again. After the musical some would doubtless buy it a third time. The Book Club sales were enormous and the leatherbound Baby Hutchmeyer Memorial Edition with gold tooling sold out in a week. All over the country *Pause* left its mark. Elderly women emerged from the seclusion of bridge clubs and beauty parlours to inveigle young men into bed. The vasectomy index fell rapidly. And finally, to crown Hutchmeyer's success, Sonia announced that she was pregnant.

In Bibliopolis, Alabama, things had changed too. The funeral of the victims of the unscheduled serpentizing took place among the live oaks that bordered the Ptomaine River. There were seven in all, though only two from snake bite. Three had been crushed in the stampede for the door. The Reverend Gideon had succumbed to heart failure, and Mrs Mathervitie to outraged shock on awakening from her faint to find Baby standing topless in the pulpit. Out of this terrible infestation Baby emerged with a remarkable reputation. It was due as much to the perfection of her breasts as to their immunity; taken together the two were irresistible. Never before had Bibliopolis witnessed so complete a demonstration of faith, and in the absence of the late Reverend Gideon Baby was offered the ministry. She accepted gratefully. It put an end to Piper's sexual depredations, and besides she had found her forte. From the pulpit she could denounce the sins of the flesh with a relish that endeared her to the womenfolk and excited the men, and having spent so much of her life in Hutchmeyer's company she could speak about hell from experience. Above all she was free to be what remained of herself. And so as the coffins were lowered into the ground the Reverend Hutchmeyer led the congregation in 'Shall we Gather by the River' and the little population of Bibliopolis bowed their heads and raised their voices. Even the snakes, hissing as they were emptied from the sack into the Ptomaine, had benefited. Baby had abolished serpentizing in a long sermon about Eve and The Apple in which she had pointed out that they were creatures of Satan. The relatives of the deceased tended to agree. And finally there was the problem of Piper. Having found her faith Baby felt obliged to the man who had so fortuitously led her to it.

With the advance royalties from *Pause* she restored Pellagra House to its ante-bellum glory and installed Piper there to continue work on his third version, *Postscript to a Lost Childhood*. As the days passed into weeks and the weeks into months, Piper wrote steadily on and resumed the routine of his life at the Gleneagle Guest House. In the afternoons he walked by the banks of the Ptomaine and in the evening read passages from *The Moral Novel* and the great classics it commended. With so much money at his disposal Piper had ordered them all. They lined the shelves of his study at Pellagra, icons of that literary religion to which he had dedicated his life. Jane Austen, Conrad, George Eliot, Dickens, Henry James, Lawrence, Mann, they were all there to spur him on. His one sorrow was that the only woman he could ever love was sexually inaccessible. As preacher Baby had made it plain she could no longer sleep with him.

'You'll just have to sublimate,' she told him. Piper tried to sublimate but the yearning remained as constant as his ambition to become a great novelist.

'It's no good,' he said, 'I keep thinking about you all the time. You are so beautiful, so pure, so ... so ...'

'You've too much time on your hands,' said Baby. 'Now if you had something more to do ...'

'Such as?'

Baby looked at the beautiful script upon the page. 'Like you could teach people to write,' she said.

'I can't even write myself,' said Piper. It was one of his self-pitying days.

'But you can. Look at the way you form your "f"s and this lovely tail to your "y". If you can't teach people to write, who can?'

'Oh you mean "write",' said Piper, 'I suppose I could do that. But who would want to learn?'

'Lots of people. You'd be surprised. When I was a girl there were schools of penmanship in almost every town. You'd be doing something useful.'

'Useful?' said Piper, attenuating that word with melancholy. 'All I want to do is –'

'Write,' said Baby, hurriedly forestalling his sexual suggestion. 'Well, this way you can combine artistry with education. You can hold classes every afternoon and it will take your mind off yourself.'

'My mind isn't on myself. It's on you. I love you ...'

'We must all love one another,' said Baby sententiously and left.

A week later the School of Penmanship opened and instead of brooding all afternoon by the sluggish waters of the Ptomaine River, Piper stood in front of his pupils and taught them to write beautifully. The classes were mostly of children but later adults came too and sat there pens in hand and bottles of Higgins Eternal Evaporated Ink at the ready while Piper explained that a diagonal ligature required an upstroke and that a wavy serif was obtrusive. Over the months his reputation grew and with it there came theory. To visitors from as far away as Selma and Meridian Piper expounded the doctrine of the word made perfect. He called it Logosophy, and won adherents. It was as if the process by which he had failed as a novelist had reversed itself in his writing. In the old days of his obsession with the great novel theory had preceded and indeed pre-empted practice. What *The Moral Novel* had condemned Piper had avoided. With penmanship Piper was his own practitioner and theorist. But still the old ambition to see his novel in print remained and as each newly expurgated version of *Pause* was finished he mailed it to Frensic. At first he sent it to New York to be readdressed and forwarded to Lanyard Lane but as the months passed his confidence in his new life grew and with it forgetfulness and he sent it direct. And every month he ordered *Books & Bookmen* and *The Times Literary Supplement* and scanned the lists of new novels only to be disappointed. *Search for a Lost Childhood* was never there.

Finally, late one night when the moon was full, he decided on a fresh approach and taking up his pen wrote to Frensic. His letter was blunt and to the point. Unless Frensic & Futtle as his literary agents were prepared to guarantee that his novel was published he would be forced to ask some other literary agent to handle his work in future.

'In fact I am seriously considering sending my manuscript direct to Corkadales,' he wrote. 'As you will remember I signed a contract with them to publish my second novel and I can see no good reason why this specific agreement should be negated. Your sincerely, Peter Piper.'

CHAPTER TWENTY-TWO

'The man must be out of his bloody mind,' muttered Frensic a week later. 'I can see no reason why this arrangement should be negated.' Frensic could. 'The sod can't seriously suppose I can go round to Corkadales and force them to publish a book by a corpse.'

But it was evident from the tone of the letter that Piper supposed exactly that. Over the months Frensic had received four Xeroxed and altered drafts of Piper's novel and had consigned them to a filing cabinet which he kept carefully locked. If Piper wanted to waste his own time reworking the damned book until every element that had made *Pause* the least bit readable had been eliminated he was welcome to do so. Frensic felt under no obligation to hawk his rubbish round publishing houses. But the threat to deal direct with Corkadales was, to put it mildly, a different kettle of fish. Piper was dead and buried and he was being well paid for it. Every month Frensic saw that the proceeds from the sale of *Pause* went into account number 478776, and wondered at the extraordinary inefficiency of the American tax system that didn't seem to mind that a taxpayer was supposedly dead. Doubtless Piper paid his taxes promptly or perhaps Baby Hutchmeyer had made complicated accountancy arrangements for his royalties to be laundered. That was none of Frensic's business. He took his commission and paid the rest over. But it was certainly his business when Piper made threats about going to Corkadales or another agent. That arrangement had definitely to be negated.

Frensic turned the letter over and studied the postmark on the envelope. It came from a place called Bibliopolis, Alabama. 'Just the sort of idiotic town Piper would choose,' he thought miserably and wondered how to reply. Or whether he should reply at all. Perhaps the best thing would be to ignore the threat. He certainly had no intention of committing to paper any words that could be used in court to prove that he knew of Piper's continued afterdeath. 'The next thing he'll come up with is a request for me to go and see him and discuss the matter. And fat chance there is of that.' Frensic had had his fill of pursuing phantom authors.

Miss Bogden on the other hand had not given up her pursuit of the man who had asked her to marry him. After the terrible telephone conversation she had had with Geoffrey Corkadale she had wept briefly, had made up her face, and had continued business as usual. For several weeks she had lived in hope that he would phone again, or that another bunch of red roses would suddenly appear, but those hopes had dwindled. Only the diamond solitaire gleaming on her finger kept her spirits up – that and the need to maintain the fiction before her staff that the engagement was still on. To that end she invented long weekends with her fiancé and reasons for the delayed wedding. But as weeks became months Cynthia's disappointment turned to determination. She had been had, and while being had was in some respects better than not being had at all, being made to look foolish in the eyes of her staff was infuriating. Miss Bogden applied her mind to the problem of finding her fiancé. While his disappearance was proof that he hadn't wanted her, the five hundred pounds he had spent on the ring was indication that he had wanted something else. Again Miss Bogden's business sense told her that the favours she had bestowed bodywise on her lover during the night hardly merited the expense of the engagement ring. Only a madman would make such a quixotic gesture and her pride refused the notion that the one man to propose to her since her divorce had been off his head.

No, there had to be another motive and as she recalled the events of those splendid twenty-four hours it slowly dawned on her that the one consistent theme had been the novel *Pause O Men for the Virgin*. In the first place her fiancé had posed as Geoffrey Corkadale, in the second he had reverted to the question of the typescript too frequently for it to be coincidental, and thirdly there had been the *code d'amour*. And the *code d'amour* had been the telephone number she had had to call for information while typing the novel. Cynthia Bogden called the number again but there was no reply, and when a week later she tried again the line had been disconnected. She looked up the name Piper in the phone directory but no one of that name had the number 20357. She called Directory Enquiries and asked for the address and name of the number but was refused the information. Defeated in that direction, she turned to another. Her instructions had been to forward the completed typescript to Cadwalladine & Dimkins, Solicitors and to return the handwritten draft to Lloyds Bank. Miss Bogden phoned Mr Cadwalladine and was puzzled by his apparent inability to remember having received the typescript. 'We may have done,' he said, 'but I'm afraid we handle so much business that ...'

Miss Bogden pressed him further and was finally told that it was unethical for solicitors to disclose confidential information. Miss Bogden was not satisfied with this answer. With each rebuttal her determination grew and was reinforced by the snide inquiries of her girls. Her mind worked slowly but it worked steadily too. She followed the line from the bank to her typing service and from there to Mr Cadwalladine and from Mr Cadwalladine to Corkadales, the publishers. The secrecy with which the entire transaction had been surrounded intrigued her too. An author who had to be contacted by phone, a solicitor ... With less flair than Frensic, but with as much perseverance, she followed the trail as far as she could, and late one evening she realized the full implications of Mr Cadwalladine's refusal to tell her where the typescript had been sent. And yet Corkadales had published the book. There had to be someone in between Cadwalladine and Corkadales and that someone was almost certainly a literary agent. That night Cynthia Bogden lay awake filled with a sense of discovery. She had found the missing link in the chain. The next morning she was up early and at the office at half past eight. At nine she telephoned Corkadales and asked to speak to the editor who had handled *Pause*. The editor wasn't in. She called again at ten. He still hadn't arrived. It was only at a quarter to eleven that she got through to him and by then she had had time to devise her approach. It was a straightforward one.

'I run a typing bureau,' she said, 'and I have typed a novel for a friend who is anxious to send it to a good literary agent and I wondered if ...'

'I'm afraid we can't advise you on that sort of thing,' said Mr Tate.

'Oh I do understand that,' said Miss Bogden sweetly, 'but you published that wonderful novel *Pause O Men for the Virgin* and my friend wanted to send her novel to the same agent. It would be so good of you if you could ...'

Responding to flattery Mr Tate did.

'Frensic & Futtle of Lanyard Lane?' she repeated.

'Well, Frensic now,' said Mr Tate, 'Miss Futtle is no longer there.'

Nor was Miss Bogden. She had put the phone down and was picking it up to dial Directory Enquiries. A few minutes later she had Frensic's number. Her intuition told her that she was getting close to home. She sat for a while staring into the depths of the solitaire for inspiration. Should she phone or ... Mr Cadwalladine's refusal to say where the manuscript had gone persuaded her. She got up from her typewriter, asked her senior 'girl' to take over for the day, drove to the station and caught the 11.15 to London. Two hours later she walked down Lanyard Lane to Number 36 and climbed the stairs to Frensic's office.

It was fortunate for Frensic that he was lunching with a promising new author in the Italian restaurant round the corner when Miss Bogden arrived. They came out at two-fifteen and walked back to the office. As they climbed the stairs Frensic stopped on the first landing.

'You go on up,' he said, 'I'll be with you in a moment.' He went into the lavatory and shut the door. The promising new author climbed the second flight. Frensic finished his business and came out and he was about to go on up when he heard a voice.

'Are you Mr Frensic?' it asked. Frensic stopped in his tracks.

'Me?' said the promising young author with a laugh. 'No I'm here with a book. Mr Frensic's downstairs. He'll be up in a minute.'

But Frensic wasn't. He shot down to the ground floor again and out into the street. That ghastly woman had tracked him down. What the hell to do now? He went back to the Italian restaurant and sat in a corner. How on earth had she managed to find him? Had that Cadbloodywalladine ... Never mind how. The thing was what to do about it. He couldn't sit in the restaurant all day and he was no more going to confront Miss Bogden than fly. Fly? The word took on a new significance for him. If he didn't turn up at the office the promising young author would ... To hell with promising young authors. He had asked that dreadful woman to marry him and ... Frensic signalled to a waiter.

'A piece of paper please.' He scribbled a note of apology to the author, saying he had been taken ill and handed it with a five pound note to the waiter, asking him to deliver it for him. As the man went out Frensic followed and hailed a taxi. 'Glass Walk, Hampstead,' he said and got in. Not that going home would do him any good. Miss Bogden's tracking powers would soon lead her there. All right, he wouldn't answer the door. But what then? A woman with the perseverance of Miss Bogden, a woman of forty-five who had painstakingly worked her way towards her quarry over the months ... such a woman held terrors for him. She wouldn't stop now. By the time he reached his flat he was panic-stricken. He went inside and locked and bolted the door. Then he sat down in his study and tried to think. He was interrupted by the phone. Unthinkingly he picked it up. 'Frensic here,' he said.

'Cynthia here,' said that pebbledashed voice. Frensic slammed the phone down. A moment later, to prevent her calling again, he picked it up and dialled Geoffrey's number.

'Geoffrey, my dear fellow,' he said when Corkadale answered, 'I wonder if ...'

But Geoffrey didn't let him finish. 'I've been trying to get hold of you all afternoon,' he said. 'I've had the most extraordinary manuscript sent to me. You're not going to believe this but there's some lunatic in a place called of all things Bibliopolis ... I mean can you beat that? Bibliopolis, Alabama ... Well anyway he calmly announces that he is our late Peter Piper and will we kindly quote fulfil the obligations incurred in my contract unquote and publish his novel, *Search for a Lost Childhood*. I mean it's incredible and the signature ...'

'Geoffrey dear,' said Frensic lapsing into the affectionate as a prophylactic against Miss Bogden's feminine charms and as a means of preparing Corkadale for the worst, 'I wonder if you would do me a favour ...'

He spoke fluently for five minutes and rang off. With amazing rapidity he packed two suitcases, telephoned for a taxi, left a note for the milkman cancelling his two pints a day, took his chequebook, his passport and a briefcase containing copies of all Piper's manuscripts, and half an hour later was carrying his belongings into Geoffrey Corkadale's house. Behind him the flat in Glass Walk was locked and when Cynthia Bogden arrived and rang the bell there was no reply. Frensic was sitting in Geoffrey Corkadale's withdrawing-room sipping a large brandy and implicating his host in the plot to deceive Hutchmeyer. Geoffrey stared at him with bulging eyes.

'You mean you deliberately lied to Hutchmeyer and to me for that matter and told him that this Piper madman had written the book?' he said.

'I had to,' said Frensic miserably. 'If I hadn't, the whole deal would have fallen through. Hutchmeyer would have backed out and where would we have been then?'

'We wouldn't be in the ghastly position we are now, that I do know.'

'You'd have gone out of business,' said Frensic. '*Pause* saved you. You've done very nicely out of the book and I've sent you others. Corkadales is a name to be reckoned with now.'

'Well, I suppose that's true,' said Geoffrey, slightly mollified, 'but it's going to be a name that will stink if it gets out that Piper is still alive and didn't write ...'

'It isn't going to get out,' said Frensic, 'I promise you that.' Geoffrey looked at him doubtfully. 'Your promises ...' he began.

'You'll just have to trust me,' said Frensic.

'Trust you? After this? You can rest assured that if there's one thing I'm not going to do ...'

'You'll have to. Remember that contract you signed? The one saying you had paid fifty thousand pounds advance for *Pause*?'

'You tore that up,' said Geoffrey, 'I saw you do it.'

Frensic nodded. 'But Hutchmeyer didn't,' he said. 'He had photocopies made and if this thing comes to court you're going to have a hard time explaining why you signed two contracts with the same author for the same book. It isn't going to look good, Geoffrey, not good at all.'

Geoffrey could see that. He sat down.

'What do you want?' he asked.

'A bed for the night,' said Frensic, 'and tomorrow morning I shall go to the American Embassy for a visa.'

'I can't see why you've got to spend the night here,' said Geoffrey.

'You would if you saw her,' said Frensic man-to-man. Geoffrey poured him another brandy.

'I'll have to explain to Sven,' he said, 'he's obsessively jealous. By the way, who *did* write *Pause*?' But Frensic shook his head. 'I can't tell you. There are some things it's best for you not to know. Just let's say the late Peter Piper.'

'The late?' said Geoffrey with a shudder. 'It's a curious expression to apply to the living.'

'It's a curious expression to apply to the dead,' said Frensic. 'It seems to suggest that they may yet turn up. Better late than never.'

'I wish I could share your optimism,' said Geoffrey.

Next morning, after a restless night in a strange bed, Frensic went to the American Embassy and got his visa. He visited his bank and he bought a return ticket to Florida. That night he left Heathrow. He spent the

crossing in a drunken stupor and boarded the flight from Miami to
Atlanta next day feeling hot, ill and filled with foreboding. To delay
matters he spent the night in a hotel and studied a map of Alabama. It
was a detailed map but he couldn't find Bibliopolis. He tried the desk
clerk but the man had never heard of it.

'You'd best go to Selma and ask there,' he told Frensic. Frensic caught
the Greyhound to Selma and inquired at the Post Office.

'The sticks. A wide place in the road over Mississippi way,' he was
told. 'Swamp country on the Ptomaine River. Take Route 80 about a
hundred miles and go north. Are you from New England?'

'Old England,' said Frensic, 'why do you ask?'

'Just that they don't take too kindly to Northern strangers in those
parts. Damn Yankees they call them. They're still living in the past.'

'So is the man I want to see,' said Frensic and went out to rent a car.
The man at the office increased his apprehension.

'You're going out along Blood Alley you want to take care,' he said.

'Blood Alley?' said Frensic anxiously.

'That what they call Route 80 through to Meridian. That road's seen
a whole heap of deaths.'

'Isn't there a more direct route to Bibliopolis?'

'You can go through the backwoods but you could get lost. Blood
Alley's your best route.'

Frensic hesitated. 'I don't suppose I could hire a driver?' he asked.

'Too late now,' said the man, 'Saturday afternoon this time everyone's
gone home and tomorrow being Sunday ...'

Frensic left the office and drove to a motel. He wasn't going to drive
to Bibliopolis along Blood Alley at nightfall. He would go in the morning.

Next day he was up early and on the road. The sun shone down out of
a cloudless sky and the day was bright and beautiful. Frensic wasn't. The
desperate resolution with which he had left London had faded and with
each mile westward it diminished still further. Woods closed in on the
road and by the time he reached the sign with the faded inscription
BIBLIOPOLIS 15 MILES he almost turned back. But a pinch of snuff and the
thought of what would happen if Piper continued his campaign of literary
revival gave him the courage he needed. Frensic turned right and followed
the dirt road into the woods, trying not to look at the black water and
the trees strangled with vines. And, like Piper those many months before
he was relieved when he came to the meadows and the cattle grazing in
the long grass. But still the abandoned shacks depressed him and the
occasional glimpse of the river, a brown slurry in the distance fringed by

veiled trees, did nothing for his morale. The Ptomaine looked aptly named. Finally the road veered down to the left and across the water Frensic looked at Bibliopolis. A wide place in the road, the girl in Selma had called it, but she had quite evidently never seen it. Besides, the road stopped at the river. The little town huddled round the square and looked old and unchanged from some time in the nineteenth century. And the ferry which presently moved towards him with an old man pulling on the rope was from some bygone age. Frensic thought he knew now why Bibliopolis was said to be in the sticks. By the Styx would have done as well. Frensic drove the car carefully on to the ferry and got out.

'I'm looking for a man called Piper,' he told the ferryman.

The man nodded. 'Guessed you might be,' he said. 'They come from all over to hear him preach. And if it isn't him it's the Reverend Baby up at the Church.'

'Preach?' said Frensic, 'Mr Piper preaches?'

'Sure does. Preaching and teaching the good word.'

Frensic raised his eyebrows. Piper as preacher was a new one to him. 'Where will I find him?' he asked.

'Down Pellagra.'

'Down with pellagra?' said Frensic hopefully.

'At Pellagra,' said the old man, 'the house.' He nodded in the direction of a large house fronted by tall white columns. 'There's Pellagra. Used to be the Stopes's place but they all died off.'

'Hardly surprising,' said Frensic, his intellectual compass spinning between vitamin deficiency, advocates of birth control, the Monkey Trial and Yoknapatawpha County. He gave the man a dollar and drove down the drive to an open gate. On one side a sign in large italic said THE PIPER SCHOOL OF PENMANSHIP while on the other an inscribed finger pointed to the CHURCH OF THE GREAT PURSUIT. Frensic stopped the car and stared at the enormous finger. The Church of The Great Pursuit? The Church of ... There could be no doubting that he had come to the right place. But what sort of religious mania was Piper suffering from now? He drove on and parked beside several other cars in front of the large white building with a wrought-iron balcony extending forward to the columns from the first-floor rooms. Frensic got out and walked up the steps to the front door. It was open. Frensic peered into the hall. A door to the left had painted on it THE SCRIPTORIUM while from a room on the right there came the drone of an insistent voice. Frensic crossed the marble floor and listened. There was no mistaking that voice. It was Piper's but the old hesitant quality had gone and in its place there was a new strident intensity. If the voice was familiar, so were the words.

'And we must not (the "must" here presupposing explicitly a sustained seriousness of purpose and an undeviating moral duty) allow ourselves to be deluded by the seeming naïvety so frequently ascribed by other less perceptive critics to the presentation of Little Nell. Sentiment not sentimentality as we must understand it is cognizant ...'

Frensic shied away from the door. He knew now what the Church of The Great Pursuit had for its gospel. Piper was reading aloud from Dr Louth's essay 'How We must Approach *The Old Curiosity Shop*'. Even his religion was derived. Frensic found a chair and sat down filled with a mounting anger. 'The unoriginal little sod,' he muttered, and cursed Dr Louth into the bargain. The apotheosis of that dreadful woman, the cause of all his troubles, was taking place here in the heart of the Bible belt. Frensic's anger turned to fury. The Bible belt! Bibliopolis and the Bible. And instead of that magnificent prose, Piper was disseminating her graceless style, her angular inverted syntax, her arid puritanism and her denunciations against pleasure and the joy of reading. And all this from a man who couldn't write to save his soul! For a moment Frensic felt that he was at the heart of a great conspiracy against life. But that was paranoia. There had been no conscious purpose in the circumstances that had led to Piper's missionary zeal. Only the accident of literary mutation which had turned Frensic himself from a would-be novelist into a successful agent and, by the way of *The Moral Novel*, had mutilated what little talent for writing Piper might once have possessed. And now like some carrier of literary death he was passing the infection on. By the time the droning voice stopped and the little congregation filed out, their faces taut with moral intensity, and made their way to the cars, Frensic was in a murderous mood.

He crossed the hall and entered the Church of The Great Pursuit. Piper was putting the book away with all the reverence of a priest handling the Host. Frensic stood in the doorway and waited. He had come a long way for this moment. Piper shot the cupboard and turned. The look of reverence faded from his face.

'You,' he said faintly.

'Who else?' said Frensic loudly to exorcize the atmosphere of sanctity that pervaded the room. 'Or were you expecting Conrad?'

Piper's face paled. 'What do you want?'

'Want?' said Frensic and sat down in one of the pews and took a pinch of snuff. 'Just to put an end to this bloody game of hide-and-seek.' He wiped his nose with a red handkerchief.

Piper hesitated and then headed for the door. 'We can't talk in here,' he muttered.

'Why not?' said Frensic. 'It seems as good a place as any.'

'You wouldn't understand,' said Piper and went out. Frensic blew his nose coarsely and then followed.

'For a horrid little blackmailer you've got a hell of a lot of pretensions,' he said as they stood in the hall, 'all that crap in there about *The Old Curiosity Shop.*'

'It isn't crap,' said Piper, 'and don't call me a blackmailer. You started this. And that's the truth.'

'Truth?' said Frensic with a nasty laugh. 'If you want the truth you're going to get it. That's what I've come here for.' He looked across at the door marked SCRIPTORIUM. 'What's in there?'

'That's where I teach people to write,' said Piper.

Frensic stared at him and laughed again. 'You're joking,' he said and opened the door. Inside the room was filled with desks, desks on which stood bottles of ink and pens, and each desk tilted at an angle. On the walls were framed examples of script and, in front, a blackboard. Frensic glared round.

'Charming. The Scriptorium. And I suppose you've got a Plagiarium too?'

'A what?' said Piper.

'A special room for plagiarism. Or do you combine the process in here? I mean there's nothing like going the whole hog. How do you go about it? Do you give each student a bestseller to alter and then flog it as your own work?'

'Coming from you, that a dirty crack,' said Piper. 'I do all my own writing in my study. Down here I teach my students how to write. Not what.'

'How? You teach them how to write?' He picked up a bottle of ink and shook it. The sludge moved slowly. 'Still on the evaporated ink, I see.'

'It gives the greatest density,' said Piper but Frensic had put the bottle down and turned back to the door.

'And where's your study?' he asked. Piper led the way slowly upstairs and opened another door. Frensic stepped inside. The walls were lined with shelves and a big desk stood in front of a window which looked out across the drive towards the river. Frensic studied the books. They were bound in calf. Dickens, Conrad, James ...

'The old testament,' he said and reached for *Middlemarch*. Piper took it brusquely from him and put it back.

'This year's model?' asked Frensic.

'A world, a universe beyond our tawdry imagination,' said Piper angrily. Frensic shrugged. There was a pathos about Piper's tenseness that was weakening his resolve. Frensic steeled himself to be coarse.

'Bloody cosy little billet you've got yourself here,' he said, seating himself at the desk and putting his feet up. Behind him Piper's face whitened at the sacrilege. 'Curator of a museum, counterfeiter of other people's novels, a bit of blackmail on the side – and what do you do about sex?' He hesitated and picked up a paperknife for safety's sake. If he was going to put the boot in there was no knowing what Piper might do. 'Screw the late Mrs Hutchmeyer?'

There was a hiss behind him and Frensic swung round. Piper was facing him with his pinched face and narrow eyes blazing with hatred. Frensic's grip tightened on the paperknife. He was frightened but the thing had to be done. He had come too far to go back now.

'It's none of my business, I daresay,' he said as Piper stared, 'but necrophilia seems to be your forte. First you rob dead authors, then you put the bite on me for two million dollars, what do you do to the late Mrs Hutch –'

'Don't you dare say it,' shouted Piper, his voice shrill with fury.

'Why not?' said Frensic. 'There's nothing like confession for cleansing the soul.'

'It isn't true,' said Piper. His breathing was audible.

Frensic smiled cynically. 'What isn't? The truth will out, as the saying goes. That's why I'm here.' He stood up with assumed menace and Piper shrank back.

'Stop it. Stop it. I don't want to hear any more. Just go away and leave me alone.'

Frensic shook his head. 'And have you send me yet another manuscript and tell me to sell it? Oh no, those days are over. You're going to learn the truth if I have to ram it down your snivelling –'

Piper covered his ears with his hands. 'I won't,' he shouted, 'I won't listen to you.'

Frensic reached in his pocket and took out Dr Louth's letter.

'You don't have to listen. Just read this.'

He thrust the letter forward and Piper took it. Frensic sat down in the chair. The crisis was over. He was no longer afraid. Piper might be mad but his madness was self-directed and held no threat for Frensic. He watched him read the letter with a new sense of pity. He was looking at a nonentity, the archetypal author for whom only words had any reality, and one who couldn't write. Piper finished the letter and looked up.

'What does it mean?' he asked.

'What it doesn't say,' said Frensic. 'That the great Dr Louth wrote *Pause*. That's what it means.'

Piper looked down at the letter again. 'But it says here she didn't.'

Frensic smiled. 'Quite. And why should she have written that? Ask yourself that question. Why deny what nobody had ever supposed?'

'I don't understand,' said Piper, 'it doesn't make sense.'

'If does if you accept that she was being blackmailed,' said Frensic.

'Blackmailed? But by whom?'

Frensic helped himself to snuff. 'By you. You threatened me and I threatened her.'

'But ...' Piper wrestled with this incomprehensible sequence. It was beyond his simple philosophy.

'You threatened to expose me and I passed the message on,' said Frensic. 'Dr Sydney Louth paid two million dollars not to be revealed as the author of *Pause*. The price of her sacred reputation.'

Piper's eyes were glazed. 'I don't believe you,' he muttered.

'Don't,' said Frensic. 'Believe what you bloody well like. All you've got to do is resurrect yourself and tell Hutchmeyer you're still alive and kicking and the media will do the rest. It will all come out. My role, your role, the whole damned story and at the end of it, your Dr Louth with her reputation as a critic in ruins. Mind you, you'll be in prison. And I dare say I'll be bankrupt too, but at least I won't have to put up with the impossible task of trying to sell your rotten *Search for a Lost Childhood*. That'll be some compensation.'

Piper sat down limply in a chair.

'Well?' said Frensic, but Piper simply shook his head. Frensic took the letter from him and turned to the window. He had called the little sod's bluff. There would be no more threats, no more manuscripts. Piper was broken. It was time to leave. Frensic stared out at the dark river and the forest beyond, a strange foreign landscape, dangerously lush, and far from the comfortable little world he had come to protect. He crossed to the door and went down the broad staircase and across the hall. All that was needed now was to get home as quickly as possible.

But when he got into his rented car and drove down the drive to the ferry it was to find the pontoon on the far side of the river and no one to bring it across. Frensic rang the bell but nobody answered. He stood in the bright sunlight and waited. There was a stillness in the air and only the sound of the black river slurping against the bank below him. Frensic got back into the car and drove into the square. Here too there was nobody in sight. Dark shadows under the tin roofs that served as awnings to the shop fronts, the white-painted church, a wooden bench at the foot of the statue in the middle of the square, blank windows. Frensic got out of his car and looked round. The clock on the courthouse stood at midday. Presumably everyone was at lunch, but there was still a sense of unnatural desolation which disturbed him and back beyond the river the forest, an undomesticated tangle of trees and underbush, made a close horizon above which the sky was an empty blue. Frensic walked round the square and then got back into the car. Perhaps if he tried the ferry again ... But it was still there across the water and when Frensic tried to pull on the rope there was no movement. He rang the bell again. There was no echo and his sense of unease redoubled. Finally leaving the car in the road he walked along the bank of the river following a little path. He would wait a while until the lunch hour was over and then try again. But the path led under live oaks hung with Spanish moss and ended in the cemetery. Frensic looked for a moment at the gravestones and then turned back.

Perhaps if he drove west he would find a road out of town on that side which would lead him back to Route 80. Blood Alley had an almost cheerful ring to it now. But he had no map in the car and after driving down a number of side streets that ended in culs-de-sac or uninviting tracks into the woods he turned back. Perhaps the ferry would be open now. He looked at his watch. It was two o'clock and people would be out and about again.

They were. As he drove into the little square a group of gaunt men standing on the sidewalk outside the courthouse moved across the road. Frensic stopped the car and stared unhappily through the windshield. The gaunt men had holsters on their belts and the gauntest of them all wore a star on his chest. He walked round the car to the side window and leant in. Frensic studied his yellow teeth.

'Your name Frensic?' he asked, Frensic nodded. 'Judge wants to see you,' continued the man. 'You going to come quietly or ... ?' Frensic came quietly and with the little group behind him climbed the steps to the courthouse. Inside it was cool and dark. Frensic hesitated but the tall man pointed to a door.

'Judge is in chambers,' he said. 'Go on in.'

Frensic went in. Behind a large desk sat Baby Hutchmeyer. She was dressed in a long black robe and above it her face, always unnaturally taut, was now unpleasantly white. Frensic, staring down at her, had no doubt about her identity.

'Mrs Hutchmeyer ...' he began, 'the late Mrs Hutchmeyer?'

'Judge Hutchmeyer to you,' said Baby, 'and we won't have anything

more about the late unless you want to end up the late Mr Frensic right
soon.'

Frensic swallowed and glanced over his shoulder. The sheriff was
standing with his back against the door and the gun on his belt glinted
obtrusively.

'May I ask what the meaning of this is?' he asked after a moment's
significant silence. 'Bringing me here like this and ...'

The judge looked across at the sheriff. 'What have you got on him so
far?' she asked.

'Uttering threats and menaces,' said the sheriff. 'Possession of an
unauthorized firearm. Spare tyre stashed with heroin. Blackmail. You
name it, Judge, he's got it.'

Frensic groped for a chair. 'Heroin?' he gasped. 'What do you mean
heroin? I haven't a single grain of heroin.'

'You think not?' said Baby. 'Herb'll show you, won't you, Herb?'

Behind Frensic the sheriff nodded. 'Got the automobile round at the
garage dismantling it right now,' he said, 'you want proof we'll show it
to you.'

But Frensic was in no need of proof. He sat stunned in the chair and
stared at Baby's white face. 'What do you want?' he asked finally.

'Justice,' said Baby succinctly.

'Justice,' muttered Frensic, 'you talk about justice and ...'

'You want to make a statement now or reserve your defence for court
tomorrow?' said Baby.

Frensic glanced over his shoulder again. 'I'd like to make a statement
now. In private,' he said.

Baby nodded to the sheriff. 'Wait outside, Herb,' she said, 'and stay
close. Any trouble in here and ...'

'There won't be any trouble in here,' said Frensic hastily, 'I can assure
you of that.'

Baby waved his assurances and Herb aside. As the door closed Frensic
took out his handerkchief and mopped his face.

'Right,' said Baby, 'so you want to make a statement.'

Frensic leant forward. It was in his mind to say 'You can't do this to
me,' but the cliché culled from so many of his authors didn't seem
appropriate. She *could* do this to him. He was in Bibliopolis and Bibliopolis
was off the map of civilization.

'What do you want me to do?' he asked faintly.

Judge Baby swung her chair and leant back. 'Coming from you, Mr
Frensic, that's an interesting question,' she said. 'You come into this little

town and you start uttering threats and menaces against one of our citizens and you want me to tell you what I want you to do.'

'I didn't utter threats and menaces,' said Frensic, 'I came to tell Piper to stop sending me his manuscripts. And if anyone's been uttering threats it's him, not me.'

Baby shook her head. 'If that's your defence I can tell you right off nobody in Bibliopolis is going to believe you. Mr Piper is the most peaceful non-violent citizen around these parts.'

'Well, he may be around these parts,' said Frensic, 'but from where I'm sitting in London ...'

'You ain't sitting in London now,' said Baby, 'you're sitting right here in my chambers and shaking like a hound dog pissing peach pits.'

Frensic considered the simile and found it disagreeable. 'You'd be shaking if you'd been accused of having a spare tyre filled with heroin,' he said.

Baby nodded. 'You could be right at that,' she said. 'I can give you life for that. Throw in the threats and menaces, the firearm and the blackmail and it could all add up to life plus ninety-nine years. You had better consider that before you say anything more.'

Frensic considered it and found he was shaking even harder. Hound dogs having problems with peach pits were no comparison. 'You can't mean it,' he gasped.

Baby smiled. 'You'd better believe I mean it. The warden of the penitentiary's a deacon in my church. You wouldn't have to do the ninety-nine years. Like life would be three months and you wouldn't last in the chain gang. They got snakes and things to make it natural death. You've seen our little cemetery?'

Frensic nodded, 'So we've got a little plot marked out already,' said Baby. 'It wouldn't have no headstone. No name like Frensic. Just a little mound and nobody would ever know. So that's your choice.'

'What is?' said Frensic when he could find his voice.

'Like life plus ninety-nine or you do what I tell you.'

'I think I'll do what you tell me,' said Frensic for whom this was no choice at all.

'Right,' said Baby, 'so first you make a full confession.'

'Confession?' said Frensic. 'What sort of confession?'

'Just that you wrote *Pause O Men for the Virgin* and palmed it off on Mr Piper and hoodwinked Hutch and instigated Miss Futtle to arsonize the house and –'

'No,' cried Frensic, 'never. I'd rather ...' He stopped. He wouldn't rather. There was a look on Baby's face that told him that. 'I don't see why I've got to confess to all those things,' he said.

Baby relaxed. 'You took his good name away from him. Now you're going to give it back to him.'

'His good name?' said Frensic.

'By putting it on the cover of that dirty novel,' said Baby.

'He didn't have any sort of good name till we did that,' said Frensic, 'he never published anything and now he's so-called dead he isn't going to.'

'Oh yes, he is,' said Baby leaning forward. 'You're going to give him your name. Like *Search for a Lost Childhood* by Frederick Frensic.'

Frensic stared at her. The woman was mad as a March hare. '*Search* by me?' he said. 'You don't understand. I've hawked that blasted book around every publisher in London and no one wants to know. It's unreadable.'

Baby smiled. Unpleasantly.

'That's your problem. You're going to get it published and you're going to get all his future books published under your own name. It's that or the chain gang.'

She glanced significantly out of the window at the horizon of trees and the empty sky and Frensic following her glance gazed into a terrible future and an early death. He'd have to humour her. 'All right,' he said, 'I'll do my best.'

'You'll do better than that. You'll do exactly what I say.' She took a sheet of paper from a drawer and handed him a pen. 'Now write,' she said.

Frensic hitched his chair forward and began to write very shakily. By the time he had finished he had confessed to having evaded British income tax by paying two million dollars plus royalties into account number 478776 in the First National Bank of New York and to having incited his partner, the former Miss Futtle, to arsonize the Hutchmeyer residence. The whole statement was such an amalgam of things he had done and things he hadn't that, cross-examined by a competent lawyer, he would never be able to disentangle himself. Baby read it through and witnessed his signature. Then she called Herb in and he witnessed it too.

'That should keep you on the straight and narrow,' she said as the sheriff left the room. 'One squeak out of you and one attempt to evade your obligation to publish Mr Piper's novels and this goes straight to Hutchmeyer, the insurance company, the FBI and the tax authorities, and you can wipe that smile off your face.' But Frensic wasn't smiling. He had developed a nervous tic. 'Because if you think you can worm your way out of this by going to the authorities yourself and telling them to look me up in Bibliopolis you can forget it. I've got friends round here and no one talks if I say no. You understand that?'

Frensic nodded. 'I quite understand,' he said.

Baby stood up and took off her robe. 'Well, just in case you don't, you're going to be saved,' she said. They went out into the hall where the group of gaunt men waited.

'We've got a convert, boys,' she said. 'See you all in Church.'

Frensic sat in the front row of the little Church of The Servants of The Lord. Before him, radiant and serene, Baby conducted the service. The church was packed and Herb sat next to Frensic and shared his hymnbook with him. They sang 'Telephoning to Glory' and 'Rock of Ages' and 'Shall we Gather by the River', and with Herb's nudging Frensic sang as loudly as the rest. Finally Baby delivered a virulent sermon on the text 'Behold a man gluttonous, and a winebibber, a friend of publishers and sinners,' her gaze fixed pointedly on Frensic throughout, and the congregation launched into 'Bibliopolis we Hold Thee Dear'. It was time for Frensic to be saved. He moved shakily forward and knelt. Snakes might no longer infest Bibliopolis, but Frensic was still petrified. Above him Baby's face was radiant. She had triumphed once again.

'Swear by the Lord to keep the covenant,' she said. And Frensic swore.

He was still swearing an hour later as he sat in his car and the ferry crossed the river. Frensic glanced across at Pellagra. The light was burning on the upper floor. Piper was doubtless at work on some terrible novel that Frensic would have to sell under his own name. He drove off the ferry recklessly and the hired car bucketed down the dirt road and the headlights picked out the dark water gleaming beneath the entwined trees. After Bibliopolis the grim landscape held no menace for him. It was a natural world full of natural dangers and Frensic could cope with them. With Baby Hutchmeyer there had been no coping. Frensic swore again.

In his study in Pellagra Piper sat silently at his desk. He was not writing. He was looking at the guarantee Frensic had written promising to publish *Search for a Lost Childhood* even at his own expense. Piper was going to be published at long last. Never mind that the name on the cover would be Frensic. One day the world would learn the truth. Or better still, perhaps, would be an unanswered question. After all who knew who Shakespeare was or who had written *Hamlet*? No one.

TWENTY-THREE

Nine months later *Search for a Lost Childhood* by Frederick Frensic, published by Corkadales, price £3.90, came out in Britain. In America it was published by Hutchmeyer Press. Frensic had had to apply some direct pressure in both directions and it was only the threat of exposure that had persuaded Geoffrey to accept the book. Sonia had been influenced by feelings of loyalty, and Hutchmeyer had needed no urging. The sound of a familiar female voice on the telephone had sufficed. And so the review copies had gone out with Frensic's name on the title-page and the dust jacket. A short biography at the back said he had once been a literary agent. He was one no longer. The name on the door of the office in Lanyard Lane still lingered but the office was empty and Frensic had moved from Glass Walk to a cottage in Sussex without a telephone.

There, safe from Mrs Bogden, he was Piper's amanuensis. Day after day he typed out the manuscripts Piper sent him and night after night lurked in the corner of the village pub and drowned his sorrows. His friends in London saw him seldom. From necessity he visited Geoffrey and occasionally went out to lunch with him. But for the most part he spent his days at his typewriter, cultivated his garden and went for long walks sunk in melancholy thought.

Not that his thoughts were always depressed. There remained a deep core of deviousness in Frensic which nagged at the problem of his predicament and sought ways to escape. But none came to mind. His imagination had been anaesthetized by his terrible experience and each day Piper's dreary prose reinforced the effect. Distilled from so many sources, it acted on Frensic's literary nerve and kept him in a state of disorientation so that he had no sooner recognized a sentence from Mann than he was flung a chunk of Faulkner to be followed by a *mot* from Proust or a slice of *Middlemarch*. After such a paragraph Frensic would get up and reel into the garden to escape his associations by mowing the lawn. At night before going to sleep he would excise the memory of Bibliopolis by reading a page or two of *The Wind in the Willows* and wish he could potter about in boats like the Water Rat. Anything to escape the ordeal he had been set.

And now it was Sunday and the reviews of *Search* would be in the papers. In spite of himself Frensic was drawn to the little shop in the village to buy the *Sunday Times* and the *Observer*. He bought them both and didn't wait until he got home to read the worst. It was best to get the agony over and done with. He stood in the lane and opened the *Sunday Times Review* and turned to the book page and there it was. At the top of the list. Frensic leant against a gatepost and read the review. As he read his world turned topsy-turvy once again. Linda Gormley 'loved' the book and devoted two columns to its praise. She called it 'the most honest and original appraisal of the adolescent trauma I have read for a very long time'. Frensic stared at the words in disbelief. Then he rummaged in the *Observer*. It was the same there. 'For a first novel it has not only freshness but a deeply intuitive insight into family relationships ... a masterpiece ...' Frensic shut the paper hurriedly. A masterpiece? He looked again. The word was still there, and further down there was even worse. 'If one can say of a novel that it is a great work of genius ...' Frensic clutched the gatepost. He felt weak. *Search for a Lost Childhood* was being acclaimed. He staggered on up the lane with a fresh sense of loss. His nose, his infallible nose, had betrayed him. Piper had been right all along. Either that or the plague of *The Moral Novel* had spread and the days of the novel of entertainment were over, supplanted by the religion of literature. People no longer read for pleasure. If they liked *Search* they couldn't. There wasn't an ounce of enjoyment to be got from the book. Frensic had painstakingly (and the word was precise) typed the manuscript out page by ghastly page and from those pages there had emanated a whining self-pity, an arrogantly self-directed sycophancy that had sickened him. And this wretched puke of words was what the reviewers called originality and freshness and a work of genius. Genius! Frensic spat the word. It had lost all meaning.

And as he lumbered up the lane the full portent of the book's success hit him. He would have to go through life bearing the stigma of being known as the author of a book he hadn't written. His friends would congratulate him ... For one awful moment Frensic contemplated suicide but his sense of irony saved him. He knew now how Piper had felt when he had discovered what Frensic had foisted on him with *Pause*. 'Hoist with his own petard' sprang to mind and he acknowledged Piper's triumphant revenge. The thought brought Frensic to a standstill. He had been made to look a fool and if the world now considered him a genius, one day they would learn the truth and the laughter would never cease. It was a threat he had used against Dr Louth and it had been turned against him. Frensic's fury at the thought spurred his deviousness to work. Standing in the lane between the hedgerows he saw his escape. He would turn the tables on them yet. Out of the accumulated experience of the thousand commercially successful novels he had sold he could surely concoct a story that would contain every ingredient Piper and his mentor, Dr Louth, would most detest. It would have sex, violence, sentimentality, romance – and all this without an ounce of significance. It would be a rattling good yarn, a successor to *Pause*, and on the dust jacket in bold type there would be Peter Piper's name. No, that was wrong. Piper was a mere pawn in the game. Behind him there lay a far deadlier enemy to literature. Dr Sydney Louth.

Frensic quickened his pace and hurried across the little wooden bridge that led to his cottage. Presently he was sitting at his typewriter and had inserted a sheet of paper. First he needed a title. His fingers hammered on the keys and the words appeared. 'AN IMMORAL NOVEL by DR SYDNEY LOUTH. CHAPTER ONE'. Frensic typed on and his mind flickered with fresh subtleties. He would incorporate her graceless style. And her ideas. It would be a grotesque pastiche of everything she had ever written and with it all there would be a story so sickly and vile as to deny every precept of *The Moral Novel*. He would stand the bitch on her head and shake her till her teeth rattled. And there was nothing she could do about it. As her agent, Frensic was safe. Only the truth could hurt him and she was in no position to tell the truth. Frensic stopped typing at the thought and stared into the distance. There was no need to concoct a story. The truth was far more deadly. He would tell the history of The Great Pursuit just as it had happened. His name would be mud but it was mud already in his own eyes with the success of *Search* and besides he owed a duty to English literature. To hell with English literature. To Grub Street and all those writers without pretensions who wrote for a living. A living? The ambiguity of the world held him for a moment. Who wrote for a living and the living too. Frensic tore the sheet from the typewriter and started again.

He would call it THE GREAT PURSUIT. A TRUE STORY by Frederick Frensic. The living deserved the truth, and a story, and he would give them both. He would dedicate the book to Grub Street. It had a good old eighteenth-century ring to it. Frensic's nose twitched. He knew he had just begun to write a book that would sell. And if they wanted to sue, let them. He would publish and be damned.

In Bibliopolis the publication of *Search* made no impression on Piper. He had lost his faith. It had gone with Frensic's visit and the revelation that Dr Sydney Louth had written *Pause*. It had taken some time for the truth to sink in and he had gone on writing and rewriting for a few months almost automatically. But in the end he knew that Frensic had not lied. He had written to Dr Louth and had had no reply. Piper closed the

Church of The Great Tradition. Only the School of Penmanship remained and with it the doctrine of logosophy. The age of the great novel was over. It remained only to commemorate it in manuscript. And so while Baby preached the need to imitate Christ, Piper too returned to traditional virtues in everything. Already he had abolished pens and his pupils had moved back to quills. They were more natural than nibs. They needed cutting, they were the original tools of his craft and they stood as reminders of that golden age when books were written by hand and to be a copyist was to belong to an honourable profession.

And so that Sunday morning Piper sat in the Scriptorium and dipped his quill in Higgins Eternal Evaporated Ink and began to write: 'My father's family name being Pirrip, and my Christian name Philip, my infant tongue could make of both names nothing longer or more explicit than Piper ...' He stopped. That wasn't right. It should have been Pip. But after a moment's hesitation he dipped his quill again and continued.

After all in a thousand years who the dickens would care who had written *Great Expectations*? Only a few scholars who could still read English. The printed works would have perished by then. Only Piper's own parchment manuscripts bound in the thickest leather and filled with his perfect hieroglyphic handwriting and gold illuminated lettering would stand the test of time and lie in the museums of the world, mute testimony to his dedication to literature, and to his craftsmanship. And when he had finished Dickens, he would start on Henry James and write *his* novels out in longhand too. There was a lifetime's work ahead of him just copying the great tradition out in Higgins Eternal Ink. The name of Piper would be literally immortal yet ...

PORTERHOUSE BLUE

CHAPTER ONE

It was a fine Feast. No one, not even the Praelector who was so old he could remember the Feast of '09, could recall its equal – and Porterhouse is famous for its food. There was Caviar and Soupe à l'Oignon, Turbot au Champagne, Swan stuffed with Widgeon and finally in memory of the Founder, Beefsteak from an ox roasted whole in the great fireplace of the College Hall. Each course had a different wine and each place was laid with five glasses. There was Pouilly Fumé with the fish, champagne with the game and the finest burgundy from the College cellars with the beef. For two hours the silver dishes came, announced by the swish of the doors in the Screens as the waiters scurried to and fro, bowed down by the weight of the food and their sense of occasion. For two hours the members of Porterhouse were lost to the world, immersed in an ancient ritual that spanned the centuries. The clatter of knives and forks, the clink of glasses, the rustle of napkins and the shuffling feet of the College servants dimmed the present. Outside the Hall the winter wind swept through the streets of Cambridge. Inside all was warmth and conviviality. Along the tables a hundred candles ensconced in silver candelabra cast elongated shadows of the crouching waiters across the portraits of past Masters that lined the walls. Severe or genial, scholars or politicians, the portraits had one thing in common: they were all rubicund and plump. Porterhouse's kitchen was long established. Only the new Master differed from his predecessors. Seated at the High Table, Sir Godber Evans picked at his swan with a delicate hesitancy that was in marked contrast to the frank enjoyment of the Fellows. A fixed dyspeptic smile lent a grim animation to Sir Godber's pale features as if his mind found relief from the present discomforts of the flesh in some remote and wholly intellectual joke.

'An evening to remember, Master,' said the Senior Tutor sebaceously.

'Indeed, Senior Tutor, indeed,' murmured the Master, his private joke enhanced by this unsought prediction.

'This swan is excellent,' said the Dean. 'A fine bird and the widgeon gives it a certain *gamin* flavour.'

'So good of Her Majesty to give Her permission for us to have swan,' the Bursar said. 'It's a privilege very rarely granted, you know.'

'Very rare,' the Chaplain agreed.

'Indeed, Chaplain, indeed,' murmured the Master and crossed his knife and fork. 'I think I'll wait for the beefsteak.' He sat back and

studied the faces of the Fellows with fresh distaste. They were, he thought
once again, an atavistic lot, and never more so than now with their
napkins tucked into their collars, an age-old tradition of the College, and
their foreheads greasy with perspiration and their mouths interminably
full. How little things had changed since his own days as an undergraduate
in Porterhouse. Even the College servants were the same, or so it seemed.
The same shuffling gait, the adenoidal open mouths and tremulous lower
lips, the same servility that had so offended his sense of social justice as
a young man. And still offended it. For forty years Sir Godber had
marched beneath the banner of social justice, or at least paraded, and if
he had achieved anything (some cynics doubted even that) it was due to
the fine sensibility that had been developed by the social chasm that
yawned between the College servants and the young gentlemen of
Porterhouse. His subsequent career in politics had been marked by the
highest aspirations and the least effectuality, some said, since Asquith,
and he had piloted through Parliament a series of bills whose aim, to
assist the low-paid in one way or another, had resulted in that middle-
class subsidy known as the development grant. His 'Every Home a
Bathroom' campaign had led to the sobriquet Soapy and a knighthood,
while his period as Minister of Technological Development had been
rewarded by an early retirement and the Mastership of Porterhouse. It
was one of the ironies of his appointment that he owed it to the very
institution for which he professed most abhorrence, Royal Patronage,
and it was perhaps this knowledge that had led him to the decision to
end his career as an initiator of social change by a real alteration in the
social character and traditions of his old College. That and the awareness
that his appointment had met with the adamant opposition of almost all
the Fellows. Only the Chaplain had welcomed him, and that was in all
likelihood due to his deafness and a mistaken apprehension of Sir Godber's
full name. No, he was Master by default even of his own convictions and
by the failure of the Fellows to agree among themselves and choose a
new Master by election. Nor had the late Master with his dying breath
named his successor, thus exercising the prerogative Porterhouse tradition
allows; failing these two expedients it had been left to the Prime Minister,
himself in the death throes of an administration, to rid himself of a
liability by appointing Sir Godber. In Parliamentary circles, if not in
academic ones, the appointment had been greeted with relief. 'Something
to get your teeth into at last,' one of his Cabinet colleagues had said to
the new Master, a reference less to the excellence of the College cuisine
than to the intractable conservatism of Porterhouse. In this respect the
College is unique. No other Cambridge college can equal Porterhouse in

its adherence to the old traditions and to this day Porterhouse men are distinguished [*sic*] by the cut of their coats and hair and by their steadfast allegiance to gowns. 'County come to Town', and 'The Squire to School', the other colleges used to sneer in the good old days, and the gibe has an element of truth about it still. A sturdy self-reliance except in scholarship is the mark of the Porterhouse man, and it is an exceptional year when Porterhouse is not Head of the River. And yet the College is not rich. Unlike nearly all the other colleges, Porterhouse has few assets to fall back on. A few terraces of dilapidated houses, some farms in Radnorshire, a modicum of shares in run-down industries, Porterhouse is poor. Its annual income amounts to less that £50,000 per annum and to this impecuniosity it owes its enduring reputation as the most socially exclusive college in Cambridge. If Porterhouse is poor, its undergraduates are rich. Where other colleges seek academic excellence in their freshmen, Porterhouse more democratically ignores the inequalities of intellect and concentrates upon the evidence of wealth. *Dives In Omnia*, reads the college motto, and the Fellows take it literally when examining the candidates. And in return the College offers social cachet and an enviable diet. True, a few scholarships and exhibitions exist which must be filled by men whose talents do not run to means, but those who last soon acquire the hallmarks of a Porterhouse man.

To the Master the memory of his own days as an undergraduate still had the power to send a shudder through him. A scholar in his day, Sir Godber, then plain G. Evans, had come to Porterhouse from a grammar school in Brierley. The experience had affected him profoundly. From his arrival had dated the sense of social inferiority which more than natural gifts had been the driving force of his ambition and which had spurred him on through failures that would have daunted a more talented man. After Porterhouse, he would remind himself on these occasions, a man has nothing left to fear. And certainly the College had left him socially resilient. To Porterhouse he owed his nerve, the nerve a few years later, while still a Parliamentary Private Secretary to the Minister of Transport, to propose to Mary Lacey, the only daughter of the Liberal Peer, the Earl of Sanderstead: the nerve to repeat the proposal yearly and to accept her annual refusal with a gracelessness that had gradually convinced her of the depth of his feelings. Yes, looking back over his long career Sir Godber could attribute much to Porterhouse and nothing more so than his determination to change once and for all the character of the college that had made him what he was. Looking down the hall at the faces florid in the candlelight and listening to the loud assertions that passed for conversation, he was strengthened in his resolve. The beefsteak and the burgundy came and went, the brandy trifle and the stilton followed, and finally the port decanter made the rounds. Sir Godber observed and abstained. Only when the ritual of wiping one's forehead with a napkin dipped in a silver bowl had been performed did he make his move. Rapping his knife handle on the table for silence, the new Master of Porterhouse rose to his feet.

In the Musicians' Gallery Skullion watched the Feast. Behind him in the darkness the lesser College servants clustered backwardly and gaped at the brilliant scene below them, their pale faces gleaming dankly in the reflected glory of the occasion. As each new dish appeared a muted sigh went up. Their eyes glittered momentarily and glazed again. Only Skullion, the Head Porter, sat surveying the setting with an air of critical propriety. There was no envy in his eyes, only approval at the fitness of the arrangements and the occasional unexpressed rebuke when a waiter spilled the gravy or failed to notice an empty glass waiting to be refilled. It was all as it should be, as it had been since Skullion first came to the College as an under-porter so many years ago. Forty-five Feasts there had been since then and at each Skullion had watched from the Musicians' Gallery just as his ancestors had watched since the college began. 'Skullion eh? That's an interesting name, Skullion,' old Lord Wurford had said when he first stopped by the lodge in 1928 and saw the new porter there. 'A very interesting name. Skullion. A no nonsense damn-my-soul name. There've been skullions at Porterhouse since the Founder. You take that from me, there have. It's in the first accounts. A farthing to the skullion. You be proud of it.' And Skullion had been proud of it as though he had been newly christened by the old Master. Yes those were the days and those were the men. Old Lord Wurford, a no nonsense damn-my-soul master. He'd have enjoyed a feast like this. He wouldn't have sat up there fiddling with his fork and sipping his wine. He'd have spilt it down his front like he always used to and he'd have guzzled that swan like it was a chicken and thrown the bones over his shoulder. But he'd been a gentleman and a rowing man and he'd stuck to the old Boat Club traditions.

'A bone for the eight in front,' they used to shout.

'What eight? There ain't no eight in front.'

'A bone for the fish in front.' And over their shoulders the bones would go and if it was a good evening there was meat on them still and damned glad we was to get it. And it was true too. There was no eight in front in those days. Only the fish. In the darkness of the Musicians' Gallery Skullion smiled at his memories of his youth. All different now. The young gentlemen weren't the same. The spirit had gone out of them since the war. They got grants now. They worked. Who had ever heard of a Porterhouse man working in the old days? They were too busy drinking and racing. How many of this lot took a cab to Newmarket these days and came back five hundred to the bad and didn't turn a hair? The Honourable Mr Newland had in '33. Lived on Q staircase and got himself killed at Boulogne by the Germans. Skullion could remember a score or more like him. Gentlemen they were. No nonsense damn-my-soul gentlemen.

Presently when the main courses were finished and the stilton had made its appearance, the Chef climbed the stairs from the kitchen and took his seat next to Skullion.

'Ah, Chef, a fine Feast. As good as any I can remember,' Skullion told him.

'It's good of you to say so, Mr Skullion,' said the Chef.

'Better than they deserve,' said Skullion.

'Someone has to keep up the old traditions, Mr Skullion.'

'True, Chef, very true,' Skullion nodded. They sat in silence watching the waiters clearing the dishes and the port moving ritually round.

'And what is your opinion of the new Master, Mr Skullion?' the Chef asked.

Skullion raised his eyes to the painted timbers of the ceiling and shook his head sadly.

'A sad day for the College, Chef, a sad day,' he sighed.

'Not a very popular gentlemen?' the Chef hazarded.

'Not a gentlemen,' Skullion pronounced.

'Ah,' said the Chef. Sentence on the new Master had been passed. In the kitchen he would ever be the victim of social obloquy. 'Not a gentleman, eh? And him with his knighthood too.'

Skullion looked at him sternly. 'Gentlemen don't depend on knighthoods, Cheffy. Gentlemen is gentlemen,' Skullion told him, and the Chef, suitably rebuked, nodded. Mr Skullion wasn't somebody you argued with, not about matters of social etiquette, not in Porterhouse. Not if you knew what was good for you. Mr Skullion was a power in the College.

They sat silently mourning the passing of the old Master and the debasement of college life which the coming of a new Master, who was not a gentlemen, brought with it.

'Still,' said Skullion finally, 'it was a fine Feast. I can't remember a better.' He said it half-grudgingly, out of respect for the past, and was about to go downstairs when the Master rapped on the High Table for silence and stood up. In the Musicians' Gallery Skullion and the Chef stared in horror at the spectacle. A speech at the Feast? No. Never. The precedence of five hundred and thirty-two Feasts forbade it.

Sir Godber stared down at the heads turned toward him so incredulously. He was satisfied. The stunned silence, the stares of disbelief, the tension were what he had wanted. And not a single snigger. Sir Godber smiled.

'Fellows of Porterhouse, members of College,' he began with the practised urbanity of a politician, 'as your new Master I feel that this is a suitable occasion to put before you some new thoughts about the role of institutions such as this in the modern world.' Calculated, every insult delicately calculated. Porterhouse an institution, new, modern, role. The words, the clichés defiled the atmosphere. Sir Godber smiled. His sense of grievance was striking home. 'After such a meal' (in the gallery the Chef shied), 'it is surely not inappropriate to consider the future and the changes that must surely be made if we are to play our part in the contemporary world ...'

The platitudes rolled out effortlessly, meaninglessly but with effect. Nobody in the hall listened to the words. Sir Godber could have announced the Second Coming with demur. It was enough that he was there, defying tradition and consciously defiling his trust. Porterhouse could remember nothing to equal this. Not even sacrilege but utter blasphemy. And awed by the spectacle, Porterhouse sat in silence.

'And so let me end with this promise,' Sir Godber wound up his appalling peroration, 'Porterhouse will expand. Porterhouse will become what it once was – a house of learning. Porterhouse will change.' He stopped and for the last time smiled and then, before the tension broke, turned on his heel and swept out into the Combination Room. Behind him with a sudden expiration of breath the Feast broke up. Someone laughed nervously, the short bark of the Porterhouse laugh, and then the benches were pushed back and they flooded out of the hall, their voices flowing out before them into the Court, into the cold night air. It had begun to snow. On the Fellows' lawn Sir Godber Evans increased his pace. He had heard that bark and the sounds of the benches and the nervous energy he had expended had left him weak. He had challenged the College deliberately. He had said what he wanted to say. He had asserted himself. There was nothing they could do now. He had risked the stamping feet and the hisses and they had not come but now, with the snow falling round him on the Fellows' lawn, he was suddenly afraid. He hurried on and closed the door of the Master's Lodge with a sigh of relief.

As the hall emptied and as even the Fellows drifted through the door of the Combination Room, the Chaplain rose to say Grace. Deaf to the world and the blasphemies of Sir Godber, the Chaplain gave thanks. Only Skullion, standing alone in the Musicians' Gallery, heard him and his face was dark with anger.

CHAPTER TWO

In the Combination Room the Fellows digested the Feast dyspeptically. Sitting in their high-backed chairs, each with an occasional table on which stood coffee cups and glasses of brandy, they stared belligerently into the fire. Gusts of wind in the chimney blew eddies of smoke into the room to mingle with the blue cirrus of their cigars. Above their heads grotesque animals pursued in plaster evidently plastered nymphs across a pastoral landscape strangely formal, in which flowers and the College crest, a Bull Rampant, alternated, while from the panelled walls glowered the gross portraits of Thomas Wilkins, Master 1618–39, and Dr Cox, 1702–40. Even the fireplace, itself surrounded by an arabesque of astonishing grapes and well-endowed bananas, suggested excess and added an extra touch of flatulence to the scene. But if the Fellows found difficulty in coming to terms with the contents of their stomachs, the contents of Sir Godber's speech were wholly indigestible.

'Outrageous,' said the Dean, discreetly combining protest with eructation. 'One might have imagined he was addressing an electoral meeting.'

'It was certainly a very inauspicious start,' said the Senior Tutor. 'One would have expected a greater regard for tradition. When all is said and done we are an old college.'

'All may have been said, though I doubt your optimism,' said the Dean, 'but it has certainly not been done. The Master's infatuation with contemporary fashions of opinion may lead him to suppose that we are flattered by his presence. It is an illusion the scourings of party politics too naturally assume. I for one am unimpressed.'

'I must admit that I find his nomination most curious,' said the Praelector. 'One wonders what the Prime Minister had in mind.'

'The Government's majority is not a substantial one,' said the Senior Tutor. 'I should imagine he was ridding himself of a liability. If this evening's lamentable speech was anything to go by, Sir Godber's statements in the Commons must have raised a good many hackles on the back benches. Besides, his record of achievement is not an enviable one.'

'It still seems odd to me,' said the Praelector, 'that we should have been chosen for his retirement.'

'Perhaps his bark is worse than his bite,' said the Bursar hopefully.

'Bite?' shouted the Chaplain. 'But I've only just finished dinner. Not another morsel, thank you all the same.'

'One must assume that it was a case of any port in a storm,' said the Dean.

The Chaplain looked appalled.

'Port?' he screamed. 'After brandy? I can't think what this place is coming to.' He shuddered and promptly fell asleep again.

'I can't think what the Chaplain is coming to, come to that,' said the Praelector sadly. 'He gets worse by the day.'

'Anno domini,' said the Dean, 'anno domini, I'm afraid.'

'Not a particularly happy expression, Dean,' said the Senior Tutor, who still retained some vestiges of a classical education, 'in the circumstances.'

The Dean looked at him lividly. He disliked the Senior Tutor and found his allusions distinctly trying.

'The year of our Lord,' the Senior Tutor explained. 'I have the notion that our Master sees himself in the role of the creator. We shall have our work cut out preventing him from overexerting himself. We have our faults I daresay but they are not ones I would wish to see Sir Godber Evans remedy.'

'I am sure the Master will allow himself to be guided by our advice,' said the Praelector. 'We have had some obdurate Masters in the past. Canon Bowel had some ill-advised notions about altering the Chapel services, I seem to recall.'

'He wanted compulsory Compline,' said the Dean.

'A fearful thought,' the Senior Tutor agreed. 'It would have interfered with the digestive process.'

'The point was made to him,' the Dean continued, 'after a particularly good dinner. We had had devilled crabs with jugged hare to follow. I think it was the cigars that did it. That and the zabaglione.'

'Zabaglione?' shouted the Chaplain, 'it's a little late but I daresay . . .'

'We were talking about Canon Bowel,' the Bursar explained to him.

The Chaplain shook his head. 'Couldn't abide the man,' he said. 'Used to live on poached cod.'

'He had a peptic ulcer.'

'I'm not surprised,' said the Chaplain. 'With a name like that he should have known better.'

'To return to the present Master,' the Senior Tutor said, 'I am not prepared to sit back and allow him to alter our present admissions policy.'

'I don't see how we can afford to,' the Bursar agreed. 'We are not a rich college.'

'The point will have to be made to him,' the Dean said. 'We look to you, Bursar, to see that he understands it.' The Bursar nodded dutifully. His was not a strong constitution and the Dean overawed him.

'I shall do my best,' he said.

'And as far as the College Council is concerned I think the best policy will be one of . . . er . . . amiable inertia,' the Praelector suggested. 'That has always been one of our strong points.'

'There's nothing like prevarication,' the Dean agreed, 'I have yet to meet a liberal who can withstand the attrition of prolonged discussion of the inessentials.'

'You don't think the Bowel treatment, to coin a phrase?' the Senior Tutor asked.

The Dean smiled and stubbed out his cigar.

'There are more ways of killing a cat than stuffing it with . . .'

'Hush,' said the Praelector, but the Chaplain slept on. He was dreaming of the girls in Woolworths.

They left him sitting there and went out into the Court, their gowns wrapped round them against the cold. Like so many black puddings, they made their way to their rooms. Only the Bursar lived out with his wife. Porterhouse was still a very old-fashioned college.

In the Porter's Lodge Skullion sat in front of the gas fire polishing his shoes. A tin of black polish stood on the table beside him and every few minutes he would dip the corner of his yellow duster into the tin and smear the polish on to the toe of his shoe with little circular movements. Round and round his finger would go inside the duster while the toecap dulled momentarily and grew to a new and deeper shine. Every now and then Skullion would spit on the cap and then rub it again with an even lighter touch before picking up a clean duster and polishing the cap until it shone like black japan. Finally he would hold the shoe away from him so that it caught the light and he could see deep in the brilliant polish a dark distorted reflection of himself. Only then would he put the shoe to one side and start on the other.

It was something he had learnt to do in the Marines so many years ago and the ritual still had the satisfying effect it had had then. In some obscure way it seemed to ward off the thought of the future and all the threats implicit in that future, as if tomorrow was always a Regimental

Sergeant-Major and an inspection and change could be propitiated by
a gleaming pair of boots. All the time his pipe smoked out of the corner
of his mouth and the mantles of the gas fire darkened or glowed in the
draught and the snow fell outside. And all the time Skullion's mind,
protected by the ritual and the artefacts of habit, digested the import of
the Master's speech. Change? There was always change and what good
did it do? Skullion could think of nothing good in change. His memory
ranged back over the decades in search of certainty and found it only in
the assurance of men. Men no longer living or, if not dead, distant and
forgotten, ignored by a world in search of effervescent novelty. But he
had seen their assurance in his youth and had been infected by it so that
now, even now, he could call it up like some familiar from the past to
calm the seething uncertainties of the present. Quality, he had called it,
this assurance that those old men had. Quality. He couldn't define it or
fix it to particulars. They had had it, that was all, and some of them had
been fools or blackguards come to that but when they'd spoken there'd
been a harshness in their voices as if they didn't give a damn for anything.
No doubts, that's what they'd had, or if they had them kept them to
themselves instead of spreading their uncertainites about until you were
left wondering who or where you were. Skullion spat on his shoe in
memory of such men and their assurance and polished his reflection by
the fire. Above him the tower clock whirred and rumbled before striking
twelve. Skullion put on his shoes and went outside. The snow was falling
still and the Court and all the College roofs were white. He went to the
postern gate and looked outside. A car slushed by and all the way up
King's Parade the lamps shone orange through the falling snow. Skullion
went in and shut the door. The outside world was none of his affair. It
had a bleakness that he didn't want to know.

   He went back into the Porter's Lodge and sat down again with his
pipe. Around him the paraphernalia of his office, the old wooden clock,
the counter, the rows of pigeonholes, the keyboard and the blackboard
with 'Message for Dr Messmer' scrawled on it, were reassuring relics of
his tenure and reminders that he was still needed. For forty-five years
Skullion had sat in the Lodge watching over the comings and goings of
Porterhouse until it seemed he was as much a part of the College as the
carved heraldic beasts on the tower above. A lifetime of little duties easily
attended to while the world outside stormed by in a maelstrom of change
had bred in Skullion a devotion to the changelessness of Porterhouse
traditions. When he'd first come there'd been an Empire, the greatest
Empire that the world had known, a Navy, the greatest Navy in the
world, fifteen battleships, seventy cruisers, two hundred destroyers, and

Skullion had been a keyboard sentry on the *Nelson* with her three for'ard turrets and her arse cut off to meet the terms of some damned treaty. And now there was nothing left of that. Only Porterhouse was still the same. Porterhouse and Skullion, relics of an old tradition. As for the intellectual life of the College, Skullion neither knew nor cared about it. It was as incomprehensible to him as the rigmarole of a Latin mass to some illiterate peasant. They could say or think what they liked. It was the men he worshipped, some at least and fewer these days, their habits and the trappings he associated with that old assurance. The Dean's 'Good morning, Skullion', Dr Huntley's silk shirts, the Chaplain's evening stroll around the Fellows' Garden, Mr Lyons's music evening every Friday, the weekly parcel from the Institute for Dr Baxter. Chapel, Hall, the Feast, the meeting of the College Council, all these occasions like internal seasons marked the calendar of Skullion's life and all the time he looked for that assurance that had once been the hallmark of a gentleman.

Now sitting there with the gas fire hissing before him he searched his mind for what it was those old men signified. It wasn't that they were clever. Some were, but half were stupid, more stupid than the young men coming up these days. Money? Some had a lot and others hadn't. That wasn't what had made the difference. To him at least. Perhaps it had to them. A race apart they were. Helpless half of them. Couldn't make their beds, or wouldn't. And arrogant. 'Skullion this and Skullion that.' Oh, he'd resented it at the time and done it all the same and hadn't minded afterwards because ... because they'd been gentlemen. He spat into the fire affectionately and remembered an argument he'd had once with a young pup in a pub who'd heard him going on about the good old days.

'What gentlemen?' the lad had said. 'A lot of rich bastards with nothing between their ears who just exploited you.'

And Skullion had put down his pint and said, 'A gentleman stood for something. It wasn't what he was. It was what he knew he ought to be. And that's something you will never know.' Not what they were but what they ought to be, like some old battle standard that you followed because it was a symbol of the best. A ragged tattered piece of cloth that stood for something and gave you confidence and something to fight for.

He got up and walked across the Court and through the Screens and down the Fellows' Garden to the back gate. Everywhere the snow had submerged the details of the garden. Skullion's feet on the gravel path were soundless. In a few rooms lights still burned. The Dean's windows were still alight.

'Brooding on the speech,' Skullion thought and glanced reproachfully at the Master's Lodge where all was dark. At the back gate he stood looking up at the rows of iron spikes that topped the wall and the gate. How often in the old days he had stood there in the shadow of the beech-trees watching young gentlemen negotiate those spikes only to step out and take their names. He could remember a good many of those names still and see the startled faces turned towards his as he stepped out into the light.

'Good morning, Mr Hornby. Dean's report in the morning, sir.'

'Oh damn you, Skullion. Why can't you go to bed sometimes?'

'College regulations, sir.'

And they had gone off to their rooms cursing cheerfully. Now no one climbed in. Instead they knocked you up at all hours. Skullion didn't know why he bothered to come and look at the back wall any more. Out of habit. Old habit. He was just about to turn and trudge back to his bed in the Lodge when a scuffling noise stopped him in his tracks. Someone in the street was trying to climb in.

Zipser walked down Free School Lane past the black clunch walls of Corpus. The talk on 'Population Control in the Indian Subcontinent' had gone on longer than he had expected, partly due to the enthusiasm of the speaker and partly to the intractable nature of the problem itself. Zipser had not been sure which had been worse, the delivery, if that was an appropriate word to use about a speech that concerned itself with abortion, or the enthusiastic advocacy of vasectomy which had prolonged the talk beyond its expected limits. The speaker, a woman doctor with the United Nations Infant Prevention Unit in Madras, who seemed to regard infant mortality as a positive blessing, had disparaged the coil as useless, the pill as expensive, female sterilization as complicated, had described vasectomy so seductively that Zipser had found himself crossing and re-crossing his legs and wishing to hell that he hadn't come. Even now as he walked back to Porterhouse through the snow-covered streets he was filled with foreboding and a tendency to waddle. Still, even if the world seemed doomed to starvation, he had had to get out of Porterhouse for the evening. As the only research graduate in the College he found himself isolated. Below him the undergraduates pursued a wild promiscuity which he envied but dared not emulate, and above him the Fellows found compensation for their impotence in gluttony. Besides he was not a Porterhouse man, as the Dean had pointed out when he had been accepted. 'You'll have to live in College to get the spirit of the place,' he had said, and while in other colleges research graduates lived in cheap and comfortable digs, Zipser found himself occupying an exceedingly expensive suite of rooms in Bull Tower and forced to follow the regime of an undergraduate. For one thing he had to be in by twelve or face the wrath of Skullion and the indelicate inquiries next morning of the Dean. The whole system was anachronistic and Zipser wished he had been accepted by one of the other colleges. Skullion's attitude he found particularly unpleasant. The Porter seemed to regard him as an interloper, and lavished a wealth of invective on him normally reserved for tradesmen. Zipser's attempts to mollify him by explaining that Durham was a university and that there had been a Durham College in Oxford in 1380 had failed hopelessly. If anything, the mention of Oxford had increased Skullion's antipathy.

'This is a gentleman's college,' he had said, and Zipser, who didn't claim to be even a putative gentleman, had been a marked man ever since. Skullion had it in for him.

As he crossed Market Hill he glanced at the Guildhall clock. It was twelve thirty-five. The main gate would be shut and Skullion in bed. Zipser slackened his pace. There was no point in hurrying now. He might just as well stay out all night now. He certainly wasn't going to knock Skullion up and get cursed for his pains. It wouldn't have been the first time he had wandered about Cambridge all night. Of course there was Mrs Biggs the bedder to be taken care of. She came to wake him every morning and was supposed to report him if his bed hadn't been slept in but Mrs Biggs was accommodating. 'A pound in the purse is worth a flea in the ear,' she had explained after his first stint of nights wandering, and Zipser had paid up cheerfully. Mrs Biggs was all right. He was fond of her. There was something almost human about her in spite of her size.

Zipser shivered. It was partly the cold and partly the thought of Mrs Biggs. The snow was falling heavily now and it was obvious he couldn't stay out all night in this weather. It was equally clear that he wasn't going to wake Skullion. He would have to climb in. It was an undignified thing for a graduate to do but there was no alternative. He crossed Trinity Street and went past Caius. At the bottom he turned right and came to the back gate in the lane. Above him the iron spikes on top of the wall looked more threatening than ever. Still, he couldn't stay out. He would probably freeze to death if he did. He found a bicycle in front of Trinity Hall and dragged it up the lane and put it against the wall. Then he climbed up until he could grasp the spikes with his hands. He paused for a moment and then with a final kick he was up with one knee on the wall and his foot under the spikes. He eased himself up and swung the other leg over, found a foothold and jumped. He landed softly in the flowerbed and scrambled to his feet. He was just moving off down the path under the beech-trees when something moved in the shadow and a hand fell on his shoulder. Zipser reacted instinctively. With a wild flurry he struck out at his attacker and the next moment a bowler hat was in mid-air and Zipser himself, ignoring the College rules which decreed that only Fellows could walk on the lawns, was racing across the grass towards New Court. Behind him on the gravel path Skullion lay breathing heavily. Zipser glanced over his shoulder as he dashed through the gate into the Court and saw his dark shape on the ground. Then he was in O staircase and climbing the stairs to his rooms. He shut the door and stood in the darkness panting. It must have been Skullion. The bowler hat told him that. He had assaulted a College porter, bashed his face and chopped him down. He went to the window and peered out and it was then that he realized what a fool he had been. His footsteps in the snow would give him away. Skullion would follow them to the Bull Tower. But there was no sign of the Porter. Perhaps he was still lying out there unconscious. Perhaps he had knocked him out. Zipser shuddered at this fresh indication of his irrational nature, and its terrible consequences for mankind. Sex and violence, the speaker had said, were the twin poles of the world's lifeless future, and Zipser could see now what she had meant.

Anyway, he could not leave Skullion lying out there to freeze to death even if going down to help him meant that he would be sent down from the University for 'assaulting a college porter', his thesis on the Pumpernickel as A Factor in the Politics of 16th-Century Westphalia uncompleted. He went to the door and walked slowly downstairs.

Skullion got to his feet and picked up his bowler, brushed the snow off it and put it on. His waistcoat and jacket were covered with patches of snow and he brushed them down with his hands. His right eye was swelling. Young bastard had caught him a real shiner. 'Getting too old for this job,' he muttered, muddled feelings of anger and respect competing in his mind. 'But I can still catch him.' He followed the footsteps across the lawn and down the path to the gate into New Court. His eye had swollen now so that he could hardly see out of it, but Skullion wasn't thinking about his eye. He wasn't thinking about catching the culprit. He was thinking back to the days of his youth. 'Fair's fair. If you can't catch 'em, you can't report 'em,' old Fuller, the Head Porter at Porterhouse had said to him when he first came to the College and what was true then was true now. He turned left at the gate and went down the Cloister to the Lodge and went through to his bedroom. 'A real shiner,' he said examining the swollen eye in the mirror behind the door.

It could do with a bit of beefsteak. He'd get some from the College kitchen in the morning. He took off his jacket and was unbuttoning his waistcoat when the door of the Lodge opened. Skullion buttoned his waistcoat again and put on his jacket and went out into the office.

Zipser stood in the doorway of O staircase and watched Skullion cross the Court to the Cloisters. Well, at least he wasn't lying out in the snow. Still he couldn't go back to his room without doing something. He had better go down and see if he was all right. He walked across the Court and into the Lodge. It was empty and he was about to turn away and go back to his room when the door at the back opened and Skullion appeared. His right eye was black and swollen and his face, old and veined, had a deformed lop-sided look about it.

'Well?' Skullion asked out of the side of his mouth. One eye peered angrily at Zipser.

'I just came to say I'm sorry,' Zipser said awkwardly.

'Sorry?' Skullion asked as if he didn't understand.

'Sorry about hitting you.'

'What makes you think you hit me?' The lop-sided face glared at him. Zipser scratched his forehead.

'Well, anyway I'm sorry. I thought I had better see if you were all right.'

'You thought I was going to report you, didn't you?' Skullion asked contemptuously. 'Well, I'm not. You got away.'

Zipser shook his head.

'It wasn't that. I thought you might be ... well ... hurt.'

Skullion smiled grimly.

'Hurt? Me hurt? What's a little hurt matter?' He turned and went back into the bedroom and shut the door. Zipser went out into the Court. He didn't understand. You knocked an old man down and he didn't mind. It wasn't logical. It was all so bloody irrational. He walked back to his room and went to bed.

CHAPTER THREE

The Master slept badly. The somatic effects of the Feast and the psychic consequences of his speech had combined to make sleep difficult. While his wife slept demurely in her separate bed, Sir Godber lay awake reliving the events of the evening with an insomniac's obsessiveness. Had he been wise to so offend the sensibilities of the College? It had been a carefully calculated decision and one which his political eminence had seemed to warrant. Whatever the Fellows might say about him, his reputation for moderate and essentially conservative reform would absolve him of the accusation that he was the advocate of change for change's sake. As the Minister who had made the slogan 'Alteration without Change' so much a part of the recent tax reforms, Sir Godber prided himself on his conservative liberalism or, as he had put it in a moment of self-revelation, authoritarian permissiveness. The challenge he had thrown down to Porterhouse had been deliberate and justified. The College was absurdly old-fashioned. Out of touch with the times, and to a man whose very life had been spent keeping in touch with the times there could be no greater dereliction. An advocate of comprehensive education at no matter what cost, chairman of the Evans Committee on Higher Education which had introduced Sixth Form Polytechnics for the Mentally Retarded, Sir Godber prided himself on the certain knowledge that he knew what was best for the country, and he was supported in this by Lady Mary, his wife, whose family, now staunchly Liberal, still retained the Whig traditions enshrined in the family motto *Laisser Mieux*. Sir Godber had taken the motto for his own, and associating it with Voltaire's famous dictum had made himself the enemy of the good wherever he found it. 'Be good, sweet maid, and let who will be clever' had no appeal for Sir Godber's crusading imagination. What sweet maids required was a first-rate education and what sleeping dogs needed was a kick up the backside. This was precisely what he intended to administer to Porterhouse.

Lying awake through the still hours of the night listening to the bells of the College clocks and the churches toll the hours, a sound he found medieval and unnecessarily premonitory, Sir Godber planned his campaign. In the first instance he would order a thorough inventory of the College's resources and make the economies needed to finance the alterations he had in mind. In themselves such economies would effect some changes in Porterhouse. The kitchen staff could well do with some thinning out and since so much of the ethos of Porterhouse emanated from the kitchen and the endowments lavished upon it by generations of Porterhouse men, a careful campaign of retrenchment there would do much to alter the character of the College. And such savings would be justified by the building programme and the expansion of numbers. With the experience of hundreds of hours in committees behind him, the Master anticipated the arguments that would be raised against him by the Fellows. Some would object to any changes in the kitchen. Others would deny the need for expansion in numbers. In the darkness Sir Godber smiled happily. It was precisely on such divisions of opinion that he thrived. The original issue would get lost in argument and he would emerge as the arbiter between divided factions, his role as the initiator of dissension quite forgotten. But first he would need an ally. He ran through the Fellows in search of a weak link.

The Dean would oppose any increase in the numbers of undergraduates on the specious grounds that it would destroy the Christian community which he supposed Porterhouse to be and, more accurately, would make discipline difficult to impose. Sir Godber put the Dean to one side. There was no help to be found there except indirectly from the very obduracy of his conservatism, which irritated some of the other Fellows. The Senior Tutor? A more difficult case to assess. A rowing man in his day, he might be inclined to favour a larger intake on the grounds that it would add weight to the College boat and improve Porterhouse's chances in the Bumps. On the other hand he would oppose any changes in the kitchen for fear that the diet of the Boat Club might be diminished. The Master decided a compromise was in order. He would give an absolute assurance that the Boat Club would continue to get its quota of beefsteak no matter what other economies were made in the kitchen. Yes, the Senior Tutur could be persuaded to support expansion. Sir Godber balanced him against the Dean and turned his attention to the Bursar. Here was the key, he thought. If the Bursar could be enlisted on the side of change, his assistance would be invaluable. His advocacy of the financial benefits to be gained from an increase of undergraduate contributions, his demand for frugality in the kitchens, would carry immense weight. Sir Godber considered the Bursar's character and, with that insight into his own nature which had been the cornerstone of his success, recognized opportunism when he saw it. The Bursar, he had no doubt, was an ambitious man and unlikely to be content with the modest attainments of College life. The opportunity to serve on a Royal Commission – Sir Godber's retirement from the Cabinet was sufficiently recent for him to know of several pending – would give him a chance to put this nonentity at the service of the public and give him the recognition which would make amends for his lack of achievement. Sir Godber had no doubt that he could arrange his invitation. There was always a place for a man of the Bursar's contingent character on Royal Commissions. He would concentrate his attention on the Bursar. Satisfied with this plan of campaign, the Master turned on his side and fell asleep.

At seven he was woken by his wife whose insistence that early to bed and early to rise makes a man healthy, comfortably off and wise had never ceased to irritate him. As she bustled about the bedroom with a lack of concern for the feelings of other people which characterized her philanthropy, Sir Godber studied once more those particulars of his wife which had been such a spur to his political ambitions. Lady Mary was not an attractive woman. Her physical angularity made manifest the quality of her mind.

'Time to get up,' she said, spotting Sir Godber's open eye.

'Ours not to reason why, ours but to do or die,' thought the Master, sitting up and fumbling for his slippers.

'How did the Feast go?' Lady Mary asked, adjusting the straps of her surgical corset with a vigour that reminded Sir Godber of a race meeting.

'Tolerably, I suppose,' he said with a yawn. 'We had swan stuffed with some sort of duck. Very indigestible. Kept me awake half the night.'

'You should be more careful about what you eat.' Lady Mary sat down and swung one leg over the other to put on her stockings. 'You don't want to have a stroke.'

'It's called Porterhouse Blue.'

'What is?'

'A stroke,' said Sir Godber.

'I thought it was something you got for rowing,' said Lady Mary. 'That or a cheese. Something on the order of a Stilton – blue and veined –'

Sir Godber lowered his eyes from her legs. 'Well, it isn't,' he said hurriedly, 'it's an apoplectic fit brought on by over-indulgence. An old College tradition, and one I intend to eradicate.'

'And about time too,' said Lady Mary. 'I think it's utterly disgraceful in this day and age that all this good food should go to waste just to satisfy the greed of some old men. When I think of all those ...'

Sir Godber went into the bathroom and shut the door and turned the tap on in the hand basin. Dimly through the door and through the noise of running water he could hear his wife lamenting starving children in India. He looked at himself in the mirror and sighed. Just like the bloody cockcrow, he thought. Starts the day with a dirge. Wouldn't be happy if someone wasn't dying of starvation or drowning in a hurricane or dropping dead of typhus.

He shaved and dressed and went down to breakfast. Lady Mary was reading the *Guardian* with an avidity that suggested a natural disaster of considerable magnitude. Sir Godber refrained from inquiring what it was and contented himself with reading one or two bills.

'My dear,' he said when he had finished, 'I shall be seeing the Bursar this morning and I was thinking of inviting him to dinner on Wednesday.'

Lady Mary looked up. 'Wednesday's no good. I have a meeting on. Thursday would be better,' she said. 'Do you want me to invite anyone else. He's a rather common little man, isn't he?'

'He has his good points,' said the Master. 'I'll see if Thursday suits him.' He went to his study with *The Times*. There were days when his wife's moral intensity seemed to hang like a pall over his existence. He wondered what the meeting on Wednesday was about. Battered babies probably. The Master shuddered.

In the Bursar's office the telephone rang.

'Ah, Master. Yes, certainly. No, not at all. In five minutes then.' He put down the phone with a smile of quiet satisfaction. The bargaining was about to begin and the Master had not invited anyone else. The Bursar's office overlooked the Fellows' Garden and nobody else had taken the path under the beech-trees to the Master's Lodge. As he left his office and walked across the lawn the Bursar reviewed the strategy he had decided on during the night. He had been tempted to put himself at the head of the Fellows in their opposition to any change. There were after all advantages to be gained in the climate of the seventies from adherence to the principles of strict conservatism, and in the event of the Master's retirement or early death the Fellows might well elect him Master in his place out of gratitude. The Bursar rather fancied not. He lacked the carnivorous bonhomie that Porterhouse sought in its Masters. Old Lord Wurford for instance, Skullion's touchstone, or Canon Bowel, whose penchant for Limburger cheese and rugby fanaticism had in a sinister way been interrelated. No, the Bursar could not see himself among their number. It was wiser to follow in his Master's footsteps. He knocked on the door of the Master's Lodge and was admitted by the French au pair.

'Ah, Bursar, so good of you to come,' said the Master, rising from his chair behind the large oak desk that stood in front of the fire. 'Some madeira? Or would you prefer something a little more contemporary?' The Master chuckled. 'A campari, for instance. Something to keep the cold out.' In the background the radiators gurgled gently. The Bursar considered the question.

'I think something contemporary would be fitting, Master,' he said at last.

'So do I, Bursar, so I do indeed,' said the Master, and poured the drinks.

'Now then,' he said when the Bursar had seated himself in an armchair, 'to business.'

'To business,' said the Bursar raising his glass in the mistaken belief that a toast had been proposed. The Master eyed him cautiously.

'Yes. Well,' he said, 'I've asked you here this morning to discuss the College finances. I understand from the Praelector that you and I share responsibility in this matter. Correct me if I am wrong?'

'Quite right, Master,' said the Bursar.

'But of course as Bursar you are the real power. I quite appreciate that,' the Master continued. 'I have no desire to impinge upon your authority in these matters, let me assure you of that.' He smiled genially on the Bursar.

'My purpose in asking you here this morning was to reassure you that the changes I spoke of last night were of a purely general nature. I seek no alterations in the administration of the College.'

'Quite,' said the Bursar, nodding with approval. 'I entirely agree.'

'So good of you to say so, Bursar,' said the Master. 'I had the impression that my little sally had a not altogether unmixed reception from the less ... er ... contemporary Senior Fellows.'

'We are a very traditional college, Master,' said the Bursar.

'Yes, so we are, but some of us, I suspect, are rather less traditional than others, eh, Bursar?'

'I think it's fair to say so, Master,' the Bursar assented.

Like two elderly dogs they circled warily in search of the odour of agreement, sniffing each hesitation for the nuance of complicity. Change was inevitable. Indeed, indeed. The old order. Quite so. Quite so. Those of us in authority. Ah yes. Ah yes. On the mantelpiece the alabaster clock ticked on. It was an hour before the preliminary skirmishes were done and with a second, larger campari Sir Godber relaxed the role of Master.

'It's the sheer animality of so many of our undergraduates I object to,' he told the Bursar.

'We tend to attract the less sensitive, I must admit.' The Bursar puffed his cigar contentedly.

'Academically our results are deplorable. When did we last get a first?'

'In 1956,' said the Bursar.

The Master raised his eyes to heaven.

'In Geography,' said the Bursar, rubbing salt in the wound.

'In Geography. One might have guessed.' He got up and stood looking out of the french windows at the garden covered in snow. 'It is time to change all that. We must return to the Founder's intentions "studiously to engage in learning". We must accept candidates who have good academic records instead of the herd of illiterates we seem to cater for at present.'

'There are one or two obstacles to that,' the Bursar sighed.

'Quite so. The Senior Tutur for one. He is in charge of admissions.'

'I was thinking rather of our, how shall I say, dependence on the endowment subscriptions,' said the Bursar.

'The endowment subscriptions? I've never heard of them.'

'Very few people have, Master, except of course the parents of our less academic undergraduates.'

Sir Godber frowned and stared at the Bursar. 'Do you mean to say that we accept candidates without academic qualifications if their parents subscribe to an endowment fund?' he asked.

'I'm afraid so. Frankly, the College could hardly continue without their contributions,' the Bursar told him.

'But this is monstrous. Why, it's tantamount to selling degrees.'

'Not tantamount, Master. Identical.'

'But what about the Tripos examinations?'

The Bursar shook his head. 'Ah I'm afraid we don't aspire to such heights. Specials are more our mark. Ordinary degrees. Just good plain old-fashioned BAs. We put up the names and they're accepted without question.'

Sir Godber sat down dumbfounded.

'Good God, and you mean to tell me that without these ... er ... contributions ... dammit, these bribes, the College couldn't carry on?'

'In a nutshell, Master,' said the Bursar. 'Porterhouse is broke.'

'But why? What do other colleges do?'

'Ah,' said the Bursar, 'well that's rather different. Most of them have enormous resources. Shrewd investments over the years. Trinity, for instance, is to the best of my knowledge the third largest landowner in the country. Only the Queen and the Church of England exceed Trinity's holdings. King's had Lord Keynes as Bursar. We unfortunately had Lord Fitzherbert. Where Keynes made a fortune, Fitzherbert lost one. You've heard of the man who broke the bank at Monte Carlo?'

The Master nodded miserably.

'Lord Fitzherbert,' said the Bursar.

'But he must have made a fortune,' said the Master.

The Bursar shook his head. 'It wasn't the bank of Monte Carlo he broke, Master, but the bank at Monte Carlo, our bank, the Anglian Lowland Bank. Two million on the spin of the wheel. Never recovered from the blow.'

'I'm not in the least surprised,' said the Master, 'I wonder he didn't blow his brains out on the spot.'

'The bank, Master, not Lord Fitzherbert. He came back and eventually was elected Master,' said the Bursar.

'Elected Master? It seems an odd thing to elect a man who has bankrupted the place. I should have thought he'd have been lynched.'

'Frankly, the College had to depend on him for some time. The revenue from his estate saw us through bad times, I'm told.' The Bursar sighed. 'So you see, Master, while I support you in principle, I'm afraid the ... er ... exigencies of our financial position do impose certain restraints in the way of effecting the changes you have in mind. A case of cutting our coats to suit our cloth.' The Bursar finished his campari and stood up. The Master sat staring out into the garden. It had started to snow again but the Master was not aware of it. His mind was on other things. Looking back over his long career, he was suddenly conscious that the situation he was now facing was a familiar one. The Bursar's arguments had been those of the Treasury and the Bank of England. Sir Godber's ideals had always foundered on the rocks of financial necessity. This time it would be different. The frustrations of a lifetime had come to a head. Sir Godber had nothing left to lose. Porterhouse would change or bust. Inspired by the example of Lord Fitzherbert, Sir Godber stood up and turned to the Bursar. But the Bursar was no longer there. He had tiptoed from the room and could be seen waddling gently across the Fellows' Garden.

CHAPTER FOUR

Zipser overslept. His exertions, both mental and physical, had left him exhausted. By the time he woke, Mrs Biggs was already busy in his outer room, moving furniture and dusting. Zipser lay in bed listening to her. Like something out of Happy Families, he thought. Mrs Biggs the Bedder. Skullion the Head Porter. The Dean. The Senior Tutor. Relics of some ancient childish game. Everything about Porterhouse was like that. Masters and Servants.

Lying there listening to the ponderous animality of Mrs Biggs' movements, Zipser considered the curious turn of events that had forced him into the role of a master while Mrs Biggs maintained an aggressive servility quite out of keeping with her personality and formidable physique. He found the relationship peculiar, and further complicated by the sinister attractions she held for him. It must be that in her fullness Mrs Biggs retained a natural warmth which in its contrast to the artificiality of all else in Cambridge made its appeal. Certainly nothing else could explain it. Taken in her particulars, and Zipser couldn't think of any other way of taking her, the bedder was quite remarkably without attractions. It wasn't simply the size of her appendages that was astonishing but the sheer power. Mrs Biggs' walk was a thing of menacing maternity, while her face retained a youthfulness quite out of keeping with her volume. Only her voice declared her wholly ordinary. That and her conversation, which hovered tenuously close to the obscene and managed to combine servility with familiarity in a manner he found unanswerable. He got out of bed and began to dress. It was one of the ironies of life, he thought, that in a college that prided itself on its adherence to the values of the past, Mrs Biggs' manifest attractions should go unrecognized. In paleolithic times she would have been a princess and he was just wondering at what particular moment of history the Mrs Biggses had ceased to represent all that was finest and fairest in womanhood when she knocked on the door.

'Mr Zipser, are you decent?' she called.

'Hang on. I'm coming,' Zipser called back.

'I shouldn't be at all surprised,' Mrs Biggs muttered audibly.

Zipser opened the door.

'I haven't got all day,' Mrs Biggs said brushing past him provocatively.

'I'm sorry to have kept you,' said Zipser sarcastically.

'Kept me indeed. Listen to who's talking. And what makes you think I'd mind being kept?'

Zipser blushed. 'That's hardly what I meant,' he said hotly.

'Very complimentary I'm sure,' said Mrs Biggs, regarding him with arch disapproval. 'Got out of bed the wrong side this morning, did we?'

Zipser noted the plural with a delicious shudder and lowered his eyes. Mrs Biggs' boots, porcinely tight, entranced him.

'Mr Skullion's got a black eye this morning,' the bedder continued. 'A right purler. Not before time either. I says to him, "Somebody's been taking a poke at you". You know what he says?' Zipser shook his head.

'He says, "I'll thank you to keep your comments to yourself, Mrs Biggs."
That's what he says. Silly old fool. Don't know which century he's living
in.' She went into the other room and Zipser followed her. He put a
kettle on to make coffee while Mrs Biggs bustled about picking things up
and putting them down again in a manner which suggested that a great
deal of work was being done but which merely helped to emphasize her
feelings. All the time she rattled on with her daily dose of inconsequential
information while Zipser dodged about the room like a toreador trying
to avoid a talkative bull. Each time she brushed past him he was aware
of an animal magnetism that overrode considerations of taste and that
aesthetic sensibility his education was supposed to have given him. Finally
he stood in the corner, hardly able to contain himself, and watched her
figure as it walloped about the room. Her words lost all meaning, became
mere soothing sounds, waves of accompaniment to the surge of her thighs
and the great rollers of her buttocks dimpled and shimmering beneath
her skirt. 'Well I says, "You know what you can do ..."' Mrs Biggs'
voice echoed Zipser's terrible thought. She bent over to plug in the
vacuum-cleaner and her breasts plunged in her blouse and undulated
with a force of attraction Zipser found almost irresistible. He felt himself
moved out of his corner like a boxer urged forward by unnatural passion
for an enormous opponent. Words crowded into his mouth. Unwanted
words. Unspeakable words.

'I want you,' he said and was saved the final embarrassment by the
vacuum-cleaner which roared into life.

'What's that you said?' Mrs Biggs shouted above the din. She was
holding the suction pipe against a cushion on the armchair. Zipser turned
purple.

'Nothing,' he bawled, and fell back into his corner.

'Bag's full,' said Mrs Biggs, and switched the machine off.

In the silence that followed Zipser leant against the wall, appalled at
his terrible avowal. He was about to make a dash for the door when Mrs
Biggs bent over and undid the clips on the back of the vacuum-cleaner.
Zipser stared at the backs of her knees. The boots, the creases, the swell
of her thighs, the edge of her stockings, the crescent ...

'Bag's full,' Mrs Biggs said again. 'You can't get any suction when the
bag's full.'

She straightened up holding the bag grey and swollen ... Zipser shut
his eyes. Mrs Biggs emptied the bag into the wastepaper basket. A cloud
of grey dust billowed up into the room.

'Are you feeling all right, dearie?' she asked, peering at him with
motherly concern. Zipser opened his eyes and stared into her face.

'I'm all right,' he managed to mutter trying to take his eyes off her lips. Mrs Biggs' lipstick gleamed thickly. 'I didn't sleep well. That's all.'

'Too much work and not enough play makes Jack a dull boy,' said Mrs Biggs holding the bag limply. To Zipser the thing had an erotic appeal he dared not analyse. 'Now you just sit down and I'll make you some coffee and you'll feel better.' Mrs Biggs' hand grasped his arm and guided him to a chair. Zipser slumped into it and stared at the vacuum-cleaner while Mrs Biggs, bending once again and even more revealingly now that Zipser was sitting down and closer to her, inserted the bag into the back of the machine and switched it on. A terrible roar, and the bag was sucked into the interior with a force which corresponded entirely to Zipser's feelings. Mrs Biggs straightened up and went through to the gyp room to make coffee while Zipser shifted feebly in the chair. He couldn't imagine what was happening to him. It was all too awful. He had to get away. He couldn't go on sitting there while she was in the room. He'd do something terrible. He couldn't control himself. He'd say something. He was about to get up and sneak out when Mrs Biggs came back with two cups of coffee.

'You do look funny,' she said, putting a cup into his hand. 'You ought to go and see a doctor. You might be going down with something.'

'Yes,' said Zipser obediently. Mrs Biggs sat down opposite him and sipped her coffee. Zipser tried to keep his eyes off her legs and found himself gazing at her breasts.

'Do you often get taken queer?' Mrs Biggs inquired.

'Queer?' said Zipser, shaken from his reverie by the accusation. 'Certainly not.'

'I was only asking,' said Mrs Biggs. She took a mouthful of coffee with a schlurp that was distinctly suggestive. 'I had a young man once,' she continued, 'just like you. Got took queer every now and then. Used to throw himself about and wriggle something frightful. Took me all my time to hold him down, it did.'

Zipser stared at her frenziedly. The notion of being held down while wriggling by Mrs Biggs was more than he could bear. With a sudden lurch that spilt his coffee Zipser hurled himself out of the chair and dashed from the room. He rushed downstairs and out into the safety of the open air. 'I've got to do something. I can't control myself. First Skullion and now Mrs Biggs.' He walked hurriedly out of Porterhouse and through Clare towards the University Library.

Alone in Zipser's room, Mrs Biggs switched on the vacuum-cleaner and poked the handle round the room. As she worked she sang to herself loudly, 'Love me tender, love me true.' Her voice, raucously off key, was drowned by the roar of the Electrolux.

The Dean spent the morning writing letters to members of the Porterhouse Society. As the Society's secretary he attended the annual dinners in London and Edinburgh and corresponded regularly with members, a great many of whom lived in Australia or New Zealand, and for whom the Dean's letters formed a link with their days at Porterhouse on which they had traded socially ever since. For the Dean himself the very remoteness of most of his correspondents, and particularly their tendency to assume that nothing had changed since their undergraduate days, was a constant reassurance. It allowed him to pretend to an omnipotent conservatism that had little connection with reality. After the new Master's speech it was not easy to maintain that pretence, and the Dean's pen held in his mottled hand crawled slowly across the paper like some literate but decrepit tortoise. Every now and then he would lift his head and look for inspiration into the clear-cut features of the young men whose photographs cluttered his desk and stared with sepia arrogance from the walls of his room. The Dean recalled their athleticism and youthful indiscretions, the shopgirls they had compromised, the tailors they had bilked, the exams they had failed, and from his window he could look down on to the fountain where they had ducked so many homosexuals. It had all been so healthy and naturally violent, so different from the effete aestheticism of today. They hadn't fasted for the good of the coolies in India or protested because an anarchist was imprisoned in Brazil or stormed the Garden House Hotel because they disapproved of the government in Greece. They'd acted in high spirits. Wholesomely. The Dean sat back in his chair remembering the splendid riot on Guy Fawkes Night in 1948. The bomb that blew the Senate House windows out. The smoke bomb down the lavatory in Market Square that nearly killed an old man with high blood pressure. The lamp glass littering the streets. The bus being pushed backwards. The coppers' helmets flying. The car they'd overturned in King's Parade. There'd been a pregnant woman in it, the Dean recalled, and afterwards they'd all chipped in to pay her for the damage. Good-hearted lads. They didn't make them like that any more. Quickened by the recollection, his pen scrawled swiftly across the page. It would take more than Sir Godber Evans to change the character of Porterhouse. He'd see to that. He had just finished a letter and was addressing the envelope when there was a knock on the door.

'Come in,' the Dean called. The door opened and Skullion came in, holding his bowler hat in one hand.

'Morning, sir,' Skullion said.

'Good morning, Skullion,' the Dean said. The ritual of twenty years, the porter's daily report, always began with pleasantries. 'Heavy fall of snow during the night.'

'Very heavy, sir. Three inches at least.'

The Dean licked the envelope and fastened it down.

'Nasty eye you've got there, Skullion.'

'Slipped on the path, sir. Icy,' Skullion said. 'Very slippery.'

'Slippery? Got away, did he?' the Dean asked.

'Yes, sir.'

'Good for him,' said the Dean. 'Nice to know there are still some undergraduates with spirit about. Nothing else to report?'

'No, sir. Nothing to report. Nothing except Cheffy, sir.'

'Cheffy? What's the matter with him?'

'Well, it's not just him, sir. It's all of us. Very upset about the Master's speech,' Skullion said carefully, treading the tightrope between speaking out of turn and rightful protest. There were things you could say to the Dean and there were things you couldn't. Reporting the Chef's sense of outrage seemed a safe way of expressing his own feelings.

The Dean swung his chair round and looked out of the window to evade the difficulty. He relied on Skullion's information but there was always the danger of condoning insubordination or at least encouraging a familiarity detrimental to good discipline. But Skullion wasn't the man to take advantage of the situation. The Dean trusted him.

'You can tell the Chef there'll be no changes,' he said finally. 'The Master was just feeling his way. He'll learn.'

'Yes sir,' said Skullion doubtfully. 'Very upsetting that speech, sir.'

'Thank you, Skullion,' said the Dean dismissively.

'Thank you, sir,' Skullion said and left the room.

The Dean swung his chair round to his desk and took up his pen again. Skullion's resentment had inspired him with a new determination to block Sir Godber's schemes. There were all the OPs, for instance. Their opinion and influence could be decisive properly organized. It might be as well to inform that opinion now.

Skullion went back to the Lodge and sorted out the second mail. His conversation with the Dean had only partially restored his confidence. The Dean was getting old. His voice didn't carry the same weight any more in the College Council. It was the Bursar who was listened to, and

Skullion had his doubts about *him*. He took the *New Statesman* and the *Spectator* and read *The Times*, not the *Telegraph* like the other dons. 'Neither fish, flesh, fowl nor good red herring,' Skullion summed him up with his usual political acumen. If the Master got at him there was no saying which way he'd jump. Skullion began to think it might be time for him to pay a visit to General Sir Cathcart D'Eath at Coft. He usually went there on the first Tuesday of every month, a ritual visit with news of the College and also to have a word with a reliable stable boy in Sir Cathcart's racing stables whose information had in the past done much to supplement Skullion's meagre income. Sir Cathcart had been one of Skullion's Scholars and the debt had never been wholly repaid. 'Taking the afternoon off,' he told Walter the under-porter when he finished sorting the mail and Walter had put Dr Baxter's weekly issue of *The Boy* back into its plain envelope.

'What? Going fishing?' Walter asked.

'Never you mind where I'm going,' Skullion told him. He lit his pipe and went into the back room to fetch his coat and presently was cycling with due care and attention over Magdalene Bridge towards Coft.

Zipser sat on the third floor of the north wing of the University Library trying to bring his mind to bear on The Influence of Pumpernickel on the Politics of 16th-Century Osnabruck but without success. He no longer cared that it had been known as *bonum paniculum* and his interest in Westphalian local politics had waned. The problem of his feelings for Mrs Biggs was more immediate.

He had spent an hour in the stacks browsing feverishly through textbooks of clinical psychology in search of a medical explanation of the symptoms of irrational violence and irrepressible sexuality which had manifested themselves in his recent behaviour. From what he had read it had begun to look as if he were suffering from a multitude of different diseases. On the one hand his reaction to Skullion suggested paranoia, 'violent behaviour as a result of delusions of persecution', while the erotic compulsion of his feelings for Mrs Biggs was even more alarming and seemed to indicate schizophrenia with sado-masochistic tendencies. The combination of the two diseases, paranoid schizophrenia, was apparently the worst possible form of insanity and quite incurable. Zipser sat staring out of the window at the trees in the garden beyond the footpath and contemplated a lifetime of madness. He couldn't imagine what had suddenly occasioned the outbreak. The textbooks implied that heredity had a lot to do with it, but apart from an uncle who had a passion for concrete dwarves in his front garden and who his mother had said was a bit touched in the head, he couldn't think of anyone in the family who was actually and certifiably insane.

The explanation had to lie elsewhere. His feelings for the bedder deviated from every known norm. So for that matter did Mrs Biggs. She bulged where she should have dimpled and bounced when she should have been still. She was gross, vulgar, garrulous and, Zipser had no doubt in his mind, thoroughly insanitary. To find himself irresistibly attracted to her was the worst thing he could think of. It was perfectly all right to be queer. It was positively fashionable. To have constant and insistent sexual desires for French au pair girls, Swedish language students, girls in Boots, even undergraduates at Girton, was normality itself, but Mrs Biggs came into the category of the unmentionable. And the knowledge that but for the fortuitous intervention of the vacuum-cleaner he would have revealed his true feelings for her threw him into a panic. He left his table and went downstairs and walked back into town.

As he reached Great St Mary's the clock was striking twelve. Zipser stopped and studied the posters on the railings outside the church which announced forthcoming sermons.

CHRIST AND THE GAY CHRISTIAN Rev. F. Leaney.

HAS SALT LOST ITS SAVOUR? Anglican attitudes to disarmament. Rev. B. Tomkins.

JOB, A MESSAGE FOR THE THIRD WORLD Right Reverend Sutty, Bishop of Bombay.

JESUS JOKES Fred Henry by permission of ITA & the management of the Palace Theatre, Scunthorpe.

BOMBS AWAY A Christian's attitude to Skyjacking by Flight Lieutenant Jack Piggett, BOAC.

Zipser stared at the University Sermons with a sudden sense of loss. What had happened to the old Church, the Church of his childhood, the friendly Vicar and the helping hand? Not that Zipser has ever been to church, but he had seen them on television and had been comforted by the knowledge that they were still there in *Songs of Praise* and *Saints Alive* and *All Gas and Gaiters*. But now when he needed help there was only this pale parody of the daily paper with its mishmash of politics and sensationalism. Not a word about evil and how to cope with it. Zipser felt betrayed. He went back into Porterhouse in search of help. He'd go and see the Senior Tutor. There was just time before lunch. Zipser climbed the stairs to the Tutor's rooms and knocked on the door.

'The trouble with the Feast,' said the Dean, munching a mouthful of cold beef, 'is that it does tend to run on. Cold beef today. Cold beef tomorrow. Cold beef on Thursday. After that I suppose we'll have stewed beef on Friday and Saturday and cottage pie on Sunday. By next week we should be getting back to normal.'

'Difficult to eat an entire ox at one sitting,' said the Bursar. 'One suspects our predecessors had, shall we say, grosser appetites.'

'I always said it was a mistake to make him Prime Minister,' said the Chaplain.

The Senior Tutor took his place at table. He was looking more than usually austere.

'Talking of gross appetites,' he said grimly, 'I have the gravest doubts about some of our younger members. I have just had a visit from a young man who claims to be under some compulsion to sleep with his bedder.' He helped himself to horseradish.

The Bursar sniggered. 'Which one?' he asked.

'Zipser,' said the Senior Tutor.

'Which bedder?'

'I didn't inquire,' said the Senior Tutor. 'It didn't seem a particularly relevant question.'

The Bursar considered the problem.

'Isn't he in the Tower?' he asked the Dean.

'Who?'

'Zipser.'

'Yes. I think he is,' said the Dean.

'Then it must be Mrs Biggs.'

The Senior Tutor, who had been debating what to do with a long piece of gristle, swallowed it.

'Dear me. Mrs Biggs. I must say I did young Zipser an injustice,' he said with alarm.

'Impossible to do an injustice to anyone with such depraved tastes,' said the Dean firmly.

'Mrs Biggs hardly comes within the category of forbidden fruit,' tittered the Bursar.

'Thank you,' answered the Chaplain, 'I think I will have an apple.'

'Mrs Biggs,' muttered the Tutor. 'No wonder the poor fellow imagined he was going mad.'

'Not really,' said the Chaplain. 'This one is all right at any rate.'

'What advice did you give him?' the Bursar asked.

The Senior Tutor looked at him disbelievingly. 'Advice?' he asked. 'It is hardly my position to offer advice on such questions. I am the Senior Tutor, not a Marriage Guidance Counsellor. As a matter of fact I advised him to see the Chaplain.'

'It's a noble calling,' said the Chaplain, helping himself to a pear. The Senior Tutor sighed and finished his cold beef.

'It only goes to show what happens when you open the doors of the College to research graduates. In the old days such a thing would have been unheard of,' said the Dean.

'Unheard of perhaps but not I think unknown,' said the Bursar.

'With bedders?' the Dean asked angrily. 'With *bedders?* Maintain some sense of proportion, I beg you.'

'No thank you, Dean. I've had quite enough already,' the Chaplain replied.

The Dean was about to say something about old fools when the Senior Tutor intervened. 'In the case of Mrs Biggs,' he said, 'it is precisely the question of proportion that is at stake.'

'We had that last night,' said the Chaplain.

'Oh for God's sake,' the Senior Tutor snarled. 'How the hell can one conduct a serious discussion with him around.'

'My dear fellow,' the Praelector sighed, 'that is a question that has been bothering me for years.'

They finished the meal in silence, each occupied with his own thoughts. It was only when they were assembled in the Combination Room for coffee and the Chaplain had been persuaded to go to his room to write a note inviting Zipser to tea that the discussion began again.

'I think that we should view this matter in the wider context,' the Dean said. 'The Master's speech last night indicated only too clearly that he has in mind an extension of precisely that permissiveness of which this latest incident is indicative. I understand, Bursar, that you had a *tête-à-tête* with Sir Godber this morning.'

The Bursar looked at him unpleasantly. 'The Master phoned to ask me to discuss the College finances with him,' he said. 'I think you might give me credit for having done my best to disabuse him of the changes his speech suggested.'

'You explained that our resources do not allow us to indulge in the liberal extravagances of King's or Trinity?' the Senior Tutor asked. The Bursar nodded.

'And was the Master satisfied?' the Dean asked.

'Stunned, I think, would be the more accurate description of his reaction,' said the Bursar.

'Then we are all agreed that whatever he suggests at the meeting of the College Council tomorrow we shall oppose on principle,' said the Dean.

'I think it would be best to wait to hear what he proposes before deciding on a definite policy,' the Praelector said.

The Senior Tutor nodded. 'We must not appear too inflexible. An appearance of open-mindedness has in my experience a tendency to disarm the radical left. They seem to feel the need to reciprocate. I've often wondered why but it has worked to keep the country on the right lines for years.'

'Unfortunately this time we are dealing with a politician,' the Dean objected. 'I have a shrewd idea the Master is rather more experienced in these affairs than we give him credit for. I still think an undivided front is the best policy.'

They finished their coffee and went about their business. The Senior Tutor went down to the Boathouse to coach the first boat, the Dean slept until teatime, and the Bursar spent the afternoon doodling in his office wondering if he had been wise to tell Sir Godber about the endowment subscriptions. There had been a strength of feeling in the Master's reaction that had surprised the Bursar and had made him wonder if he had gone too far. Perhaps he had misjudged Sir Godber and the vehemence of his ideals.

CHAPTER FIVE

Skullion cycled out along the Barton Road towards Coft. His bowler hat set squarely on his head, his cycle clips and his black overcoat buttoned against the cold gave him an intransigently episcopalian air in the snow-covered landscape. He cycled slowly but relentlessly, his thoughts as dark as his habit and as bitter as the wind blowing unchecked from the Urals. The few bungalows he passed looked insubstantial beside him, transient and rootless in contrast to the black figure on the bicycle in whose head centuries of endured servitude had bred a fierce bigotry nothing would easily remove. Independence he called it, this hatred for change whether for better or worse. In Skullion's view there was no such thing as change for the better. That came under the heading of improvement. He was prepared to give his qualified approval to improvements provided there was no suggestion that it was the past that had been improved upon. That was clearly out of the question and if at the back of his mind he recognized the illogicality of his own argument, he refused to admit it even to himself. It was one of the mysteries of life which he accepted as unquestioningly as he did the great metal spiders's webs strung out across the fields beside the road to catch the radio evidence of stars that had long since ceased to exist. The world of Skullion's imagination was as remote as those stars but it was enough for him that, like the radio telescopes, he was able to catch echoes of it in men like General the Honourable Sir Cathcart D'Eath, KCMG, DSO.

The General had influence in high places and Royalty came to stay at Coft Castle. Skullion had once seen a queen mother dawdling majestically in the garden and had heard royal laughter from the stables. The General could put in a good word for him and more importantly a bad one for the new Master and, as an undergraduate, the then just Hon Cathcart D'Eath had been one of Skullion's Scholars.

Skullion never forgot his Scholars and there was little doubt that though they might have liked to, none of them forgot him. They owed him too much. It had been Skullion who had arranged the transactions and had acted as intermediary. On the one hand idle but influential undergraduates like the Hon Cathcart and on the other impecunious research graduates eking out a living giving supervision and grateful for the baksheesh Skullion brought their way. The weekly essay regularly handed in and startingly original for undergraduates so apparently ill-informed. Two pounds a week for an essay had served to subsidize some very important research. More than one doctorate owed everything to those two pounds. And finally Tripos by proxy, with Skullion's Scholars lounging in a King Street pub while in the Examination School their substitutes wrote answers to the questions with a mediocrity that was unexceptional. Skullion had been careful, very careful. Only one or two a year and in subjects so popular that there would be no noticing an unfamiliar face in the hundreds writing the exams. And it had worked. 'No one will be any the wiser,' he had assured the graduate substitutes to allay their fears before slipping five hundred, once a thousand, pounds into their pockets. And no one had been any the wiser. Certainly the Honourable Cathcart D'Eath had gone down with a two two in History with his ignorance of Disraeli's influence on the Conservative Party unimpaired in spite of having to all appearances written four pages on the subject. But what he had gained on the roundabout he had also gained on the swings and the study of horseflesh he had undertaken during those three years at Newmarket served him well in the future.

His use of cavalry in the Burmese jungle had unnerved the Japanese by its unadulterated lunacy and, combined with his name, had suggested a kamikaze element in the British army they had never suspected. Sir Cathcart had emerged from the campaign with twelve men and a reputation so scathed that he had been promoted to General to prevent the destruction of the entire army and the loss of India. Early retirement and his wartime experience of getting horses to attempt the impossible had encouraged Sir Cathcart to return to his first love and to take up training. His stables at Coft were world-famous. With what appeared to be a magical touch but owed in fact much to Skullion's gift for substitution, Sir Cathcart could transform a broken-winded nag into a winning two-year-old and had prospered accordingly. Coft Castle, standing in spacious grounds, was surrounded by a high wall to guard against intruding eyes and cameras and by an ornate garden in a remote corner of which was a small canning factory where the by-products of the General's stables were given discreet anonymity in Cathcart's Tinned Catfood. Skullion dismounted at the gate and knocked on the lodge door. A Japanese gardener, a prisoner of war, whom Sir Cathcart kept carefully ignorant of world news and who was, thanks to the language barrier, incapable of learning it for himself, opened the gate for him and Skullion cycled on down the drive to the house.

In spite of its name there was nothing remotely ancient about Coft Castle. Staunchly Edwardian, its red brick bespoke a lofty disregard for style and a concern for comfort on a grand scale. The General's Rolls-Royce, RIP 1, gleamed darkly on the gravel outside the front door. Skullion dismounted and pushed his bicycle round to the servants' entrance.

'Come to see the General,' he told the cook. Presently he was ushered into the drawing-room where Sir Cathcart was lolling in an armchair before a large coal fire.

'Not your usual afternoon, Skullion,' he said as Skullion came in, bowler hat in hand.

'No, sir. Came special,' said Skullion. The General waved him to a kitchen chair the cook brought in on these occasions and Skullion sat down and put his bowler hat on his knees.

'Carry on smoking,' Sir Cathcart told him. Skullion took out his pipe and filled it with black tobacco from a tin. Sir Cathcart watched him with grim affection.

'That's filthy stuff you smoke, Skullion,' he said as blue smoke drifted towards the chimney. 'Must have a constitution like an elephant to smoke it.'

Skullion puffed at his pipe contentedly. It was at moments like this, moments of informal subservience, that he felt happiest. Sitting smoking his pipe on the hard kitchen chair in Sir Cathcart D'Eath's drawing-room he felt approved. He basked in the General's genial disdain.

'That's a nice black eye you've got there,' Sir Cathcart said. 'You look as if you've been in the wars.'

'Yes, sir,' said Skullion. He was quite pleased with that black eye.

'Well, out with it, man, what have you come about?' Sir Cathcart said.

'It's the new Master. He made a speech at the Feast last night,' Skullion told him.

'A speech? At the Feast?' Sir Cathcart sat up in his chair.

'Yes, sir. I knew you wouldn't like it.'

'Disgraceful. What did he say?'

'Says he's going to change the College.'

Sir Cathcart's eyes bulged in his head. 'Change the College? What the devil does he mean by that? The damned place has been changed beyond all recognition already. Can't go in the place without seeing some long-haired lout looking more like a girl than a man. Swarming with bloody poofters. Change the College? There's only one change that's needed and that's back to the old ways. The old traditions. Cut their hair off and duck them in the fountain. That's what's needed. When I think what Porterhouse used to be and see what it's become, it makes my blood boil. It's the same with the whole damned country. Letting niggers in and keeping good white men out. Gone soft, that's what's happened. Soft in the head and soft in the body.' Sir Cathcart sank back in his chair limp from his denunciation of the times. Skullion smiled inwardly. It was just such bitterness he had come to hear. Sir Cathcart spoke with an authority Skullion could never have but which charged his own intransigence with a new vigour.

'Says he wants Porterhouse to be an open college,' he said, stoking the embers of the General's fury.

'Open college?' Sir Cathcart responded to the call. 'Open? What the devil does he mean by that? It's open enough already. Half the scum of the world in as it is.'

'I think he means more scholars,' Skullion said.

Sir Cathcart grew a shade more apoplectic.

'Scholars? That's half the trouble with the world today, scholarship. Too many damned intellectuals about who think they know how things should be done. Academics, bah! Can't win a war with thinking. Can't run a factory on thought. It needs guts and sweat and sheer hard work.

If I had my way I'd kick every damned scholar out of the College and put in some athletes to run the place properly. Anyone would think Varsity was some sort of school. In my day we didn't come up to learn anything, we came up to forget all the damned silly things we'd had pumped into us at school. My God, Skullion, I'll tell you this, a man can learn more between the thighs of a good woman than he ever needs to know. Scholarship's a waste of time and public money. What's more, it's iniquitous.' Exhausted by his outburst, Sir Cathcart stared belligerently into the fire.

'What's Fairbrother say?' he asked finally.

'The Dean, sir? He doesn't like it any more than you do, sir,' Skullion said, 'but he's not as young as he used to be, sir.'

'Don't suppose he is,' Sir Cathcart agreed.

'That's why I came to tell you, sir,' Skullion continued. 'I thought you'd know what to do.'

Sir Cathcart sniffed. 'Do? Don't see what I can do,' he said presently. 'I'll write to the Master, of course, but I've no influence in the College these days.'

'But you have outside, sir,' Skullion assured him.

'Well perhaps,' Sir Cathcart assented. 'All right I'll see what I can do. Keep me informed, Skullion.'

'Yes, sir. Thank you, sir.'

'Get Cook to give you some tea before you go,' Sir Cathcart told him and Skullion went out with his chair and took it back to the kitchen. Twenty minutes later he cycled off down the drive, spiritually resuscitated. Sir Cathcart would see there were no more changes. He had influence in high places. There was only one thing that puzzled Skullion as he rode home. Something Sir Cathcart had said about learning more between the thighs of a good woman than ... but Sir Cathcart had never married. Skullion wondered how an unmarried man got between the thighs of a good woman.

Zipser's interview with the Senior Tutor had left him with a sense of embarrassment that had unnerved him completely. His attempt to explain the nature of his compulsion had been fraught with difficulties. The Senior Tutor kept poking his little finger in his ear and wriggling it around and examining the end of it when he took it out while Zipser talked, as if he held some waxy deposit responsible for the flow of obscene information that was reaching his brain. When he finally accepted that his ears were not betraying him and that Zipser was in fact confessing to being attracted by his bedder, he had muttered something to the effect that the Chaplain would expect him for tea that afternoon and that, failing that, a good psychiatrist might help. Zipser had left miserably and had spent the early part of the afternoon in his room trying to concentrate on his thesis without success. The image of Mrs Biggs, a cross between a cherubim in menopause and booted succubus, kept intruding. Zipser turned for escape to a book of photographs of starving children in Nagaland but in spite of this mental flagellation Mrs Biggs prevailed. He tried Hermitsch on *Fall Out & the Andaman Islanders* and even *Sterilization, Vasectomy and Abortion* by Allard, but these holy writs all failed against the pervasive fantasy of the bedder. It was as if his social conscience, his concern for the plight of humanity at large, the universal and collective pity he felt for all mankind, had been breached in some unspeakably personal way by the inveterate triviality and egoism of Mrs Biggs. Zipser, whose life had been filled with a truly impersonal charity – he had spent holidays from school working for SOBB, the Save Our Black Brothers campaign – and whose third worldliness was impeccable, found himself suddenly the victim of a sexual idiosyncrasy which made a mockery of his universalism. In desperation he turned to *Syphilis, the Scourge of Colonialism*, and stared with horror at the pictures. In the past it had worked like a charm to quell incipient sexual desires while satisfying his craving for evidence of natural justice. The notion of the Conquistadores dying of the disease after raping South American Indians no longer had its old appeal now that Zipser himself was in the grip of a compulsive urge to rape Mrs Biggs. By the time it came for him to go to the Chaplain's rooms for tea, Zipser had exhausted the resources of his theology. So too, it seemed, had the Chaplain.

'Ah my boy,' the Chaplain boomed as Zipser negotiated the bric-à-brac that filled the Chaplain's sitting-room. 'So good of you to come. Do make yourself comfortable.' Zipser nudged past a gramophone with a paper-mâché horn, circumvented a brass-topped table with fretsawed legs, squeezed beneath the fronds of a castor-oil plant and finally sat down on a chair by the fire. The Chaplain scuttled backwards and forwards between his bathroom and the teatable muttering loudly to himself a liturgy of things to fetch. 'Teapot hot. Spoons. Milk jug. You do take milk?' 'Yes, thank you,' said Zipser. 'Good. Good. So many people take lemon, don't they? One always forgets these things. Teacosy. Sugar basin.' Zipser looked round the room for some indication of the Chaplain's interests but the welter of conflicting objects, like the addition of random numbers to a code, made interpretation impossible. Apart from senility the furnishings had so little in common that they seemed to indicate a wholly catholic taste.

'Crumpets,' said the Chaplain scurrying out of the bathroom. 'Just the thing. You toast them.' He speared a crumpet on the end of a toasting-fork and thrust the fork into Zipser's hand. Zipser poked the crumpet at the fire tentatively and felt once again that dissociation from reality that seemed so much a part of life in Cambridge. It was as if everyone in the College sought to parody himself, as if a parody of a parody could become itself a new reality. Behind him the Chaplain stumbled over a footrest and deposited a jar of honey with a boom on the brass-topped table. Zipser removed the crumpet, blackened on one side and ice cold on the other, and put it on a plate. He toasted another while the Chaplain tried to spread butter on the one he had half done. By the time they had finished Zipser's face was burning from the fire and his hands were sticky with a mixture of melted butter and honey. The Chaplain sat back in his chair and filled his pipe from a tobacco jar with the Porterhouse crest on it.

'Do help yourself, my dear boy,' said the Chaplain, pushing the jar towards him.

'I don't smoke.'

The Chaplain shook his head sadly. 'Everyone should smoke a pipe,' he said. 'Calms the nerves. Puts things in perspective. Couldn't do without mine.' He leant back, puffing vigorously. Zipser stared at him through a haze of smoke.

'Now then where were we?' he asked. Zipser tried to think. 'Ah yes, your little problem, that's right,' said the Chaplain finally. 'I knew there was something.'

Zipser stared into the fire resentfully.

'The Senior Tutor said something about it. I didn't gather very much but then I seldom do. Deafness, you know?'

Zipser nodded sympathetically.

'The affliction of the elderly. That and rheumatism. It's the damp, you know. Comes up from the river. Very unhealthy living so close to the Fens.' His pipe percolated gently. In the comparative silence Zipser tried to think what to say. The Chaplain's age and his evident physical disabilities made it difficult for Zipser to conceive that he could begin to understand the problem of Mrs Biggs.

'I really think there's been a misunderstanding,' he began hesitantly and stopped. It was evident from the look on the Chaplain's face that there was no understanding at all.

'You'll have to speak up,' the Chaplain boomed. 'I'm really quite deaf.'

'I can see that,' Zipser said. The Chaplain beamed at him.

'Don't hesitate to tell me,' he said. 'Nothing you say can shock me.'

'I'm not surprised,' Zipser said.

The Chaplain's smile remained insistently benevolent. 'I know what we'll do,' he said, hopping to his feet and reaching behind his chair. 'It's something I use for confession sometimes.' He emerged holding a loudhailer and handed it to Zipser. 'Press the trigger when you're going to speak.'

Zipser held the thing up to his mouth and stared at the Chaplain over the rim. 'I really don't think this is going to help,' he said finally. His words reverberated through the room and set the teapot rattling on the brass table.

'Of course it is,' shouted the Chaplain, 'I can hear perfectly.'

'I didn't mean that,' Zipser said desperately. The fronds of the castor-oil plant quivered ponderously. 'I meant I don't think it's going to help to talk about . . .' He left the dilemma of Mrs Biggs unspoken.

The Chaplain smiled in absolution and puffed his pipe vigorously. 'Many of the young men who come to see me,' he said, invisible in a cloud of smoke, 'suffer from feelings of guilt about masturbation.'

Zipser stared frantically at the smoke screen. 'Masturbation? Who said anything about masturbation?' he bawled into the loudhailer. It was apparent someone had. His words, hideously amplified, billowed forth from the room and across the Court outside. Several undergraduates by the fountain turned and stared up at the Chaplain's windows. Deafened by his own vociferousness, Zipser sat sweating with embarrassment.

'I understood from the Senior Tutor that you wanted to see me about a sexual problem,' the Chaplain shouted.

Zipser lowered the loudhailer. The thing clearly had disadvantages.

'I can assure you I don't masturbate,' he said.

The Chaplain looked at him incomprehendingly. 'You press the trigger when you want to speak,' he explained. Zipser nodded dumbly. The knowledge that to communicate with the Chaplain at all he had to announce his feelings for Mrs Biggs to the world at large presented him with a terrible dilemma made no less intolerable by the Chaplain's shouted replies.

'It often helps to get these things into the open,' the Chaplain assured him. Zipser had his doubts about that. Admissions of the sort he had to make broadcast through a loudhailer were not likely to be of any help at all. He might just as well go and propose to the wretched woman straightaway and be done with it. He sat with lowered head while the Chaplain boomed on.

'Don't forget that anything you tell me will be heard in the strictest

confidence,' he shouted. 'You need have no fears that it will go any
further.'

'Oh sure,' Zipser muttered. Outside in the Quad a small crowd of
undergraduates had gathered by the fountain to listen.

Half an hour later Zipser left the room, his demoralization quite
complete. At least he could congratulate himself that he had revealed
nothing of his true feelings and the Chaplain's kindly probings, his
tentative questions, had elicited no response. Zipser had sat silently
through a sexual catechism only bothering to shake his head when the
Chaplain broached particularly obscene topics. In the end he had listened
to a lyrical description of the advantages of au pair girls. It was obvious
that the Chaplain regarded foreign girls as outside the sexual canons of
the Church.

'So much less danger of a permanently unhappy involvement,' he had
shouted, 'and after all I often think that's what they come here for. Ships
that pass in the night and not on one's own doorstep you know.' He
paused and smiled at Zipser salaciously. 'We all have to sow our wild
oats at some time or other and it's much better to do it abroad. I've
often thought that's what Rupert Brooke had in mind in that line of his
about some corner of a foreign field. Mind you, one can hardly say that
he was particularly healthy, come to think of it, but there we are. That's
my advice to you, dear boy. Find a nice Swedish girl, I'm told they're
very good, and have a ball. I believe that's the modern idiom. Yes,
Swedes or French, depending on your taste. Spaniards are a bit difficult,
I'm told, and then again they tend to be rather hairy. Still, buggers can't
be choosers as dear old Sir Winston said at the queer's wedding. Ha, ha.'

Zipser staggered from the room. He knew now what muscular
Christianity meant. He went down the dark staircase and was about to
go out into the Court when he saw the group standing by the fountain.
Zipser turned and fled up the stairs and locked himself in the lavatory
on the top landing. He was still there an hour later when First Hall
began.

CHAPTER SIX

Sir Godber dined at home. He was still recovering from the gastric consequences of the Feast and in any case the Bursar's revelations had disinclined him to the company of the Fellows until he had formulated his plans more clearly. He had spent the afternoon considering various schemes for raising money and had made several telephone calls to financial friends in the City to ask their advice and to put up proposals of his own but without success. Blomberg's Bank had been prepared to endow several Research Fellowships in Accountancy but even Sir Godber doubted if such generosity would materially alter the intellectual climate of Porterhouse. He had even considered offering the American Phosgene Corp. facilities for research into nerve gas, facilities they had been denied by all American universities, in return for a really large endowment but he suspected that the resultant publicity and student protest would destroy his already tenuous liberal reputation. Publicity was much on his mind. At five o'clock the BBC phoned to ask if he would appear on a panel of leading educationalists to answer questions on financial priority in Education. Sir Godber was sorely tempted to agree but refused on the grounds that he had hardly acquired much experience. He put the phone down reluctantly and wondered what effect his announcement to several million viewers that Porterhouse College was in the habit of selling degrees to rich young layabouts would have had. It was a pleasing thought and gave rise in the Master's mind to an even more satisfying conclusion. He picked up the phone again and spoke to the Bursar.

'Could we arrange a College Council meeting for tomorrow afternoon? Say two-thirty?' he asked.

'It's rather short notice, Master,' the Bursar replied.

'Good. Two-thirty it is then,' Sir Godber said with iron geniality and replaced the receiver. He sat back and began to draw up a list of innovations. Candidates to be chosen by academic achievement only. The kitchen endowment to be cut by three-quarters and the funds reallocated to scholarships. Women undergraduates to be admitted as members. Gate hours abolished. College playing fields open to children from the town. Sir Godber's imagination raced on compiling proposals with no thought for the financial implications. They would have to find the money somewhere and he didn't much care where. The main thing was that he had the Fellows over a barrel. They might protest but there was nothing they could do to stop him. They had placed a weapon in his hands. He smiled to himself at the thought of their faces when he explained the alternatives tomorrow. At six-thirty he went through to the drawing-room where Lady Mary, who had been chairing a committee on Teenage Delinquency, was writing letters.

'Be with you in a minute,' she said when Sir Godber asked her if she would like a sherry. He looked at her dubiously. There were times when he wondered if his wife was ever with him. Her mind followed a wholly independent course and was ever concentrated on the more distressing aspects of other people's lives. Sir Godber poured himself a large whisky.

'Well, I think I've got them by the short hairs,' he said when she finally stopped tapping at her typewriter.

Lady Mary's lean tongue lubricated the flap of an envelope. 'Nonspecific urethritis is reaching epidemic proportions among school-leavers,' she said. Sir Godber ignored the interjection. He couldn't for the life of him see what it had to do with the College. He pursued his own topic. 'I'm going to show them that I'm not prepared to be a cipher.'

'Surveys show that one in every five children has ...'

'I haven't ended my career in politics only to be pushed into a sinecure,' Sir Godber contended.

'That's not the problem,' Lady Mary agreed.

'What isn't?' Sir Godber asked momentarily interested by her assertion.

'Cure. Easy enough. What we've got to get at is the moral delinquency ...'

Sir Godber drank his whisky and tried not to listen. There were times when he wondered if he would ever have succeeded as a politician without the help of his wife. Without her incessant preoccupation with unsavoury statistics and sordid social problems, late-night sittings in the House might have had less appeal and committees less utility. Would he have made so many passionate speeches or spoken with such urgency if Lady Mary had been prepared to listen to one word he said at home? He rather doubted it. They went into dinner and Sir Godber passed the time as usual by counting the number of times she said Must and Our Duty. The Musts won by fifty-four to forty-eight. Not bad for the course.

After he had heard the Chaplain go down to Hall, Zipser slipped out of the lavatory and went to his room. There was no sign of the little crowd of undergraduates who had been gathered in the Court when he first went down and he hoped no one would find out who had been talking, if that was the right word, to the Chaplain. The tendency he shared with the Master's wife to think in wholly impersonal terms about world issues had quite deserted him. During his hour in the lavatory he had taken the Chaplain's advice and had attempted to interpose the image of a Swedish girl between himself and Mrs Biggs. Every time Mrs Biggs intruded he concentrated on the slim buttocks and breasts of a Swedish actress he had seen once in *Playboy* and to some extent the practice had worked. Not entirely. The Swede tended to swell and to assume unnatural proportions until she was displaced by a smiling Mrs Biggs, but the series of little respites was encouraging and suggested that a substantial Swede might be even more effective. He would take the Chaplain's advice and find an au pair girl or a language student and ... and ... well ... and. Zipser's lack of sexual experience prevented him from formulating at all clearly what he would do then. Well, he would copulate with her. Having arrived at this neat if somewhat abstract conclusion he felt better. It was certainly preferable to raping Mrs Biggs, which seemed the only alternative. As usual Zipser had no doubts about rape. It was a brutal, violent act of assertive masculinity, a loosening of savage instinctual forces, passionate and bestial. He would hurl Mrs Biggs to the floor and thrust himself ... With an effort of will he dragged his imagination back from the scene and thought aseptically about copulating with a Swede.

A number of difficulties immediately presented themselves. First and foremost he knew no Swedes, and secondly he had never copulated with anyone. He knew a great many intense young women who shared his concern for the fate of mankind and who were prepared to talk about birth control into the early hours of the morning but they were all English and their preoccupation with mankind's problems had seemed to preclude any interest in him. In any case Zipser had scruples on aesthetic grounds about asking any of them to act as a substitute Mrs Biggs, and rather doubted their efficacy in the role. It would have to be a Swede. With the abstract calculation that was implicit in his whole approach Zipser decided that he would probably be able to find a promiscuous Swede in the Cellar Bar. He wrote it down and put as an alternative the Ali Baba Discothèque. That dealt with the first problem. He would fill her up with wine, Portuguese white would do, and bring her back to his room. All quite simple. With her cooperation the sexual spectre of Mrs Biggs would lose its force. He went to bed early having set the alarm for seven o'clock so as to be up and out before the bedder arrived – and before he fell asleep realized that he had forgotten an important detail. He would need some contraceptives. He'd go and have his hair cut in the morning and get some.

Skullion sat in front of the gas fire in the Porter's Lodge and smoked his pipe. His visit to Coft Castle had eased his mind. The General would use his influence to see that the Master didn't make any changes. You could rely on the General. One of the old brigade, and rich too. The sort that always gave you a big tip at the end of term. Skullion had had some big tips in his time and he had put them all away in his bank with the shares old Lord Wurford had left him in his will and had never touched them. He lived off his salary and what he earned on his night off as a steward at the Fox Club. There had been some big takings there too in his time; the Maharajah of Indpore had once given him fifty quid after a day at the races, when a tip from Sir Cathcart's stable-boy had paid off. Skullion considered the Maharahjah quite a gent, a compliment he paid to few Indians, but then a Maharahah wasn't a proper Indian, was he? Maharajahs were Princes of the Empire and as far as Skullion was concerned wogs in the Empire were quite different from wogs outside it and wogs in the Fox Club wasn't wogs at all or they wouldn't be members. The intricate system of social classification in Skullion's mind graded everyone. He could place a man within a hair's breadth in the social scale by the tone of his voice or even the look in his eye. Some people thought you could depend on the cut of a man's coat but Skullion knew better. It wasn't externals that mattered, it was something much more indefinable, an inner quality which Skullion couldn't explain but which he recognized immediately. And responded to. It had something to do with assurance, a certainty of oneself which nothing could shake. There were lots of intermediate stages between this ineffable superiority and the manifest inferiority of, say, the kitchen staff, but Skullion could sense them all and put them in the right place. There was money by itself, brash and full of itself but easily deflated. There was two-generation money with a bit of land. Usually a bit pompous, that was. There was County rich and poor. Skullion noted the distinction but tended to ignore it. Some of the best families had come down in the world and so long as the confidence was there, money didn't count, not in Skullion's eyes anyway. In fact confidence without money was preferable, it indicated a genuine quality and was accordingly revered. Then there were various degrees of uncertainty, nuances of self-doubt that went unnoticed by most people but which Skullion spotted immediately. Flickers of residual deference immediately suppressed – but too late to be missed by Skullion. Doctors' and lawyers' sons. Professional classes and treated respectfully. Still public school anyway, and graded from Eton and Winchester downwards. Below public school Skullion lost all interest, according only slight respect if there was money in it for him. But at the top of the scale above all these distinctions there was an assurance so ineffable that it seemed almost to merge into its opposite Real quality, Skullion called it, or even the old aristocracy to distinguish it from mere titular nobility. These were the saints of his calendar, the touchstone against which all other men were finally judged. Even Sir Cathcart was not of their number. In fact Skullion had to admit that he was fundamentally of the fourth rank, though near the top of it, and that was high praise considering how many ranks Skullion had in his mind. No, the real quality were without Sir Cathcart's harshness. There was often an unassuming quality about the saints which less perceptive porters than Skullion mistook for timidity and social insecurity but which he knew to be a sign of breeding, and not to be taken advantage of. It accorded his servility the highest accolade, this helplessness that was quite unforced, and gave him the sure knowledge that he was needed. Under the cover of that helplessness Skullion could have moved mountains, and frequently had to in the way of luggage and furniture, humping it up staircases and round corners and arranging it first here and then there while its owner, graciously indecisive, tried to make up what there was of his mind where it would look best. From such expeditions Skullion would emerge with a temporary lordliness as if touched by grace and would recall such services rendered in years to come with the feeling that he had been privileged to attend an almost spiritual occasion. In Skullion's social hagiography two names stood out as the epitome of the effeteness he worshipped, Lord Pimpole and Sir Launcelot Gutterby, and at moments of contemplation Skullion would repeat their names to himself like some repetitive prayer. He was in the process of this incantation and had reached his twentieth 'Pimpole and Gutterby' when the Lodge door opened and Arthur, who waited at High Table, came in.

'Evening, Arthur,' said Skullion condescendingly.

'Evening,' said Arthur.

'Going off home?' Skullion inquired.

'Got something for you,' Arthur told him, leaning confidentially over the counter.

Skullion looked up. Arthur's attendance at High table was a source of much of his information about the College. He rose and came over to the counter. 'Oh ah,' he said.

'They're in a tizz whizz tonight,' Arthur said. 'Proper tizz-whizz.'

'Go on,' said Skullion encouragingly.

'Bursar come in to dinner all flushed and flummoxy and the Dean's got them high spots on his cheeks he gets when his gander's up and the Tutor don't eat his soup. Not like him to turn up his soup,' Arthur said.

Skullion grunted his agreement. 'So I know something's up.' Arthur paused for effect. 'Know what it is?' he asked.

Skullion shook his head. 'No. What is it?' he said.

Arthur smiled. 'Master's called a College Council for tomorrow. The Bursar said it wasn't convenient and the Master said to call it just the same and they don't like it. They don't like it at all. Put them off their dinner it did, the new Master acting all uppity like that, telling them what to do just when they thought they'd got him where they wanted him. Bursar said he'd told the Master they hadn't got the money for all the changes he has in mind and the Master seemed to have taken it, but then he rings the Bursar up and tells him to call the meeting.'

'Can't call a College Council all of a sudden,' Skullion said, 'Council meets on the first Thursday of every month.'

'That's what the Dean said and the Tutor. But the Master wouldn't have it. Got to be tomorrow. Bursar rang him up and said Dean and Tutor wouldn't attend like they'd told him and Master said that was all right with him but that the meeting would be tomorrow whether they were there or not.' Arthur shook his head mournfully over the Master's wilfulness. 'It ain't right all this telling people what to do.'

Skullion scowled at him. 'The Master come to dinner?' he asked.

'No,' said Arthur, 'he don't stir from the Lodge. Just telephones his orders to the Bursar.' He glanced significantly at the switchboard in the corner. Skullion nodded pensively.

'So he's going ahead with his changes,' he said at last.

'And they thought they'd got him where they wanted him, eh?'

'That's what they said,' Arthur assured him. 'Bursar said he wasn't going to do nothing and then he suddenly calls the meeting.'

'What's the Dean say to all this?' Skullion asked.

'Says they've all got to stick together. Mind you, he didn't have much to say tonight. Too upset by the look of him. But that's what he's said before.'

'Don't suppose the Tutor agrees with him,' Skullion suggested.

'He do now. Didn't before but this being told to attend the meeting has got him on the raw. Don't like that at all, the Tutor don't.'

Skullion nodded. 'Ah well, that's something,' he said. 'It isn't like him to side with the Dean. Bursar agree?'

'Bursar says he does but you never can tell with him, can you?' Arthur said. 'He's a slippery sod, he is. One moment this, the next moment something else. You can't rely on him.'

'Got no bottom, the Bursar,' said Skullion, drawing on the language of the late Lord Wurford for his judgement.

'Ah, is that what it is?' Arthur said. He gathered up his coat. 'Got to be getting along now.'

Skullion saw him to the door. 'Thank you, Arthur,' he said. 'Very useful that is.'

'Glad to be of service,' Arthur said, 'besides I don't want any changes in the College any more than you do. Too old for changes, I am. Twenty-five years I've waited at High Table and fifteen years before that I was ...'

Skullion shut the door on old Arthur's reminiscences and went back to the fire. So the Master was going ahead with his plans. Well it wasn't a bad thing he'd ordered the College Council for tomorrow. It had got the Dean and the Senior Tutor to agree for the first time in years. That was something in itself. They had hated one another's guts for years, ever since the Dean had preached a sermon on the text, 'Many that are first shall be last', when the Tutor had first begun to coach the Porterhouse Boat. Skullion smiled to himself at the memory. The Tutor had come storming out of Chapel with his gown billowing behind him like the wrath of God and had worked the eight so hard they were past their peak by the time of the May Bumps. Porterhouse had been bumped three times that year and had lost the Head of the River. He'd never forgiven the Dean that sermon. Never agreed with him about anything since and now the Master had got their backs up. Well, it was an ill wind that blew no good. And anyway there was always Sir Cathcart in the wings to put his oar in if the Master went too far. Skullion went out and shut the gate and went to bed. Outside it was snowing again. Damp flakes flicked against the windows and ran in runnels of water down the panes. 'Pimpole and Gutterby,' murmured Skullion for the last time, and fell asleep.

Zipser slept fitfully and was awake before the alarm clock went off at seven. He dressed and made himself some coffee before going out and he was just cutting himself some bread in the gyp room when Mrs Biggs arrived.

'You're up early for a change,' she said, easing herself through the door of the tiny gyp room.

'What are you doing here now?' Zipser demanded belligerently. 'You shouldn't come till eight.'

Mrs Biggs, fulsome in a red mackintosh, smiled dreadfully. 'I can come any time I want to,' she said with quite unnecessary emphasis. Zipser needed no telling. He writhed against the sink and stared helplessly into the acres of her smile. Mrs Biggs unbuttoned her mac slowly with one hand like a gargantuan stripper and Zipser's eyes followed her down. Her breasts swarmed in her blouse as she slipped the mac over her shoulders. Zipser's eyes salivated over them.

'Here, help me with the arms,' Mrs Biggs said, wedging herself round so that she had her back to him. Zipser hesitated a moment and then, impelled by a fearful and uncontrollable urge, lunged forward.

'Here,' said Mrs Biggs somewhat surprised by the frenzy of his assistance and the unusual whinnying sounds Zipser was making, 'the arms I said. What do you think you're doing?' Zipser floundered in the folds of her mac unable to think at all let alone what he was doing. His mind was ablaze with overwhelming desire. As he thrust himself into the red inferno of Mrs Biggs's raincoat, the bedder hunched herself and then heaved. Zipser fell back against the sink and Mrs Biggs issued into the hall. Between them on the gyp-room floor, like the plastic afterbirth of some terrible delivery, the disputed raincoat slowly subsided.

'Goodness gracious me,' said Mrs Biggs recovering her composure, 'you want to be more careful. You might give people the wrong idea.'

Zipser huddled in the corner of the gyp room breathing heavily hoped desperately that Mrs Biggs didn't get the right idea.

'I'm sorry,' he mumbled, 'I must have slipped. Don't know what came over me.'

'Wonder you didn't come all over me,' Mrs Biggs said coarsely. 'Throwing yourself about like that.' She plummeted over and picked up the raincoat and, trailing it behind her like a bull fighter's cape, marched into the other room. Zipser stared at her boots with a fresh surge of longing and hurried downstairs. The need for a girl his own age to take his body off the bedder had become imperative. He had to do something to escape the temptation presented by Mrs Biggs's extensive charms or he would find himself before the Dean. Zipser could think of nothing worse than being sent down from Porterhouse for 'the attempted rape of a bedder'. Or only one thing. The successful accomplishment of rape. That would be a police-court matter. He would kill himself sooner than face that humiliation.

'Good morning, sir,' Skullion called out as he passed the Lodge.

'Good morning,' said Zipser and went out of the gate. He had over an hour to wait before the barbers' shops opened. He walked along the river to kill time and envied the ducks, sleeping on the banks, their uncomplicated existence.

Mrs Biggs tucked the sheets under the mattress of Zipser's bed with a practised hand and plumped his pillow with a mitigated force that was almost tender. She was feeling rather pleased with herself. It had been some years since Mr Biggs had passed on, consigned to an early grave by his wife's various appetites, and even longer since anyone had paid her the compliment of finding her attractive. Zipser's clumsy advances had not escaped her attention. The fact that he followed her about from room to room as she worked and that his eyes were seldom off her were signs too obvious to be ignored. 'Poor boy misses his mum,' she had thought at first and had noted Zipser's solitariness as an indication of homesickness. But his recent behaviour had suggested less remote causes for his interest. The bedder's fancy ignored the weather and lumbered to thoughts of love. 'Don't be silly,' she told herself. 'What would he see in you?' But the notion remained and Mrs Biggs' sense of propriety began to adapt itself to the incongruities of the situation. She had begun to dress accordingly and to pay more attention to her looks and even, as she went from room to room and bed to bed, to indulge her imagination a little. The episode in the gyp room had confirmed her best suspicions. 'Fancy now,' she said to herself, 'and him such a nice young fellow too. Who'd have guessed?' She looked at herself in the mirror and primped her hair with a heavy hand.

At nine-fifteen Zipser took his seat in the barber's chair.

'Just a trim,' he told the barber.

The man looked at his head doubtfully.

'Wouldn't like a nice short back and sides, I don't suppose?' he asked mournfully.

'Just a trim, thank you,' Zipser told him.

The barber tucked the sheet into his collar. 'Don't know why some of you young fellows bother to have your hair cut at all,' he said. 'Seem determined to put us out of business.'

'I'm sure you still get lots of work,' Zipser said.

The barber's scissor clicked busily round his ears. Zipser stared at himself in the mirror and wondered once again at the disparity between his innocent apperance and the terrible passion which surged inside him. His eyes moved sideways to the rows of bottles, Eau de Portugal, Dr Linthrop's Dandruff Mixture, Vitalis, a jar of Pomade. Who on earth used Pomade? Behind him the barber was chattering on about football but Zipser wasn't listening. He was eyeing the glass case to his left where a box in one corner suggested the reason for his haircut. He couldn't move his head so that he wasn't sure what the box contained but it looked the right sort of box. Finally when the man moved forward to pick up the clippers Zipser turned his head and saw that he had been eyeing with quite pointless interest a box of razor blades. He turned his head further and scanned the shelves. Shaving creams, razors, lotions, combs, all were there in abundance but not a single carton of contraceptives.

Zipser sat on in a trance while the clippers buzzed on his neck. They must keep the damned things somewhere. Every hairdresser had them. His face in the mirror assumed a new uncertainty. By the time the barber had finished and was powdering his neck and waving a handmirror behind him, Zipser was in no mood to be critical of the result. He got out of the chair and waved the barber's brush away impatiently.

'That'll be thirty pence, sir,' the barber said, and made out a ticket. Zipser dug into his pocket for the money. 'Is there anything else?' Now was the moment he had been waiting for. The open invitation. That 'anything else' of the barber had covered only too literally a multitude of sins. In Zipser's case it was hopelessly inadequate not to say misleading.

'I'll have five packets of Durex,' Zipser said with a strangled bellow.

'Afraid we can't help you,' said the man. 'Landlord's a Catholic. It's in the lease we're not allowed to stock them.'

Zipser paid and went out into the street, cursing himself for not having looked in the window to see if there were any contraceptives on display. He walked into Rose Crescent and stared into a chemist's shop but the place was full of women. He tried three more shops only to find that they were all either full of housewives or that the shop assistants were young females. Finally he went into a barber's shop in Sidney Street where the window display was sufficiently broad-minded.

Two chairs were occupied and Zipser stood uncertainly just inside the door waiting for the barber to attend to him. As he stood there the door behind him opened and someone came in. Zipser stepped to one side and found himself looking into the face of Mr Turton, his supervisor.

'Ah, Zipser, getting your hair cut?' It seemed an unnecessarily inquisitive remark to Zipser. He felt inclined to tell the wretched man to mind his own busines. Instead he nodded dumbly and sat down.

'Next one,' said the barber. Zipser feigned politeness.

'Won't you ...?' he said to Mr Turton.

'Your need is greater than mine, my dear fellow,' the supervisor said and sat down and picked up a copy of *Titbits*. For the second time that morning Zipser found himself in a barber's chair.

'Any particular way?' the barber asked.

'Just a trim,' said Zipser.

The barber bellied the sheet out over his knees and tucked it into his collar.

'If you don't mind my saying so, sir,' he said, 'but I'd say you'd already had your hair cut this morning.'

Zipser, staring into the mirror, saw Mr Turton look up and his own face turn bright red.

'Certainly not,' he muttered. 'What on earth makes you think that?' It was not a wise remark and Zipser regretted it before he had finished mumbling.

'Well, for one thing,' the barber went on, responding to this challenge to his powers of observation, 'you've still got powder on your neck.' Zipser said shortly that he'd had a bath and used talcum powder.

'Oh quite,' said the barber sarcastically, 'and I suppose all these clipper shavings ...'

'Listen,' said Zipser conscious that Mr Turton has still not turned back to *Titbits* and was listening with interest, 'if you don't want to cut my hair ...' The buzz of the clippers interrupted his protest. Zipser stared angrily at his reflection in the mirror and wondered why he was being dogged by embarrassing situations. Mr Turton was eyeing the back of his head with a new interest.

'I mean,' said the barber putting his clippers away, 'some people like having their hair cut.' He winked at Mr Turton and in the mirror Zipser saw that wink. The scissors clicked round his ears and Zipser shut his eyes to escape the reproach he saw in them in the mirror. Everything he did now seemed tinged with catastrophe. Why in God's name should he fall in love with an enormous bedder? Why couldn't he just get on with his work, read in the library, write his thesis and go to meetings of CUNA?

'Had a customer once,' continued the barber remorselessly, 'who used to have his hair cut three times a week. Mondays, Wednesdays and Fridays. Regular as clockwork. I asked him once, when he'd been coming for a couple of years mind you, I said to him, "Tell me, Mr Hattersley, why do you come and have your hair cut so often?" Know what he said? Said it was the one place he could think. Said he got all his best ideas in the barber's chair. Weird when you think about it. Here I stand all day clipping and cutting and right in front of me, under my hand you might say, there's all those thoughts going on unbeknown to me. I mean I must have cut the hair on over a hundred thousand heads in my time. I've been cutting hair for twenty-five years now and that's a lot of customers. Stands to reason some of them must have been having some pretty peculiar thoughts at the time. Murderers and sex maniacs I daresay. I mean there would be, wouldn't there in all that number? Stands to reason.'

Zipser shrank in the chair. Mr Turton had lost all interest in *Titbits* now.

'Interesting theory,' he said encouragingly. 'I suppose statistically you're right. I've never thought of it that way before.'

Zipser said it took all sorts to make a world. It seemed the sort of trite remark the occasion demanded. By the time the barber had finished, he had given up all thought of asking for contraceptives. He paid the thirty pence and staggered out of the shop. Mr Turton smiled and took his place in the chair.

It was almost lunchtime.

CHAPTER SEVEN

'I think we can dispense with formalities,' the Master said sitting forward in his chair and looking down the long mahogany table. On his left the Bursar fiddled with his pen while on his right the Chaplain, accorded this position by virtue of his deafness, nodded his agreement. Down the long table the faces of the Council reflected their displeasure at this sudden meeting.

'It would appear to me,' said the Dean, 'that we have already dispensed with such formalities as we are used to. I can see no virtue in ridding ourselves of the few that are left.'

The Master regarded him closely. 'Bear with me, Dean,' he said, aware that he was relapsing from his carefully rehearsed down-to-earth manner into the vernacular of academic bitchiness. He pulled himself up. 'I have called this meeting,' he continued with a nasty smile, 'to discuss in detail the changes in the College I mentioned in my speech on Tuesday night. I shan't keep you long. When I have finished you can go away and think about my suggestions.' A ripple of indignation at the effrontery of his remark ran round the table. The Dean in particular lost his cool.

'The Master seems to be under some misapprehension as to the purpose of the College Council,' he said. 'May I remind him that it is the governing body of the College. We have been summoned here this afternoon at short notice and we have come at considerable inconvenience to ourselves . . .' The Master yawned. 'Quite so. Quite so,' he murmured. The Dean's face turned a deeper shade of puce. A virtuoso in the art of the discourteous aside, he had never been subjected to such disrespect.

'I think,' said the Senior Tutor stepping into the breach, 'that it should be left to the Council to decide whether or not the Master's proposals merit discussion this afternoon.' He smiled unctuously at the Master.

'As you wish,' said Sir Godber. He looked at his watch. 'I shall be here until three. If after that you have things you wish to discuss, you will have to do so without me.' He paused. 'We can meet again tomorrow or the next day. I shall be available in the afternoon.'

He looked down the table at the suffused faces of the Fellows and felt satisfied. The atmosphere was just what he had wanted for the announcement of his plans. They would react predictably and with a violence that would disarm them. Then when it would appear to be all over he would nullify all their protests with a threat. It was a charming prospect made all the more pleasing by the knowledge that they would misinterpret his motives. They would, they would. Obtuse men, small men for whom Porterhouse was the world and Cambridge the universe. Sir Godber despised them, and it showed.

'If we are all agreed then,' he continued, ignoring the titubation of the Dean who had been nerving himself to protest at the Master's incivility and leave the meeting, 'let me outline the changes I have in mind. In the first place, as you are all aware, Porterhouse's reputation has declined sadly since ... I believe the rot set in in 1933. I have been told there was a poor intake of Fellows in that year. Correct me if I'm wrong.'

It was the turn of the Senior Tutor to stiffen in his seat. 1933 had been the year of his election.

'Academically our decline seems to have set in then. The quality of our undergraduates has always seemed to me to be quite deplorable. I intend to change all that. From now on, from this year of Grace, we shall accept candidates who possess academic qualifications alone.' He paused to allow the information to sink in. When the Bursar ceased twitching in his chair, he continued. 'That is my first point. The second is to announce that the College will become a co-educational institution from the beginning of the forthcoming academic year. Yes, gentlemen, from the beginning of next year there will be women living in Porterhouse.' A gasp, almost a belch of shock, broke from the Fellows. The Dean buried his face in his hands and the Senior Tutor put both his hands on the edge of the table to steady himself. Only the Chaplain spoke.

'I heard that,' he bellowed, his face radiant as if with divine revelation, 'I heard it. Splendid news. Not before time either.' He relapsed into silence. The Master beamed. 'I accept your approval, Chaplain,' he said, 'with thanks. It is good to know that I have support from such an unexpected quarter. Thirdly ...'

'I protest,' shouted the Senior Tutor, half rising to his feet. Sir Godber cut him short.

'Later,' he snapped and the Senior Tutor dropped back into his seat. 'Thirdly, the practice of dining in Hall will be abandoned. A self-service canteen run by an outside catering firm will be established in the Hall. There will be no High Table. All forms of academic segregation will disappear. Yes Dean . . . ?'

But the Dean was speechless. His face livid and congested he had started to protest only to slump in his chair. The Senior Tutor hurried to his side while the Chaplain, always alert to the possibilities provided by a stricken audience, bellowed words of comfort into the insensible Dean's ear. Only the Master remained unmoved.

'Not, I trust, another Porterhouse Blue,' he said audibly to the Bursar, and looked at his watch, with calculated unconcern. To the Dean Sir Godber's manifest lack of interest in his demise came as a stimulant. His face grew pale and his breathing less sibilant. He opened his eyes and stared with loathing down the table at the Master.

'As I was saying,' continued Sir Godber, picking up the threads of his speech, 'the measures I have proposed will transform Porterhouse at a stroke.' He paused and smiled at the appositeness of the phrase. The Fellows stared at this fresh evidence of gaucherie. Even the Chaplain, imbued with the spirit of goodwill and deaf to the world's wickedness, was appalled by the Master's sang-froid.

'Porterhouse will regain its rightful place in the forefront of colleges,' the Master went on in a manner now recognizably political. 'No longer will we stumble on hamstrung by the obsolescence of outmoded tradition and class prejudice, by the limitations of the past and the cynicism of the present, but inspired by confidence in the future we shall prove ourselves worthy of the great trust that has been bequeathed us.' He sat down, inspired by his own brief eloquence. It was clear that nobody else present shared his enthusiasm for the future. When at last someone spoke it was the Bursar.

'There do appear to be one or two problems involved in this . . . er . . . transformation,' he pointed out. 'Not insuperable, I daresay, but nevertheless worth mentioning before we all become too enthusiastic.'

The Master surfaced from his reverie. 'Such as?' he said shortly.

The Bursar pursed his lips. 'Quite apart from the foreseeable difficulties of getting this . . . er . . . legislation accepted by the Council, I use the term advisedly you understand, there is the question of finance to consider. We are not a rich college . . .' He hesitated. The Master had raised an eyebrow.

'I am not unused to the argument,' he said urbanely. 'In a long career in government I had heard it put forward on too many occasions to be wholly convinced that the plea of poverty is as formidable as it sounds. It is precisely the rich who use it most frequently.'

The Bursar was driven to interrupt. 'I can assure you ...' he began but the Master overrode him.

'I can only invoke the psalmist and say Cast thy bread upon the waters.'

'Not to be taken literally,' snapped the Senior Tutor.

'To be taken how you wish,' Sir Godber snapped back. The members of the Council stared at him with open belligerence.

'It is precisely that we have no bread to throw,' said the Bursar, trying to pour oil on troubled waters.

The Senior Tutor ignored his efforts. 'May I remind you,' he snarled at the Master, 'that this Council is the governing body of the College and ...'

'The Dean reminded me earlier in the meeting,' the Master interrupted.

'I was about to say that policy decisions affecting the running of the College are taken by the Council as a whole,' continued the Senior Tutor. 'I should like to make it quite clear that I for one have no intention of accepting the changes outlined in the proposals that the Master has submitted to us. I think I can speak for the Dean,' he glanced at the speechless Dean before continuing, 'when I say we are both adamantly opposed to any changes in College policy.' He sat back. There were murmurs of agreement from the other Fellows. The Master leant forward and looked round the table.

'Am I to understand that the Senior Tutor has expressed the general feelings of the meeting?' he asked. There was a nodding of heads round the table. The Master looked crestfallen.

'In that case, gentlemen, there is little I can say,' he said sadly. 'In the face of your opposition to the changes in College policy that I have proposed, I have little choice but to resign the Mastership of Porterhouse.' A gasp came from the Fellows as the Master rose and gathered his notes. 'I shall announce my resignation in a letter to the Prime Minister, an open letter, gentlemen, in which I shall state the reasons for my resignation, namely that I am unable to continue as Master of a college that augments its financial resources by admitting candidates without academic qualifications in return for large donations to the Endowment Subscription Fund and selling degrees.' The Master paused and looked at the Fellows who sat stunned by his announcement. 'When I was nominated by the Prime Minister, I had no idea that I was accepting the Mastership of an academic auction-room nor that I was ending a career marked, I am proud to say, by the utmost adherence to the rules of probity in public life by becoming an accessory to a financial scandal of national proportions. I have the facts and figures here, gentlemen, and I shall include them in my letter to the Prime Minister, who will doubtless pass them on to the Director of Public Prosecutions. Good afternoon, gentlemen.'

The Master turned and stalked out of the room. Behind him the Fellows of Porterhouse sat rigid like embalmed figures round the table, each absorbed in calculating his own complicity in a scandal that must bring ruin to them all. It took little imagination to foresee the public outcry that would follow Sir Godber's resignation and the publication of his open letter, the wave of indignation that would sweep the country, the execrations that would fall on their heads from the other colleges in Cambridge, the denunciations of the other, newer universities. The Fellows of Porterhouse had little imagination but they could foresee all this and more, the demand for public accountability, possibly even prosecutions, even perhaps an inquiry into the sources and size of College funds. What would Trinity and King's say to that? The Fellows of Porterhouse knew the odium they could expect for having precipitated a public inquiry that could put, would put, in jeopardy the vast wealth of the other colleges and they shrank from the prospect. It was the Dean who first broke the silence with a strangled cry.

'He must be stopped,' he gurgled.

The Senior Tutor nodded sympathetically. 'We have little alternative.'

'But how?' demanded the Bursar, who was desperately trying to banish from his mind the knowledge that he had inadvertently provided the Master with the information he was now threatening to disclose. If the other Fellows should ever learn who had provided Sir Godber with this material for blackmail his life in College would not be worth living.

'At all costs the Master must be persuaded to stay on,' said the Senior Tutor. 'We simply cannot afford the scandal that would ensue from the publication of his letter of resignation.'

The Praelector looked at him vindictively. 'We?' he asked. 'I beg not to be included in the list of those responsible for this disgraceful disclosure.'

'And what precisely do you mean by that?' asked the Senior Tutor.

'I should have thought that it was obvious,' said the Praelector. 'Most of us have had nothing to do with the administration of College finances nor with the admissions procedure. We cannot be held responsible for ...'

'We are all responsible for College policy,' shouted the Senior Tutor.

'You are responsible for admissions,' the Praelector shouted back. 'You are responsible for the choice of candidates. You are ...'

'Gentlemen,' the Bursar interposed, 'let us not bicker about individual responsibilities. We are all responsible as members of the Council for the running of the College.'

'Some of us are more responsible than others,' the Praelector pointed out.

'And we shall all share the blame for the mistakes that have been made in the past,' continued the Bursar.

'Mistakes? Who said anything about mistakes?' demanded the Dean breathlessly.

'I think that in the light of the Master's ...' began the Senior Tutor.

'Damn the Master,' the Dean snarled, struggling to his feet. 'Damn the man. Let us stop talking about mistakes. I said he must be stopped. I didn't say we had to surrender to the swine.' He waddled to the head of the table, portly, belligerent and stubborn, like some crimson toad and with all that creature's resilience to the challenges of climate. The Senior Tutor hesitated in the face of his colleague's revitalized obstinacy. 'But ...' he began. The Dean raised a hand for silence.

'He must be stopped,' he said. 'For the time being perhaps we must accept his proposals, but for the time being only. In the short run we must use the tactics of delay, but only in the short run.'

'And then?' the Senior Tutor asked.

'We must buy time,' continued the Dean. 'Time to bring influence to bear upon Sir Godber and time to subject his own career to the scrutiny he has seen fit to apply to the customs and traditions of the College. No man who has spent as long as Sir Godber Evans in public life is wholly without fault. It is our business to discover the extent of his weaknesses.'

'Are you saying that we should ...' the Praelector began.

'I am saying that the Master is vulnerable,' the Dean went on, 'that he is corrupt and that he is open to influence from the powers that be. The tactics he has used this afternoon, tactics of blackmail, are a symptom of the corruption I am referring to. And let us not forget that we have powerful friends.'

The Senior Tutor pursed his lips and nodded. 'True. Very true, Dean.'

'Yes, Porterhouse can justly claim its share of eminent men. The Master may dismiss our protests but we have powerful allies,' said the Dean.

'And in the meantime we must eat humble pie and ask the Master to reconsider his resignation in the light of our acceptance of the changes he has proposed?' said the Senior Tutor.

'Precisely.' The Dean looked round the table at the Fellows for a sign of hesitancy. 'Has anyone here any doubts as to the wisdom of the course I have proposed?' he asked.

'We seem to be left with little choice,' said the Bursar.

'We have no choice at all,' the Dean told him.

'And if the Master refuses to withdraw his resignation?' the Praelector asked.

'There is no possible reason why he should,' the Dean said. 'I propose that we go now in a body to the Master's Lodge and ask him to reconsider.'

'In a body? Is that really wise? Wouldn't it look ... rather ... well ... obsequious?' the Senior Tutor asked doubtfully.

'I don't think this is any time to be thinking about appearances,' said the Dean. 'I am only concerned with results. Humble pie, you said yourself. Very well, if Sir Godber requires humble pie to retract his threat he shall have it. I shall see to it that he eats it himself later on. Besides I should not like him to think that we are in any way divided.' He stared fiercely at the Bursar. 'At a time of crisis it is vital that we present a united front. Don't you agree, Bursar?'

'Oh yes. Absolutely, Dean,' the Bursar assured him.

'Very well, let us go,' said the Dean and led the way out of the Council Chamber. The Fellows trooped after him into the cold.

Skullion listened to their footsteps on the floor above his head and climbed off the chair he had been standing on. It was hot in the boiler-room, hot and dusty, a dry heat that had irritated his nose and made it difficult not to sneeze while he stood on the chair with his ear pressed to a pipe listening to the voices raised in anger in the Council Chamber. He brushed the dust off his sleeve and spread an old newspaper on the seat of the chair and sat down. It wouldn't do to be seen coming out of the boiler-room just yet and besides he wanted to think.

The central heating system wasn't the best conductor of conversations in the world, it tended to parenthesize its own gurgles at important moments, but Skullion had heard enough to startle him. The Master's threat to resign he had greeted with delight, only to feel the sting in its tail with an alarm that equalled that of the Fellows. His thoughts flew to his Scholars and the threat that public exposure of the sort Sir Godber was proposing would do to them. Sir Cathcart must hear this new danger at once – but then the Dean had proposed his own solution and Skullion's heart had warmed to the old man. 'There's life in the old Dean yet,' he said to himself and chuckled at the thought of Sir Godber retracting his resignation only to find that he had been outsmarted. Powerful allies, the Dean had said and Skullion wondered if the old man knew just how powerful some of those allies were, or what a threat the Master's disclosure would pose to them. Cabinet ministers ranked among Skullion's Scholars, cabinet ministers, civil servants, directors of the Bank of England, eminent men indeed. It began to dawn on Skullion that the Master was in a stronger position than he knew. A public inquiry into the academic antecedents of so many public figures would have appalling consequences, and the powerful allies the Dean evidently had in mind were hardly likely to put up more than token opposition to the changes at Porterhouse the Master wanted, if the alternative was a national scandal in which they would figure so prominently. The Dean was barking up the wrong tree after all, and Skullion's premature optimism gave way to a deep melancholy. At this rate there would be women in Porterhouse before the year was out. It was a prospect that infuriated him. 'Over my dead body,' he muttered darkly, and pondered ways and means of frustrating Sir Godber.

CHAPTER EIGHT

Zipser was drunk. Eight pints of bitter, each drunk in a different pub, had changed his outlook on life. The narrow confines of his compulsion had given way to a brighter, broader, more expansive frame of mind. True, his haircuts had left him shorn and practically bald and with an aversion for the company of barbers which would last him a lifetime, but his eyes sparkled, his cheeks had a ruddier, rosier look, and he was in a mood to run the gauntlet of a hundred middle-aged housewives and to face the disapproval of as many chemists in search of an immaculate misconception. In any case a flash of inspiration had robbed him of the need to publicize his requirements. As he had wandered up Sidney Street after his second haircut he had suddenly recalled having seen a contraceptive dispenser in the lavatory of a pub in Bermondsey, and while Bermondsey was rather too far to go in search of a discreet anonymity, it occurred to him that Cambridge pubs must surely offer a similarly sophisticated service for lovers caught as it were on the hop. Zipser's spirits rose with the thought. He went into the first pub he came to and ordered a pint. Ten minutes later he left that pub empty-handed and found another only to be similarly disappointed. By the time he had been to six pubs and had drunk six pints of bitter he was in a mood to point out the deficiency of their service to the bartenders. At the seventh pub he struck gold. Waiting until two elderly men had finished a protracted pee Zipser fumbled with his change and put two coins into the machine. He was about to pull the handle when an undergraduate came in. Zipser went out and finished his seventh pint keeping an eagle eye on the door of the Gents. Two minutes later he was back and tugging at the handle. Nothing happened. He pulled and pushed but the dispenser refused to dispense. He peered into the Money Returned slot and found it empty. Finally he put two more coins in and pulled the handle again. This time his money dropped into the slot and Zipser took it out and looked at it. The damned dispenser was empty. Zipser went back to the bar and ordered an eighth pint.

'That machine in the toilet,' he said conspiratorially to the barman.

'What about it?' the barman asked.

'It's empty,' said Zipser.

'That's right,' said the barman. 'It's always empty.'

'Well, it's got some of my money in it.'

'You don't say.'

'I do say.'

'A gin and tonic,' said a man with a moustache next to Zipser.

'Coming up,' said the barman. Zipser sipped his pint while the barman poured a gin and tonic. Finally when the man with the moustache had taken his drink back to a table by the window, Zipser raised the subject of faulty dispensers again. He was beginning to feel distinctly belligerent.

'What are you going to do about my money?' he asked.

The barman looked at him warily.

'How do I know you put any in?' he asked. 'How do I know you're not just trying it on?'

Zipser considered the question.

'I don't see how I can,' he said finally. 'I haven't got it.'

'Very funny,' said the barman. 'If you've got any complaints to make about that dispenser, you take them to the suppliers.' He reached under the bar and produced a card and handed it to Zipser. 'You go and tell them your problems. They stock the machines. I don't. All right?' Zipser nodded and the man went off down the other end of the counter to serve a customer. Zipser left the pub with the card and went down the road. He found the suppliers in Mill Road. There was a young man with a beard behind the counter. Zipser went in and put the card down in front of him.

'I've come from the Unicorn,' he said. 'The dispenser is empty.'

'What already?' the man said. 'Don't know what happens to them, they go so quickly.'

'I want . . .' Zipser began thickly but the young man had disappeared through a door to the back. Zipser was beginning to feel distinctly light-headed. He tried to think what he was doing discussing wholesale contraceptive sales with a young man with a beard in an office in Mill Road.

'Here you are. Two gross. Sign here,' said the clerk reappearing from the back with two cartons which he plonked on the counter. Zipser stared at the cartons, and was about to explain that he had merely come to ask for his money back when a woman came in. Zipser suddenly felt sick. He picked up the ballpen and signed the slip and then, clutching the two cartons, stumbled from the shop.

By the time he got back to the Unicorn the pub was shut. Zipser tried knocking on the door without result and finally gave it up and went back to Porterhouse.

He weaved his way past the Porter's Lodge and headed across the Court towards his staircase. Ahead of him a line of black figures emerged from the door of the Council Chamber in solemn processional and moved towards him. At the head of them waddled the Dean. Zipser hiccupped and tried to focus on them. It was very difficult. Almost as difficult as trying to stop the world going around. Zipser hiccupped again and was sick on the snow as the column of figures advanced on him.

'Beg your pardon,' he said. 'Shouldn't have done that. Had too much to drink.'

The column stopped and Zipser peered down into the Dean's face. It kept going in and out of focus alarmingly.

'Do you . . . do you . . . know how red your face is?' he asked, waving his head erratically at the Dean. 'Shouldn't have a red face, should you?'

'Out of the way,' snapped the Dean.

'Shertainly,' said Zipser and sat down in the snow. The Dean loomed over him menacingly.

'You, sir, are drunk. Disgustingly drunk,' he said.

'Quite right,' said Zipser. 'Full marks for perspic . . . perspicac . . . ity. Hit the nail on the head firsht time.'

'What is your name?'

'Zhipsher shir, Zhipsher.'

'You're gated for a week, Zipser,' snarled the Dean.

'Yesh,' said Zipser happily, 'I am gated for a week. Shertainly, shir.' He struggled to his feet, still clutching his cartons, and the column of dons moved on across the Court. Zipser wobbled off to his room and collapsed on the floor.

*

Sir Godber watched the deputation of Fellows from his study window. 'Canosssa,' he thought to himself as the procession trudged through the snow to the front door and rang the bell. For a moment it crossed his mind to let them wait but better judgement prevailed. Pope Gregory's triumph had after all been a temporary one. He went out into the hall and let them in.

'Well, gentlemen,' he said when they had filed into his study, 'and what can I do for you now?'

The Dean shuffled forward. 'We have reconsidered our decision, Master,' he said.

Behind him the members of the College Council nodded obediently. Sir Godber looked round their faces and was satisfied. 'You wish me to remain as Master?'

'Yes, Master,' the Dean said.

'And this is the general wish of the Council?'

'It is.'

'And you accept the changes in the College that I have proposed without any reservations?' the Master asked.

The Dean mustered a smile. 'Naturally, we have reservations,' he said. 'It would be asking rather much to expect us to abandon our ... er ... principles without retaining the right to have private reservations, but in the interest of the College as a whole we accept that there may be a need for compromise.'

'My conditions are final,' said the Master. 'They must be accepted as they stand. I am not prepared to attenuate them. I think I should make that plain.'

'Quite so, Master. Quite so.' The Dean smiled weakly.

'In that case I shall postpone my decision,' said Sir Godber, 'until the next meeting of the College Council. That will give us all time to consider the matter at our leisure. Shall we say next Wednesday at the same time?'

'As you wish, Master,' said the Dean. 'As you wish.'

They trooped out and Sir Godber, having seen them to the door, stood at the window watching the dark procession disappear into the winter evening with a new sense of satisfaction. 'The iron fist in the iron glove,' he murmured to himself, conscious that for the first time in a long career of political manoeuvring and compromise he had at long last achieved a clear-cut victory over an apparently intransigent opposition. There had been no doubting the Fellows' obeisance. They had crawled to him and Sir Godber indulged himself in the recollection before going on to consider the implications of their surrender. No one – and who should know better than Sir Godber – crawled quite so submissively without good reasons.

The Fellows' obeisance had been too complete to be without ulterior motive. It was not enough to suppose that his threat had been utter. It had been sufficient to force them to come to heel but there had been no need for the Dean, of all people, to wag his tail so obsequiously. Sir Godber sat down by the fire and considered the character of the Dean for a hint of his motive. And the more he thought the less cause he found for premature self-congratulation. Sir Godber did not underestimate the Dean. The man was an ignorant bigot, with all the persistence of bigotry and all the cunning of the ignorant. 'Buying time,' he thought shrewdly, 'but time for what?' It was an unpleasant notion. Not for the first time since his arrival at Porterhouse, Sir Godber felt uneasy, aware, if only subliminally, that the facile assumptions about human nature upon which his liberal ideals were founded were somehow threatened by a devious scholasticism whose origins were less rational and more obscure than he preferred to think. He got up and stared out into the night at the medieval buildings of the College silhouetted against the orange sky. It had begun to snow again and the wind had risen, blowing the snowflakes hither and thither in sudden ungovernable flurries. He pulled the curtains to shut out the sight of nature's lack of symmetry and settled himself in his chair with his favourite author, Bentham.

At High Table the Fellows dined in moody silence. Even the Chef's poached salmon failed to raise their spirits, dampened by the obduracy of the Master and the memory of their capitulation. Only the Dean remained undaunted, shovelling food into his mouth as if to fuel his determination and mouthing imprecations on Sir Godber simultaneously, his forehead greasy and his eyes bright with the cunning Sir Godber had recognized.

In the Combination Room, as they took their coffee, the Senior Tutor broached the topic of their next move. 'It would appear that we have until Wednesday to circumvent the Master's proposals,' he said, sipping brandy fastidiously.

'A relatively short time, if you don't mind my saying so.'

'Short but enough,' said the Dean tersely.

'I must say I find your confidence a little surprising, Dean,' said the Bursar nervously.

The Dean looked at him with a sudden ferocity. 'No more surprising than I find your lack of discretion, Bursar,' he snapped. 'I hardly imagine that this unfortunate turn of events would have occurred without your disclosure of the financial state of the College.'

The Bursar reddened. 'I was simply trying to point out to the Master that the changes he was proposing would place an intolerable strain on our resources,' he protested. 'If my memory serves me right you were the first to suggest that the finances should be brought to his attention.'

'Certainly I suggested that. I didn't however suggest that he should be made privy to the details of our admissions policy,' the Dean retorted.

'Gentlemen,' said the Senior Tutor, 'the mistake has been made. Nothing is to be gained by post-mortem. We are faced by an urgent problem. It is not in our best interest to apportion blame for past mistakes. If it comes to that we are all culpable. Without the divisions that prevented the election of Dr Siblington as Master, we should have avoided the nomination of Sir Godber.'

The Dean finished his coffee. 'There is some truth in that,' he admitted, 'and a lesson to be learnt. We must remain united in the face of the Master. In the meantime I have already made a move. I have arranged a meeting with Sir Cathcart D'Eath for this evening. His car should be waiting for me now.' He rose to his feet and gathered his gown about him.

'May one inquire the purpose of this meeting?' the Praelector asked. The Dean looked down at the Bursar. 'I should not like to think that our plans are likely to reach Sir Godber's ears,' he said deliberately.

'I can assure you ...' began the Bursar.

'I have requested this meeting because Sir Cathcart as you all know is President of the OPs. I think he should know what changes the Master proposes. Furthermore I think he should know the manner in which the Master has conducted himself in the matter. I fancy that there will be an extraordinary meeting of the Porterhouse Society next Tuesday to discuss the situation and I have high hopes that at that meeting a resolution will be passed censoring Sir Godber for the dictatorial attitude he has adopted in his dealings with the College Council and calling for his immediate resignation from the Mastership.'

'But, Dean, surely that is most unwise,' protested the Senior Tutor thoroughly alarmed. 'If a motion of that sort is passed, the Master is bound to resign and to publish his confounded letter. I really don't see what that is going to accomplish.'

The Bursar put down his coffee-cup with unwonted violence. 'For God's sake, Dean,' he said, 'consider what you are doing.'

The Dean smiled grimly. 'If Sir Godber can threaten us,' he said, 'we can threaten him.'

'But the scandal, think of the scandal. It will involve us all,' muttered the Bursar desperately.

'It will also involve Sir Godber. That is precisely the point of the exercise. We shall get in first by demanding his resignation. The force of his letter to the PM will be dulled by the fact that the College authorites and the Porterhouse Society have both demanded his resignation on the grounds of incompetence and his letter to the press with its so-called disclosures will have the appearance of being the action of a slighted and bitter man. Besides I rather think you over-estimate Sir Godber's political courage. Faced with the ultimatum we shall present at the Council meeting on Wednesday I doubt if he will risk a further confrontation.'

'But if the call for his resignation has already been published ...'

'It won't have been. The motion will have been passed, I trust unanimously, but its publication will be dependent on Sir Godber's attitude. If he persists in demanding the changes in the College, then we shall publish.'

'And if he resigns without warning?'

'We shall publish all the same,' said the Dean. 'We shall muddy the issue until it is uncertain whether we forced his resignation or not. Oh, we shall stir the pot, gentlemen. Have no fear of that. If there must be dirt let there be lots of it.' The Dean turned and went out, his gown billowing darkly behind him. In the Combination Room the Fellows looked at one another ruefully. Whatever changes the Master proposed appeared minor by comparison with the uproar the Dean seemed bent on provoking.

It was the Chaplain who broke the silence. 'I must say,' he shouted, 'that the Chef excelled himself tonight. That soufflé was delicious.'

Outside the main gate Sir Cathcart's Rolls-Royce waited ostentatiously as the Dean, swaddled in a heavy coat and wearing his blackest hat, hurried past the Porter's Lodge.

Skullion opened the car door for him.

'Good evening, Skullion.'

'Good evening to you, sir,' Skullion murmured humbly.

The Dean clambered in and the car moved off, its wheels slushing through the snow. In the back the Dean stared through the window at the flurries of snowflakes and the passers-by with their heads bent against the driving wind. He felt warm and contented, with none of the uneasy feelings that had driven the Master to his Bentham. This was weather he appreciated, cold bitter weather with the river rising and the biting wind creating once again the divisions of his youth, that hierarchy of rich and poor, good and bad, the comfort and the misery which he longed to preserve and which Sir Godber would destroy in his search for soulless uniformity. 'The old order changeth,' he muttered to himself, 'but damned slowly if I have anything to do with it.'

*

Skullion went back into the Porter's Lodge.

'Going to supper,' he told the under-porter and trudged across the Court to the kitchen. He went down the stone stairs to the kitchen where the Chef had laid a table for two in his pantry. It was hot and Skullion took off his coat before sitting down.

'Snowing again they tell me,' said the Chef taking his seat.

Skullion waited until a younger waiter with a gaping mouth had brought the dishes before saying anything.

'Dean's gone to see the General,' he said finally.

'Has he now?' said the Chef, helping himself to the remains of the poached salmon.

'Council meeting this afternoon,' Skullion continued.

'So I heard.'

Skullion shook his head.

'You aren't going to like this,' he said. 'The Master's changes aren't going to suit your book, I can tell you.'

'Never supposed they would, Mr Skullion.'

'Worse than I expected, Chef, much worse.' Skullion took a mouthful of Ockfener Herrenberg 1964 before going on.

'Self-service in Hall,' he said mournfully.

The Chef put down his knife and fork. 'Never,' he growled.

'It's true. Self-service in Hall.'

'Over my dead body,' said the Chef. 'Over my bloody dead body.'

'Women in College too.'

'What? Living in College?'

'That's it. Living in College.'

'That's unnatural, Mr Skullion. Unnatural.'

'You don't have to tell me that, Chef. You don't have to tell me. Unnatural and immoral. It isn't right, Chef, it's downright wicked.'

'And self-service in Hall,' the Chef muttered. 'What's the world coming to? You know, Mr Skullion, when I think of all the years I've been Chef to the College and all the dinners I've cooked for them, I sometimes wonder what's the meaning of it all. They've got no right to do it.'

'It's not them that's doing it,' Skullion told him. 'It's him that says it's got to change.'

'Why don't they stop him? They're the Council. He can't do it without their say-so.'

'They can't stop him. Threatened to resign if they didn't agree.'

'Why didn't they let him? Good riddance to bad rubbish.'

'Threatened to write to the papers and tell them we've been selling degrees,' Skullion said.

The Chef looked at him with alarm.

'You don't mean he knows about your ...'

'I don't know what he knows and what he don't,' Skullion said. 'I don't think he knows about them. I think he's talking about the ones they let in because they've got money. I think that's what he means.'

'But we've a right to let in who we like,' the Chef protested. 'It's our college. It's not anyone else's.'

'That's not the way he sees it,' Skullion said. 'He's threatened them with a national scandal if they don't toe the line and they've agreed.'

'What did the Dean say? He must have said something.'

'Said they'd got to buy time by seeming to agree. He's gone to see the General now. They'll think of something.'

Skullion finished his wine and smiled to himself. 'He don't know what he's tackled,' he said more cheerfully.

'Thinks he's dealing with the pipsqueaks in Parliament, he does. Wordmongers, that's what MPs are. Think you've only got to say a thing for it to be there next day. They don't know nothing about doing and they don't have nothing to lose, but the Dean's a different kettle of fish. He and the General, they'll do him down. See if they don't.' He grinned knowingly and winked his unblacked eye. The Chef nibbled a grape moodily.

'Don't see how they can,' he said.

'Digging for dirt,' said Skullion. 'Digging for dirt in his past, that's what the Dean said.'

'Dirt? What sort of dirt?'

'Women,' said Skullion.

'Ah,' said the Chef. 'Disreputable women.'

'Precisely, Chef, them and money.'

The Chef pushed his hat back on his head. 'He wasn't what you might call a rich undergrad, was he?'

'No,' said Skullion, 'he wasn't.'

'And he's rich now.'

'Married it,' Skullion told him. 'Lacey money, that's what it is. Lady Mary's money. That's the sort of man he is, Sir Godber.'

'Bony woman. Not my cup of tea,' said the Chef. 'Like something with a bit more meat to it myself. Wouldn't be surprised if he hadn't got a fancy woman somewhere.'

Skullion shook his head doubtfully. 'Not him. Not enough guts,' said Skullion.

'You don't think they'll find anything then?'

'Not that sort of thing. They'll have to bring pressure. Influential friends the College has got, the Dean said. They'll use them.'

'They'd better use something. I'm not staying on to run a self-service canteen and have women in my Hall,' said the Chef.

Skullion got up from the table and put on his coat. 'The Dean'll see to it,' he said and climbed the stairs to the Screens. The wind had blown snow on to the steps and Skullion turned up the collar of his coat. 'Got no right to change things,' he grumbled to himself, and went out into the night.

At Coft Castle the Dean and Sir Cathcart sat in the library, a decanter of brandy half empty on the table beside them and their thoughts bitter with memories of past greatness.

'England's ruin, damned Socialists,' growled Sir Cathcart. 'Turned the country into a benevolent society. Seem to think you can rule a nation with good intentions. Damned nonsense. Discipline. That's what the country needs. A good dose of unemployment to bring the working classes to their senses.'

'Doesn't seem to work these days,' said the Dean with a sigh. 'In the old days a depression seemed to have a very salutary effect.'

'It's the dole. Man can earn more not working than he can at his job. All wrong. A bit of genuine starvation would soon put that right.'

'I suppose the argument is that the wives and children suffer,' said the Dean.

'Can't see much harm in that,' the General continued. 'Nothing like a hungry woman to put some pep into a man. Reminds me of a painting I saw once. Lot of fellows sitting round a table waiting for their dinner and the lady of the house comes in and lifts the cover of the dish. Spur inside, what? Sensible woman. Fine painting. Have some more brandy?'

'That's very kind of you,' said the Dean, proffering his glass.

'Trouble with this Godber Evans fellow is he comes from poor stock,' continued Sir Cathcart when he had filled their glasses. 'Doesn't understand men. Hasn't got generations of county stock behind him. No leadership qualities. Got to have lived with animals to understand men, working men. Got to train them properly. A whack on the arse if they do something wrong and a pat on the head if they get it right. No use filling their heads with a whole lot of ideas they can't use. Bloody nonsense, half this education lark.'

'I quite agree,' said the Dean. 'Educating people above their station has been one of the great mistakes of this century. What this country requires is an educated elite. What it's had in fact, for the past three hundred years.'

'Three meals a day and a roof over his head and the average man has nothing to grumble about. Stout fellows. The present system is designed to create layabouts. Consumer society indeed. Can't consume what you don't make. Damned tommyrot.'

The Dean's head nodded on his chest. The fire, the brandy and the ubiquitous central heating in Coft Castle mingled with the warmth of Sir Cathcart's sentiments to take their toll of his concentration. He was dimly aware of the rumble of the General's imprecations, distant and receding like some tide going out across the mudflats of an estuary where once the fleet had lain at anchor. All empty now, the ships gone, dismantled, scrapped, the evidence of might deplenished, only a sandpiper with Sir Godber's face poking its beak into the sludge. The Dean was asleep.

CHAPTER NINE

Zipser stirred on the floor of his room. His face in contact with the carpet felt sore and his head throbbed. Above all he was cold and stiff. He turned on his side and stared at the window, where an orange glow from the sky over Cambridge shone dimly through the falling snow. Slowly he gathered himself together and got to his feet. Feeling distinctly weak and sick he went to the door and turned on the light and stood blinking at the two large cartons on the floor. Then he sat down hurriedly in a chair and tried to remember what had happened to him and why he was the possessor of two gross of guaranteed electronically tested three-teat vending machine pack contraceptives. The details of the day's events slowly returned to him and with them the remembrance of his misunderstanding with the Dean. 'Gated for a week,' he murmured and realized the implications of his predicament. He couldn't deliver the beastly things to the Unicorn now and he had signed the slip at the wholesale office. Inquiries would be made. The barman at the Unicorn would identify him. So would the wretched clerk at the wholesale office. The police would be informed. There would be a search. He'd be arrested. Charged with being in felonious possession of two gross of ... Zipser clutched his head in his hands and tried to think what to do. He'd have to get rid of the things. He looked at his watch. Eleven o'clock. Got to hurry. Burn them? He looked at the gas fire and gave up the idea. Out of the question. Flush them down the lavatory? Better idea. He threw himself at the cartons and began to open them. First the outer carton, then the inner one, then the packet itself and finally the foil wrapper. It was a laborious job. He'd never do it. He'd got to do it.

Beside him on the carpet a pile of empty packets slowly grew and with it a pile of foil and a grotesque arrangement of latex rings looking like flattened and translucent button mushrooms. Lubricated with sensitol, his hands were sticky, which made it even more difficult to tear the foil. Finally after an hour he had emptied one carton. It was twelve o'clock. He gathered the contraceptives up and took a handful out on to the landing and into the lavatory. He dropped them into the pan and pulled the chain. A rush of water, swirls, bubbles, gone? The water subsided and he stared down at two dozen rubber rings floating defiantly in the pan. 'For God's sake,' said Zipser desperately and waited until the cistern had filled again. He waited a minute after the water had stopped running and pulled the chain again. Two dozen contraceptives smiled up at him. One or two had partially unfurled and were filled with air. Zipser stared at the things frantically. Got to get them to go down somehow. He reached behind the pan and grabbed the cleaning brush and shoved it down on them. One or two disappeared round the U bend but for the most part they resisted his efforts. Three even had the audacity to adhere to the brush itself. Zipser picked them off with fastidious disgust and dropped them back into the water. By this time the cistern had filled again, gurgling gently and ending with a final swish. Zipser tried to think what to do. If buying the damned things had been fraught with appalling difficulties, getting rid of them was a nightmare.

He sat down on the lavatory seat and considered the intractability of matter. A tin of lavatory cleanser caught his attention. He picked it up and wondered if it would dissolve rubber. Then he got off the seat and emptied the contents on to the rings floating in the water. Whatever chemical action the cleanser promised failed altogether. The contraceptives remained unaffected. Zipser grabbed the brush again and plunged it into the pan. Wafts of disinfectant powder irritated his nose. He sneezed loudly and clutched the chain. For the third time the cistern flushed and Zipser was just studying the subsidence and counting the six contraceptives which remained immune to chemistry and the rush of water when someone knocked on the door.

'What the hell's going on in there?' a voice asked. It was Foxton, who lived in the room next door.

Zipser looked hauntedly at the door. 'Got diarrhoea,' he said weakly.

'Well, must you pull the bloody chain so often?' Foxton asked. 'Making a bloody awful noise and I'm trying to sleep.' He went back to his room and Zipser turned back to the pan and began fishing for the six contraceptives with the lavatory brush.

Twenty minutes later he was still searching for some method of disposing of his incriminating evidence. He had visited six lavatories on neighbouring staircases and had found a method of getting the things to disappear by first filling them with water from a tap and tying the ends. It was slow and cumbersome and above all noisy and when he had tried six at a time on J staircase he had to spend some time unblocking the U pipe. He went back to his room and sat shivering with cold and anxiety. It was one o'clock and so far he had managed to rid himself of thirty-eight. At this rate he would still be flushing lavatories all over the College when Mrs Biggs arrived in the morning. He stared at the pile of foil and the packets. Got to get rid of them too. Put them behind the gas fire and burn them he thought and he was just wrestling with the gas fire and trying to make space behind it when the howling draught in the chimney gave him a better idea. He went to the window and looked out into the night. In the darkness outside snowflakes whirled and scattered while the wind battered at the window pane. Zipser opened the window and poked his head out into the storm before wetting his finger and holding it up to the wind. 'Blowing from the East,' he muttered and shut the window with a smile of intense satisfaction. A moment later he was kneeling beside the gas fire and undoing the hose of his gas ring and five minutes afterwards the first of 250 inflated contraceptives bounced buoyantly against the sooty sides of the medieval chimney and disappeared into the night sky above. Zipser rushed to the window and gazed up for a glimpse of the winsome thing as it whirled away carrying its message of abstinence far away into the world, but the sky was too dark and there was nothing to see. He went back and fetched a torch and shone it up the chimney but apart from one or two errant snowflakes the chimney was clear. Zipser turned cheerfully back to the gas ring and inflated five more. Once again the experiment was entirely successful. Up the chimney they floated, up and away. Zipser inflated twenty and popped them up the chimney with equal success. He was just filling his hundredth when the gas gave out, with a hideous wheeze the thing deflated. Zipser rummaged in his pockets for a shilling and finally found one. He put it into the meter and the contraceptive assumed a new and satisfactory shape. He tied the end and stuffed it up the chimney. The night wore on and Zipser acquired a wonderful dexterity. On to the tube, gas on, gas off, a knot in the end and up the chimney. Beside him on the floor the cartons filled with discarded foil and Zipser was just wondering if there were schoolchildren who collected used contraceptive containers like milk-bottle tops when he became aware that something had gone wrong in the chimney. The bloated and strangulated rear of his last contraceptive was hanging suspended in the fireplace. Zipser gave it a shove of encouragement but the poor thing merely bulged dangerously. Zipser pulled it out and peered up the chimney. He couldn't peer very far. The chimney was crowded with eager contraceptives. He extracted another, smeared with soot, and put it down on the floor. He extracted a third and thrust it behind him. Then a fourth and a fifth, both deeply encrusted with soot. After that he gave up. The rest were too high to reach. He clambered out of the fireplace and sat on the floor wondering what to do. At least he had disposed of all two gross, even if some were lodged in the chimney stack. They were well hidden there – or would be once he had put the gas fire back in place. He would think of some way of disposing of them in the morning. He was too tired to think of anything now. He turned to reach for the five he had managed to extract only to find that they had disappeared. 'I put them down on the carpet. I'm sure I did,' he muttered lightheadedly to himself and was about to look under the bookcase when his eye caught sight of a movement on the ceiling. Zipser looked up. Five sooty contraceptives had lodged themselves in a corner by the door. Little bits of soot marked the ceiling where they had touched.

Zipser got wearily to his feet and climbed on to a chair and reached up. He could just manage to get his fingers on to the belly of one of the things but the sensitol made it impossible to get a grip. Zipser squeezed and with a coy squeak the contraceptive evaded his grasp and lumbered away across the room, leaving a track of soot behind it. Zipser tried again on another with the same result. He moved the chair across the room and reached up. The contraceptive waddled gently into the corner by the window. Zipser moved the chair again but the contraceptive rolled away. Zipser climbed down and stared maniacally at his ceiling. It was covered in delicate black trails as if some enormous snail had called after a stint of coal-heaving. The self-control Zipser had been exercising began to slip. He picked up a book and lobbed it at a particularly offensive-looking contraceptive, but apart from driving it across the room to join the flock in the corner by the door the gesture was futile. Zipser crossed to the desk and pushed it over to the door. Then he fetched the chair and stood it on the desk and climbed precariously up and seized a contraceptive by its knotted tail. He climbed down and thrust it up the last one still protruded below the lintel, when he pushed the gas fire back into position it was invisible. Zipser collapsed on to his sofa and stared at the ceiling. All that remained was to clean the soot off the plaster. He went out into the gyp room and fetched a duster and spent the next half hour pushing his desk round the room and climbing on to it to dust the ceiling. Traces of soot still remained but they were less noticeable now. He pushed the desk back into its corner and looked round the room. Apart from a noticeable smell of gas and the more intransigent stains on the ceiling there was nothing to connect him with two gross of contraceptives fraudulently obtained from the wholesalers. Zipser opened the window to clear the room of gas and went through to his bedroom and went to bed. In the eastern sky the first light of dawn was beginning to appear, but Zipser had no eyes for the beauties of nature. He fell into a restless sleep haunted by the thought that the logjam in his chimney might break during the coming day to issue with shocking ebullience above the unsuspecting College. He need not have worried. Porterhouse was already infested. The falling snow had seen to that. As each porcine sensitol-lubricated protective had emerged from the chimney stack the melting snow had ended its night flight almost abruptly. Zipser had not foreseen the dangers of icing.

The Dean arrived back at Porterhouse in Sir Cathcart's Rolls-Royce at two o'clock. He was spiritually restored though physically taxed by the day's excitements and Sir Cathcart's brandy. He knocked on the main gate and Skullion, who had been waiting up obediently for him, opened the postern and let him in.

'Need any help, sir,' Skullion asked as the Dean tottered through.

'Certainly not,' said the Dean thickly and set off across the Court. Skullion followed him at a distance like a good dog and saw him through the Screens before turning back to his Porter's Lodge and bed. He had already shut the door and gone through into his backroom when the Dean's strangled cry sounded from the New Court. Skullion heard nothing. He took off his collar and tie and climbed between the sheets. 'Drunk as a lord,' he thought fondly, and closed his eyes.

The Dean lay in the snow and cursed. He tried to imagine what he had slipped on. It certainly wasn't the snow. Snow didn't squash like that. Snow certainly didn't explode like that and even in these days of air pollution snow didn't smell of gas like that. The Dean eased himself on to a bruised hip and peered into the darkness. A strange rustling sound in which a sort of wheeze and the occasional squeak were intermingled came from all sides. The Court seemed to be alive with turgid and vaguely translucent shapes which gleamed in the starlight. The Dean reached out tentatively towards the nearest one and felt it bounce delicately away from him. He scrambled to his feet and kicked another. A ripple of rustling, squeaking, jostling shapes issued across the Court. 'That damned brandy,' muttered the Dean. He waded through the mass to the door of his staircase and stumbled upstairs. He was feeling distinctly ill. 'Must be my liver,' he thought, and slumped into a chair with the sudden resolution to leave brandy well alone in future. After a bit he got up and went to the window and looked out. Seen from above the Court looked empty, white with snow but otherwise normal. The Dean shut the window and turned back into the room. 'I could have sworn there were . . .' He tried to think just what he could have sworn the Court was filled with, but couldn't think of anything appropriate. Balloons was as near as he could get, but balloons didn't have that awful translucent ectoplasmic quality about them.

He went into his bedroom and undressed and put on his pyjamas and got into bed but sleep was impossible. He had dozed too long at Sir Cathcart's, and besides, he was haunted by his recent experience. After an hour the Dean got out of bed again and put on his dressing-gown and went downstairs. At the bottom he peered out into the Court. There was the same indelicate squeaking sound but apart from that the night was too dark to see anything clearly. The Dean stepped out into the Court and banged into one of the objects. 'They *are* there after all,' he muttered and reached down to pick whatever it was up. The thing has a soft vaguely oily feel about it and scuttled away as soon as the Dean's finger's tightened on it. He tried another and missed and it was only at the third attempt that he managed to obtain a grip. Holding the thing by its tail the Dean took it into the lighted doorway and looked at it with a growing sense of disgust and outrage. He held it head down and the thing righted itself and turned head up. Holding it thus he went out into the Court and through the Screens to Old Court and the Porter's Lodge.

To Skullion, emerging sleepily from his backroom, the sight of the Dean in his dressing-gown holding the knotted end of an inflated contraceptive had about it a nightmare quality that deprived him of his limited amount of speech. He stood staring wild-eyed at the Dean while on the periphery of his vision the contraceptive wobbled obscenely.

'I have just found this in New Court, Skullion,' said the Dean, suddenly conscious that there was a certain ambiguity about his appearance.

'Oh ah,' said Skullion in the tone of one who has his private doubts. The Dean let go of the contraceptive hurriedly.

'As I was saying …' he began only to stop as the thing slowly began to ascend. Skullion and the Dean watched it, hypnotized. The contraceptive reached the ceiling and hovered there. Skullion lowered his eyes and stared at the Dean.

'There seem to be others of that ilk,' continued the Dean.

'Oh ah,' said Skullion.

'In the New Court,' said the Dean. 'A great many others.'

'In the New Court?' said Skullion slowly.

'Yes,' said the Dean. In the face of Skullion's evident doubts he was beginning to feel rather heated. So was the contraceptive. The draught from the door had nudged it next to the light bulb in the ceiling and as the Dean opened his mouth to say that the New Court was alive with the things, the one above their heads touched the bulb and exploded. In fact there were three explosions. First the contraceptive blew. Then the bulb, and finally and most alarmingly of all the gas ignited. Blinded momentarily by the flash and bereft of the light of the bulb, the Dean and Skullion stood in darkness while fragments of glass and rubber descended on them.

'There are more where that one came from,' said the Dean finally, and led the way out into the night air. Skullion groped for his bowler and put it on. He reached behind the counter for his torch and followed the Dean. They passed through the Screens and Skullion shone his torch into New Court.

Huddled like so many legless animals, some two hundred contraceptives gleamed in the torchlight. A light dawn breeze had risen and with it some of the more inflated contraceptives, so that it seemed as though they were attempting to mount their less active neighbours while the whole mass seethed and rippled. One or two were to be seen nudging the windows on the first floor.

'Gawd,' said Skullion irreverently.

'I want them cleared away before it gets light, Skullion,' said the Dean. 'No one must hear about this. The College reputation, you understand.'

'Yes, sir,' said Skullion. 'I'll clear them away. Leave it to me.'

'Good, Skullion,' said the Dean and with one last disgusted look at the obscene flock went up the stairs to his rooms.

Mrs Biggs had a bath. She had poured bath salts into the water and the pink suds matched the colour of her frilly shower cap. Bath night for Mrs Biggs was a special occasion. In the privacy of her bathroom she felt

liberated from the constraints of commonsense. Standing on the pink
bath mat surveying her reflection in the steamed-up mirror it was almost
possible to imagine herself young again. Young and fancy free, and she
fancied Zipser. There was no doubt about it and no doubt too that Zipser
fancied her. She dried herself lovingly and put on her nightdress and
went through to her bedroom. She climbed into bed and set the alarm
clock for three. Mrs Biggs wanted to be up early. She had things to do.

In the early hours she left the house and cycled across Cambridge. She
locked the bicycle by the Round Church and made her way on foot
down Trinity Street to the side entrance of Porterhouse ·and let herself
in with a key she had used in the old days when she had bedded for the
Chaplain. She passed through the passage by the Buttery and came out
by the Screens and was about to make her way across New Court when
a strange sound stopped her in her tracks. She peered round the archway.
In the early morning light Skullion was chasing balloons. Or something.
Not chasing. Dancing seemed more like it. He ran. He leapt. He cavorted.
His outstretched arms reached yearningly towards whatever it was that
floated jauntily beyond his reach as if to taunt the Porter. Backwards
and forwards across the ancient court the strange pursuit continued until
just as it seemed the thing was about to escape over the wall into the
Fellows' Garden there was a loud pop and whatever it was or had been
hung limp and tatterdemalion upon the branches of a climbing rose like
some late-flowering bloom. Skullion stopped, panting, and stared up at
the object of his chase and then, evidently inspired by its fate, turned
and hurried towards the Screens. Mrs Biggs retreated into the darkness
of the Buttery passage as Skullion hurried by and then, when she could
see him heading for the Porter's Lodge, emerged and tiptoed through
the contraceptives to the Bull Tower. Around her feet the contraceptives
squeaked and rustled. Mrs Biggs climbed the staircase to Zipser's room
with a fresh sense of sexual excitement brought on by the presence of so
many prophylactics. She couldn't remember when she had seen so many.
Even the American airmen with whom she had been so familiar in the
past had never been quite so prolific with their rubbers, and they'd been
generous enough in all conscience if her memory served her aright. Mrs
Biggs let herself into Zipser's room and sported the oak. She had no
intention of being disturbed. She crossed to Zipser's bedroom and went
inside. She switched on the bedside light.

Zipser awoke from his troubled sleep and blinked. He sat up in bed
and stared at Mrs Biggs brilliant in her red coat. It was evidently
morning. It didn't feel like morning but there was Mrs Biggs so it must

be morning. Mrs Biggs didn't come in the middle of the night. Zipser levered himself out of bed.

'Sorry,' he mumbled groping for his dressing-gown. 'Must have overslept.' Zipser's eye caught the alarm clock. It seemed to indicate half-past three. Must have stopped.

'Shush,' said Mrs Biggs with a terrible smile. 'It's only half-past three.'

Zipser looked at the clock again. It certainly said half-past three. He tried to equate the time with Mrs Biggs's arrival and couldn't. There was something terribly wrong with the situation.

'Darling,' said Mrs Biggs, evidently sensing his dilemma. Zipser looked up at her open-mouthed. Mrs Biggs was taking off her coat. 'Don't make any noise,' she continued, with the same extraordinary smile.

'What the hell is going on?' asked Zipser. Mrs Biggs went into the other room.

'I'll be with you in a minute,' she called out in a hoarse whisper.

Zipser stood up shakily. 'What are you doing?' he asked.

There was a rustle of clothes in the other room. Even to Zipser's befuddled mind it was evident that Mrs Biggs was undressing. He went to the door and peered out into the darkness.

'For God's sake,' he said, 'you mustn't do that.'

Mrs Biggs emerged from the shadows. She had taken off her blouse. Zipser stared at her enormous brassière.

'Darling,' she said. 'Go back to bed. You mustn't stand and watch me. It's embarrassing.' She gave him a push which sent him reeling on to the bed. Then she shut the door. Zipser sat on his bed shaking. The sudden emergence of Mrs Biggs at half-past three in the morning from the shadows of his own private fantasies into a real presence terrified him. He tried to think what to do. He couldn't shout or scream for help. Nobody would believe he hadn't invited her to ... He'd be sent down. His career would be finished. He'd be disgraced. They'd find the French letters up the chimney. Oh God. Zipser began to weep.

In the front room Mrs Biggs divested herself of her bra and panties. It was terribly cold. She went to the window to shut it when a faint popping noise from below startled her. Mrs Biggs peered out. Skullion was running round the Court with a stick. He appeared to be spearing the contraceptives. 'That'll keep him busy,' Mrs Biggs thought happily, and shut the window. Then she crossed to the gas fire and lit it. 'Nice to get dressed in the warm,' she thought, and went into the bedroom. Zipser had got back into bed and had switched off the light.

'Wants to spare me,' Mrs Biggs thought tenderly and climbed into bed. Zipser shrank from her but Mrs Biggs had no sense of his reluctance.

Grasping him in her arms she pressed him to her vast breasts. In the darkness Zipser squeaked frantically and Mrs Biggs's mouth found his. To Zipser it seemed that he was in the grip of a great white whale. He fought desperately for air, surfaced for a moment and was engulfed again.

Skullion, who had returned from the Porter's Lodge armed with a broom handle to which he had taped a pin, hurled himself into the shoal and struck about him with a fury that was only partially explained by having to work all night. It was rather the effrontery of the things that infuriated him. Skullion had little use for contraceptives at the best of times. Unnatural, he called them, and placed them in the lower social category of things along with elastic-sided boots and made-up bow ties. Not the sort of attire for a gentleman. But even more than their humble origins, he was infuriated by the insult to Porterhouse that the presence of so great and so inflated a number represented. The Dean's admonition that news of the infestation must not leak out was wasted on Skullion. He needed no telling. 'We'd be the laughing-stock of the University,' he thought, lancing a particularly large one. By the time dawn broke over Cambridge Skullion had cleared New Court. One or two had escaped into the Fellows' Garden and he went through the archway in the wall and began spiking the remainder. Behind him the Court was littered with tattered latex, almost invisible against the snow. 'I'll wait until it's a bit lighter to pick them up,' he muttered. 'Can't see them now.' He had just run a small but agile one to earth in the rose garden when a dull rumbling noise at the top of the Tower made him turn and look up. Something was going on in the old chimney. The chimney pot at the top was shaking. The brickwork silhouetted against the morning sky appeared to be bulging. The rumbling stopped, to be succeeded by an almighty roar as a ball of flame issued from the chimney and billowed out before ascending above the College. Below it the chimney toppled sideways, crashed on to the roof of the Tower and with a gradually increasing rumble of masonry the fourteenth-century building lost its entire façade. Behind it the rooms were clearly visible, their floors tilted horribly and sagging. Skullion stood mesmerized by the spectacle. A bed on the first floor slid sideways and dropped on to the masonry below. Desks and chairs followed suit. There were shouts and screams. People poured out of doorways and windows opened all round the Court. Skullion ignored the screams for help. He was busy chasing the last few remaining contraceptives when the Master, clad in his dressing-gown, emerged from the Master's Lodge and hurried to the scene of the disaster. As he rushed across the garden he found Skullion trying to spear a contraceptive floating in the fishpond.

'Go and open the main gates,' the Master shouted at him.

'Not yet,' said Skullion taciturnly.

'What do you mean, not yet?' the Master demanded. 'The ambulance men and the fire brigade will want to get in.'

'Not having any strangers in College till I've cleared these things up. Wouldn't be right,' said Skullion.

The Master stared at the floating contraceptive furiously. Skullion's obstinacy enraged him. 'There are injured people in there,' he screamed.

'So there are,' said Skullion, 'but there's the College reputation to be thought of too.' He leant across the pond and burst the floating bubble. Sir Godber turned and ran on to the scene of the accident. Skullion turned and followed him slowly. 'Got no sense of tradition,' he said sadly, and shook his head.

CHAPTER TEN

'These sweetbreads are delicious,' said the Dean at dinner. 'The coroner's inquest has given me a considerable appetite.'

'Very tactfully handled,' said the Senior Tutor. 'I must admit I had anticipated a less magnanimous verdict. As it is, suicide never hurt anyone.'

'Suicide?' shouted the Chaplain. 'Did I hear someone say suicide?' He looked up expectantly. 'Now there's a topic we could well consider.'

'The Coroner has already done so at some length, Chaplain,' the Bursar bawled in his ear.

'Very good of him too,' said the Chaplain.

'The Senior Tutor has just made that point,' the Bursar explained.

'Has he now? Very interesting,' said the Chaplain, 'and about time too. Haven't had a decent suicide in College for some years now. Most regrettable.'

'I must say I can't see why the decline of the fashion should be so regrettable, Chaplain,' said the Bursar.

'I think I'll have a second helping of sweetbreads,' said the Dean.

The Chaplain leant back in his chair and looked at them over his glasses. 'In the old days hardly a week went by without some poor fellow taking the easy way out. When I first came here as Chaplain I used to spend half my time attending inquests. Come to think of it, there was a time when we were known as the Slaughterhouse.'

'Things have changed for the better since then,' said the Bursar.

'Nonsense,' said the Chaplain. 'The fall in the number of suicides is the clearest indication of the decline of morality. Undergraduates don't seem to be as conscience-stricken as they were in my young days.'

'You don't think it has to do with the introduction of natural gas?' asked the Senior Tutor.

'Natural gas? No such thing,' said the Dean. 'I agree with the Chaplain. Things have gone to pot.'

'Pot,' shouted the Chaplain. 'Did I hear somebody say pot?'

'I was merely saying . . .' began the Dean.

'At least nobody has suggested that young Zipser was on drugs,' interrupted the Bursar. 'The police made a very thorough investigation, you know, and they found nothing.'

The Dean raised his eyebrows. 'Nothing?' he asked. 'To the best of my knowledge they took away an entire sackful of . . . er . . . contraceptives.'

'I was talking of drugs, Dean. There was the question of motive, you understand. The police seemed to think Zipser was in the grip of an irrational impulse.'

'From what I heard he was in the grip of Mrs Biggs,' said the Senior Tutor. 'I suppose you can call Mrs Biggs an irrational impulse. Certainly a very tasteless one. And as for the other things, I must admit I find a predilection for gas-filled contraceptives quite unaccountable.'

'According to the police, there were two hundred and fifty,' said the Bursar.

'No accounting for tastes,' said the Dean, 'though for my part I prefer . . . to regard the whole deplorable affair as being politically motivated. This fellow Zipser was clearly an anarchist. He had a lot of left-wing literature in his rooms.'

'I understood him to be doing research into pumpernickel,' said the Bursar. 'Its origins in sixteenth-century Germany.'

'He also belonged to a number of subversive societies,' the Dean continued.

'I'd hardly call the United Nations Association subversive, Dean,' the Bursar protested.

'I would,' said the Dean. 'All political societies are subversive. Must be. Stands to reason. Wouldn't exist if they weren't trying to subvert something or other.'

'Certainly a most extraordinary way of going about things,' said the Bursar. 'And it still doesn't explain the presence of Mrs Biggs.'

'I'm inclined to agree with the Dean,' said the Senior Tutor. 'Anyone who could go to bed with Mrs Biggs must have been either demented or motivated by a grossly distorted sense of social duty and to have launched two hundred and fifty lethal contraceptives on an unsuspecting world argues a fanaticism ...'

'On the other hand,' said the Bursar, 'he had been to see you about his ... er ... compulsion for the good woman. You mentioned it at the time.'

'Yes, well, perhaps he did,' the Senior Tutor admitted, 'though I'd question your use of good as far as Mrs Biggs was concerned. In any case, I sent him on to the Chaplain.'

They looked at the Chaplain questioningly. 'Mrs Biggs good?' shouted the Chaplain. 'I should say so. Splendid woman.'

'We were wondering if Zipser gave you any hint as to his motives,' the Bursar explained.

'Motives?' said the Chaplain. 'Perfectly obvious. Good old-fashioned lust.'

'That hardly explains the explosive nature of his end,' said the Senior Tutor.

'You can't put new wine in old bottles,' said the Chaplain.

The Dean shook his head. 'Whatever his motives,' he said, 'Zipser has certainly made our own position extremely awkward. It is difficult to argue against the need for change when members of the College make such an exhibition of themselves. The meeting of the Porterhouse Society has been cancelled.'

The Fellows looked at him in amazement.

'But I understood the General had agreed to call it,' said the Senior Tutor. 'He's surely not backing down now.'

'Cathcart has proved himself a broken reed,' said the Dean mournfully. 'He phoned me this morning to say that he thought we should wait until this whole affair had blown over. An unfortunate phrase but one sees his point. The College can hardly afford another scandal just yet.'

'Damn Zipser,' said the Senior Tutor. The Fellows finished their dinner in silence.

In the Master's Lodge Sir Godber and Lady Mary mourned the passing of Zipser more austerely over scrambled eggs. As was ever the case, tragedy had lent Lady Mary a fresh vitality, and the strange circumstances of Zipser's end had given a fillip to her interest in psychology.

'The poor boy must have had a fetish,' she said, peeling a banana with a dispassionate interest that reminded Sir Godber of his honeymoon. 'Just like that case of the boy who was found inside a plastic bag in the lavatory on a railway train.'

'Seems an odd place to be,' said Sir Godber, helping himself to some tinned raspberries.

'Of course, that was a much clearer case of the mother complex at work,' continued Lady Mary. 'The plastic bag was obviously a substitute placenta.'

Sir Godber pushed his plate away. 'I suppose you're going to tell me that filling contraceptives with gas is a sure indication that the poor fellow had penis envy,' he said.

'Boys don't have penis envy, Godber,' said Lady Mary austerely. 'That's a girls' complaint.'

'Is it? Well, perhaps the bedder suffered from it then. I mean there's no indication that Zipser was actually responsible for stuffing them up the chimney. We know that he obtained the things, but for all we know Mrs Biggs filled them with gas and put them up the chimney.'

'And that's another thing,' Lady Mary said. 'The Dean's remarks about Mrs Biggs were in the worst of taste. He seemed to find the fact that the boy was having an affair with his bedder proof that Zipser was insane. A more glaring example of class prejudice it would be hard to imagine, but then I've always thought the Dean was a singularly common little man.'

Sir Godber looked at his wife with open admiration. The illogicality of her attitudes never ceased to amaze him. Lady Mary's egalitarianism stemmed from a sense of innate superiority which not even her marriage to Sir Godber had diminished. There were times when he wondered if her acceptance of his proposal had not been yet another political decision, a demonstration of her liberal pretensions. He brushed aside this domestic reverie and thought about the consequences of Zipser's death.

'It's going to be very difficult to quell the Dean now,' he said thoughtfully. 'He's already maintaining that this whole affair is a result of sexual permissiveness.'

Lady Mary snorted. 'Absolute nonsense,' she snapped predictably. 'If there had been women in College this thing would never have happened.'

'In the Dean's view, it was precisely the presence of Mrs Biggs in Zipser's rooms that caused the disaster,' Sir Godber pointed out.

'The Dean,' said Lady Mary with feeling, 'is a male chauvinist pig. A sensible policy of coeducation would avoid the sexual repressions that result in fetishism. You must make the point at the next Council meeting.'

'My dear,' said Sir Godber wearily, 'you don't seem to understand the difficulty I am in. I can hardly resign the Mastership now. It would look as if I was admitting some responsibility for what has happened. As it is my time is going to be taken up raising money for the Restoration Fund. It's going to cost a quarter of a million to repair the Tower.'

Lady Mary regarded him sternly. 'Godber,' she said, 'you must not weaken now. You must not compromise your principles. You must stick to your guns.'

'Guns, my dear?'

'Guns, Godber, guns.'

Sir Godber raised his eyebrows doubtfully. What guns he had had, and, in the light of Lady Mary's pacifism, he doubted if the metaphor was morally appropriate, appeared to have been effectively spiked by Zipser's tragic act.

'I really can't see what I can do,' he said finally.

'Well, in the first place, you can see that contraceptives are freely available in the College.'

'I can what?' shouted Sir Godber.

'You heard me,' snapped his wife. 'King's College has a dispenser in the lavatory. So do some of the other colleges. It seems a most wholesome precaution.'

The Master shuddered. 'King's has them, eh? Well I daresay it needs them. The place is a hotbed of homosexuality.'

'Godber,' said Lady Mary warningly. Sir Godber stopped short. He knew Lady Mary's views on homosexuals. She held them in the same sort of esteem as foxes, and her views on foxhunting were intemperate to say the least.

'All I meant was that King's have them for a purpose,' he said.

'I hardly imagine that ...' Lady Mary began when the French au pair girl brought in coffee.

'As I was saying ...'

'Pas devant les domestiques,' said his wife.

'Oh quite,' said Sir Godber hastily. 'All I meant was that they have them pour encourager les autres.'

The girl went out and Lady Mary poured coffee.

'What others?' she asked.

'Others?' said Sir Godber, who by this time had lost the thread of the conversation.

'You were saying that King's had installed a dispenser to encourage the others.'

'Precisely. I know how you feel about homosexuality, my dear, but one can have enough of a good thing,' he explained.

'Godber, you are prevaricating,' said Lady Mary firmly. 'I insist that for once in your life you do what you say you're going to do. When I marrried you, you were filled with splendid ideals. Now when I look at you, I sometimes wonder what happened to the man I married.'

'My dear, you seem to forget that I have spent a lifetime in politics,' Sir Godber protested. 'One learns to compromise. It's a depressing fact but there it is. Call it the death of idealism if you will, at least it saves a lot of people's lives.' He took his coffee cup and went through to his study and sat morosely by the fire and wondered at his own pusillanimity.

He could remember a time when he had shared his wife's enthusiasm for social justice, but time had dimmed ... or rather since Lady Mary remained vigorous over the years, not time itself but something had dimmed his zeal – if zeal could be dimmed. Sir Godber wondered about it and was struck by his preoccupation with the question. If not time then what? The intractability of human nature. The sheer inertia of Englishmen for whom the past was always sacred and inviolable and who prided themselves on their obstinacy. 'We didn't win the war,' thought Sir Godber, 'we just refused to lose it.' Stirred to a new belligerency, he reached for the poker and poked the fire angrily and watched the sparks fly upwards into the darkness. He was damned if he was going to be put upon by the Dean. He hadn't spent a lifetime in high office to be frustrated by an ageing academic with a taste for port. He got up and poured himself a stiff whisky and paced the room. Lady Mary was right. A dispenser would be a move in the right direction. He'd speak to the Bursar in the morning. He glanced out of the window towards the Bursar's rooms and saw the lights burning. It wasn't late. He'd pay him a social call now. He finished his drink and went out into the hall and put on his overcoat.

The Bursar lived out. He dined in College as frequently as possible, thanks to his wife's cooking, and it was only by chance that he had stayed on in his rooms after dinner. He had things to think about. The Dean's pessimism, for one thing, and his failure to solicit the help of Sir Cathcart. It might be as well, he thought, to consider transferring his tenuous loyalties to Sir Godber after all. The Master had already shown himself to be a man of some determination – the Bursar had not forgotten his ultimatum to the College Council – and properly handled might well reward him for services rendered. After all it had been the Bursar who had given him the information which Sir Godber had used to browbeat the Council. It was worth considering. He got up to put on his coat and go home when footsteps on the stairs suggested a late caller. The Bursar sat down at his desk again and pretended business. There was a knock on the door.

'Come in,' said the Bursar. Sir Godber peered round the door.

'Ah, Bursar,' he said. 'I hope I'm not disturbing you. I was crossing the Court when I saw your light and I thought I would pop up.'

The Bursar rose to greet him with warm obsequiousness. 'How good of you to come, Master,' he said, hurrying to take Sir Godber's coat. 'I was about to drop you a line asking if I could see you.'

'In that case, I am delighted to have saved you the trouble,' said Sir Godber.

'Do take a seat.' Sir Godber sat in an armchair by the fire and smiled genially. The warmth of the Bursar's welcome and the atmosphere of indigence in the furnishings of his rooms were to his taste. He looked round approvingly at the worn carpet and the second-rate prints on the walls, from an almanac by the look of them, and felt the broken spring in the chair beneath him. Sir Godber recognized the importunity of it all. His years in office had given him a nose for dependency, and Sir Godber was not a man to withhold favours.

'Would you care for a little something?' the Bursar asked, hovering uncertainly near a decanter of indifferent port. Sir Godber hesitated a moment. Port on top of whisky? He thrust the considerations of his liver aside in favour of policy.

'Just a small glass, thank you,' he said, taking out his pipe and filling it from a worn pouch. Sir Godber was not an habitual pipe smoker; he found it burnt his tongue, but he had learnt the value of the common touch.

'A bad business about poor Zipser,' said the Bursar bringing the port. 'It's going to be a costly business restoring the Tower.'

Sir Godber lit his pipe. 'One of the topics I wanted to consult you about, Bursar. We'll have to set up a Restoration Fund, I imagine.'

'I'm afraid so, Master,' the Bursar said sadly.

Sir Godber sipped his port. 'In the ordinary way,' he said, 'and if the College were only less ... er shall we say ... less antiquated in its attitudes, I daresay I could use my influence in the City to raise a substantial sum, but as it is I find myself in an ambiguous position.' He trailed off airily, leaving the Bursar with a sense of infinite financial connections. 'No, we shall simply have to fall back on our own resources.'

'We have so few,' said the Bursar.

'We shall have to make what use we can of them,' Sir Godber continued, 'until such time as the College decides to give itself a more contemporary image. I'll do what I can of course, but I'm afraid it will

be an uphill battle. If only the Council would see the importance of
change.' He smiled and looked at the Bursar. 'But then I daresay you
agree with the Dean?'

It was the moment the Bursar had been waiting for. 'The Dean has
his own views, Master,' he said, 'and they are not ones I share.'

Sir Godber's eyebrows expressed encouragement with reservations.

'I have always felt that we were falling behind the times,' continued
the Bursar, anxious to win the full approval of those eyebrows, 'but as
Bursar I have been concerned with administration and it does tend to
leave little time for policy. The Dean's influence is quite remarkable, you
know, and of course there is Sir Cathcart.'

'I gather Sir Cathcart intends to call a meeting of the Porterhouse
Society,' said Sir Godber.

'He's cancelled it since the Zipser affair,' the Bursar told him.

'That's interesting. So the Dean is on his own, is he?'

The Bursar nodded. 'I think some of the Council have had second
thoughts too. The younger Fellows would like to see changes, but they
don't carry much weight. So few of them too, but then we've never been
noted for our Research Fellowships. We have neither the money nor the
reputation to attract them. I have suggested ... but the Dean ...' he
waved his hands helplessly.

Sir Godber gulped his port. In spite of it he was glad he had come.
The Bursar's change of tune was encouraging and Sir Godber was
satisfied. It was time to talk frankly. He knocked out his pipe and leant
forward.

'Between ourselves I think we can circumvent the Dean,' he said,
tapping the Bursar on the knee with a forefinger with a vulgar assurance.
'You mark my words. We'll have him where we want him.'

The Bursar stared at Sir Godber in startled fascination. The man's
crudity, the change from an assumed urbanity to this backstair forcefulness
took him by surprise, and Sir Godber noted his astonishment with
satisfaction. The years of calling working men whom he despised 'Brother'
had not been wasted. There was no doubting the menace in his grim
bonhomie. 'He won't know his arse from his elbow by the time we've
finished with him,' he continued. The Bursar nodded meekly. Sir Godber
hitched his chair forward and began to outline his plans.

Skullion stood in the Court and wondered at the lights burning in the
Bursar's room.

'He's staying late,' he thought. 'Usually home by nine, he is.' He
walked through to the back gate and locked it, glancing hopefully at the

spiked wall as he did so. Then he turned and made his way through the Fellows' Garden to New Court. He walked slowly and with a slight limp. The exertions of the chase had left him stiff and aching and he had still not recovered from the shock of the explosion in the Tower. 'Getting old,' he muttered and stopped to light his pipe, and as he stood in the shadow of a large elm the light in the Bursar's room went out. Skullion sucked at his pipe thoughtfully and tamped the tobacco down with his thumb. He was about to leave the shelter of the elm when a crunch of gravel on the path caused him to hesitate. Two figures had emerged from New Court and were coming towards him deep in conversation. Skullion recognized the Master's voice. He moved back into the shadows as the two figures passed him.

'No doubt the Dean will object,' Sir Godber was saying, 'but faced with a *fait accompli* there won't be anything he can do about it. I think we can take it that the days of the Dean's influence are numbered.'

'Not before time,' said the Bursar. The two figures disappeared round the side of the Master's Lodge. Skullion emerged from the shadow and stood on the path peering after them, his mind furiously occupied. So the Bursar had gone over to Sir Godber. Skullion wasn't surprised. He had never had much time for the Bursar. The man wasn't out of the top drawer for one thing and for another he was responsible for the wages of the College servants. Skullion regarded him more as a foreman than a genuine Fellow, a paymaster, and a mean one at that, and held him responsible for the pittance he received. And now the Bursar had gone over to Sir Godber. Skullion turned and made his way into New Court with a fresh sense of grievance and some perplexity. The Dean should be told but Skullion knew better than to tell him. The Dean didn't approve of eavesdropping. He was a proper gentleman. Skullion wondered what a fate accomplee was. He'd have to think of some way of warning the Dean in the morning. He went through the Screens and across to the Porter's Lodge and made himself some cocoa. 'So the Dean's days are numbered, are they?' he thought bitterly. 'We'll see about that.' It would take more than Sir Godber Evans and the miserable Bursar to change things. There was always Sir Cathcart. He'd see they didn't get their way. He had great faith in Sir Cathcart. At midnight he got up and went outside to close the front gate. During the day the thaw had set in and the snow had begun to melt but the wind had changed during the evening and it had begun to freeze again. Skullion stood in the doorway for a moment and stared out into the street. A middle-aged man slipped on the pavement opposite and fell. Skullion regarded his fall without interest. What happened outside Porterhouse was none of his affair. With a sudden wish that the Master would slip and break his neck, Skullion went back into the College and shut the door. Above him in the Tower the clock struck twelve.

CHAPTER ELEVEN

On the towpath by the river the Dean stood huddled in his overcoat against the wind. Behind him the willows shuddered and shook and the hedgerow rustled. In front the eights rowed through choppy water, each with its coterie of coaches and supporters splashing through the puddles on their bicycles and shouting orders and encouragement. On every stroke the coxes jerked backwards and the boats leapt forwards, each in pursuit of the eight ahead and each in turn in flight from the eight behind. Occasionally a sudden burst of cheering signalled a bump as one eight touched the boat in front and the two pulled into the side of the river and the victors broke off a willow branch and stuck it into the bow. There were gaps in the procession where bumps had been achieved, spaces of empty water and then another eight would appear round the bend still trying desperately to catch the boat at least two lengths ahead and overbump. Jesus. Porterhouse. Lady Margaret. Pembroke. Trinity. St Catherine's. Christ's. Churchill. Magdalene. Caius. Clare. Peterhouse. Historic names, hallowed names like so many prayers on a rosary of racing boats to be repeated twice yearly at Lent and after Easter. To the Dean the ritual was holy, a sacred occasion to be attended, no matter how cold or wet the weather, in memory of the healthy athleticism of the past and the certainties of his youth ... The Bumps were a time of renewal for him. Standing on the towpath he felt once more the innocence, the unquestioning innocence of his own rowing days and the fitness of things then. Yes, fitness, a fitness not simply of body, or even of mind, but of things in general, an acceptance of life as it was without the insidious subversion of questions or the dangerous speculations which had gained momentum since. A guiltless time, that, a golden age of assurance before the Great War when there was honey still for tea and a servant to bring it too. In memory of that time the Dean braved the wind and the cold and stood on the towpath while the bicycles splashed mud on to his shoes and the eights rowed by. When it was all over he turned and trudged back to the Pike and Eel where his car was parked. Behind him and in front, strung out along the path, old men like himself turned up the collars of their overcoats and headed home, their heads bent against the wind but with a new sprightliness in their step. The Dean had reached the railway bridge when he was aware of a familiar figure in front. 'Afternoon, Skullion. We rowed over again,' he said. Skullion nodded. 'Jesus never looked like catching us,' the Dean said, 'and we should bump Trinity tomorrow. It was the choppy water that stopped us today.'

They walked on in silence while the Dean recalled other Bumps and famous crews and Skullion tried to think of some way of broaching the subject of the Bursar's treachery without offending the Dean's sense of what was proper for College servants to say. It wasn't easy even to walk beside the Dean. Not his place, and presently Skullion gave up the unequal struggle with his conscience and gradually fell back a pace or two behind the old man. At the Pike and Eel the Dean, still lost in thought, unlocked his car and climbed in. Skullion fetched his bicycle and wheeled it across the footbridge. Behind him the Dean sat in his car and waited for the traffic to clear. He had forgotten Skullion. He had forgotten even the Bumps and the youth they had recalled to him. He was thinking about Sir Godber and the glibness of his modernity and the threat to Porterhouse he represented. His feet were cold and the joints in his knees ached. He was an old man, bitter at the loss of his power. When the last of the other cars had gone he started the engine and drove home through the factory workers coming out of Pye's television factory. Cars pulled out of the factory gates in front of him. Men on bicycles ignored him and girls ran across the road to catch their buses. The Dean eyed them angrily. In the old days he would have blown his horn and cleared them off the road. Now he had to sit and wait. He found himself staring at an advertisement. 'Watch with Carrington on Pye', it said and a face smiled at him from a television screen. A familiar face. A face he knew. 'Carrington on Conservation. The Nation's Heritage at Stake.' The Dean stared at the face and was suddenly conscious of new hope. Behind him someone hooted importunately and the Dean put his car in gear and moved forward. He drove steadily home, unaware now of the traffic and of the present.

He left his car in the garage behind Phipps Building and went up to his room and presently he was sitting at his desk checking the Porterhouse Register for Cornelius Carrington's name. There it was, 1935–8. The Dean closed the book and sat back contentedly. A nasty piece of work, Cornielius Carrington, but effective for all that. The Jeremiah of the BBC, they called him, and certainly his romantic Toryism was popular. Not even politically divisive, just good-hearted nostalgia for the best that was British and with immense family appeal. The Dean did not often watch television but he had heard of Cornelius Carrington's programmes.

'Jewels of the Empire' had been one such series, with the ubiquitous Carrington expatiating on the architectural treasures of Poona and Lucknow. Another programme had been devoted to the need to preserve the rum ration in the Royal Navy, and Carrington had made himself the spokesman for past privileges wherever they were threatened. He was, the Dean felt sure, capable of extolling the virtues of any subject you chose and certainly there was no doubting the effectiveness of his appearance. Elicit Cornelius Carrington's interest and you were sure of an audience. And the wretched fellow was a Porterhouse man. The Dean smiled to himself at the thought of Carrington's publicizing the threat that Sir Godber's innovations posed to the College. It was a nice thought. He would have to speak to Sir Cathcart about it. It would depend on the outcome of the College Council meeting in the morning.

Skullion was at his waterpipe in the boiler-room when the meeting began. With the usual interruptions from the central heating system he could hear much of what was said. Most of the discussion centred on the cost of repairing the damage done to the Tower by Zipser's experiment in the mass disposal of prophylactics. Sir Godber, it seemed, had very definite views on the subject.

'It is time,' he was saying, 'that the College recognized the need to act in accordance with the principles which appear to have motivated the members of this Council in the past. The changes which I proposed at our last meeting met with opposition on the grounds that Porterhouse is a self-sufficient and independent college, a self-governing body whose interests are internal and without reference to the world at large. For myself as you know, that view is without foundation, but I am prepared to accept it since it appears to represent the views of the majority of this Council.' The Master paused, evidently looking round the Fellows for approval. In the boiler-room Skullion tried to digest the import of his words without much success. It seemed too much to hope that Sir Godber had changed his mind.

'Are we to understand that you have conceded that there is no need for the changes you proposed at our last meeting?' the Dean asked.

'The point I am conceding, Dean,' continued the Master, 'is that the College is responsible for its own internal affairs. I am prepared to accept the views of the Council that we should not look for guidance or assistance from the public.'

'I should certainly hope not,' said the Senior Tutor fervently.

'That is all I am conceding and since that is the case the full responsibility for the recent tragic events must be borne by the College.

In particular the cost of the repairs to the Tower must be met out of our own resources.'

A murmur of astonishment greeted the Master's statement.

'Impossible,' said the Dean angrily, 'out of the question. In the past we have had recourse to a Restoration Fund. There seems to be no good reason why we should not set up such a fund in this case.'

In the boiler-room Skullion followed the argument with difficulty. The Master's tactics evaded him.

'I must say, Dean, that I find your attitude a little difficult to understand,' Sir Godber continued. 'On the one hand you are opposed to any changes that would bring Porterhouse into line with contemporary standards of education ...' There was an angry interjection from the Dean. '... and on the other you seem only too ready to appeal to public subscription to avoid the necessary economies required to rebuild the Tower ...' At this point the central heating system interjected and it was some time before Skullion could catch the drift of the discussion again. By then they had got on to the details of the economies Sir Godber had in mind. Not surprisingly they seemed to embody just those changes in College policy he had suggested at the previous meeting but this time the Master was arguing less from policy than from financial necessity.

Through the gurgles in the pipe Skullion caught the words 'Self-service system in Hall ... coeducation ... and the sale of College properties.' He was about to climb down from his perch when Rhyder Street was mentioned. Skullion lived in Rhyder Street. Rhyder Street was College property. In the boiler-room Skullion's interest in the proceedings taking place above his head took on a new and more personal touch.

'The Bursar and I have calculated that the cost of the repairs can be met by the economies I have outlined,' Skullion heard. 'The sale of Rhyder Street in particular will provide something in the region of £150,000 at today's inflated prices. It is slum property, I know, but ...' Skullion slid down the pipe and sat on the chair. Slum property, he called it. Rhyder Street where he lived in Number 41. Slum property. The Chef lived there too. The street was filled with the houses of College servants. They couldn't sell it. They'd got no right to. A new fury possessed Skullion, a bitterness against Sir Godber that was no longer a concern for the traditions of the College he had served so long but a sense of personal betrayal. He'd been going to retire to Rhyder Street. It had been one of the conditions of his employment. The College had provided a house at a nominal rent. Skullion hadn't worked for forty-five years at a pittance a week to be evicted from a house that had been sold over his head by Sir Godber. Without waiting to hear more he got

up from the chair and lurched out of the boiler-room into the Old Court
in search of the Chef. Above his head a new violence of debate had
broken out in the Council Chamber. Sir Godber had announced the
proposed installation of a contraceptive dispenser.

The Dean erupted from the meeting with a virulence that stemmed from
the knowledge that he had been outmanoeuvred. The Master's appeal
to principle had placed him in a false position and the Dean was conscious
that his arguments against the Master's proposed economies had lacked
the force of conviction. 'To cap it all,' he muttered to himself as he swept
from the room, 'a damned contraceptive machine.' The Bursar's sudden
change of allegiance had infuriated him too. With his support Sir Godber
could manipulate the College finances as he pleased, and the Dean cursed
the Bursar viciously as he climbed the stairs to his room. There remained
only Sir Cathcart and already he had shown himself pusillanimous in
the matter of calling a meeting of the Porterhouse Society. Well, there
were others who could be relied on to bring influence to bear. 'I'll see
Sir Cathcart this afternoon,' he decided, and poured himself a glass of
sherry.

Sir Godber left the meeting with the Bursar. He was feeling distinctly
pleased with his morning's work.

'Why don't you lunch with us at the Lodge?' he said with a sudden
generosity. 'My wife has been asking to meet you.'

'That's very kind of you,' said the Bursar, glad to escape the hostile
reception he was likely to meet at High Table. They strolled across the
lawn past a group of Fellows who were conferring at the entrance to the
Combination Room. In the Screens they saw Skullion scowling darkly
in the shadows.

'I must say I find Skullion's manner a trifle taciturn,' Sir Godber said
when they were out of earshot. 'Even as an undergraduate I found him
unpleasant to deal with, and age hasn't improved his manners.'

The Bursar sympathized with Sir Godber. 'Not a very likeable fellow
but he's very conscientious and he is a great favourite of the Dean.'

'I can imagine that they get on well together,' said Sir Godber. 'All
the same, Porterhouse may be the name of the College but it doesn't
mean that the Head Porter is in charge. On the night of the ... er ...
accident Skullion was distinctly disrespectful. I told him to open the main
gates for the ambulancemen and he refused. One of these days I daresay
I shall have to ask you to give him notice.'

The Bursar blanched at the thought. 'I think that would be most inadvisable, Master,' he said. 'The Dean would be most upset.'

'Well,' said Sir Godber, 'the next time I have any insolence from him out he goes and no mistake.' With the silent thought that it was time such relics of the past got their marching orders, the Master led the way into the Lodge.

Lady Mary was waiting in the drawing-room. 'I've asked the Bursar to lunch, my dear,' said Sir Godber, his voice a shade less authoritative in the presence of his wife.

'I'm afraid you'll just have to take pot luck,' Lady Mary told the Bursar. 'My husband tells me that you treat yourselves lavishly at High Table.'

The Bursar simpered apologetically. Lady Mary ignored these signs of submission. 'I find it quite deplorable that so much good money should be wasted on maintaining the ill-health of a number of elderly scholars.'

'My dear,' Sir Godber intervened, 'you'll be glad to hear that the Council has accepted our proposals.'

'And not before time,' said Lady Mary, studying the Bursar with distaste. 'One of the most astonishing things about the educational institutions of this country is the way they have resisted change. When I think how long we've been urging the abolition of private education I'm amazed. The public schools seem to go from strength to strength.'

To the Bursar, himself the product of a minor public school on the South Downs, Lady Mary's words verged on the blasphemous. 'You're surely not suggesting public schools should be abolished,' he said. From the table where Sir Godber was pouring sherry there came the sound of rattled glass. Lady Mary assumed a new hauteur.

'Am I to infer from that remark that you are in favour of private education?' she asked.

The Bursar groped for a conciliatory reply. 'Well, I think there is something to be said for it,' he mumbled finally.

'What?' asked Lady Mary.

But before the Bursar could think of anything to recommend the Public School system without offending his hostess, Sir Godber had come to his rescue with a glass of sherry. 'Very good of you, Master,' he said gratefully and sipped his drink. 'And a very pleasant sherry, if I may say so.'

'We don't drink South African sherry,' Lady Mary said. 'I hope the College doesn't keep any in stock.'

'I believe we have some for the undergraduates,' said the Bursar, 'but I know the Senior Members don't touch the stuff.'

'Quite right too,' said Sir Godber.

'I was not thinking of the question of taste,' Lady Mary continued, 'so much as the moral objections to buying South African products. I have always made a point of boycotting South African goods.'

To the Bursar, long accustomed to the political opinions expressed at High Table by the Dean and the Senior Tutor, Lady Mary's views were radical in the extreme and the fact that they were expressed in a tone of voice which suggested that she was addressing a congregation of unmarried mothers unnerved him. He stumbled through the thorny problems of world poverty, the population explosion, abortion, the Nicaraguan earthquake, strategic arms limitation talks, and prison reform until a gong sounded and they went into lunch. Over a sardine salad that would have served as an *hors d'oeuvre* in Hall his discomfiture took a more personal turn.

'You're not by any chance related to the Shropshire Shrimptons?' Lady Mary asked.

The Bursar shook his head sorrowfully.

'My family came originally from Southend,' he said.

'How very unusual,' said Lady Mary. 'I only asked because we used to stay with them at Bognorth before the war. Sue Shrimpton was up with me at Somerville and we served together on the Needham Commission.'

The Bursar acknowledged Lady Mary's social distinction in silence. He would put his present humiliation to good use in the future. At sherry parties for years to come he would be able to say 'Lady Mary was saying to me only the other day ...' or 'Lady Mary and I ...' and establish his own superiority over lesser men and their wives. It was in such small achievements that the Bursar's satisfactions were found. Sir Godber ate his sardines in silence too. He was grateful to the Bursar for providing a target for his wife's conversation and moral rectitude. He dreaded to think what would happen if the injustices on which Lady Mary vented her moral spleen ever disappeared. 'The poor are always with us, thank God,' he thought and helped himself to a piece of cheddar.

It was left to Skullion to represent the college on the towpath that afternoon. The Dean had driven over to Coft to see Sir Cathcart and Skullion stood alone in the biting wind watching Porterhouse row over for the second day running. The terrible sense of wrong that he had felt in the boiler-room when he heard the proposed sale of Rhyder Street had not left him. It had been augmented by the news Arthur had brought him from High Table after lunch.

'He's put the cat among the pigeons now, the Master has,' Arthur said breathlessly. 'He's got under their skin something terrible this time.'

'I don't wonder,' said Skullion, thinking bitterly of Rhyder Street.

'I mean you wouldn't want one in your own home, would you? Not one of them things.'

'What things?' Skullion asked, all too conscious of the fact that he was unlikely to have a home to put anything in if Sir Godber had his way.

'Well I don't rightly know what they're called,' Arthur said. 'Not exactly, that is. You put your money in and ...'

'And what?' Skullion asked irritably.

'And you get these things out. Three I think. Not that I've ever had occasion to use them.'

'What things?'

'Frenchies,' said Arthur, looking round to make sure no one was listening.

'Frenchies?' said Skullion. 'What Frenchies?'

'The Frenchies that Zipser gentleman exploded himself with,' Arthur explained. Skullion looked at him in disgust. 'You mean to tell me they're going to bring one of those filthy things into the College?'

Arthur nodded. 'In the men's toilet. That's where it's going.'

'Over my dead body,' said Skullion. 'I'm not staying here as Head Porter with one of those things in the toilet. This isn't a bloody chemist's shop.'

'Some of the other colleges have them,' Arthur told him.

'Some of the other colleges may have them. Doesn't mean we've got to. It isn't right. Encourages immorality, French letters do. You'd have thought they'd have learnt that from what happened to that Zipser bloke. Preyed on his mind, all those FLs did.'

Arthur shook his head sorrowfully. ''Tisn't right,' he said, ''tisn't right, Mr Skullion. I don't know what the College is coming to. Senior Tutor is particularly upset. He says it will affect the rowing.'

Standing on the towpath Skullion agreed with the Senior Tutor. 'All this business about sex,' he muttered. 'It doesn't do anybody any good. It isn't right.'

When the Porterhouse Eight rowed past Skullion raised a feeble cheer and then stumped off after them. Around him bicycles churned the muddy puddles as they overtook him but, like the Dean the day before, Skullion was lost in thought and bitterness.

His anger, unlike the Dean's, was tainted with a sense of betrayal. The College whose servant he was and his ancestors before him had let him down. They had no right to let Sir Godber sell Rhyder Street. They should have stopped him. That was their duty to him, just as his duty to the College had been for forty-five years to sit in the Porter's Lodge all day and half the night for a miserable pittance a week, the guardian of privilege and of the indiscretions of the privileged young. How many drunken young gentlemen had Skullion helped to their rooms? How many secrets had he kept? How many insults had he suffered in his time? He could not begin to recall them but in the back of his mind the debits had balanced the credits and he had been secure in the knowledge that the College would always look after him now and in his old age. He had been proud of his servility, the Porter of Porterhouse, but what if the College's reputation was debased? What would he be then? A homeless old man with his memories. He wasn't having it. They'd got to see him right. It was their duty.

CHAPTER TWELVE

In the library at Coft Castle, the Dean put the same point to Sir Cathcart.

'It's our duty to see these damnable innovations are stopped,' he said. 'The man seems intent on changing the entire character of the College. For years, damn it for centuries, we've been famous for our kitchens and now he's proposing a self-service canteen and a contraceptive dispenser.'

'A what?' Sir Cathcart gasped.

'A contraceptive dispenser.'

'Good God, the man's insane!' shouted Sir Cathcart. 'Can't have one of those damned things in College. When I was an undergraduate you got sent down if your were caught riveting a dolly!'

'Quite,' said the Dean, who had a shrewd suspicion that in his time the General had been a steam-hammer if the imagery of his language was anything to go by. 'What you don't seem to appreciate, Cathcart,' he continued, before the General could indulge in any further mechanical memories, 'is that the Master is undermining something very fundamental. I'm not thinking simply of the College now. The implications are rather wider than that. Do you take my meaning?'

Sir Cathcart shook his head. 'No, I don't,' he said bluntly.

'This country,' said the Dean with a new intensity, 'has been run for the past three hundred years by an oligarchy.' He paused to see if the General understood the word.

'Quite right, old boy,' said Sir Cathcart. 'Always has been, always will be. No use denying it. Good thing.'

'An elite of gentlemen, Cathcart,' continued the Dean. 'Now don't mistake me, I'm not suggesting they started off as gentlemen. They didn't, half of them, they came from all walks of life. Take Peel for instance, grandson of a mill hand, ended up a gentleman though, and a damned fine Prime Minister. Why?'

'Can't think,' said Sir Cathcart.

'Because he had a proper education.'

'Ah. Went to Porterhouse eh?'

'No,' said the Dean. 'He was an Oxford man.'

'Good God. And still a gentleman? Extraordinary.'

'The point I'm trying to make, Cathcart,' said the Dean solemnly, 'is that the two Universities have been the forcing-house of an intellectual aristocracy with tastes and values that had nothing whatever to do with their own personal backgrounds. How many of our Prime Ministers over the last hundred and seventy years have been to Oxford or Cambridge?'

'Good Lord, don't ask me,' said the General. 'Got no idea.'

'Most of them,' said the Dean.

'Quite right too,' said Sir Cathcart. 'Can't have any Tom, Dick or Harry running the affairs of state.'

'That is precisely the point I have been trying to make,' said the Dean. 'The business of the older Universities is to take Toms and Dicks and Harrys and turn them into gentlemen. We have been doing that very successfully for the past five hundred years.'

'Mind you,' said Sir Cathcart doubtfully, 'I knew some bounders in my time.'

'I daresay you did,' said the Dean.

'Used to duck 'em in the Fountain. Did them no end of good.' Sir Cathcart reminisced cheerfully.

'What Sir Godber proposes,' the Dean continued, 'means the end of all that. In the name of so-called social justice the man intends to turn Porterhouse into a run-of-the-mill college like Selwyn or Fitzwilliam.'

Sir Cathcart snorted.

'Take more than Godber Evans to do that,' he said. 'Selwyn! Full of religious maniacs in my time, and Fitzwilliam wasn't a college at all. A sort of hostel for townies.'

'And what do you think Porterhouse will be with a self-service canteen instead of Hall and a contraceptive dispenser in every lavatory? There won't be a decent family prepared to pay a penny towards the Endowment Fund, and you know what that means.'

'Oh come now, can't be as bad as that,' said Sir Cathcart, 'I mean to say we've survived worse crises in the past. There was the business over the Bursar ... what was his name?'

'Fitzherbert.'

'Enough to ruin another college, that was.'

'Enough to ruin us,' said the Dean. 'If it hadn't been for him we wouldn't be dependent on wealthy parents now.'

'But we got over it all the same,' Sir Cathcart insisted, 'and we'll get over this present nonsense. Just fashion, all this · equality. Here today, gone tomorrow. Have a drink.' He got up and went over to the Waverley Novels. 'Scotch?' The Dean regarded the set in some bewilderment.

'Scott?' he asked. He had never regarded Sir Cathcart as a man with even remotely literary tastes and this sudden change in the conversation seemed unduly inconsequential.

'Or sherry? if you prefer,' said Sir Cathcart, indicating a handsomely bound copy of *Lavengro*. The Dean shook his head irritably. There was something extraordinarily vulgar about Sir Cathcart's travesty of a library.

'*Romany Rye* perhaps?' The Dean shook his head. 'Nothing, thank you,' he said. Sir Cathcart helped himself to *Rob Roy* and sat down.

'Proust,' he said, raising his glass. The Dean stared at him angrily. Sir Cathcart's flippancy was beginning to get on his nerves. He hadn't come out to Coft Castle to be regaled with the liquid contents of the library.

'Cathcart,' he said firmly, 'we have got to do something to stop the rot.'

The General nodded. 'Absolutely. Couldn't agree more.'

'It needs more than agreement to stop Sir Godber,' continued the Dean. 'It needs action. Public pressure. That sort of thing.'

'Difficult to get any public sympathy when you've got undergraduates running round blowing up buildings. Extraordinary thing to do really. Fill all those contraceptives with gas. Practical joke I suppose. Went wrong.'

'Very wrong,' said the Dean, who didn't want to get side-tracked.

'Mind you,' said Sir Cathcart, 'I can remember getting up to some pretty peculiar pranks. When I first went in the Army, great thing was to fill a French letter with water and stick it down someone's bed when he was out. Top bunk, you follow. Comes back. Gets into bed. Puts his toe through the thing. Fellow below gets drenched.'

'Very amusing,' said the Dean grimly.

'That's only the beginning,' said the General. 'Fellow below thinks fellow on top has wet his bed. Gets up and clobbers him. Damned funny.

Two fellows fighting like that.' He finished his whisky and got up to replenish his glass. 'Sure you won't change your mind,' he asked.

The Dean studied the shelves pensively. He was beginning to feel the need for some sort of restorative.

'A pink gin,' he said finally, with a malicious gleam in his eye.

'Zola,' said the General promptly and reached up for a copy of *Nana*. The Dean tried to collect his thoughts. Sir Cathcart's flippancy had begun to erode his fervour. He sipped his gin in silence while the General lit a cheroot.

'Trouble with you academic wallahs,' said Sir Cathcart finally, evidently sensing the Dean's confusion, 'is you take things too seriously.'

'This is a serious matter,' said the Dean.

'Didn't say it wasn't,' Sir Cathcart told him. 'What I said was you take it seriously. Bad mistake. Ever hear the joke Goering told his psychiatrist in the prison at Nuremburg?'

The Dean shook his head.

'About different nationalities. Very revealing,' Sir Cathcart went on. 'Take one German and what have you got?'

'And what have you got?'

'A good worker. Take two Germans and you've got a Bund. Three Germans and you've a war.'

The Dean smiled obediently. 'Very amusing,' he said, 'but I really don't see what this has to do with the College.'

'Haven't finished yet. Take one Italian and you've a tenor. Two Italians a retreat. Three Italians unconditional surrender. Take one Englishman and you've an idiot. Two Englishmen a club and three Englishmen an Empire.'

'Very funny,' said the Dean, 'but a little out of date, don't you think? We seem to have mislaid the Empire en route.'

'Forgot to be idiots,' said Sir Cathcart. 'Great mistake. Did bloody well when we were chinless wonders. Done bloody badly since. The Sir Godbers of this world have upset the applecart. Look serious and are fools. Different in the old days. Looked fools and were serious. Confused the foreigners. Ribbentrop came over to London. Heil Hitlered the King. Went back to Germany convinced we were decadent. Got a thrashing for his pains in '40. Hanged for that slip-up. Should have looked a bit closer. Mind you, it wouldn't have helped him. Went on appearances.' Sir Cathcart chuckled to himself and eyed the Dean.

'You may be right at that,' said the Dean grudgingly. 'And certainly the Master is a fool.'

'Clever fellows often are,' Sir Cathcart said. 'Got one-track minds.

Have to have, I suppose, to do so well. Great handicap, though. In life I mean. Get so carried away with what's going on inside their own silly heads they can't cope with what's going on outside. Don't know about life. Don't know about people. Got no nose for it.'

The Dean sipped his gin and tried to follow the train of Sir Cathcart's thoughts. A new mellowness had begun to steal over him and he had the feeling, it was no more than a mere glimmer, that somewhere in the General's rambling and staccato utterances there was a thread that was leading slowly to an idea. Something about the General's manner as he helped himself to a third whisky and the Dean to a second gin and bitters suggested it. Something like a sparkle of cunning in the bloodshot eyes and a twitch of his veined snout and the bristles of his ginger whiskers which reminded the Dean of an old animal, scarred but undefeated. The Dean began to suspect that he had underestimated Sir Cathcart D'Eath. He accepted one of the General's cheroots and puffed it slowly.

'As I was saying,' Sir Cathcart continued, settling once more into his chair, 'we've forgotten the natural advantages of idiocy. Puts the other fellow off you see. Can't take you seriously. Good thing. Then when he's off guard you give it to him in the goolies. Never fails. Out like a light. Want to do the same with this Godber fellow.'

'I really hadn't visualized going to quite such lengths,' said the Dean doubtfully.

'Shouldn't think he's got any,' said the General. 'Wife certainly doesn't look up to much. Scrawny sort of woman. Bad complexion. Not fond of boys, is he.'

The Dean shuddered. 'That at least we've been spared,' he said.

'Pity,' said Sir Cathcart. 'Useful bait, boys.'

'Bait?' asked the Dean.

'Bait the trap.'

'Trap?'

'Got to have a trap. Weak spot. Bound to have one. What?' said the General. 'Bleating of the sheep excites the tiger. *Stalky*. Great book.' He got up from his chair and crossed to the window and stared out into the darkness while the Dean, who had been trying to keep up with his train of thought, wondered if he should tell Sir Cathcart that *Lavengro* had nothing to do with Spain. On the whole he thought not. Sir Cathcart was too set in his ways.

'I forgot to mention it earlier,' he said at last, 'but the Master also intends to put Rhyder Street up for sale.'

Sir Cathcart, who had become immersed in his own reflection in the window, turned and stood glowering down at him. 'Rhyder Street?'

'He wants to use the money for the restoration of the Tower,' the Dean explained. 'It's old College property and rather run down. The College servants live there.'

The General sat down and fiddled with his moustache. 'Skullion live there?' he asked. The Dean nodded. 'Skullion, the Chef, the under-porter, the gardener, people like that.'

'Can't have that. Got to stable them somewhere,' said the General. He helped himself to a fourth whisky. 'Can't turn them out into the street. Old retainers. Wouldn't look good,' and his eyes which a moment before had been dark suddenly glittered. 'Not a bad idea either.'

'I must say, Cathcart,' said the Dean, 'I do wish you would not jump about so. What do you mean? "Wouldn't look good" and "Not a bad idea either". The two statements don't go together.'

'Looks bad for Sir Godber,' said the General. 'Bad publicity for a socialist. Headlines. See them now. Wouldn't dare. Got him.'

Slowly and dimly, through the shrapnel of Sir Cathcart's utterances, the Dean perceived the drift of his thought.

'Ah,' he said.

The General winked a dreadful eye. 'Something there, eh?' he asked.

The Dean leant forward eagerly. 'Have you ever heard of a fellow called Carrington? Cornelius Carrington? Conservationist. TV personality.'

He was aware that the infection of the General's staccato had finally taken hold of him but the thought was lost in the excitement of the moment. Sir Cathcart's eyes were gleaming brightly now and his nostrils were flared like those of a bronze warhorse.

'Just the fellow. An OP. Up his street. Couldn't do better. Nasty piece of work.'

'Right,' said the Dean. 'Can you arrange it?'

'Invite him up. Delighted to come. Snob. Give him the scent and off he'll go.'

The Dean finished his gin with a contented smile.

'It's just the sort of situation he likes,' he said, 'and although I deplore the thought of any more publicity – that wretched fellow Zipser gave us a lot of trouble in that direction you know – I rather fancy friend Carrington will give Sir Godber cause for thought. You definitely think he'll come?'

'Jump at the opportunity. I'll see to that. Same club. Can't think why. Should have been blackballed,' said the General. 'Fix it tomorrow.'

By the time the Dean left Coft Castle that evening he was a happier man. As he tottered out of his car in time for dinner and passed the

Porter's Lodge he noticed Skullion sitting staring into the gas fire. 'Must ask him how we did,' the Dean muttered and went into the Porter's Lodge.

'Ah, Skullion,' he said as the porter got to his feet, 'I wasn't able to be at the Bumps this afternoon. How did it go?'

'Rowed over, sir,' said Skullion dejectedly.

The Dean shook his head sadly.

'What a pity,' he said, 'I was rather hoping we'd do better today. Still there is always a chance in May.'

'Yes, sir,' Skullion said, but without, it seemed to the Dean, the enthusiasm that had been his wont.

'Getting old, poor fellow,' the Dean thought as he stumbled past the red lanterns that guarded the fallen debris of Zipser's climacteric.

CHAPTER THIRTEEN

Cornelius Carrington travelled to Cambridge by train. It accorded with the discriminating nostalgia which was the hallmark of his programmes that he should catch the Fenman at Liverpool Street and spend the journey in the dining-car speculating on the suddenness of Sir Cathcart's invitation, while observing his fellow travellers and indulging in British Rail's high tea. As the train rattled past the tenements and factories of Hackney and on to Ponders End, Carrington recoiled from the harshness of reality into the world of his own choosing and considered whether or not to have a second toasted tea cake. His was a soft world, fuzzy with private indecisions masked by the utterance of public verities which gave him the appearance of a lenient Jeremiah. It was a reassuring image and a familiar one, appearing at irregular but timely intervals throughout the year and bringing with it a denunciation of the present, made all the more acceptable by his approval of the recent past. If pre-stressed concrete and high-rise apartments were anathemas to Cornelius Carrington, to be condemned on social, moral and aesthetic grounds, his adulation of pebble-dash, pseudo-Tudor and crazy paving asserted the supreme virtues of the suburbs and reassured his viewers that all was well with the world in spite of the fact that nearly everything was wrong. Nor were his crusades wholly architectural. With a moral fervour which was evidently religious, without being in any way denominational, he espoused hopeless causes and gave viewers a vicarious sense of philanthropy that was eminently satisfying. More than one meths drinker had been elevated to the status of an alcoholic thanks to Carrington's intervention, while several heroin addicts had served an unexpected social purpose by suffering withdrawal symptoms in the company of Carrington, the camera crew, and several million viewers. Whatever the issue, Cornelius Carrington managed to combine moral indignation with entertainment and to extract from the situation just those elements which were most disturbing, without engendering in his audience a more than temporary sense of hopelessness which his own personality could render needless. There was about the man himself a genuinely comforting quality, epitomizing all that was sure and certain and humane about the British way of life. Policemen might be shot (and if his opinion was anything to go by they were being massacred daily across the country) but the traditions of the law remained unimpaired and immune to the rising tide of violence. Like some omniscient Teddy Bear, Cornelius Carrington was ultimately comforting.

As he sat in the dining car savouring the desultory landscape of Broxbourne, Carrington's thoughts turned from teacakes to the ostensible reasons for his visit. Sir Cathcart's invitation had come too abruptly both in manner and in time to convince him that it was wholly ingenuous. Carrington had listened to the General's description of the recent events in Porterhouse with interest. His ties with his old college had been tenuous, to put it mildly, and he shared with Sir Godber some unpleasant memories of the place and his time as an undergraduate. At the same time he recognized that the changes Sir Cathcart regretted in other colleges and feared in Porterhouse might have a value for a series on Cambridge. Carrington on Cambridge. It was an excellent title and the notion of a personal view of the University by 'An Old Freshman' appealed to him. He had declined the General's invitation and had come unannounced to reconnoitre. He would visit Porterhouse, certainly, but he would stay more comfortably at the Belvedere Hotel. More comfortably and less fettered by obligation. No one should say that Cornelius Carrington had bit the hand that fed him.

By the time the train reached Cambridge, he had already begun to organize the programme in his mind. The railway station would make a good starting point and one that pointed a moral. It had been built so far from the centre of the town on the insistence of the University Authorities in 1845 who had feared its malign influence. Foresight or the refusal to accept change? The viewer could take his pick. Carrington was impartial. Then shots of College gateways. Eroded statues. Shields. Heraldic animals. Chapels and gilded towers. Gowns. Undergraduates.

The Bridge of Sighs. It was all there waiting to be explored by Carrington
at his most congenial.

He took a taxi and drove to the Belvedere Hotel. It was not what he
remembered. The old hotel, charming in a quiet opulent way, was gone
and in its place there stood a large modern monstrosity, as tasteless a
monument to commercial cupidity as any he had ever seen. Cornelius
Carrington's fury was aroused. He would definitely make the series now.
Rejecting the anonymous amenities of the Belvedere, he cancelled his
room and took the taxi to the Blue Boar in Trinity Street. Here too
things had changed, but at least from the outside the hotel looked what
it had once been, an eighteenth-century hostelry, and Carrington was
satisfied. After all, it is appearances that matter, he thought as he went
up to his room.

At any previous time in his life Skullion would have agreed with him
but now that his house in Rhyder Street was up for sale, and the College's
reputation threatened by the Master's flirtation with the commercial
aspects of birth control, Skullion was less concerned with appearances.
He skulked in the Porter's Lodge with a new taciturnity in marked
contrast to the gruff deference he had accorded callers in the past. No
longer did he appear at the door to greet the Fellows with a brisk 'Good
morning, sir' and anyone calling for a parcel was likely to be treated to
a surly indifference and a churlishness which defeated attempts at
conversation. Even Walter, the under-porter, found Skullion difficult. He
had never found him easy but now his existence was made miserable by
Skullion's silence and his frequent outbursts of irritation. For hours
Skullion would sit staring at the gas fire mulling over his grievances and
debating what to do. 'Got no right to do it,' he would suddenly say out
loud with a violence that made Walter jump.

'No right to do what?' he asked at first.

'None of your business,' Skullion snapped back and Walter gave up
the attempt to discuss whatever it was that had put the Head Porter's
back up. Even the Dean, never the most sensitive of men when it came
to other people's feelings, noticed the change in Skullion when he called
each morning to make his report. There was a hangdog look about the
Porter that caused the Dean to wonder if it wasn't time he was put down
before recalling that Skullion was after all a human being and that he
had been misled by the metaphor. Skullion would sidle into the room
with his hat in his hand and mutter, 'Nothing to report, sir,' and sidle
out again leaving the Dean with a sense of having been rebuked in some
unspoken way. It was an uncomfortable feeling after so many years of

approval and the Dean felt aggrieved. If Skullion couldn't be put down, it was perhaps time he retired before this new churlishness tarnished his previously unspotted reputation for deference. Besides, the Dean had enough to worry about in Sir Godber's plans without being bothered with Skullion's private grievances.

If Skullion accorded the Dean scant respect, his attitude to the other Fellows was positively mutinous. The Bursar in particular suffered at his hands, or at least his tongue, whenever he had the misfortune to have to call in at the Porter's Lodge for some unavoidable reason.

'What do you want?' Skullion would ask in a tone that suggested that he would like the Bursar to ask for a black eye. It was the only thing Skullion, it appeared, was prepared to give him. His mail certainly wasn't. It regularly arrived two days late and Skullion's inability on the telephone switchboard to put the Bursar's calls through to the right number exacerbated the Bursar's sense of isolation. Only the Master seemed happy to see him now and the Bursar spent much of his time in consultation with Sir Godber in the Master's Lodge, conscious that even here he was not wholly welcome, if Lady Mary's manner was anything to go by. Between the Scylla of Skullion and the Charybdis of Lady Mary, not to mention the dangers of the open sea in the shape of the Fellows at High Table, the Bursar led a miserable existence made no less difficult by Sir Godber's refusal to accept the limitations placed on his schemes by the financial plight of the College. It was during one of their many wrangles about money that the Bursar mentioned Skullion's new abruptness.

'Skullion costs us approximately a thousand pounds a year,' he said. 'More if you take the loss on the house in Rhyder Street. Altogether the College servants mean an annual outflow of £15,000.'

'Skullion certainly isn't worth that,' said the Master, 'and besides I find his attitude decidedly obnoxious.'

'He has become very uncivil,' agreed the Bursar.

'Not only that but I dislike the proprietary attitude he takes to the College,' the Master said. 'Anyone would think he owns the place. He'll have to go.'

For once the Bursar did not disagree. As far as he was concerned Porterhouse would be a pleasanter place when Skullion no longer exercised his baleful influence in the Porter's Lodge.

'He'll be reaching retiring age in a few years' time,' he said. 'Do you think we should wait ...'

But Sir Godber was adamant. 'I don't think we can afford to wait,' he said. 'It's a simple question of redundancy. There is absolutely no need for two porters, just as there is no point in employing a dozen mentally deficient kitchen servants where one efficient man could do the job.'

'But Skullion is getting on. He's an old man,' said the Bursar, who saw looming before him the dreadful task of telling Skullion that his services were no longer required.

'Precisely my point. We can hardly sack the under-porter, who is young, simply to satisfy Skullion, who, as you say yourself, will be retiring in a few years' time. We really cannot afford to indulge in sentimentality, Bursar. You must speak to Skullion. Suggest that he look around for some other form of employment. There must be something he can do.'

The Bursar had no doubts on that score and he was about to suggest deferring Skullion's dismissal until they should see what the sale of Rhyder Street raised by way of additional funds when Lady Mary put a spoke in his wheel.

'I can't honestly see why the porter's job shouldn't be done by a woman,' she said. 'It would mark a significant break with tradition and really the job is simply that of a receptionist.'

Both Sir Godber and the Bursar turned and stared at her.

'Godber, don't goggle,' said Lady Mary.

'My dear ...' Sir Godber began, but Lady Mary was in no mood to put up with argument.

'A woman porter,' she insisted, 'will do more than anything else to demonstrate the fact that the College has entered the twentieth century.'

'But there isn't a college in Cambridge with a female porter,' said the Bursar.

'Then it's about time there was,' Lady Mary snapped. The Bursar left the Master's Lodge a troubled man. Lady Mary's intervention had ended once and for all his hopes of deferring the question of Skullion until the Porter had either made himself unpopular with the other Fellows by his manner or had come to his senses. The thought of having to tell the Head Porter that his services were no longer required daunted the Bursar. For a brief moment he even considered consulting the Dean but he was hardly likely to get any assistance from that quarter. He had burnt his bridges by siding with the Master. He could hardly change sides again. He entered his office and sat at his desk. Should he send Skullion a letter or speak to him personally? He was tempted by the idea of an impersonal letter but his better feelings prevailed over his natural timidity. He picked up the phone and dialled the Porter's Lodge.

'Best to get it over with quickly,' he thought, waiting patiently for Skullion to answer.

The summons to the Bursar's office caught Skullion in a rare mood of melancholy and self-criticism. The melancholy was not rare, but for once Skullion was not thinking of himself so much as of the College. Porterhouse had come down in the world since he had first come to the Porter's Lodge and in his silent commune with the gas fire Skullion had come to feel that he had been a little unjust in his treatment of the Dean and Fellows. They couldn't help what Sir Godber did. It was all the Master's fault. No one else was to blame. It was in this brief mood of contrition that he answered the phone.

'Wonder what he wants?' he muttered as he crossed the Court and knocked on the Bursar's door.

'Ah, Skullion,' said the Bursar with a nervous geniality, 'good of you to come.'

Skullion stood in front of the desk and waited. 'You wanted to see me,' he said.

'Yes, yes. Do sit down,' Skullion chose a wooden chair and sat down.

The Bursar shuffled some papers and then looked fixedly at the doorknob which he could see slightly to the left of the porter.

'I don't really know how to put this,' he began, with a delicacy of feeling that was wasted on Skullion.

'What?' said the Porter.

'Well to put the matter in perspective, Skullion, the College financial resources are not all that they should be,' the Bursar said.

'I know that.'

'Yes. Well, for some years now we've been considering the advisability of making some essential economies.'

'Not in the kitchen I hope.'

'No. Not in the kitchen.'

Skullion considered the matter. 'Wouldn't do to touch the kitchen,' he said. 'Always had a good kitchen the College has.'

'I can assure you that I am not talking about the kitchen,' said the Bursar, still apparently addressing the doorknob.

'You may not be talking about it but that's what the Master has in mind,' said Skullion. 'He's going to have a self-service canteen. Told the College Council he did.'

For the first time the Bursar looked at Skullion. 'I really don't know where you get your information from ...' he began.

'Never you mind about that,' said Skullion. 'It's true.'

'Well ... perhaps it is. There may be something in what you say but that's not ...

'Right,' interrupted Skullion. 'And it's all wrong. He shouldn't be allowed to do it.'

'To be perfectly honest, Skullion,' said the Bursar, 'there are some changes envisaged on the catering side.'

Skullion scowled. 'Told you so,' he said.

'But I really didn't ask you here to discuss ...'

'Could always raise money in the old days by asking the Porterhouse Society. Haven't tried that yet, have you?'

The Bursar shook his head.

'Lot of rich gentlemen still,' Skullion assured him. 'They wouldn't want to see changes in the kitchen. They'd chip in if they knew he was going to put a canteen in. You ask them before you do anything.'

The Bursar tried to think how to bring the conversation back to its original object.

'It isn't simply the kitchen, you know. There are other economies we have to make.'

'Like selling Rhyder Street I suppose,' said Skullion.

'Well, there's that and ...'

'Wouldn't have done that in Lord Wurford's time. He wouldn't have stood for it.'

'We simply haven't got the money to do anything else,' said the Bursar lamely.

'It's always money,' Skullion said. 'Everything gets blamed on money.' He got up and walked to the door. 'Doesn't mean you've got the right to sell my home. Wouldn't have happened in the old days.' He went out and shut the door behind him. The Bursar sat at his desk and stared after him. He sighed. 'I'll simply have to write him a letter,' he thought miserably and wondered what it was about Skullion that was so daunting. He was still sitting there ten minutes later when there was a knock on the door and the Head Porter reappeared.

'Yes, Skullion?' the Bursar asked.

Skullion sat down again on the wooden chair. 'I've been thinking about what you said.'

'Really?' said the Bursar, trying to think what he had said. He had been under the impression that Skullion had done all the talking.

'I'm prepared to help the College,' Skullion said.

'Well, that's very good of you, Skullion,' said the Bursar, 'but ...'

'It isn't very much but it's all I can do,' Skullion continued. 'You'll have to wait till tomorrow for it till I've been to the bank.'

The Bursar looked at him in astonishment.

'The bank? You don't mean ...'

'Well it's college property really. Lord Wurford left it to me in his will. It's only a thousand pounds but if it ...'

'My dear Skullion, really this is ... Well, it's extremely good of you but I ... we couldn't possibly accept a gift from you,' the Bursar stuttered.

'Why not?' said Skullion.

'Well ... well it's out of the question. You'll need it yourself. For your retirement ...'

'I ain't retiring,' Skullion said firmly.

The Bursar stood up. The situation was getting quite beyond him. He must take a firm line.

'It's about your retirement that I wanted to see you,' he said with a determined harshness. 'It has been decided that it would be in your own interest if you were to seek other employment.' He stopped and stared out of the window. Behind him Skullion had sagged on the chair.

'Sacked,' he said, with a hiss of air that sounded as if he were expiring with disbelief.

The Bursar turned reassuringly.

'Not sacked, Skullion,' he said cheerfully. 'Not sacked, just ... well ... for your own sake, for everyone's sake it would be better if you looked around for another job.'

Skullion stared at him with an intensity that alarmed the Bursar. 'You can't do it,' he said, rising to his feet. 'You've got no right. No right at all.'

'Skullion,' the Bursar began warningly.

'You've sacked me,' Skullion roared, and his face which had been briefly pale flushed to a new and terrible red. 'After all these years I've given to the College you've sacked me.'

To the Bursar it seemed that Skullion had swollen to a fearful size which filled his office and threatened him. 'Now, Skullion,' he began, as the Porter loomed at him, but Skullion only stared a moment and then turned on his heel and rushed from the office slamming the door behind him. The Bursar subsided into his chair limp and exhausted.

To Skullion, stumbling blindly across the Court, the Bursar's words were impossible. Forty years. Forty-five years he had served the College. He reeled into the Screens and stood clutching the lintel of the Buttery counter for support. The sense of being needed, of being as much a support to the College as the stone lintel he clutched was to the wall above it, all this had left him or was leaving him as waves of realization swept over him and eroded his absolute conviction that he was still and would forever be the Porter of Porterhouse. Breathing deeply Skullion heaved himself on down the steps into the Old Court and walked woodenly towards the Porter's Lodge and the consolation of his gas fire. There he brushed past Walter and sat slumped in his chair, unable even now to accept the enormity of the Bursar's words. There had been Skullions at Porterhouse since the College was founded. He had Lord Wurford's word for it and with such a continuity of possession behind him, it was as though he stood upon the edge of the world with only an abyss before him. Skullion recoiled from the oblivion. It was impossible to conceive. In a state of numbed disbelief he heard Walter moving about the Lodge as if it were somewhere distant.

'Gutterby and Pimpole,' Skullion muttered, invoking the saints of his calendar almost automatically in his agony.

'Yes, Mr Skullion?' said Walter. 'Did you say something?' But Skullion said nothing and presently Walter went out leaving the Head Porter muttering dimly to himself.

'Going off his head, old bugger,' he thought without regret. But Skullion was mad only in a figurative sense. As the full extent of his deprivation dawned on him, the anger which had been gathering in him since Sir Godber became Master broke through the barrier of his deference and swept like a flash flood down the arid watercourse of his feelings. For years, for forty years, he had suffered the arrogance and the impertinent assumptions of privileged young men and had accorded them in turn a quite unwarranted respect and now at last, released from all his obligations, the anger he had suppressed at so many humiliations added to the momentum of his present fury. It was almost as though Skullion welcomed the ruin of his pretensions, had secretly hoarded the memories of his afflictions against such an eventuality so that his freedom, when and if it came, should be complete and final. Not that it was or could be. The habits of a lifetime remained unaltered. An undergraduate came in for a parcel and Skullion rose obediently and brought it to the counter but without the rancour that had been the emblem of his servitude. His anger was all internal. Outwardly Skullion seemed subdued and old, shuffling about his office in his bowler hat and muttering to himself, but inwardly all was altered. The deep divisions in his mind, like the two separate lobes of his brain, his allegiance to the College and his self-interest, were sundered and Skullion's anger at his lot in life could run unchecked.

When Walter returned at six o'clock, Skullion put on his overcoat.

'Going out,' he said and left Walter dumbfounded. It wasn't his night on duty. Skullion went out of the gate and turned down Trinity Street towards the Round Church. On the corner he hesitated and looked down towards the Baron of Beef but it wasn't the pub for his present mood. He wanted something less tainted by change. He walked on down Sidney Street towards King Street. The Thames Boatman was better. He hadn't been there for some time. He went in and ordered a Guinness and sat at a table in the corner and lit his pipe.

CHAPTER FOURTEEN

Cornelius Carrington spent the day in rehearsal. With a cultivated eccentricity he wandered through the colleges singling out the architectural backdrops against which his appearance would be most effective. He adored King's College Chapel though only briefly. It was too well-known, hackneyed he thought and, more important, it dwarfed his personality. Conscious of his own limitations he sought the less demanding atmosphere of Corpus Christi and stood in the Old Court admiring its medieval charms. He pottered on through St Catherine's and Queens' over the wooden bridge and shuddered at the desecration of concrete that had been erected over the river. In Pembroke he lamented Waterhouse's library for its Victorian vulgarity before changing his mind and deciding that it was an ornamental classic of its time. Glazed brick was preferable to concrete after all, he thought, as he made his way down Little St Mary's Lane towards the Graduate Centre.

He had morning coffee in the Copper Kettle, lunch in the Whim, and all the time his mind revolved around the question which had been bothering him since his arrival. The programme as he visualized it lacked the human touch. It was not enough to conduct a million viewers on a guided tour of Cambridge colleges. There had to be a moral in it somewhere, a human tragedy that touched the heart and raised the Carrington Programme from the level of aesthetic nostalgia to the heights of drama. He'd find it somewhere, somehow. He had a nose for the undiscovered miseries of life.

In the afternoon he continued his pilgrimage through Trinity and John's and fulminated at the huge new building there. He minced through Magdalene and it wasn't until half-past three that he found himself in Porterhouse. Here, if anywhere in Cambridge, time stood still. No hint of concrete here. The blackened walls of brick and clunch were as they had been in his day. The cobbled court with its chapel in the Gothic style, its lawns and the great Hall through whose stained-glass windows the winter sun glowed richly: all was as he remembered. And with the

memory there came the uneasy feeling of his own inadequacy, which had
been his mood in those days, and which, in spite of his renown, he had
never wholly eradicated. Steeling himself against this recrudescence of
inferiority he climbed the worn steps to the Screens and stood for a
moment studying the notices posted in the glass cases there. Here too
nothing had changed. The Boat Club. Rugger. Squash. Fixture lists.
With a shudder Carrington turned away from this reminder that
Porterhouse was a rowing college and stood in the archway looking down
into New Court with astonishment. Here things had changed. Plastic
sheeting covered the front of the Tower and broken masonry lay heaped
on the flags below. Carrington gaped at the extent of the destruction and
was about to go down to make a closer examination when a small figure,
heavily muffled in an overcoat, panted up the steps behind him and he
turned to find himself face to face with the Dean.

'Good afternoon,' Carrington said, relapsing suddenly into a deference
he thought he had outgrown. The Dean stopped and looked at him.

'Good afternoon,' he said, suppressing the glint of recognition in his
eye. Carrington's face was familiar from the hoardings, but the Dean
preferred to pretend to an infallible memory for Porterhouse men. 'We
haven't seen you for a long time, have we?'

Carrington shrank a little at the supposition that his viewers, however
numerous elsewhere, did not include the Senior Members of his old
college.

'To my knowledge you haven't been back since ... um ... er,' the
Dean fabricated a tussle with his memory, 'nineteen ... er thirty-eight,
wasn't it?'

Carrington agreed humbly that it was, and the Dean, secure now in
his traditional role as the ward of an ineffable superiority, led the way
towards his rooms.

'You'll join me for tea,' he asked and Carrington, already reduced to
a submissiveness that infuriated him, thanked him for the offer.

'I'm told,' said the Dean as they climbed the narrow staircase, 'by
those who know about these things, that you have made something of a
name for yourself in the entertainment industry.'

Carrington found himself simpering a polite denial.

'Come, come, you're too modest,' said the Dean, rubbing salt into the
wound. 'Your opinion matters, you know.'

Carrington doubted it.

'You must be one of the few distinguished members the College has
produced in recent years,' the Dean continued, leading the way down
the corridor from whose walls there stared the faces of Porterhouse men

whose expressions left Carrington in little doubt that whatever they might think of him distinguished was not the word.

'You just sit down while I put the kettle on,' said the Dean and Carrington left for a moment tried hard to restore the dykes of his self-esteem. The room did not help. It was filled with reminders of past excellence in which he had no share. As an undergraduate Carrington had shone at nothing and even the knowledge that these peers of his youth who stared unwrinkled from their frames, singly or in teams, had failed to sustain the promise of their early brilliance did nothing to console him. They were probably substantial men, if hardly known, and Carrington for all his assumed arrogance was conscious of the ephemeral nature of his own reputation. He was not and would never be a substantial man, a man with Bottom, as the eighteenth century and no doubt the Dean would phrase it, and Carrington was enough of an Englishman to resent his inadequacy. It was probably this sense of having failed as a good fellow, a solid dependable sort of a chap, which give to his practised nostalgia for the twenties and thirties its quality of genuine emotion as if he pined for a time as mediocre as himself. He was rescued from his self-pity by the Dean who emerged with a tray from his tiny kitchen.

'Harrison,' said the Dean of the photograph Carrington had been studying self-critically.

'Ah,' he agreed noncommittally.

'Brilliant scrum-half. Scored that try at Twickenham in ... now when was it?'

'I've no idea,' said Carrington.

'Thirty-six? About your time. I'm surprised you don't remember.'

'I was never a great rugby man.'

The Dean looked at him critically. 'No, now I come to think of it you weren't, were you? Was it rowing, you were interested in?'

'No,' said Carrington, uncomfortably aware that the Dean knew it already.

'You must have done something in your years in College. Mind you, a lot of the young fellows who come up these days don't do anything very much. I sometimes wonder what they come to University for. Sex, I suppose, though why they can't indulge their sordid appetites somewhere else I can't imagine.' He shuffled into his kitchen and returned with a plate of rock cakes.

'I was looking at the damage to the Tower,' Carrington began when the Dean had poured tea.

'Come to make capital out of our misfortunes, I suppose,' said the

Dean. 'You journalist fellows seem to be the carrion crows of contemporary civilization.' He sat back smiling at the happy alliteration of his insult.

'I wouldn't really regard myself as a journalist,' Carrington demurred.

'Wouldn't you? How every interesting,' said the Dean.

'I see myself more as a commentator.'

The Dean smiled. 'Of course. How stupid of me. One of the lords of the air. A maker of opinion. How very interesting.' He paused to allow Carrington to savour his indifference. 'Don't you often feel embarrassed at the amount of influence you wield? I know I should. But then of course nobody listens to what I have to say. I suppose you might say I lack the common touch. Do have some more tea.'

In his chair Carrington regarded the old man angrily. He had had enough of the Dean's hospitality, the polite insults and the delicate depreciation of everything he had achieved. Porterhouse had not changed. Not one iota. The place, the man, were anachronisms beyond the compassion of his nostalgia.

'One of the things that amazes me,' he said finally, 'is to find that in a University that prides itself on scholarship and research, Porterhouse remains so resolutely a sporting college. I was glancing at the notices just now. No mention of scholarships or academic work. Just the old rugby lists ...'

'And what did you get? A double first, was it?' the Dean inquired sweetly.

'A two two,' said Carrington.

'And look where it's got you,' said the Dean. 'It speaks for itself really. Let's just say that we haven't succumbed to the American infection yet.'

'The American infection?'

'Doctoratitis. The assumption that a man's worth is to be measured by mere diligence. A man spends three years minutely documenting documents if you understand my meaning, anyway investigating issues that have escaped the notice of more discriminating scholars, and emerges from the ordeal with a doctorate which is supposed to be proof of his intelligence. Than which I can think of nothing more stupid. But there you are, that's the modern fashion. It comes, I suppose, from a literal acceptance of the ridiculous dictum that genius is an infinite capacity for taking pains. These fellows seem to think that if you can demonstrate an appetite for indigestible and trivial details for three years you must be a genius. In my opinion genius is by definition a capacity to jump the whole process of taking infinite pains, but then as I say, nobody listens to me. I mean there must be millions of people taking whatever these infinite pains are without a spark of intelligence let alone genius between them. And then again you have a silly fellow like Einstein who can't even count ... it depresses me, it really does, but it's the fashion.'

The Dean waved his hands as if to exorcize the evil spirit of his time and Carrington ventured to intervene.

'But surely research does pay off ...' he suggested.

'Pay?' said the Dean, 'I daresay it does. It certainly earns some colleges a great deal of money. Again you have this absurd assumption that provided you purchase enough sows' ears one of them is bound to turn into a silk purse. Utter nonsense, of course. It's the quality that counts not the quantity but then I don't expect you to sympathize with my old-fashioned point of view. When all's said and done it's quantity that's made your reputation, isn't it?'

'Quantity?'

'Megaviewers,' said the Dean. 'It seems an appropriate if nasty expression.'

By the time Cornelius Carrington left the Dean's rooms the erosion of his self-respect was almost complete and the comfortable acceptance of himself as the spokesman of a wholesome public concern quite gone. In the Dean's eyes he was clearly a parvenu, a jack in the box, he had suggested with a smile, and Carrington had found himself sharing the Dean's opinion. He walked out of Porterhouse envying the man his assurance and cursing himself for his inability to cope. What concrete and system-built housing was for him, he clearly was for the Dean, evidence of a facile and ugly commercialism. What had the Dean said? That he found the ephemeral distasteful, and there had been no doubt that of all ephemera he found television commentators the least to his liking. Carrington walked down Senate House Lane debating the source of the Dean's assurance. The man's lifetime spanned the coming of pebble-dash and the mock-Tudor suburbs Carrington found so appealing. He belonged to an earlier tradition. The Toby Jug Englishman, Squarsons and squires who didn't give a tuppenny damn what the world thought of them and bloodied the world's nose when it got in their way. In this mood of self-recrimination at his unalterable deference to such men, Carrington found himself in King Street. He wasn't at all sure how he had got there and at first found it difficult to recognize. King Street had changed more than any other part of Cambridge. The houses and shops that had stood huddled together down the narrow street were gone. A concrete multi-storied car park, a row of ugly brick arcades. And where were all the pubs? Walking down the street Carrington forgot his own demolition. A sense of righteous anger gripped him. The old King Street had been shabby and dishevelled but it had been entertaining. Now it was bleak, impersonal and grim. A little further on he came to some remnants. An antique shop that had odds and ends of vases and bad paintings in its windows. A coffee-shop cluttered with percolators and the more intricate jugs that undergraduates still evidently cultivated. But for the most part the developers had done their damnedest. Finally he came to the Thames Boatman and grateful to find it still standing he went inside.

'A pint of bitter, please,' he told the barman with his usual sense of place. Gin and tonic in a King Street pub would have been unthinkable. He took his beer to a table by the window.

'Seem to have been a lot of changes since I was here last,' he said, having taken a large swig from his beer glass. He didn't usually take large swigs. In fact he didn't usually drink beer at all, but beer in large swigs was, he remembered, customary in King Street.

'Knocking the whole street down,' said the barman laconically.

'Must be bad for business,' Carrington suggested.

''Tis and it isn't,' the barman agreed.

Carrington gave up the attempt to make conversation and turned his attention to the more responsive decorations of the bar-room.

A short time later a man in a bowler hat entered the bar and ordered a Guinness. Carrington studied his back and found a vague familiarity there. The dark overcoat, the highly polished shoes, the solid neck and above all the square set of the bowler hat, all these were tokens of a college porter. But it was the pipe, the jutting bulldog pipe, that woke his memory and told him this was Skullion. The porter paid for his Guinness and took it to the table in the corner and lit his pipe. A waft of blue smoke reached Carrington. He sniffed, and in that sniff the years receded and he was back in the Porter's Lodge in Porterhouse. Skullion. He had forgotten the man and his stiff, wooden almost military ways. Skullion standing like some heraldic beast at the College gate or seen from his rooms above the Hall, a dark helmeted figure marching across the Court in the early morning, his attendant shadow jutting above the crenellations cast by the morning sunlight on the lawn. The pipe at the gates of dawn, Carrington had once called him but there was nothing of the dawn about the Porter now. He sat over his Guinness and sucked his pipe and scowled unseeingly. Carrington studied the heavy features and was struck by the grim strength of the face below the brim of the bowler hat. If the Dean had prompted the thought of Toby Jugs, Skullion called to mind an older type that than. Something almost Chaucerian about the man, Carrington thought, relying for his assessment on vague memories of *The Prologue*. Certainly medieval. But above all it was the impressiveness of the man that struck him most. Impressive was the word for the face that stared out across the bar. Carrington drank his beer and ordered another. As he waited for it he crossed to the table where Skullion sat.

'It's Skullion, isn't it?' he asked. Skullion looked up at him doubtfully. 'What if it is?' he asked, adopting the impersonal pronoun as if to avoid an intrusion on his privacy.

'I thought I recognized you,' Carrington went on. 'You probably wouldn't remember me, Carrington. I was up at Porterhouse in the thirties.'

'Yes, I remember you. You had rooms over the Hall.'

'Let me get you another drink. Guinness, isn't it?' And before Skullion could say anything Carrington had returned back to the barman and was ordering a Guinness. Skullion regarded him morosely. He remembered Carrington all right. Bertie they used to call him. Flirty Bertie. Not a gentleman. He'd been something in the Footlights. Skullion hadn't approved of him.

Carrington brought the glasses across and sat down. 'I suppose you've retired now,' he asked presently.

'Not what you might call retired,' Skullion said grimly.

'You mean you're still Head Porter after all these years? My goodness, you have been there a long time.' He spoke with the affected eagerness of an interviewer, and indeed something about Skullion had awoken in him the feeling that there was a story here. Carrington had a nose for these things.

'Forty-five years,' said Skullion and drank his stout.

'Forty-five years,' echoed Carrington. 'Remarkable.'

Skullion grunted and lifted a bushy eyebrow. There was nothing remarkable about it to him.

'And now you've retired?' Carrington persisted. Skullion sucked his pipe slowly and said nothing. Carrington drank another mouthful of beer, and changed the subject.

'I don't suppose they have the King Street Run anymore,' he said. 'Now that they've knocked down so many of the old pubs.'

Skullion nodded. 'Used to be fourteen and a pint in every one in half an hour. Took some doing.' He relapsed into silence. Carrington had caught the mood. The old ways were passed and with them the Head Porter. That partially explained the old man's grim expression but there was something more behind it. Carrington changed his tack.

'The College doesn't seem to have changed much anyway.'

Skullion's scowl deepened. 'Changed more than you know,' he grunted.

'Going to change out of recognition now.' He made a move as if to spit on the floor but turned back and smelt the bowl of his pipe.

'You mean the new Master?' Carrington inquired.

'Him and all the rest of them. Women in college. Self-service canteen in Hall. And what about us as served the College all our lives! Out on the street like dogs.' Skullion drank his beer and banged the glass down on the table. Carrington was silent. He sat still almost invisible with interest like a predator that sees its prey. Skullion lit his pipe and blew smoke.

'Forty-five years I've been a porter,' he said presently. 'A lifetime, wouldn't you say?' Carrington nodded solemnly. 'I've sat in that Lodge and watched the world go by. When I was a boy we used to wait at the Catholic Church for the young gentlemen's cabs to come by from the station. "Carry your bags, sir," we'd shout and run beside the horses all the way to the College and carry their trunks up to their rooms for sixpence. That's how we earned some money in those days. Running a mile and carrying trunks into College. For sixpence.' Skullion smiled at the memory and for a moment it seemed to Carrington that the intensity had gone out of him. But there was something more than mere memory there, a sense of wrong that Carrington could sense and which in a remote way matched his own feelings. And his own feelings? It was difficult to define them, to say precisely what it was that he had found so monstrous in the Dean's delicate contempt. Except an insufferable arrogance that viewed him distantly as if he had been a microbe squirming convulsively upon a slide. Carrington acknowledged his own infirmity of spirit but his anger remained. He turned to Skullion as to an ally.

'And now they've turned you out?' he asked.

'Who said they had?' Skullion asked belligerently. Carrington prevaricated. 'I thought you said something about being made redundant,' he murmured.

'Got no right to do it,' he said almost to himself. 'They wouldn't have done it in the old days.'

'I seem to remember in my day that the College had rather a good reputation among the servants.'

Skullion looked at him with new respect. 'Yes, sir,' he said, 'Porterhouse was known for its fairness.'

'That's what I thought,' said Carrington, adopting the lordly manner which was evidently what Skullion required of him.

'Old Lord Wurford wouldn't have dreamt of turning the Head Porter into the streets,' Skullion continued. 'When he died he left me a thousand pounds. Offered it to the Bursar, I did, to help the College out. Turned me down. Would you believe it? Turned my offer down.'

'You offered him a thousand pounds to help the College out?' Carrington asked.

Skullion nodded. 'I did that. "Oh no," he says, "wouldn't dream of taking it" and the next second he gives me notice. It's not credible is it?'

To Carrington credibility hardly mattered. The story was enough.

'They're selling Rhyder Street too,' Skullion went on.

'Rhyder Street?'

'Where all the College servants live. Turning us all out.'

'Turning you out? They can't do that.'

'They are,' Skullion said. 'Chef, the head gardener, Arthur, all of us.'

Carrington finished his beer and bought two more. He had the human touch he had been seeking and with it the knowledge that his visit had not been wasted after all. He had his story now.

CHAPTER FIFTEEN

The Dean smiled. He had enjoyed his tea with Carrington. It was seldom nowadays that he had the opportunity to put his gifts for malice to good use. 'Nothing like a goad for making a man prove himself,' he thought, recalling his happy days as coach to the Porterhouse crew, and the insults he had used to drive the Eight to victory. And Carrington had suffered the gibes in silence. They would fester in him and give him the edge that was needed. He would do the programme on Porterhouse. His coming to Cambridge had proved his interest in the College in spite of his refusal of Sir Cathcart's invitation. And that refusal was an advantage too. Nobody could say now that he had been put up to it. As for the content of the programme, the Dean felt secure in the knowledge that Carrington was the high priest of nostalgia. Sir Godber's plans would be the bait. Tradition sullied. The old and proven ways under threat. The curse of modernism. The Dean could hear the clichés now, rolling off Carrington's tongue to stir the millions hungry for the good old days. And what of Sir Godber himself? Carrington would make mincemeat of the man's pretensions. The Dean helped himself to sherry with the air of a man well content, if not with the world, at least with that corner of it over which he was guardian. He went down to dinner in high spirits. They were having Caneton à l'orange and the Dean was fond of duck. He entered the Combination Room and was surprised to find the Master already there talking to the Senior Tutor. The Dean had forgotten that Sir Godber dined in Hall occasionally.

'Good evening, Master,' he said.

'Good evening, Dean,' Sir Godber replied. 'I have just been discussing this business of the restoration fund with the Senior Tutor. It seems that we've had an offer for Rhyder Street from Mercantile Properties. They've offered one hundred and fifty thousand. I must say I'm inclined to accept. What's your opinion?'

The Dean grasped his gown and frowned. His objections to the sale of Rhyder Street were tactical. He opposed what Sir Godber proposed on principle but now it was useful that the Master should commit himself to an act whose lack of charity Cornelius Carrington could emphasize.

'Opinion? Opinion?' he said finally. 'I have no opinions on the matter. I regard the sale of Rhyder Street as a betrayal of our trust to the College servants. That is not an opinion. It is a matter of fact.'

'Ah well,' said Sir Godber, 'we shall just have to differ, won't we?'

The Senior Tutor was conciliatory. 'It's a hard decision to make. I do see that,' he said. 'On the one hand the servants have to be considered and on the other there is no doubt that the restoration fund needs the money. A difficult decision.'

'Not one that I apparently am called to make,' said the Dean. They trooped into Hall and in the absence of the Chaplain, whose deafness had in no way improved since the explosion in the tower, the Dean said grace. They ate in silence for a while, Sir Godber munching his duck and congratulating himself on the change in the Senior Tutor's attitude, due possibly to the poor showing of the College in the Bumps, and one or two unfortunate remarks by the Dean. Eager to exploit the rift, Sir Godber set out to cultivate the Senior Tutor. He passed the salt without being asked for it. He told two amusing stories about the Prime Minister's secretary and finally, when the Senior Tutor ventured the opinion that he thought such goings-on were due to the entry into the Common Market, launched into a detailed account of an interview he had once had with de Gaulle. Throughout it all the Dean remained patently uninterested, his eyes fixed on tables where the undergraduates sat talking noisily, and his mind entertained by the fuse that had been lit in Cornelius Carrington. Towards the end of the meal the Master, having exhausted the eccentricities of de Gaulle, turned the monologue to matters nearer home.

'My wife is most anxious that you should dine with us one evening,' he fabricated. 'She is concerned to know your views on the question of lady tutors for our female undergraduates.'

'Lady tutors?' said the Senior Tutor. 'Lady tutors?'

'Naturally as a coeducational college we shall require some female Fellows,' the Master explained.

'Charming,' said the Dean nastily.

'This comes as something of a shock, Master,' said the Senior Tutor.

Sir Godber helped himself to stilton. 'There are some matters, Senior Tutor, that are essentially feminine if you see what I mean. You would hardly want a young woman coming to you for advice about an abortion.'

The Senior Tutor disengaged himself from a mango precipitately. 'Certainly not,' he spluttered.

'It's an eventuality we have to consider, you know,' continued Sir Godber. 'These things do happen, and since they do it would be as well to have a Lady Tutor.'

Down the table the Dean smiled happily. 'And possibly a resident surgeon?' he suggested.

The Master flushed. 'You find the topic amusing, Dean?' he inquired.

'Not the topic, Master, so much as the contortions of the liberal conscience,' said the Dean, settling back in his chair with relish. 'On the one hand we have an overwhelming urge to promote the equality of the sexes. We admit women to a previously all-male college on the grounds that their exclusion is clearly discriminatory. Having done so much we find it necessary to provide a contraceptive dispenser in the Junior lavatory and an abortion centre doubtless in the Matron's room. Such a splendid prospect for parents to know that the welfare of their daughters is so well provided for. No doubt in time there will be a College crèche and a clinic.'

'Sex is not a crime, Dean.'

'In my view pre-marital intercourse comes into the category of breaking and entering,' said the Dean. He pushed back his chair and they stood while he said grace.

As he walked back through the Fellows' Garden the Master felt again that sense of unease which dining in Hall always seemed to give him. There had been a confidence about the Dean that he distrusted. Sir Godber couldn't put his finger on it exactly but the feeling persisted. It wasn't simply the Dean's manner. It had something to do with the Hall itself. There was something vaguely barbarous about the Hall, as if it were a shrine to appetite and hallowed by the usage of five hundred years. How many carcases had been devoured within its walls? And what strange manners had those buried generations had? Pre-Renaissance men, pre-scientific men, medieval men had sat and shouted and thought ...

Sir Godber shuddered at the superstitions they had entertained as if he could undo the thread of time that linked him to their animality. He willed his separation from them. He was a rational man. The contradiction in the phrase alarmed him suddenly. A rational man, free of the absurd and ignorant restrictions that had limited those men whose speculations on the nature of angels and devils, on alchemy and Aristotle, seemed now to verge on the insane. Sir Godber halted in the garden, astonished at the idea that he was the product of such a strange species. They were as remote to him as prehistoric animals and yet he inhabited buildings which they had built. He ate in the same Hall in which they had eaten and even now was standing on ground where they had walked. Alarmed at this new apprehension of his pedigree, Sir Godber peered around him in the darkness and hurried down the path to the Master's Lodge. Only when he had closed the door and was standing in the hall beneath the electric light did he feel reassured. He went into the drawing-room where Lady Mary was watching a film on television about the problems of senility. Sir Godber allowed himself to be conducted through several geriatric wards before becoming uncomfortably aware that his simple equation of progress with improvement did not apply to the ageing process of the human body. With the silent thought that if that was what the future held in store for him he would prefer to return to the past, he took himself up to bed.

Skullion returned from the Thames Boatman at closing time. He had had no supper and eight pints of Guinness had done nothing to improve his opinion that he had been shamefully treated. He staggered into the Porter's Lodge and, ignoring Walter's protest that his wife had been expecting him home for supper at seven o'clock and it was now eleven and what was he supposed to tell her, stumbled through to the back room and lay on the bed. It was a long time since he had had eight pints of anything and it was this more than his innate sense of duty that got him off the bed to close the front gate at twelve o'clock. In the intervals between tottering through to the lavatory Skullion lay in the darkness, while the room revolved around him, trying to sort out what he should do from what that television chap had said to him. Go and see the General in the morning. Apppear on the box with Carrington. Programme on Cambridge. Finally he got to sleep and woke late for the first time in forty-five years. It no longer mattered. His days as Head Porter of Porterhouse were over.

By the time Walter arrived Skullion had made up his mind. He took his coat down from the hook and put it on. 'Going out,' he told the astonished under-porter (Skullion hadn't been known to go out in the morning since he had been his assistant) and fetched his bicycle. The thaw had set in and this time as Skullion pedalled out to Coft the fields around him were piebald. Head bent against the wind, Skullion concentrated on what he was going to say and failed to notice the Dean's car as it swept past him. By the time he reached Coft Castle the bitterness that had been welling in him since his interview with the Bursar had bred in him an indifference to etiquette. He left his bicycle beside the front door of the house and knocked heavily on the door knocker. Sir Cathcart answered the door himself and was too astonished to find Skullion glowering at him from the doorstep to remind him that he was expected to use the kitchen door. Instead he found himself following the Porter into his drawing-room where the Dean, already ensconced in an armchair in front of the fire, had been telling him the news about Cornelius Carrington. Skullion stood inside the door and stared belligerently at the Dean while Sir Cathcart wondered if he should ring for the cook to bring a kitchen chair.

'Skullion, what on earth are you doing here?' asked the Dean. There was nothing hangdog about the Porter now.

'Come to tell the General about being sacked,' said Skullion grimly.

'Sacked? What do you mean? Sacked?' The Dean rose to his feet, and stood with his back to the fire. It was a good traditional stance for dealing with truculent servants.

'What I say,' said Skullion, 'I've been sacked.'

'Impossible,' said the Dean. 'You can't have been sacked. Nobody's told me anything about this. What for?'

'Nothing,' said Skullion.

'There must be some mistake,' said the General. 'You've got hold of the wrong end of ...'

'Bursar sent for me. Told me I'd got to go,' Skullion insisted.

'Bursar? He's got no authority to do a thing like that,' said the Dean.

'Well, he's done it. Yesterday afternoon,' Skullion continued. 'Told me to find other employment. Says the College can't afford to keep me on. Offered him money too, to help out. Wouldn't take it. Just gave me the sack.'

'This is scandalous. We can't have College servants treated in this high-handed fashion,' said the Dean. 'I'll have a word with the Bursar when I get back.'

Skullion shook his head sullenly. 'That won't do any good. The Master put him up to it.'

The Dean and Sir Cathcart looked at one another. There was in that glance a hint of triumph which grew as Skullion went on. 'Turned out of my own house. Sacked after all the years I've given to the College. It isn't right. Not standing for it, I'm not. I'm going to complain.'

'Quite right,' said the General. 'Absolutely scandalous behaviour on the part of the Master.'

'I want my job back now or else,' Skullion muttered. The Dean turned and warmed his hands at the fire. 'I'll put in a good word for you, Skullion. You need have no fear on that score.'

'I'm sure the Dean will do his best for you, Skullion,' said Sir Cathcart, opening the door for him. But Skullion stood his ground.

'Going to need more than words,' he said defiantly. The Dean turned round sharply. He wasn't used to being spoken to in that tone of voice by servants.

'You heard what I said, Skullion,' he said peremptorily. 'We'll do what we can for you. Can't promise more than that.'

Still Skullion stood where he was.

'Got to do better than that,' he muttered.

'I beg your pardon, Skullion,' said the Dean. But Skullion was not to be intimidated.

'It's my right to be porter,' he maintained. 'I've not done anything wrong. Forty-five years ...'

'Yes, we know all that, Skullion,' said the Dean.

'I'm sure this is just a misunderstanding,' interposed Sir Cathcart. 'The Dean and I will see what we can do to put the matter right. I'll see the Master personally if necessary. Can't have this sort of thing going on in a college like Porterhouse.'

Skullion looked at him gratefully. The General would see him right. He turned to the door and went out. The General followed him into the hall. 'Ask Cook to give you some tea before you go,' he said, reverting to his old routine, but Skullion had already gone. Planting his bowler hat firmly on his head he mounted his bicycle and pedalled off down the drive.

Sir Cathcart went back into the drawing-room. 'What price Sir Godber now?' he said.

The Dean rubbed his hands happily. 'I think we've got the rod we need,' he said. 'The Master is going to rue the day he sacked Skullion. That's one of the nice things about these damned socialists. The first people to get hurt by their rage for social justice are the working classes.'

'He's certainly got old Skullion's back up,' said Sir Cathcart. 'Well, I suppose we had better get in touch with the Bursar and see what we can do.'

'Do? My dear Cathcart, we do precisely nothing. If Sir Godber is fool enough to have the Bursar sack Skullion, I for one am not going to rescue him from his folly.'

Sir Cathcart stared uneasily at the receding figure of the Porter. Seen through the glass of the mullioned window Skullion had assumed a new amorphous aspect, dwindling but at the same time unsettling. He wondered briefly how much the Dean knew about Skullion's amendment of the examination process. It seemed a question better left unasked. Doubtless the whole business would blow over.

'After all, Cathcart,' said the Dean, 'you were the one who said the bleating of the sheep excites the tiger. Carrington is going to love this. He's staying at the Blue Boar. I think I'll drop in and have a word with him on the way back. Invite him to dine in Hall.'

General Sir Cathcart D'Eath sighed. It was one of the few good things about the affair that he didn't have to share his house with Cornelius Carrington.

CHAPTER SIXTEEN

Cornelius Carrington spent the morning in his room organizing his thoughts. It was one of his characteristics as a spokesman for his times that he seldom knew what to think about any particular issue. On the other hand he had an unerring instinct about what not to think. It was for instance unthinkable to approve of capital punishment, of government policy, or of apartheid. These were always beyond the pale and on a par with Stalin, Hitler and the Moors murderers. It was in the middle ground that he found most difficulty. Comprehensive schools were terrible but then so was the eleven-plus. Grammar schools were splendid but he despised their products. The unemployed were shiftless unless they were redundant. Miners were splendid fellows until they went on strike, and the North of England was the heart of Britain to be avoided at all costs. Finally Ireland and Ulster. Cornelius Carrington's mind boggled when he tried to find an opinion on the topic. And since his existence depended upon his capacity to appear to hold inflexible opinions on nearly every topic under the sun without at the same time offending more than half his audience at once, he spent his life in a state of irresolute commitment.

Even now, faced with the simple case of Skullion's sacking, he needed to decide which side the angels were on. Skullion was irrelevant, the object of an issue and superbly telegenic, but otherwise unimportant. He would be paraded before the cameras, encouraged to say a few inarticulate

but moving sentences, and sent home with his fee to be forgotten. It was
the issue that bothered Carrington. Who to blame for the injustice done
to the old retainer? What aspect of Cambridge life to deplore? The old
or the new? Sir Godber, who was evidently doing his best to turn
Porterhouse into an academic college with modern amenities in an
atmosphere of medieval monasticism? Or the Dean and Fellows, whose
athletic snobbery Carrington found personally so insufferable? On the
surface Sir Godber was the culprit but there was much to be said for
lambasting the Dean without whose obstinacy the economies which
necessitated sacking the Head Porter could have been avoided. He would
have to see Sir Godber. It was necessary in any case to get his permission
to do the programme. Carrington picked up the phone and dialled the
Master's Lodge.

'Ah, Sir Godber,' he said when the Master answered, 'my name is
Carrington, Cornelius Carrington.' He paused and listened to the Master's
voice change tone from indifference to interest. Sir Godber was evidently
a man who knew his media, and rose accordingly in Carrington's
estimation.

'Of course. Come to lunch. We can have it here or in Hall as you
prefer,' Sir Godber gushed. Carrington said he'd be delighted to. He left
the Blue Boar and walked towards Porterhouse.

Sir Godber sat in his study invigorated. A programme on Porterhouse
by Cornelius Carrington. It was an unexpected stroke of luck, a chance
for him to appear once more in the public eye, and a golden opportunity
to propound his philosophy of education. Come to think of it, he cut a
good figure on television. He rather doubted if the Dean would come
across as well, always supposing the old fool was prepared to appear on
anything quite so new fangled. He was still engrossed in composing an
unrehearsed account of the changes he had in mind for the College when
the doorbell rang and the au pair girl announced Cornelius Carrington.
The Master rose to greet him.

'How very nice of you to come,' he said warmly and led Carrington
into the study. 'I had no idea you were an old Porterhouse man and to
be perfectly honest I still find it hard to believe. I don't mean that in
any derogatory sense, I assure you. I'm a great admirer of yours. I
thought that thing you did on Epilepsy in Flintshire was excellent. It's
just that I've come to associate the College with a rather less concerned
approach to contemporary problems.' Conscious that he was perhaps
being a little too effusive, the Master offered him a drink. Carrington
looked round the room appreciatively. There were no photographs here

to remind him of the insignificance of his own youth and Sir Godber's adulation came as a pleasant change from the Dean's polite asperity.

'This programme of yours on the College is a splendid idea,' Sir Godber continued when they were seated. 'Just the sort of thing the College needs. A critical look at old traditions and an emphasis on the need for change. I imagine you have something of that sort in mind?' Sir Godber looked at him expectantly.

'Quite,' said Carrington. Sir Godber's generalities left every option open. 'Though I don't imagine the Dean will approve.'

Sir Godber looked at him keenly. The hint of malice he detected was most encouraging. 'A wonderful character, the Dean,' he said, 'though a trifle hidebound.'

'A genuine eccentric,' agreed Carrington drily. It was evident from his manner that the Dean did not command his loyalty. Reassured, the Master launched into an analysis of the function of the college system in the modern world while Carrington toyed with his glass and considered the invincible gullibility of all politicians. Sir Godber's faith in the future was almost as insufferable as the Dean's condescension and Carrington's erratic sympathies veered back towards the past. Sir Godber had just finished describing the advantages of coeducation, a subject that Carrington found personally distasteful, when Lady Mary arrived.

'My dear,' said Sir Godber, 'I'd like you to meet Cornelius Carrington.'

Carrington found himself gazing into the arctic depths of Lady Mary's eyes.

'How do you do?' said Lady Mary, her sympathies strained by the evident ambiguities of Carrington's sexual nature.

'He's thinking of doing a programme on the College,' Sir Godber said, pouring the driest of sherries.

'How absolutely splendid,' Lady Mary barked. 'I found your programme on spina bifida most invigorating. It really is time we put some backbone into those people at the Ministry of Health.'

Carrington shivered at the forcefulness of Lady Mary's enthusiasm. It filled him with that nostalgia for the nursery that was the hidden counterpart of his own predatory nature. The nursery with Lady Mary as the nanny. Even the thin mouth thrilled him, and the yellow teeth.

'Of course it's the same with the dental service,' Lady Mary snarled telepathically. 'We should put some teeth into it.' She smiled and Carrington glimpsed the dry tongue.

'I imagine you must find this a great change from London,' he said.

'It's quite extraordinary,' said Lady Mary still blossoming under the warmth of his asexual attention. 'Here we are only fifty miles from

London and it seems like a thousand.' She pulled herself together. He was still a man for all that.

'What sort of thing were you thinking of doing on the College?' she asked. On the sofa Sir Godber blended with the loose cover.

'It's really a question of presentation,' Carrington said vaguely. 'One has to show both sides, naturally . . .'

'I'm sure you'll do that very well,' said Lady Mary.

'And leave it to the viewers to make up their own minds,' Carrington went on.

'I think you'll have difficulty persuading the Dean and the Fellows to cooperate. You've no idea what a reactionary lot they are,' Lady Mary said. Carrington smiled.

'My dear,' said Sir Godber. 'Carrington is a Porterhouse man himself.'

'Really,' said Lady Mary, 'in that case I must congratulate you. You've come out of it very well.' They went in to lunch and Lady Mary talked enthusiastically about her work with the Samaritans over a pilchard salad while Carrington slowly wilted. By the time he left the Lodge carrying with him their benediction on the programme Carrington had begun to feel he understood the Master's longing for a painless, rational and fully automated future free from disease, starvation and the miseries of war and personal incompatibility. There would be no place in it for Lady Mary's terrifying philanthropy.

He dawdled throughout the College grounds, gazed at the goldfish in the pond, patted the busts in the library, and posed in front of the reredos in the chapel. Finally he made his way to the Porter's Lodge to reassure himself that Skullion was still agreeable to stating his grievances before three million viewers. He found the Porter less pessimistic than he'd hoped.

'I told them,' he said, 'I told them they'd got to do something.'

'Told whom?' Carrington asked, grammatically influenced by his surroundings.

'Sir Cathcart and the Dean.'

Carrington breathed a sigh of relief. 'They should certainly see that you're reinstated,' he said, 'but just in case they don't, you can always find me at the Blue Boar.'

He left the office and made his way to the hotel. There was really nothing to worry about. An appeal by the Dean to Sir Godber's better feelings was hardly likely to advance the Porter's cause but, just in case, Carrington phoned the *Cambridge Evening News* and announced that the Head Porter of Porterhouse had been dismissed for objecting to the proposed installation of a contraceptive dispenser in the Junior lavatory.

'You can confirm it with the Domestic Bursar,' he told the sub-editor, and replaced the receiver.

A second call to the Students Radical Alliance announcing the victimization of a college servant for joining a trade union, and a third to the Bursar himself, conducted this time in pidgin English, and complaining that the UNESCO expert on irrigation in Zaire expected his diplomatic immunity to protect him from being ejected with obscenities by the guardian of the Porterhouse gate, completed the process of ensuring that Skullion's dismissal should become public knowledge, the centre of left-wing protest, and irrevocable. Feeling fully justified, Carrington lay back on his bed with a smile. It had been a long time since he had been ducked in the fountain in New Court but he had never forgotten it. In the Bursar's office the telephone rang and rang again. The Bursar answered, refused to comment, demanded to know where the sub-editor had got his information, denied that a contraceptive dispenser had been installed in the Junior lavatory, admitted that one was going to be, refused to comment, denied any knowledge of sexual orgies, agreed that Zipser's death had been caused by the explosion of gas-filled prophylactics, asked what that had to do with the Head Porter's dismissal, admitted that he had been sacked and put the phone down. He was just recovering when the Students Radical Alliance phoned. This time the Bursar was brief and to the point. Having relieved his feelings by telling the Radical Students what he thought of them he replaced the receiver with a bang only to hear it ring again. The ensuing conversation with the delegate from Zaire, marked as it was by frequent references to the Secretary of State for Foreign Affairs and the Race Relations Board and punctuated by apologies from the Bursar and the assurance that the porter in question had been dismissed, completed his demoralization. He put the phone down, picked it up again and sent for Skullion. He was waiting for him when the Dean entered.

'Ah, Bursar,' he said, 'just wanted a word with you. What's all this I hear about Skullion being sacked?' The Bursar looked at him vindictively. He had had about all he could take of Skullion for one afternoon.

'It would appear that you have been misinformed,' he said with considerable restraint, 'Skullion has not been sacked. I have merely suggested to him that it is time he looked round for other employment. He's getting on and he's due for retirement shortly. If he can find another job in the meantime it would be sensible for him to take it.' He paused for a moment to allow the Dean to digest this version before continuing. 'However, that was yesterday. What has happened today puts the matter in an entirely different light. I have sent for Skullion and I do intend to sack him.'

'You do?' said the Dean, who had never before seen the Bursar so forthright.

'I have just received a complaint from a diplomat from Zaire who says that he was thrown out of the College by Skullion, who, if I understood him aright, called him among other things a nigger.'

'Quite right and proper,' said the Dean, who had been trying to figure out where Zaire was. 'The College is private property and Skullion doubtless had good reasons for chucking the blighter out. Probably committing a public nuisance.'

'He called him a nigger,' said the Bursar.

'If the man is a nigger, I see no reason why Skullion shouldn't call him one.'

'The Race Relations Board might not view the matter quite so leniently.'

'Race Relations Board? What the devil has it got to do with them?' asked the Dean.

'The fellow said he was going to complain to them. He also mentioned the Foreign Secretary.'

The Dean capitulated. 'Dear me,' he muttered, 'we can't have the College involved in a diplomatic incident.'

'We certainly can't,' said the Bursar. 'Skullion will just have to go.'

'I suppose you're right,' said the Dean, and took his leave. Outside in the Court he found the Porter waiting in the rain.

'This is a bad business, Skullion,' he said mournfully. 'A very bad business. There's nothing I can do for you now I'm afraid. A bad business,' and still shaking his head he made his way across the lawn to his staircase. Behind him Skullion stood in the falling dusk with a new and terminal sense of betrayal. There was evidently no point in seeing the Bursar. He turned and plodded back to the Porter's Lodge and began to pack his odds and ends.

The Bursar sat on in his office waiting. He phoned the Porter's Lodge but there was no reply. Finally he typed a letter to Skullion and posted it on the way home.

It was still raining when Skullion left the Porter's Lodge with his few belongings in a battered suitcase. The rain gathered on his bowler and flecked his face so that it was difficult even for him to know if there were tears running down his nose or not. If there were they were not for himself but for the past whose representative he had ceased to be. He stopped every now and then to make sure that none of the labels on the suitcase had come off in the rain. The bag had belonged to Lord Wurford and the stickers from Cairo and Cawnpore and Hong Kong were like relics from some Imperial pilgrimage. He crossed the Market Square, where the stalls were empty for the night. He went down Petty Curie and through Bradwell's Court and across Christ's Piece towards Midsummer Common. It was already dark and his feet squelched in the mud of the cycle track. Like the wind that blew in his face, swerved to left and right and suddenly propelled him forward, Skullion's feelings seemed to have no fixed direction. There was no calculation in them; the years of his subservience had robbed him of self-interest. He was a servant with nothing left to serve. No Master, no Dean, not even an undergraduate to whom he could attach himself, grudgingly, rudely, to disguise from himself the totality of his dependence. Above all, no College to protect him from the welter of experience. It wasn't the physical college that mattered. It was the idea and that had gone with his dismissal and the betrayal it represented.

Skullion crossed the iron footbridge and came to Rhyder Street. A tiny street of terraced houses hidden among the large Victorian villas of Chesterton so that even here Skullion could feel himself not far removed from the boathouses and the homes of professors. He went inside and took off his coat and put the suitcase on the kitchen table. Then he sat down and took his shoes off. He made a pot of tea and sat at the kitchen table wondering what to do. He'd go and see the bank manager in the morning about his legacy from Lord Wurford. He fetched a tin of boot polish and a duster and began to polish the toecaps of his shoes. And slowly, as each toecap began to gather lustre under the gentle circling of his finger, Skullion lost the sense of hopelessness that had been with him since the Dean had left him standing in New Court. Finally, taking a clean duster, he gave a final polish to the shoes and held them up to the light and saw reflected in their brilliance something remote that he knew to be his face. He got up and put the duster and the tin of polish away and made himself some supper. He was himself again, the Porter of Porterhouse and with this restoration of his own identity there came a new stubbornness. He had his rights. They couldn't turn him out of his own home and his job. Something would happen to stop them. As he moved about the house his mind became obsessed with Them. They had always been there hedged with respect and carrying an aura of authority and trust so that he had felt himself to be safe from Them but it was different now. The old loyalty was gone and Skullion had lost all sense of obligation to Them. Looking back over the years since the war he could see that there'd been a steady waning of respect. There'd been no real gentlemen since then, none that he'd had much time for, but if each succeeding year had disillusioned him a little more with the present, it had added a deal of deference to the more distant past. It was as though the war had been the fulcrum of his regard. Lord Wurford, Dr Robson, Professor Dunstable, Dr Montgomery, they had gained in lustre out of sheer contrast with the men who had come after them. And Skullion himself had been exalted with them because he had known and served them.

At ten o'clock he went to bed and lay in the darkness unable to sleep. At midnight he got up and shuffled downstairs almost automatically and opened the front door. It had stopped raining and Skullion shut the door again after peering up and down the street. Then, reassured by this act of commemoration, he lit the gas fire in the front room and made himself a pot of tea. At least he had still got his legacy. He'd go to the bank in the morning.

The bank manager saw Skullion at ten o'clock. 'Shares?' he said. 'We have an investment department and we could advise you of course.' He looked down at the details of Skullion's deposit account. 'Yes, five thousand pounds is quite sufficient but don't you think it would be wiser to put the money into something less speculative?'

Skullion shifted his hat on his knees and wondered why no one seemed to listen to what he said. 'I don't want to buy any shares. I want to buy a house,' he said.

The manager looked at him approvingly. 'A much better idea. Put your money in property especially in these days of inflation. You have a property in mind?'

'It's in Rhyder Street,' said Skullion.

'Rhyder Street?' The manager raised his eyebrows and pursed his mouth. 'That's a different matter. It's being sold as a lot, you know. You can't buy individual houses in Rhyder Street, and quite frankly I don't suppose your five thousand would match some of the other bids.' He permitted himself a chuckle. 'In fact it's doubtful if five thousand would get you anything in Cambridge. You'd have to raise a mortgage, and at your age that's not an easy matter.'

Skullion produced the envelope containing his shares. 'I know that,' he said. 'That's why I want to sell these shares. There are ten thousand. I think they're worth a thousand pounds.'

The manager took the envelope. 'We must just hope they're worth a little more than that,' he said. 'Now then ...' His condescendingly cheerful tone stuttered out. 'Good God!' he said, and stared at the sheaf of shares before him. Skullion shifted guiltily on his chair, as if he personally took the blame for whatever it was about the pieces of paper that caused the manager to stare in such amazement. 'Amalgamated Universal Stores. But this is quite extraordinary. How many did you say?' the manager was on his feet now twittering.

'Ten thousand,' said Skullion.

'Ten thousand?' The manager sat down again. He picked up the phone and rang the investment department. 'Amalgamated Universal Stores. What's the current selling price?' There was a pause while the manager studied Skullion with a new incredulous respect. 'Twenty five and a half?' He put the phone down and stared at Skullion.

'Mr Skullion,' he said at last, 'this may come as something of a shock to you. I don't quite know how to put it, but you are worth a quarter of a million pounds.'

Skullion heard the words, but they had no visible effect upon him. He sat unmoved upon his chair and stared numbly at the bank manager. It was the manager himself who seemed most affected by the sudden change in Skullion's status. He laughed nervously and with a slight hysteria.

'I don't think there's much doubt that you can make a bid for Rhyder Street now,' he said at last but Skullion wasn't listening. He was a rich man. It was something he had never dreamed of being.

'There must have been dividends,' said the manager. Skullion nodded. 'In the building society.' He got up and put the chair back against the wall. He looked at the shares which represented his fortune. 'You'd better put them back into the safe,' he said.

'But ...' began the manager. 'Now Mr Skullion, sit down and let's discuss this matter. Rhyder Street? There's no need to think of Rhyder Street now. We can sell these shares and ... or at least some of them and you can purchase a decent property and settle down to a new life.'

Skullion considered the suggestion. 'I don't want a new life,' he said grimly, 'I want my old one back.'

He left the manager standing behind his desk and went out into Sydney Street. In his office the bank manager sat down, his mind crowded with cheap images of wealth, cruises and cars and bright suburban bungalows, ideas he had thought disreputable before. To Skullion, standing on the pavement, such things meant nothing. He was a rich man and the knowledge did nothing to ease his resentment. If anything it increased it. He had been cheated somehow. Cheated by his own ignorance and the loyalty he had given Porterhouse. The Master, the Dean, even General Sir Cathcart D'Eath, were the legatees of his new bitterness.

They had misused him. He was free now, without the fear of dismissal or unemployment to mitigate his hatred. He went down Green Street towards the Blue Boar.

CHAPTER SEVENTEEN

During the next two days Cornelius Carrington was intensely busy. His dapper figure trotted across lawns and up staircases with a retinue of cameramen and assistants. Corners of Porterhouse that had remained obscure for centuries were suddenly illuminated by the brightest of lights as Carrington adorned his commentary with architectural trimmings. Everyone cooperated. Even the Dean, convinced that he was heaping coals of fire on the Master's head, consented to discuss the need for conservatism in the intellectual climate of the present day. Standing beneath a portrait of Bishop Firebrace, Master 1545–52, who had, as Carrington was at some pains to point out in his added commentary, played a notable role in suppressing Kett's Rebellion, the Dean launched into a ferocious attack on permissive youth and extolled the celibacy of previous generations of undergraduates. In contrast, the Chaplain was driven to admit that what many supposed to have been a nunnery before it was burnt down in 1541 had in fact been a brothel during the fifteenth century. The camera dwelt at length on foundations of the 'nunnery' still visible in parts in the Fellows' Garden while Carrington expressed surprise that a college like Porterhouse should have allowed such sexual laxity so many centuries before. The Senior Tutor was filmed cycling along the towpath by Fen Ditton coaching an eight, and was then interviewed in Hall on the dietary requirements of athletes. Carrington wheedled out of him the fact that the annual Feast cost over £2,000 and then went on to ask if the College made any contribution to Oxfam. At this point, forgetful of his electronic audience, the Senior Tutor told him to mind his own business and stalked out of the Hall trailing the broken lead of his throat microphone. Sir Godber was treated more gently. He was allowed to stroll across New Court and through the Screens discoursing on the need for a progressive and humanitarian role for Porterhouse. Pausing to look far-sightedly across the thirty feet that separated him from the end wall of the library, the Master spoke of the emotional-intellectual symbiosis that was a part of university experience, he lowered his head and addressed a crocus on the catharsis of sexual union, he raised his eyes to a fifteenth-century chimney and esteemed the compassion of the young, their energetic concern and the rightness of their revulsion at the outmoded traditions that ... He waxed eloquent on meaningful relationships and urged the abolition of exams. Above all he praised youth. The elderly, by which he evidently meant anyone over thirty-five, must not stand in the way of young men and women whose minds and bodies were open ... Even Sir Godber faltered at this point and Carrington steered him back to the subject of social compassion, which he saw as the true benefit of a university education. The Master agreed that a sense of social justice was indeed the hallmark of the educated mind. Carrington stopped the cameras and Sir Godber made his way back to the Master's Lodge, certain that he had ended on the right note. Carrington thought so too. While his cameramen took close-ups of the heraldic beasts on the front of the main gate and panned along the spikes that guarded the back wall, Carrington drove over to Rhyder Street and spent an hour closeted with Skullion. 'All I want you to do is to come back to the College and talk about your life as Head Porter,' he told him. Skullion shook his head. Carrington tried again. 'We'll take some shots of you outside the main gate and then you can stand in the street and I'll ask you a few questions. You don't have to go into the College itself.' Skullion remained adamant.

'You'll do me in London or you won't do me at all,' he insisted.

'In London?'

'Haven't been to London for thirteen years,' said Skullion.

'We can take you up to London for a day if you like but it would be much better if we filmed the interview here. We can do it here in your own home.' Carrington looked round the dingy kitchen approvingly. It had just that element of pathos he required.

'Wouldn't look good,' said Skullion. Under his breath Carrington cursed the old fool.

'I'm not having myself on film either,' Skullion continued.

'Not having yourself on film?'

'I want to go out live,' said Skullion.

'Live?'

'In a studio. Like they do on *Panorama*. Always wanted to see what it was like in a studio,' Skullion went on. 'It's more natural, isn't it?'

'No,' said Carrington, 'it's extremely unnatural. It's hot and you have large cameras ...'

'That's the way I want it,' Skullion said, 'I'm not doing it any other way. Live.'

'All right,' Carrington said finally, 'if you insist. We'll have to rehearse it first, of course. I'll put questions to you and you'll reply. We'll run through it so that there aren't any mistakes.' He left the house in some annoyance, troubled by Skullion's persistence and conscious that without Skullion the programme would lack dramatic impact. If Skullion wanted to go to London and if, in his superstitious way, he objected to being 'put on film' he would have to be placated. In the meantime the cameramen could film Rhyder Street and at least the exterior of the Head Porter's home. He drove back to Porterhouse and collected the camera crew. Only one interview left now, that with General Sir Cathcart D'Eath at Coft Castle.

A week later Carrington and Skullion travelled to London together. Carrington had spent the week editing the film and adding his commentary but all the time he had been harassed by a nagging suspicion that there was something wrong, not with the programme as he had finally concocted it but with Skullion. The petulance that had attracted Carrington to him in the first place had gone out of him. In its stead there was a stillness and an impression of strength. It was as though Skullion had gained in stature since his dismissal and was pursuing interests he knew to be his own and no one else's. Carrington did not mind the change. In its own way it would heighten the effect Skullion would have on the millions who would watch him. Carrington had even found reason to congratulate himself on the Porter's insistence that he appear live in the studio. His rugged face, with its veined nose and heavy eyebrows, would stand out against the artificiality of the studio and give his appearance a sense of immediacy that was lacking in the interviews filmed in Cambridge. Above all, Skullion's inarticulate answers would stir the hearts of his audience. Across the country men and women would sit forward in their chairs to listen to his pitiable story, conscious that they were witnessing an authentic human drama. Coming after the radical platitudes of Sir Godber and the reactionary vehemence of the Dean, Skullion's transparent honesty would emphasize the homely virtues in which they and Cornelius Carrington placed so much faith. And finally there would come the master-stroke. From the gravel drive in front of Coft Castle, General Sir Cathcart D'Eath would offer Skullion a home and the camera would pan to a bungalow where the Head Porter could see his days out in peace. Carrington was proud of that scene. Coft Castle was suburbia inflated and transplanted to the countryside and the General himself the epitome of a modern English gentleman. It had taken a good deal of editing to achieve that result, but Carrington's good sense had prevailed over Sir Cathcart's wilder flights of abuse. He had to admit that the Sealyham had helped to inject a note of sympathy into Sir Cathcart's conversation.

Carrington had spotted the dog playing on the lawn and had asked the General if he was fond of dogs.

'Always been fond of 'em,' Sir Cathcart had replied. 'Loyal friend, obedient, go anywhere with you. Nothing to touch 'em.'

'If you found a stray you'd give him a home?'

'Certainly,' said Sir Cathcart. 'Glad to. Couldn't leave him to starve. Plenty of room here. Have the run of the place. Decent quarters.'

Since in the edited version Sir Cathcart's hospitality appeared to refer to Skullion, Carrington felt that he could congratulate himself on a brilliant performance. All it had needed had been the substitution of 'If Skullion needed a place to live you'd offer him a home?' for 'If you found a stray you'd give him a home?' The General was unlikely to deny his invitation. The consequences to his image as a public benefactor would be too enormous.

As they drove to London Carrington coached Skullion in his role. 'Remember to look straight into the camera. Just answer my questions simply.' In the darkness Skullion nodded silently.

'I'll say "When did you first become a porter?" and you'll say "In 1928". You don't have to elaborate. Do you understand?'

'Yes,' said Skullion.

'Then I'll say, "You've been the Head Porter of Porterhouse since 1945?" and you'll say "Yes".'

'Yes,' said Skullion.

'Then I'll go on, "So you've been a College servant for forty-five years?" and you'll say "Yes". Is that clear?'

'Yes,' said Skullion.

'Then I'll say, "And now you've been sacked?" and you'll say "Yes". I'll say "Have you any idea why you've been sacked?" What will you say to that?'

'No,' said Skullion. Carrington was satisfied. The General might just as well have been talking about Skullion when he said that dogs were obedient. Carrington relaxed. It was going to go well.

They crossed London to the studio and Skullion was shepherded by an assistant to the entertainment room in the basement while Carrington disappeared into a lift. Skullion looked around him suspiciously. The room looked like a rather large air-raid shelter.

'Do sit down, Mr Skullion,' said the young man. Skullion sat on the plastic sofa and took off his bowler hat, while the young man unlocked what looked like a built-in wardrobe and wheeled out a large box. Skullion scowled at the box.

'What's that?' he inquired.

'It's a sort of portable bar. It helps to have a drink before one goes up to the studio.'

'Ah,' said Skullion and watched the young man unlock the box. A formidable array of bottles gleamed in the interior.

'What would you care for? Whisky, gin?'

'Nothing,' said Skullion.

'Really,' twittered the young man. 'That's most unusual. Most people need a drink especially if they're going on live.'

'You have one if you want one,' Skullion said. 'Mind if I smoke?' He took out his pipe and filled it slowly. The young man looked doubtfully at the portable bar.

'Are you sure you wouldn't care for a drink?' he asked. 'It does help, you know.'

Skullion shook his head. 'Have one afterwards,' he said, and lit his pipe. The young man locked the bar and put it back into the wardrobe.

'Is this your first time?' he asked, evidently anxious to put Skullion at his ease.

Skullion nodded and said nothing.

He was still saying nothing when Cornelius Carrington came down to collect him. The room was filled with the acrid smoke from Skullion's pipe and the young man was sitting at the far end of the plastic sofa in a state of considerable agitation.

'He won't drink anything,' he whispered. 'He won't say anything. He just sits there smoking that filthy pipe.' Carrington looked at Skullion with some alarm. Visions of Skullion drying up in the middle of the interview began to seem a distinct possibility.

'Are you all right?' he asked.

Skullion looked at him sourly. 'Never felt better,' he said. 'But I can't say I like the company.' He glowered at the young man.

Carrington escorted him out into the corridor. 'Poofter,' said Skullion as they went up in the lift. Carrington shuddered. There was something disturbing about the Head Porter's new attitude. He lacked the eagerness to please that seemed to affect most people who came to be interviewed, a nervous geniality that made them pliable and stimulated in Carrington a dominance he was unable to satisfy outside the artificial environs of the studio. If anyone was likely to dry up, he admitted to himself, it seemed more likely to be Cornelius Carrington than Skullion. He ushered the Porter into the brilliantly lit studio and sat him in the chair before hurrying out and having two quick slugs of whisky. By the time he had returned Skullion was telling a young make-up woman to keep her paws to herself.

Carrington took his seat and smiled at Skullion. 'One thing you must try to avoid is kicking the mike,' he said. Skullion said he'd try not to. The cameras moved round him. Young men came and went. In the next room behind a large darkened window the producer and the technicians arranged themselves at the console. Carrington on Cambridge was on the air. 9.25. Peak-hour viewing.

In Porterhouse dinner was over. It had, for a change, been an equable affair without any of the verbal infighting that usually occurred whenever the Fellows were gathered together. Instead a strange goodwill prevailed. Even the Master dined in Hall and the Dean sitting on his right managed to refrain from being offensive. It was as though a truce had been declared.

'I've done my best to see that more influential members of the Porterhouse Society have been informed about the programme,' he told the Master.

'Excellent,' said Sir Godber. 'I'm sure we all owe you a debt of gratitude, Dean.' The Dean forebore from sniggering. 'One does one's best,' he said. 'After all it's for the good of the College. We should get one or two fairly healthy subscriptions for the restoration fund as a result of young Carrington's efforts.'

'I found him a most sympathetic man,' said Sir Godber. 'Unusually perceptive, I thought, for ...' He was about to say an old Porterhouse man but thought better of it.

'Flirty Bertie, they used to call him, when he was an undergraduate,' shouted the Chaplain.

'Ah well, he seems to have changed a good deal since those days,' said Sir Godber.

'They ducked him in the fountain,' the Chaplain continued. It was the only ominous remark of the whole meal.

Afterwards they sat in the Combination Room over coffee and cigars, glancing occasionally at the large colour television set that had been installed for the occasion. At nine they switched it on and watched the news, while Arthur, the waiter, was told to bring some more brandy. Sir Cathcart arrived at the invitation of the Dean and when the Carrington Programme began all those who had some part in it were present in the Combination Room. All except Skullion, who sat in the studio with the suggestion of a smile softening imperceptibly the harsh lines of his face.

In the Combination Room Cornelius Carrington's voice broke through the last bars of the Eton Boating Song which had accompanied the opening shots of the Backs and King's College Chapel. 'To many people

Cambridge is one of the great centres of learning, the birthplace of science and of culture. Here the great English poets had their education. Milton was a scholar of Christ's College.' The interior of Milton's room appeared upon the screen. 'Wordsworth and Tennyson, Byron and Coleridge were all Cambridge men.' The camera skipped briefly from an upper window in St John's to Trinity and Jesus, before settling on the seated figure of Tennyson in Trinity Chapel. 'Here Newton,' Newton's statue glowed on the screen, 'first discovered the laws of gravity, and Rutherford, the father of the atom bomb, first split the atom.' A corner of the Cavendish Laboratory, discreetly photographed to avoid any sign of modernity, appeared.

'I must say friend Carrington has a way of leaping the centuries fairly rapidly,' said the Dean.

'What's the Eton Boating Song got to do with King's?' asked Sir Cathcart.

Carrington continued. Cambridge was the Venice of the Fens. Shots of the Bridge of Sighs. Punts. Grantchester. Undergraduates pouring out of the lecture rooms in Mill Lane. Carrington's emollient voice proclaimed the glory that was Cambridge.

'But tonight we are going to look at a college that is unique even in the unchanging world of Cambridge.'

The Master sat forward and stared at the College crest on the tower above the main gate. Around him the Fellows stirred uneasily in their chairs. The invasion of their privacy had begun. And it continued. Carrington asked his audience to consider the anachronism that was his old college. The balm had left his voice. A new strident note of alarm had crept in suggesting to his audience that what they were about to see might well shock and surprise them. There was an implication that Porterhouse was something more than a mere college and that the crisis which had developed there was somehow symbolic of the choice that confronted the country. In the Combination Room the Fellows gaped at the screen in amazement. Even Sir Godber shivered at the new emphasis. Malaise was hardly a word he'd expected to hear applied to the condition of the College and when, after floating through Old Court and the Screens, the camera zoomed in on the plastic sheeting of the Tower there was a unanimous gasp in the Combination Room.

'What drove a brilliant young scholar to take his life and that of an elderly woman in this strange fashion?' Carrington asked, and proceeded to describe the circumstances of Zipser's death in a manner which fully justified his earlier warning that viewers must expect to be shocked and surprised.

'Good God,' shouted Sir Cathcart, 'what's the bastard trying to do?' The Dean closed his eyes and Sir Godber took a gulp of brandy.

'I asked the Dean his opinion,' Carrington continued and the Dean opened his eyes to peer at his own face as it appeared on the screen.

'It's my opinion that young men come up today with their heads filled with anarchist nonsense. They seem to think they can change the world by violent means,' the Dean heard himself telling the world.

'He did nothing of the sort,' shouted the Dean. 'He never mentioned Zipser!'

Carrington issued his denial. 'So you see this as an act of self-destructive nihilism on the part of a young man who had been working too hard?' he asked.

'Porterhouse has always been a sporting college. In the past we have tried to achieve a balance between scholarship and sport,' the Dean replied.

'He never put that question to me,' yelled the real Dean. 'He's taking my words out of context.'

'You don't see this as an act of sexual aberration?' Carrington interrupted.

'Sexual promiscuity plays no part in college life,' the Dean asserted.

'You've certainly changed your tune, Dean,' shouted the Chaplain. 'The first time I've heard you say that.'

'I didn't say that,' screamed the Dean. 'I said ...'

'Hush,' said Sir Godber, 'I'm trying to hear what you did say.'

The Dean turned purple in the darkness as Carrington continued.

'I interviewed the Chaplain of Porterhouse in the Fellows' Garden,' he told the world. The Dean and Bishop Firebrace had disappeared to be replaced by the rockeries and elms and two tiny figures walking on the lawn.

'I never realized the Fellows' Garden was so large,' said the Chaplain, peering at his remote figure.

'It's distorted by the wide-angle lens ...' Sir Cathcart began to explain.

'Distorted?' snarled the Dean. 'Of course it's distorted, the whole bloody programme's a distortion.'

The camera zoomed in on the Chaplain.

'The College used to have a brothel, you know. People like to pretend it was a nunnery but it was actually a whorehouse. In the fifteenth century it was quite the normal thing,' the Chaplain's voice echoed across the lawn. 'Burnt down in 1541. A great pity really. Mind you I'm not saying there weren't nuns. The Catholics have always been broadminded about such things.'

'So much for the ecumenical movement,' muttered the Senior Tutor.

'So you don't agree with the Dean that ...' Carrington began.

'Agree with the Dean, dear me no,' the Chaplain shouted. 'Never did. Peculiar fellow, the Dean. All those photographs of young men in his room. And he's getting on in years now. We all are. We all are.' The camera moved away slowly, leaving the Chaplain a distant figure in a landscape with his voice growing fainter like the distant cawing of rooks.

The Chaplain turned to the Senior Tutor. 'That was rather nice. Seeing oneself on the screen like that. Most enlightening.' In the corner a strangled sound issued from the Dean. The Senior Tutor was breathing hard too, and staring at the river at Fen Ditton. An eight was swinging round Grassy Corner and an aged youth in a blazer and cap cycled busily after them. As the eight approached and disappeared the screen filled with the perspiring face of the Senior Tutor. He stopped and dismounted his bicycle. Carrington's voice interrupted his panting.

'You've been coach now for twenty years and in that time you must have seen some extraordinary changes in Porterhouse. What do you think of the type of young man coming up to Cambridge today?'

'I've seen some lily-livered swine in my time,' the Senior Tutor bawled, 'but nothing to equal this. A more disgraceful exhibition of gutlessness I've never seen.'

'Would you put this down to pot-smoking?' Carrington inquired.

'Of course,' said the Senior Tutor, and promptly disappeared from the screen.

In the Combination Room the Senior Tutor was speechless with rage. 'He didn't ask me any questions like that. He wasn't even there,' he managed to gasp. 'He told me they were simply going to film me on the river.'

'It's poetic licence,' said the Chaplain, and relapsed into silence as Carrington and the Senior Tutor reappeared in Hall and strolled between the tables. The camera focused on the several portraits of obese Masters before returning to the Senior Tutor.

'Porterhouse has enjoyed a long reputation for good living,' Carrington said. 'Would you say that the sort of expense involved in providing caviar and truffled duck paté was really necessary for scholastic achievement?'

'I think much of our success has been due to the balanced diet we provide in Porterhouse,' said the Senior Tutor. 'You can't expect people to do well unless they are adequately fed.'

'But I understand that you spend fairly large sums on the annual Feast. Would you say that £2,000 on a single meal was a fair estimate?' Carrington inquired.

'We do have an endowed kitchen,' the Senior Tutor admitted.

'And I suppose the College makes a large contribution to Oxfam,' said Carrington.

'That's none of your damned business,' shouted the Senior Tutor. The camera followed his figure out of Hall.

As the devastating disclosures continued the Fellows sat dumbfounded in the Combination Room. Carrington waxed eloquent on Porterhouse's academic shortcomings, interviewed several undergraduates who sat with their backs to the camera to preserve their anonymity and claimed that they were afraid they would be sent down if their identities were known to the Senior Members of the College. They accused the College authorities of being hidebound and violently reactionary in their politics, and ... On and on it went. Sir Godber put his case for social compassion as the hallmark of the educated mind and suddenly the scene changed. The images of Cambridge disappeared and the Fellows found themselves staring lividly at Skullion who sat firmly in his seat in the studio. The camera switched to Carrington. 'In the interviews we have already shown tonight we have heard a good deal to justify, and some would say to condemn, the role of institutions such as Porterhouse. We have heard the old traditions defended. We have heard privilege attacked by the progressive young and we have heard a great deal about social compassion, but now we have in the studio a man who more than any other has an intimate knowledge of Porterhouse and whose knowledge extends over four decades. Now you, Mr Skullion, have been for some forty years the Porter of Porterhouse.'

Skullion nodded. 'Yes,' he said.

'You first became a porter in 1928?'

'Yes.'

'And in 1945 you were made Head Porter?'

'That's right.'

'So really you've been in the College long enough to have seen some quite remarkable changes?' Skullion nodded obediently.

'And now I understand you've been sacked?' said Carrington. 'Have you any idea why this has happened?'

Skullion paused while the camera moved in for a close-up.

'I have been dismissed because I objected to the installation of a contraceptive dispenser in the College for the use of the young gentlemen,' Skullion told three million viewers. There was a pause while the camera swung back to Carrington, who was looking suitably shocked and surprised.

'A contraceptive dispenser?' he asked. Skullion nodded. 'A contraceptive dispenser. I don't think it's right and proper for Senior Members of a college like Porterhouse to encourage young men to behave like that.'

'Oh my God,' said the Master. Beside him the Senior Tutor was staring at the screen with bulging eyes while the Dean appeared to be in the throes of some appalling paroxysm. Throughout the Combination Room the Fellows gazed at Skullion as if they were seeing him for the first time, as if the caricature that they had known had suddenly come alive by virtue of the very apparatus which separated him from them. Skullion's presence filled the room. Even Sir Cathcart took note of the change and sat rigidly to attention. Beside him the Bursar whimpered. Only the Chaplain remained unmoved. 'Skullion's remarkably fluent,' he said, 'and making some interesting points too.'

Carrington too seemed to have shrunk to a less substantial role. 'You think the attitude of the authorities is wrong?' he asked lamely.

'Of course it's wrong,' said Skullion. 'Young people shouldn't be taught to think that they've a right to do what they want. Life isn't like that. I didn't want to be a porter. I had to be one to earn my living. Just because a man's been to Cambridge and got a degree doesn't mean life's going to treat him any different. He's still got to earn a living, hasn't he?'

'Quite,' said Carrington, desperately trying to think of some way of getting the discussion back to the original topic. 'And you think –'

'I think they've lost their nerve,' said Skullion. 'They're frightened. They call it permissiveness. It isn't that. It's cowardice.'

'Cowardice?' Carrington had begun to dither.

'It's the same all over. Give them degrees when they haven't done any work. Let them walk about looking like unwashed scarecrows. Don't send them down when they take drugs. Let them come in at all hours of the night and have women in their rooms. When I first started as a porter they'd send an undergrad down as soon as look at him and quite right too, but now, now they want them to have an FL machine in the gents to keep them happy. And what about queers?' Carrington blanched.

'You ought to know about that,' said Skullion. 'Used to duck them in the fountain, didn't they? Yes I remember the night they ducked you. And quite right too. It's all cowardice. Don't talk to me about permissiveness.' Carrington gazed frantically at the programme controller behind the dark glass but the programme remained on the air.

'And what about me?' Skullion asked the camera in front of him. 'Worked for a pittance for forty years and they sack me for nothing. Is that fair? You want permissiveness? Well, why can't I be permitted to work? A man's got a right to work, hasn't he? I offered them money to keep me on. You ask the Bursar if I didn't offer him my savings to help the College out.'

Carrington grasped at the straw. 'You offered the Bursar your life savings to help the College out?' he asked with as much enthusiasm as the recent revelations about his sex life had left him.

'He said they couldn't afford to keep me on as Porter,' Skullion explained. 'He said they were having to sell Rhyder Street to pay for the repairs to the Tower.'

'And Rhyder Street is where you live?'

'It's where all the College servants live. They've got no right to turn us out of our own homes.'

In the Combination Room the Master and Fellows of Porterhouse watched the reputation of the College disintegrate as Skullion pressed on with his charges. This was no longer Carrington on Cambridge. Skullion had taken over with a truer and more forceful nostalgia. While Carrington sat pale and haggard beside him, Skullion ranged far and wide. He spoke of the old virtues, of courage and loyalty, with an inarticulate eloquence that was authentically English. He praised gentlemen long dead and castigated men still alive. He asserted the value of tradition in college life against the shoddy innovations of the present. He expressed his admiration for scholarship and deplored research. He extolled wisdom and refused to confuse it with knowledge. Above all he claimed the right to serve and with it the right to be treated fairly. There was no petulant whine about Skullion's appeal. He held a mirror up to a mythical past and in a million homes men and women responded to the appeal.

By the time the programme ended, the switchboard at the BBC was jammed with calls from people all over the country supporting Skullion in his crusade against the present.

CHAPTER EIGHTEEN

In the Combination Room the Fellows sat looking at the blank screen long after Skullion's terrible image had disappeared and the Bursar had switched the set off. It was the Chaplain who finally broke the appalled silence.

'Very interesting point of view, Skullion's,' he said, 'though I must admit to having some doubts about the effect on the restoration fund. What did you think of the programme, Master?'

Sir Godber suppressed a torrent of oaths. 'I don't suppose,' he said with a desperate attempt at composure, 'that many people will take much note of what a college porter has to say. The public have very short memories, I'm glad to say.'

'Damned scoundrel,' snarled Sir Cathcart. 'Ought to be horsewhipped.'

'What? Skullion?' asked the Senior Tutor.

'That swine Carrington,' shouted the General.

'It was your idea in the first place,' said the Dean.

'Mine?' screamed Sir Cathcart. 'You put him up to this.'

The Chaplain intervened. 'I always thought it was a mistake to duck him in the fountain,' he said.

'I shall consult my solicitor in the morning,' said the Dean. 'I think we have adequate grounds for suing. There's such a thing as slander.'

'I must say I can hardly see any justification for going to law,' said the Chaplain. Sir Godber shuddered at the prospect.

'He deliberately fabricated questions to answers I had already given,' said the Senior Tutor.

'He may have done that,' the Chaplain agreed, 'but I think you'll have difficulty in proving it. In any case if I were asked I should have to say that he did manage to convey the spirit of our opinions if not the actual letter. I mean you do think the modern generation of undergraduates are ... what was the expression? ... a lot of lily-livered swine. The fact that you have now said it in public may be regrettable but at least it's honest.'

They were still fulminating an hour later when the Master, exhausted by the programme and by the terrible animosity it had provoked among his colleagues, finally left the Combination Room and made his way across the Fellows' Garden to the Master's Lodge. As he stumbled across the lawn he was still uncertain what effect the programme would have.

He tried to console himself with the thought that public opinion was essentially progressive and that his record as a reforming politician would carry him safely through the outcry that was bound to follow. He tried to recall what it was about his own appearance on the screen that had so alarmed him. For the first time in his life he had seen himself as others saw him, an old man mouthing clichés with a conviction that was wholly unconvincing. He went into the Lodge and shut the door.

Upstairs in the bedroom Lady Mary disembarked from her corset languidly. She had watched the programme by herself and had found it curiously stimulating. It had confirmed her opinion of the College while at the same time she had been aroused once again by the warm hermaphroditism of Cornelius Carrington himself. Age and the Rubicon of menopause had stimulated Lady Mary's appetite for such men and she found herself moved by his vulnerable mediocrity. As ever with Lady Mary's affections, distance lent enchantment to the view, and for one brief self-indulgent moment she saw herself the intimate patroness of this idol of the media. Sir Godber, she had to admit, was a spent force whereas Carrington was still an influence. She smothered the impulse with cold cream but there was enough vivacity left to surprise Sir Godber when he came to bed.

'I thought it went rather well, didn't you?' she asked as the Master wearily untied his shoes. Sir Godber lifted his head balefully.

'Well of course there was that awful creature at the end,' Lady Mary conceded. 'I can't imagine why he had to appear.'

'I can,' said Sir Godber.

'Otherwise I enjoyed it. It showed the Dean up in a very foolish light.'

'It showed us all up in a perfectly terrible light,' said Sir Godber.

'He gave you fair warning,' Lady Mary pointed out. 'He said he had to show both sides of the problem.'

'He didn't say he had to show it from underneath,' Sir Godber snapped. 'He made us all look like complete idiots and as for Skullion, anybody would think we had done the damned man an injustice.'

'Aren't you being a bit extreme?' Lady Mary said. 'After all anyone could see he was a dreadful oaf.'

Sir Godber went through to the bathroom and did his teeth while Lady Mary settled down comfortably with the latest statistics on juvenile crime.

At Shepherd's Bush Skullion sat on smoking his pipe and drinking whisky while Carrington screamed at the programme producer.

'You had no right to let him continue,' he shouted. 'You should have cut him off.'

'It's your programme, sweetie,' said the producer. The telephone rang. 'Anyway I don't know what you're worried about,' said the producer, 'the public loved him. The phone's been ringing non-stop.' He listened for a moment and turned to Carrington. 'It's Elsie. She wants to know if he's available for an interview.'

'Elsie?'

'Elsie Controp. The *Observer* woman,' said the producer.

'No, he isn't,' shouted Carrington.

'Yes, he is still here,' the producer said into the phone. 'If you come over now you'll probably get him.' He put the phone down.

'Do you realize he is likely to involve us in a legal action,' Carrington asked. The phone rang. 'Yes,' said the controller. He turned to Carrington. 'They want him for *Talk-In* on Monday. Is that all right?'

'For God's sake,' shouted Carrington.

'He says that's fine,' said the producer.

Skullion sat in the entertainment room with Elsie Controp. It was past eleven but Skullion was not feeling tired. His appearance had invigorated him and the whisky was helping. 'You mean the College authorities accept candidates who have taken no entrance examination and who have no A-levels?' Miss Controp asked. Skullion drank some more whisky and nodded.

'And their parents subscribe to an Endowment Fund?' Skullion nodded again. Miss Controp's pencil flitted across her pad.

'And this is quite a normal procedure at Porterhouse?' she asked. Skullion agreed that it was.

'And other colleges admit candidates in the same way?'

'If you're rich enough you can usually get into a college,' Skullion told her. 'I don't say they subscribe to any funds like in Porterhouse but they get in all the same.'

'But how do they get degrees if they can't pass the exams?'

Skullion smiled. 'Oh, they fail the Tripos. Then they give them pass degrees. College recommends someone for a pass degree and they get it. It's a fiddle.'

'You can say that again,' said Miss Controp fervently. Skullion spent the night in a hotel in Bayswater. On Saturday he went to the Zoo and on Sunday he stayed in bed reading the *News of the World* and then went down to Greenwich to look at the *Cutty Sark*.

*

Sir Godber came down to breakfast on Sunday to find Lady Mary engrossed in the *Observer*. He could see from her expression that a disaster had struck some part of the world.

'Where is it this time?' he asked wearily. Lady Mary did not reply. 'It must be a simply appalling catastrophe,' Sir Godber thought and helped himself to toast. He sat munching noisily and looking out of the window. Saturday had been an unpleasant day. There had been a number of calls from old Porterhouse men who wanted to say how much they resented the sacking of Skullion and who hoped that the Master would think again before making any changes to the College. He had been asked for his opinions by several leading London papers. He had been approached by the BBC to appear on *Talk-In*. He had even received a phone call from the League of Contraception complimenting him on his stand. Altogether the Master was in no mood to face Lady Mary's sympathy for some wretched population stricken by disease, destitution, or natural disaster at the other end of the globe. He could have done with some sympathy himself.

He looked up from a piece of toast to find her regarding him with unusual severity.

'Godber,' she said, 'this is simply dreadful.'

'I rather imagined it must be,' said the Master.

'You've got to do something about it immediately.'

Sir Godber put down his piece of toast. 'My dear,' he said, 'my capacity for doing anything about the inhumanity of man to man or of nature to man or of man to nature is strictly limited. That much I have learnt. Now whatever it is that's causing you such exquisite pain and suffering for the plight of mankind this morning, I am not in any position to do anything about it. I have enough trouble trying to do something about this College –'

'I am talking about the College,' Lady Mary interrupted. She thrust the paper across the table to him and Sir Godber found himself staring at headlines that read, CAMBRIDGE COLLEGE SELLS DEGREES. PORTER ALLEGES CORRUPTION, by Elsie Controp. A photograph of Skullion appeared below the headlines and several columns were devoted to an analysis of Porterhouse's financial affairs. The Master breathed deeply and read.

'Porterhouse College, one of Cambridge's socially more exclusive colleges, has been in the habit of selling pass degrees to unqualified sons of wealthy parents, according to the college porter, Mr James Skullion.'

'Well?' said Lady Mary before Sir Godber could read any further.

'Well what?' said the Master.

'You've got to do something about it. It's outrageous.'

The Master peered vindictively at his wife. 'If you would give me time to read the article I might be able to think of something to do about it. As it is I have had time neither to digest its import nor what little breakfast –'

'You must issue a press statement denying the allegations,' said Lady Mary.

'Quite,' said Sir Godber. 'Which, since as far as I have been able to read, seem to be perfectly true, would do nobody least of all me, any good whatsoever. I suppose Skullion might benefit by being awarded damages for being called a liar.'

'Are you trying to tell me that you've been condoning the sale of degrees?'

'Condoning?' shouted the Master. 'Condoning? What the hell do you –'

'Godber,' said Lady Mary threateningly. The Master lapsed into a stricken silence and tried to finish the article while Lady Mary launched into a sermon on the iniquities of bribery and corruption, public schools and the commercial ethics, or lack of them, of the middle classes. By the end of breakfast the Master was feeling like a battered baby.

'I think I'll take a walk,' he said, and left the table. Outside the sun was shining and in the Fellows' Garden the daffodils were out. So were the pickets. Outside the main gate several youths were sitting on the pavement with placards which read REINSTATE SKULLION. The Master walked past them with his head lowered and headed for the river wondering why it was that his well-meaning efforts to effect a radical change should always provoke the opposition of those in whose interests he was acting. Why should Skullion, whose ideas were archaic in the extreme and who would have chased those long-haired youths away from the main gate, elicit their sympathy now? There was something perverse about English political attitudes that defeated logic. Looking back over his lifetime Sir Godber was filled with a sense of injustice. 'It's the Right wot gets the power. It's the Left wot gets the blame,' he thought. 'Ain't it all a blooming shame?' He wandered on along the path across Sheep's Green towards Lammas Land, dreaming of a future in which all men would be happy and all problems solved. Lammas Land. The land of the day that would never come.

The Dean didn't read the *Observer*. He found its emphasis on the malfunction of the body politic and the body physical not at all to his taste. In fact none of the Sunday papers appealed to him. He preferred his agnosticism straight and accordingly attended morning service in the

College chapel where the Chaplain could be relied upon to maintain the formalities of religious observance in a tone loud enough to make good the deficiency of his congregation and with an irrelevance to the ethical needs of those few who were present that the Dean found infinitely reassuring. He was therefore somewhat surprised to find that the Chaplain had chosen his text from Jeremiah 17:11. 'As the partridge sitteth on eggs, and hatcheth them not; so he that getteth riches, and not by right, shall leave them in the midst of his days, and at his end shall be a fool.' Fortunately for the Dean, he was so preoccupied with the problem of the continuing existence of partridges in spite of their evident shortcomings as parents that he missed a great deal of what the Chaplain had to say. He awoke from his reverie towards the end of the sermon to find the Chaplain in a strangely outspoken way criticizing the college for admitting undergraduates whose only merit was that they belonged to wealthy families. 'Let us remember our Lord's words, "It is easier for a camel to go through the eye of a needle, than for a rich man to enter into the Kingdom of God",' shouted the Chaplain. 'We have too many camels in Porterhouse.' He climbed down from the pulpit and the service ended with 'As pants the hart ...' The Dean and the Senior Tutor left together.

'A most peculiar service,' said the Dean. 'The Chaplain seemed obsessed with various forms of wild life.'

'I think he misses Skullion,' said the Senior Tutor.

They walked down the Cloisters with a speculative air. After that dreadful programme I would hardly go so far as to say that I missed him,' the Dean said, 'though I daresay he's a great loss to the College.'

'In more ways than one,' said the Senior Tutor. 'I dined in Emmanuel last night.' He shuddered at the recollection.

'Very commendable,' said the Dean. 'I try to avoid Emmanuel. I had some cutlets there once that disagreed with me.'

'I hardly noticed the food,' said the Senior Tutor. 'It was the conversation I found disagreeable.'

'Carrington, I suppose?'

'There was some mention,' said the Senior Tutor. 'I did my best to play it down. No, what I really had in mind was something old Saxton there told me. Apparently there is a not unsubstantial rumour going around that Skullion's assertion that he offered the College his life savings was not without foundation.'

The Dean waded through the morass of double negatives towards some sort of assertion. 'Ah,' he said finally, uncertain how far to commit himself.

'I understood Saxton to say he had it on the highest authority that Skullion was worth a good deal more than one might have supposed.'

'I always said Skullion was invaluable,' said the Dean.

'The sum mentioned was in the region of a quarter of a million pounds,' said the Senior Tutor.

'Out of the question to accept ... What?' said the Dean.

'A quarter of a million pounds.'

'Good God!'

'Lord Wurford's legacy to him,' explained the Senior Tutor.

'And the bloody Bursar turned it down,' stuttered the Dean.

'It puts a rather different complexion on the matter, doesn't it?'

It had certainly put a different complexion on the Dean who stood in the Cloister trying to get his breath.

'My God, a quarter of a million pounds. And the Master sacked him,' he gasped. The Senior Tutor helped him down the Cloisters.

'Come and have a little something in my rooms,' he said. They passed the main gate where a youth was holding a placard.

'Reinstate Skullion,' said the Dean. 'For once I think the protestors are right.'

'The danger is that some other college will bag him before we get the chance,' said the Senior Tutor.

'Do you really think so?' asked the Dean anxiously. 'The dear old fellow was ... is such a loyal College servant.' Even to the Dean's ears the word 'servant' had a hollow ring to it now.

In the Senior Tutor's rooms the bric-à-brac of a rowing man hung like ancient weapons on the walls, an arsenal of trophies. The Dean sipped his sherry pensively.

'I blame Carrington entirely,' he said. 'The programme was a travesty. Cathcart should never have invited him.'

'I had no idea he had,' said the Senior Tutor. The Dean changed direction.

'As a matter of fact I found myself agreeing with a great deal of what Skullion had to say. Most of his accusations applied only to the Master. And Sir Godber is entirely responsible for the whole disgraceful affair. He should never have been nominated. He has done irreparable damage to the reputation of the College.'

The Senior Tutor stared out of the window at the damage done to the Tower. The animosity he had felt for the Dean, an antagonism which had taken the place of the transitory attachments of his youth, had quite left him. Whatever the Dean's faults, and over the years the Senior Tutor had catalogued them all meticulously, no one could accuse him of being an intellectual. Together, though never in unison, they had steered Porterhouse away from the academic temptations to which all other Cambridge colleges had succumbed and had preserved that integrity of ignorance which gave Porterhouse men the confidence to cope with life's complexities which men with more educated sensibilities so obviously lacked. Unlike the Dean, whose lack of scholarship was natural and unforced, the Senior Tutor had once possessed a mind and it had only been by the most rigorous discipline that he had suppressed his academic leanings in the interests of the College spirit. His had been an intellectual decision founded on his conviction that if a little knowledge was a dangerous thing, a lot was lethal. The damage done to the Tower by Zipser's researches confirmed him in his belief.

'Has it occurred to you,' he said, at last turning from his contemplation of the dangers of intellectualism, 'that it might be possible to turn this affair of Carrington's programme and Skullion's sacking to some advantage?'

The Dean agreed that he had hoped it might unnerve the Master. 'It's too late for that now,' he said. 'We have been exposed to ridicule. All of us. It may be College policy to suffer fools gladly but I am afraid the public has other views about university education.'

The Senior Tutor shook his head. 'I think you may be unduly pessimistic,' he said. 'My reading of the situation differs from yours. We have certain advantages on our side. For one thing we have Skullion.' The Dean began to protest but the Senior Tutor held up his hand. 'Hear me out, Dean, hear me out. However ludicrous we may have been made to appear by friend Carrington, Skullion made an extremely favourable impression.'

'At our expense,' the Dean pointed out.

'Certainly, but the fact remains that public sympathy is on his side. Let us assume for a moment that we – and by we I mean the College Council – all excepting the Master, agree to demand Skullion's reinstatement. Sir Godber would naturally resist and would be seen to resist such a move. We should appear as the champions of the underdog and the Master would find himself in an extremely difficult position. If further we present a reasoned case for our admissions policy –'

'Impossible,' said the Dean. 'No one is going to –'

'I haven't finished,' said the Senior Tutor. 'There is a sound case to be made for admitting candidates without suitable academic qualifications. We provide a natural outlet for those without apparent ability. No other college performs such a necessary function. Only the clever people get in to King's or Trinity. Certainly New Hall admits candidates under, to put it mildly, peculiar circumstances, but that's a women's college.'

The Dean sniffed disparagingly.

'Quite,' said the Senior Tutor. 'My point is this: that a properly articulated appeal on behalf of the scholastically crippled might win a great deal of public support. Couple it to demands on our part for Skullion's reinstatement and we could well turn what appears to be defeat into victory.' The Senior Tutor fetched the decanter and poured more sherry while the Dean considered his words.

'There may something in what you say,' he admitted. 'It has always seemed to me to be decidedly inequitable that only the intelligent minority should be allowed to benefit from a university education.'

'My point exactly,' said the Senior Tutor. 'We cease to be the college of privilege, we become the college of the intellectually deprived. It is simply a question of emphasis. What is more, since we are not dependent on grant-assisted undergraduates, it is self-evident that we are saving public money. The question remains how to present this new image to the public. I confess the problem baffles me.'

'The first essential is to call an urgent meeting of the College Council and get some degree of unanimity about reinstating Skullion,' said the Dean.

The Senior Tutor picked up the telephone.

CHAPTER NINETEEN

The College Council met at ten on Monday morning. Several Fellows were unable to attend but signified their readiness to vote by proxy through the Dean. Even the Master, who was not fully informed of the agenda, welcomed the meeting. 'We must thrash this affair out once and for all,' he told the Bursar, as they made their way to the Council Chamber. 'The allegations in yesterday's *Observer* have made it essential to make a clean break with the past.'

'They've certainly made things very awkward for us,' said the Bursar.

'They've made it a damned sight more awkward for the old fogeys,' said Sir Godber.

The Bursar sighed. It was evidently going to be an acrimonious meeting.

It was. The Senior Tutor led the attack.

'I am proposing that we issue a statement rescinding the dismissal of Skullion,' he told the Council when the preliminaries had been dealt with.

'Out of the question,' snapped the Master. 'Skullion has chosen to draw the attention of the public to facts about College policy which I am sure we all agree have put the reputation of Porterhouse in jeopardy.'

'I can't agree,' said the Dean.

'I certainly don't,' said the Senior Tutor.

'But the whole world knows now that we sell degrees,' Sir Godber insisted.

'That portion of the world that happens to read the *Observer*, perhaps,' said the Senior Tutor, 'but in any case allegations are not facts.'

'In this case they happen to be facts,' said the Master. 'Unadulterated facts. Skullion was speaking no more than the truth.'

'In that case I can't see why you should object to his reinstatement,' said the Senior Tutor.

They argued for twenty minutes but the Master remained adamant.

'I suggest we put the motion to the vote,' said the Dean finally. Sir Godber looked round the table angrily.

'Before we do,' he said, 'I think you should consider some further matters. I have been examining the College statutes over the past few days and it appears that as Master I am empowered, should I so wish, to take over admissions. In the light of your refusal to agree to a change in College policy regarding the sort of candidates we admit, I have decided to relieve the Senior Tutor of his responsibilities in this sphere. From now on I shall personally choose all Freshmen. It also lies within my power to select College servants and to dismiss those I consider unsatisfactory. I shall do just that. However you may vote in Council, I shall not, as Master, reinstate Skullion.'

In the Council Chamber a momentary silence followed the Master's announcement. Then the Senior Tutor spoke.

'This is outrageous,' he shouted. 'The statutes are out of date. The position of the Master is a purely formal one.'

'I admire your consistency,' snapped the Master. 'As the upholder of outmoded traditions you should be the first to congratulate me for reassuming powers that are a legacy of the past.'

'I am not prepared to stand by and see College traditions flouted,' shouted the Dean.

'They are not being flouted, Dean,' said Sir Godber, 'they are being applied. As to your standing by, if by that you mean that you wish to resign your fellowship, I shall be happy to accept your resignation.'

'I did not say anything ...' stuttered the Dean.

'Didn't you?' interrupted the Master, 'I thought you did. Am I to understand that you withdraw your –'

'He never made it,' the Senior Tutor was on his feet now. 'I find your behaviour quite unwarranted. We, sir, are not some pack of schoolboys that you can dictate to –'

'If you behave like schoolboys, you may expect to be treated like schoolboys. In any case the analogy was yours not mine. Now if you would be so good as to resume your seat the meeting may continue.' The Master looked icily at the Fellows and the Senior Tutor sat down.

'I shall take this opportunity, gentlemen,' said Sir Godber after a long pause, 'to enlighten you on my views about the function of the College in the modern world. I must confess that I am astonished to find that you seem unaware of the changes that have taken place in recent years. Your attitude suggests that you regard the College as part of a private domain of which you are custodians. Let me disabuse you of that notion. You are part of the public realm, with public duties, obligations and public functions. The fact that you choose to ignore them and to conduct the affairs of the College as though they are your personal property indicates to me that you are acting in abuse of your powers. Either we live in a society that is free, open and wholly equalitarian or we do not. As Master of this College I am determined that we shall extend the benefits of education to those who merit it by virtue of ability, irrespective of class, sex, financial standing or race. The days of rotten boroughs are over.' Sir Godber's voice was strident with idealism and threat. Not since the days of the Protectorate had the Council Chamber of Porterhouse known such vehemence, and the Fellows sat staring at the Master as at some strange animal that had assumed the shape of a man. By the time he had exhausted his theme he had left them in no doubt as to his intentions. Porterhouse would never be the same again. To the long catalogue of changes he had proposed at earlier meetings, he had now added the creation of a student council, with executive powers to decide College appointments and policy. He left the Council Chamber emotionally depleted but satisfied that he had made his point. Behind him the Fellows sat aghast at the crisis they had precipitated. It was a long time before anyone spoke.

'I don't understand,' said the Dean pathetically, 'I simply don't understand what these people want.' It was clear that in his mind Sir Godber's eloquence had elevated or possibly debased him from an individual to a class.

'Their own way,' said the Senior Tutor bitterly.

'The Kingdom of Heaven,' shouted the Chaplain.

The Bursar said nothing. His multiple allegiances left him speechless.

Lunch was a mournful occasion. It was the end of term and the Fellows at High Table ate in a silence made all the more noticeable by the lack of conversation from the empty tables below them. To make matters worse, the soup was cold and there was cottage pie. But it was the knowledge of their own dispensability that cast gloom over them. For five hundred years they and their predecessors had ordained at least some portion of the elite that had ruled the nation. It had been through the sieve of their indulgent bigotry that young men had squeezed to become judges and lawyers, politicians and soldiers, men of affairs, all of them imbued with a corporate complacency and an intellectual scepticism that desiccated change. They were the guardians of political inertia and their role was done. They had succumbed at last to the least effectual of politicians.

'A student council to run the College. It's monstrous,' said the Senior Tutor, but there was no hope in his protest. Despite his cultivated mediocrity of mind, the Senior Tutor had seen change coming. He blamed the sciences for reestablishing the mirage of truth, and still more the pseudomorph subjects like anthropology and economics whose adepts substituted inapplicable statistics for the ineptness of their insights. And finally there was sociology with its absurd maxim, The Proper Study of

Mankind is Man, which typically it took from a man the Senior Tutor would have rejected as unfit to cox the rugger boat. And now with Sir Godber triumphant, and the Senior Tutor, at least privately, admitted the Master's victory, Porterhouse would lose even the semblance of the College he had loved. Sickly unisex would replace the healthy cheerful louts who had helped to preserve the inane innocence and the athleticism that were his only safeguards against the terrors of thought.

'There must be something we can do,' said the Dean.

'Short of murder I can think of nothing,' the Senior Tutor answered.

'Is he really entitled by statute to take over admissions?'

The Senior Tutor nodded. 'Tradition has it so,' he answered mournfully.

'There's only one thing they can do now,' said Sir Godber to Lady Mary over coffee.

'And what is that, dear?'

'Surrender,' said the Master. Lady Mary looked up. 'How very martial you do sound, Godber,' she said, invoking the ancient spirit of Sir Godber's pacifism. The Master resisted the call.

'I sounded a good deal more belligerent in the Council,' he said.

'I'm sure you did, dear,' Lady Mary parried.

'I should have thought you would have approved,' Sir Godber said. 'After all, if they had their way the College would continue to sell degrees, and exclude women.'

'Oh, don't think for a moment I am criticizing you,' said Lady Mary. 'It's just that power changes one.'

'It has been said before,' Sir Godber replied wearily. His wife's insatiable dissatisfaction subdued him. Looking into her earnest face he sometimes wondered what she saw in him. It must be something pretty harrowing, he thought. They'd been happily married for twenty-eight years.

'I'll leave you to your little victory,' Lady Mary said, getting up and putting her cup on the tray. 'I shan't be in this evening for dinner. It's my night as a Samaritan.' She went out and Sir Godber poked the fire lethargically. He felt depressed. As usual there had been something in what his wife had said. Power did change one, even the power to dominate a group of elderly Fellows in a fourth-rate college. And it was a little victory after all. Sir Godber's humanity prevailed. It wasn't their fault that they opposed the changes that he wanted. They were creatures of habit, comfortable and indulgent habits. Bachelors too – he was thinking of the Dean and the Senior Tutor – without the goad of an empty marriage to spur them to attainment. Good-hearted in their way. Even their personal animosities and petty jealousies sprang from a too constant companionship. When he examined his own motives he found them rooted in inadequacy and personal pique. He would go and speak to the Senior Tutor again and try to establish a more rational ground for disagreement. He got up and carried the coffee cups through to the kitchen and washed up. It was the au pair's day off. Then he put on his coat and went out into the spring sunshine.

Skullion lay in bed and stared at the pale blue ceiling of his hotel room. He felt uncomfortable. For one thing the bed was strange and the mattress too responsive to his movements. It wasn't hard enough for him. There was something indefinite about the whole room which left him feeling uneasy and out of place. It wasn't anything he could put his finger to but it reminded him of a whore he'd once had in Pompey. Too eager to please so that what had started out as a transaction, impersonal and hard, had turned into an encounter with his own feelings. It was the same with this room. The carpet was too thick. The bed too soft. There was too much hot water in the basin. There was nothing to grumble about and in the absence of anything particular to assert himself against, Skullion's resentment was turned in on himself. He was out of place.

His tour of monuments had unsettled him too. He wasn't interested in the *Cutty Sark* or even in *Gypsy Moth*. They too were out of place, set high and dry for kids to run about on and pretend that they were sailors. Skullion had no such romantic illusions. He couldn't pretend even for a moment that he was other than he was, a college servant out of work. The knowledge that he was a rich man only aggravated his sense of loss. It seemed to justify his dismissal by robbing him of his right to feel hard done by. Skullion even regretted his appearance on the Carrington Programme. They'd said how good he was but who were they? A lot of brown-hatters and word-merchants he had no time for, giggling and squeaking and rushing about like blue-arsed flies. They could keep their bleeding compliments to themselves, Skullion didn't need them.

He got out of bed and went through to the bathroom and shaved. They had even bought him a new razor and aerosol of shaving foam and the very ease with which he shaved robbed him of his own ritual in the matter. He put on his collar and tie and did up his waistcoat. He'd had enough. He'd said his piece and he'd been inside a television studio. That was sufficient, he decided. He'd go back to Cambridge. They could have their talk-in without him. He collected his things together and went down to the desk and paid his bill. Two hours later Skullion was sitting in the train smoking his pipe and looking out at the flat fields of Essex. The

monotony of the landscape pleased him and reminded him of the Fens.
He could buy a bit of land in the Fens now if he wanted to, and grow
vegetables like his stepfather had done. Skullion considered the idea only
to reject it. He didn't want a new life. He wanted his old one back.

When the train stopped at Cambridge Station Skullion had made up
his mind. He would make one last appeal, this time not to the Dean or
Sir Cathcart. He'd speak to the Master himself. He walked out of the
station and down Station Road wondering why he hadn't thought of it
before. He had his pride, of course, and he'd put his trust in the Dean
but the Dean had let him down. Besides, he despised Sir Godber,
according him only that automatic respect that went with the Mastership.
At the corner of Lensfield Road he hesitated under the spire of the
Catholic Church. He could turn right across Parker's Piece to Rhyder
Street or left to Porterhouse. It was only twelve o'clock and he hadn't
eaten. He'd walk into town and have a bite to eat in a pub and think
about it. Skullion trudged on down Regent Street and went into the
Fountain and ordered a pint of Guinness and some sandwiches. Sitting
at a table by the door he drank his beer and tried to imagine what the
Master would say. He could only turn him down. Skullion considered
the prospect and decided it was worth trying even if it meant risking his
self-respect. But was he risking it? All he was asking for was his rights
and besides he had a quarter of a million pounds to his name. He didn't
need the job. Nobody could accuse him of grovelling. It was simply that
he wanted it, wanted his good name back, wanted to go on doing what
he had always done for forty-five years, wanted to be the Porter of
Porterhouse. Buoyed by the good sense of his own argument Skullion
finished his beer and left the pub. He threaded his way through the
shoppers towards the Market Hill, his mind still mulling over the wisdom
of his action. Perhaps he should wait a day or two. Perhaps they had
already changed their mind and a letter was waiting for him at home
offering him his job back. Skullion dismissed the idea. And all the time
there was the nagging fear that he was putting in jeopardy his self-respect
by asking. He silenced the fear but it remained with him, as constant as
the natural tendency of his steps to lead towards Porterhouse. Twice he
decided to go home and twice changed his mind, postponing the decision
by walking down Sydney Street towards the Round Church instead of
going on down Trinity Street. He tried to fortify his resolve by thinking
about Lord Wurford's legacy but the idea of all that money was as unreal
to him as the experience of the past few days. There was no consolation
to be found in money. It couldn't replace the cosiness of his Porter's
Lodge with its pigeonholes and switchboard and the sense that he was

needed. The sum was almost an affront to him, its fortuity robbing his years of service of their sense. He needn't have been a porter. He could have been anything he wanted, within reason. The realization increased his sense of purpose. He would speak to the Master. He hesitated at the Round Church. He wouldn't go in the Main Gate, he'd knock at the Master's Lodge. He turned and went back the way he'd come.

The Master's sudden decision to seek some ground of understanding with the Senior Tutor left him almost as soon as he had crossed the Fellows' Garden. Any sort of overture now would be misinterpreted, he realized, taken as evidence of weakness on his part. He had established his authority. It would not do to weaken it now. But having come out he felt obliged to continue his walk. He went into town and browsed in Heffer's for an hour before buying Butler's *Art of the Possible*. It was not a maxim with which he had much sympathy. It smacked of cynicism but Sir Godber was sufficient of a politician still to appreciate the author's sense of irony. He wandered on debating his own choice of a title for his autobiography. *Future Perfect* was probably the most appropriate, combining as it did his vision with a modicum of scholarship. Catching sight of this reflection in a shop window he found it remarkable that he was as old as he looked. It was strange that his ideals had not altered with his appearance. The methods of their attainment might mellow with experience but the ideals remained constant. That was why it was so important to see that the undergraduates who came up to Porterhouse should be free to form their own judgements, and more important still that they should have some judgements to form. They should rebel against the accepted tenets of their elders and, in Sir Godber's opinion, their worse. He stopped at the Copper Kettle for tea and then made his way back to Porterhouse and sat in his study reading his book. Outside the sky darkened, and with it the College. Out of term it was empty and there were no room lights on to brighten the Court. At five the Master got up and pulled the curtains and he was about to sit down again when a knock at the front door made him stop and go down the corridor into the hall. He opened the door and peered out into the darkness. A dark familiar shape stood on the doorstep.

'Skullion?' said Sir Godber as if questioning the existence of the shape. 'What are you doing here?'

To Skullion the question emphasized his misery. 'I'd like a word,' he said.

Sir Godber hesitated. He didn't want words with Skullion. 'What about?' he asked. It was Skullion's turn to hesitate. 'I've come to apologize,' he said finally.

'Apologize? What for?' Skullion shook his head. He didn't know what for. 'Well, man? What for?'

'It's just that . . .'

'Oh for goodness sake,' said Sir Godber, appalled at Skullion's inarticulate despair. 'Come on in.' He turned and led the way to his study with Skullion treading gently behind him.

'Well now, what is it?' he asked when they were in the room.

'It's about my dismissal, sir,' Skullion said.

'Your dismissal?' Sir Godber sighed. He was a sympathetic man who had to steel himself with irritation. 'You should see the Bursar about that. I don't deal with matters of that sort.'

'I've seen the Bursar,' said Skullion.

'I don't see that I can do anything,' the Master said. 'And in any case I really don't think that you can expect much sympathy after what you said the other night.'

Skullion looked at him sullenly. 'I didn't say anything wrong,' he muttered. 'I just said what I thought.'

'It might have paid you to consider what you did think before . . .' Sir Godber gave up. The situation was most unfortunate. He had better things to do with his time than argue with college porters. 'Anyway there's nothing more to be said.'

Skullion stirred resentfully. 'Forty-five years I've been a porter here,' he said.

Sir Godber's hand brushed the years aside. 'I know. I know,' he said. 'I'm aware of that.'

'I've given my life to the College.'

'I daresay.'

Skullion glowered at the Master. 'All I ask is to be kept on,' he said.

The Master turned his back on him and kicked the fire with his foot. The man's maudlin appeal annoyed him. Skullion had exercised a baleful influence on the College ever since he could remember. He stood for everything Sir Godber detested. He'd been rude, bullying and importunate all his life and the Master hadn't forgotten his insolence on the night of the explosion. Now here he was, cap in hand, asking to be taken back. Worst of all he made the Master feel guilty.

'I understand from the Bursar that you have some means,' he said callously. Skullion nodded. 'Enough to live on?'

'Yes.'

'Well then, I really can't see what you're complaining about. A lot of people retire at sixty. Haven't you got a family?' Skullion shook his head. Again Sir Godber felt a tremor of unreasonable disgust. His contempt showed in his face, contempt as much for his own vulnerable sensibilities as for the pathetic man before him. Skullion saw that contempt and his little eyes darkened. He had swallowed his pride to come and ask but it rode up in him now in the face of the Master's scorn. It rose up out of the distant past when he'd been a free man and it overwhelmed the barriers of his reference. He hadn't come to be insulted even silently by the likes of Sir Godber. Without knowing what he was doing he took a step forward. Instinctively Sir Godber recoiled. He was afraid of Skullion and, like his contempt a moment before, it showed. He'd been afraid of Skullion all his life, the little Skullions who lived in drab streets he'd had to pass to go to school, who chased him and threw stones and wore grubby clothes.

'Now look here,' he said with an attempt at authority, but Skullion was looking. His bitter eyes stared at Sir Godber and he too was in the grip of the past and its violent instincts. His face was flushed and unknown to him his fists were clenched.

'You bastard!' he shouted and lunged at the Master. 'You bloody bastard!' Sir Godber staggered backwards and tripped against the coffee table. He fell against the mantelpiece and clutched at the edge of the armchair and the next moment he had fallen back into the fireplace. Beneath his feet a rug gently slid away and Sir Godber subsided on to the study floor. His head had hit the corner of the iron grate. Above him Skullion stood dumbfounded. Blood oozed on to the parquet. Skullion's fury ebbed. He stared down at the Master for a moment and turned and ran. He ran down the passage and out the front door into the street. It was empty. Skullion turned to the right and hurried along the pavement. A moment later he was in Trinity Street. People passed him but there was nothing unusual about a college porter in a hurry.

In the Master's Lodge Sir Godber lay still in the flickering light of his fire. The blood running fast from his scalp formed in a pool and dried. An hour passed and Sir Godber still bled, though more slowly. It was eight before he recovered consciousness. The room was blurred and distant and clocks ticked noisily. He tried to get to his feet but couldn't. He knelt against the fireplace and reached for the armchair. Slowly he crawled across the room to the telephone. He'd got to ring for help. He reached up and pulled the phone down on to the floor. He started to dial emergency but the thought of scandal stopped him. His wife? He put the receiver back and reached for the pad with the number of the

Samaritans on it. He found it and dialled. While he waited he stared at
the notice Lady Mary had pinned on the pad. 'If you are in Despair or
thinking of Suicide, Phone the Samaritans.'

The dialling tone stopped. 'Samaritans here, can I help you?' Lady
Mary's voice was as stridently concerned as ever.

'I'm hurt,' said Sir Godber indistinctly.

'You're what? You'll have to speak up.'

'I said I'm hurt. For God's sake come ...'

'What's that?' Lady Mary asked.

'Oh God, oh God,' Sir Godber moaned feebly.

'All right now, tell me all about it,' said Lady Mary with interest. 'I'm
here to help you.'

'I've fallen in the grate,' Sir Godber explained.

'Fallen from grace?'

'Not grace,' said Sir Godber desperately. 'Grate.'

'Great?' Lady Mary inquired, evidently convinced she was dealing
with a disillusioned megalomaniac.

'The hearth. I'm bleeding. For God's sake come ...' Exhausted by his
wife's lack of understanding Sir Godber fell back upon the floor. Beside
him the phone continued to squeak and gibber with Lady Mary's
exhortations.

'Are you there?' she asked. 'Are you still there? Now there's no need
to despair.' Sir Godber groaned. 'Now don't hang up. Just stay there
and listen. Now you say you've fallen from grace. That's not a very
constructive way of looking at things, is it?' Sir Godber's stentorian
breathing reassured her. 'After all what is grace? We're all human. We
can't expect to live up to our own expectations all the time. We're bound
to make mistakes. Even the best of us. But that doesn't mean to say we've
fallen from grace. You mustn't think in those terms. You're not a Catholic,
are you?' Sir Godber groaned. 'It's just that you mentioned bleeding
hearts. Catholics believe in bleeding hearts, you know.' Lady Mary was
adding instruction to exhortation now. It was typical of the bloody
woman, Sir Godber thought helplessly. He tried to raise himself so that
he could replace the receiver and shut out forever the sound of Lady
Mary's implacable philanthropy but the effort was too much for him.

'Get off the line,' he managed to moan. 'I need help.'

'Of course you do and that's what I'm here for,' Lady Mary said. 'To
help.'

Sir Godber crawled away from the receiver, spurred on by her
obtuseness. He had to get help somehow. His eye caught the trays of
drinks near the door. Whisky. He crawled towards it and managed to

get the bottle. He drank some and still clutching the bottle reached the side door. Somehow he opened it and dragged himself out into the Fellows' Garden. If only he could reach the Court, perhaps he could call out and someone would hear him. He drank some more whisky and tried to get to his feet. There was a light on in the Combination Room. If only he could get there. Sir Godber raised himself on his knees and fell sideways on to the path.

CHAPTER TWENTY

It was Sir Cathcart's birthday and as usual there was a party at Coft Castle. On the gravel forecourt the sleek cars bunched in the moonlight like so many large seals huddled on the foreshore. Inside the animal analogy continued. In the interests of several Royal guests and uninhibited debauchery, masks were worn if little else. Sir Cathcart typically adopted the disguise of a horse, its muzzle suitably foreshortened to facilitate conversation and his penchant for fellatio. Her Royal Highness the Princess Penelope sought anonymity as a capon and deceived no one. A judge from the Appellate Division was a macaw. There was a bear, two gnus, and a panda wearing a condom. The Loverley sisters sported dildos with stripes and claimed they were zebras and Lord Forsyth, overzealous as a labrador, urinated against a standard lamp in the library and had to be resuscitated by Mrs Hinkle, who was one of the judges at Crufts. Even the detectives mingling with the crowd were dressed as pumas. Only the Dean and the Senior Tutor came as humans, and they were not invited.

'Cathcart's the only man I know who could do it,' the Dean had said suddenly during dinner in the empty Hall.

'Do what?' asked the Senior Tutor.

'See the PM,' said the Dean. 'Get him to rescind the Master's nomination.'

The Senior Tutor lacerated a shinbone judiciously and wiped his fingers. 'On what grounds?'

'General maladministration,' said the Dean.

'Difficult to prove,' said the Senior Tutor.

The Dean helped himself to devilled kidneys and Arthur replenished his wine glass. 'Let us review the facts. Since his arrival the College has seen the deaths of one undergraduate, a bedder, the total destruction of a building classified as a national monument, charges of peculation and a scandal involving the admission of unqualified candidates, the sacking of Skullion and now, to cap it all, the assumption of dictatorial powers by the Master.'

'But surely –'

'Bear with me,' said the Dean. 'Now you and I may know that the Master is not wholly responsible, but the general public thinks otherwise. Have you seen today's *Telegraph?*'

'No,' said the Senior Tutor, 'but I think I know what you mean. *The Times* has three columns of letters, all of them supporting Skullion's statement on the box.'

'Exactly,' said the Dean. 'The *Telegraph* also has a leading article calling for a stand against student indiscipline and a return to the values Skullion so eloquently advocated. Whatever the merits of the Carrington Programme, it has certainly provoked a public reaction against the dismissal of Skullion. Porterhouse may have been blackguarded but it is Sir Godber who takes the blame.'

'As Master, you mean?'

'Precisely,' continued the Dean. 'He may claim –'

'As Master he must accept full responsibility,' said the Senior Tutor. 'Still, I don't see that the Prime Minister would willingly dismiss him. It would reflect poorly on his own judgement in the first place.'

'The Government's position is not a particularly healthy one just at the moment,' said the Dean. 'It only needs a nudge ...'

'A nudge? From whom?'

The Dean smiled and signalled to Arthur to make himself scarce. 'From me,' he said when the waiter had shuffled off into the darkness of the lower hall.

'You?' said the Senior Tutor. 'How?'

'Have you ever heard of Skullion's Scholars?' the Dean asked. His bloated face glowed in the light of the candles.

'That old story,' said the Senior Tutor. 'An old chestnut surely?'

The Dean shook his head. 'I have the names and the dates and the sums involved,' he said. 'I have the names of the graduates who wrote the papers. I have even some examples of their work.' He put the tips of his fingers together and nodded. The Senior Tutor stared at him.

'No,' he muttered.

'Yes,' the Dean assured him.

'But how?'

The Dean withdrew a little. 'Let's just say that I have,' he said. 'There was a time when I disapproved of the practice. I was young in those days and full of foolishness but I changed my mind. Fortunately I did not destroy the evidence. You see now what I mean by a nudge?'

The Senior Tutor gulped some wine in his amazement. 'Not the PM?' he muttered.

'Not,' admitted the Dean, 'but one or two of his colleagues.' The Senior Tutor tried to think which ministers were Porterhouse men.

'I have some eighty names,' said the Dean, 'some eighty *eminent* names. I think they're quite sufficient.'

The Senior Tutor mopped his forehead. There was no doubt in his mind about the sufficiency of the Dean's information. It would bring the Government down. 'Could you rely on Skullion to substantiate,' he asked.

The Dean nodded. 'I hardly think it will come to that,' he said, 'and if it does I am prepared to stand as scapegoat. I am an old man. I no longer care.'

They sat in silence. Two old men together in the isolated candlelight under the dark rafters of the Hall. Arthur, standing obediently by the green baize door, watched them fondly.

'And Sir Cathcart?' asked the Senior Tutor.

'And Sir Cathcart,' agreed the Dean.

They stood up and the Dean said grace, his voice tremulous in the vastness of the silent Hall. They went out into the Combination Room and Arthur shuffled softly up to the High Table and began to collect the dishes.

Half an hour later they drove out of the College car park in the Senior Tutor's car. Coft Castle was blazing with Edwardian brilliance when they arrived.

'It seems an inopportune moment,' said the Senior Tutor doubtfully surveying the shoal of cars.

'We must strike while the iron is hot,' said the Dean. Inside they were accosted by a puma.

'Do we look like gatecrashers?' the Dean asked severely. The puma shook its head.

'We have urgent business with General Sir Cathcart D'Eath,' said the Senior Tutor. 'Be so good as to inform him that the Dean and Senior Tutor have arrived. We shall wait for him in the library.'

The puma nodded dutifully and they pushed their way through a crush of assorted beasts to the library.

'I must say I find this sort of thing extremely distasteful,' said the Dean. 'I am surprised that Cathcart allows such goings on at Coft Castle. One would have thought he had more taste.'

'He always did have something of a reputation,' said the Senior Tutor. 'Of course he was before my time but I did hear one or two rather unsavoury stories.'

'Youthful excess is one thing,' said the Dean, 'but mutton dressed as lamb is another.'

'They say the leopard doesn't change its spots,' said the Senior Tutor. He sat down in a club easy while the Dean idly examined a nicely bound copy of Stendhal. It contained, as he had expected from the title, a bottle of liqueur.

Outside the puma stalked Sir Cathcart. He found it extremely difficult. He tried the billiard-room, the smoking-room, the morning-room, and the dining-room without success. In the kitchen he asked the cook if she had seen him.

'I wouldn't know him if I had,' the cook said primly. 'All I know is that he's gone as a horse.'

The detective went back into the menagerie and asked several guests who were wearing horsey masks if they were Sir Cathcart. They weren't. He helped himself to champagne and tried again. Finally he ran Sir Cathcart to ground in the conservatory with a well-known jockey. The detective surveyed the scene with disgust.

'Two gentlemen to see you in the library,' he said. Sir Cathcart got to his feet.

'What do you mean?' he said indistinctly. 'What are they doing there? I said nobody was to go in the library.' He staggered off down the passage and into the library where the Dean had just discovered a copy of *A Man and A Maid* inside an early edition of *Great Expectations*.

'What the hell . . .?' Sir Cathcart began before realizing who they were.

'Cathcart?' inquired the Dean, staring doubtfully at the General.

'Who?' said Sir Cathcart.

'We are waiting to speak to Sir Cathcart D'Eath,' said the Dean.

'Isn't here. Gone to London,' said the General, slurring his voice deliberately and hoping that his mask was a sufficient proof against identity. The Dean was unpersuaded. He recognized the General's fetlocks.

'I am prepared to accept the explanation,' he said grimly. 'We have not come here to pry.' He returned to copy of *Great Expectations* to its place. 'We simply wanted to inform Sir Cathcart that the matter of Skullion's Scholars is about to receive a public airing.'

'Damnation,' shouted the General, 'how the hell did . . .?' He stopped and regarded the Dean bitterly.

'Quite,' said the Dean. He sat down behind the desk and the General sank into a chair. 'The matter is urgent, otherwise we shouldn't be here. We have no desire to abuse your hospitality, if that were possible, any longer than we have to. Let us assume that Sir Cathcart is in London for the moment.'

The General nodded his agreement with this tactful proposition. 'What do you want?' he asked.

'Things have reached a crisis,' said the Senior Tutor rising from his club easy. 'We simply want the Prime Minister to be informed that Sir Godber's Mastership must be rescinded.'

'Must?' said the General. The word had an authoritarian ring about it that he was unused to.

'Must,' said the Dean.

Sir Cathcart inside his mask looked doubtful. 'It's a tall order.'

'No doubt,' said the Dean. 'The alternative is possibly the fall of the Government. I am prepared to place my information in the hands of the press. I think you follow the likely consequences.'

Sir Cathcart did. 'But why, for God's sake?' he asked. 'I don't understand. If this got out it would ruin the College.'

'If the Master stays there will be no college to ruin,' said the Dean. 'There will be a hostel. I have some eighty names, Cathcart.'

Sir Cathcart peered through his mask bitterly. '*Eighty*? And you're prepared to put their reputations at risk?'

The Dean's mouth curved upwards in a sneer. 'In the circumstances I find that question positively indecent,' he said.

'Oh, come now,' said the General. 'We all have our little peccadilloes. A fellow's entitled to a little fun.'

On the way out they were importuned by a fowl. 'These gentlemen are just leaving,' said Sir Cathcart hurriedly.

'Before me?' cackled the capon. 'It's against protocol.'

They drove back to Porterhouse in silence. What they had just witnessed had left them with a new sense of disillusionment.

'The whole country is going to the dogs,' said the Senior Tutor as they crossed New Court. As if in answer there was a low moan from the Fellows' Garden.

'What on earth was that?' said the Dean. They turned and peered into the darkness. Under the elms a shadow darker than the rest struggled to its feet and collapsed. They crossed the lawn cautiously and stood staring down at the figure on the ground.

'A drunk,' said the Senior Tutor. 'I'll fetch the Porter,' but the Dean

had already struck a match. In the small flare of light they looked down
into the ashen face of Sir Godber.

'Good God,' said the Dean, 'it's the Master.'

They carried him slowly and with difficulty down the gravel path to
the Master's Lodge and laid him on the sofa.

'I'll get an ambulance,' said the Senior Tutor, and picked the phone
off the floor and dialled. While they waited the Dean sat staring down
into the Master's face. It was evident Sir Godber was dying. He struggled
to speak but the words wouldn't come.

'He's trying to tell us something,' said the Senior Tutor softly. There
was no bitterness now. In extremis the Master had regained the Senior
Tutor's loyalty.

'He must have been drunk,' said the Dean, who could smell the whisky
on Sir Godber's feeble breath.

The Master shook his head. An indefinite future awaited him now in
which he would only be a memory. It must not be sullied by false report.

'Not drunk,' he managed to mutter, gazing pitifully into the Dean's
face. 'Skullion.'

The Dean and Senior Tutor looked at one another. 'What about
Skullion?' the Senior Tutor asked but the Master had no answer for him.

They waited for the ambulance before leaving. It had been impossible
to contact Lady Mary. She was on the phone to a depressive who was
threatening to end his life. On the way back through the Fellows' Garden
the Dean retrieved the whisky bottle.

'I don't think we need mention this to the police,' he said. 'He was
obviously drunk and fell into the fireplace. A tragic end.'

The Senior Tutor was lost in thought. 'You realize what he's done?'
he asked.

'Only too well,' said the Dean. 'I'll phone Sir Cathcart and tell him
to cancel the ultimatum. There's no need for it now. We shall have to
elect a new Master. Let us see to it that he has the true interests of the
College at heart. We mustn't make another mistake.'

The Senior Tutor shook his head. 'There can be no question of an
election, Dean,' he said. 'The Master has already nominated his own
successor.'

In the darkness the two old men stared at one another digesting the
extraordinary import of Sir Godber's last word. it was unthinkable but
yet ...

They went into the Combination Room to deliberate. The ancient panelled walls, the plaster ceiling decorated with heraldic devices and grotesque animals, the portraits of past Masters, and the silver candlesticks all combined to urge considerations of the past upon their present dilemma.

'There are precedents,' said the Senior Tutor. 'Thomas Wilkins was a pastrycook.'

'He was also an eminent theologian,' said the Dean.

'Dr Cox began his career as a barber,' the Senior Tutor pointed out. 'He owed his election to his wealth.'

'I take your point,' said the Dean. 'In the present cicumstances it is one that cannot be ignored.'

'There is also the question of public opinion to consider,' the Senior Tutor continued. 'In the present climate it would not be an unpopular appointment. It would disarm our critics entirely.

'So it would,' said the Dean. 'It would indeed. But the College Council –'

'Have no say in the matter,' said the Senior Tutor. 'Tradition has it that the Master's dying words constitute an unalterable decision.'

'If uttered in the presence of two or more of the Senior Fellows,' agreed the Dean. 'So it is up to us.'

'There is little doubt that he would be malleable,' the Senior Tutor continued after a long pause. The Dean nodded. 'I confess to finding the argument unanswerable,' he said. They rose and snuffed the candles.

Skullion sat in the darkness of his kitchen, shivering. It was a cold night but Skullion was unconscious of the cold. His tremors had other causes. He had threatened the Master. He had in all probability killed him. The memory of Sir Godber lying in a pool of blood in the fireplace haunted Skullion. He could not think of sleep. He sat there at the kitchen table shivering with fright. He couldn't begin to think what to do. The law would find him. Skullion's innate respect for authority rejected the possibility that his crime would go undetected. It was almost as monstrous a thought as the knowledge that he was a murderer. He was still there when the Dean and the Senior Tutor knocked on his door at eight o'clock. They had brought the Praelector with them. As usual his was a supernumerary role.

Skullion listened to the knocking for some minutes before his instincts as a porter got the better of him. He got up and went down the dingy hall and opened the door. He stood blinking in the sunlight, his face purple with strain but with a solemnity that befitted the occasion.

'If we could just have a word with you, Mr Skullion,' the Dean said.

To Skullion the addition of the title had the effect of confirming his worst fears. It suggested the polite formalities of the hangman. He turned and led the way into his front parlour where the sun, shining through the lace curtains, dappled the antimacassars with a fresh embroidery.

The three Fellows removed their hats and sat awkwardly on the Victorian chairs. Like most of the furniture in the house they had been salvaged from the occasional refurbishment of Porterhouse.

'I think it would be better if you sat down,' said the Dean when Skullion continued to stand before them. 'What we are about to tell you may come as something of a shock.'

Skullion sat down obediently. Nothing that they could tell him would comee as a shock, he felt sure. He had prepared himself for the worst.

'We have come here this morning to tell you that the Master has died,' said the Dean. Skullion's face remained impassively suffused. To the three Fellows his evident self-control augured well for the future.

'On his deathbed Sir Godber named you as his successor,' said the Dean slowly. Skullion heard the words but his expectations deprived them of their meaning. What had seemed unthinkable to the Dean and Senior Tutor at first hearing was inconceivable to Skullion. He stared uncomprehendingly at the Dean.

'He nominated you as the new Master of Porterhouse,' continued the Dean. 'We have come here this morning on behalf of the College Council to ask you to accept this nomination.' He paused to allow the Porter to consider the proposal. 'Naturally we understand that this must come as a very great surprise to you, as indeed it did to us, but we would like to know your answer as soon as possible.'

In the silence that followed this announcement, Skullion underwent a terrible change. A tremor ran down his body and his face, already purple, became darker still. He wrestled with the terrible inconsequentiality of it all. He had murdered the Master and they were offering him the Mastership. There were no just rewards in life, only insane inversions of the scheme of things in which he had trusted. It seemed for a moment that he was going mad.

'We must have your answer,' said the Dean. Skullion's body acted uncontrollably as he went into apoplexy. His head nodded frantically.

'Then we may take it that you accept?' asked the Dean. Skullion's head nodded without stop.

'Then let me be the first to congratulate you, Master,' said the Dean and seizing Skullion's hand shook it convulsively. The Praelector and the Senior Tutor followed suit.

*

'The poor fellow was quite overcome,' said the Dean as they climbed back into the car. 'It seemed to leave him speechless.'

'Hardly surprising, Dean,' said the Praelector, 'I find it difficult to voice my feelings even now. Skullion as the Master of Porterhouse. That it should come to this.'

'At least we shan't have any speeches at the Feast,' said the Senior Tutor.

'I suppose there is that to be said for it,' said the Praelector.

In the front parlour of his old home the new Master of Porterhouse lay still in his chair and stared calmly at the linoleum. A new peace had come to Skullion out of the chaos of the last few minutes. There were no contradictions now between right and wrong, master and servant, only a strange inability to move his left side.

Skullion had suffered a Porterhouse Blue.

CHAPTER TWENTY-ONE

'A stroke of luck really,' said the Dean at lunch after the formal ceremony in the Council Chamber at which the new Master had presided before being wheeled back by Arthur to the Master's Lodge.

'I must say I don't follow you, Dean,' said the Praelector with distaste. 'If you are referring to the Master's affliction –'

'I was merely trying to draw your attention to the advantages of the situation,' said the Dean. 'The Master is not without his comforts after all, and we ...'

'Enjoy the administration of policy?' the Senior Tutor suggested.

'Precisely.'

'I suppose that is one way of looking at it. Certainly Sir Godber's reforms have been frustrated. I thought Lady Mary behaved extremely badly.'

The Dean sighed. 'Liberals tend to overreact, in my experience. There seems to be something inherently hysterical about progressive opinion,' he said. 'Still, there was no excuse whatsoever for accusing the police of incompetence. Nothing could be more absurd than her suggestion that Sir Godber had been murdered. For one moment I thought she was going to accuse the Senior Tutor and myself.'

'I suppose he was drunk,' said the Praelector.

'Not according to the coroner,' said the Bursar.

The Dean sniffed. 'I have never placed much faith in expert opinion,' he said. 'I smelt the fellow's breath. He was as drunk as a lord.'

'It's certainly the only rational explanation of his choice of Skullion,' said the Praelector. 'To my knowledge he loathed the man.'

'I'm afraid I have to agree with you,' said the Bursar. 'Lady Mary –'

'Accused us of lying,' said the Dean and the Senior Tutor simultaneously.

'As you said yourself, Dean, she was hysterical,' said the Praelector. 'She wasn't herself.'

The Dean scowled down the table. Lady Mary's accusation still rankled. 'Damned woman,' he said, 'she's a disgrace to her sex.' He took his irritation out on the new waiter. 'These potatoes are burnt.'

'Now you come to mention it,' said the Senior Tutor, 'what went wrong at the crematorium? There seemed an inordinately long delay.'

'There was a power cut,' the Dean said, 'on account of the strike.'

'Ah, was that it?' said the Senior Tutor. 'A sympathy strike no doubt.'

They finished their meal and took coffee in the Combination Room.

'There's still the question of Sir Godber's portrait to be considered,' said the Senior Tutor. 'I suppose we should decide on a suitable artist.'

'There's only Bacon,' said the Dean, 'I can think of no one else who could portray a more exact likeness.'

The Fellows of Porterhouse had regained their vivacity.

In the Master's Lodge Skullion's life followed its inexorable pattern. He was wheeled from room to room to catch the sun so that it was possible to tell the time of day from his position at the windows, and every afternoon Arthur would take him out through the Fellows' Garden and across New Court to the main gate. Occasionally late at night the wheel chair, with its dark occupant wearing his bowler hat, could be seen in the shadows by the back gate waiting and watching with an implacable futility of purpose the spiked wall over which the undergraduates no longer climbed. But if Skullion's horizons were limited to the narrow confines of the College they were celestial in time. Each corner of Porterhouse held memories for him that made good the infirmities of the present. It was as if his stroke had sutured the gaps in his memory so that in his immobility he was left free at last to haunt the years as once he had patrolled the courtyards and the corridors of Porterhouse. Sitting in New Court he would recall the occupants of every room, their names and faces, even the counties they came from, so that the Court assumed a new dimension, at once recessional and mute. Each staircase was a warren in his mind alive with men no longer living who had once conferred the honour of their disregard upon him. 'Skullion,' they had shouted, and the shouts still echoed in his mind with their call to a service he would never know again. Instead they called him Master now and Skullion suffered their respect in silence.

Around him the life of the College went on unaltered. Lord Wurford's legacy helped to restore the Tower and Skullion had signed the papers with his thumbprint unprotestingly. As a sop to scholarship there were a few research fellows, mainly in law and the less controversial sciences, but apart from these concessions, little changed. The undergraduates kept later hours, grew longer hair and sported their affectations of opinion as trivially as ever they had once seduced the shopgirls. But in essentials they were just the same. In any case, Skullion discounted thought. He'd known too many scholars in his time to think that they would alter things. It was the continuity of custom and character that counted. What men were, not what they said, and looking round him he was reassured. The faces that he saw and the voices he heard, though now obscured by hair and the borrowed accents of the poor, had still the recognizable attributes of class, and if the old unfeeling arrogance had been replaced by a kindliness and gentle quality that he despised, it was still Them and Us even in the privilege of sympathy. And when an undergraduate would offer to wheel the Master for a walk, he would be deterred by the glint in Skullion's eyes which betrayed a contempt that made a mockery of his dependence.

Occasionally the Senior Tutor would smother his revulsion for the physically inadequate and visit the Master for tea to tell him how the Eight was doing or what the Rugger fifteen had won, and every day the Dean would waddle to the Master's Lodge to report the day's events. Skullion did not enjoy this strange reversal of roles but it seemed to afford the Dean some little satisfaction. It was as if this mock subservience assuaged his sense of guilt.

'We owe it to him,' he told the Senior Tutor who asked him why he bothered.

'But what do you find to say to him?'

'I ask after his health,' said the Dean gaily.

But he can't reply,' the Senior Tutor pointed out.

'I find that most consoling,' said the Dean. 'And after all no news is good news isn't it?'

On Thursday nights the Master dined in Hall, wheeled in by Arthur at the head of the Fellows to sit at the end of the table and watch the ancient ritual of Grace and the serving of the dishes with a critical eye.

While the Fellows gorged themselves, Skullion was fed a few, choice morsels by Arthur. It was his worst humiliation. That, and the fact that his shoes lacked the brilliance that his patient spit and polish had once given them.

It was left to the Dean, unfeeling to the end, to say the last word in the Combination Room after one such meal. 'He may not have been born with a silver spoon in his mouth, but by God he's going to die with one.'

In his corner by the fire the Master was seen to twitch deferentially at this joke at his own expense, but then Skullion had always known his place.

BLOTT
ON THE
LANDSCAPE

CHAPTER ONE

Sir Giles Lynchwood, Member of Parliament for South Worfordshire, sat in his study and lit a cigar. Outside his window tulips and primroses bloomed, a thrush pecked at the lawn and the sun shone down out of a cloudless sky. In the distance he could see the cliffs of the Cleene Gorge rising above the river.

But Sir Giles had no thoughts for the beauties of the landscape. His mind was occupied with other things; with money and Mrs Forthby and the disparity between things as they were and things as they might have been. Not that the view from his window was one of uninterrupted beauty. It held Lady Maud, and whatever else she might be, nobody in his right mind would ever have described her as beautiful. She was large and ponderous and possessed a shape that someone had once aptly called Rodinesque – certainly Sir Giles, viewing her as dispassionately as six years of marriage allowed, found her monumentally unattractive. Sir Giles was not particularly fussy about external appearances. His fortune had been made by recognizing potential advantage in unprepossessing properties and he could justly claim to have evicted more impecunious tenants than any other anonymous landlord in London. Maud's appearance was the least of his marital problems. It was rather the cast of her mind, her outspoken self-assurance, that infuriated him. That, and the fact that for once in his life he was lumbered with a wife he could not leave and a house he could not sell.

Maud was a Handyman and Handyman Hall had always been her family home. A vast rambling building with twenty bedrooms, a ballroom with a sprung floor, a plumbing system that held fascinations for industrial archaeologists but which kept Sir Giles awake at night, and a central heating system that had been designed to consume coke by the ton, and now seemed to gulp oil by the megagallon, Handyman Hall had been built in 1899 to make manifest in bricks, mortar and the more hideous furnishings of the period the fact that the Handyman family had arrived. Theirs had been a brief social season. Edward the Seventh had twice paid visits to the house, on each occasion seducing Mrs Handyman in the mistaken belief that she was a chambermaid (a result of the diffidence which left her speechless in the presence of Royalty). In recompense for this royal gaffe, and for services rendered, her husband Bulstrode was raised to the Peerage. From that brief moment of social acceptance the Handymans had sunk to their present obscurity. Borne to prominence on a tide of ale – Handyman Pale, Handyman Triple XXX and Handyman West Country had been famous in their time – they had succumbed to a taste for brandy. The first earl of Handyman had died, a suspicious husband and an understandably ardent republican, in time to achieve posthumous fame as the first cadaver to incur Lloyd George's exorbitant death duties. He had been followed almost immediately by his eldest son Bartholomew, whose reaction to the taxman's summons had been to drink himself to death on two bottles of his father's Trois Six de Montpellier.

The outbreak of the First World War had completed the decline in the family fortunes. Boothroyd, the second son, had returned from France with his taste buds so irreparably impaired by taking a swig from a bottle of battery acid to steady his nerves before going over the top that his efforts to restore Handyman Ale to its pre-war quality and popularity had quite the contrary effect. For the first time the title 'Brewers Extraordinary to his Majesty the King' accurately reflected the character of the beer dispensed by the Handyman Brewery. During the twenties and thirties sales dropped until they were confined to a dozen tied houses in Worfordshire whose patrons were forced to consume Boothroyd's appalling concoctions out of a sense of loyalty to the family and by the refusal of the local magistrates (Boothroyd among them) to grant licences to sell spiritous liquors to anyone else. By that time the Handymans had been reduced to living in one wing of the great house and had celebrated the outbreak of the Second World War by offering the rest of their home to the War Office. Boothroyd had died on Home Guard duty to be succeeded by his brother Busby, Maud's father, and the Hall had served first as a home for General de Gaulle's chief of staff and the entire Free French army of that time and later as an Italian prisoner-of-war camp. The fourth Earl had done what he could to restore Handyman Ale to its previous popularity by reverting to the original recipe, and to restore the family fortune by using his influence to see that the War Office paid a quite disproportionately high rent for a building they didn't want.

It had been that influence, the Handyman influence, which had persuaded Sir Giles that he could do worse than marry Lady Maud and through her acquire a seat in Parliament. Looking back over the years Sir Giles was inclined to think that he had paid too high a price for the Hall and social acceptance. A marriage of convenience he had called it at the time, but the term had proved singularly inappropriate. Nothing about Maud's appearance had suggested an unduly fastidious attitude to sex and Sir Giles had been surprised, not to say pained, by her too literal interpretation of his suggestion on their honeymoon that she should tie him to the bed and beat him. Sir Giles' screams had been audible a quarter of a mile along the Costa Brava and had led to an embarrassing interview with the hotel manager. Sir Giles had stood all the way home and ever since had sought refuge in a separate bedroom and in Mrs Forthby, in whose flat in St John's Wood he could at least be assured of moderation. To make matters worse there was no possibility of a divorce. Their marriage settlement included a reversionary clause whereby the Hall and the Estate, for which he had had to pay one hundred thousand pounds to Maud, would revert to her in the event of his death without heirs or of misconduct on his part leading to a divorce case. Sir Giles was a rich man but one hundred thousand pounds was too high a price to pay for freedom.

He sighed and glanced out of the window. Lady Maud had disappeared but the scene was no pleasanter for her going. Her place had been taken by Blott, the gardener, who was plodding across the lawn towards the kitchen garden. Sir Giles studied the squat figure with distaste. For a gardener, for an Italian gardener *and* an Ex-PoW, Blott had an air of contentment that grated on Sir Giles' nerves. He liked his servants to be obsequious and there was nothing obsequious about Blott. The wretched fellow seemed to think he owned the place. Sir Giles watched him disappear through the door in the wall of the kitchen garden and considered ways and means of getting rid of Blott, Lady Maud and Handyman Hall. He had just had an idea.

So had Lady Maud. As she lumbered about the garden, uprooting here a dandelion and there a chickweed, her mind was occupied with thoughts of maternity.

'It's now or never,' she murmured as she squashed a slug. Between her legs she could see Sir Giles in his study and wondered once again why it was that she should have married a man with so little sense of duty. In her view there was no higher virtue. It was out of duty to her family that she had married him. Left to herself she would have chosen a younger, more attractive man, but young attractive men with fortunes were in short supply in Worfordshire and Maud too plain to seek them out in London.

'Coming out?' she had shouted at her mother when Lady Handyman had suggested she should be presented at court. 'Coming out? But I've already been.'

And it was true. Lady Maud's moment of beauty had been premature. At fifteen she had been lovely. At twenty-one the Handyman features, the prominent nose in particular, had made themselves and her plain.

At thirty-five she was a Handyman all over and only acceptable to someone with Sir Giles' depraved taste and eye for hidden advantage. She had accepted his proposal without illusions, only to discover too late that his long bachelorhood had left him with a set of habits and fantasies which made it impossible for him to fulfil his part of the bargain. Whatever else Sir Giles was cut out for it was not paternity. After the unfortunate experience of their honeymoon, Maud had attempted a reconciliation, but without result. She had resorted to drink, to spicy foods, to oysters and champagne, to hard-boiled eggs, but Sir Giles had remained obdurately impotent. Now on this bright spring day when everything about her was breaking out or sprouting or proclaiming the joys of parenthood from every corner of the estate, Lady Maud felt distinctly wanton. She would make one more effort to make Sir Giles see reason. Straightening her back she marched across the lawn to the house and went down the passage.

'Giles,' she said entering the study without knocking, 'it's time we had this thing out.'

Sir Giles looked up from his *Times*. 'What thing?' he asked.

'You know very well what I'm talking about. There's no need to beat about the bush.'

Sir Giles folded the paper. 'Bush, dear?' he said doubtfully.

'Don't prevaricate,' said Lady Maud.

'I'm not prevaricating,' Sir Giles protested, 'I simply don't know what you are talking about.'

Lady Maud put her hands on the desk and leant forward menacingly. 'Sex,' she snarled.

Sir Giles curdled in his chair. 'Oh that,' he murmured. 'What about it?'

'I'm not getting any younger.'

Sir Giles nodded sympathetically. It was one of the few things he was grateful for.

'In another year or two it will be too late.'

Thank God, thought Sir Giles, but the words remained unspoken. Instead he selected a Ramon Allones from his cigarbox. It was an unfortunate move. Lady Maud leant forward and twitched it from his fingers.

'Now you listen to me, Giles Lynchwood,' she said, 'I didn't marry you to be left a childless widow.'

'Widow?' said Sir Giles flinching.

'The operative word is childless. Whether you live or die is of no great moment to me. What is important is that I have an heir. When I married you it was on the clear understanding that you would be a father to my children. We have been married six years now. It is time for you to do your duty.'

Sir Giles crossed his legs defiantly. 'We've been through all this before,' he muttered.

'We have never been through it at all. That is precisely what I am complaining about. You have steadfastly refused to act like a normal husband. You have—'

'We all have our little problems, dear,' Sir Giles said.

'Quite,' said Lady Maud, 'so we do. Unfortunately my problem is rather more pressing than yours. I am over forty and as I have already pointed out, in a year or two I will be past the childbearing age. My family has lived in the Gorge for five hundred years and I do not intend to go to my grave with the knowledge that I am the last of the Handymans.'

'I don't really see how you can avoid that whatever happens,' said Sir Giles. 'After all, in the unlikely event of our having children, their name would be Lynchwood.'

'I have always intended,' said Lady Maud, 'changing the name by deed poll.'

'Have you indeed? Well then let me inform you that there will be no need,' said Sir Giles. 'There will be no children by our marriage and that's final.'

'In that case,' said Lady Maud, 'I shall take steps to get a divorce. You will be hearing from my solicitors.'

She left the room and slammed the door. Behind her Sir Giles sat in his chair shaken but content. The years of his misery were over. He would get his divorce and keep the Hall. He had nothing more to worry about. He reached for another cigar and lit it. Upstairs he could hear his wife's heavy movements in her bedroom. She was no doubt going out to see Mr Turnbull of Ganglion, Turnbull and Shrine, the family solicitors in Worford. Sir Giles unfolded *The Times* and read the letter about the cuckoo once again.

CHAPTER TWO

Mr Turnbull of Ganglion, Turnbull and Shrine was sympathetic but unhelpful. 'If you initiate proceedings on grounds as evidently insubstantial as those you have so vividly outlined,' he told Lady Maud, 'the reversionary clause becomes null and void. You might well end up losing the Hall and the Estate.'

'Do you mean to sit there and tell me that I cannot divorce my husband without losing my family home?' Lady Maud demanded.

Mr Turnbull nodded. 'Sir Giles has only to deny your allegations,' he explained, 'and frankly I can hardly see a man in his position admitting them. I'm afraid the Court would find for him. The difficulty about this sort of case is that you can't produce convincing proof.'

'I should have thought my virginity was proof enough,' Lady Maud told him bluntly. Mr Turnbull suppressed a shudder. The notion of Lady Maud presenting her maidenhead as Exhibit A was not one that appealed to him.

'I think we should need something a little more orthodox than that. After all, Sir Giles could claim that you had refused him his conjugal rights. It would simply be his word against yours. Of course, you could still get your divorce, but the Hall would remain legally his.'

'There must be something I can do,' Lady Maud protested. Looking at her, Mr Turnbull rather doubted it but he was tactful enough not to say so.

'And you say you have attempted a reconciliation?'

'I have told Giles that he must do his duty by me.'

'That's not quite what I meant,' Mr Turnbull told her. 'Marriage is after all a difficult relationship at the best of times. Perhaps a little tenderness on your part would ...'

'Tenderness?' said Lady Maud. 'Tenderness? You seem to forget that my husband is a pervert. Do you imagine that a man who finds satisfaction in being—'

'No,' said Mr Turnbull hurriedly. 'I take your point. Perhaps tenderness is the wrong word. What I meant was ... well ... a little understanding.'

Lady Maud looked at him scornfully.

'After all *tout comprendre, c'est tout pardonner*,' continued Mr Turnbull, relapsing into the language he associated with sophistication in matters of the heart.

'I beg your pardon,' said Lady Maud.

'I was merely saying that to understand all is to pardon all,' Mr Turnbull explained.

'Coming from a legal man I find that remark astonishing,' said Lady Maud, 'and in any case I am not interested in either understanding or in pardon. I am simply interested in bearing a child. My family have lived in the Gorge for five hundred years and I have no intention of being responsible for their not living there for another five hundred. You may find my insistence on the importance of my family romantic. I can only say that I regard it as my duty to have an heir. If my husband refuses to do his duty by me I shall find someone who will.'

'My dear Lady Maud,' said Mr Turnbull, suddenly conscious that he might be in danger of becoming the first object of her extramarital attentions, 'I beg you not to do anything hasty. An act of adultery on your part would certainly allow Sir Giles to obtain a divorce on grounds which would invalidate the reversionary clause. Perhaps you would like me to have a word with him. It sometimes helps to have a third party, someone entirely impartial you understand, to bring about a reconciliation.'

Lady Maud shook her head. She was thinking about adultery.

'If Giles were to commit adultery,' she said finally, 'would I be right in supposing that the Estate would revert to me?'

Mr Turnbull beamed at the prospect. 'No difficulties at all in that case,' he said. 'You would have an absolute right to the Estate. It's in the settlement. No difficulties at all.'

'Good,' said Lady Maud, and stood up. She went downstairs, leaving Mr Turnbull with the distinct impression that Sir Giles Lynchwood was in for a nasty surprise and, better still, that the firm of Ganglion, Turnbull and Shrine could look forward to a protracted case with substantial fees.

Outside Blott was waiting in the car.

'Blott,' said Lady Maud climbing into the back seat, 'what do you know about telephone tapping?'

Blott smiled and started the car. 'Easy,' he said, 'all you need is some wire and a pair of headphones.'

'In that case stop at the first radio shop you come to and buy the necessary equipment.'

By the time they returned to Handyman Hall, Lady Maud had laid her plans.

So had Sir Giles. The first moment of elation at the prospect of a divorce had worn off and Sir Giles, weighing the matter up in his mind, had recognized some ugly possibilities. For one thing he did not relish the thought of being cross-examined about his private life by some eminent barrister. The newspapers, particularly one or two of the Sundays, would have a ball with Lady Maud's description of their honeymoon. Worse still, he would be unable to issue writs for libel. The story could be verified by the hotel manager and while Sir Giles might well win the divorce case and retain the Hall he would certainly lose his public reputation. No, the matter would have to be handled in some less conspicuous manner. Sir Giles picked up a pencil and began to doodle.

The problem was a simple one. The divorce, if and when it came, must be on the grounds on his own choosing. He must be free from any breath of scandal. It was too much to hope that Lady Maud would find a lover, but desperation might drive her to some act of folly. Sir Giles rather doubted it, and besides, her age, shape and general disposition made it seem unlikely. And then there was the Hall and the one hundred thousand pounds he had paid for it. He drew a cat and was just considering that there were more ways of making a profit from property than selling it or burning it to the ground when the shape of his drawing, an eight with ears and tail, put him in mind of something he had once seen from the air. A flyover, a spaghetti junction, a motorway.

A moment later he was unfolding an ordnance survey map and studying it with intense interest. Of course. Why hadn't he thought of it before? The Cleene Gorge was the ideal route. It lay directly between Sheffingham and Knighton. And with motorways there came compulsory purchase orders and large sums paid in compensation. The perfect solution. All it needed was a word or two in the right ear. Sir Giles picked up the phone and dialled. By the time Lady Maud returned from Worford he was in excellent humour. Hoskins at the Worfordshire Planning Authority had been most helpful, but then Hoskins had always been helpful. It paid him to be and it certainly paid for a rather larger house than his salary would have led one to expect. Sir Giles smiled to himself. Influence was a wonderful thing.

'I'm going down to London this afternoon,' he told Lady Maud as they sat down to lunch. 'One or two business things to fix up. I daresay I shall be tied up for a couple of days.'

'I shouldn't be at all surprised,' said Lady Maud.

'If you need me for anything, leave a message with my secretary.'

Lady Maud helped herself to cottage pie. She was in a good humour. She had no doubt whatsoever that Sir Giles indulged his taste for restrictive practices with someone in London. It might take time to find out the name of his mistress but she was prepared to wait.

*

'Extraordinary woman, Lady Maud,' Mr Turnbull said as he and Mr Ganglion sat in the bar of the Four Feathers in Worford.

'Extraordinary family,' Mr Ganglion agreed. 'I don't suppose you remember her grandmother, the old Countess. No, you wouldn't. Before your time. I remember drawing up her will in ... now when can it have been ... must have been in March 1936. Let's see, she died in June of that year so it must have been in March. Insisted on my inserting the fact that her son, Busby, was of partially royal parentage. I did point out that in that case he was not entitled to inherit but she was adamant. "Royal Blood," she kept saying. In the end I got her to sign several copies of the will but it was only in the top one that any mention was made of the royal bastardy.'

'Good Lord,' said Mr Turnbull, 'do you think there was anything in it?'

Mr Ganglion looked over the top of his glasses at him. 'Between ourselves, I must admit it was not outside the bounds of possibility. The dates did match. Busby was born in 1905 and the Royal visit took place in '04. Edward the Seventh had quite a reputation for that sort of thing.'

'It certainly goes some way to explain Lady Maud's looks,' Mr Turnbull admitted. 'And her arrogance, come to that.'

'These things are best forgotten,' said Mr Ganglion sadly. 'What did she want to see you about?'

'She's seeking a divorce. I dissuaded her, at least temporarily. Seems that Lynchwood has a taste for flagellation.'

'Extraordinary what some fellows like,' said Mr Ganglion. 'It's not as though he went to public school either. Most peculiar. Still, I should have thought Maud could have satisfied him if anyone could. She's got a forearm like a navvy.'

'I got the impression that she had rather overdone it,' Mr Turnbull explained.

'Splendid. Splendid.'

'The main trouble seems to be non-consummation. She wants an heir before it's too late.'

'The perennial obsession of these old families. What did you advise? Artificial insemination?'

Mr Turnbull finished his drink. 'Certainly not,' he muttered. 'Apparently she's still a virgin.'

Mr Ganglion sniggered. 'There was an old virgin of forty, whose habits were fearfully naughty. She owned a giraffe whose terrible laugh ... or was it distaff? I forget now.'

They went into lunch.

*

Blott finished his lunch in the greenhouse at the end of the kitchen garden. Around him early geraniums and chrysanthemums, pink and red, matched the colour of his complexion. This was the inner sanctum of Blott's world where he could sit surrounded by flowers whose beauty was proof to him that life was not entirely without meaning. Through the glass windows he could look down the kitchen garden at the lettuces, the peas and beans, the redcurrant bushes and the gooseberries of which he was so proud. And all around the old brick walls cut out the world he mistrusted. Blott emptied his thermos flask and stood up. Above his head he could see the telephone wires stretching from the house. He went outside and fetched a ladder and presently was busily engaged in attaching his wires to the line above. He was still there when Sir Giles left in the Bentley. Blott watched him pass without interest. He disliked Sir Giles intensely and it was one of the advantages of working in the kitchen garden that they seldom came into contact. He finished his work and fitted the headphones and bell. Then he went into the house. He found Lady Maud washing up in the kitchen.

'It's ready,' he said, 'we can test it.'

Lady Maud dried her hands, 'What do I do?'

'When the bell rings put the headphones on,' Blott explained.

'You go into the study and ring a number and I'll listen,' said Lady Maud. Blott went into the study and sat behind the desk. He picked up the phone and tried to think of someone to call. There wasn't anyone he knew to call. Finally his eye fell on a number written in pencil on the pad in front of him. Beside it there was some doodles and a drawing of a cat. Blott dialled the number. It was rather a long one and began with 01 and he had to wait for some time for an answer.

'Hullo, Felicia Forthby speaking,' said a woman's voice.

Blott tried to think of something to say. 'This is Blott,' he said finally.

'Blott?' said Mrs Forthby. 'Do I know you?'

'No,' said Blott.

'Is there anything I can do for you?'

'No,' said Blott.

There was an awkward silence and then Mrs Forthby spoke. 'What do you want?'

Blott tried to think of something he wanted. 'I want a ton of pig manure,' he said.

'You must have the wrong number.'

'Yes,' said Blott and put the phone down.

In the greenhouse Lady Maud was delighted with the experiment. 'I'll soon find out who's beating him now,' she thought and took the headphones off. She went back to the house.

'We shall take it in turns to monitor all telephone calls my husband makes,' she told Blott. 'I want to find out who he's visiting in London. You must write down the name of anyone he talks to. Do you understand?'

'Yes,' said Blott and went back to the kitchen garden happily. In the kitchen Lady Maud finished washing up. She'd meant to ask Blott who he had been talking to. Never mind, it wasn't important.

CHAPTER THREE

Sir Giles got back from London rather sooner than he had expected. Mrs Forthby's period had put her in a foul mood and Sir Giles had enough on his plate without having to put up with the side-effects of Mrs Forthby's menstrual tension. And besides, Mrs Forthby in the flesh was a different kettle of fish to Mrs Forthby in his fantasies. In the latter she had a multitude of perverse inclinations, which corresponded exactly with his own unfortunate requirements, while possessing a discretion that would have done credit to a Trappist nun. In the flesh she was disappointingly different. She seemed to think, and in Sir Giles opinion there could be no greater fault in a woman, that he loved her for herself alone. It was a phrase that sent a shudder through him. If he loved her at all, and it was only in her absence that his heart grew even approximately fonder, it was not for Mrs Forthby's self. It was precisely because as far as he could make out she lacked *any* self that he was attracted to her in the first place.

Externally Mrs Forthby had all the attributes of desirable womanhood, rather too many for more fastidious tastes, and all confined with corsets, panties, suspender belts and bras that inflamed Sir Giles' imagination and reminded him of the advertisements in women's magazines on which his sexual immaturity had first cut its teeth. Internally Mrs Forthby was a void if her inconsequential conversation was anything to go by and it was this void that Sir Giles, ever hopeful of finding a lover with needs as depraved as his own, sought to fill. And here he had to admit that Mrs Forthby fell far short of his expectations. Broad-minded she might be, though he sometimes doubted that she had a mind, but she still lacked enthusiasm for the intricate contortions and strangleholds that constituted Sir Giles' notions of foreplay. And besides she had an unfortunate habit of giggling at moments of his grossest concentration and of interjecting reminiscences of her Girl Guide training while tightening the granny knots which so affected him. Worst of all was her absent-mindedness (and here he had no quarrel with the term). She had been known to leave him trussed to the bed and gagged for several hours while she entertained friends to tea in the next room. It was at such moments of enforced contemplation that Sir Giles was most conscious of the discrepancies between his public and his private posture and hoped to hell the two wouldn't be brought closer together by some damned woman looking for the lavatory. Not that he wouldn't have welcomed some intervention into his fantasy world if only he could be certain that he wouldn't be the laughing-stock of Westminster. After one such episode he had threatened to murder Mrs Forthby and had only been restrained by his inability to stand upright even after she had untied him.

'Where the hell have you been?' he shouted when she returned at one o'clock in the morning.

'Covent Garden,' Mrs Forthby said. '*The Magic Flute*. A divine performance.'

'You might have told me. I've been lying here in agony for six hours.'

'I thought you liked that,' Mrs Forthby said. 'I thought that's what you wanted.'

'Wanted?' Sir Giles screamed. 'Six hours? Nobody in his right mind wants to be trussed up like a spring chicken for six hours.'

'No, dear,' Mrs Forthby said agreeably. 'It's just that I forgot. Shall I get you your enema now?'

'Certainly not,' shouted Sir Giles, in whom some measure of self-respect had been induced by his confinement. 'And don't meddle with my leg.'

'But it shouldn't be there, dear. It looks unnatural.'

Sir Giles stared violently out of the corner of his right eye at his toes. 'I know it shouldn't be there,' he yelled. 'And it wouldn't be if you hadn't been so damned forgetful.'

Mrs Forthby had tidied up the straps and buckles and had made a pot of tea. 'I'll tie a knot in my handkerchief next time,' she said tactlessly, propping Sir Giles up on some pillows so that he could drink his tea.

'There won't be a next time,' he had snarled and had spent a sleepless night trying desperately to assume a less contorted posture. It had been an empty promise. There was always a next time. Mrs Forthby's absent shape and her ready acceptance of his revolting foibles made good the lapses of her memory and Sir Giles returned to her flat whenever he was in London, each time with the fervent prayer that she wouldn't leave him hooded and bound while she spent a month in the Bahamas.

*

But if Sir Giles had difficulties with Mrs Forthby there were remarkably few as far as the motorway was concerned. The thing was already on the drawing board.

'It's designated the Mid-Wales Motorway, the M101,' he was told when he made discreet inquiries of the Ministry of the Environment. 'It has been sent up for Ministerial approval. I believe there have been some doubts on conservation grounds. For God's sake don't quote me.' Sir Giles put the phone down and considered his tactics. Ostensibly he would have to oppose the scheme if only to keep his seat as member for South Worfordshire but there was opposition and opposition. He invested heavily in Imperial Cement, who seemed likely to benefit from the demand for concrete. He had lunch with the Chairman of Imperial Motors, dinner with the Managing Director of Motorway Manufacturers Limited, drinks with the Secretary of the Amalgamated Union of Roadworkers, and he pointed out to the Chief Whip the need to do something to lower the rate of unemployment in his constituency.

In short he was the catalyst in the chemistry of progress. And with it all no money passed hands. Sir Giles was too old a dog for that. He passed information. What companies were on the way to making profits, what shares to buy, and what to sell, these were the tender of his influence. And to insure himself against future suspicions he made a speech at the annual dinner of the Countryside Conservation League in which he urged eternal vigilance against the depredations of the property speculator. He returned to Handyman Hall in time to be outraged by the news of the proposed motorway.

'I shall demand an immediate inquiry,' he told Lady Maud when the requisition order arrived. He reached for the phone.

In the greenhouse Blott had his time cut out listening to Sir Giles' telephone calls. He had no sooner settled down to deal with some aphids on the ornamental apple trees that grew against the wall than the bell rang. Blott dashed in and listened to General Burnett fulminating from the Grange about blackguards in Whitehall, red tape, green belts and blue-stockings, none of which he fully understood. He went back to his aphids when the phone rang again. This time it was Mr Bullett-Finch phoning to find out what Sir Giles intended to do about stopping the motorway.

'It's going to take half the garden,' he said. 'We have spent the last six years getting shipshape and now for this to happen. It's too much. It's not as though Ivy's nerves can stand it.'

Sir Giles sympathized unctuously. He was, he said, organizing a protest committee. There was bound to be an Inquiry. Mr Bullett-Finch could rest assured that no stone would be left unturned. Blott returned to the aphids puzzled. The English language still retained its power to baffle him, and Blott occasionally found himself trapped in some idiom. Shipshape? There was nothing vaguely in the shape of a ship about Mr Bullett-Finch's garden. But then Blott had to admit that the English themselves remained a mystery to him. They paid people more when they were unemployed than when they had to work. They paid bricklayers more than teachers. They raised money for earthquake victims in Peru while old-age pensioners lived on a pittance. They refused Entry Permits to Australians and invited Russians to come and live in England. Finally they seemed to take particular pleasure in being shot at by the Irish. All in all they were a source of constant astonishment to him and of reassurance. They were only happy when something dreadful happened to them, be it flood, fire, war or some appalling disaster, and Blott, whose early life had been a chapter of disasters, took comfort from the fact that he was living in a community that actually enjoyed misfortunes.

Born when, of whom, where, he had no idea. The date of his discovery in the Ladies Room in the Dresden railway station was as near as he could get to a birthday and since the lady cleaner had disclaimed any responsibility for his appearance there, although hard pressed by the authorities to do so, he had no idea who his mother was – let alone his father. He couldn't even be sure his parents had been Germans. For all he and the authorities knew they might have been Jews, though even the Director of the Race Classification Bureau had had the illogical grace to admit that Jews did not make a habit of abandoning their offspring in railway cloakrooms. Still, the notion lent a further element of uncertainty to Blott's adolescence in the Third Reich and he had got no help from his appearance. Dark, hook-nosed pure Aryans there doubtless were, but Blott, who had taken an obsessive interest in the question, found few who were happy to discuss their pedigree with him. Certainly no one was prepared to adopt him, and even the orphanage tended to push him into the background when there were visitors. As for the Hitler Youth ... Blott preferred to forget his adolescence and even the memory of his arrival in England still filled him with uneasiness.

It had been a dark night and Blott, who had been put in to stiffen the resolve of the crew of an Italian bomber, had taken the opportunity to emigrate. Besides, he had a shrewd suspicion that his squadron leader had ordered him to volunteer as navigator to the Italians in the hope that he would not return. It seemed the only explanation for his choice and Blott, whose previous experience had been as a rear-gunner where his only contribution to the war effort had been to shoot down two Messerschmidt 109s that were supposed to be escorting his bomber squadron, had fulfilled his squadron leader's expectations to the letter. Even the Italian airmen, pusillanimous to a man, had been surprised by Blott's insistence that Margate was situated in the heart of Worcestershire. After a heated argument they dropped their bombs over Exmoor and headed back for Pas de Calais across the Bristol Channel before running out of fuel over the mountains of North Wales. It was at this point that the Italians decided to bale out and were attempting to explain the urgency of the situation to Blott, whose knowledge of Italian was negligible, when they were saved the bother by the intervention of a mountain which, according to Blott's bump of direction, should not have been there. In the ensuing holocaust Blott was the sole survivor and since he was discovered naked in the wreckage of an Italian bomber by a search party next morning it was naturally assumed that he must be Italian. The fact that he couldn't speak a word of his native tongue deceived nobody, least of all the Major in charge of the prisoner-of-war camp to which Blott was sent, for the simple reason that he couldn't speak Italian either and Blott was his first prisoner. It was only much later, with the arrival of some genuine Italian prisoners from North Africa, that doubts were cast on his nationality, but by that time Blott had established his bona fides by displaying no interest in the course of the war and by resolutely demonstrating a reluctance to escape that was authentically Italian. Besides, his claim to have been born the son of a shepherd in the Tyrol explained his lack of Italian.

In 1942 the camp had been moved to Handyman Hall and Blott had made the place his home. The Hall and the Handyman family appealed to him. They were both the epitome of Englishness and in Blott's view there could be no higher praise. To be English was the supreme virtue and being a prisoner in England was better than being free anywhere else. If he had had his way the war would have continued indefinitely. He lived in a great house, he had a park to walk in, a river to fish in, a kitchen garden to grow things in, and the run of an idyllic countryside full of woods and hills and fair women whose husbands were away fighting to save the world from people like Blott. Even at night when the camp gates were closed it was perfectly easy to scale the walls and go where he liked. There were no air-raids, no sudden alarms and the whole question of earning a living was taken care of. Even the food was good, supplemented as it was by his poaching and his husbandry in the kitchen garden. To Blott the place was paradise and his only worry was that Germany might win the war. It was an eventuality he dreaded. It had been bad enough being a German in Germany. He couldn't imagine what it would be like to be an Italian who was a German who looked like a Jew in conquered Britain, and the notion of trying to explain how he came to be what he was where he was to the German occupying authorities appalled him. It was one of the nicest things about the English that they didn't seem to worry about such details, but he knew his own countrymen too well to imagine that they would be satisfied with his evasions. Layer by layer, they would peel off his equivocations until the nothing that was the essential Blott was revealed quite naked and then they would shoot what was left for desertion. Blott had no doubt about his fate, and what made matters worse was that as far as he could tell the British were quite incapable of winning the war. Half the time they seemed oblivious of the fact that there was a war on, and for the rest conducted it with an inefficiency that astonished him. Shortly after his arrival at the Hall, Western Command had conducted manoeuvres in the Cleene Forest and Blott had watched the chaos that ensued with horror. If these were the men on whose fighting qualities he had to depend for his captivity, he would have to look for his salvation elsewhere. He found it in a nearby ammunition dump which was, quite typically, unguarded and Blott, determined that if the English wouldn't defend him he would, slowly acquired a small arsenal which he buried in the forest. Two-inch mortars, Bren guns, rifles, boxes of ammunition, all disappeared without notice and were cached, carefully greased and watertight, under the bracken in the hills behind the Hall. By 1945 Blott was in a position to fight a guerrilla war in South Worfordshre. And then the war ended and new problems arose.

The prospect of being repatriated to Italy was not one that appealed to him and he couldn't see himself settling down in Naples after so many agreeable years in England. On the other hand he had no intention of returning to what remained of Dresden. It was in the Russian Zone and Blott had no desire to swop the comforts of life in Worfordshire for the rigours of existence in Siberia. Besides, he rather doubted if even a defeated Fatherland would welcome home a man who had spent five years masquerading as an Italian PoW. It seemed far wiser to stay where he was, and here his devotion to the Handyman family paid off.

Lord Handyman had been a man of enthusiasms. Long before it was generally fashionable he had conceived the notion that the world's resources were on the verge of extinction and had sought to avoid the personal consequences by saving everything. He had been particularly keen on compost and Blott had dug enormous pits in the kitchen garden into which all household refuse of an organic sort was thrown.

'Nothing must be wasted,' the Earl had declared, and nothing was. Under his direction the Hall's sewage system had been diverted to empty into the compost pits and Blott and the Earl had spent happy hours observing the layers of cabbage stalks, potato peelings, and excrement which made up the day's leavings. As each pit filled Blott dug another one and the process began again. The results were quite astonishing. Enormous cabbages and alarming marrows and cucumbers proliferated. So, in summer, did the flies until the situation became intolerable and Lady Handyman, who had lost her appetite since the recycling began, put her foot down and insisted that either the flies went or she would. Blott diverted the sewage system back to its proper place while the Earl, evidently inspired by the rate of reproduction of the flies, turned his attention to rabbits. Blott had constructed several dozen hutches built one above the other on the lines of apartment buildings in which the Earl installed the largest rabbits he could buy, a breed called Flemish Giants. Like all the Earl's schemes, the rabbits had not been an unqualified success. They consumed enormous quantities of vegetation and the family had developed an aversion for rabbit pie, roast rabbit, rabbit stew and lapin à l'orange, while Blott had been driven to distraction trying to keep pace with their voracious appetites. To add to his problems Maud, then ten, had identified her father with Mr McGregor and had aided and abetted the rabbits to escape. As peace broke out in Europe the Gorge was overrun with Flemish Giants. By then Lord Handyman's enthusiasm had waned. He turned to ducks and particularly to Khaki Campbells, a species which had the advantage that they were largely self-supporting and produced an abundance of eggs.

'Can't go wrong with ducks,' he had said cheerfully as the family switched from a diet of rabbit to duck eggs. As usual with his prophecies this one had proved unfounded. It was all too easy to go wrong with ducks, as the family found out when the Earl succumbed to a lethal egg that had been laid too close to one of his old compost pits. Passing away as peacefully as ptomaine poisoning allowed, he had left Maud and her mother to manage alone. It was largely thanks to his death that Blott had been allowed to stay on at the Hall.

CHAPTER FOUR

Over the next few weeks Lady Maud was intensely active. She took legal advice from Mr Turnbull daily. She canvassed opposition to the proposed motorway from every quarter of South Worfordshire and she sat almost continuously on committees. In particular she made her considerable presence felt on the Committee for the Preservation of the Cleene Gorge. General Burnett of the Grange, Guildstead Carbonell, was elected President but as Secretary Lady Maud was the driving force. Petitions were organized, protest meetings held, motions proposed, seconded and passed, money raised and posters printed.

'The price of justice is eternal publicity,' she said with an originality that startled her hearers, but which in fact she had found in *Bartlett's Familiar Quotations*. 'It is not enough to protest, we must make our protest known. If the Gorge is to be saved it will not be by words alone but by action.' On the platform beside her Sir Giles nodded his apparent approval, but inwardly he was alarmed. Publicity was all very well, and justice was fine when it applied to other people but he didn't want public attention focused too closely on his role in the affair. He had expected the motorway to upset Lady Maud; he had not foreseen that she would turn into a human tornado. He certainly hadn't supposed that his seat would be jeopardized by the uproar she seemed bent on provoking.

'If you don't see that the Hall is saved,' Lady Maud told him, 'I'll see to it that you don't sit for South Worfordshire at the next election.' Sir Giles took the threat seriously and consulted Hoskins at the Planning Authority in Worford.

'I thought you wanted the thing to go through the Gorge,' Hoskins told him as they sat in the bar of the Handyman Arms.

Sir Giles nodded unhappily. 'I do,' he admitted, 'but Maud has gone berserk. She's threatening ... well, never mind.'

Hoskins was reassuring. 'She'll get over it. They always do. Got to give them time to get used to the idea.'

'It's all very well for you to talk,' said Sir Giles, 'but I have to live with the beastly woman. She's up half the night thundering about the bloody house and I'm having to cook for myself. Besides, I don't like the way she keeps cleaning her father's shotgun in the kitchen.'

'You know she took a potshot at one of the surveyors last week,' Hoskins said.

'Can't you have her charged?' Sir Giles asked eagerly. 'That would take the heat off for a bit. Haul her up before the local beaks.'

'She *is* a local magistrate,' Hoskins pointed out, 'and anyway there's no proof. She would just claim she was shooting rabbits.'

'And that's another thing. She's got the house full of bloody great Alsations. Hired them from some damned security firm. I tell you I can't go down the passage for a pee in the night without running the risk of being bitten.' He ordered another two whiskies and considered the problem. 'There'll have to be an Inquiry,' he said finally. 'Promise them an Inquiry and they'll calm down a bit. Secondly, offer the Inquiry a totally unacceptable alternative. Like we did with the block of flats in Shrewton.'

'You mean give planning permission for a sewage farm?'

'That's what we did there. Worked like a charm,' Sir Giles said. 'Now if we could come up with an alternative route which nobody in his right mind would accept ...'

'There's always Ottertown,' said Hoskins.

'What about Ottertown?'

'It's ten miles out of the way and you'd have to go through a council estate.'

Sir Giles smiled. 'Right through the middle?'

'Right through the middle.'

'It sounds promising,' Sir Giles agreed. 'I think I shall be the first to advocate the Ottertown route. You're quite sure it's unacceptable?'

'Quite sure,' said Hoskins. 'And, by the way, I'll take my fee in advance.'

Sir Giles looked round the bar. 'My advice is to buy ...' he began.

'Cash this time,' said Hoskins, 'I lost on United Oils.'

Sir Giles returned to Handyman Hall in a fairly good humour. He disliked parting with money but Hoskins was worth it and the Ottertown idea was the sort of strategy he liked. It would take Maud's mind off eternal publicity. Tempers would cool and the Inquiry would decide in favour of the Gorge. By then it would be too late to inflame public opinion once again. Inquiries were splendid soporifics. He ran the gauntlet of the guard dogs and spent the evening in his study writing a letter to the Minister of the Environment demanding the setting up of an Inquiry. No one could say that the Member of Parliament for South Worfordshire had not got the interests of his constituents at heart.

While Sir Giles connived and Lady Maud committeed, Blott in the kitchen garden had his work cut out trying to do his conflicting duties.

He would settle down to weed the lettuces only to be interrupted by the bell in the greenhouse. Blott spent hours listening to long conversations between Sir Giles and officials at the Ministry, between Sir Giles and members of his constituency or his stockbroker or his business partners, but never between Sir Giles and Mrs Forthby. Sir Giles had been forewarned. Mrs Forthby's remark that she had received a call from someone called Blott who had ordered a ton of pig manure had alarmed Sir Giles. There was obviously some mistake though how Blott could have got hold of the number in the first place he couldn't imagine. It wasn't in the telephone index on his desk. He kept it in his private diary and the diary was in his pocket. Sir Giles memorized the number and then erased it from the diary. There would be no more calls to Mrs Forthby from Handyman Hall.

When Sir Giles wasn't on the telephone, Lady Maud was, issuing orders, drumming up support or hurling defiance at the authorities with a self-assurance that amazed and delighted Blott. You knew where you were with her and Blott, who prized certainty above all else, emerged from the greenhouse after listening to her with the feeling that all was well with the world and would remain so. Handyman Hall, the Park, the Lodge, a great triumphal arch at the bottom of the drive where Blott lived, the kitchen garden, all those things to which he had grafted his own anonymity in a hostile world, would remain safe and secure if Lady Maud had anything to do with it. Sir Giles' calls left a different impression. His protests were muted, too polite and too equivocal to satisfy Blott, so that he came away with the feeling that something was wrong. He couldn't put his finger on it, but whenever he took the earphones off after listening to Sir Giles he felt uneasy. There was too much talk about money for Blott's liking, and in particular about ample compensation for the Hall. The sum most frequently mentioned was a quarter of a million pounds. As he went down the rows of lettuces with his hoe, Blott shook his head. 'Money talks,' Sir Giles had told his caller but it had said nothing to Blott. There were more important words in his vocabulary. On the other hand his hours of listening to Sir Giles had done wonders for his accent. With the headphones on Blott had sat practising Sir Giles' pronunciation. In his study Sir Giles said, 'Of course, my dear fellow, I absolutely agree with you ...' In the greenhouse Blott repeated the words. By the end of a week his imitation was so exact that Lady Maud, coming into the kitchen garden to collect some radishes and spring onions for lunch one day, had been astonished to hear Sir Giles' voice issuing from among the geraniums. 'I looked upon the whole thing as an infringement of the rules of conservation,' he was saying. 'My dear General, I shall do my damnedest to see that the matter is raised in the House.' Lady Maud stood and gazed into the greenhouse and was just considering the possibility that Blott had rigged up a loudspeaker there when he emerged, beaming triumphantly.

'You like it, my pronunciation?' he asked.

'Good heavens, was that you? You gave me quite a start,' Lady Maud said.

Blott smirked proudly. 'I have been practising correct English,' he said.

'But you speak English perfectly.'

'I don't. Not like an Englishman.'

'Well, I'd be glad if you didn't go round speaking like my husband,' said Lady Maud. 'It's bad enough having one of him about the place.'

Blott smiled happily. These were his sentiments exactly.

'Which reminds me,' she continued, 'I must see that the TV people cover the Inquiry. We must get the maximum publicity.'

Blott collected his hoe and went back to his lettuces while Lady Maud, having collected her radishes, returned to the kitchen. He was rather pleased with himself. It wasn't often he got a chance to demonstrate his ability to mimic people. It was a skill that had developed from his earliest days at the orphanage. Not knowing who he was, Blott had tried out other people's personalities. It had come in handy poaching, too. More than one gamekeeper had been startled to hear his employer's voice issuing from the darkness to tell him to stop making an ass of himself while Blott made good his escape. Now as he worked away at the weeds he tried out Sir Giles again. 'I demand that there be an Inquiry into this whole business,' he said. Blott smiled to himself. It sounded quite authentic. And there was going to be an Inquiry too. Lady Maud had said so.

CHAPTER FIVE

The Inquiry was held in the Old Courthouse in Worford. Everyone was there – everyone, that is, whose property stood on the proposed route through the Cleene Gorge. General Burnett, Mr and Mrs Bullett-Finch, Colonel and Mrs Chapman, Miss Percival, Mrs Thomas, the Dickinsons, all seven of them, and the Fullbrooks who rented a farm from the General. There were also a few other influential families who were quite unaffected by the motorway but who came to support Lady Maud. She sat in front with Sir Giles and Mr Turnbull and behind them the seats were all filled. Blott stood at the back. On the other side of the aisle the seats were empty except for a solicitor representing the Ottertown Town Council. It was quite clear that nobody seriously supposed that Lord Leakham would decide in favour of Ottertown. The thing was a foregone conclusion – or would have been but for the intervention of Lady Maud and the intransigence of Lord Leakham, whose previous career as a judge had been confined to criminal cases in the High Court. The choice of venue was unfortunate, too. The Old Courthouse resembled too closely the courtrooms of Lord Leakham's youth for the old man to deal at all moderately with Lady Maud's frequent interruption of the evidence.

'Madam, you are trying the court's patience,' he told her when she rose to her feet for the tenth time to protest that the scheme as outlined by Mr Hoskins for the Planning Board was an invasion of individual liberty and the rights of property. Lady Maud bristled in tweeds.

'My family has held land in the Cleene Gorge since 1472,' she shouted. 'It was entrusted to us by Edward the Fourth who designated the Handyman family custodians of the Gorge—'

'Whatever His Majesty Edward the Fourth may have done,' said Lord Leakham, 'in 1472 has no relevance to the evidence being presented by Mr Hoskins. Be so good as to sit down.'

Lady Maud sat down. 'Why don't you two men do something?' she demanded loudly. Sir Giles and Mr Turnbull shifted uncomfortably in their seats.

'You may continue, Mr Hoskins,' said the judge.

Mr Hoskins turned to a large relief model of the county which stood on a table. 'As you can see from this model South Worfordshire is a particularly beautiful county,' he began.

'Any fool with eyes in his head can see that,' Lady Maud commented loudly. 'It doesn't require a damnfool model.'

'Continue, Mr Hoskins, continue,' Lord Leakham said with a restraint that suggested he had in mind giving Lady Maud rope to hang herself with.

'Bearing this in mind the Ministry has attempted to preserve the natural amenities of the area to the greatest possible extent—'

'My foot,' said Lady Maud.

'We have here,' Mr Hoskins went on, pointing to a ridge of hills that ran north and south of the Gorge, 'the Cleene Forest, an area of designated natural beauty noted for its wild life . . .'

'Why is it,' Lady Maud inquired of Mr Turnbull, 'that the only species that doesn't seem to be protected is the human?'

By the time the Inquiry adjourned for lunch Mr Hoskins had presented the case for the Ministry. As they went downstairs Mr Turnbull had to admit that he was not optimistic.

'The snag as I see it lies in those seventy-five council houses in Ottertown. If it weren't for them I think we would stand a good chance, but quite frankly I can't see the Inquiry deciding in favour of demolishing them. The cost would be enormous and in any case there is the additional ten miles to be taken into account. Frankly, I am not hopeful.'

It was market day in Worford and the town was full. Outside the courtroom two TV cameras had been set up.

'I have no intention of being evicted from my home,' Lady Maud told the interviewer from the BBC. 'My family have lived in the Cleene Gorge for five hundred years and ...'

Mr Turnbull turned away sadly. It was no good. Lady Maud might say what she liked, it would make no difference. The motorway would still come through the Gorge. In any case Lady Maud had made a bad impression on Lord Leakham. He waited for her to finish and then they made their way through the market stalls to the Handyman Arms.

'I wonder where Giles has got to,' she said as they entered the hotel.

'I think he's gone over to the Four Feathers with Lord Leakham,' Mr Turnbull told her. 'He said something about putting him in a more mellow mood.'

Lady Maud looked at him furiously. 'Did he indeed? Well, I'll see about that,' she snapped and leaving Mr Turnbull in the foyer she went into the manager's office and phoned the Four Feathers. When she came out there was a new glint of malice in her eye.

They went into the dining-room and sat down.

At the Four Feathers Sir Giles ordered two large whiskies in the lounge before sending for the menu.

Lord Leakham took his whisky doubtfully.

'I really shouldn't at this time of the day,' he said. 'Peptic ulcer you know. Still, it's been a tiring morning. Who was that ghastly woman in the front row who kept interrupting?'

'I think I'll have prawns to start with,' said Sir Giles hurriedly.

'Reminded me of the assizes in Newbury in '28,' Lord Leakham continued. 'Had a lot of trouble with a woman there. Kept getting up in the dock and shouting. Now what was her name?' He scratched his head with a mottled hand.

'Lady Maud is rather outspoken,' Sir Giles agreed. 'She has something of a reputation in this part of the world.'

'I can well believe it,' said the Judge.

'She's a Handyman, you know.'

'Really?' said Lord Leakham indifferently. 'I should have thought she could have afforded to employ one.'

'The Handyman family have always been very influential,' Sir Giles explained. 'They own the brewery and a number of licensed premises. This is a Handyman House, as a matter of fact.'

'Elsie Watson,' said Lord Leakham abruptly. 'That's the name.' Sir Giles looked doubtful.

'Poisoned her husband. Kept shouting abuse from the dock. Didn't make the slightest difference. Hanged her just the same.' He smiled at the recollection. Sir Giles studied the menu wistfully and tried to think what to recommend for someone with a peptic ulcer. Oxtail à la Handyman or consommé? On the other hand, he was delighted at the way things had gone at the Inquiry. Maud's display had clinched the matter. Finally he ordered Tournedos Handyman for himself, and Lord Leakham ordered fish.

'Fish is off,' said the head waiter.

'Off?' said Sir Giles irritably.

'Not on, sir,' the man explained.

'What on earth is Bal de Boeuf Handyman?' asked the Judge.

'Faggot.'

'I beg your pardon.'

'Meatball.'

'And Brandade de Handyman?' Lord Leakham inquired.

'Cod balls.'

'Cod? That sounds all right. Yes I think I'll have that.'

'Cod's off,' said the waiter.

Lord Leakham looked desperately at the menu. 'Is anything on?'

'I can recommend the Poule au Pot Edward the Fourth,' said Sir Giles.

'Very appropriate,' said Lord Leakham grimly. 'Oh well I suppose I'd better have it.'

'And a bottle of Chambertin,' Sir Giles said indistinctly. He wasn't very happy with his French.

'Extraordinary way to run an hotel,' said Lord Leakham. Sir Giles ordered two more whiskies to hide his irritation.

In the kitchen the chef took their order. 'You can forget the chicken,' he said. 'He can have Lancashire hotpot or faggots à la me.'

'But it's Lord Leakham and he ordered chicken,' the waiter protested. 'Can't you do something?'

The chef took a bottle of chilli powder off the shelf. 'I'll fix something,' he said.

The wine waiter meanwhile was having difficulty finding a Chambertin. In the end he took the oldest bottle he could find. 'Are you sure you want me to serve him this?' he asked the manager, holding up a bottle filled with a purple cloudy fluid that looked like a post-mortem specimen.

'That's what her ladyship instructed,' said the manager. 'Just change the label.'

'It seems a bloody peculiar thing to do.'

The manager sighed. 'Don't blame me,' he muttered. 'If she wants to poison the old bugger that's her affair. I'm just paid to do what she tells me. What is it anyway?'

The wine waiter wiped the bottle. 'It says it's crusted port,' he said doubtfully.

'Crusted's about the word,' said the manager and went back to the kitchen, where the chef was crumbling some leftover faggots on to half a fried chicken. 'For God's sake don't let anyone else have a taste of that stuff,' he told the chef.

'Serve him right for poking his nose into our affairs,' said the chef, and poured sauce from the Lancashire hotpot on to the dish. The manager went upstairs and signalled to the head waiter. Sir Giles and Lord Leakham finished their whiskies and went through into the dining-room.

At the Handyman Arms Lady Maud finished her lunch and ordered coffee. 'One can place too much reliance on the law,' she said. 'My family didn't get where they did by appealing to the courts.'

'My dear Lady Maud,' said Mr Turnbull, 'I implore you not to do anything foolish. The situation is already fraught with difficulty and quite frankly your interruptions this morning didn't help. I'm afraid Lord Leakham may have been prejudiced against us.'

Lady Maud snorted. 'If he isn't he soon will be,' she said. 'You don't seriously suppose that I intend to accept his judgement? The man is a buffoon.'

'He is also a retired judge of considerable reputation,' said Mr Turnbull doubtfully.

'His reputation is only just beginning,' Lady Maud replied. 'It has been perfectly obvious from the beginning that he was going to decide to recommend that the motorway be put through the Gorge. The Ottertown route is not an alternative. It's a red herring. Well, I for one am not going to put up with that.'

'I don't really see what you can do.'

'That, Henry Turnbull, is because you are a lawyer and hold the law in high regard. I don't. And since the law is an ass I intend to see that everyone is aware of the fact.'

'I wish I could see some way out of the situation,' said Mr Turnbull sadly.

Lady Maud stood up. 'You will, Henry, you will,' she said. 'There are more ways of killing a cat than choking it with cream.' And leaving Mr Turnbull to meditate on the implications of this remark she stalked out of the dining-room.

At the Four Feathers Lord Leakham would have understood at once, though given the choice he would have chosen cream every time. The prawn cocktail which he had not ordered but which had been thrust on him by the head waiter appeared to have been marinated in tabasco, but it was as nothing to the Poule au Pot Edward the Fourth. His first mouthful left him speechless and with the absolute conviction that he had swallowed some appalling corrosive substance like caustic soda.

'That chicken looks good,' said Sir Giles as the Judge struggled to get his breath. 'It's a speciality of the maison, you know.'

Lord Leakham didn't know. With starting eyes he reached for his glass of wine and took a large swig. For a moment he cherished the illusion that the wine would help. His hope was short-lived. His palate, in spite of being cauterized by the Poule au Pot, was still sufficiently sensitive to recognize that whatever it was he was in the process of swallowing it most certainly wasn't Chambertin '64. For one thing it appeared to be filled with some sort of gravel which put him in mind of ground glass and for another what he could taste of the muck seemed to be nauseatingly sweet. Stifling the impulse to vomit he held the glass up to the light and stared into its opaque depths.

'Anything the matter?' asked Sir Giles.

'What did you say this was?' asked the Judge.

Sir Giles looked at the label on the bottle. 'Chambertin '64', he muttered. 'Is it corked or something?'

'It's certainly something,' said Lord Leakham who wished the stuff had never been bottled, let alone corked.

'I'll get another bottle,' said Sir Giles and signalled to the wine waiter. 'Not on my account I beg you.'

But it was too late. As the wine waiter hurried away Lord Leakham, distracted by the strange residue under his upper dentures, absent-mindedly took another mouthful of Poule au Pot.

'I thought it looked a bit dark myself,' said Sir Giles ignoring the desperate look in Lord Leakham's bloodshot eyes. 'Mind you I have to admit I'm not a connoisseur of wines.'

Still gasping for air, Lord Leakham pushed his plate away. For a moment he resisted the temptation to quench the flames with crusted port but the certain knowledge that unless he did something he would never speak again swept aside all considerations of taste. Lord Leakham drained his glass.

In the public bar of the Handyman Arms Lady Maud announced that drinks were on the house. Then she crossed the Market Square to the Goat and Goblet and repeated the order before making her way to the Red Cow. Behind her the bars filled with thirsty farmers and by two o'clock all Worford was drinking Lady Maud's health and damnation to the motorway. Outside the Old Courthouse she stopped to chat with the TV men. A crowd had assembled and Lady Maud was cheered as she went inside.

'I must say we do seem to have the public on our side,' said General Burnett as they went upstairs. 'Mind you I thought things looked pretty grim this morning.'

Lady Maud smiled to herself. 'I think you will find they liven up this afternoon,' she said and swept majestically into the courtroom where Colonel and Mrs Chapman were chattering with the Bullett-Finches.

'Leakham has a fine record as a judge,' Colonel Chapman was saying. 'I think we can rely on him to see our point of view.'

By the time he had finished his lunch Lord Leakham was incapable of seeing anyone's point of view but his own. What prawns tabasco and Poule au Pot had begun, the Chambertin '64 and its successor, a refined vinegar that Sir Giles chose to imagine was a Chablis, had completed. That and the Pêche Maud with which Lord Leakham had attempted to soothe the spasms of his peptic ulcer. The tinned peaches had been all right but the ice cream had been larded with a mixture of cloves and nutmeg, and as for the coffee ...

As he hobbled down the steps of the Four Feathers in the vain hope of finding his car waiting for him – it had been moved on by a traffic warden – as he limped up Ferret Lane and across Abbey Close accompanied by his loathsome host, Lord Leakham's internal organs sounded the death knell of what little restraint he had shown before lunch. By the time he reached the Old Courthouse to be booed by a large crowd of farmers and their wives he was less a retired judge than an active incendiary device.

'Have those damned oafs moved on,' he snarled at Sir Giles. 'I will not be subject to hooliganism.'

Sir Giles phoned the police station and asked them to send some men over to the Courthouse. As he took his seat beside Lady Maud it was clear that things were not proceeding as he had expected. Lord Leakham's complexion was horribly mottled and his hand shook as he rapped the gavel on the bench.

'The hearing will resume,' he said huskily. 'Silence in court.' The courtroom was crowded and the Judge had to use his gavel a second time before the talking stopped. 'Next witness.'

Lady Maud rose to her feet. 'I wish to make a statement,' she said. Lord Leakham looked at her reluctantly. Lady Maud was not a sight for sore stomachs. She was large and her manner suggested something indigestible.

'We are here to take evidence,' said the Judge, 'not to listen to statements of opinion.'

Mr Turnbull stood up. 'My lord,' he said deferentially. 'my client's opinion is evidence before this Inquiry.'

'Opinion is not evidence,' said Lord Leakham. 'Your client whoever she may be . . .'

'Lady Maud Lynchwood of Handyman Hall, my lord,' Mr Turnbull informed him.

'. . . is entitled to hold what opinions she may choose,' Lord Leakham continued, staring at the author of Poule au Pot Edward the Fourth with undisguised loathing, 'but she may not express them in this court and expect them to be accepted as evidence. You should know the rules of evidence, sir.'

Mr Turnbull adjusted his glasses defiantly. 'The rules of evidence do not, with due deference to your lordship's opinion, apply in the present circumstances. My client is not under oath and—'

'Silence in court,' snarled the Judge, addressing himself to a drunken farmer from Guildstead Carbonell who was discussing swine fever with his neighbour. With a pathetic look at Lady Maud Mr Turnbull sat down.

'Next witness,' said Lord Leakham.

Lady Maud stood her ground. 'I wish to protest,' she said with a ring of authority that brought a hush to the courtroom. 'This Inquiry is a travesty . . .'

'Silence in court,' shouted the Judge.

'I will not be silenced,' Lady Maud shouted back. 'This is not a courtroom—'

'It most certainly is,' snarled the Judge.

Lady Maud hesitated. The courtroom was obviously a courtroom. There was no denying the fact.

'What I meant to say ...' she began.

'Silence in court,' screamed Lord Leakham whose peptic ulcer was in the throes of a new crisis.

Lady Maud echoed the Judge's private thoughts. 'You are not fit to conduct this Inquiry,' she shouted, and was supported by several members of the public. 'You are a senile old fool. I have a right to be heard.'

In his chair Lord Leakham's mottled head turned a plum colour and his hand reached for the gavel. 'I hold you in contempt of court,' he shouted banging the gavel. Lady Maud lurched towards him menacingly. 'Officer, arrest this woman.'

'My lord,' Mr Turnbull said, 'I beg you to ...' but it was too late. As Lady Maud advanced two constables, evidently acting on the assumption that an ex-judge of the High Court knew his law better than they did, seized her arms. It was a terrible mistake. Even Sir Giles could see that. Beside him Mr Turnbull was shouting that this was an unlawful act, and behind him pandemonium had broken out as members of the public rose in their seats and surged forward. As his wife was frogmarched, still shouting abuse, from the courtroom, as Lord Leakham bellowed in vain for the court to be cleared, as fighting broke out and windows were broken, Sir Giles sat slumped in his seat and contemplated the ruin of his plans.

Downstairs the TV cameramen, alerted by the shouts and the fragments of broken glass raining on their heads from the windows above, aimed their cameras on the courtroom door as Lady Maud emerged dishevelled and suddenly surprisingly demure between two large policemen. Somewhere between the courtroom and the cameras her twinset had been quite obscenely disarranged, a shoe had been discarded, her skirt was torn suggestively and she appeared to have lost two front teeth. With a brave attempt at a smile she collapsed on the pavement, and was filmed being dragged across the market square to the police station. 'Help,' she screamed as the crowd parted. 'Please help.' And help was forthcoming. A small dark figure hurtled out of the Courthouse and on to the larger of the two policemen. Inspired by Blott's example several stallholders threw themselves into the fray. Hidden by the crowd from the cameras Lady Maud reasserted her authority. 'Blott,' she said sternly, 'let go of the constable's ears.' Blott dropped to the ground and the stallholders fell back obediently. 'Constables, do your duty,' said Lady Maud and led the way to the police station.

Behind her the crowd turned its attention to Lord Leakham's Rolls-Royce. Apples and tomatoes rained on the Old Courthouse. To roars of approval from the onlookers Blott attempted single-handed to turn the car over and was immediately joined by several dozen farmers. When Lord Leakham, escorted by a posse of policemen, emerged from the Courthouse it was to find his Rolls on its side. It took several baton charges to clear a way through the crowd and all the time the cameras recorded faithfully the public response to the proposed motorway through the Cleene Gorge. In Ferret Lane shop windows were broken. Outside the Goat and Goblet Lord Leakham was drenched with a pail of cold water. In the Abbey Close he was concussed by a portion of broken tombstone, and when he finally reached the Four Feathers the Fire Brigade had to be called to use their hoses to disperse the crowd that besieged the hotel. By that time the Rolls-Royce was on fire and groups of drunken youths roamed the streets demonstrating their loyalty to the Handyman family by smashing street lamps.

In her cell in the police station Lady Maud removed her dentures from her pocket and smiled at the sounds of revelry. If the price of justice was eternal publicity she was assured of a fair trial. She had done what she had set out to do.

CHAPTER SIX

In London the Cabinet, meeting to cope with yet another turn for the worse in the balance of payments crisis, greeted the news of the disturbances in Worford less enthusiastically. The evening papers had headlined the arrest of an MP's wife but it was left to the television news to convey to millions of homes the impression that Lady Maud was the victim of quite outrageous police brutality.

'Oh my God,' said the Prime Minister as he watched her on the screen. 'What the hell do they think they've been doing?'

'It rather looks as if she's lost a couple of teeth,' said the Secretary of State for Foreign Affairs. 'Is that a teat hanging out there?'

Lady Maud smiled bravely and collapsed on to the pavement.

'I shall institute a full investigation at once,' said the Home Secretary.

'Who the hell appointed Leakham in the first place?' snarled the Prime Minister.

'It seemed a suitably impartial appointment at the time,' murmured the Minister of the Environment. 'As I remember it was thought that an Inquiry would satisfy local opinion.'

'Satisfy ...?' began the Prime Minister, only to be interrupted by a phone call from the Lord Chancellor who complained that the rule of law was breaking down and even after it was explained to him that Lord Leakham was a retired judge muttered mysteriously that the law was indivisible.

The Prime Minister put the phone down and turned on the Minister of the Environment. 'This is your pigeon. You got us into this mess. You get us out. Anyone would think we had an absolute majority.'

'I'll see what I can do,' said the Minister.

'You'll do better than that,' said the Prime Minister grimly. On the screen Lord Leakham's Rolls-Royce was burning brilliantly.

The Minister of the Environment hurried from the room and phoned the home number of his Under-Secretary. 'I want a troubleshooter sent to Worford to sort this mess out,' he said.

'A troubleshooter?' Mr Rees, who was in bed with flu and whose temperature was 102, was in no state to deal with Ministerial requests for troubleshooters.

'Someone with a flair for public relations.'

'Public relations?' said Mr Rees, searching his mind for a subordinate who knew anything about public relations. 'Can I let you know by Wednesday?'

'No,' said the Minister, 'I need to be able to tell the Prime Minister that we have the situation in hand. I want someone despatched tomorrow morning by the latest. We need to have someone up there who will take charge of negotiations. I look to you to pick someone with initiative. None of your run-of-the-mill old fogies. Someone different.'

Mr Rees put the phone down with a sigh. 'Someone different indeed,' he muttered. 'Troubleshooters.' He felt aggrieved. He disliked being phoned at home, he disliked being ordered to make rapid decisions, he disliked the Minister and he particularly disliked the suggestion that his department consisted of run-of-the-mill old fogies.

He took another spoonful of cough mixture and considered a suitable candidate to send to Worford. Harrison was on leave. Beard was engaged on the Tanker Terminal at Scunthorpe. Then there was Dundridge. Dundridge was clearly unsuitable. But the Minister had specified someone different and Dundridge was decidedly different. There was no denying that. Mr Rees lay back in his bed, his head fuzzy with flu and recalled some of Dundridge's initiatives. There had been the one-way system for

Central London, of an inflexibility that would have made it impossible
to drive from Hyde Park Corner to Piccadilly except by way of Tower
Bridge and Fleet Street. Then there was his pilot project for installing
solid-state traffic lights in Clapham, a scheme so aptly named that it had
isolated that suburb from the rest of London for almost a week. In
practical terms Dundridge was clearly a disaster. On the other hand he
did have a flair for public relations. His schemes sounded good and year
by year Dundridge had been promoted, carried upward by an ineluctable
wave of inefficiency and the need to save the public the practical
consequences of his latest idea until he had reached that rarefied zone of
administration where, thanks to the inertia of his subordinates, his projects
could never be implemented.

   Mr Rees, semi-delirious and drugged with cough medicine, decided on
Dundridge. He went downstairs and dictated his instructions by phone
to the tape recorder on his secretary's desk at the Ministry. Then he
poured himself a large whisky and drank to the thought of Dundridge
in Worford. 'Troubleshooter,' he said and went back to bed.

Dundridge travelled to work by tube. It was in his opinion the rational
way to travel and one that avoided the harsh confusion of reality. Seated
in the train he was able to concentrate on essentials and to find some
sense of order in the world above by studying the diagram of the Northern
Line on the wall opposite. Far above him there was chaos. Streets, houses,
shops, blocks of flats, bridges, cars, people, a welter of disparate and
perverse phenomena which defied easy categorization. By looking at the
diagram he could forget that confusion. Chalk Farm followed Belsize
Park and was itself followed by Camden Town in a perfectly logical
sequence so that he knew exactly where he was and where he was going.
Then again, the diagram showed all the stations as equidistant from their
neighbours and while he knew that in fact they weren't, the schematic
arrangement suggested that they should be. If Dundridge had had
anything to do with it they would have been. His life had been spent in
pursuit of order, and abstract order that would have supplanted the
perplexities of experience. As far as he was concerned variety was not
the spice of life but gave it a very bitter flavour. In Dundridge's philosophy
everything conformed to a norm. On one side there was chance, nature
red in tooth and claw and everything haphazard; on the other science,
logic and numeration.

   Dundridge particularly favoured numeration and his flat in Hendon
conformed to his ideal. Everything he possessed was numbered and
marked on a chart above his bed. His socks for instance were 01/7, the

01 referring to Dundridge himself and the 7 to the socks and were to be found in the top drawer left (1) of his chest of drawers 23 against the wall 4 of his bedroom 3. By referring to the chart and looking for 01/7/1/23/4/3 he could locate them almost immediately. Outside his flat things were less amenable and his attempts to introduce a similar system into his office at the Ministry had met with considerable – grade 10 on the Dundridge scale – resistance and contributed to his frequent transfers from one department to another.

He was therefore not in the least surprised to find that Mr Joynson wanted to see him in his office at 9.15. Dundridge arrived at 9.25.

'I got held up in the tube,' he explained bitterly. 'It's really most irritating. I should have got here by 9.10 but the train didn't arrive on time. It never does.'

'So I've noticed,' said Mr Joynson.

'It's the irregularity of the stops that does it,' said Dundridge. 'Sometimes it stops for half a minute and at other times for a minute and a half. Really, you know, I do think it's time we gave serious consideration to a system of continuous flow underground transportation.'

'I don't suppose it would make any difference,' said Mr Joynson wearily. 'Why don't you just catch an earlier train?'

'I'd be early.'

'It would make a change. Anyway I didn't ask you here to discuss the deficiencies of the Underground system.' He paused and studied Mr Rees' instructions. Quite apart from the incredible choice of Dundridge to handle a situation which demanded intelligence, flexibility and persuasiveness, there was an unusually garbled quality about the syntax that surprised him. Still, there was a lot to be said for getting Dundridge out of London for a while and he couldn't be held personally responsible for his appointment.

'I have here,' he said finally, 'details of your new job. Mr Rees wants you ...'

'My new job?' said Dundridge. 'But I'm with Leisure Activities.'

'And very appropriate too,' said Mr Joynson. 'And now you are with Motorways Midlands. Next month I daresay we'll be able to find you a niche in Parks and Gardens.'

'I must say I find all this moving around very disturbing. I don't see how I can be expected to get anything constructive done when I'm being shifted from one Department to another all the time.'

'There is that to be said for it,' Mr Joynson agreed. 'However, in this case there is nothing constructive for you to do. You will merely be required to exercise a moderating influence.'

'A moderating influence?' Dundridge perked up.

Mr Joynson nodded. 'A moderating influence,' he said and consulted his instructions again. 'You have been appointed the Minister's trouble-shooter in Worford.'

'What?' said Dundridge, now thoroughly alarmed. 'But there's just been a riot in Worford.'

Mr Joynson smiled. He was beginning to enjoy himself. 'So there has,' he said. 'Well now, your job is to see that there are no more riots in Worford. I'm told it is a charming little town.'

'It didn't look very charming on the news last night,' said Dundridge.

'Oh well, we mustn't go by appearances now, must we? Here is your letter of appointment. As you can see it gives you full powers to conduct negotiations—'

'But I thought Lord Leakham was heading the Inquiry,' said Dundridge.

'Well, yes he is. But I understand he's a little indisposed just at the moment and in any case he appears to be under some misapprehension as to his role.'

'You mean he is in hospital, don't you?' said Dundridge.

Mr Joynson ignored the question. He turned to a map on the wall behind him. 'The issue you will have to consider is really quite simple,' he said. 'The M101, as you can see here, has two possible routes. One through the Cleene Gorge here, the other through Ottertown. The Ottertown route is out of the question for a number of reasons. You will see to it that Leakham decides on the Cleene Gorge route.'

'Surely it's up to him to decide,' said Dundridge.

Mr Joynson sighed. 'My dear Dundridge, when you have been in public service as long as I have you will know that Inquiries, Royal Commissions and Boards of Arbitration are only set up to make recommendations that concur with decisions already taken by the experts. Your job is to see that Lord Leakham arrives at the correct decision.'

'What happens if he doesn't?'

'God alone knows. I suppose in the present climate of opinion we'll have to go ahead and build the bloody thing through Ottertown, and then there would be hell to pay. It is up to you to see it doesn't. You have full powers to negotiate with the parties involved and I daresay Leakham will cooperate.'

'I don't see how I can negotiate when I've got nothing to negotiate with,' Dundridge pointed out plaintively. 'And in any case what does it mean by troubleshooter?'

'Presumably whatever you choose to make it,' said Mr Joynson.

Dundridge took the file on the M101 back to his office.

'I'm the Minister's troubleshooter in the Midlands division,' he told his secretary grandly and phoned the transport pool for a car. Then he read his letter of authority once again. It was quite clear that his abilities had been recognized in high places. Dundridge had power, and he was determined to use it.

At Handyman Hall Lady Maud congratulated herself on her skill in disrupting the Inquiry. Released from custody against her own better judgement at the express command of the Chief Constable, she returned to the Hall to be deluged by messages of support. General Burnett called to offer his congratulations. Mrs Bullett-Finch phoned to see if there was anything she needed after the ordeal of her confinement, a term Lady Maud found almost as offensive as Colonel Chapman's comment that she was full of spunk. Even Mrs Thomas wrote to thank her on behalf, as she modestly put it, of the common people. Lady Maud accepted these tributes abruptly. They were she felt quite unnecessary. She had only been doing her duty after all. As she put it to the reporter from the *Observer*, 'Local interests can only be looked after by local authorities,' a sufficiently ambiguous expression to satisfy the correspondent while stating very precisely Lady Maud's own view of her role in South Worfordshire.

'And do you intend to sue the police for unlawful arrest?' the reporter asked.

'Certainly not. I have the greatest respect for the police. They do a magnificent job. I hold Lord Leakham entirely responsible. I am taking legal counsel as to what action I should take against him.'

In the Worford Cottage Hospital Lord Leakham greeted the news that she was considering legal proceedings against him with a show of indifference. He had more immediate problems, the state of his digestive system for one thing, six stitches in his scalp for another, and besides he was suffering from concussion. In his lucid moments he prayed for death and in his delirium shouted obscenities.

But if Lord Leakham was too preoccupied with his own problems to think at all clearly about the disruption of the Inquiry, Sir Giles could think of little else.

'The whole situation is extremely awkward,' he told Hoskins when they conferred at the latter's office the next morning. 'That bloody woman has put the cat among the pigeons and no mistake. She's turned the whole thing into an issue of national interest. I've been inundated with calls from conservationists from all over the country, all supporting our stand. It's bloody infuriating. Why can't they mind their own confounded business?'

Hoskins lit his pipe moodily. 'That's not all,' he said, 'they're sending some bigwig up from the Ministry to take charge of the negotiations.'

'That's all we need, some damned bureaucrat to come poking his nose into our affairs.'

'Quite,' said Hoskins, 'so from now on no more phone calls to me here. I can't afford to be connected with you.'

'Do you think he's going to choose the Ottertown route?'

Hoskins shrugged. 'I've no idea. All I do know is that if I were in his shoes I'm damned if I'd recommend the Gorge.'

'Let me know what the blighter suggests,' said Sir Giles and went out to his car.

CHAPTER SEVEN

To Dundridge, travelling up the M1, the underlying complexities of the situation in South Worfordshire were quite unknown. For the first time in his life he was armed with authority and he intended to put it to good use. He would make a name for himself. The years of frustration were over. He would return to London with his reputation for swift, decisive action firmly established.

At Warwick he stopped for lunch, and while he ate he studied the file on the motorway. There was a map of the district, the outline of the alternative routes, and a list of those people through whose property the motorway would run and the sums they would receive as compensation. Dundridge concentrated his attention on the latter. A single glance was enough to explain the urgency of his appointment and the difficulty of his mission. The list read like a roll-call of the upper class in the county. Sir Giles Lynchwood, General Burnett, Colonel Chapman, Mr Bullett-Finch, Miss Percival. Dundridge peered uncomfortably at the names and incredulously at the sums they were being offered. A quarter of a million pounds for Sir Giles. One hundred and fifty thousand to General Burnett. One hundred and twenty thousand to Colonel Chapman. Even Miss Percival whose occupation was listed as schoolteacher was offered fifty-five thousand. Dundridge compared these sums with his own income and felt a surge of envy. There was no justice in the world and Dundridge (whose socialism was embodied in the maxim 'To each according to his abilities, from each according to his needs', the 'his' in both cases referring to Dundridge himself) found his thoughts wandering in the direction of money. It had been Dundridge's mother who had instilled in him the saying 'Don't marry money, go where money is' and since this had been easier said than done, Dundridge's sex life had been largely confined to his imagination. There, safe from the disagreeable complexities of real life, he had indulged his various passions. In his imagination Dundridge was rich, Dundridge was powerful and Dundridge was the possessor of an entourage of immaculate women – or to be precise of one woman, a composite creature made up of bits and pieces of real woman who had once partially attracted him but without any of their concomitant disadvantages. Now for the first time he was going where money was. It was an alluring prospect. He finished his lunch and drove on.

And as he drove he became increasingly aware that the countryside had changed. He had left the motorway and was on a minor road that twisted and turned. The hedgerows grew taller and more rank. Hills rose up and fell away into empty valleys and woods took on a rougher, less domesticated air. Even the houses had lost the comfortable homogeneous look of the North London suburbs. They were either large and isolated, standing in their own grounds, or stone-built farmhouses surrounded by dark corrugated iron sheds and barns. Every now and again he passed through villages, strange conglomerations of cottages and shops, buildings that loomed misshapenly over the road or retreated behind hedges with an eccentricity of ornaments he found disturbing. And finally there were churches. Dundridge disliked churches most of all. They reminded him of death and burial, guilt and sin and the hereafter. Archaic reminders of a superstitious past. And since Dundridge lived if not for the present at least the immediate future, these memento mori held no attractions for him. They cast horrid doubts on the rational nature of existence. Not that Dundridge believed in reason. He placed his faith in science and numeration.

Now as he drove northwards he had to admit that he was entering a world far removed from his ideal. Even the sky had changed with the landscape and the shadows of large clouds slid erratically across the fields and hills. By the time he reached South Worfordshire he was distinctly perturbed. If Worford was anything like the surrounding countryside it must be a horrid place filled with violent, irrational creatures swayed by strange emotions. It was. As he drove over the bridge that spanned the Cleene he seemed to have moved out of the twentieth century into an earlier age. The houses below the town gate were huddled together higgledy-piggledy and only their scrubbed doorsteps redeemed their squalid lack of uniformity. The gate, a great stuccoed tower with a dark narrow entrance, loomed up before him. He drove nervously through and emerged into a street lined with eighteenth-century houses. Here he felt temporarily more at home but his relief evaporated when he reached the town centre. Dark narrow alleyways, half-timbered medieval houses jutting over the pavement, cobbled streets, and shopfronts which retained the format of an earlier age. Pots and pans, spades and sickles hung outside an ironmongers. Duffel coats, corduroy trousers and breeches were displayed outside an outfitters. A mackerel gleamed on a fishmonger's marble slab while a saddler's was adorned with bits and bridles and leather belts. Worford was in short a perfectly normal market town but to Dundridge, accustomed to the soothing anonymity of supermarkets, there was a disturbing, archaic quality about it. He drove into the Market Square and asked the car-park attendant for the Regional Planning Office. The attendant didn't know or if he did, Dundridge was none the wiser. The accents of Wales and England met in South Worfordshire, met and mingled incomprehensibly. Dundridge parked his car and went into a telephone kiosk. He looked in the Directory and found the Planning Office in Knacker's Yard.

'Where's Knacker's Yard?' he asked the car-park attendant.

'Down Giblet Walk.'

'Very informative,' said Dundridge with a shudder. 'And where's Giblet Walk?'

'Well now, let's see, you can go down past the Goat and Goblet or you can take a short cut through the Shambles,' said the old man and spat into the gutter.

Dundridge considered this unenticing alternative. 'Where are the Shambles?' he asked finally.

'Behind you,' said the attendant.

Dundridge turned round and looked into the shadow of a narrow alley. It was cobbled and led down the hill and out of sight. He walked down it uncomfortably. Several of the houses were boarded up and one or two had actually fallen down and the alleyway had a peculiar smell that he associated with footpaths and tunnels under railway lines. Dundridge held his breath and hurried on and came out into Knacker's Yard where a sign in front of a large red-brick building said Regional Planning Board. He opened an iron gate and went down a path to the door.

'Planning Board's on the second floor,' said a dentist's assistant who emerged from a room holding a metal bowl in which a pair of false teeth rested pinkly. 'You'll be lucky if you find it open though. You looking for anyone in particular?'

'Mr Hoskins,' said Dundridge.

'Try the Club,' said the woman. 'He's usually there this time of day. It's on the first floor.'

'Thank you,' said Dundridge and went upstairs. On the first landing there was a door marked Worford and District Gladstone Club. Dundridge looked at it doubtfully and went on up. As the woman had said, the Regional Planning Board was shut. Dundridge went downstairs and stood uncertainly on the landing. Then, reminding himself that he was the Minister's plenipotentiary and troubleshooter, he opened the door and looked inside.

'You looking for someone?' asked the large red-faced man who was standing beside a billiard table.

'I'm looking for Mr Hoskins, the Planning Officer,' said Dundridge. The red-faced man put down his cue and stepped forward.

'Then you've come to the right place,' he said. 'Bob, there's a bloke wants to see you.'

Another large red-faced man who was sitting at the bar in the corner turned round and stared at Dundridge. 'What can I do for you?' he asked.

'I'm from the Ministry of the Environment,' said Dundridge.

'Christ,' said Mr Hoskins and got down from his bar stool. 'You're early aren't you? Wasn't expecting you till tomorrow.'

'The Minister is most anxious that I should get down to work as rapidly as possible.'

'Quite right,' said Mr Hoskins more cheerfully now that he could see that Dundridge wasn't sixty, didn't wear gold rimmed glasses and didn't carry an air of authority about him. 'What will you have?'

Dundridge hesitated. It wasn't his habit to drink in the middle of the afternoon. 'A half of bitter,' he said finally.

'Make it two pints,' Hoskins told the barman. They took their glasses across to a small table in the corner and sat down. At the billiard table the men resumed their game.

'Awkward business this,' said Mr Hoskins, 'I don't envy you your job. Local feeling's none too good.'

'So I've noticed,' said Dundridge sipping his beer. It tasted, as he had anticipated, both strong and unpleasantly organic. On the wall opposite a portrait of Mr Gladstone glared relentlessly down on this dereliction of the licensing laws. Spurred on by his example, Dundridge attempted to explain his mission. 'The Minister is particularly anxious that the negotiations should be handled tactfully. He has sent me to see that the outcome of these negotiations has the backing of all the parties involved.'

'Has he?' said Mr Hoskins. 'Well, all I can say is that you'll have your
work cut out.'

'Now as I see it, the best approach would be to propose an alternative
route,' Dundridge continued.

'We've done that already. Through Ottertown.'

'Out of the question,' said Dundridge.

'I couldn't agree more,' said Mr Hoskins. 'Which leaves the Cleene
Gorge.'

'Or the hills to the south?' suggested Dundridge hopefully.

Mr Hoskins shook his head. 'Cleene Forest is an area of natural beauty,
a designated area. Not a hope in hell.'

'Well that doesn't leave us with many alternatives, does it?'

'It doesn't leave us with any,' said Mr Hoskins.

Dundridge drank some more beer. The mood of optimism with which
he had started the day had quite left him. It was all very well to talk
about negotiating but there didn't seem any negotiations to conduct. He
was faced with the unenviable task of enforcing a thoroughly unpopular
decision on a group of extremely influential and hostile landowners. It
was not a prospect he relished. 'I don't suppose there is any chance of
persuading Sir Giles Lynchwood and General Burnett to drop their
opposition,' he said without much hope.

'Not a hope in hell,' Hoskins told him, 'and anyway if they did it
wouldn't make the slightest difference. It's Lady Maud you've got to
worry about. And she isn't going to budge.'

'I must say you make it all sound extremely difficult,' said Dundridge
and finished his beer. By the time he left the Gladstone Club he had a
clear picture of the situation. The stumbling block was Handyman Hall
and Lady Maud. He would explore the possibilities of that more fully in
the morning. He walked back up the Shambles and Giblet Walk to the
Market Square and booked in at the Handyman Arms.

At the Hall Sir Giles spent the day sequestered in his study. This seclusion
was only partly to be explained by the presence in the house and grounds
of half a dozen guard dogs who seemed to feel that he was an intruder
in his own home. More to the point was the fact that Lady Maud had
expressed herself very forcibly on the matter of his lunch with Lord
Leakham. If the Judge regretted that lunch, and from the reports of the
doctors at the Cottage Hospital he had cause to, so did Sir Giles.

'I was only trying to help,' he had explained. 'I thought if I gave him
a good lunch he might be more prepared to see our side of the case.'

'Our side of the case?' Lady Maud snorted. 'If it comes to that we didn't have a case at all. It was perfectly obvious he was going to recommend the route through the Gorge.'

'There is the Ottertown alternative,' Sir Giles pointed out.

'Alternative my foot,' said Lady Maud. 'If you can't see a red herring when it's thrust under your nose, you're a bigger fool than I take you for.'

Sir Giles had retreated to his study cursing his wife for her perspicacity. There had been a very nasty look in her eye at the mention of Ottertown, and one or two unpleasant cracks about property speculators and their ways over breakfast had made him wonder if she had heard anything about Hoskins' new house. And now there was this damned official from Whitehall to poke his nose into the affair. Finally and most disturbing of all there had been the voices. Or rather one voice: his own. While putting the car away before lunch he had distinctly heard himself assuring nobody in particular that they could look to him to see that nothing was done that would in any way jeopardize ... Sir Giles had stared round the yard with a wild surmise. For a moment he had supposed that he had been talking to himself but the presence in his mouth of a cigar had ended that explanation. Besides the voice had been quite distinct. It had been a most disturbing experience and one for which there was no rational explanation. It had taken two stiff whiskies to convince him that he had imagined the whole thing. Now to take his mind off the occurrence he sat at his desk and concentrated on the motorway.

'Red herring indeed,' he muttered to himself. 'I wonder what she would have said if Leakham had decided in favour of Ottertown.' It was an idle thought and quite out of the question. They would never build a motorway through Ottertown. Old Francis Puckerington would have another heart attack. Old Francis Puckerington ... Sir Giles stopped in his tracks, amazed at his own intuitive brilliance. Francis Puckerington, the Member for Ottertown, was a dying man. What had the doctors said? That he'd be lucky to live to the next general election. There had been rumours that he was going to resign his seat. And his majority at the last election had been a negligible one, somewhere in the region of fifty. If Leakham had decided on the Ottertown route it would have killed old Francis. And then there would have to be a bye-election. Sir Giles' devious mind catalogued the consequences. A bye-election fought on the issue of the motorway and the demolition of seventy-five council houses with a previous majority of fifty. It wasn't to be thought of. The Chief Whip would go berserk. Leakham's decision would be reversed. The motorway would come through the Cleene Gorge after all. And best of all not a shred of suspicion would rest on Sir Giles. It was a brilliant stratagem. It would put him in the clear. He was about to reach for the phone to call Hoskins when it occurred to him that he had better wait to hear what the man from the Ministry had to say. There was no point in rushing things now. He would go and see Hoskins in the morning. Imbued with a new spirit of defiance he left the study and selecting a large walking-stick from the rack in the hall he went out into the garden for a stroll.

It was a glorious afternoon. The sun shone down out of a cloudless sky. Birds sang. The flowering cherries by the kitchen garden flowered and Sir Giles himself blossomed with smug self-satisfaction. He paused for a moment to admire the goldfish in the ornamental pond and was just considering the possibility of pushing up the compensation to three hundred thousand when for the second time that day he heard himself speaking. 'I'm damned if I'm going to allow the countryside to be desecrated by a motorway. I shall take the earliest opportunity of raising the matter in the House.' Sir Giles stared round the garden panic-stricken, but there was no one in sight. He turned and looked at the Hall but the windows were all shut. To his right was the wall of the kitchen garden. Sir Giles hurried across the lawn to the door in the wall and peered inside. Blott was busy in a cucumber frame.

'Did you say anything?' Sir Giles asked.

'Me?' said Blott. 'I didn't say anything. Did you?'

Sir Giles hurried back to the house. It was no longer a glorious afternoon. It was a quite horrible afternoon. He went into his study and shut the door.

CHAPTER EIGHT

Dundridge spent a perfectly foul night at the Handyman Arms. His room there had a sloping floor, a yellowed ceiling, an ochre chest of drawers and a wardrobe whose door opened of its own accord ten minutes after he had shut it. It did so with a hideous wheeze and would then creak softly until he got out of bed and shut it again. He spent half the night trying to devise some method of keeping it closed and the other half listening to the noises coming from the next room. These were of a most disturbing sort and suggested an incompatibility of size and temperament that played havoc with his imagination. At two o'clock he managed to get to sleep, only to be woken at three by a sudden eruption in the drainpipe of his washbasin which appeared to be most unhygienically connected to the one next door. At half past three a dawn breeze rattled the signboard outside his window. At four the man next door asked if someone wanted it again. 'For God's sake,' Dundridge muttered and buried his head under the pillow to shut out this evidence of sexual excess. At ten past four the wardrobe door, responding to the seismic tremors from the next room, opened again and creaked softly. Dundridge let it creak and turned for relief to his composite woman. With her assistance he managed to get back to sleep to be woken at seven by a repulsive-looking girl with a tea-tray.

'Is there anything else you wanted?' she asked coyly.

'Certainly not,' said Dundridge wondering what there was about him that led only the most revolting females to offer him their venereal services. He got up and went along to the bathroom and wrestled with the intricacies of a gas-fired geyser which had evidently set its mind on asphyxiating him or blowing him up. In the end he had a cold wash.

By the time he had finished breakfast he was in a thoroughly bad mood. He had been unable to formulate any coherent strategy and had no idea what to do next. Hoskins had advised him to have a word with Sir Giles Lynchwood and Dundridge decided he would do that later. To begin with he would pay a call on Lord Leakham at the Cottage Hospital.

After wandering down narrow lanes and up a flight of steps behind the Worford Museum he found the hospital, a grey gaunt stone building that looked as though it had once been a workhouse. It fronted on to the Abbey and in the small front garden a number of geriatric patients were sitting around in dressing-gowns. Stifling his disgust, Dundridge went inside and asked for Lord Leakham.

'Visiting hours are two to three,' said the nurse at Admissions.

'I'm here on Government business,' said Dundridge feeling that it was about time someone understood he was not to be trifled with.

'I'll have to ask Matron,' said the nurse. Dundridge went outside into the sunshine to wait. He didn't like hospitals. They were not, he felt, his forte, particularly hospitals which overlooked graveyards, stank of disinfectant and had the gall to call themselves Cottage Hospitals when they were situated in the middle of towns. He was just considering the awful prospect of being treated for a serious complaint in such a dead-and-alive hole when the Matron appeared. She was gaunt, grey-haired and grim.

'I understand you want to see Lord Leakham,' she said.

'On Government business,' said Dundridge pompously.

'You can have five minutes,' said the Matron and led the way down the passage to a private room. 'He's still suffering from concussion and shock.' She opened the door and Dundridge went inside. 'Now nothing controversial,' said the Matron. 'We don't want to have a relapse, do we?'

On the bed, ashen-faced and with his head swathed in bandages, Lord Leakham regarded her venomously. 'There's nothing the matter with me apart from food poisoning,' he said. Dundridge sat down beside his bed.

'My name is Dundridge,' he said. 'The Minister of the Environment has asked me to come up to see if I can do something to ... er ... well to negotiate some sort of settlement in regard to the motorway.'

Lord Leakham looked at him vindictively over the top of his glasses. 'Has he indeed? Well let me tell you what I intend to do about the motorway first and then you can inform him,' he said. He raised himself on his pillows and leant towards Dundridge. 'I was appointed to head the Inquiry into the motorway and I do not intend to relinquish my responsibility.'

'Oh quite,' said Dundridge.

'Furthermore,' said the Judge, 'I have no intention whatsoever of allowing myself to be influenced by hooliganism and riot from doing my duty as I see it.'

'Oh definitely,' said Dundridge.

'As soon as these damnfool doctors get it into their thick heads that there is nothing wrong with me except a peptic ulcer, I shall re-open the Inquiry and announce my decision.' Dundridge nodded.

'Quite right too,' he said. 'And what will your decision be? Or is it too early to ask that?'

'It most certainly isn't,' shouted Lord Leakham. 'I intend to recommend that the motorway goes through the Cleene Gorge, plumb through it, you understand. I intend to see that that damned woman's home is levelled to the ground, brick by brick. I intend ...' He sank back on to the bed exhausted by his outburst.

'I see,' said Dundridge, wondering what possible use there was in trying to negotiate a compromise between an irresistible force and an immovable object.

'Oh no you don't,' said Lord Leakham. 'That woman deliberately sent her husband to poison me. She interrupted the proceedings. She insulted me in my own court. She incited to riot. She made a mockery of the legal process and she shall rue the day. The law shall not be mocked, sir.'

'Oh quite,' said Dundridge.

'So you go and negotiate all you want but just remember the decision to go through the Gorge is mine and I do not for one moment intend to forgo the pleasure of making it.'

Dundridge went out into the passage and conferred with the Matron.

'He seems to think someone tried to poison him,' he said carefully skirting the law of libel. The Matron smiled gently.

'That's the concussion,' she said. 'He'll get over that in a day or two.'

Dundridge went out into the Abbey Close past the geriatric patients and wandered disconsolately down the steps and out into Market Street. It didn't seem likely to him that Lord Leakham would get over his conviction that Lady Maud had tried to poison him and he had a shrewd suspicion that the Judge had in some perverse way enjoyed the contretemps in court and was looking forward to pursuing his vendetta as soon as he was up and about. He was just considering what to do next when he caught sight of his reflection in a shop window. It was not that of a man of authority. There was a sort of dispirited look about it, a hangdog look quite out of keeping with his role as the Minister's troubleshooter. It was time to take the bull by the horns. He straightened his back, marched across the road to the Post Office and telephoned Handyman Hall. He got Lady Maud and explained that he would like to see Sir Giles.

'I'm afraid Sir Giles is out just at present,' she said modulating her tone to suggest a secretary. 'He'll be back shortly. Would eleven o'clock be convenient?'

Dundridge said it would. He left the Post Office and threaded his way through the market stalls to the car park to collect his car.

At Handyman Hall Lady Maud congratulated herself on her performance. She was rather looking forward to a private chat with the man from the Ministry. Dundridge, he had said his name was. From the Ministry. Sir Giles had mentioned the fact that someone had been sent up from London on a factfinding mission. And since Giles had said he would be out until late in the afternoon this seemed an ideal opportunity to provide this Mr Dundridge with facts that would suit her book. She went upstairs to change, and to consider her tactics. She had spiked Lord Leakham's guns by frontal assault but Dundridge on the phone had sounded far less self-assured than she had expected. It might be better to try persuasion, perhaps even a little charm. It would confuse the issue. Lady Maud selected a cotton frock and dabbed a little Lavender Water behind her ears. Mr Dundridge would get the meek treatment, the helpless little girl approach. If that didn't work she could always revert to sterner methods.

In the greenhouse Blott put down the earphones and went back to the broad beans. So an official was coming to see Sir Giles, was he? An official. Blott felt strongly about officials. They had made his early life a misery and he had no time for them. Still, Lady Maud had invited this one to the Hall so presumably she knew what she was doing. It was a pity. Blott would have liked to have been ordered to give this Dundridge the reception he deserved and he was just considering what sort of reception he would have organized for him when Lady Maud came into the garden. Blott straightened up and stared at her. She was wearing a cotton frock and to Blott at least she looked quite beautiful. It was not a notion anyone else would have shared but Blott's standards of beauty were not determined by fashion. Large breasts, enormous thighs and hips were attributes of a good or at least ample mother, and since Blott had never had a good, ample or even *any* mother in a post-natal sense he placed great emphasis on these outward signs of potential maternity. Now, standing among the broad beans, he was filled with a sudden sense of desire. Lady Maud in a cotton frock dappled with a floral pattern combined botany with biology. Blott goggled.

'Blott,' said Lady Maud, oblivious of the effect she was having, 'there's a man from the Ministry of the Environment coming to lunch. I want some flowers in the house. I want to make a good impression on him.'

Blott went into the greenhouse and looked for something suitable while Lady Maud bent low to select a lettuce for lunch. As she did so Blott glanced out of the greenhouse door. It was the turning point in his life. The silent devotion to the Handyman family which had been the passive mainspring of his existence for so long was gone, to be replaced by an active urgency of feeling.

Blott was in love.

CHAPTER NINE

Dundridge left Worford by the town gate, crossed the river and took the Ottertown road. On his left the Cleene wandered through meadows and on his right the Cleene Hills rose steeply to a wooded crest. He drove for three miles and turned up a side road that was signposted Guildstead Carbonell and found himself in evidently hostile territory. Every barn had the slogan 'Save the Gorge' whitewashed on it and there were similar sentiments painted on the road itself. At one point an avenue of beeches had been daubed with letters that spelt out 'No to the Motorway' so that as he drove down it Dundridge was left in no doubt that local feeling was against the scheme.

Even without the slogans Dundridge would have been alarmed. The Cleene Forest was nature undomesticated. There was none of that neatness that he found so reassuring in Middlesex. The hedges were rank, the few farmhouses he passed looked medieval, and the forest itself dense with large trees, humped and gnarled with bracken growing thickly underneath. He was relieved when the road ran into an open valley with hedges and little fields. The respite was brief. At the top of the next hill he came to a crossroads marked by nothing more informative than a decayed gibbet.

Dundridge stopped the car and consulted his map. According to his calculations Guildstead Carbonell lay to the left while in front was the Gorge and Handyman Hall. Dundridge wished it wasn't. Below him the forest lay thicker than before and the road less metalled, with moss and grass growing down the middle. He drove on for a mile and was beginning to wonder if the map had misled him when the trees thinned and he found himself looking down into the Gorge itself.

He stopped the car and got out. Below him the Cleene tumbled between cliffs overgrown with brambles, ivy and creepers. Ahead lay Handyman Hall. It stood, an amalgam in stone and brick, timber and tile and turret, a monument to all that was most eclectic and least attractive in English architecture. To Dundridge, himself a devotee of function, for whom simplicity was all, it was a nightmare. Ruskin and Morris, Gilbert Scott, Vanbrugh, Inigo Jones and Wren to name but a few had all lent their influence to a building that combined the utility of a water-tower with the homeliness of Wormwood Scrubs. Around it lay a few acres of parkland, a wall, and beyond the wall a circle of hills, heavily wooded. Over the whole scene there lay a sense of isolation. Somewhere to the west there were presumably towns and houses, shops and buses, but to Dundridge it seemed that he was standing on the very edge of civilization if not actually beyond it. With the sinking feeling that he was committing himself to the unknown he got back into the car and drove on, down the hill into the Gorge. Presently he came to a small iron suspension bridge across the river which rattled as he drove over. On the far side something large and strange loomed through the trees. It was the Lodge. Dundridge stopped the car and gaped at the building through the windshield.

Constructed in 1904 to mark the occasion of the visit of Edward the Seventh, the Lodge, in deference to the King's Francophilia, had been modelled on the Arc de Triomphe. There were differences. The Lodge was slightly smaller, its frieze did not depict scenes of battle, but for all that the resemblance was remarkable and to Dundridge its existence in the heart of Worfordshire came as final proof that whoever had built Handyman Hall had been an architectural kleptomaniac. Above all the Lodge bespoke a lofty arrogance which, coming so shortly after Lord Leakham's outburst, made a tactful approach all the more necessary. As he stood looking up at it Dundridge was recalled to his task. Some sort of compromise was clearly necessary to avoid his becoming embroiled in an extremely nasty situation. If the Ottertown route was out of the question and he had it on the highest authority that it was, and if the Gorge ... There was no if about the Gorge, Dundridge had seen enough to convince him of that, then a third route was imperative. But there was no third route. Dundridge got back into his car and drove thoughtfully through the great arch and as he did so a vision of the third route dawned upon him. A tunnel. A tunnel under the Cleene Hills. A tunnel had all the merits of simplicity, of straightness and, best of all, of leaving undisturbed the hideous landscape that so many irate and influential people inexplicably admired. There would be no more wrangles about property rights, no compensation, no trouble. Dundridge had discovered the ideal solution.

In the entrance hall Lady Maud, radiant in Tootal, lurked among the ferns. High above her head the stained-glass rooflight cast a reddish glow upon the marble staircase and lent a fresh air of apoplexy to the ruddy faces of her ancestors glowering down from the walls. Lady Maud patted her hair in readiness. She had laid her plans. Mr Dundridge would get the gracious treatment at least to begin with. After that she would see how he responded. As his car crunched on the gravel outside she adjusted her step-in and gave a practice smile to a vase of snapdragons. Then she stepped forward and opened the door.

'Nincompoop? Nincompoop? Did you say nincompoop?' said Sir Giles. In his constituency office situated conveniently close to Hoskins' Regional Planning Board the word had a reassuring ring to it.

'A perfect nincompoop,' said Hoskins.

'Are you sure?'

'Positive. A first rate, Grade A nincompoop.'

'It sounds too good to be true,' said Sir Giles doubtfully. 'You can't always go by appearances. I've known some very slippery customers in my time who looked like idiots.'

'I'm not going by appearances,' Hoskins said. 'He doesn't look an idiot. He is one. Wouldn't know one end of a motorway from the other.'

Sir Giles considered the statement. 'I'm not sure I would come to that,' he said.

'You know what I mean,' said Hoskins. 'He's no more an expert on motorways than I am.'

Sir Giles pursed his lips. 'If he's such a dimwit why did the Minister send him up? He's given him full authority to negotiate.'

'Don't look a gift horse in the mouth, is what I say.'

'I daresay there's something in that,' said Sir Giles. 'So you don't think there's anything to worry about?'

Hoskins smiled. 'Not a thing in the world. He'll nosey around a bit and then he will do just what we want. I tell you this bloke takes the biscuit. Butter wouldn't melt in his mouth.'

Sir Giles considered this mixture of metaphors and found it to his taste. 'I hear Lord Leakham's still foaming at the mouth.'

'He can't wait to re-open the Inquiry. Says he's going to put the motorway through the Gorge if it's the last thing he does.'

'It probably will be if Maud has anything to do with it,' said Sir Giles. 'She's in a very nasty frame of mind.'

'There's nothing much she can do about it once the decision is taken,' said Hoskins.

'I wouldn't be too sure about that.'

Sir Giles got up and stared out of the window and considered his alternative plan. 'You don't think this fellow Dundridge will advise against the Gorge?' he asked finally.

'Lord Leakham wouldn't listen to him if he did. He's got it into his head you tried to poison him,' said Hoskins and went back to his office leaving Sir Giles to ponder on the best-laid plans of mice and men. It was all very well for Hoskins to talk confidently about nincompoops from the Ministry. He had nothing to lose. Sir Giles had. His seat in Parliament for one thing. Well, if the worst came to the worst and Maud carried out her threat he could always get another. It was worth the risk. Reassured by the thought that Lord Leakham had made up his mind to route the motorway through the Gorge Sir Giles went out to lunch.

At Handyman Hall Lady Maud's gracious approach had worked wonders. Like some delicate plant in need of water, Dundridge had blossomed out. He had come expecting to meet Sir Giles but, after the first shock of finding himself alone in a large house with a large woman had worn off, Dundridge began to enjoy himself. For the first time since he had arrived in Worfordshire he was being taken seriously. Lady Maud treated him as a person of consequence.

'It is so good to know that you have come to take over from Lord Leakham,' Lady Maud said as she led him down a corridor to the drawing-room.

Dundridge said he hadn't actually come to take over. 'I'm simply here in an advisory capacity,' he said modestly.

Lady Maud smiled knowingly. 'Oh quite, and we all know what that means, don't we?' she murmured, drawing Dundridge into a warm complicity he found quite delightful.

Dundridge relaxed on the sofa. 'The Minister is most anxious that the proposed motorway should fit in with the needs of local residents as much as possible.'

Maud smothered a snarl with another smile. The notion that she was a local resident made her blood boil, but she had set out to humour this snivelling civil servant and humour him she would. 'And there is the landscape to consider too,' she said. 'The Cleene Forest is one of the few remaining examples of virgin woodland left in England. It would be a terrible shame to spoil it with a motorway, don't you think?'

Dundridge didn't think anything of the sort but he knew better than to say so, and besides this seemed as good an opportunity as any to test out his theory of a tunnel. 'I think I've found a solution to the problem,' he said. 'Of course it's only an idea, you understand, and it has no official standing, but it should be possible to build a tunnel under the Cleene Hills.' He stopped. Lady Maud was staring at him intently. 'Of course, as I say, it's only an idea ...'

Lady Maud had risen and for one terrible moment Dundridge thought she was about to assault him. She lurched forward and took his hand. 'Oh how wonderful,' she said. 'How absolutely brilliant. You dear, dear man,' and she sat down beside him on the sofa and gazed into his face ecstatically. Dundridge blushed and looked down at his shoes. He was quite unused to married women taking his hand, gazing into his face ecstatically and calling him their dear, dear man. 'It's nothing. Only an idea.'

'A splendid idea,' said Lady Maud, engulfing him in a blast of Lavender Water. Out of the corner of his eye Dundridge could see her bosom quivering beneath a nosegay of marigolds. He shrank into the sofa.

'Of course, there would have to be a feasibility study ...' he began but Lady Maud brushed his remark aside.

'Of course there would, but that would take time wouldn't it?'

'Months,' said Dundridge.

'Months!'

'Six months at least.'

'Six months!' Lady Maud relinquished his hand with a sigh and contemplated a respite of six months. In six months so much could happen and if she had anything to do with it a great deal would. Giles would throw his weight behind the tunnel or she would know the reason why. She would drum up support from conservationists across the country. In six months she would do wonders. And she owed it all to this insubstantial little man with plastic shoes. Now that she came to look at him she realized she had misjudged him. There was something almost appealing about his vulnerability. 'You'll stay to lunch,' she said.

'Well ... er ... I really ...'

'Of course you will,' said Lady Maud. 'I insist. And you can tell Giles all about the tunnel when he gets back this afternoon.' She rose and, leaving Dundridge to wonder how it was that Sir Giles who had been coming back at eleven had delayed his return until the afternoon, Lady Maud swept from the room. Left to himself, Dundridge sat stunned by the enthusiasm his suggestion had unleashed. If Sir Giles' reaction was as favourable as that of his wife he would have made some influential friends. And rich ones. He ran his fingers appreciatively over the moulding of a rosewood table. So this was how the other half lived, he thought, before realizing that the cliché was inappropriate. The other two per cent. Useful people to know.

Sir Giles returned from Worford at four to find Lady Maud in a remarkably good mood.

'I had a visit from such a strange young man,' she told him when he inquired what the matter was.

'Oh really?'

'He was called Dundridge. He was from the Ministry of the—'

'Dundridge? Did you say Dundridge?'

'Yes. Such a very interesting man ...'

'Interesting? I understood he was a nincom ... oh never mind. What did he have to say for himself?'

'Oh, this and that,' said Lady Maud, gratified by her husband's agitation.

'What do you mean "this and that"?'

'We talked about the absurdity of putting a motorway through the Gorge,' said Lady Maud.

'I suppose he's in favour of the Ottertown route.'

Lady Maud shook her head, 'As a matter of fact he isn't.'

'He isn't?' said Sir Giles, now thoroughly alarmed. 'What the hell is he in favour of then?'

Lady Maud savoured his concern. 'He has in mind a third route,' she said. 'One that avoids both Ottertown and the Gorge.'

Sir Giles turned pale. 'A third route? But there isn't a third route. There can't be. He's not thinking of going through the Forest, is he? It's an area of designated public beauty.'

'Not through it. Under it,' said Lady Maud triumphantly.

'Under it?'

'A tunnel. A tunnel under the Cleene Hills. Don't you think that's a marvellous idea.'

Sir Giles sat down heavily. He was looking quite ill.

'I said "Don't you think that's a marvellous idea",' said Lady Maud.

Sir Giles pulled himself together. 'Er ... What ... oh yes ... splendid,' he muttered. 'Quite splendid.'

'You don't sound very enthusiastic,' said Lady Maud.

'It's just that I wouldn't have thought it was financially viable,' Sir Giles said. 'The cost would be enormous. I can't see the Ministry taking to the idea at all readily.'

'I can,' said Lady Maud, 'with a little prodding.' She went out through the french windows on to the terrace and looked lovingly across the park. With Dundridge's help she had solved one problem. The house had been saved. There remained the question of an heir and it had just occurred to her that here again Dundridge might prove invaluable. Over lunch he had waxed quite eloquent about his work. Once or twice he had mentioned cementation. The word had struck a chord in her. Now as she leant over the balustrade and stared into the depths of the pinetum it returned to her insistently. 'Sementation,' she murmured, 'sementation.' It was a new word to her and strangely technical for such an intimate act, but Lady Maud was in no mood to quibble.

Sir Giles was. He waddled off to the study and phoned Hoskins. 'What's all this about that bastard Dundridge being a nincompoop?' he snarled. 'Do you know what he's come up with now? A tunnel. You heard me. A bloody tunnel under the Cleene Hills.'

'A tunnel?' said Hoskins. 'That's out of the question. They can't put a tunnel under the Forest.'

'Why not? They're putting one under the blasted Channel. They can put tunnels wherever they bloody well want to these days.'

'I know that, but it would be cost-prohibitive,' said Hoskins.

'Cost-prohibitive my arse. If this sod goes round bleating about tunnels he'll whip up support from every environmental crank in the country. He's got to be stopped.'

'I'll do my best,' said Hoskins doubtfully.

'You'll do better than that,' Sir Giles snarled. 'You get him on to the idea of Ottertown.'

'But what about the seventy-five council houses—'

'Bugger the seventy-five council houses. Just get him off the bloody tunnel.' Sir Giles put down the phone and stared out of the window vindictively. If he didn't do something drastic he would be saddled with Handyman Hall. And with Lady Maud to boot. He got up and kicked the wastepaper basket into the corner.

CHAPTER TEN

Dundridge drove back to Worford with no thought for the landscape. His encounter with Lady Maud had left him stunned and with his sense of self-importance greatly inflated. Lunch had been most enjoyable and Dundridge with two large gins inside him had found Lady Maud a most appreciative audience. She had listened to his exposition of the theory of non-interruptive constant-flow transportation with an evident fervour usually quite absent in his audience and Dundridge had found her enthusiasm extraordinarily refreshing. Moreover she exuded confidence, a supreme self-confidence which was contagious and which exerted an enormous fascination over him. In spite of her lack of symmetry, of beauty, in spite of the manifest discrepancy between her physique and that of the ideal woman of his imagination, he had to admit that she held charms for him. After lunch she had shown him over the house and garden and Dundridge had followed her from room to room with a quite inexplicable sense of weak-kneed excitement. Once when he had stumbled in the rockery Lady Maud had taken his arm and Dundridge had felt limp with pleasure. Again when he had squeezed past her in the doorway of the bathroom he had been conscious of a delicious passivity. By the time he left the house he felt quite childishly happy. He was appreciated. It made all the difference.

He got back to the Handyman Arms to find Hoskins waiting for him in the lounge.

'Just thought I'd drop in to see how you were getting on.'

'Fine. Fine. Just fine,' said Dundridge.

'Got on all right with Leakham?'

The warm glow in Dundridge cooled. 'I can't say I like his attitude,' he said. 'He seems determined to go ahead with the Gorge route. He has evidently developed a quite irrational hatred for Lady Maud. I must say I find his attitude inexplicable. She seems a perfectly charming woman to me.'

Hoskins stared at him incredulously. 'She does?'

'Delightful,' said Dundridge, the warm glow returning gently.

'Delightful?'

'Charming,' said Dundridge dreamily.

'Good God,' said Hoskins unable to contain his astonishment any longer. The notion that anyone could find Lady Maud charming and delightful was quite beyond him. He looked at Dundridge with a new interest. 'She's a bit large, don't you think?' he suggested.

'Comely,' said Dundridge benevolently. 'Just comely.'

Hoskins shuddered and changed the subject. 'About this tunnel,' he began. Dundridge looked at him in surprise.

'How did you hear about that?'

'News travels fast in these parts.'

'It must,' said Dundridge, 'I only mentioned it this morning.'

'You're not seriously proposing to recommend the construction of a tunnel under the Cleene Hills, are you?'

'I don't see why not,' said Dundridge, 'it seems a sensible compromise.'

'A bloody expensive one,' said Hoskins, 'it would cost millions and take years to put through.'

'At least it would avoid another riot. I came up here to try to find a solution that would be acceptable to all parties. It seems to me that a tunnel would be a very sensible alternative. In any case the plan is still in the formative stage.'

'Yes, but ...' Hoskins began but Dundridge had risen and with an airy remark about the need for vision had gone up to his room. Hoskins went back to the Regional Planning Board in a pensive mood. He had been wrong about Dundridge. The man wasn't such a nincompoop after all. On the other hand he had found Lady Maud charming and delightful. 'Bloody pervert,' Hoskins muttered as he picked up the phone. Sir Giles wasn't going to like this.

Nor was Blott. He had had a relatively phone-free day in the kitchen garden. There had been Dundridge's call in the morning but for the most part he had been left in peace. At half past four he had heard Sir Giles call Hoskins and tell him about the tunnel. At half past five he was watering the tomatoes when Hoskins called back to say that Dundridge was serious about the tunnel.

'He can't be,' Sir Giles snarled. 'It's an outrageous idea. A gross waste of taxpayers' money.'

Blott shook his head. The tunnel sounded a very good idea to him.

'You try telling him that,' said Hoskins.

'What about Leakham?' Sir Giles asked. 'He's not going to buy it, is he?'

'I wouldn't like to say. Depends what sort of weight this fellow Dundridge carries in London. The Ministry may bring pressure to bear on Leakham.'

There was a silence while Sir Giles considered this. In the greenhouse Blott wrestled with the intricacies of the English language. Why should Lord Leakham buy the tunnel? How could Dundridge carry weight in London? And in any case why should Sir Giles dislike the idea of a tunnel? It was all very odd.

'I've got another bit of news for you,' Hoskins said finally. 'He's keen on your missus.'

There was a strangled sound from Sir Giles. 'He's what?' he shouted.

'He has taken a fancy to Maud,' Hoskins told him. 'He said he found her charming and delightful.'

'Charming and delightful?' said Sir Giles. 'Maud?'

'And comely.'

'Good God. No wonder she's looking like the cat that's swallowed the canary,' said Sir Giles.

'I just thought you ought to know,' said Hoskins. 'It might give us some sort of lever.'

'Kinky?'

'Could be,' said Hoskins.

'Meet me at the Club at nine,' said Sir Giles, suddenly making up his mind. 'This needs thinking about.' He rang off.

In the greenhouse Blott stared lividly into the geraniums. If Sir Giles had been surprised, Blott's reaction was stronger still. The sudden discovery that he was in love with Lady Maud had coloured his day. The thought of Dundridge sharing his feelings for her infuriated him. Sir Giles he discounted. It was quite clear that Lady Maud despised her husband and from what she had said Blott had gathered that there was another woman in London. Dundridge was another matter. Blott left the greenhouse, tidied up and went home.

Home for Blott was the Lodge. The architect of the arch had managed to combine monumentality with utility and at one time the Lodge had housed several families of estate workers in rather cramped and insanitary conditions. Blott had the place to himself and found it quite adequate. The arch had its little inconveniences; the windows were extremely small and hidden among the decorations on the exterior; there was only one door so that to get from one side of the arch to the other one had to climb the staircase to the top and then cross over, but Blott had made himself very comfortable in a large room that spanned the arch. Through a circular window on one side he could keep an eye on the Hall and through another he could inspect visitors crossing the bridge. He had converted one small room into a bathroom and another into a kitchen, while he stored apples in some of the others so that the whole place had a pleasant smell to it. And finally there was Blott's library filled with books that he had picked up on the market stalls in Worford or in the second-hand bookshop in Ferret Lane. There were no novels in Blott's library, no light reading, only books on English history. In its way it was a scholar's library born of an intense curiosity about the country of his adoption. If the secret of being an Englishman was to be found anywhere it was to be found, Blott thought, in the past. Through the long winter evenings he would sit in front of his fire absorbed in the romance of England. Certain figures loomed large in his imagination, Henry VIII, Drake, Cromwell, Edward I, and he intended to identify if not himself at least other people with the heroes and villains of history. Lady Maud, in spite of her marriage, he saw as the Virgin Queen, while Sir Giles seemed to have the less savoury aspects of Sir Robert Walpole.

But that was for winter. During the summer he was out and about. Twice a week he cycled over to Guildstead Carbonell to the Royal George and sat in the bar until it was time for bed, the bed in question belonging to Mrs Wynn who ran the pub and whose husband had obligingly left her a widow as a result of enemy action on D-Day. Mrs Wynn was the last of Blott's wartime customers and the affair had lingered on owing more to habit than to affection. Mrs Wynn found Blott useful, he dried glasses and carried bottles, and Blott found Mrs Wynn comfortable, undemanding and accommodating in the matter of beer. He had a weakness for Handyman Brown.

But now as he washed his neck – it was Friday night and Mrs Wynn was expecting him – he was conscious that he no longer felt the same way about her. Not that he had ever felt very much, but that little had been swept aside by his sudden surge of feeling for Maud. He was sensible enough not to entertain any expectations of being able to do anything about it. It just didn't seem right to go off to Mrs Wynn any more. In any case it was all most peculiar. He had always had a soft spot for Lady Maud but this was different and it occurred to him that he might be sickening for something. He stuck out his tongue and studied it in the bathroom mirror but it looked all right. It might be the weather. He had once heard someone say something about spring and young men's fancies but Blott wasn't a young man. He was fifty. Fifty and in love. Daft.

He went downstairs and got on his bicycle and cycled off across the bridge towards Guildstead Carbonell. He had just reached the crossroads when he heard a car coming up fast behind him. He got off the bike to let it go by. It was Sir Giles in the Bentley. 'Going to the Golf Club to see Hoskins,' he thought, and looked after the car suspiciously. 'He's up to something.' He got back on to his bike and freewheeled reluctantly down the hill towards the Royal George and Mrs Wynn. Perhaps he ought to tell Maud what he had heard. It didn't seem a good idea and in any case he wasn't going to let her know that Dundridge fancied her. 'He can sow his own row,' he said to himself and was pleased at his command of the idiom.

In the Worford Golf Club, Sir Giles and Hoskins discussed tactics.

'He's got to have a weakness,' said Sir Giles. 'Every man has his price.'

'Maud?' said Hoskins.

'Be your age,' said Sir Giles. 'She isn't going to fartarse around with some tinpot civil servant with that reversionary clause in the contract at stake. Besides, I don't believe it.'

'I distinctly heard him say he found her charming. And comely.'

'All right, so he likes fat women. What else does he like? Money?'

Hoskins shrugged. 'Hard to tell. You need time to find that out.'

'Time is what we haven't got. He's only got to start blabbing about that bleeding tunnel and the fat's in the fire. No, we've got to act fast.'

Hoskins looked at him suspiciously. 'What's all this "We" business?' he asked. 'It's your problem, not mine.'

Sir Giles gnawed a fingernail thoughtfully. 'How much?'

'Five thousand.'

'For what?'

'Whatever you decide.'

'Make it five per cent of the compensation. When it's paid.'

Hoskins did a quick calculation and made it twelve and half thousand. 'Cash on the nail,' he said.

'You're a hard man, Hoskins, a hard man,' Sir Giles said sorrowfully.

'Anyway what do you want me to do? Sound him out?'

Sir Giles shook his head. His little eyes glittered. 'Kinky,' he said. 'Kinky. What made you say that?'

'I don't know. Just wondered,' said Hoskins.

'Boys, do you think?'

'Difficult to know,' said Hoskins. 'These things take time to find out.'

'Drink, drugs, boys, women, money. There's got to be some damned thing he's itching for.'

'Of course, we *could* frame him,' said Hoskins. 'It's been done before.'

Sir Giles nodded. 'The unsolicited gift. The anonymous donor. It's been done before all right. But it's too risky. What if he goes to the police?'

'Nothing ventured nothing gained,' said Hoskins. 'In any case there would be no indication where it came from. My bet is he'd take the bait.'

'If he didn't we would have lost him. No, it's got to be something foolproof.'

They sat in silence and considered a suitably compromising future for Dundridge.

'Ambitious would you say?' Sir Giles asked finally. Hoskins nodded.

'Very.'

'Know any queers?'

'In Worford? You've got to be joking,' said Hoskins.

'Anywhere.'

Hoskins shook his head. 'If you're thinking what I'm thinking ...'

'I am.'

'Photos?'

'Photos?' Sir Giles agreed. 'Nice compromising photos.'

Hoskins gave the matter some thought. 'There's Bessie Williams,' he said. 'Used to be a model, if you know what I mean. Married a photographer in Bridgeminster. She'd do it if the money was right.' He smiled reminiscently. 'I can have a word with her.'

'You do that,' said Sir Giles. 'I'll pay up to five hundred for a decent set of photos.'

'Leave it to me,' Hoskins told him. 'Now then, about the cash.'

By the time Sir Giles left the Golf Club the matter was fixed. He drove home in a haze of whisky. 'The stick first and then the carrot,' he muttered. Tomorrow he would go to London and visit Mrs Forthby. It was just as well to be out of the way when things happened.

CHAPTER ELEVEN

Dundridge spent the following morning at the regional Planning Board with Hoskins poring over maps and discussing the tunnel. He was rather surprised to find that Hoskins had undergone a change of heart about the project and seemed to favour it. 'It's a brilliant idea. Pity we didn't think of it before. Would have saved no end of trouble,' he said, and while Dundridge was flattered he wasn't so sure. He had begun to have doubts about the feasibility of a tunnel. The Ministry wouldn't exactly like the cost, the delay would be considerable and there was still Lord Leakham to be persuaded. 'You don't think we could find an alternative route,' he asked but Hoskins shook his head.

'It's either the Cleene Gorge or Ottertown or your tunnel.' Dundridge, studying the maps, had to concede that there wasn't any other route. The Cleene Hills stretched unbroken save for the Gorge from Worford to Ottertown.

'Ridiculous fuss people make about a bit of forest,' Dundridge complained. 'Just trees. What's so special about trees?'

They had lunch at a restaurant in River Street. At the next table a couple in their thirties seemed to find Dundridge quite fascinating and more than once Dundridge looked up to find the woman looking at him with a quiet smile. She was rather attractive, with almond eyes.

In the afternoon Hoskins took him on a tour of the proposed route through Ottertown. They drove over and inspected the council houses and returned through Guildstead Carbonell, Hoskins stopping the car every now and again and insisting that they climb to the top of some hill to get a better view of the proposed route. By the time they got back to Worford Dundridge was exhausted. He was also rather drunk. They had stopped at several pubs along the way and, thanks to Hoskins' insistence that pints were for men and that only boys drank halves – he put rather a nasty inflection on boys – Dundridge had consumed rather more Handyman Triple XXX than he was used to.

'We're having a little celebration party at the Golf Club tonight,' Hoskins said as they drove through the town gate. 'If you'd care to come over ...'

'I think I'll get an early night,' said Dundridge.

'Pity,' Hoskins said. 'You'd meet a number of influential local people. Doesn't do to give the locals the idea you're hoity-toity.'

'Oh all right,' said Dundridge grudgingly. 'I'll have a bath and something to eat and see how I feel.'

'See you later, old boy,' said Hoskins as Dundridge got out of the car and went up to his room in the Handyman Arms. A bath and a meal and he'd probably feel all right. He fetched a towel and went down the passage to the bathroom. When he returned having immersed himself briefly in a lukewarm bath – the geyser still refused to operate at all efficiently – he was feeling better. He had dinner and decided that Hoskins was probably right. It might be useful to meet some of the more influential local people. Dundridge went out to his car and drove over to the Golf Club.

'Delighted you could make it,' said Hoskins when Dundridge made his way through the crush to him. 'What's your poison?'

Dundridge said he'd have a gin and tonic. He'd had enough beer for one day. Around him large men shouted about doglegs on the third and water hazards on the fifth. Dundridge felt out of it. Hoskins brought him his drink and introduced him to a Mr Snell. 'Glad to meet you, squire,' said Mr Snell heartily from behind a large moustache. 'What's your handicap?' Suppressing his immediate reaction to tell him to mind his own damned business, Dundridge said that as far as he knew he didn't have one. 'A Beginner, eh? Well, never mind. Give it time. We've all got to start somewhere.' He drifted away and Dundridge wandered in the opposite direction. Looking round the room at the veined faces of men and hennaed hair of the women Dundridge cursed himself for coming. If this was Hoskins' idea of local influence he could keep it. Presently he went out on to the terrace and stared resentfully down the eighteenth. He'd finish his drink and then go home. He drained his glass and was about to go inside when a voice at his elbow said, 'If you're going to the bar, you could get me another one.' It was a soft seductive voice. Dundridge turned and looked into a pair of almond eyes. Dundridge changed his mind about leaving. He went through to the bar and got two more drinks.

'These affairs are such a bore,' said the girl. 'Are you a great golfer?'

Dundridge said he wasn't a golfer at all.

'Nor am I. Such a boring game.' She sat down and crossed her legs. They were really very nice legs. 'And anyway I don't like sporty types. I prefer intellectuals.' She smiled at Dundridge. 'My name is Sally Boles. What's yours?'

'Dundridge,' said Dundridge and sat down where he could see more of her legs. Ten minutes later he got another two drinks. Twenty minutes later two more. He was enjoying himself at last.

Miss Boles, he learnt, was visiting her uncle. She came from London too. She worked for a firm of beauty consultants. Dundridge said he could well believe it. She found the country so boring. Dundridge said he did too. He waxed lyrical about the joys of living in London and all the time Miss Boles' almond eyes smiled seductively at him and her legs crossed and recrossed in the gathering dusk. When Dundridge suggested another drink Miss Boles insisted on getting it.

'It's my turn,' she said, 'and besides I want to powder my nose.' She left Dundridge sitting alone on the terrace in a happy stupor. When she returned with the drinks she was looking thoughtful.

'My uncle's gone without me,' she said, 'I suppose he thought I had gone home already. Would it be too much for you to give me a lift?'

'Of course not. I'd be delighted,' said Dundridge and sipped his drink. It tasted extraordinarily bitter.

'I'm so sorry, I got Campari,' Miss Boles said by way of explanation. Dundridge said it was quite all right. He finished his drink and they wandered off the terrace towards the car park. 'It's been such a lovely evening,' Miss Boles said as she climbed into Dundridge's car. 'You must look me up in London.'

'I'd like to,' said Dundridge. 'I'd like to see a lot more of you.'

'That's a promise,' said Miss Boles.

'You really mean that?'

'Call me Sally,' said Miss Boles and leant against him.

'Oh Sally . . .' Dundridge began, and suddenly felt quite extraordinarily tired, '. . . I do want to see so much more of you.'

'You will, my pet, you will,' said Miss Boles and took the car keys out of his inert fingers. Dundridge had passed out.

In London Sir Giles lay back supine on the bed while Mrs Forthby tightened the straps. Occasionally he struggled briefly for the look of the thing and whimpered hoarsely but Mrs Forthby was, at least superficially, implacable. The scenario of Sir Giles' fantasy called for a brutal implacability and Mrs Forthby did her best. She wasn't very good, being a kindhearted soul and not given to tying people up and whipping them, and as a matter of fact she disapproved of corporal punishment on principle. It was largely because she was so progressive that she was prepared to indulge Sir Giles in the first place. 'If it gives the poor man pleasure who am I to say him nay,' she told herself. Cetainly she had to say nay a great many times to Sir Giles in the throes of his ritual. But if Mrs Forthby wasn't naturally brutal, with the lights down low it was possible to imagine that she was and she had the merit of being strong and wearing her constume – there were several – most convincingly. Tonight she was Cat Woman, Miss Dracula, the Cruel Mistress Experimenting On Her Helpless Victim.

'No, no,' whimpered Sir Giles.

'Yes, yes,' insisted Mrs Forthby.

'No, no.'

'Yes, Yes.'

Mrs Forthby's fingers forced his mouth open and inserted the gag. 'No ...' it was too late. Mrs Forthby inflated the gag and smiled maliciously down at him. Her breasts loomed above him, heavy with menace. Her gloved hands ...

Mrs Forthby went into the kitchen and made a pot of tea. While she waited for the kettle to boil she nibbled a digestive biscuit thoughtfully. There were times when she tired of Sir Giles' desultory attachment and longed for a more permanent arrangement. She would have to speak to him about it. She warmed the teapot, put in two teabags and then a third for the pot and poured the boiling water in. After all she was getting on and she rather fancied the idea of being Lady Lynchwood. She looked round the kitchen. Now where had she put the lid of the teapot?

On the bed Sir Giles struggled with his bonds and was still. He lay back happily exhausted and waited for his cruel mistress. He had to wait a long time. In between spasms of excitement his mind went back to Dundridge. He hoped Hoskins hadn't made a bloody mess of things. That was the trouble with subordinates, you couldn't trust them. Sir Giles preferred to attend to matters himself but he had too much to lose to be closely involved in the actual details of this particular operation. First the stick and then the carrot. He wondered how much the carrot would have to be. Two, three, four thousand pounds? Expensive. Add Hoskins' five thousand. Still, it was worth it. A profit of £150,000 was worth it. So was the prospect of Maud's fury when she realized that the motorway was coming through the Gorge. Teach the stupid bitch. But where was Mrs Forthby? Why didn't she come back?

Mrs Forthby finished her cup of tea and poured another. She was getting rather hot in her tight costume. Perhaps she would go and have a bath. She got up and went into the bathroom and turned on the tap before remembering that there was something she still had to do. 'Silly old me: talk about forgetful,' she said to herself and picked up the thin cane. The Cruel Mistress, Miss Dracula, went through to the bedroom and closed the door.

In the library in the Lodge Blott sat reading Sir Arthur Bryant, but his mind wasn't on the Age of Elegance. It kept slipping away to Maud, Mrs Wynn, Dundridge, Sir Giles. Besides, he didn't much care for the Prince Regent. Nasty piece of goods in Blott's opinion. But then Blott had no time for any of the Georges. His sympathies were all with the Jacobites. The lost cause and Bonnie Prince Charlie. In his present mood of romantic devotion he felt a longing to kneel before Lady Maud and confess his love. It was an absurd notion. She would be furious with him. Worse still, she might laugh. The thought of her contemptuous laughter made him put the book down and go downstairs. It was a lovely evening. The sun had set over the hills to the west but the sky was still bright. Blott felt like a beer. He wasn't going over to Guildstead Carbonell for one. Mrs Wynn would expect him to spend the night and Blott didn't feel like another night with her. He had spent the previous evening wrestling with his conscience and trying to make up his mind to tell her it was all over between them. In the end his sense of realism had prevailed. Lady Maud wasn't for the likes of Blott. He would just have to dream about her. He had done so while making love to Mrs Wynn, who had been amazed at his renewed fervour. 'Just like the old days,' she had said wistfully as Blott got dressed to cycle back to the Lodge. No, he definitely didn't feel like another night at the Royal George. He would go for a walk. There were some rabbits over by the pinetum. Blott fetched his shotgun and set off across the Park. Beside him the river murmured gently and there was a smell of summer in the air. A blackbird called from a bush. Blott ignored his surroundings. He was dreaming of changed circumstances, of Lady Maud in peril, an act of heroism on his part that would reveal his true feelings for her and bring them together in love and happiness. By the time he reached the pinetum it was too dark to see any rabbits. But Blott wasn't interested in rabbits any more. A light had come on in Lady Maud's bedroom. Blott crept across the lawn and stood looking up at it until it went out. Then he walked home and went to bed.

CHAPTER TWELVE

Dundridge woke in a lay-by on the London road. He had a splitting headache, he was extremely cold and the gear lever was sticking into his ribs. He sat up, untangled his legs from under the steering wheel and wondered where the hell he was, how he had got there and what the devil had happened. He had an extremely clear memory of the party at the Golf Club. He could remember talking to Miss Boles on the terrace. He could even recall walking back to his car with her. After that nothing.

He got out of the car to try to get the circulation moving in his legs and discovered that his trousers were undone. He did them up hurriedly and reached up automatically to tighten the knot of his tie to hide his embarrassment only to find that he wasn't wearing a tie. He felt his open shirt collar and the vest underneath. It was on back to front. He pulled the vest out a bit and looked down at the label. St Michael Combed Cotton it said. It was definitely on back to front. Now he came to think of it, his Y-fronts felt peculiar too. He took a step forward and tripped over a shoelace. His shoes were untied. Dundridge staggered against the car, seriously alarmed. He was in the middle of nowhere at ... He looked at his watch. At six a.m. with his shoes untied, his vest and pants on back to front, and his trousers undone, and all he could remember was getting into the car with a girl with almond eyes and lovely legs.

And suddenly Dundridge had a horrid picture of the night's events. Perhaps he had raped the girl. A sudden brainstorm. That would explain the headache. The years of self-indulgence with his composite woman had come home to roost. He had gone mad and raped Miss Boles, possibly killed her. He looked down at his hands. At least there wasn't any blood on them. He could have strangled her. There was always that possibility. There were any number of awful possibilities. Dundridge bent over painfully and did up his shoes and then, having looked in the ditch to make sure that there was no body there, he got back into the car and wondered what to do. There was obviously no point in sitting in the lay-by. Dundridge started the car and drove on until he came to a signpost which told him he was going towards London. He turned the car round and drove back to Worford, parked in the yard of the Handyman Arms and went quietly up to his room. He was in bed when the girl brought him tea.

'What time is it?' he asked sleepily. The girl looked at him with a nasty smile.

'You ought to know,' she said, 'you've only just come in. I saw you sneaking up the stairs. Been having a night on the tiles, have you?'

She put the tray down and went out, leaving Dundridge cursing himself for a fool. He drank some tea and felt worse. There was no point in doing anything until he felt better. He turned on his side and went to sleep. When he awoke it was midday. He washed and shaved, studying his face in the mirror for some sign of the sexual mania he suspected. The face that stared back at him was a perfectly ordinary face but Dundridge was not reassured. Murderers tended to have perfectly ordinary faces. Perhaps he had simply had a blackout or amnesia. But that wouldn't explain his vest being on back to front, nor his Y-fronts. At some time during the night he had undressed. Worse still, he had dressed in such a hurry that he hadn't noticed what he was doing. That suggested panic or at least an extraordinary urgency. He went downstairs and had lunch. After lunch he would get hold of a telephone directory and look up Boles. Of course her uncle might not be called Boles but it was worth a try. If that didn't work he would try Hoskins or the Golf Club. On second thoughts, that might not be such a good idea. There was no point in drawing attention to the fact that he had taken Miss Boles home. Or hadn't.

In the event there was no need to look in the telephone directory. As he passed the hotel desk, the clerk handed him a large envelope. It was addressed to Mr Dundridge and marked Private and Confidential. Dundridge took it up to his room before opening it and was extremely thankful that he hadn't opened it in the foyer. Dundridge knew now how he had spent the night.

He dropped the photographs on to the bed and slumped into a chair. A moment later he was up and locking the door. Then he turned back and stared at the pictures. They were 10 by 8 glossies and quite revolting. Taken with a flash, they were extremely clear and portrayed Dundridge with an unmistakable clarity, naked and all too evidently unashamed, engaged in a series of monstrous activities beyond his wildest imaginings with Miss Boles. At least he supposed it was Miss Boles. The fact that she seemed ... Not seemed, *was* wearing a mask, a sort of hood, made identification impossible. He thumbed through the pictures and came to the hooded man. Dundridge hurriedly put them back in the envelope and sat sweating on the edge of the bed. He'd been framed. The word seemed wholly inappropriate. Nothing on God's earth would get him to frame these pictures. Someone was trying to blackmail him.

Trying? They had bloody well succeeded, but Dundridge had no money. He couldn't pay anything. Dundridge opened the envelope again and stared at the evidence of his depravity. Miss Boles? Miss Boles? It obviously wasn't her real name. Sally Boles. He had heard that name before somewhere. Of course, Sally Bowles in *I am a Camera*. Dundridge didn't need telling. He'd been had in many more ways than one. In many more ways if the photos were anything to go by.

He was just wondering what to do next when the telephone rang. Dundridge grabbed it. 'Yes,' he said.

'Mr Dundridge?' said a woman's voice.

'Speaking,' said Dundridge shakily.

'I hope you like the proofs.'

'Proofs, you bitch?' Dundridge snarled.

'Call me Sally,' said the voice. 'There's no need to be formal with me now.'

'What do you want?'

'A thousand pounds ... to be going on with.'

'A thousand pounds? I haven't got a thousand pounds.'

'Then you had better get it, hadn't you sweetie?'

'I'll tell you what I'm going to get,' shouted Dundridge, 'I'm going to get the police.'

'You do that,' said a man's voice roughly, 'and you'll end up with your face cut to ribbons. You're not playing with small fry, mate. We're bigtime, understand.'

Dundridge understood all too well. The woman's voice came back on the line. 'If you do go to the police remember we've had one or two customers there. We'll know. You just start looking for your thousand pounds.'

'I can't—'

'Don't call us. We'll call you,' said Miss Boles, and put the phone down. Dundridge replaced his receiver more slowly. Then he leant forward and held his head in his hands.

Sir Giles returned from London in excellent spirits. Mrs Forthby had excelled herself and he was still tingling with satisfaction. Best of all had been Hoskins' cryptic message over the phone. 'The fish is hooked,' he had said. All that was required now was to provide a net in which Mr Dundridge could flounder. Sir Giles parked his car and went up to his constituency office and sent for Hoskins.

'Here they are. As nice a set of prints as you could wish for,' Hoskins said, laying the photographs out on the desk.

Sir Giles studied them with an appreciative eye. 'Very nice,' he said finally. 'Very nice indeed. And what does lover-boy have to say for himself now?'

'They've asked him for a thousand pounds. He says he hasn't got it.'

'He'll have it, never fear,' said Sir Giles. 'He'll have his thousand pounds and we'll have him. There won't be any more talk about tunnels in future. From now on it's going to be Ottertown.'

'Ottertown?' said Hoskins, thoroughly puzzled. 'But I thought you wanted it through the Gorge. I thought—'

'The trouble with you, Hoskins,' said Sir Giles, putting the photographs back into the envelope and the envelope into his briefcase, 'is that you can't see further than the end of your nose. You don't really think I want to lose my lovely house and my beautiful wife, do you? You don't think I haven't got the interests of my constituents like General Burnett and Mr Bullett-Bloody-Finch at heart, do you? Of course I have. I'm honest Sir Giles the poor man's friend,' and leaving Hoskins completely confused by this strange change of tack, he went downstairs.

There was nothing like throwing people off the scent. Killing two birds with one stone, he thought as he got into the Bentley. The decision to go through Ottertown would kill Puckerington for sure. Sir Giles looked forward to his demise with relish. Puckerington was no friend of his. Snobby bastard. Well, he was bird number one. Then the bye-election in Ottertown and they would have to change the route to the Gorge and Handyman Hall would go. Bird number two. By that time he would be able to claim even more compensation and no one, least of all Maud, could say he hadn't done his damnedest. There was only one snag. That old fool Leakham might still insist on the Gorge route. It was hardly a snag. Maud would create a bit more. He might lose his seat in Parliament but he would be £150,000 richer and Mrs Forthby was waiting. Swings or roundabouts, Sir Giles couldn't lose. The main thing was to see that the tunnel scheme was scotched. Sir Giles parked outside the Handyman Arms, went inside and sent a message up to Dundridge's room to say that Sir Giles Lynchwood was looking forward to his company in the lounge.

Dundridge went downstairs gloomily. The last person he wanted to see was the local MP. He could hardly consult him about blackmail. Sir Giles greeted him with a heartiness Dundridge no longer felt that his position warranted. 'My dear fellow, I'm delighted to see you,' he said shaking Dundridge's limp hand vigorously. 'Been meaning to look you up and have a chat about this motorway nonsense. Had to go to London unfortunately. Looking after you all right here? It's one of our houses, you know. Any complaints, just let me know and I'll see to it. We'll have tea in the private lounge.' He led the way up some steps into a small lounge with a TV set in the corner. Sir Giles plumped into a chair and took out a cigar. 'Smoke?'

Dundridge shook his head.

'Very wise of you. Still they do say cigars don't do one any harm and a fellow's entitled to one or two little vices, eh, what?' said Sir Giles and pierced the end of the cigar with a silver cutter. Dundridge winced. The cigar reminded him of something that had figured rather too largely in his activities with Miss Boles, and as for vices ...

'Now then, about this business of the motorway,' said Sir Giles, 'I think it's as well to put our cards on the table. I'm a man who doesn't

beat about the bush I can tell you. Call a spade a bloody shovel. I don't
let the grass grow under my feet. Wouldn't be where I was if I did.' He
paused briefly to allow Dundridge to savour this wealth of metaphors
and the bluff dishonesty of his approach. 'And I don't mind telling you
that I don't like this idea of your building a motorway through my
damned land one little bit.'

'It was hardly my idea,' said Dundridge.

'Not yours personally,' said Sir Giles, 'but you fellows at the Ministry
have made up your mind to slap the bloody thing smack through the
Gorge. Don't tell me you haven't.'

'Well, as a matter of fact ...' Dundridge began.

'There you are. What did I tell you? Told you so. Can't pull the wool
over my eyes.'

'As a matter of fact I'm against the Gorge route,' Dundridge said when
he got the opportunity. Sir Giles looked at him dubiously.

'You are?' he said. 'Damned glad to hear it. I suppose you favour
Ottertown. Can't say I blame you. Best route by far.'

'No,' said Dundridge. 'Not through Ottertown. A tunnel under the
Cleene Hills ...'

Sir Giles feigned astonishment. 'Now wait a minute,' he said, 'the
Cleene Forest is an area of designated public beauty. You can't start
mucking around with that.' His accent, as variable as a weathercock,
had veered round to Huddersfield.

'There's no question of mucking about ...' Dundridge began but Sir
Giles was leaning across the table towards him with a very nasty look on
his face.

'You can say that again,' he said poking his forefinger into Dundridge's
shirt front. 'Now you just listen to me, young man. You can forget all
about tunnels and suchlike. I want a quick decision one way or t'other.
I don't like to be kept hanging about while lads like you dither about
talking a lot of airy twaddle about tunnels. That's all right for my missus,
she being a gullible woman, but it won't wash with me. I want a straight
answer. Yes or No. Yes to Ottertown and No to the Gorge.' He sat back
and puffed his cigar.

'In that case,' said Dundridge stiffly, 'you had better have a word with
Lord Leakham. He's the one who makes the final decision.'

'Leakham? Leakham? Makes the final decision?' said Sir Giles. 'Don't
try to have me on, lad. The Minister didn't send you up so that that dry
old stick could make decisions. He sent you up to tell him what to say.
You can't fool me. I know an expert when I see one. He'll do what you
tell him.'

Dundridge felt better. This was the recognition he had been waiting for. 'Well I suppose I do have some influence,' he conceded.

Sir Giles beamed. 'What did I say? Top men don't grow on trees and I've got a nose for talent. Well, you won't find me ungenerous. You pop round and see me when you've had your little chat with Lord Leakham. I'll see you right.'

Dundridge goggled at him. 'You don't mean—'

'Name your own charity,' said Sir Giles with a prodigious wink. 'Mind you, I always say "Charity begins at home". Eh? I'm not a mean man. I pays for what I gets.' He drew on his cigar and watched Dundridge through a cloud of smoke. This was the moment of truth. Dundridge swallowed nervously.

'That's very kind of you ...' he began.

'Say no more,' said Sir Giles. 'Say no more. Any time you want me I'll be in my constituency office or out at the Hall. Best time to catch me is in the morning at the office.'

'But what am I going to say to Lord Leakham?' Dundridge said. 'He's adamant about the Gorge route.'

'You tell him from me that my good lady wife intends to take him to the cleaners about that unlawful arrest unless he decides for Ottertown. You tell him that.'

'I don't think Lord Leakham would appreciate that very much,' said Dundridge nervously. He didn't much like the idea of uttering threats against the old judge.

'You'll tell him I'll sue him for every brass farthing he's got. And I've got witnesses, remember. Influential witnesses who'll stand up in court and swear that he was drunk and disorderly at that Inquiry, and abusive too. You tell him he won't have a reputation and he won't have a penny by the time we've finished with him. I'll see to that.'

'I doubt if he'll like it,' said Dundridge, who certainly didn't.

'Don't suppose he will,' said Sir Giles, 'I'm not a man to run up against.'

Dundridge could see that. By the time Sir Giles left Dundridge had no doubts on that score at all. As Sir Giles drove away Dundridge went up to his room and looked at the photographs again. Spurred on by their obscenity he took an aspirin and went slowly round to the Cottage Hospital. He'd make Lord Leakham change his mind about the Gorge. Sir Giles had said he would pay for what he got and Dundridge intended to see that he got something to pay for. He didn't have any choice any longer. It was either that or ruin.

On the way back to Handyman Hall, Sir Giles stopped and unlocked his briefcase and took out the photographs. They were really very interesting. Mrs Williams was an imaginative woman. No doubt about it. And attractive. Most attractive. He might look her up one of these days. He put the photographs away and drove back to the Hall.

CHAPTER THIRTEEN

At the Cottage Hospital Dundridge had some difficulty in finding Lord Leakham. He wasn't in his room. 'It's very naughty of him to wander about like this,' said the Matron. 'You'll probably find him in the Abbey. He's taken to going over there when he shouldn't. Says he likes looking at the tombstones. Morbid, I call it.'

'You don't think his mind has been affected, do you?' Dundridge asked hopefully.

'Not so's you'd notice. All lords are potty in my experience,' the Matron told him.

In the end Dundridge found him in the garden discussing the merits of the cat o'nine tails with a retired vet who had the good fortune to be deaf.

'Well what do you want now?' Lord Leakham asked irritably when Dundridge interrupted.

'Just a word with you,' said Dundridge.

'Well, what is it?' said Lord Leakham.

'It's about the motorway,' Dundridge explained.

'What about it? I'm re-opening the Inquiry on Monday. Can't it wait till then?'

'I'm afraid not,' said Dundridge. 'The thing is that as a result of an in-depth on-the-spot investigative study of the socio-environmental and geognostic ancillary factors ...'

'Good God,' said Lord Leakham, 'I thought you said you wanted a word ...'

'It is our considered conclusion,' continued Dundridge, manfully devising a jargon to suit the occasion, 'that given the—'

'Which is it to be? Ottertown or the Cleene Gorge? Spit it out, man.'

'Ottertown,' said Dundridge.

'Over my dead body,' said Lord Leakham.

'I trust not,' said Dundridge, disguising his true feelings. 'There's just one other thing I think you ought to know. As you are probably aware the Government is most anxious to avoid any further adverse publicity about the motorway ...'

'You can't expect to demolish seventy-five brand-new council houses without attracting adverse publicity,' Lord Leakham pointed out.

'And,' continued Dundridge, 'the civil action for damages which Lady Lynchwood intends to institute against you is bound—'

'Against *me*?' shouted the Judge. 'She intends to—'

'For unlawful arrest,' said Dundridge.

'That's a police matter. If she has any complaints let her sue those responsible. In any case no sane judge would find for her.'

'I understand she intends to call some rather eminent people as witnesses,' said Dundridge. 'Their testimony will be that you were drunk.'

Lord Leakham began to swell.

'And personally abusive,' said Dundridge gritting his teeth. 'And disorderly. In fact that you were not in a fit state ...'

'WHAT?' yelled the Judge, with a violence that sent several elderly patients scurrying for cover and a number of pigeons fluttering off the hospital roof.

'In short,' said Dundridge as the echo died away across the Abbey Close, 'she intends to impugn your reputation. Naturally the Minister has to take all these things into account, you do see that?'

But it was doubtful if Lord Leakham could see anything. He had slumped on to a bench and was staring lividly at his bedroom slippers.

'Naturally too,' continued Dundridge, pursuing his advantage, 'there is a fairly widespread feeling that you might be biased against her in the matter of the Gorge.'

'Biased?' Lord Leakham snuffled. 'The Gorge is the logical route.'

'On the grounds of the civil action she intends to take. Now if you were to decide on Ottertown ...' Dundridge left the consequences hanging in the air.

'You think she might reconsider her decision?'

'I feel sure she would,' said Dundridge. 'In fact I'm positive she would.'

Dundridge walked back to the Handyman Arms rather pleased with his performance. Desperation had lent him a fluency he had never known before. In the morning he would go and see Sir Giles about a thousand pounds. He had an early dinner and went up to his room, locked the door and examined the photographs again. Then he turned out the light and considered several things he hadn't done to Miss Sally Boles but which on reflection he wished he had. Strangled the bitch for one thing.

At Handyman Hall Sir Giles and Lady Maud dined alone. Their

conversation seldom sparkled and was usually limited to an exchange of acrimonious opinions but for once they were both in a good mood at the same time. Dundridge was the cause of their good humour.

'Such a sensible young man,' Lady Maud said helping herself to asparagus. 'I'm sure that tunnel is the right answer.'

Sir Giles rather doubted it. 'My bet is he'll go for Ottertown,' he said.

Lady Maud said she hoped not. 'It seems such a shame to turn those poor people out of their homes. I'm sure they would feel just as strongly as I do about the Hall.'

'They build them new houses,' said Sir Giles. 'It's not as if they turn them out into the street. Anyway, people who live on council estates deserve what they get. Sponging off public money.'

Lady Maud said some people couldn't help being poor. They were just built that way like Blott. 'Dear Blott,' she said. 'You know he did such a strange thing this morning, he brought me a present, a little figure he had carved out of wood.'

But Sir Giles wasn't listening. He was still thinking about people who lived in council houses. 'What the man in the street doesn't seem able to get into his thick head is that the world doesn't owe him a living.'

'I thought it was rather sweet of him,' said Lady Maud.

Sir Giles helped himself to cheese soufflé. 'What people don't understand is that we're just animals,' he said. 'The world is a bloody jungle. It's dog eat dog in this life and no mistake.'

'Dog?' said Lady Maud, roused from her reverie by the word. 'That reminds me. I suppose I'll have to send all those Alsatians back now. Just when I was getting fond of them. You're quite sure Mr Dundridge is going to advise Ottertown?'

'Positive,' said Sir Giles, 'I'd stake my life on it.'

'Really,' said Lady Maud wistfully, 'I don't see how you can be so certain. Have you spoken to him?'

Sir Giles hesitated. 'I have it on the best authority,' he said.

'Hoskins,' said Lady Maud, 'that horrid man. I wouldn't trust him any further than I could throw him. He'd say anything.'

'He also says that this fellow Dundridge has taken a fancy to you,' Sir Giles said. 'It seems you had a considerable effect on him.'

Lady Maud considered the remark and found it intriguing. 'I'm sure that can't be true. Hoskins is making things up.'

'It might explain why he is in favour of the Ottertown route,' Sir Giles said. 'You bowled him over with your charm.'

'Very funny,' said Lady Maud.

But afterwards as she washed up in the kitchen she found herself thinking about Dundridge, if not fondly, at least with a renewed interest. There was something rather appealing about the little man, a vulnerability that she found preferable to Sir Giles' disgusting self-sufficiency ... and Dundridge had taken a fancy to her. It was useful to know these things. She would have to cultivate him. She smiled to herself. If Sir Giles could have his little affairs in London, there was no reason why she shouldn't avail herself of his absence for her own purposes. But above all there was an anonymity about Dundridge that appealed to her. 'He'll do,' she said to herself and dried her hands.

Next morning Dundridge went round to Sir Giles' constituency office at eleven. 'I've had a word with Lord Leakham and I think he'll be amenable,' he said.

'Splendid, my dear fellow, splendid. Delighted to hear it. I knew you could do it. A great weight off my mind, I can tell you. Now then is there anything I can do for you?' Sir Giles leant back in his chair expansively. 'After all, one good turn deserves another.'

Dundridge braced himself for the request. 'As a matter of fact, there is,' he said, and hesitated before going on.

'I'll tell you what I'll do,' said Sir Giles coming to his rescue. 'I don't know if you're a betting man but I am. I'll bet you a thousand pounds to a penny that old Leakham says the motorway has to go through Ottertown. How about that? Couldn't ask for anything fairer, eh?'

'A thousand pounds to a penny?' said Dundridge, hardly able to believe his ears.

'That's right. A thousand pounds to a penny. Take it or leave it.'

'I'll take it,' said Dundridge.

'Good man. I thought you would,' said Sir Giles, 'and just to show my good faith I'll put the stake up now.' He reached down to a drawer in the desk and took out an envelope. 'You can count it at your leisure.' He put the envelope on the desk. 'No need for a receipt. Just don't spend it until Leakham gives his decision.'

'Of course not,' said Dundridge. He put the envelope in his pocket.

'Nice meeting you,' said Sir Giles. Dundridge went out and down the stairs. He had accepted a bare-faced bribe. It was the first time in his life. Behind him Sir Giles switched off the tape recorder. It was just as well to have a receipt. Once the Inquiry was over he would burn the tape but in the meantime better safe than sorry.

CHAPTER FOURTEEN

Lord Leakham's announcement that he was recommending the Ottertown route provoked mixed reactions. In Worford there was open rejoicing and the Handyman pubs dispensed free beer. In Ottertown the Member of Parliament, Francis Puckerington, was inundated with telephone calls and protest letters and suffered a relapse as a result. In London the Prime Minister, relieved that there hadn't been another riot in Worford, congratulated the Minister of the Environment on the adroit way his department had handled the matter, and the Minister congratulated Mr Rees on his choice of a troubleshooter. No one in the Ministry shared his enthusiasm.

'That bloody idiot Dundridge has dropped us in it this time,' said Mr Joynson. 'I knew it was a mistake to send him up there. The Ottertown route is going to cost an extra ten million.'

'In for a penny in for a pound,' said Rees. 'At least we've got rid of him.'

'Got rid of him? He'll be back tomorrow crowing about his success as a negotiator.'

'He won't you know,' Rees told him. 'He got us into this mess, he can damned well get us out. The Minister had approved his appointment as Controller Motorways Midlands.'

'Controller Motorways Midlands? I didn't know there was such a post.'

'There wasn't. It's been specially created for him. Don't ask me why. All I know is that Dundridge has found favour with one or two influential people in South Worfordshire. Wheels within wheels,' said Mr Rees.

In Worford Dundridge greeted the news of his appointment with consternation. He had spent an anxious weekend confined to his room at the Handyman Arms partly because he was afraid of missing the telephone call from Miss Boles and partly because he had no intention of leaving the money he had received from Sir Giles in his suitcase or of carrying it around on his person. But there had been no phone call. To add to his troubles, there was the knowledge that he had accepted a bribe. He tried to persuade himself that he had merely taken a bet on, but it was no use.

'I could get three years for this,' he said to himself, and seriously considered handing the money back. He was deterred by the photographs.

He couldn't imagine how many years he could get for doing what they suggested he had done.

By the time the Inquiry re-opened on Monday, Dundridge's nerves were frayed to breaking point. He had taken his seat inconspicuously at the back of the courtroom and had hardly listened to the evidence. The presence of a large number of policemen, brought in to ensure that there was no further outbreak of violence, had done nothing to reassure him. Dundridge had misconstrued their role and had finally left the courtroom before Lord Leakham announced his decision. He was standing in the hall downstairs when a burst of cheering indicated that the Inquiry was over.

Sir Giles and Lady Maud were the first to congratulate him. They issued from the courtroom and down the stairs followed by General Burnett and Mr and Mrs Bullet-Finch.

'Splendid news,' said Sir Giles. Lady Maud seized Dundridge's hand.

'I feel we owe you a great debt of gratitude,' she said staring into his face significantly.

'It was nothing,' murmured Dundridge modestly.

'Nonsense,' said Lady Maud, 'you have made me very happy. You must come and see us before you leave.'

Sir Giles had winked prodigiously – Dundridge had come to loathe that wink – and had whispered something about a bet being a bet and Hoskins had insisted on their going to have a drink together to celebrate. Dundridge couldn't see anything to celebrate about.

'You've got friends at court,' Hoskins explained.

'Friends at court?' said Dundridge. 'What on earth do you mean?'

'A little bird has told me that someone has put in a good word for you. You wait and see.'

Dundridge had waited in the hope (though that was hardly the right word) that Miss Boles would call but instead of a demand for a thousand pounds he had received a letter of appointment. 'Controller Motorways Midlands with responsibility for co-ordinating ... Good God!' he muttered. He made a number of frantic phone calls to the Ministry threatening to resign unless he was brought back to London, but the enthusiasm with which Mr Rees endorsed his decision was enough to make him retract it.

Even Hoskins, who might have been expected to resent Dundridge's appointment as his superior, seemed relieved. 'What did I tell you, old boy,' he said when Dundridge told him the news. 'Friends at court. Friends at court.'

'But I don't know anything about motorway construction. I'm an administrator not an engineer.'

'All you have to do is see that the contractors keep to schedule,' Hoskins explained. 'Nothing to it. You leave all the rest of it to me. Basically yours is a public-relations role.'

'But I'm responsible for coordinating construction work. It says so here,' Dundridge protested, waving his letter of appointment, '"and in particular problems relating to environmental factors and human ecology". I suppose that means dealing with the tenants of those council houses in Ottertown.'

'That sort of thing,' said Hoskins. 'I shouldn't worry about that too much. Cross your bridges when you come to them is my motto.'

'Oh well, I suppose I'll just have to get used to the idea.'

'I'll fix you up an office here. You'd better set about finding somewhere to live.'

Dundridge had spent two days looking at flats in Worford before settling on an apartment overlooking Worford Castle. It wasn't a prospect he found particularly pleasing, but the flat had the merit of being comparatively modern and was certainly better than some of the squalid rooms he had looked at elsewhere. And besides it had a telephone and was partly furnished. Dundridge placed particular emphasis upon the telephone. He didn't want Miss Boles to get the false idea that he wasn't prepared to pay a thousand pounds for the photographs and negatives. But as the days passed and there was still no demand from her he began to relax. Perhaps the whole thing had been some sort of filthy practical joke. He even asked Hoskins if he knew anything about the girl at the party but Hoskins said he couldn't remember much about the evening and hadn't known half the people who were there.

'My mind's a blank on the whole evening, old chap,' he said. 'Had a good time, though. I do remember that. Why? Are you thinking of looking her up again?'

'Just wondered who she was,' said Dundridge and went back to his office to draw up plans for the opening ceremony to mark the start of the construction of the motorway. It was going to be a grand affair, he had decided.

So had Lady Maud, though the affair she had in mind was of quite a different sort. She waited until Sir Giles said he was going to spend a fortnight in London before inviting Dundridge to dinner. She sent a formal invitation.

Dundridge hired a dinner-jacket **and** expected to find a number of other guests. He was extremely nervous and had fortified himself in advance with two stiff gins. In the event he need not have bothered. He arrived to find Lady Maud dressed, if not to kill, at least to seriously endanger anyone who came near her.

'I'm so glad you could come,' she said taking his arm almost as soon as he had entered the front door. 'I'm afraid my husband has had to go to London on business. I hope you don't mind having to put up with me.'

'Not at all,' said Dundridge, conscious once again of that weakness in his legs that Lady Maud's presence seemed to induce in him. They went into the drawing-room and Lady Maud mixed drinks. 'I did think of inviting General Burnett and the Bullett-Finches but the General does tend to monopolize the conversation and Ivy Bullett-Finch is a bit of a wet blanket.'

Dundridge sipped his drink and wondered what the hell she had put into it. It looked innocuous, but clearly wasn't. Lady Maud's dress, on the other hand, practised no such deception. A thing of silk designed to emphasize the curvature of the female form, it had evidently been created with someone more lissom in mind. It bulged where it should have hung and wheezed when it should have rustled. Above all it was so clearly breathtaking in its constriction that Dundridge found himself almost panting in empathy. Besides Lady Maud's voice had undergone a strange alteration. It was curiously husky.

'How do you like your new flat?' she asked, sitting down beside him with a squeak of pre-stressed silk.

'Flat?' said Dundridge momentarily unable to make the transition between adjective and noun. 'Oh flat. Yes. Very pleasant.'

'You must let me come up and see it some time,' said Lady Maud. 'Unless you feel I might be compromising you.' She sighed, and her great bosom heaved like an approaching breaker.

'Compromising?' said Dundridge, who couldn't imagine that he was likely to be compromised by being alone in his flat with her any more than he was already by those beastly photographs. 'I'd be delighted to have you.'

Lady Maud tittered coyly. 'I'm afraid you're going to miss the excitement of life in London,' she murmured. 'We must do what we can to see that you don't get bored.'

It seemed a remote prospect to Dundridge. He sat rigid on the sofa and tried to keep his eyes averted from the incomprehensible fascinations of her body.

'Let me get you another drink,' she breathed softly, and once again he was conscious of a feeling of being overcome. It was partly the drink, partly the waft of perfume, but it was mostly the strength of her self-assurance that held him fascinated. In spite of her size, in spite of her assertiveness, in spite of everything about her that conflicted with his idea of a beautiful woman, Lady Maud was wholly confident. And Dundridge, who wasn't (or at best only partially and whose completeness, depending on achievement and money, lay in the future) was intoxicated by her presence. If the past could confer such assurance there was more to be said for it than Dundridge had previously admitted. Dundridge sipped his drink and smiled at her. Lady Maud smiled back.

By the time they went in to dinner, Dundridge was incongruously gay. He opened the door for her; he held her arm; he pulled back her chair and nudged it forward against her thighs meaningfully; he opened the champagne with a nonchalance that suggested he seldom drank anything else and laughed debonairly as the cork tinkled among the glass lustres of the chandelier. And through the meal, oysters followed by cold duck, Dundridge no longer cared what the world might think of him. Lady Maud's appreciative smile, half yawn and half abyss, beckoned him on to be himself. And Dundridge was. For the first time in his life he lived up to his own expectations, up to and far beyond. The champagne cork flew a second time into the upper reaches of the room, the duck disappeared to be followed by strawberries and cream, and Dundridge lost the last vestiges of inhibition or even the apprehension that there was anything at all unusual about dining alone with a married woman whose husband was away on business. All such considerations vanished in the bubble of his gaiety and in the light of Lady Maud's approval. Under the table her knee confirmed the implications of her smile; on top her hand lay heavily on his and traced the contours of his fingers; and when, their coffee finished, she took his arm and suggested that they dance Dundridge heard himself say he would be delighted to. Arm-in-arm they went down the passage to the ballroom with the sprung floor. Only then, with the chandeliers lighting the great room brilliantly and a record on the turntable, did he realize what he had let himself in for. Dundridge had never danced in his life.

Blott walked down the hill from Wilfrid's Castle. For a week he had been avoiding the Royal George in Guildstead Carbonell and Mrs Wynn's favours. He had taken to going over to a small pub on the lane leading from the church to the Ottertown Road. It wasn't up to the standard of the Royal George, merely a room with benches round the walls and a barrel of Handyman beer in one corner, but its dismal atmosphere suited

Blott's mood. By the time he had silently consumed eight pints he was ready for bed. He wobbled up the hill past the church and stood gazing down at the Hall in amazement. The great ballroom lights were on. Blott couldn't remember when he had last seen them on, certainly not since Lady Maud's marriage. They cast yellow rectangles on to the lawn, and the conservatory which opened out of the ballroom glowed green with ferns and palms. He stumbled down the path and across the bridge into the pinetum. Here it was pitch-dark but Blott knew his way instinctively. He came out at the gate and crossed the lawn to the terrace. Music, old-fashioned music, floated out towards him. Blott went round the corner and peered through the window.

Inside Lady Maud was dancing. Or learning to dance. Or teaching someone to dance. Blott found difficulty in making up his mind. Under the great chandeliers she moved with a tender gracelessness that took his breath away. Up and down, round and about, in great sweeps and double turns she went, the floor moving visibly beneath her, and in her arms she held a small thin man with an expression of intense concentration on his face. Blott recognized him. He was the man from the Ministry who had stayed to lunch the previous week. Blott hadn't liked the look of him then and he liked it even less now. And Sir Giles was away. Sick with disgust Blott blundered off the flower bed and away from the window. He had half a mind to go in and say what he thought. It wouldn't do any good. He walked unsteadily round the front of the house. There was a car standing there. He peered at it. The man's car. Serve him right if he had to walk home, the bastard. Blott knelt by the front tyre and undid the valve. Then he went round to the boot and let the air out of the spare tyre. That would teach the swine to come messing about with other people's wives. Blott staggered off down the drive to the Lodge and climbed into bed. Through the circular window he could see the lights of the Hall. They were still on when he fell asleep and through the night air there came the faint sound of trombones.

CHAPTER FIFTEEN

What drinks, dinner and Lady Maud's assiduous coquetry had done for Dundridge, dancing had undone. In particular her interpretation of the hesitation waltz – Dundridge considered the probability of a slipped disc – while her tango had threatened hernia. All his attempts to get her to do something a little less complicated had been ignored.

'You're doing splendidly,' she said treading on his toes. 'All you need is a little practice.'

'What about something modern?' said Dundridge.

'Modern dancing is so unromantic,' said Maud, changing the record to a quickstep. 'There's no intimacy in it.'

Intimacy was not what Dundridge had in mind. 'I think I'll sit this one out,' he said limping to a chair. But Lady Maud wouldn't hear of it. She whirled him on to the floor and strode off through a series of half-turns clasping him to her bosom with a grip that brooked no argument. When the record stopped Dundridge put his foot down politely.

'I really think it is time I was off,' he said.

'What? So early? Just one more teeny weeny glass of champers,' said Lady Maud, relapsing rather prematurely into the language of the nursery.

'Oh all right,' said Dundridge choosing the devil of drink to the deep blue sea of the dance floor. They took their glasses through to the conservatory and stood for a moment among the ferns.

'What a wonderful night. Let's go out on the terrace,' said Lady Maud and took his arm. They leant on the stone balustrade and looked into the darkness of the pinetum.

'All we need now is a lover's moon,' Lady Maud murmured and turned to face him. Dundridge looked up into the night sky. It was long past his bedtime and besides not even the champagne could disguise the fact that he was in an ambiguous situation. He had had enough of ambiguous situations lately to last him a lifetime and he certainly didn't relish the thought of Sir Giles returning home unexpectedly to find him on the terrace drinking champagne with his wife at one o'clock in the morning.

'It looks as if it's going to rain,' he said to change the topic from lovers' moons.

'Silly boy,' cooed Lady Maud. 'It's a lovely starlit night.'

'Yes. Well, I really do think I must be getting along,' Dundridge insisted. 'It's been a lovely evening.'

'Oh well if you must go ...' They went indoors again.

'Just one more glass ...?' Lady Maud said but Dundridge shook his head and limped on down the passage.

'You must look me up again,' said Lady Maud as he climbed into his car. 'The sooner the better. It's been ages since I had so much fun.' She waved goodbye and Dundridge drove off down the drive. He didn't get very far. There was something dreadfully wrong with the steering. The car seemed to veer to the left all the time and there was a thumping sound. Dundridge stopped and got out and went round to the front.

'Damn,' said Dundridge feeling the flat tyre. He went to the boot and got the jack out. By the time he had jacked the car up and taken the left front wheel off, the lights in the Hall had gone out. He fetched the spare wheel from the boot and bolted it into place. He let the jack down and stowed it away. Then he got back into the car and started the engine and drove off. There was a thumping noise and the car pulled to the left. Dundridge stopped with a curse.

'I must have put the flat tyre on again,' he muttered and got out the jack.

In the Hall Lady Maud switched off the ballroom lights sadly. She had enjoyed the evening and was sorry it has ended so tamely. There had been a moment earlier in the evening when she had thought Dundridge was going to prove amenable to her few charms.

'Men,' she said contemptuously as she undressed and stood looking at herself dispassionately in the mirror. She was not, and she was the first to admit it, a beautiful woman by contemporary standards of beauty but then she didn't pay much heed to contemporary standards of any sort. The world she lived for had admired substantial things, large women, heavy furniture, healthy appetites and strong feelings. She had no time for the present with its talk of sex, its girlish men and boyish women, and its reducing diets. She longed to be swept off her feet by a strong man who knew the value of bed, board and babies. She wasn't going to find him in Dundridge.

'Silly little goose doesn't know what he's missing,' she said and climbed into bed.

Outside the silly little goose knew only too well what he was missing. An inflated tyre. He had changed the wheel again and let down the jack only to find that his spare tyre had been flat after all. He got back into the car and tried to think what to do. Nearby something moved heavily through the grass and a night bird called. Dundridge shut the door. He couldn't sit there all night. He got out of the car and trudged back up the drive to the house and rang the doorbell.

Upstairs Lady Maud climbed out of bed and turned on the light. So the silly little goose had come back after all. He had caught her unprepared. She grabbed a lipstick and daubed her lips hastily, powdered her face and put a dollop of Chanel behind each ear. Finally she changed out of her pyjamas and slid into a see-through nightdress and went downstairs and opened the door.

'I'm sorry to bother you like this but I'm afraid I've had a puncture,' said Dundridge nervously. Lady Maud smiled knowingly.

'A puncture?'

'Yes, two as a matter of fact.'

'Two punctures?'

'Yes. Two,' said Dundridge conscious that there was something rather improbable about having two punctures at the same time.

'You had better come in,' said Lady Maud eagerly. Dundridge hesitated.

'If I could just use the phone to call a garage ...'

But Lady Maud wouldn't hear of it. 'Of course you can't,' she said, 'it's far too late for anyone to come out now.' She took his arm and led him into the house and closed the door.

'I'm terribly sorry to be such a nuisance,' said Dundridge but Lady Maud shushed him.

'What a silly boy you are,' she cooed. 'Now come upstairs and we'll see about a bed.'

'Oh really ...' Dundridge began but it was no good. She turned and led the way, a perfumed spinnaker, up the marble staircase. Dundridge followed miserably.

'You can have this room,' she said as they stood on the landing and she switched on the light. 'Now you go down to the bathroom and have a wash and I'll make the bed up.'

'The bathroom?' said Dundridge gazing at her astonished. In the dim light of the hall Lady Maud had been a mere if substantial shape but now he could see the full extent of her abundant charms. Her face was extraordinary too. Lady Maud smiled, a crimson gash with teeth. And the perfume!

'It's down the corridor on the left.'

Dundridge stumbled down the corridor and tried several doors before he found the bathroom. He went inside and locked the door. When he came out he found the corridor in darkness. He groped his way back to the landing and tried to remember which room she had given him. Finally he found one that was open. It was dark inside. Dundridge felt for the switch but it wasn't where he had expected.

'Is there anyone there?' he whispered but there was no reply. 'This must be the room,' he muttered and closed the door. He edged across the room and felt the end of the bed. A faint light came from the window. Dundridge undressed and noticed that Lady Maud's perfume still lingered heavily on the air. He went across to the window and opened it and then, moving carefully so as not to stub his toes, he went back and got into bed. As he did so he knew there was something terribly wrong. A blast of Chanel No. 5 issued from the bedclothes overpoweringly. So did Lady Maud. Her arms closed round him and with a husky, 'Oh you wicked boy,' her mouth descended on his. The next moment Dundridge was engulfed. Things seemed to fold round him, huge hot terrible things, legs, arms, breasts, lips, noses, thighs, bearing him up, entwining him, and bearing him down again in a frenzy of importunate flesh. He floundered frantically while the waves of Lady Maud's mistaken response broke over him. Only his mind remained untrammelled, his mind and his inhibitions. As he writhed in her arms his thoughts raced to a number of ghastly conclusions. He had chosen the wrong room; she was in love with him; he was in bed with a nymphomaniac; she was providing her husband with grounds for divorce; she was seducing him. There was no question about the last. She was seducing him. Her hands left him in no doubt about that, particularly her left hand. And Dundridge, accustomed to the wholly abstract stimulus of his composite woman, found the inexperience of a real woman – and Lady Maud was both real and inexperienced – hard to put up with.

'There's been a terr—' he managed to squeak as Lady Maud surfaced for air, but a moment later her mouth closed over his, silencing his protest while threatening him with suffocation. It was this last that gave him the desperation he needed. With a truly Herculean revulsion Dundridge hurled himself and Lady Maud, still clinging limpetlike to him, out of the bed. With a crash the bedside table fell to the floor as Dundridge broke free and leapt to his feet. The next moment he was through the door and running down the corridor. Behind him Lady Maud staggered to the bed and pulled the light cord. Stunned by the vigour of his rejection and by the bedside table which had caught her on the side of the head, she lumbered into the corridor and turned on the light but there was no sign of Dundridge.

'There's no need to be shy,' she called but there was no reply. She went into the next room and switched on the light. No Dundridge. The next room was empty too. She went from room to room switching on lights and calling his name, but Dundridge had vanished. Even the bathroom was unlocked and empty and she was just wondering where to look next when a sound from the landing drew her attention. She went back and switched on the hall light and caught him in the act of tiptoeing down the stairs. For an instant he stood there, a petrified satyr, and turned pathetic eyes towards her and then he was off down the stairs and across the marble floor, his slender legs and pale feet twinkling among the squares. Lady Maud leant over the balustrade and laughed.

She was still laughing as she went down the staircase, laughing and holding on to the banister to keep herself from falling. Her laughter echoed in the emptiness of the hall and filtered down the corridors.

In the darkness by the kitchen Dundridge listened to it and shuddered. He had no idea where he was and there was a demented quality about that laughter that appalled him. He was just wondering what to do when, silhouetted against the hall light at the end of the passage he saw her bulky outline. She had stopped laughing and was peering into the gloom.

'It's all right, you can come out now,' she called, but Dundridge knew better. He understood now why his car had two flat tyres, why he had been invited to the Hall when Sir Giles was away. Lady Maud was a raving nymphomaniac. He was alone in a huge house in the middle of the back of beyond with no clothes on, a disabled car and an enormously powerful and naked female lunatic. Nothing on God's earth would induce him to come out now. As Lady Maud lumbered down the passage Dundridge turned and fled, collided with a table, lurched into some iron banisters and was off up the servants' stairs. Behind him a light went on. As he reached the landing he glanced back and saw Lady Maud's face staring up at him. One glance was enough to confirm his fears. The smudged lipstick, the patches of rouge, the disordered hair ... mad as a hatter. Dundridge scampered down another corridor and behind him came the final proof of her madness.

'Tally ho,' shouted Lady Maud. 'Gone away.' Dundridge went away as fast as he could.

In the Lodge, Blott woke up and stared out through the circular window. Dimly below the rim of the hills he could see the dark shape of the Hall and he was about to turn over and go back to sleep when a light came on in an upstairs room to be followed almost immediately by another and then a third. Blott sat up in bed and watched as one room after another lit up. He glanced at his clock and saw it was ten past two. He looked back towards the house and saw the stained glass roof-light above the hall glowing. He got up and opened the window and stared out and as he did so there came the faint sound of hysterical laughter. Or crying. Lady Maud. Blott pulled on a pair of trousers, put on his slippers, took his twelve-bore and ran downstairs. There was something terribly wrong up at the house. He ran up the drive, almost colliding in the darkness with Dundridge's car. The bastard was still around. Probably chasing her from room to room. That would explain the lights going on and the hysterical laughter. He'd soon put a stop to that. Clutching his shotgun he went through the stable yard and in the kitchen door. The lights were on. Blott went across to the passage and listened. There was no sound now. He went down the passage to the hall and stood there. Must be upstairs. He was halfway up when Lady Maud emerged from a corridor on to the landing breathlessly. She ran across the landing to the top of the stairs and stood looking down at Blott naked as the day she was born. Blott gaped up at her open mouthed. There above him was the woman he loved. Clothed she had been splendid. Naked she was perfection. Her great breasts, her stomach, her magnificent thighs, she was everything Blott had ever dreamed of and, to make matters even better, she was clearly in distress. Tear-stains ran down her daubed cheeks. His moment of heroism on her behalf had arrived.

'Blott,' said Lady Maud, 'what on earth are you doing here? And what are you doing with that gun?'

'I am here at your service,' said Blott gallantly assuming the language of history.

'At my service?' said Lady Maud, oblivious of the fact that she wasn't exactly dressed for discussions about service with her gardener. 'What do you mean by my service? You're here to look after the garden, not to wander about the house in the middle of the night in your bedroom slippers armed with a shotgun.'

On the staircase Blott bowed before the storm. 'I came to protect your honour,' he murmured.

'My honour? You came to protect my honour? With a shotgun? Are you out of your mind?'

Blott was beginning to wonder. He had come up expecting to find her lying raped and murdered, or at least pleading for mercy, and here she was standing naked at the top of the stairs dressing him down. It didn't seem right. It didn't seem exactly right to Lady Maud now that she came to think of it. She turned and went into her bedroom and put on a dressing-gown.

'Now then,' she said with a renewed sense of authority, 'what's all this nonsense about my honour?'

'I thought I heard you call for help,' Blott mumbled.

'Call for help indeed,' she snorted. 'You heard nothing of the sort. You've been drinking. I've spoken to you about drinking before and I don't want to mention it again. And what's more when I need any help protecting my so-called honour, which God knows I most certainly don't, I won't ask you to come up here with a twelve-bore. Now then go back to the Lodge and go to bed. I don't want to hear any more about this nonsense, do you understand?'

Blott nodded and slunk down the staircase.

'And you can turn the lights off down there as you go.'

'Yes, ma'am,' said Blott and went down the passage to the kitchen filled with a new and terrible sense of injustice. He turned the kitchen light off and went back to the ballroom and switched off the chandeliers. Then he made his way through the conservatory to the terrace and was about to shut the door when he glimpsed a figure cowering among the ferns. It was the man from the Ministry, and like Lady Maud he was naked. Blott slammed the door and went off down the terrace steps, his mind seething with dreams of revenge. He had come up to the house with the best of intentions to protect his beloved mistress from the sexual depravity of that beastly little man and instead he had been blamed and abused and told he was drunk. It was all so unfair. In the middle of the park he paused and aimed the shotgun into the air and fired both barrels. That was what he thought of the bloody world. That was all that the bloody world understood. Force. He stamped off across the field to the Lodge and went upstairs to his room.

To Dundridge, still cowering in the conservatory, the sound of the shotgun came as final proof that Lady Maud's intentions towards him were homicidal. He had been lured to the Hall, his tyres had been punctured, he had suffered attempted rape, he had been chased naked around the house by a laughing and demented woman and now he was being hunted by a man with a gun. And finally he was in danger of freezing to death. He stayed in the conservatory for twenty minutes anxiously listening for any sounds that might indicate pursuit, but the house was silent. He crept out from his hiding-place and went through the door to the terrace and peered outside. There was no sign of the man with the gun. He would have to take a chance. There was a light look about the eastern sky which suggested the coming of dawn and he had to get away while it was still dark. He ran across the terrace and scampered down the steps towards his car.

Two minutes later he was in the driver's seat and had started the engine. He drove off as fast as the flat tyre would allow, crouching low and waiting for the blast of the shotgun. But nothing came and he passed under the Lodge and into the darkness of the wood. He switched on the headlights, negotiated the suspension bridge and headed up the hill, his flat tyre thumping on the road and the steering pulling violently to the left. Around him the Cleene Forest closed in, his headlights picked out monstrous shapes and weird shadows but Dundridge had lost his terror of the wild landscape. Anything was preferable to the human horrors he had left behind and even when two miles further on the tyre finally came away from the rim and he had to jack the car up and change it for the other flat spare he did so with hesitation. After that he drove more slowly and reached Worford as dawn broke. He parked his car on the double yellow line outside his flat, made sure there was nobody about and flitted across the pavement and down the alley to the outside stairs that led up to his apartment. Even here he was baulked. The key to his flat was in the pocket of his dinner-jacket.

Dundridge stood on the landing outside his door, naked, shivering and livid. Deprived of dignity, pretensions, authority and reason, Dundridge was almost human. For a moment he hesitated and then with a sudden ferocity he hurled himself against the door. At the second attempt the lock gave. He went inside slamming it to behind him. He had made up his mind. Come hell or high water he would do his damnedest to see that the route of the motorway was changed. They could bribe him and blackmail him for all they were worth but he'd get his own back. By the time he had finished that fat insane bitch would laugh on the other side of her filthy face.

CHAPTER SIXTEEN

His opportunity came sooner than he had expected and from an unforeseen quarter. Overwhelmed by the volume of complaints arriving at his office from the tenants of the seventy-five council houses due for demolition, harried by the Ottertown Town Council, infuriated by the refusal of the Minister of the Environment to re-open the Inquiry, and warned by his doctors that unless he curtailed most of his activities his heart would end them all, Francis Puckerington resigned his seat in Parliament. Sir Giles was the first to congratulate him on the wisdom of his withdrawal from public life. 'Wish I could do the same myself,' he said, 'but you know how things are.'

Mr Puckerington didn't but he had a shrewd idea that lurking behind Sir Giles' benevolent concern there was financial advantage. Lady Maud shared his suspicion. Ever since the Inquiry there had been something strange about Giles' manner, an air of expectation and suppressed excitement about him which she found disturbing. Several times she had noticed him looking at her with a smile on his face and when Sir Giles smiled it usually meant that something unpleasant was about to happen. What it was she couldn't imagine and since she took no interest in politics the likely consequences of Mr Puckerington's resignation escaped her. Hoskins was understandably more informed. He realized at once why Sir Giles had agreed so readily to the Ottertown route. 'Brilliant,' he told him when he saw him at the Golf Club. Sir Giles looked mystified.

'I don't know what you're talking about. I had no idea the poor fellow was so ill. A great loss to the party.'

'My eye and Betty Martin,' said Hoskins.

'I'd rather have your Bessie Williams myself,' Sir Giles said, relaxing a little. 'I trust she is keeping well?'

'Very well. She and her husband took a holiday in Majorca I believe.'

'Sensible of them,' Sir Giles said. 'So our young friend Dundridge must be a little puzzled by now. No harm in keeping him hanging in the wind, as someone once put it.'

'He's probably blown that money you gave him.'

'I gave him?' said Sir Giles who preferred not to let his right hand know what his left hand was doing.

'Say no more,' said Hoskins. 'I'll tell you one thing though. He's lost all interest in your wife.'

Sir Giles sighed. 'Such a pity,' he said. 'There was a time when I entertained the hope that he would ... One can't expect miracles. Still, it was a nice thought.'

'He's got it in for her now, anyway. Hates her guts.'

'I wonder why,' said Sir Giles thoughtfully. 'Ah well, it happens to us all in the end. Still, it couldn't have come at a better time.'

'That's what I thought,' said Hoskins. 'He's already sent three memoranda to the Ministry asking for the motorway to be re-routed through the Gorge.'

'Quite the little weathercock isn't he? I trust you tried to dissuade him.'

'Every time. Every time.'

'But not too hard, eh?'

Hoskins smiled. 'I try to keep an open mind on the matter.'

'Very wise of you,' said Sir Giles. 'No point in getting yourself involved. Well, things seem to be moving.'

Things certainly were. In London Francis Puckerington's resignation had immediate repercussions.

'Seventy-five council houses due for demolition in a constituency with a bye-election pending?' said the Prime Minister. 'And what did you say his last majority was?'

'Forty-five,' said the Chief Whip. 'A marginal seat.'

'Marginal be damned. It's lost.'

'It does rather look that way,' the Chief Whip agreed. 'Of course if the motorway could be re-routed ...'

The Prime Minister reached for the phone.

Ten minutes later Mr Rees sent for Mr Joynson.

'Done it,' he said beaming delightedly.

'Done what?'

'Pulled the fat out of the fire. The Ottertown scheme is dead and buried. The M101 is going ahead through the Cleene Gorge.'

'Oh, that is good news,' said Mr Joynson. 'How on earth did you do it?'

'Just a question of patience and gentle persuasion. Ministers may come and Ministers may go but in the end they do tend to see the errors of their ways.'

'I suppose this means you'll be recalling Dundridge,' said Mr Joynson, who was inclined to look on the dark side of things.

'Not on your Nelly,' said Mr Rees, 'Dundridge is coping very well. I look forward to his perpetual absence.'

Dundridge received the news with mixed emotions. On the one hand here was his golden opportunity to teach that bitch Lady Maud a lesson. On the other the knowledge that he had accepted a bribe from Sir Giles bothered him. He looked forward to Lady Maud's misery when she learnt that Handyman Hall was going to be demolished after all but he didn't relish the thought of her husband's reaction. He need not have worried. Sir Giles, anxious to be out of the way when the storm broke, had taken the precaution of being tied up in London in advance of the announcement. In any case Hoskins was reassuring.

'You don't have to worry about Giles,' he told Dundridge. 'It's Maud who'll be out for blood.'

Dundridge knew exactly what he meant, 'If she calls I'm not in,' he told the girl on the switchboard. 'Remember that. I am never in to Lady Maud.'

While Hoskins concentrated on the actual details of the new route and arranged for the posting of advance notices of compulsory purchase, Dundridge spent much of his time on field work, which meant in fact sitting in his flat and not answering the telephone. To occupy his mind and to lend some sort of credence to his title of Controller Motorways Midlands, he set about devising a strategy for dealing with the campaign to stop construction which he was convinced Lady Maud would initiate.

'Surprise is of the essence,' he explained to Hoskins.

'She's had that already,' Hoskins pointed out. He had in his time supervised the eviction of too many obstinate householders to be daunted by the threat of Lady Maud, and besides he was relying on Sir Giles to undermine her efforts. 'She's not going to give us any trouble. You'll see. When it comes to the push she'll go. They all do. It's the law.' Dundridge wasn't convinced. From his personal experience he knew how little the law meant to Lady Maud.

'The thing is to move quickly,' he explained.

'Move quickly?' said Hoskins. 'You can't move quickly when you're building a motorway. It's a slow process.'

Dundridge waved his objections aside. 'We must hit at key objectives. Seize the commanding heights. Maintain the initiative,' he said grandly.

Hoskins looked at him doubtfully. He wasn't used to this sort of military language. 'Look, old boy, I know how you feel and all that but ...'

'You don't,' said Dundridge vehemently.

'But what I was going to say was that there's no need to go in for anything complicated. Just let things take their natural course and you'll find people will get used to the idea. It's amazing how adaptable people are.'

'That's precisely what's worrying me,' said Dundridge. 'Now then the essence of my plan is to make random sorties.'

'Random sorties?' said Hoskins. 'What on earth with?'

'Bulldozers,' said Dundridge and spread out a map of the district.

'Bulldozers? You can't have bulldozers roaming the countryside making random sorties,' said Hoskins, now thoroughly alarmed. 'What the hell are they going to randomly sort?'

'Vital areas of control,' said Dundridge, 'lines of communication. Bridgeheads.'

'Bridgeheads? But—'

'As I see it,' Dundridge continued implacably, 'the main centre of resistance is going to be here.' He pointed to the Cleene Gorge. 'Strategically this is the vital area. Seize that and we've won.'

'Seize it? You can't suddenly go in and seize the Cleene Gorge!' shouted Hoskins. 'The motorway has to proceed by deliberate stages. Contractors work according to a schedule and we have to keep to that.'

'That is precisely the mistake you're making,' said Dundridge. 'Our tactics must be to alter the schedule just when the enemy least expects it.'

'But that's impossible,' Hoskins insisted. 'You can't go about knocking people's houses down without giving them fair warning.'

'Who said anything about knocking houses down?' said Dundridge indignantly. 'I certainly didn't. What I have in mind is something entirely different. Now then what we'll do is this.'

For the next half hour he outlined his grand strategy while Hoskins listened. When he had finished Hoskins was impressed in spite of himself. He had been quite wrong to call Dundridge a nincompoop. In his own peculiar way the man had flair.

'All the same I just hope it doesn't have to come to that,' he said finally.

'You'll see,' said Dundridge. 'That bitch isn't going to sit back and let us put a motorway through her wretched house without putting up a struggle. She's going to fight to the bitter end.'

Hoskins went back to his office thoughtfully. There was nothing illegal about Dundridge's plan in spite of the military jargon. In a way it was extremely shrewd.

The Committee for the Preservation of the Cleene Gorge met under the Presidency of General Burnett at Handyman Hall. Lady Maud was the first speaker.

'I intend to fight this project to the bitter end,' she said, fulfilling Dundridge's prediction. 'I have no intention of being driven from my own home simply because a lot of bureaucratic dunderheads in London take it into their thick skulls to ignore the recommendations of a properly constituted Inquiry. It's outrageous.'

'It's so unfair,' said Mrs Bullett-Finch, 'particularly after what Lord Leakham said about preserving the wildlife of the area. What I can't understand is why they changed their minds so suddenly.'

'As I see it,' said General Burnett, 'the change is a direct consequence of Puckerington's resignation. I have it on the hightest authority that the Government felt that the new candidate was bound to lose the bye-election if they went ahead with the route through Ottertown.'

'Why did Puckerington resign?' asked Miss Percival.

'Ill-health,' said Colonel Chapman. 'He's got a dicky heart.'

Lady Maud said nothing. What she had just heard explained a great many things and suggested more. She knew now why Sir Giles had smiled so secretively at her and why he had had that air of expectation. Everything suddenly fell into place in her mind. She understood why he had been so alarmed about the possibility of a tunnel, why he had insisted on Ottertown, why he had been so pleased at Lord Leakham's decision. Above all, she realized for the first time the full enormity of his betrayal. Colonel Chapman put her thoughts into numbers.

'I suppose there is this to be said for it. I've heard a rumour that we are going to get increased compensation,' he said. 'The figure mentioned was twenty per cent. That makes your sum, Lady Maud, something in the region of three hundred thousand pounds.'

Lady Maud sat rigid in her chair. Three hundred thousand pounds. It was not her share. Sir Giles owned the Hall. Owned it and had put it up for sale in the only way legally available to him. Faced with such treachery there was nothing left for her to say. She shook her head wearily and while the discussion continued round her she stared out of the window to where Blott was mowing the lawn.

The meeting broke up without any decision being taken on the next move.

'Poor old Maud seems quite broken up about this dreadful business,' General Burnett said to Mrs Bullett-Finch as they walked across the drive to their cars. 'It's knocked all the spirit out of her. Bad business.'

'One does feel so terribly sorry for her,' Mrs Bullett-Finch agreed.

Lady Maud watched them leave and then went back into the house to think. Committees would achieve nothing now. They would talk and pass resolutions but when the time for taking action came they would still be talking. Colonel Chapman had given the game away by talking about money. They would settle.

She went down the passage to the study and stood there looking round the room. It was here that Giles had thought the whole thing out, in this sanctum, at this desk where her father and grandfather had sat, and it was here that she would sit and think until she had planned some way of stopping the motorway and of destroying him. In her mind the two things were inextricably linked. Giles had conceived the idea of the motorway, he would be broken by it. There was no compunction left in her. She had been outwitted and betrayed by a man she had always despised. She had sold herself to him to preserve the house and the family and the knowledge of her own guilt added force to her determination. If need be she would sell herself to the devil to stop him now. Lady Maud sat down behind the desk and stared at the filigree of her grandfather's silver inkstand for inspiration. It was shaped like a lion's head. An hour later she had found the solution she was looking for. She reached for the phone and was about to pick it up when it rang. It was Sir Giles calling from London.

'I just thought I had better let you know I shan't be back this weekend,' he said. 'I know it is a damned inconvenient time for me to be away with all this motorway business going on, but I really can't get away.'

'That's all right,' said Lady Maud, feigning her usual degree of indifference, 'I daresay I'll be able to cope without you.'

'How are things going?'

'We've just had a committee meeting to discuss the next move. We are thinking of organizing protest meetings round the county.'

'That's the sort of thing we need,' said Sir Giles. 'I'm doing my damnedest down here to get the Ministry to reconsider. Keep up the good work at your end.' He rang off. Lady Maud smiled grimly. She would keep up the good work all right. And he could go on doing his damnedest. She picked up the phone and dialled. In the next two hours she spoke to her bank manager, the Head Keeper at Whipsnade Zoo, the Game Warden at Woburn Wildlife Park, the managers of five small private Zoos and a firm of fencing experts in Birmingham. Finally she went outside to look for Blott.

Ever since the night of Dundridge's visit she had been worried by Blott's attitude. It hadn't been like him to behave like that and she had been alarmed by the sound of the shotgun going off outside. She rather regretted what she had said about his drinking too. It certainly hadn't had any good effect. If anything he had taken to going off to the Royal George more often and late one night she had heard him singing in the pinetum. 'Typically Italian,' she thought, confusing 'Wir Fahren Gegen England' with *La Traviata*. 'Probably pining for Naples.' But Blott stumbling through the park was merely drunk and if he was pining for anything it was for her innocence which Dundridge's visit had destroyed.

She found him, as she had expected, in the kitchen garden. 'Blott,' she said, 'I want you to do something for me.'

Blott grunted morosely. 'What?'

'You know the wall safe in the study?' Blott nodded. 'I want you to open it for me.'

Blott shook his head and went on weeding the onion bed. 'Not possible without the combination,' he said.

'If I had the combination I wouldn't have to ask you to open it,' Lady Maud said tartly. Blott shrugged. 'If I don't know the combination,' he said, 'how do I open it?'

'You blow it open,' said Lady Maud. Blott straightened up and looked at her.

'Blow it open?'

'With explosive. Use a ... what are those things with flames ... oxy ...'

'Acetylene torch,' said Blott. 'It wouldn't work.'

'I don't mind how you do it. You can pull it out of the wall and drop it from the roof for all I care but I want that safe opened. I've got to know what is inside it.'

Blott pushed back his hat and scratched his head. This was a new Lady Maud speaking. 'Why don't you ask him for the combination?' he said.

'Him?' said Lady Maud with a new contempt. 'Because I don't want him to know. That's why.'

'He'll know it if we blow it open,' Blott pointed out.

Lady Maud thought for a moment. 'We can always say it was burglars,' she said finally.

Blott considered the implications of this remark and found them to his liking. 'Yes, we could do that. Let's go and have a look at it.'

They went into the house and stood in the study examining the safe which was set into the wall behind some books.

'Difficult,' said Blott. He went into the dining-room next door and looked at the wall on that side. 'It's going to do a lot of damage,' he said when he came back.

'Do whatever damage you have to. The house is coming down if we don't do something. What does it matter if we do some damage to it now? It can always be repaired.'

'Ah,' said Blott, who had begun to understand. 'Then I'll use a sledgehammer.' He went round to the workshop in the yard and returned with a sledgehammer, a metal wedge and a crowbar.

'You're quite sure?' he asked. Lady Maud nodded. Blott swung the sledgehammer against the dining-room wall. Half an hour later the safe was out of the wall. Together they carried it outside and laid it on the drive. It was quite small. Blott twiddled the knob idly and tried to think what next to do.

'What we need is some high-explosive,' he said. 'Dynamite would do it.'

'We haven't got any dynamite,' Lady Maud pointed out. 'And you can't go into a shop and buy it. You couldn't bore a hole in it and hoik things out with a wire?'

'Too thick and the steel is too hard,' said Blott. 'It's like armour-plate on a tank.' He stopped. Like a tank. Somewhere among the armoury of weapons he had collected during the war there was a rocket-launcher. It was in a long wooden box and labelled PIAT. Projectile Infantry Anti-Tank. Now where had he buried it?

CHAPTER SEVENTEEN

As dusk fell over the Cleene Gorge Blott left the Lodge with a spade. He had had his supper, sausages and mashed potatoes, and was comfortably full. Above all he was happy. As he followed the park wall round to the west and found the exact spot where he had climbed over as a prisoner of war he was boyishly excited. There had been a piece of iron fencing which he had propped against the wall to give himself a leg-up. It was still there, rusting in a patch of stinging nettles. Blott dragged it out and leant it against the wall and climbed up. The barbed-wire had gone but as he straddled the top of the wall and dropped down on the other side he had the same feeling of freedom he had experienced night after night over thirty years before. Not that he had disliked life in the camp. He had felt freer then than at any time before. To sneak out at night and roam the woods on his own was to escape from the orphanage in Dresden and all the petty restrictions of his dreadful childhood. It had been to cock a snook at authority and to be himself.

And so it was now as he pushed through the bracken and began to climb through the trees. He was doing the forbidden thing again and he exulted in it. Half a mile up the hillside he came to a clearing. You turned left here. Blott turned left, following the old instinct as surely as if there had been a path there, and came out into the setting sunlight behind a mound of stones that had once been a cottage. Here he turned up the hill again until he found the tree he was looking for. It was a large old oak. Blott went round the trunk and found the slash he had made in the bark. He walked away from the tree, counting his paces. Then he took off his jacket and began to dig. It took him an hour to get down to the cache but it was there exactly where he had recalled. He pulled out a box and prised the lid open with a hammer. Inside caked in grease and wrapped in oilskin was a two-inch mortar. He dragged out another box. Mortar bombs. Finally he found what he was looking for. The long box and the four cases of armour-piercing rockets. He sat down on the box and wondered what to do next. Now that he came to think about it, all he needed were the rockets. All he had to do was to tie a piece of string to the fin and drop it from a height on to the safe. That would do the trick just as well as firing the rocket at the safe.

Still, he had come so far, he might as well take the PIAT home with him and clean it up. It would make an interesting souvenir. Blott put the mortar back with the cases of bombs, and covered them with earth. Then he went back down the hill with the long box. It was very heavy and he had to stop fairly frequently to rest. By the time he got back to the Lodge it was dark. He humped the box up to his room and went back for the rockets. He didn't take those up to his room but left them in the grass outside. He didn't feel like sleeping beside some rockets that were thirty years old.

In the morning he was up early and busy in the Gorge. He fetched the safe down on a wheelbarrow and stood it upright at the bottom of the cliff. Then he took a long piece of twine and tied it to the knob of the combination lock before going back up the cliff with it and attaching it to an overhanging branch so that it ran in a straight line some fifty feet down to the safe. Finally he fetched two of the finned projectiles and tied a short length of string to the fin of the first. At the other end of the string he tied a small ring, undid the twine and fitted the ring over it and tied it back on to the branch. Then he lay down at the top of the cliff and removed the cap from the detonator on the nose of the rocket. Blott peered over the edge. There was the safe directly below. He held the PIAT bomb out and let go and watched as it plummeted down the twine. The next moment there was a flash and a roar. Blott shut his eyes and pulled his head back and as he did so something hurtled past him into the air above. He looked up. The fin of the rocket reached its peak, curved over and fell into the road behind him. Blott got up and went down to the safe. The bomb had missed the combination lock but it had done its job. A small hole the size of a pencil was blown in the front of the safe and the door was loose.

Lady Maud was having breakfast when the blast came. For a moment she thought Blott was out shooting rabbits but there had been a concussion and an echo about the explosion that had suggested something more powerful than a shotgun. She went outside and saw Blott coming down the cliff path on the other side of the river. Of course, the safe. He had sworn he would blow it open and that's what he had done. She ran across the lawn and through the pinetum and over the footbridge.

Blott was bending over the safe when she came up.

'Have you done it?' she asked.

'Yes, it's open,' said Blott, 'but there's nothing much in it.' Lady Maud could see that. The safe was much smaller inside than she had expected and it appeared to be filled with burnt, charred and torn fragments of paper. She reached in and picked one out. It was a portion of what had once been a photograph. She held it up and looked at it. It appeared to be the legs of a naked man. She reached in and took out another piece, this time an arm, a bare arm and what looked like a woman's breast. She peered into the safe again but apart from the shreds of photographs there was nothing inside.

'I'll go and get an envelope,' Lady Maud said. 'Don't touch anything until I get back.' She walked off thoughtfully towards the Hall while Blott went back to the top of the cliff and collected the unused PIAT bomb. At least he knew now that they worked. 'Might come in handy,' he said to himself and took it back to the Lodge.

An hour later the safe was buried under some bushes at the base of the cliff and Blott had gone back to the kitchen garden. In the study Lady Maud sat at the desk and examined the fragments of photographs, trying to sort out which portion of anatomy fitted the next. It was a difficult task and an unedifying one. The photographs were too charred and torn to be reassembled properly and besides the force of the explosion had decapitated the participants in what even on this slender evidence appeared to be a series of extremely unnatural acts. And slender was the word. Certainly in the case of the man. That ruled out Sir Giles. It was a pity. She could have done with some photographic proof of his obscene habits. She picked up another fragment and was about to look for the appropriate place in the jigsaw puzzle where it would fit when she suddenly realized where she had seen those slender legs and pale feet. Of course. Twinkling across the marble floor of the hall. She looked again at the portion of leg, at the arm. She was certain now. Dundridge. Dundridge engaged in ... It was unthinkable. She was just trying to work out what this extraordinary idea implied when the front doorbell rang. She went out and opened the door. It was the manager of the high-security fencing company.

'Ah, good,' said Lady Maud. 'Now then, to business. I'll show you exactly what I want.' They went inside to the billiard room and Lady Maud unrolled a map of the estate. 'I am opening a wildlife park,' she explained. 'I want a fence extending the entire perimeter of the park. It must be absolutely secure and proof against any sort of animal.'

'But I understood ...' the manager began.

'Never mind what you understood,' said Lady Maud. 'Just understand that I am opening a wildlife park in three weeks' time.'

'In three weeks? That's out of the question.'

Lady Maud rolled up the map. 'In that case I shall employ someone else,' she said. 'Some enterprising firm that can erect a suitable fence ...'

'You won't get any firm to do it in three weeks,' said the manager. 'Not unless you pay a fortune.'

'I am prepared to pay a fortune,' said Lady Maud.

The manager looked at her and rubbed his jaw. 'Three weeks?' he said.

'Three weeks,' said Lady Maud.

The manager took out a notebook and made some calculations. 'This is simply a rough estimate,' he said finally, 'but I would say somewhere in the region of twenty-five thousand pounds.'

'Say thirty and be done with it,' said Lady Maud. 'Thirty thousand pounds for the fence to be completed in three weeks from today with a bonus of one thousand a day for every day under three weeks and a penalty clause of two thousand pounds for every day after three weeks.'

The manager gaped at her. 'I suppose you know what you're doing,' he muttered.

'I know precisely what I'm doing, thank you very much,' said Lady Maud. 'What is more you will work day and night. You will bring your materials in at night. I don't want any lorries coming here during the day and you will house your men here. I will provide accommodation. You will see to their bedding and their food. This whole operation must be done in the strictest secrecy.'

'If you don't mind,' said the manager and sat down in a chair. Lady Maud sat down opposite him.

'Well?'

'I don't know,' said the manager. 'It *can* be done ...'

'It will be,' Lady Maud assured him. 'Either by you or someone else.'

'You realize that if we were to finish the job in a fortnight the cost would have risen to thirty-seven thousand pounds.'

'And I should be delighted. And if you can finish in a week I shall be happy to pay forty-two thousand pounds,' she said. 'Are we agreed?' The manager nodded. 'Right, in that case I shall make out a cheque to you for ten thousand now and two post-dated cheques for the same amount. I trust that will be a sufficient earnest of my good faith.' She went through to the study and wrote the cheques. 'I shall expect the arrival of materials tonight and work to begin at once. You can bring the contract tomorrow for me to sign.'

The manager went out and got into his car in a state of shock. 'Mad as a March bloody hare,' he muttered as he drove down the drive.

Behind him Lady Maud went back to the study and sat down. It was costing more than she had anticipated but it was worth every penny. And then there was the price of the animals. Lions didn't come cheap. Nor did a rhinoceros. And finally there was the puzzle of the photographs. What were obscene pictures of Mr Dundridge doing in Giles' safe? She got up and went out into the garden and walked up and down the path by the wall of the kitchen garden. And suddenly it dawned on her. It explained everything and in particular why Dundridge had changed his mind about the tunnel. The wretched little man had been blackmailed. Well, two could play at that game. By God they could. She went through the door into the kitchen garden.

'Has my husband ever put through a call to a woman in London?' she asked Blott.

'His secretary,' said Blott. Lady Maud shook her head. Sir Giles' secretary wasn't the sort of woman who would take kindly to the suggestion that she should tie her employer to a bed and beat him and in any case she was happily married.

'Anyone else?'

'No.'

'Has he ever mentioned a woman in any of his conversations on the phone?'

Blott tried to remember. 'No, I don't think so.'

'In that case, Blott,' she said, 'you and I are going to London tomorrow.'

Blott gazed at her in astonishment. 'To London?' He had never been to London.

'To London. We shall be away for a few days.'

'But what shall I wear?' said Blott.

'A suit of course.'

'I haven't got one,' said Blott.

'Well then,' said Lady Maud, 'we had better go into Worford and get you one. And while we're about it we'll get a camera as well. I'll pick you up in ten minutes.'

She went back into the house and put the photographs into an envelope and hid it behind a set of Jorrocks on the bookshelf. It might be worth paying Mr Dundridge a visit while she was in Worford.

CHAPTER EIGHTEEN

But Dundridge was not to be found in Worford. 'He's out,' said the girl at the Regional Planning Board.

'Where?' said Lady Maud.

'Inspecting the site,' said the girl.

'Well, kindly tell him when he comes back that I have some sights I would like him to inspect.'

The girl looked at her. 'I'm sure I don't know what you mean,' she said nastily. Lady Maud suppressed the reaction to tell the little hussy exactly what she did mean.

'Tell Mr Dundridge that I have a number of photographs in which I feel sure he will take a particular interest. You had better write it down before you forget it. Tell him that. He knows where he can find me.'

She went back to the outfitters where Blott was trying on a salmon-pink suit of Harris Tweed. 'If you think I'm going to be seen with you in London in that revolting article of menswear, you've got another think coming,' she snorted. She ran an eye over a number of less conspicuous suits and finally selected a dark grey pinstripe. 'That'll do.' By the time they left the shop Blott was fitted out with shirts, socks, underwear and ties. They called at a shoe shop and bought a pair of black shoes.

'And now all we need is a camera,' said Lady Maud as they stowed Blott's new clothes in the back of the Land-Rover. They went into a camera shop.

'I want a camera with an excellent lens,' she told the assistant, 'one that can be operated by a complete idiot.'

'You need an automatic camera,' said the man.

'No, she doesn't,' said Blott who resented being called a complete idiot in front of strangers. 'She means a Leica.'

'A Leica?' said the man. 'But that's not a camera for a novice. That's a ...'

'Blott,' said Lady Maud, taking him out on to the pavement, 'do you mean to say that you know how to take photographs?'

'In the Luft ... before the war I was trained in photography. I was ...'

Lady Maud beamed at him. 'Oh Blott,' she said, 'you're a godsend. An absolute godsend. Go and buy whatever you need to take good clear photographs.'

'What of?' asked Blott. Lady Maud hesitated. Oh well, he would have to know sooner or later. She took the plunge. 'Him in bed with another woman.'

'Him?'

'Yes.'

It was Blott's turn to beam now. 'We'll need flash and a wide-angle lens.' They went back into the shop and came out with a second-hand Leica, an enlarger, a developing tank, an electronic flash, and everything they needed. As they drove back to Handyman Hall Blott was in his seventh heaven.

*

Dundridge, on the other hand, was in the other place. The girl at the switchboard had phoned him as soon as Lady Maud had left.

'Lady Maud's been,' she told him. 'She's left a message for you.'

'Oh yes,' said Dundridge. 'I hope you didn't tell her where I was.'

'No, I didn't,' said the girl. 'She's a horrid old bag isn't she? I wouldn't wish her on my worst enemy.'

'You can say that again,' Dundridge agreed. 'What was the message?'

'She said "Tell Mr Dundridge that I have a number of photographs in which I feel sure he will take a particular interest". She made me write it down. Hullo, are you still there? Mr Dundridge. Hullo. Hullo. Mr Dundridge, are you there?' But there was no reply. She put the phone down.

In his flat Dundridge sat in a state of shock. He still clutched the phone but he was no longer listening. His thoughts were concentrated on one terrible fact, Lady Maud had those ghastly photographs. She could destroy him. There was nothing he could do about it. She would use them if the motorway went ahead and there was absolutely no way he could stop it now. The fucking bitch had arranged the whole thing. First the photographs, then the bribe, and finally the attempt to murder him. The woman was insane. There could be no doubt about it now. Dundridge put down the phone and tried desperately to think what to do. He couldn't even go to the police. In the first place they would never believe him. Lady Maud was a Justice of the Peace, a respected figure in the community and what had that Miss Boles told him? 'We'll know if you tell the police. We've had customers in the police.' And in any case he had no proof that she was involved. Only the word of the girl at the Planning Board and Lady Maud would claim she had been talking about photographs of the Hall or something like that. He needed proof but above all he needed legal advice. A good lawyer.

He picked up the telephone directory and looked in the yellow pages under Solicitors. 'Ganglion, Turnbull and Shrine.' Dundridge dialled and asked to speak to Mr Ganglion. Mr Ganglion would see him in the morning at ten o'clock. Dundridge spent the evening and most of the night pacing his room in an agony of doubt and suspense. Several times he picked up the phone to call Lady Maud only to put it down again. There was nothing he could say to her that would have the slightest effect and he dreaded what she would have to say to him. Towards dawn he fell into a restless sleep and awoke exhausted at seven.

At Handyman Hall Lady Maud and Blott slept fitfully too; Blott because he was kept awake by the rumble of lorries through the arch; Lady Maud because she was superintending the whole operation and explaining where she wanted things put.

'Your men can sleep in the servants' quarters,' she told the manager. 'I shall be away for a week. Here is the key to the back door.'

When she finally got to bed in the early hours Handyman Hall had assumed the aspect of a construction camp. Concrete mixers, posts, lorries, fencing wire, bags of cement and gravel were arranged in the park and work had already begun by the light of lamps and a portable generator.

She lay in bed listening to the voices and the rumble of the machines and was well satisfied. When money was no object you could still get things done quickly even in England. 'Money no object,' she thought and smiled to herself at the oddity of the phrase. She would have to do something about money before very long. She would think about it in the morning.

At seven she was up and had breakfasted. Through the window of the kitchen she was pleased to note that several concrete posts had already been installed and that a strange machine that looked like a giant corkscrew was boring holes for some more. She went along to the study and spent an hour going through Sir Giles' filing-cabinets. She paid particular attention to a file marked Investments and took down the details of his shareholdings and the correspondence with his stockbroker. Then she went carefully through his personal correspondence, but there was no indication to be found there of any mistress with a penchant for whips and handcuffs.

At nine she signed the contract and went up to her room to pack and at ten she and Blott, now dressed in his pinstripe suit and wearing a blue polka-dot tie, drove off in the Land-Rover for Hereford and the train to London. Behind them in the study the phone was off the stand. There would be no phone calls to Handyman Hall from Sir Giles.

Dundridge arrived promptly at the offices of Ganglion, Turnbull and Shrine and was kept waiting for ten minutes. He sat in an outer office clutching his briefcase and looking miserably at the sporting prints on the walls. They didn't suggest the sophisticated modern approach to life that he felt an understanding of his particular case required. Nor did Mr Ganglion, who finally deigned to see him. He was an elderly man with gold-rimmed glasses over which he looked at Dundridge critically. Dundridge sat down in front of his desk and tried to think how to begin.

'And what did you wish to consult me about, Mr Dundridge?' Mr Ganglion inquired. 'I think you should know in advance that if this has anything to do with the motorway we are not prepared to handle it.'

Dundridge shook his head. 'It hasn't got anything to do with the motorway, well not exactly,' he said. 'The thing is that I'm being blackmailed.'

Mr Ganglion put the tips of his fingers together and tapped them. 'Blackmailed? Indeed. An unusual crime in this part of the world. I can't remember when we last had a case of blackmail. Still it does make a change, I must say. Yes, blackmail. You interest me, Mr Dundridge. Do go on.'

Dundridge swallowed nervously. He hadn't come to interest Mr Ganglion or at least not in the way his smile suggested. 'It's like this,' he said. 'I went to a party at the Golf Club and I met this girl ...'

'A girl, eh?' said Mr Ganglion and drew his chair up to the desk. 'An attractive girl I daresay.'

'Yes,' said Dundridge.

'And you went home with her, I suppose,' said Mr Ganglion, his eyes alight with a very genuine interest now.

'No,' said Dundridge. 'At least I don't think so.'

'You don't think so?' said Mr Ganglion. 'Surely you know what you did?'

'That's the whole point,' Dundridge said, 'I don't know what I did.' He stopped. He did know what he had done. The photographs proclaimed his actions all too clearly. 'Well actually ... I know what I did and all that ...'

'Yes,' Mr Ganglion said encouragingly.

'The thing is I don't know where I did it.'

'In a field perhaps?'

Dundridge shook his head. 'Not in a field.'

'In the back of a car?'

'No,' said Dundridge. 'The thing is that I was unconscious.'

'Were you really? Extraordinary. Unconscious?'

'You see, I had a Campari before we left. It tasted bitter but then Campari does, doesn't it?'

'I have no idea,' said Mr Ganglion, 'what Campari tastes like but I'll take your word for it.'

'Very bitter,' said Dundridge, 'and we got into the car and that's the last thing I remember.'

'How very unfortunate,' said Mr Ganglion, clearly disappointed that he wasn't going to hear the more intimate details of the encounter.

'The next thing I knew I was sitting in my car in a lay-by.'

'A lay-by. Very appropriate. And what happened next?'

Dundridge shifted nervously in his chair. This was the part he had been dreading. 'I got some photographs.'

Mr Ganglion's flagging interest revived immediately. 'Did you really? Splendid. Photographs indeed.'

'And a demand for a thousand pounds.'

'A thousand pounds? Did you pay it?'

'No,' said Dundridge. 'No I didn't.'

'You mean they weren't worth it?'

Dundridge chewed his lip. 'I don't know what they're worth,' he muttered bitterly.

'Then you've still got them,' said Mr Ganglion. 'Good. Good. Well I'll soon tell you what I think of them.'

'I'd rather ...' Dundridge began but Mr Ganglion insisted.

'The evidence,' he said, 'let's have a look at the evidence of blackmail. Most important.'

'They're pretty awful,' said Dundridge.

'Bound to be,' said Mr Ganglion. 'For a thousand pounds they must be quite revolting.'

'They are,' said Dundridge. Encouraged by Mr Ganglion's broad-mindedness, he opened his briefcase and took out the envelope. 'The thing is you've got to remember I was unconscious at the time.'

Mr Ganglion nodded understandingly. 'Of course, my dear fellow, of course.' He reached out and took the envelope and opened it. 'Good God,' he muttered as he looked at the first one. Dundridge squirmed in his chair and stared at the ceiling, and listened while Mr Ganglion thumbed through the photographs, grunting in an ecstasy of disgust and astonishment.

'Well?' he asked when Mr Ganglion sat back exhausted in his chair. The solicitor was staring at him incredulously.

'A thousand pounds? Is that really all they asked?' he said. Dundridge nodded. 'Well, all I can say is that you got off damned lightly.'

'But I didn't pay,' Dundridge reminded him. Mr Ganglion goggled at him.

'You didn't? You mean to tell me you baulked at a mere thousand pounds after having ...' he stopped at a loss for words while his finger wavered over a particularly revolting photograph.

'I couldn't,' said Dundridge feeling hard done by.

'Couldn't?'

'They never called me back. I had one phone call and I've been waiting for another.'

'I see,' said Mr Ganglion. He looked back at the photograph. 'And you've no idea who this remarkable woman is?'

'None at all. I only met her the once.

'Once is enough by the look of things,' Mr Ganglion said. 'And no more phone calls? No letters?'

'Not until last night,' said Dundridge, 'and then I got a message from the girl at the desk at the Regional Planning Board.'

'The girl at the desk at the Regional Planning Board,' said Mr Ganglion, eagerly reaching for a pencil. 'And what's her name?'

'She's got nothing to do with it,' Dundridge said, 'she was simply phoning to give me the message. It said Lady Maud Lynchwood had called and wanted me to know that she had some photographs of particular interest to me ...' He stopped. Mr Ganglion had half risen from his seat and was glaring at him furiously.

'Lady Maud?' he yelled. 'You come in here with this set of the most revolting photographs I've ever set eyes on and have the audacity to tell me that Lady Maud Lynchwood has something to do with them. My God, sir, I've half a mind to horse-whip you. Lady Maud Lynchwood is one of our most respected clients, a dear sweet lady, a woman of the highest virtues, a member of one of the best families ...' He fell back into his chair, speechless.

'But—' Dundridge began.

'But me no buts,' said Mr Ganglion, trembling with rage. 'Get out of my office. If I have one more word out of you, sir, I shall institute proceedings for slander immediately. Do you hear me? One more word here or anywhere else. One breath of rumour from you and I won't hesitate, do you hear me?'

Dundridge could still hear him fulminating as he dashed downstairs and into the street clutching his briefcase. It was only when he got back to his apartment that he realized he had left his photographs on Mr Ganglion's desk. They could stay there for all he cared. He wasn't going back for the beastly things.

Behind him Mr Ganglion simmered down. On the desk in front of him Dundridge and the masked woman lay frozen in two-dimensional contortions. Mr Ganglion adjusted his bifocals and studied them with interest. Then he put the photographs into the envelope and the envelope into his safe. The good name of the Handymans was safe with him. Mind you, come to think of it, he wouldn't put anything past her. Remarkable woman, Maud, quite remarkable.

By the time they reached London Lady Maud had explained Blott's new duties to him.

'You will hire a taxi and wait outside his flat until he comes out and then you will follow him wherever he goes. Particularly in the evening. I want to know where he spends his nights. If he goes into a block of flats, go in after him and make a note of the floor the lift stops at. Do you understand?'

Blott said he did.

'And on no account let him catch sight of you.' She studied him critically. In his dark grey suit Blott was practically unrecognizable anyway. Still, it was best to be careful. She would buy him a bowler at Harrods. 'If you see him with a woman follow them wherever they go and if they separate follow the woman. We have got to find out who she is and where she is and where she lives.'

'And then we break in and take the photographs of them?' said Blott eagerly.

'Certainly not,' said Lady Maud. 'When we find out who the woman is we'll decide what we're going to do.'

They took a taxi to an hotel in Kensington, stopping on the way to buy Blott's bowler, and at five o'clock Blott was sitting in a taxi outside Sir Giles' flat in Victoria.

'I suppose you know what you're doing,' said the driver when they had been sitting there for an hour with the meter running. 'This is costing you a packet.' Blott, with a hundred pounds in his pocket, said he knew what he was doing. He was enjoying himself watching the traffic go by and studying the pedestrians. He was in London, the capital of Great Britain, the heart of what had been the world's greatest Empire, the seat of those great Kings and Queens he had read so much about and all the romance in Blott's nature thrilled at the thought. What was even better he was tracking down him – Blott had never deigned to call him anything else – him and his mistress. He was doing Lady Maud a service after all.

At seven Sir Giles came out and drove to his Club for dinner. Behind him Blott's taxi followed relentlessly. At eight he came out and drove across to St John's Wood, Blott's taxi still behind. He parked in Elm Road and went into a house while Blott stared out of the taxi and noticed that he pressed the second bell. As soon as Sir Giles had gone inside, Blott got out and walked across the road and took a note of the name on the doorbell. It read Mrs Forthby. Blott went back to the taxi.

'Mrs Forthby, Mrs Forthby,' said Lady Maud when Blott reported to her. 'Elm Road.' She looked Mrs Forthby up in the telephone directory. 'That's very clever of you, Blott. Very clever indeed. And you say he didn't come out?'

'No. But the taxi-driver wouldn't wait any longer. He said it was time for his supper.'

'Never mind. You've done very well. Now the only thing to do is to find out what sort of woman she is. I would like to get to know Mrs Forthby a little better. I wonder how I can do that.'

'I can follow her,' said Blott.

'I don't see what good that would do,' said Lady Maud. 'And in any case how would you know her to follow?'

'She's the only woman living in the house,' Blott said. 'There's a Mr Sykes on the top floor and a Mr Billington on the ground floor.'

'Excellent,' said Lady Maud. 'You are an observant man. Now then how can I get to know her? There must be some way of arranging a meeting.'

'I could,' said Blott, adopting the voice of Sir Giles, 'ring her up and pretend I was him and ask her to meet me somewhere ...' he said.

Lady Maud gazed at him. 'Of course. Oh Blott what would I do without you?' Blott blushed. 'But no, that wouldn't do,' Lady Maud continued. 'She would tell him. I'll have to think of something else.'

Blott went up to his room and went to bed. He was tired and very hungry but these little inconveniences counted for nothing beside the knowledge that Lady Maud was pleased with him. Blott fell asleep blissfully happy.

So did Lady Maud, though her happiness was more practical and centred on the solution to a problem that had been worrying her. Money. The fence for the Wildlife Park was going to cost at least thirty thousand pounds and the animals she had ordered came to another twenty. Fifty thousand pounds was a lot of money to pay to save the Hall and besides there was no guarantee that it would work. If anybody should be paying it was Giles, who was responsible for the whole wretched business. And she had found a way of making him pay. She would ruin him yet.

Next morning at eight o'clock she and Blott were sitting in a taxi at the end of Elm Road. At nine they saw Sir Giles leave. Lady Maud paid the taxi-driver and with Blott at her heels strode down to number six.

'Now remember what to say,' Lady Maud told Blott as she pressed the bell. There was a buzz.

'Who is it?' Mrs Forthby asked.

'It's me. I've left my car keys,' said Blott in the accents of Sir Giles.

'And I thought I was the forgetful one,' said Mrs Forthby.

The door opened. Blott and Lady Maud went upstairs. Mrs Forthby opened the door of her flat. She was dressed in a housecoat and was holding a yellow duster.

'Good morning,' said Lady Maud and walked past her into the flat.

'But I thought ...' Mrs Forthby began.

'Do let me introduce myself,' said Lady Maud. 'I am Lady Maud Lynchwood and you must be Mrs Forthby.' She took Mrs Forthby's hand. 'I've been looking forward to meeting you. Giles has told me so much about you.'

'Oh dear,' said Mrs Forthby. 'How frightfully embarrassing.' Behind her Blott closed the door. Lady Maud took stock of the furniture, including Mrs Forthby in the process, and then sat down in an armchair.

'Quite the little love nest,' she said finally. Mrs Forthby stood plumply in front of her wringing the duster.

'Oh this is awful,' she said, 'simply awful.'

'Nonsense. It's nothing of the sort. And do stop twisting that duster. You make me nervous.'

'I'm so sorry,' said Mrs Forthby. 'It's just that I feel ... well ... just that I owe you an apology.'

'An apology? What on earth for?' said Lady Maud.

'Well ... you know ...' Mrs Forthby shook her head helplessly.

'If you imagine for one moment that I have anything against you, you're mightily mistaken. As far as I am concerned you have been a positive godsend.'

'A godsend?' Mrs Forthby mumbled and sat down on the sofa.

'Of course,' said Lady Maud. 'I have always found my husband a positively disgusting man with the very vilest of personal habits. The fact that you appear to be prepared, presumably out of the goodness of your heart, to satisfy his obscene requirements leaves me very much in your debt.'

'It does?' said Mrs Forthby, her world being stood on its head by this extraordinary woman who sat in her armchair and addressed her in her own flat as if she were a servant.

'Very much so,' Lady Maud continued. 'And where do these absurdities take place? In the bedroom I suppose.' Mrs Forthby nodded. 'Blott, have a look in the bedroom.'

'Yes, ma'am,' said Blott and went through first one door and then another. Mrs Forthby sat and stared at Lady Maud, hypnotized.

'Now then, you and I are going to have a little chat,' Lady Maud continued. 'You seem to be a sensible sort of woman with a head on your shoulders. I'm sure we can come to some mutually advantageous arrangement.'

'Arrangement?'

'Yes,' said Lady Maud, 'arrangement. Tell me, have you ever been a co-respondent in a divorce case?'

'No, never,' said Mrs Forthby.

'Well my dear,' Lady Maud went on, 'unless you are prepared to do exactly what I tell you down to the finest detail I'm afraid you are going to find yourself involved in quite the most sordid divorce case this country has seen for a very long time.'

'Oh dear,' Mrs Forthby whimpered, 'how simply awful. What would Cedric think of me?'

'Cedric?'

'My first husband. My late husband I should say. The poor dear would be absolutely furious. He'd never speak to me again. He was very particular, you know. Doctors have to be.'

'Well, we wouldn't want to upset Cedric, would we?' said Lady Maud. 'And there will be absolutely no need to if you do what I say. First of all I want you to tell me what Giles likes you to do.'

'Well ...' Mrs Forthby began only to be interrupted by Blott who emerged from the bedroom with the Miss Dracula, the Cruel Mistress, costume.

'I found this,' he announced.

'Oh dear, how frightfully embarrassing,' said Mrs Forthby.

'Not half as embarrassing, my dear, as it will be when we produce that in court as an exhibit. Now then, the details.'

Mrs Forthby got up. 'It's all written down,' she said. 'He writes it all down for me. You see I'm terribly forgetful and I do tend to get things wrong. I'll get you the game plan.' She went through to the bedroom and returned with a notebook. 'It's all there.'

Lady Maud took the book and studied a page. 'And what were you last night?' she asked finally. 'Miss Catheter, the Wicked Nurse, or Sister Florinda, the Nymphomaniac Nun?'

Mrs Forthby blushed. 'Doris, the Schoolgirl Sexpot,' she tittered.

Lady Maud looked at her doubtfully. 'My husband must have a truly remarkable imagination,' she said, 'but I find his literary style rather limited. And what are you going to be tonight?'

'Oh he doesn't come tonight. He's had to go to Plymouth for a business conference. He's coming again the day after tomorrow. That's Nanny Whip's night.'

Lady Maud put the book down. 'Now then, this is the arrangement,' she said. 'In return for your co-operation I will settle for a divorce on the grounds of incompatibility. There will be no mention of you at all

and Sir Giles need know nothing about the help you have given me. All
I want you to do is to go out for a little while on Thursday night so that
I can have a little chat with him.'

Mrs Forthby hesitated. 'He'll be awfully cross,' she said.

'With me,' Lady Maud assured her. 'I don't think he'll worry about
you by the time I've had my say. He'll have other things on his mind.'

'You won't do anything nasty to him, will you?' said Mrs Forthby. 'I
wouldn't want him to be hurt or anything. I know he's not very nice
but I'm really quite fond of him.'

'I won't touch him,' Lady Maud said. 'I give you my word of honour
I won't so much as lift a little finger to him. And let me say I think your
feelings do you great credit.'

Mrs Forthby began to weep. 'You're very kind,' she said.

Lady Maud stood up. 'Not at all,' she said truthfully. 'And now if
you'll be so good as to give me the key of the flat I'll send Blott to get
a duplicate cut.'

By the time they left the flat Mrs Forthby was feeling better. 'It's been
so nice meeting you and getting things straightened out,' she said. 'It's
taken a great weight off my mind. I do hate deception so.'

'Quite,' said Lady Maud. 'Unfortunately men seem to live in a fantasy
world and as the weaker sex we have to follow suit.'

'That's what I keep telling myself,' Mrs Forthby said. 'Felicia, I say,
you may find it peculiar but if it makes him happy you can't afford to
be choosey.'

'My sentiments exactly,' said Lady Maud. She and Blott went
downstairs. They took a taxi across London to Sir Giles' flat in Victoria.
On the way Lady Maud coached Blott in his new role.

CHAPTER NINETEEN

In Worford Dundridge asserted himself. Now that he came to think about
it, he could see that he had been wise to visit Mr Ganglion. The old
man's reaction might have been violent but at least it had been genuine
and served to indicate that the solicitor was far too respectable to be a
party to a blackmail attempt by one of his clients no matter how
influential she might be. And Mr Ganglion could do one of two things:
he could let Lady Maud know that Dundridge had visited him and had
accused her of blackmail, or, more likely, since it was unprofessional to
disclose one client's business to another, he could keep silent. In either

case Dundridge was in a fairly strong position. If Ganglion spoke to Lady Maud she would not dare to repeat her threat. If he kept silent ... Dundridge considered the most likely consequence. There would be another message from her. Dundridge got up and went out and bought himself a tape recorder. The next time he visited Mr Ganglion he would tape evidence, solid evidence that Lady Maud was involved. That was the thing to do.

Having arrived at that conclusion he felt better. He had spiked the bitch's guns. Operation Overland could proceed. He went round to the Regional Planning Board and sent for Hoskins.

'We are going ahead,' he told him.

'Of course we are,' said Hoskins. 'Work has already started at Bunnington.'

'Never mind that,' said Dundridge, 'I want a task force to begin work in the Gorge.'

Hoskins consulted his schedule. 'We're not due there until October.'

'I know that but all the same I want work to begin there at once. Just a token force, you understand.'

'At Handyman Hall? A token force?'

'Not at the Hall. In the Gorge itself,' said Dundridge.

'But we haven't even served a compulsory purchase order on the Lynchwoods yet,' Hoskins protested.

'In that case it is about time we did. I want orders out to Miss Percival, General Burnett, and the Lynchwoods at once. We've got to bring pressure to bear on them as quickly as possible. Do you understand?'

'Well, I understand that,' said Hoskins who was beginning to resent Dundridge's authoritarian manner, 'but quite frankly I can't see what all the hurry is about.'

'You wouldn't,' said Dundridge, 'but I'm telling you to do it so get it done. In any case we don't need a compulsory purchase order for the entrance to the Gorge. It's common land. Move men in there tomorrow.'

'And what the hell do you expect them to do? Storm the bloody Hall under cover of darkness?'

'Hoskins,' said Dundridge, 'I'm getting a little tired of your sarcasm. You seem to forget that I am Controller Motorways Midlands and what I say goes.'

'Oh all right,' said Hoskins. 'Just remember that if anything goes wrong you'll have to take the can back. What do you want the task force to do?'

Dundridge looked at the plans for construction. 'It says here that the cliffs have to be cleared and the Gorge widened. They can start work on that.'

'That means dynamiting,' Hoskins pointed out.

'Excellent,' said Dundridge, 'that ought to serve notice on the old bag that we mean business.'

'It will do that all right,' said Hoskins. 'She'll probably be round here like a flash.'

'And I shall be only too glad to see her,' Dundridge said. Hoskins went back to his office puzzled. The more he saw of the Controller Motorways Midlands the odder he found him.

'I never thought he would stand up to Lady Maud like this,' he muttered. 'Well, better him than me.'

In his office Dundridge smiled to himself. Dynamite. That was just the thing to bring Lady Maud rushing into the trap he had set. He took the tape recorder out of his briefcase and tested it. The thing worked perfectly.

In Sir Giles' flat in Victoria, Lady Maud and Blott sat down by the desk. In front of her were the details of Sir Giles' shareholdings. In front of Blott the telephone and the script of his part.

'Ready?' said Lady Maud.

'Ready,' said Blott and dialled.

'Schaeffer, Blodger and Vaizey,' said the girl at the stockbrokers.

'Mr Blodger please,' said Blott.

'Sir Giles Lynchwood on the line for you, Mr Blodger,' he heard the girl say.

'Ah Lynchwood,' said Blodger, 'good morning.'

'Good morning Blodger,' said Blott. 'Now then, I want to sell the following at best. Four thousand President Rand. One thousand five hundred ICM. Ten thousand Rio Pinto. All my Zinc and Copper ...'

At the other end of the line there was a choking sound. Mr Blodger was evidently having some difficulty coming to terms with Sir Giles' orders. 'I say, Lynchwood,' he muttered, 'are you all right?'

'All right? What the devil do you mean? Of course I'm all right,' snarled Blott.

'It's just that ... well ... I mean the market's rock bottom just at the moment. Wouldn't it be better to wait ...'

'Listen Blodger,' said Blott, 'I know what I'm doing and when I say sell I mean sell. And if you'll take my advice you'll get out now too.'

'You really think ...' Mr Blodger began.

'Think?' said Blott. 'I know. Now then see what you can get and call me back. I'll be here at the flat for the next twenty minutes.'

'Well if you say so,' said Mr Blodger.

Blott put the phone down.

'Brilliant, Blott, absolutely brilliant. For a moment even I thought it was Giles talking,' said Lady Maud. 'Well that should put the cat among the pigeons. Or the bulls among the bears. Now, when he calls back give him the second list.'

At the offices of Schaeffer, Blodger and Vaizey there was consternation. Blodger consulted Schaeffer and together they sent for Vaizey.

'Either he's gone out of his mind or he knows something,' shouted Blodger. 'He's dropping eighty thousand on the President Rand.'

'What about Rio Pinto?' Schaeffer yelled. 'He bought in at twenty-five and he's selling at ten.'

'He's usually right,' said Vaizey. 'In all the years we've handled his account he hasn't put a foot wrong.'

'A foot! He's putting his whole damned body wrong if you ask me.'

'Unless he knows something,' said Vaizey.

They looked at one another. 'He must know something,' said Schaeffer.

'Do you want to speak to him?' asked Blodger.

Schaeffer shook his head. 'My nerves couldn't stand it,' he muttered.

Blodger picked up the phone. 'Get me Sir Giles Lynchwood,' he told the girl on the switchboard. 'No, come to think of it, don't. I'll use the outside line.' He dialled Sir Giles' number.

Ten minutes later he staggered through to Schaeffer's office whitefaced. 'He wants out,' he said and slumped into a chair.

'Out?'

'Everything. The whole damned lot. And today. He knows something all right.'

'Well,' said Lady Maud, 'that's taken care of that. We had better spend another hour or two here in case they phone back. It's a great pity we can't do the same thing with some of his property. Still, there's no point in overdoing things.'

At two o'clock Blodger phoned again to say that Sir Giles' instructions had been carried out.

'Good,' said Blott. 'Send the transfers round tomorrow. I'm going to Paris overnight. And by the way, I want the money transferred to my current account at Westlands in Worford.'

Sir Giles returned from Plymouth the following afternoon by car. He was in a good humour. The conference had gone well and he was looking forward to an evening with Nanny Whip. He went to his flat, had a bath, dined in a restaurant and drove round to Elm Road to find Mrs Forthby already dressed for the part.

'Now then you naughty boy,' she said with just that touch of benign menace he found most affecting, 'off with your clothes.'

'No, no,' said Sir Giles.

'Yes, yes,' said Nanny Whip.

'No, no.'

'Yes, yes.'

Sir Giles succumbed to the allure of her apron. It smelt of childhood. Nanny Whip's breath, on the other hand, suggested something more mature but Sir Giles was too intoxicated with her insistence that he behave himself while she fixed his nappy that he took no notice. It was only when he was finally strapped down and was having his bonnet adjusted that he caught a full whiff. It was brandy.

'You've been drinking,' he spluttered.

'Yes, yes,' said Mrs Forthby and stuffed a dummy into his mouth. Sir Giles stared up at her incredulously. Mrs Forthby never drank. The bloody woman was a teetotaller. It was one of the things he liked about her. She didn't cost much to entertain. She might be absent-minded but she was . . . My God, if she was absent-minded sober what the hell was she going to be like drunk? Sir Giles writhed on the bed and realized that he was tied down rather more firmly than he had expected. Nanny Whip had excelled herself. He could hardly move.

'I'm just going to pop downstairs for some fish fingers,' she said, 'I won't be a moment.'

Sir Giles stared lividly at her while she took off her cap and put on a coat over her costume. What in God's name did the bloody woman want with fish fingers at this time of night? A moment? Sir Giles knew her moments. He was liable to be left strapped up in baby clothes and with a dummy in his mouth until the small hours while she went to some fucking concert. Sir Giles gnawed frantically at the dummy but the damned thing was tied on too tightly.

'Now you be a good boy while I'm away,' said Nanny Whip, 'and don't do anything I wouldn't do. Ta, ta.'

She went out and shut the door. Sir Giles subsided. There was no point in worrying now. He might as well enjoy his impotence while he could. There would probably be plenty of time later on for genuine concern. With the necessarily silent prayer that she hadn't been given tickets for the Ring Cycle he settled down to be Naughty Boy and he was just beginning to get into the role when the front doorbell rang. Sir Giles assumed an even greater rigidity. A moment later he was petrified.

'Is anyone at home?' a voice called. Sir Giles knew that voice. It was the voice of hell itself. It was Lady Maud.

'Oh well, the key's in the door,' he heard her say, 'so we might as well go in and wait.'

On the bed Sir Giles had palpitations. The thought of being discovered in this ghastly position by Lady Maud was bad enough but the fact that she had somebody with her was utterly appalling. He could hear them moving about the next room. If only they would stay there. And what the hell was Lady Maud doing there anyway? How on earth had she discovered about Mrs Forthby? And just at that moment the door opened and Lady Maud stood framed in it.

'Ah there you are,' she said cheerfully, 'I had an idea we'd find you here. How very convenient.'

From under his frilled bonnet Sir Giles peered up at her venomously, his face the colour of the sheet on which he was lying and his legs jerking convulsively in the air. Convenient! Convenient! The fucking woman was out of her mind. The next moment he was certain of it.

'You can come in, Blott,' she said, 'Giles won't mind.' Blott came into the room. He was carrying a camera and a flash gun.

'And now,' said Lady Maud, 'we're going to have a little chat.'

'What about the pictures?' said Blott. 'Shouldn't we take them first?'

'Do you think he would prefer the pictures first?' she asked. Blott nodded his head vigorously while Sir Giles shook his. For the next five minutes Blott went round the room taking photographs from every conceivable angle. Then he changed the film and took some close-ups. 'That will do for now,' he announced finally. 'We should have enough.'

'I'm sure we have,' said Lady Maud and drew up a chair beside the bed. 'Now then we are going to have our little chat about your future, my dear.' She bent over and took out the comforter.

'Don't touch me,' squealed Sir Giles.

'I have no intention of touching you,' said Lady Maud with evident disgust. 'It has been one of the few compensations for our wholly unsatisfactory marriage that I don't have to. I am simply here to arrange terms.'

'Terms? What terms?' squawked Sir Giles. Lady Maud rummaged in her handbag.

'The terms of our divorce,' she said and produced a document. 'You will simply append your signature here.'

Sir Giles stared up at it blankly. 'I need my reading-glasses,' he muttered.

Lady Maud perched them on his nose. Sir Giles read the document. 'You expect me to sign that?' he yelled. 'You really think I'm going to—'

Lady Maud replaced the dummy. 'You unspeakable creature,' she snarled, 'you'll sign this document if it's the last thing you do. And this.' She waved another piece of paper in front of him. 'And this.' Another. 'And this.'

On the bed Sir Giles struggled with the straps convulsively. Nothing on God's earth would make him sign a document that was an open confession that he had made a habit of deceiving his lawful wife, had denied her her conjugal rights, had committed adultery on countless occasions and had subjected her for six years to mental and physical cruelty. Lady Maud read his thoughts.

'In return for your signature I will not distribute copies of the photographs we have just taken to the Prime Minister, the Chief Whip, the members of your constituency party or the press. You will sign that document, Giles, and you will see that the motorway is stopped within a month. A month, do you hear me? Those are my terms. What do you say to that?' She removed the dummy.

'You filthy bitch.'

'Quite,' said Lady Maud, 'so you agree to sign?'

'I do not,' screamed Sir Giles and was promptly silenced.

'I don't know if you know your Shakespeare,' she said, 'but in *Edward the Second* . . .'

Sir Giles didn't know his Marlowe either but he did know about Edward the Second.

'Blott,' said Lady Maud, 'go into the kitchen and see if you can find—'

But already Sir Giles was nodding his head. He would sign anything now.

While Blott untied his right hand Lady Maud took a fountain pen out of her handbag. 'Here,' she said pointing to a dotted line. Sir Giles signed. 'Here,' and 'Here.' Sir Giles signed and signed. When he had finished Blott witnessed his signatures. Then he was tied down again.

'Good,' said Lady Maud, 'I will institute proceedings for divorce at once and you will stop the motorway or face the consequences. And don't you dare to set foot on my property again. I will have your things sent down to you.' She took out the dummy. 'Have you anything to say?'

'If I do manage to stop the motorway will you guarantee to let me have the photographs and negatives back?'

'Of course,' said Lady Maud, 'we Handymans may have our faults, but breaking our promises isn't one of them.' She stuffed the dummy back into his mouth and tied it behind his head. Then, having removed his glasses, she adjusted his bonnet and left the room.

On the staircase they met Mrs Forthby in a dither. 'You didn't do anything horrid, did you?' she asked.

'Of course not,' Lady Maud assured her, 'just got him to sign a document consenting to divorce.'

'Oh dear, I do hope he isn't too cross. He gets into such terrible tantrums.'

'Come, come, Nanny Whip, be your true self,' said Lady Maud. 'You must be firm.'

'Yes, you're quite right,' said Mrs Forthby. 'But it's very difficult. It's not in my nature to be unkind.'

'And before I forget, here's a little honorarium for your assistance.' Lady Maud produced a cheque from her bag but Mrs Forthby shook her head.

'I may be a silly woman and not very nice but I do have my standards,' she said. 'And besides I'd probably forget to cash it.' She went upstairs a little wistfully.

'That woman,' said Lady Maud as they drove to Paddington to catch the train to Worford, 'is far too good for Giles. She deserves something better.' On the way they stopped to post the share transfers to Messrs Schaeffer, Blodger and Vaizey.

CHAPTER TWENTY

By the time they reached Handyman Hall it was two o'clock in the morning but the park was well lit. Under the floodlights men were busily engaged in erecting the fencing posts and already one side of the park was fenced in. Lady Maud drove round to have a look and congratulated Mr Firkin, the manager, on the progress.

'I'm afraid you're going to have to pay the bonus,' he told her. 'At this rate we'll be finished in ten days.'

'Make it a week,' said Lady Maud. 'Money's no problem.' She went into the house and up to bed well content. Money was no object now.

In the morning she would withdraw every penny from their joint account at Westland Bank in Worford and deposit it in her own private account at the Northern. Sir Giles would scream blue murder but there was nothing he could do. He had signed the share transfer certificates if not of his own free will at least in circumstances which made it impossible for him to argue otherwise. And besides she still held one card up her sleeve, the photographs of Dundridge. She would call on the little goose and force him to admit that he had been blackmailed by Giles. Once she had proof of that there would be no question of the motorway continuing. She wouldn't even have to bother with her own awful photographs. Giles would be in jail, his seat in Parliament empty, a bye-election, and the whole wretched business finished.

Whatever happened now she was safe and so was the Hall. 'Fight fire with fire,' she thought and lay in bed considering the strange set of circumstances that had turned her from a plain, simple home-loving woman, a Justice of the Peace and a respectable member of the community, into a blackmailer dealing in obscene photographs and extorting signatures under threat of torture. Evidently the blood of her ancestors who had held the Gorge (by fair means and foul) against all comers still ran in her veins.

'You can't make omelettes without breaking eggs,' she murmured, and fell asleep.

In Mrs Forthby's flat one of the eggs in question lay in his frilly bonnet desperately trying to think of some way out of both his predicaments and promising himself that he would murder Nanny Fucking Whip as soon as he got free. Not that there seemed much chance of that before morning. Nanny Whip was snoring loudly on the sofa in the sitting-room. One look at Sir Giles' suffused face had been enough to persuade her that Naughty Boy's naughtiness had not diminished during her absence. A policy of continued restraint seemed called for. Nanny Whip went into the kitchen and hit the bottle of cooking brandy. 'A drop will give me some Dutch courage,' she thought and poured herself a large glass. By the time she had finished it she had forgotten what she had been taking it for. 'A little of what you fancy does you good,' she murmured, and collapsed on to the sofa.

A little of what Sir Giles fancied wasn't doing him any good at all. Besides, eight hours wasn't a little. As the clock on the mantelpiece chimed the hours Sir Giles' thoughts turned from murder to the more lurid forms of slow torture and in between he tried to think what the hell to do about Maud. There didn't seem anything he could do short of applying for the Chiltern Hundreds, resigning from all his clubs, realizing his assets and taking a quick trip to Brazil where the extradition laws didn't apply. And even then he wasn't sure he had any assets to realize. At about four in the morning it dawned on him that some of those pieces of paper he had signed had looked remarkably like share transfer certificates. At the time he hadn't been in any shape to consider them at all carefully. Not that he was in any better shape now but at least the threat of following Edward the Second to an agonizing death had been removed. Finally exhausted by his ordeal he fell into a semi-coma, waking every now and then to consider new and more awful fates for that absent-minded old sot in the next room.

Mrs Forthby woke with a hangover. She staggered off the sofa and ran a bath and it was only when she was drying herself that she remembered Sir Giles.

'Oh dear, he will be cross,' she thought, and went through to the kitchen to make a pot of tea. She carried the tray through to the bedroom and put it down on the bedside table. 'Wakey, wakey, rise and shine,' she said cheerfully and untied the straps. Sir Giles spat the dummy out of his mouth. This was the moment he had been waiting twelve hours for but there was no rising and shining for Sir Giles. He slithered sideways off the bed and crawled towards Mrs Forthby like a crab with rheumatoid arthritis.

'No, no, you naughty boy,' said Mrs Forthby horrified at his colour. She rushed out of the room and locked herself in the bathroom. There was no need to hurry. Behind her Sir Giles was stuck in the bedroom door and one of his legs had attached itself inextricably to a standard lamp.

In his office at the Regional Planning Board the Controller Motorways Midlands was having second thoughts about his plan for proving that Lady Maud was a blackmailer. The wretched woman had phoned the switchboard to say that she was coming in to Worford and wanted a word in private with him. Dundridge could well understand her desire for privacy but he did not share it. He had seen more than enough of Lady Maud in private and he had no intention of seeing any more. On the other hand she was hardly likely to threaten him with blackmail in front of a large audience. Dundridge paced up and down his office trying to find some way out of the quandary. In the end he decided to use Hoskins as a bodyguard. He sent for him.

'We've flushed the old cow out with that dynamiting,' he said.

'We've done what?' said Hoskins.

'She's coming to see me this morning. I want you to be present.'

Hoskins had his doubts. 'I don't know about that,' he muttered. 'And anyway, we haven't started dynamiting yet.'

'But the task force has moved in, hasn't it?'

'Yes, though I do wish you wouldn't call it a task force. All this military jargon is getting on my nerves.'

'Never mind that,' said Dundridge. 'The point is that she's coming. I want you to conceal yourself somewhere where you can hear what she has to say and make an appearance if she turns nasty.'

'*Turns* nasty?' said Hoskins. 'The bloody woman *is* nasty. She doesn't have to turn it.'

'I mean if she becomes violent,' Dundridge explained. 'Now then, we've got to find somewhere for you to hide. He looked hopefully at a filing cabinet but Hoskins was adamant.

'Why can't I just sit in the corner?' he asked.

'Because she wants to see me in private.'

'Well then see her in private for God's sake,' said Hoskins. 'She isn't likely to assault you.

'That's what you think,' said Dundridge. 'And in any case I want you as a witness. I have reason to believe that she is going to make an attempt to blackmail me.'

'Blackmail you?' said Hoskins turning pale. He didn't like that 'reason to believe'. It smacked of a policeman giving evidence.

'With photographs,' said Dundridge.

'With photographs?' echoed Hoskins, now thoroughly alarmed.

'Obscene photographs,' said Dundridge, with a deal more confidence than Hoskins happened to know was called for.

'What are you going to do?' he asked.

'I'm going to tell her to go jump in a lake,' said Dundridge.

Hoskins looked at him incredulously. To think that he had once described this extraordinary man as a nincompoop. The bastard was as tough as nails.

'I'll tell you what I'll do,' he said finally, 'I'll stand outside the door and listen to what she says. Will that do?'

Dundridge said it would have to and Hoskins hurried back to his office and phoned Mrs Williams.

'Sally,' he said, 'this is you-know-who.'

'I don't, you know,' said Mrs Williams, who had had a hard night.

'It's me. Horsey, horsey catkins,' snarled Hoskins desperately searching for a pseudonym that would deceive anyone listening in on the switchboard.

'Horsey horsey catkins?'

'Hoskins, for God's sake,' whispered Hoskins.

'Oh, Hoskins, why didn't you say so in the first place?'

Hoskins controlled his frayed temper. 'Listen carefully,' he said, 'the gaff's blown. The gaff. Gee for Gifuckingraffe. A for Animal. F for Freddie.'

'What's it mean?' interrupted Mrs Williams.

'The fuzz,' said Hoskins. 'It means the balloon's going to go up. Burn the lot, you understand. Negatives, prints, the tootee. You've never heard of me and I've never heard of you. Get it. No names, no pack drill. And you've never been near the Golf Club.'

By the time he had put the phone down Mrs Williams had got the message. So had Hoskins. If Mrs Williams was going to be nabbed, he could be sure that he would be standing in the dock beside her. She had left him in no doubt about that.

He went back to Dundridge's office and was there to open the door for Lady Maud when she arrived. Then he stationed himself outside and listened.

Inside Dundridge nerved himself for the ordeal. At least with Hoskins outside the door he could always call for help and in any case Lady Maud seemed to be rather better disposed towards him than he had expected.

'Mr Dundridge,' she said, taking a seat in front of his desk, 'I would like to make it quite clear that I have come here this morning in no spirit of animosity. I know we've had our little contretemps in the past but as far as I am concerned all is forgiven and forgotten.'

Dundridge looked at her balefully and said nothing. As far as he was concerned nothing was ever likely to be forgotten and certainly he wasn't in a forgiving mood.

'No, I have come here to ask for your co-operation,' she went on, 'and I want to assure you that what I am about to say will go no further.'

Dundridge glanced at the door and said he was glad to hear it.

'Yes, I rather thought you might,' said Lady Maud. 'You see I have reason to believe that you have been the subject of a blackmail attempt.'

Dundridge stared at her. She knew damned well he had been subject to blackmail.

'What makes you think that?'

'These photographs,' said Lady Maud and, producing an envelope from her handbag, she spread the torn and charred fragments of the photographs out on the desk. Dundridge studied them carefully. Why the hell were they torn and charred? He sorted through them looking for his face. It wasn't there. If she thought she was going to blackmail him with this lot she was very much mistaken.

'What about them?' he asked.

'You know nothing about them?'

'Certainly not,' said Dundridge, thoroughly confident now. He knew what had happened. He had left these photographs on Mr Ganglion's desk. Ganglion had torn them up and thrown them in the fire and had then changed his mind. He had taken them out and had visited Lady Maud and explained that he, Dundridge, had accused her of blackmail. And here she was trying to wriggle out of it. Her next remark confirmed this theory.

'Then my husband has never tried to influence you in any of your decisions by using these photographs,' she said.

'Your husband? Your husband?' said Dundridge indignantly. 'Are you suggesting that your husband has attempted to blackmail me with these ... obscene photographs?'

'Yes,' said Lady Maud, 'that is exactly what I am suggesting.'

'Then all I can say is that you are mistaken. Sir Giles has always treated me with the greatest consideration and courtesy, which is,' he glanced at the door before continuing courageously, 'more than I can say for you.'

Lady Maud looked at him, mystified. 'Is that all you have to say?'

'Yes,' said Dundridge, 'except this. Why don't you take those photographs to the police?'

Lady Maud hesitated. She hadn't bargained on this attitude from Dundridge. 'I don't think that would be very sensible, do you?'

'Yes,' said Dundridge, 'as a matter of fact I do. Now then I am a busy man and you are wasting my time. You know your way out.'

Lady Maud rose from her chair wrathfully. 'How dare you speak to me like that?' she shouted.

Dundridge leapt out of his chair and opened the door. 'Hoskins,' he said, 'show Lady Maud Lynchwood out.'

'I will find my own way,' said Lady Maud, and stormed past them and down the corridor. Dundridge went back into his office and collapsed into his chair. He had called her bluff. He had shown her the door. Nobody could say the Controller Motorways Midlands wasn't master in his own house. He was astonished at his own performance.

So was Hoskins. He stared at Dundridge for a moment and staggered back to his own office shaken by what he had just heard. She had confronted Dundridge with those awful photographs and he had had the nerve to tell her to take them to the police. My God, a man who could do that was capable of doing anything. The fat was really in the fire now. On the other hand she had said it wouldn't be sensible. Hoskins agreed with her wholeheartedly. 'She must be protecting Sir Giles,' he thought and wondered how the hell she had got hold of the photographs in the first place. For a moment he thought of phoning Sir Giles but decided against it. The best thing to do was to sit tight and keep his mouth shut and hope that things would blow over.

He had just reached this comforting conclusion when the bell rang. It was Dundridge again. Hoskins went back down the corridor and found the Controller in a jubilant mood.

'Well that's put paid to that little scheme,' he said. 'You heard her threatening me with filthy photographs. She thought she was going to get me to use my influence to change the route of the motorway. I told her.'

'You most certainly did,' said Hoskins deferentially.

'Right,' said Dundridge turning to a map he had pinned on the wall, 'we must strike while the iron is hot. Operation Overland will proceed immediately. Have the compulsory purchase orders been served?'

'Yes,' said Hoskins.

'And the task force has begun demolition work in the Gorge?'

'Demolition work?'

'Dynamiting.'

'Not yet. They've only just moved in.'

'They must start at once,' said Dundridge. 'We must keep the initiative and maintain the pressure. I intend to establish a mobile HQ here.' He pointed to a spot on the map two miles east of Guildstead Carbonell.

'A mobile HQ?' said Hoskins.

'Arrange for a caravan to be set up there. I intend to supervise this operation personally. You and I will move our offices out there.'

'That's going to be frightfully inconvenient,' Hoskins pointed out.

'Damn the inconvenience,' said Dundridge, 'I mean to have that bitch out of Handyman Hall before Christmas come hell or high water. She's on the run now and by God I mean to see she stays there.'

'Oh all right,' said Hoskins gloomily. He knew better than to argue with Dundridge now.

Lady Maud drove back to the Hall pensively. She could have sworn that the thin legs in the photographs were the legs she had seen twinkling across the marble floor but evidently she had been wrong. Dundridge's self-righteous indignation had been wholly convincing. She had expected the wretched little man to blush and stammer and make excuses but instead he had stood up to her and ordered her out of his office. He had even suggested she should take the photographs to the police and, considering his pusillanimity in other less threatening circumstances, it was impossible to suppose he had been bluffing. No, she had been wrong. It was a pity. She would have liked to have seen Sir Giles in court, but it hardly mattered. She had enough to be going on with. Sir Giles would move heaven and earth to see that the motorway was stopped now and if he failed she would force him to resign his seat. There would have to be another bye-election and what had worked in the case of Ottertown would work again in the case of the Gorge. The Government would cancel the motorway. And finally if that too failed there was always the Wildlife Park. It was one thing to demolish half a dozen houses and evict the families that lived there, but it was quite a different kettle of fish to deprive ten lions, four giraffes, a rhinoceros and a dozen ostriches of their livelihood. The British public would never stand for cruelty to animals. She arrived at the Hall to find Blott busy washing his films in the kitchen.

'I've turned the boiler-room into a darkroom,' he explained, and held up a film for her to look at. Lady Maud studied it inexpertly.

'Have they come out all right?' she asked.

'Very nicely,' said Blott. 'Quite lovely.'

'I doubt if Giles would share your opinion,' said Lady Maud and went out into the garden to pick a lettuce for lunch. Blott finished washing his films in the sink and took them down to the boiler-room and hung them up to dry. When he came back lunch was ready on the kitchen table.

'You'll eat in here with me,' said Lady Maud. 'I'm very pleased with you, Blott, and besides, it's nice to have a man about the house.'

Blott hesitated. It seemed an illogical remark. There appeared to be a great many men about the house, tramping up and down the servants' stairs to their bedrooms and working day and night on the fencing. Still, if Lady Maud wanted him to eat with her, he was not going to argue. Things were looking up. She was going to get a divorce from her husband. He was in love and while he had no hope of ever being able to do anything about it, he was happy just to sit and eat with her. And then there was the fence. Blott was delighted by the fence. It brought back memories of the war and his happiness as a prisoner. It would shut out the world and he and Maud would live singly but happily ever after.

They had just finished lunch and were washing-up when there was a dull boom in the distance and the windows rattled.

'I wonder what that was,' said Lady Maud.

'Sounds like blasting,' said Blott.

'Blasting?'

'In a quarry.'

'But there aren't any quarries round here,' said Lady Maud. They went out on to the lawn and stood looking at a cloud of dust rising slowly into the sky a mile or two to the east.

Operation Overland had begun.

CHAPTER TWENTY-ONE

And Operation Overland continued. Day after day the silence of the Gorge was broken by the rumbling of bulldozers and the dull thump of explosions as the cliffs were blasted and the rocks cleared. Day after day the contractors complained to Hoskins that the way to build a motorway was to start at the beginning and go on to the end, or at least to stick to some sort of predetermined schedule and not go jumping all over the place digging up a field here and rooting out a wood there, starting a bridge and then abandoning construction to begin a flyover. And day after day Hoskins took their complaints and some of his own to Dundridge, and was overruled.

'The essential feature of Operation Overland lies in the random nature of our movements,' Dundridge explained. 'The enemy never knows where we are going to be next.'

'Nor do I, come to that,' said Hoskins bitterly. 'I had a job finding this place this morning. You might have warned me you were going to move it before I went home last night.'

Dundridge looked round the Mobile Headquarters. 'That's odd,' he said, 'I thought *you* had it moved.'

'Me? Why should I do that?'

'I don't know. To be nearer the front line I suppose.'

'Nearer the front line?' said Hoskins. 'All I want is to be back in my bloody office, not traipsing round the countryside in a fucking caravan.'

'Well anyway, whoever had it moved had a good idea,' said Dundridge. 'We are nearer the scene of action.'

Hoskins looked out of the window as a giant dumper rumbled past.

'Nearer?' he shouted above the din. 'We're bloody well in it if you ask me.' As if to confirm his words there was a deafening roar and two hundred yards away a portion of cliff collapsed. As the dust settled Dundridge surveyed the scene with satisfaction. This was nature as man, and in particular Dundridge, intended. Nature conquered, nature subdued, nature disciplined. This was progress, slow progress but inexorable. Behind them cuttings and embankments, concrete and steel, ahead the Gorge and Handyman Hall.

'By the way,' said Hoskins when he could hear himself speak, 'we've had a complaint from General Burnett. He says one of our trucks damaged his garden wall.'

'So what?' said Dundridge. 'He won't have a garden or a wall in two months' time. What's he complaining about?'

'And Mr Bullett-Finch phoned to say—'

But Dundridge wasn't interested. 'File all complaints,' he said dismissively, 'I haven't got time for details.'

In London Sir Giles didn't share his opinion. He was obsessed with details, particularly those concerned with the sale of his shares and what Lady Maud was going to do with those damned photographs.

'I lost half a million on those shares,' he yelled at Blodger. 'Half a bleeding million.'

Blodger commiserated. 'I said at the time I thought you were being a little hasty,' he said.

'You thought? You didn't think at all,' Sir Giles screamed. 'If you'd thought you would have known that wasn't me on the phone.'

'But it sounded like you. And you asked me to call you back at your flat.'

'I did nothing of the sort. You don't seriously imagine I would sell four thousand President Rand when the market was at rock bottom. I'm not fucking insane you know.'

Blodger looked at him appraisingly. The thought had crossed his mind. It was Schaeffer who brought the altercation to an end.

'If you must swear,' he said, 'I can only suggest that you would do so more profitably before a Commissioner of Oaths.'

'And what would I want with a Commissioner of Fucking Oaths?'

'A sworn statement that the signatures on the share transfer certificates were forgeries,' said Schaeffer coldly.

Sir Giles picked up his hat. 'Don't think this is the end of the fucking matter,' he snarled. 'You'll be hearing from me again.'

Schaeffer opened the door for him. 'I can only hope fucking not,' he said.

But if his stockbrokers were not sympathetic, Mrs Forthby was.

'It's all my fault,' she wailed squinting at him through the two black eyes he had given her for her pains. 'If only I hadn't gone out for those fish fingers this would never have happened.'

'Fish fucking . . .' he began and pulled himself up. He had to keep a grip on his sanity and Mrs Forthby's self-denunciations didn't help. 'Never mind about that. I've got to think what to do. That bloody wife of mine isn't going to get away with this if I can help it.'

'Well, if all she wants is a divorce . . .'

'A divorce? A divorce? If you think that's all she wants . . .' He stopped again. Mrs Forthby mustn't hear anything about those photographs. Nobody must hear about them. The moment that information got out he would be a ruined man and he had just three weeks to do something about them. He went back to his flat and sat there trying to think of some way of stopping the motorway. There wasn't much he could do in London. His request to discuss the matter with the Minister of the Environment had been turned down, his demand for a further Inquiry denied. And his private source in the Ministry had been adamant that it was too late to do anything now.

'The thing is under construction already. Barring accidents nothing can stop it.'

Sir Giles put down the phone and thought about accidents, nasty accidents, like Maud falling downstairs and breaking her neck or having a fatal car crash. It didn't seem very likely somehow. Finally he thought about Dundridge. If Maud had something on him, he had something on the Controller Motorways Midlands. He telephoned Hoskins at the Regional Planning Board.

'He's out at SHMOCON,' said the girl on the switchboard.

'Shmocon?' said Sir Giles desperately trying to think of a village by that name in South Worfordshire.

'Supreme Headquarters Motorway Construction,' said the girl. 'He's Deputy Field Commander.'

'What?' said Sir Giles. 'What the hell's going on up there?'

'Don't ask me,' said the girl, 'I'm only a field telegraphist. Shall I put you through?'

'Yes,' said Sir Giles. 'It sounds batty to me.'

'It is,' said the girl. 'It's a wonder I don't have to use morse code.'

Certainly Hoskins sounded peculiar when Sir Giles finally got through to him. 'Deputy Field—' he began but Sir Giles interrupted.

'Don't give me that crap, Hoskins,' he shouted. 'What the hell do you think you're playing at? Some sort of war game?'

'Yes,' said Hoskins looking nervously out of the window. There was a deafening roar as a charge of dynamite went off.

'What the hell was that?' yelled Sir Giles.

'Just a near miss,' said Hoskins as small fragments of rock rattled on the roof of the caravan.

'You can cut the wisecracks,' said Sir Giles, 'I didn't call you to talk nonsense. There's been a change of plan. The motorway has got to be stopped. I've decided ...'

'Stopped?' Hoskins interrupted him. 'You haven't a celluloid rat's hope in hell of stopping this little lot now. We're advancing into the Gorge at the rate of a hundred yards a day.'

'Into the Gorge?'

'You heard me,' said Hoskins.

'Good God,' said Sir Giles. 'What the hell's been going on? Has Dundridge gone off his head or something?'

'You could put it like that,' said Hoskins hesitantly. The Controller Motorways Midlands had just come into the caravan covered in dust and was taking off his helmet.

'Well, stop him,' shouted Sir Giles.

'I'm afraid that is impossible, sir,' said Hoskins modulating his tone to indicate that he was no longer alone. 'I will make a note of your complaint, and forward it to the appropriate authorities.'

'You'll do more than that,' bawled Sir Giles, 'you'll use those photographs. You will—'

'I understand the police deal with these matters, sir,' said Hoskins. 'As far as we are concerned I can only suggest that you use an incinerator.'

'An *incinerator*? What the hell do I want with an incinerator?'

'I have found that the best method is to burn that sort of rubbish. The answer is in the negative.'

'In the negative?'

'Quite, sir,' said Hoskins. 'I have found that it avoids the health risk to incinerate inflammable material. And now if you'll excuse me, I have someone with me.' Hoskins rang off and Sir Giles sat back and deciphered his message.

'Incinerators. Police. Negative. Health risks.' These were the words Hoskins had emphasized and it dawned on Sir Giles that all hope of influencing Dundridge had gone up in flames. He was particularly alarmed by the mention of the police. 'Good God, that little bastard Dundridge has been to the cops,' he muttered, and suddenly recalled that his safe at Handyman Hall contained evidence that hadn't been incinerated. Maud was sitting on a safe containing photographs that could send him to prison. 'Inflammable material. That bitch can get me five years,' he thought. 'I'd like to incinerate her.' Incinerate her? Sir

Giles stared into space. He had suddenly seen a way out of all his problems.

He picked up a pencil and detailed the advantages. Number One, he would destroy the evidence of his attempt to blackmail Dundridge. Number Two, he would get rid of those photographs Blott had taken of him in Mrs Forthby's flat. Number Three, by acting before Maud could divorce him he would still be the owner of the ashes of Handyman Hall and liable for the insurance money and possibly the compensation from the motorway. Number Four, if Maud were to die ... Number Four was a particularly attractive prospect and just the sort of accident he had been hoping for.

He picked up the sheet of paper and carried it across to the fireplace and lit a match. As the paper flared up Sir Giles watched it with immense satisfaction. There was nothing like a good fire for cleansing the past. All he needed now was a perfect alibi.

At Handyman Hall Lady Maud surveyed her handiwork with equal satisfaction. The fence had been finished in ten days, the lions, giraffes, and the rhinoceros had been installed and the ostriches were accommodated in the old tennis court. It was really very pleasant to wander round the house and watch the lions padding across the park or lying under the trees.

'It gives one a certain sense of security,' she told Blott, whose movements had been restricted to the kitchen garden and who complained that the rhinoceros was mucking up the lawn.

'It may give you a sense of security,' said Blott, 'but the postman has other ideas. He won't come further than the Lodge and the milkman won't either.'

'What nonsense,' said Lady Maud. 'The way to deal with lions is to put a bold front on and look them squarely in the eyes.'

'That's as maybe,' said Blott, 'but that rhino needs spectacles.'

'The thing with rhinos,' said Lady Maud, 'is to move at right angles to their line of approach.'

'That didn't work with the butcher's van. You've no idea what it did to his back mudguard.'

'I have a very precise idea. Sixty pounds worth of damage but it didn't charge the van.'

'No,' said Blott, 'it just leant up again it and scratched its backside.'

'Well at least the giraffes are behaving themselves,' said Lady Maud.

'What's left of them,' said Blott.

'What do you mean "What's left of them"?'

'Well, there's only two left.'

'Two? But there were four. Where have the other two got to?'

'You had better ask the lions about that,' Blott told her. 'I have an idea they rather like giraffes for dinner.'

'In that case we had better order another hundredweight of meat from the butchers. We can't have them eating one another.'

She strode off across the lawn imperiously, stopping to prod the rhinoceros with her shooting stick. 'I won't have you in the rockery,' she told it. Outside the kitchen door a lion was snoozing in the sun. 'Be off with you, you lazy beast.' The lion got up and slunk away.

Blott watched with admiration and then shut the door of the kitchen garden. 'What a woman,' he murmured and went back to the tomatoes. He was interrupted five minutes later by a dull thump from the Gorge. Blott looked up. They were getting nearer. It was about time he did something about that business. So far his efforts had been confined to moving Dundridge's mobile headquarters about the countryside at night and altering the position of the pegs that marked the route so that had the motorway proceeded as the contractors desired it would have been several degrees off course. Unfortunately Dundridge's insistence on random construction had defeated Blott's efforts. His only success had been the felling of all the trees in Colonel Chapman's orchard which was a quarter of a mile away from the supposed route of the motorway. Blott was rather proud of that. The Colonel had raised Cain with the authorities and had been promised additional compensation. A few more miscalculations like that and there would be a public outcry. Blott applied his mind to the problem.

That night Blott visited the Royal George at Guildstead Carbonell for the first time in several weeks.

Mrs Wynn greeted him enthusiastically. 'I'm so glad you've come,' she said, 'I thought you'd given me up for good.'

Blott said he had been busy. 'Busy?' said Mrs Wynn. 'You're one to talk. I've been rushed off my feet with all the men from the motorway. They come in here at lunch and they're back at night. I tell you, I can't remember anything like it.'

Blott looked round the bar and could see what she meant. The pub was filled with construction workers. He helped himself to a pint of Handyman Brown and went to a table in the corner. An hour later he was deep in conversation with the driver of a bulldozer.

'Must be interesting work knocking things down,' said Blott.

'The pay's good,' said the driver.

'I imagine you've got to be a real expert to demolish a big building like Handyman Hall.'

'I don't know. The bigger they is the harder they falls is what I say,' said the driver, flattered by Blott's interest.

'Let me get you another pint,' said Blott.

Three pints later the driver was explaining the niceties of demolition to a fascinated Blott.

'It's a question of hitting the corner stone,' he said. 'Find that, swing the ball back and let it go and Bob's your uncle, the whole house is down like a pack of cards. I tell you I've done that more times than you've had hot dinners.'

Blott said he could well believe it. By closing time he knew a great deal about demolition work and the driver said he looked forward to meeting him again. Blott helped Mrs Wynn with washing the glasses and then did his duty by her but his heart wasn't in it. Mrs Wynn noticed it.

'You're not your usual self tonight,' she said when they had finished. Blott grunted. 'Mind you I can't say I'm any great shakes myself. My legs are killing me. What I need is a holiday.'

'Why don't you take a day off?' said Blott.

'How can I? Who would look after the customers?'

'I would,' said Blott.

At five he was up and cycling down the main street of Guildstead Carbonell towards Handyman Hall. At seven he had fed the lions and when Lady Maud came down to breakfast Blott was waiting for her.

'I'm taking the day off,' he announced.

'You're what?' said Lady Maud. Blott didn't take days off.

'Taking the day off. And I'll need the Land-Rover.'

'What for?' said Lady Maud who wasn't used to being told by her gardener that he needed her Land-Rover.

'Never you mind,' said Blott. 'No names, no pack drill.'

'No names, no pack drill? Are you feeling all right?'

'And a note for Mr Wilkes at the Brewery to say he's to give me Very Special Brew.'

Lady Maud sat down at the kitchen table and looked at him doubtfully. 'I don't like the sound of this, Blott. You're up to something.'

'And I don't like the sound of that,' said Blott as a dull thump came from the Gorge. Lady Maud nodded. She didn't like the sound of it either.

'Has it got anything to do with that?' she asked. Blott nodded. 'In that case you can have what you want but I don't want you getting into any trouble on my account, you understand.'

She went through to the study and wrote a note to Mr Wilkes, the manager of the Handyman Brewery in Worford, telling him to give Blott whatever he asked for.

At ten Blott was in the manager's office.

'Very Special?' said Mr Wilkes. 'But Very Special is for special occasions. Coronations and suchlike.'

'This is a special occasion,' said Blott.

Mr Wilkes looked at the letter again. 'If Lady Maud says so, I suppose I must, but it's strictly against the law to sell Very Special. It's twenty per cent proof.'

'And ten bottles of vodka,' said Blott. They went down to the cellar and loaded the Land-Rover.

'Forget you've seen me,' Blott said when they had finished.

'I'll do my best,' said the manager, 'this is all bloody irregular.'

Blott drove to the Royal George and saw Mrs Wynn on to the bus. Then he went back into the pub and set to work. By lunchtime he had emptied one barrel of Handyman Bitter down the drain and had refilled it with bottles of Very Special and five bottles of vodka. He tried it out on a couple of customers and was delighted with the result. During the afternoon he had a nap and then took a stroll through the village and up past the Bullett-Finches' house. It was a large house in mock Tudor set back from the road and with a very fine garden. Outside the gates a sign announced that Finch Grove was For Sale. The Bullett-Finches didn't fancy living within a hundred yards of a motorway. Blott didn't blame them. Then he walked back through the village and looked at Miss Percival's cottage. That wasn't for sale. It was due for demolition and Miss Percival had already vacated it. A large crane with a steel ball on the end of its arm stood nearby. Blott climbed into the driver's seat and played with the controls. Then he walked back to the pub and sat behind the bar, waiting for opening time.

CHAPTER TWENTY-TWO

Sir Giles busied himself in Mrs Forthby's flat. He altered the date on the clock on the mantelpiece. He turned the pages of the *Radio Times* to the following day and hid the newspaper. Several times he asserted that today was Wednesday.

'That just goes to show what a muddlehead I am,' said Mrs Forthby, who was busy making supper in the kitchen, 'I could have sworn it was Tuesday.'

'Tomorrow's Thursday,' said Sir Giles.

'If you say so, dear,' said Mrs Forthby. 'I'm sure I don't know what day of the week it is. My memory is simply shocking.'

Sir Giles nodded approvingly. It was on Mrs Forthby's appalling memory that his alibi depended, that and sleeping pills. 'Silly old bitch won't miss a day in her life,' he thought as he crunched six tablets up in the bottom of a glass with the handle of a toothbrush before adding a large tot of whisky. According to his doctor the lethal dose was twelve. 'Six would probably put you out for twenty-four hours,' the doctor had told him and twenty-four hours was all Sir Giles needed. He went through to the kitchen and had supper.

'What about a nightcap?' he said when they had finished.

'You know I never drink,' said Mrs Forthby.

'You did the other night. You finished half a bottle of cooking brandy.'

'That was different. I wasn't feeling myself.'

It was on the tip of Sir Giles' tongue to tell her that she wouldn't feel anything let alone herself by the time she had finished that little lot but he restrained himself. 'Cheers,' he said, and finished his glass.

'Cheers,' said Mrs Forthby doubtfully and sipped her whisky.

Sir Giles poured himself another glass. 'Down the hatch,' he said.

Mrs Forthby took another sip. 'You know I could have sworn today was Tuesday,' she said.

Sir Giles could have sworn, period. 'Today is Wednesday.'

'But I've got a hair appointment on Wednesday. If today is Wednesday I must have missed it.'

'You have,' said Sir Giles truthfully. Whatever happened, Mrs Forthby had missed her hair appointment. He raised his glass. 'Mud in your eye.'

'Mud in your eye,' said Mrs Forthby and sipped again. 'If today is

Wednesday, tomorrow must be Thursday in which case I've got a pottery class in the afternoon.'

Sir Giles poured himself another whisky hurriedly. It was on just such insignificant details that the best plans floundered. 'I was thinking of going down to Brighton for the weekend,' he improvised. 'I thought you would like that.'

'With me?' said Mrs Forthby, her eyes shining.

'Just us two together,' said Sir Giles.

'Oh, you are thoughtful.'

'A votre santé,' said Sir Giles.

Mrs Forthby finished her drink and got to her feet. 'It's Nurse Catheter tonight, isn't it?' she said moving unsteadily towards him.

'Forget it,' said Sir Giles, 'I'm not in the mood.' Nor was Mrs Forthby. He carried her through to the bedroom and put her to bed. When he left the flat five minutes later she was snoring soundly. By the time she woke up he would be back and in bed beside her. He got into his car and began the drive north.

At the Royal George in Guildstead Carbonell Blott's experiment in induced narcosis proceeded more slowly but with gayer results. By nine o'clock the pub was filled with singing dumper drivers, two fights had erupted and died down before they could get well under way, a darts match had had to be cancelled when a non-participant had been pinned by his ear to last year's calendar, and two consenting adults had been ejected from the Gents by Blott and Mrs Wynn's Alsatian. By ten o'clock Blott's promise that the Very Special was needed for a special occasion had been fulfilled to the letter. Two more fights, this time between locals and the men from the motorway, had started and had not died down but had spread to the Saloon Bar where the operator of a piledriver was attempting to demonstrate his craft to the fiancée of the secretary of the Young Conservatives, the darts match had been resumed using a portrait of Sir Winston Churchill as a dartboard, and half a dozen bulldozer drivers were giving an exhibition of clog dancing on the bar-billiards table. In between whiles Blott had coaxed Mr Edwards, who claimed to have knocked down more houses than Blott had had hot dinners, into a nicely belligerent mood.

'I can knock any damned house you like to show me down with one bloody blow,' he shouted.

Blott raised an eyebrow. 'Tell me another one.'

'I tell you I can,' Mr Edwards asserted. 'One knock in the right place and Bob's your uncle.'

'I'll believe it when I see it,' said Blott and poured him another pint of Very Special.

'I'll show you. I'll bloody show you,' said Mr Edwards and took a swig.

By closing time Very Special had cast if not a healing balm at least a soporific one on the whole proceedings. As the motorway men stumbled off to their cars and the Young Conservatives drove off nursing their wounds, Blott shut up shop and helped Mr Edwards to his feet.

'I tell you I can,' he mumbled.

'Never,' said Blott.

Together they staggered off down the street towards Miss Percival's cottage, Blott clutching a bottle of vodka and Mr Edwards' arm.

'I'll show you,' said Mr Edwards as they crossed the field to the cottage. 'I'll fucking show you.'

He climbed into the crane and started it up. Blott stood behind him and watched.

'Oh what a pity she's only one titty to bang against the wall,' Mr Edwards sang as the crane jerked forward through the hedge and into the garden. Behind them the iron ball wobbled and swung. Mr Edwards stopped the crane and adjusted the controls. The arm of the crane swung round and the ball followed. It went wide.

'I thought you said you could do it in one,' said Blott.

'That,' said Mr Edwards, 'was just a practice swing.' He lowered the crane and a sundial disintegrated. Mr Edwards raised it again.

'Never been laid, never been made, Queen of all the Fairies,' he bawled. The crane swung round and Blott darted out of the way as the iron ball lolloped past him. The next moment it hurtled into the side of the cottage. There was a roar of falling bricks, tiles, breaking glass and a great cloud of dust momentarily obscured what had once been Miss Percival's attractive home. When the dust finally cleared what remained of the cottage held few attractions. On the other hand it was not entirely demolished. A chimney still stood and the roof while hanging at a disreputable angle was still recognizably the roof. Blott regarded the result sceptically.

'I don't think much of that,' he said superciliously. 'Still I suppose there's always a first time.'

'Whadja mean always a first time?' said Mr Edwards. 'I knocked it down, didn't I?'

'No,' said Blott, 'not with one blow.'

Mr Edwards consoled himself with vodka. ''sonly a fucking cottage. Can't expect much with a cottage. Got no bulk to it. Gotta have bulk, got to have weight. Show me a house, a proper house, a big bulky house and I'll ...' He slumped over the controls. Blott climbed up into the cab and shook him.

'Wake up,' he shouted. Mr Edwards woke up.

'Show me a proper house ...'

'All right, I will,' said Blott. 'Show me how to drive this thing and I'll show you a proper house.'

Mr Edwards did his best to show him. 'You pull that lever and you press that 'celerator.' Five minutes later Guildstead Carbonell, already disturbed by the eruption of violence at the Royal George, was convulsed a second time as Blott with Mr Edwards' assistance attempted to negotiate the High Street at something over the statutory speed limit. As the mobile crane hurtled into the first of several corners at forty miles per hour Blott struggled to keep it on the road. He wasn't helped by Mr Edwards' inertia nor by that of the iron ball which, swinging behind, tended to demonstrate the attractions of centrifugal force. On the first corner it gave a glancing blow to the plate-glass window of a newly opened mini-market, bounced off the roof of a parked car, entered the front parlour of Mrs Tate's house and came out through Mr and Mrs Williams' sitting-room, decapitated the War Memorial and took a telegraph pole and fifty yards of wire in tow. On the second it took a short cut through the forecourt of Mr Dugdale's garage neatly severing the stanchions that had formerly supported the roof and demolishing four petrol pumps and a sign advertising free tumblers. By the time they had traversed the rest of the High Street, the ball had left its imprint on seven more cars and the façades of twelve splendid examples of eighteenth-century domestic architecture while the telegraph pole, not to be left out of things, had vaulted through every third window before disentangling itself from the crane and coming to rest in the vestry of the Primitive Methodist Chapel taking with it a large sign announcing the Coming of the Lord. As they left the village, the iron ball made its last contribution to the peace and tranquillity of the place by nudging an electricity transformer which exploded with a galaxy of blue sparks and plunged the entire district into darkness. At this point Mr Edwards woke up.

'Where are we?' he mumbled.

'Almost there,' said Blott, managing to slow the crane down. Mr Edwards took another swig of vodka.

'Show me the way to go home,' he sang, 'I'm tired and I want to go to bed.'

'Not yet,' said Blott and turned the crane up the drive towards the Bullett-Finches' house.

*

It was one of Mrs Bullett-Finch's pleasanter qualities from her husband's point of view that she went to bed early. 'It's the early bird that catches the worm,' she would say at nine o'clock every night and take herself upstairs, leaving Mr Bullett-Finch to sit up by himself and read about lawns in peace and quiet. And lawns interested him. They held a charm for him that Ivy Bullett-Finch had long since relinquished. Lawns improved with age, which was more than could be said for wives and what Mr Bullett-Finch didn't know about browntop and chewing fescue and velvet bent was not worth knowing. And the lawns around Finch Grove were in his opinion among the finest in the country. They stretched immaculately in front of the house down to the stream at the bottom of the garden. Not a dandelion scarred their surface, not a plantain, not a daisy. For six years Mr Bullett-Finch had nurtured his lawns, sanding, mowing, spiking, fertilizing, weedkilling, even going so far as to prohibit visitors with high heels from walking on them. And when Ivy wanted to go down to the orchard she had to wear her bedroom slippers. It may have been this insistence on his part that the front garden was sacrosanct that had contributed to her nervous disposition and sense of guilt. What the garden was to her husband, the house was to Ivy, a source of obsessive concern in which everything had its place, was dusted twice a day and polished three times a week so that she went to bed early less out of indolence than from sheer exhaustion and lay there wondering if she had turned everything off.

On this particular night Mr Bullett-Finch was deep in a chapter on hormone weedkillers when the lights went out. He got up and stumbled through to the fusebox only to find that the fuses were intact.

'Must be a power failure,' he thought and went up to bed in the dark. He had just undressed and was putting on his pyjamas when he became aware that something extremely large and powered by an enormous diesel engine appeared to be making its way up his drive. He rushed to the window and peered out into two powerful headlights. Temporarily blinded, he groped for his dressing-gown and slippers, found them and put them on and looked out of the window again. What looked like a gigantic crane had stopped on the gravel forecourt and was backing on to his lawn. With a scream of rage Mr Bullett-Finch told it to stop but it was too late. A moment later there was a winching noise and the crane began to swing. Mr Bullett-Finch pulled his head in the window and raced for the stairs. He was halfway down them when all concern for his precious lawn disappeared, to be replaced by the absolute conviction that Finch Grove was at the very centre of some gigantic earthquake. As the house disintegrated around him – Mr Edwards' claim to be a demolition expert entirely vindicated – Mr Bullett-Finch clung to the banisters and peered through a dust-storm of plaster and powdered brick while the furnishings of which his wife had been so rightly proud hurtled past him from the upstairs rooms. Among them came Mrs Bullett-Finch herself, screaming and hysterically proclaiming her innocence, which had until then never been in doubt, and he was just debating why she should assume responsibility for what was obviously a natural cataclysm when he was saved the trouble by the roof collapsing on top of him and the staircase collapsing underneath. Mr Bullett-Finch descended into the cellar and lay unconscious, surrounded by his small stock of claret. Mrs Bullett-Finch, still clinging to her mattress and the conviction that she had left the gas on, had meanwhile been catapulted into the herb-garden where she sobbed convulsively among the thyme.

From the cab of his crane Mr Edwards regarded his handiwork with pride.

'Told you I could do it,' he said and seized the bottle of vodka from Blott who had been steadying his nerves with it. Blott let him finish it. Then dragged him down from the cab and climbed back to wipe any fingerprints from the controls. Finally, hoisting Mr Edwards over his shoulder, he set off down the drive.

By the time he reached the Royal George Mrs Wynn was back from Worford, and washing glasses by candlelight.

'Look at all this mess,' she said irately, 'I leave you to look after the place for one day and what do I find when I get back. Anyone would think there had been an orgy here. And what's been going on in the village, I'd like to know? The place looks like it's been bombed.'

Blott helped with the glasses and then went out to the Land-Rover. Mr Edwards was still sleeping soundly in the back. He drove slowly out of the yard and turned towards Ottertown. It was a longer way round but Blott didn't want to be seen in the High Street. He stopped at the caravan site where the motorway workers lived and deposited Mr Edwards on the grass. Then he drove on towards the Gorge and Handyman Hall. At two o'clock he was in bed in the Lodge. All in all it had been a good day's work.

In Dundridge's flat the phone rang. He groped for it sleepily and switched on the light. It was Hoskins. 'What the hell do you want? Do you realize what time it is?'

'Yes,' said Hoskins, 'as a matter of fact I do. I just wanted to tell you that you've gone too far this time.'

'Gone too far?' said Dundridge. 'I haven't gone anywhere.'

'Don't give me that,' said Hoskins. 'You and your random sorties and your task forces and assault groups. Well you've certainly landed us in it this time. There were people living in that fucking house, you know, and it wasn't even scheduled for demolition in the first place and as for what you've done to Guildstead Carbonell ... I hope you realize that the motorway wasn't supposed to go within a mile of that village. It's a historical monument, Guildstead Carbonell is ... was. It's a fucking ruin now, a disaster area.'

'A disaster area?' said Dundridge. 'What do you mean a disaster area?'

'You know very well what I mean,' shouted Hoskins hysterically. 'I always thought you were mad but now I know it.' He slammed the phone down, leaving Dundridge mystified. He sat on the edge of his bed and wondered what to do. Clearly something had gone wrong with Operation Overland. He was just about to call Hoskins back when the phone rang again. This time it was the police.

'Is that Mr Dundridge?'

'Yes, speaking.'

'This is the Chief Constable. I wonder if I could have a word with you. It's about this business at Guildstead Carbonell ...'

Dundridge got dressed.

Sir Giles parked his car outside Wilfrid's Castle Church. It was an unfrequented spot and nobody was likely to be out and about at two o'clock in the morning. It was one of the great advantages of a Bentley that it was not a noisy car. For the last five miles Sir Giles had driven without lights, coasting past farmhouses and keeping to back roads. He had seen no other vehicles and, so far as he could tell, had been seen by nobody. So far so good. Leaving the car he made his way down the footpath to the bridge. It was dark down there under the trees and he had some difficulty in finding his way. On the far side of the bridge he came to a wire-mesh gate. Using his torch briefly he unlatched it and went through into the pinetum. The gate puzzled Sir Giles. It was a long time since he had been over the bridge, not since the day of his wedding in fact, but he felt sure there had been no gate there then. Still he hadn't time to worry about little things like that. He had to move quickly. It wasn't easy. The pinetum was dark enough by daylight. At night it was pitch black. Sir Giles shone his torch on the ground and moved forward cautiously grateful to the carpet of pine needles that deadened his footsteps. He was halfway through the wood when he became conscious that he was not alone. Something was breathing nearby.

He switched off his torch and listened. Above him the pine trees sighed in a light breeze and for a moment Sir Giles hoped he had been mistaken. The next moment he knew he hadn't. An extraordinary whistling, wheezing noise issued from the wood. 'Must be a cow with asthma,' he thought though how an asthmatic cow had got into the pinetum he couldn't imagine. A moment later he was disabused of the notion of a cow. With a horrible snort whatever it was got to its feet, a process that involved breaking a number of branches, large branches by the sound of things, and lumbered off with a singlemindedness of purpose that seemed to bring it into contact with a great many trees. Sir Giles stood and quaked, partly from fear and partly because the ground beneath his feet was also quaking, and when finally the creature smashed through the iron fence at the edge of the wood with as little regard for property as for its own health and welfare he was in two minds about going on. In the end he forced himself to continue, though more cautiously. After all, whatever he had disturbed, it *had* run away.

Sir Giles came to the gate and stared at the house. The place was in darkness. He walked quickly across the lawn and round to the front door. Then taking off his shoes he unlocked the door and stepped inside. Silence. He went down the corridor to his study and shut the door. Then he switched on his torch and shone it on the safe – or rather on the hole in the wall where the safe had been. Sir Giles stared at it in horror. No wonder Hoskins had talked so insistently about incinerators and inflammable material and health risks. It hadn't been Dundridge who had been threatening to go to the police. It was Maud. But had she been already? There was no way of telling. He switched off the torch and stood in the darkness thinking. There was certainly one way of ensuring that if she hadn't been already she wasn't going to in future. Any doubts he had had, and they were few, about the wisdom of disposing of Handyman Hall and Maud disappeared. He would make certain of the bitch. He opened the door of the study and listened for a moment before tiptoeing down the passage towards the kitchen. Kitchens were the logical place for fires to start of their own accord and besides there were the oil tanks that fed the Aga cooker. On the way he stopped to put on his Wellington boots in the cloakroom under the stairs.

The twang of the iron fence woke Lady Maud. She sat up in bed and wondered what it portended. Iron fences didn't twang of their own accord and rhinoceroses didn't go charging across rockeries in the small hours of the morning without good reason. She switched on the bedside lamp to see what time it was but thanks to the power failure at Guildstead Carbonell the light didn't come on. Peculiar. She got out of bed and went to the window and was just in time to see a shadow slip across the lawn and disappear round the side of the house. It was a distinctly furtive shadow and it came from the pinetum. For a moment she supposed it to be Blott, but there was no reason for Blott to be running furtively about the park at ... she looked at her watch ... half past two in the morning. Anyway she could always check. She picked up the phone and dialled the Lodge.

'Blott,' she whispered, 'are you there?'

'Yes,' said Blott.

'Are the gates locked?'

'Yes,' said Blott, 'why?'

'I just wanted to make sure.' She put the phone down gently and got dressed. Then she went downstairs quietly and tried the front door. It was unlocked. Lady Maud looked around. A pair of shoes on the doorstep. She picked them up and sniffed. Giles. Unmistakably Giles. Then she put the shoes down again and shutting the front door behind her went round to the workshop. So the little beast had come back. She could imagine what for. Well, come back he might but he wouldn't get away so easily. A moment later she was running, remarkably swiftly for so large a woman and so dark a night, across the lawn towards the pinetum. Even there in the pitch darkness her pace did not slacken. A life-time's familiarity with the path gave her an unerring sense of when to twist or turn through the trees. Five minutes later she was at the gate to the footbridge. She reached into her pocket and took out a large lock, fitted it to the bolt and closed the hasp. Then, having tested it to see that it was firmly fastened, she turned and made her way back towards the Hall.

In the kitchen Sir Giles took his time. The essence of successful arson lay in simplicity, and murder was best when it looked like natural death. The Aga cooker was self-igniting. It came on automatically at intervals during the night. Sir Giles shone his torch on the time switch and saw that it was set for four o'clock. Plenty of time. He took an adjustable spanner out of his pocket and undid the nut that secured the feedpipe from the oil tanks to the stove. Oil began to pour out over the floor. Sir Giles sat down on a chair and listened to it. It slurped out steadily and spread under the table. Presently it would begin to run down the passage into the hall. There were a thousand gallons of heating oil in those tanks and as Sir Giles knew they had recently been filled. He would wait until they were empty and then replace the feedpipe but not tightly. To the police and the insurance investigators it would look as though there had been a simple leak. Yes, a thousand gallons of heating oil would certainly do the trick. Handyman Hall would turn into a raging furnace in seconds. The fire brigade would take at least half an hour to come from Worford and by that time the place would be in ashes. So would Maud. Sir Giles knew her too well to suppose that she would be sensible enough to jump from her bedroom window even if she had time. She might not even wake before the flames reached the first floor and if she did her first thought would be to rush out on to the landing and try to save her precious family home. It would be Blott in the Lodge who would raise the alarm. It was a pity about Blott. Sir Giles would have liked him to be cremated too.

Outside in the garden Lady Maud stood looking at the house. Giles had come back to look for the negatives of the pictures they had taken of him. Well, he was hardly likely to find them. Blott had cut them into strips of six and had taken them back to the Lodge with him. Or perhaps he had come to get those photographs from his safe. He was going to be disappointed there too. Whichever way she looked at it he was going to be in for a nasty surprise. She went round to the front door and picked up his shoes. It might not be a bad idea to remove those while she was about it. She took them round to the garage and put them in an empty bucket and she was just coming out again when it struck her that there might be a more sinister purpose in Giles' visit. Six years of cohabitation with the brute had taught her that he was as ruthless as he was devious. It would pay her to be careful.

'I had better watch my step,' she thought, and went round to the kitchen door. She was just about to unlock it when she stepped in something slippery. She steadied herself and reached down. Oil. It was seeping out from under the kitchen door and down the steps into the yard. A moment later she understood the purpose of his visit. He was going to burn the Hall. By God, he wasn't. With a howl of rage Lady Maud hurled herself at the door, unlocked it and charged into the kitchen. For a moment she remained upright, the next she was flat on her back and sliding across the floor. So was Sir Giles though in a different direction. As Lady Maud's great bulk swept under him carrying his chair with her, Sir Giles catapulted through the air, landed on his face and slid irresistibly down the corridor and across the marble floor of the great hall. As he floundered about trying to get to his feet in a sea of oil he could hear Maud ricocheting about the kitchen. By the sound of things she had been joined by the entire complement of pots, pans, and kitchen utensils. Sir Giles slithered to the front door and managed to get to his feet on the mat. He grasped the handle and tried to turn it. The fucking thing wouldn't turn. He groped in his pocket for a handkerchief and wiped his hands and the doorknob and an instant later he was outside and reaching for his shoes. The bloody things weren't there.

There wasn't time to look for them. Behind him Maud had finally overcome the combined forces of grease and gravity and was coming down the passage promising to strangle him with her own bare hands. Sir Giles waited no longer. He galumphed off in his gumboots down the drive and across the lawn towards the pinetum. Behind him Lady Maud slithered into the downstairs lavatory and emerged with a shotgun. She went to the front door and opened it. Sir Giles was still visible across the lawn. Lady Maud raised the gun and fired. He was out of range but at least she had the satisfaction of knowing that he wouldn't come near the house again in a hurry. She put the gun back and began to clean up the mess.

CHAPTER TWENTY-THREE

In the Lodge Blott heard the shot and leapt out of bed. Lady Maud's telephone call had disturbed him. Why should she want to know if the gates were locked? And why had she whispered? Something was up. And with the sound of the shotgun Blott was certain. He dressed and went downstairs with his twelve-bore to the Land-Rover which he had parked just inside the archway. Before getting in he checked the lock on the gate. It was quite secure. Then he drove off up to the Hall and parked outside the front door and went inside.

'It's me, Blott,' he called into the darkness. 'Are you all right?'

From the kitchen there came the sound of someone sliding about and a muffled curse.

'Don't move,' Lady Maud shouted. 'There's oil everywhere.'

'Oil?' said Blott. Now that he came to think of it there was a stench of oil in the house.

'He's tried to burn the house down.'

Blott stared into the darkness and promised that if he got the chance he would kill him. 'The bastard,' he muttered. Lady Maud slithered down the passage with a squeegee.

'Now listen carefully, Blott,' she said. 'I want you to do something for me.'

'Anything,' said Blott gallantly.

'He came in through the pinetum. I've locked the gate there so he can't get out but his car must be up at Wilfrid's Castle. I want you to drive round there and remove the dis ... the thing that goes round.'

'The rotor arm,' said Blott.

'Right,' said Lady Maud. 'And while you are about it you might as well put extra locks on both the gates. We must make quite sure that innocent people don't get into the park. Do you understand?'

Blott smiled in the darkness. He understood.

'I'll take the rotor arm off the Land-Rover too,' he said.

'A wise precaution,' Lady Maud agreed. 'And when you have finished come back here. I don't think he'll return tonight but it might be as well to take precautions.'

Blott turned to the door.

'There's just one other thing,' said Lady Maud. 'I don't think we'll feed the lions in the morning. They'll just have to fend for themselves for a day or two.'

'I didn't intend to,' said Blott and went outside.

Lady Maud sighed happily. It was so nice to have a real man about the house.

At Finch Grove Ivy Bullett-Finch's feelings were quite the reverse. What was left of the house seemed to be about the man and in any case what was left of Mr Bullett-Finch was real only in a material sense. He had died, as he had lived, concerned for the welfare of his lawn. Dundridge arrived with the Chief Constable in time to pay his last respects. As firemen carried her husband's remains out of the cellar, Mrs Bullett-Finch, relieved of the burden of guilt about the oven, vented her feelings on the Controller Motorways Midlands.

'You murderer,' she screamed, 'you killed him. You killed him with your awful ball.' She was led away by a policewoman. Dundridge looked balefully at the ball and crane.

'Nonsense,' he said, 'I had nothing to do with it.'

'We have been led to understand by your deputy, Mr Hoskins, that you gave orders for random sorties to be made by task forces of demolition experts,' said the Chief Constable. 'It would rather appear that they've carried out your instructions to the letter.'

'My instructions?' said Dundridge. 'I gave no instructions for this house to be demolished. Why should I?'

'We were rather hoping you would be able to tell us,' said the Chief Constable.

'But it's not even scheduled for demolition.'

'Quite. Nor to the best of my knowledge was the High Street. But since your equipment was used in both cases—'

'It's not my equipment,' shouted Dundridge, 'it belongs to the contractors. If anyone is fucking responsible—'

'I'd be glad if you didn't use offensive language,' said the Chief Constable. 'The situation is unpleasant enough as it is. Local feeling is running high. I think it would be best if you accompanied us to the station.'

'The station? Do you mean the police station?' said Dundridge.

'It's just for your own protection,' said the Chief Constable. 'We don't want any more accidents tonight, now do we?'

'This is monstrous,' said Dundridge.

'Quite so,' said the Chief Constable. 'And now if you'll just step this way.'

As the police car wound its way slowly through the rubble that littered the High Street, Dundridge could see that Hoskins had been telling the truth when he called Guildstead Carbonell a disaster area. The transformer still smouldered in the grey dawn, the Primitive Methodist Chapel lived up to at least part of its name, while the horribly mis-shapen relics of a dozen cars crouched beside the glass-strewn pavement. What the iron ball hadn't done with the aid of the telegraph pole to end Guildstead Carbonell's reputation for old-world charm, the conflagration at Mr Dugdale's garage had. Ignited by some unidentifiable public-spirited person who had brought out a paraffin lamp to warn passers-by to watch out for the debris, the blast from the petrol storage tanks had blown in what few windows remained unbroken after Blott's passing and had set fire to the thatched roofs of several delightful cottages. The fire had spread to a row of almshouses. The simultaneous arrival of fire engines from Worford and Ottertown had added to the chaos. Working with high-pressure hoses in total darkness they had swept a number of inadequately clothed old-age pensioners who had escaped from the almshouses down the street before turning their attention to the Public Library which they had filled with foam. To Dundridge, staring miserably out of the window of the police car, the knowledge that he was held responsible for the catastrophe was intolerable. He wished now that he had never set eyes on South Worfordshire.

'I must have been mad to have come up here,' he thought.

The same thought had already occurred to Sir Giles though in his case the madness he had in mind was in no way metaphorical. As dawn broke over the Park, Sir Giles wrestled with the lock on the gate to the footbridge and tried to imagine how it had got there. It had not been on the gate when he arrived. He wouldn't have been able to enter if it had. But if the existence of the lock was bad enough, that of the fence was worse and it certainly hadn't been there when he had last been at the Hall. It was an extremely high fence with large metal brackets at the top and four strands of heavy barbed-wire overhanging the Park so that it was evidently designed to stop people getting out rather than trespassers getting in.

It was at this point that Sir Giles gave up the struggle with the lock and decided to look for some other way out. He followed the fence along the edge of the pinetum and was about to clamber over the iron railings when the sense of unreality that had come over him with the sudden appearance of a large lock where no lock had previously been took a decided turn for the worse. Against the grey dawn sky he saw a head, a small head with a long nose and knobs on it. Below the head there was a neck, a long neck, a very long neck indeed. Sir Giles shut his eyes and hoped to hell that when he opened them he wouldn't see what he thought he had seen. He opened them but the giraffe was still there. 'Oh my God,' he murmured and was about to move away when his eye caught sight of something even more terrifying. In the long grass fifty yards behind the giraffe there was another face, a large face with a mane and whiskers.

Sir Giles gave up all thought of looking for a way out in that direction. He turned and stumbled back into the pinetum. Either he had gone mad or he was in the middle of some fucking zoo. Giraffes? Lions? And what the hell was it that he had almost stumbled across during the night? An elephant? He got back to the gate and looked at the lock hopefully. But instead of one lock there were now two and the second was even larger than the first. He was just trying to think what this meant when he heard a noise on the path across the river. Sir Giles looked up. Blott was standing there with a shotgun, smiling down at him. It was a horrible smile, a smile of quiet satisfaction. Sir Giles turned and ran into the pinetum. He knew death when he saw it.

By the time Blott got back to the Hall Lady Maud was down and making breakfast in the kitchen.

'What took you so long?' she asked.

'I moved the Bentley,' Blott told her. 'I brought it round and put it in the garage. I thought it would look more natural.'

Lady Maud nodded. 'You are probably right,' she said. 'People might have started asking questions if they found it left up by the church. Besides if he did get out he might have telephoned the AA for assistance.'

'He isn't going to get out,' said Blott, 'I saw him. He's in the pinetum.'

'Well it's his own fault. He came up here to burn the house down and whatever happens now he has only himself to blame.' She handed Blott a plate of cereal. 'I'm afraid I can't give you a cooked breakfast. The electricity has been cut off. I telephoned the electricity office in Worford but they say there has been a power failure.'

Blott ate his cereal in silence. There didn't seem much point in telling her about his part in the power failure and besides she seemed in a talkative mood herself.

'The trouble with Giles was,' she said using the past tense in a way that Blott found most agreeable, 'that he liked to think of himself as a self-made man. I have always thought it an extremely presumptuous phrase and in his case particularly inappropriate. I suppose he had some right to call himself a man, though from my experience of him I wouldn't have said virility was his strong point, but as for being self-made, he was nothing of the kind. He made his money, and of course that's what he meant by self, by speculating in property, by evicting people from their homes and by obtaining planning permission to put up office blocks. At least my family made its money selling beer, and very good beer at that. And it took them generations to do it. There's nothing so splendid about that but at least they were honest men.' She was still talking and doing the washing-up when Blott left to go out to the kitchen garden.

'Is there anything else you want done about him?' he asked as he left.

Lady Maud shook her head. 'I think we can just leave nature to take its course,' she told him. 'He was a great believer in the law of the jungle.'

In Worford Police Station Dundridge was having difficulty with the law of the land. Hoskins had been no great help.

'According to him,' said the Superintendent in charge of the case, 'you gave specific orders for random sorties to be made by bulldozers on various properties. Now you say you didn't.'

'I was speaking figuratively,' Dundridge explained. 'I certainly didn't give any instructions that could lead anyone but a complete idiot to suppose that I wanted the late Mr Bullett-Finch's house demolished.'

'Nevertheless it was demolished.'

'By some lunatic. You don't seriously imagine I went out there and smashed the house up myself?'

'If you'll just keep calm, sir,' said the Superintendent, 'all I am trying to do is to establish the chain of circumstances that led up to this murder.'

'Murder?' mumbled Dundridge.

'You're not claiming it was an accident, are you? A person or persons unknown deliberately take a large crane and use it to pulverize a house in which two innocent people are sleeping. You can call that all sorts of things but not an accident. No sir, we are treating this as a case of murder.'

Dundridge thought for a moment. 'If that's the case there must have been a motive. Have you given any thought to that?'

'I'm glad you mentioned motive, sir,' said the Superintendent. 'Now I understand that Mr Bullett-Finch was an active member of the Save the Gorge Committee. Would you say that your relations with him were marked by an unusual degree of animosity?'

'Relations?' shouted Dundridge. 'I didn't have any relations with him. I never met the man in my life.'

'But you did speak to him over the telephone on a number of occasions.'

'I may have done,' said Dundridge. 'I seem to remember his phoning once to complain about something or other.'

'Would that have been the occasion on which you told him that quote "If you don't stop pestering me I'll see to it that you'll lose a bloody-sight more than a quarter of an acre of your bleeding garden" unquote?'

'Who told you that?' snarled Dundridge.

'The identity of our informant is irrelevant, sir. The question is did you or did you not say that.'

'I may have done,' Dundridge admitted, promising himself that he would make Hoskins' life difficult for him in future.

'And wouldn't you agree that the late Mr Bullett-Finch has in fact lost more than a quarter of an acre of his bleeding garden?'

Dundridge had to admit that he had.

As the morning wore on the Controller Motorways Midlands had the definite impression that a trap was closing in around him.

In Sir Giles' case there was the absolute conviction. His attempts to scale the wire fence had failed miserably. Oily gum-boots were not ideal for the purpose and Sir Giles' physical activities had been of too passive a nature to prepare him at all adequately for scrambling up wire mesh or coping with barbed-wire overhangs. What he needed was a ladder, but his only attempt to leave the pinetum to look for one had been foiled by the sight of a rhinoceros browsing in the rockery and of a lion sunning itself outside the kitchen door. Sir Giles stuck to the pinetum and waited for an opportunity. He waited a long time.

By three o'clock in the afternoon he was exceedingly hungry. So were the lions. From the lower branches of a tree over-looking the park Sir Giles watched as four lionesses stalked a giraffe, one moving upwind while the other three lay in the grass downwind. The giraffe moved off and a moment later was thrashing around in its death throes. From his eyrie Sir Giles watched in horror as the lionesses finished it off and were presently joined by the lions. Stifling his disgust and fear Sir Giles climbed down from the branch. This was his opportunity. Ignoring the rhinoceros which had its back to him he raced across the lawn towards the house as fast as his gumboots would allow. He reached the terrace and hurried round past the conservatory where Lady Maud was watering a castor-oil plant. As he ran past she looked up and for a moment he had an impulse to stop and beg her to let him in but the look on her face was enough to tell him he would be wasting his time. It expressed an indifference to his fate, almost an ignorance of his existence, which was in its way even more frightening than Blott's terrible smile. As far as Maud was concerned he simply wasn't there. She had married him to save the Hall and preserve the family. And now she was prepared to murder him by proxy for the same purpose. Sir Giles had no doubt about that. He ran on into the yard and opened the garage door. Inside stood the Bentley. He could get away at last. He pushed the doors back and got into the car. The keys were still in the ignition. He turned them and the starter whirred. He tried again but the car wouldn't start.

In the kitchen garden Blott listened to the engine turning over. He was wasting his time. He could go on till Doomsday and the car wouldn't start. Blott had no sympathy for him. 'Nature must take its course,' Lady Maud had said and Blott agreed. Sir Giles meant nothing to him. He was like the pests in the garden, the slugs or the greenfly. No that wasn't true. He was worse. He was a traitor to the England that Blott revered, the old England, the upstanding England, the England that had carved an Empire by foolhardiness and accident, the England that had built this garden and planted the great oaks and elms not for its own immediate satisfaction but for the future. What had Sir Giles done for the future? Nothing. He had desecrated the past and betrayed the future. He deserved to die. Blott took his shotgun and went round to the garage.

Lady Maud in the conservatory was having second thoughts. The look on Sir Giles' face as he hesitated outside had awakened a slight feeling of pity in her. The man was afraid, desperately afraid, and Lady Maud had no time for cruelty. It was one thing to talk in the abstract about the law of the jungle, but it was another to participate in it.

'He's learnt his lesson by now,' she thought, 'I had better let him go.' And she was about to go out and look for him when the phone rang. It was General Burnett.

'It's about this business of poor old Bertie,' said the General. 'The committee would like to come over and have a chat with you.'

'Bertie?' said Lady Maud. 'Bertie Bullett-Finch?'

'You know he's dead, of course,' said the General.

'Dead?' said Lady Maud. 'I had no idea. When did this happen?'

'Last night. House was knocked down by the motorway swine. Bertie was inside at the time.'

Lady Maud sat down, stunned by the news. 'How absolutely dreadful. Do they know who did it?'

'They've taken that fellow Dundridge in for questioning,' said the General. Lady Maud could think of nothing to say. 'Knocked half Guildstead down too. The Colonel and I thought we ought to come over and have a talk to you about it. Puts a very different complexion on the whole business of the motorway, don't you know.'

'Of course,' said Lady Maud. 'Come over at once.' She put the phone down and tried to imagine what had happened. Dundridge taken in for questioning. Mr Bullett-Finch dead. Finch Grove demolished. Guildstead Carbonell ... It was such astonishing news that it drove all thoughts of Giles from her mind.

'I must phone poor dear Ivy,' she muttered and dialled Finch Grove. Not surprisingly, she got no reply.

In the garage Sir Giles was doing his best to persuade Blott to stop pointing the twelve-bore at his chest.

'Five thousand pounds,' he said. 'Five thousand pounds. All you've got to do is open the gates.'

'You get out of here,' said Blott.

'What do you think I want to do? Stay here?'

'Out of the garage,' said Blott.

'Ten thousand. Twenty thousand. Anything you ask ...'

'I'll count to ten,' said Blott. 'One.'

'Fifty thousand pounds.'

'Two,' said Blott.

'A hundred thousand. You can't ask better than that.'

'Three,' said Blott.

'I'll make it—'

'Four,' said Blott.

Sir Giles turned and ran. There was no mistaking the look on Blott's face. Sir Giles stumbled round the house and across the lawn to the pinetum. He scrambled over the iron railings and climbed back into his tree. The lions had finished the giraffe and were licking their paws and wiping their whiskers. Sir Giles wiped the sweat off his face with an oily handkerchief and tried to think what to do next.

Dundridge was saved that trouble by the discovery of an empty vodka bottle in the cab of the crane and by eye-witnesses who testified that one of the two men seen driving the crane up the High Street had been singing bawdy songs and was very clearly intoxicated.

'There seems to have been some mistake,' the Superintendent told him apologetically. 'You're free to go.'

'But you told me you were treating the case as one of murder,' shouted Dundridge indignantly. 'Now you turn round and say it was simply drunken driving.'

'Murder in my view implies premeditation,' explained the Superintendent. 'Now, two blokes go out and have one too many. They get a bit merry and pinch a crane and knock a few houses down, well you can't feel the same about it, can you? There's no premeditation there. Just a bit of fun, that's all. Now I'm not saying I approve. Don't get me wrong. I'm as hard on vandalism and drunkenness as the next man, but there are mitigating circumstances to be taken into account.'

Dundridge left the police station unconvinced, and as far as Hoskins' behaviour was concerned he could find no mitigating circumstances whatsoever.

'You deliberately led the police to believe that I had given orders for the Bullett-Finches' house to be demolished,' he shouted at him in the Mobile HQ. 'You gave them to understand that I set out to murder Mr Bullett-Finch.'

'I only told them that you had had a row with him on the phone. I'd have said the same thing about Lady Maud if they had asked me,' Hoskins protested.

'Lady Maud doesn't happen to have been murdered,' yelled Dundridge. 'Nor does General Burnett or the Colonel and I've had rows with them too. I suppose if any of them get run over by a bus or die of food poisoning you'll tell the police I'm responsible.'

Hoskins said he didn't think that was being fair.

'Fair,' yelled Dundridge, 'fair? Now you just listen to what I've had to put up with since I've been up here. I've been threatened. I've been given doctored drinks. I've been ... Well never mind about that. I've been shot at. I've been subject to abuse. I've had my car tyres slashed.

I've been accused of murder and you have the fucking gall to stand there and talk to me about fairness. My God, I've fought clean up to now but not any longer. From now on anything goes and the first thing to go is you. Get out of here and don't come back.'

'There's just one thing I think you ought to know,' said Hoskins edging towards the door. 'You've got a new problem on your hands. Lady Maud Lynchwood is opening a Wildlife Park at Handyman Hall on Sunday.'

Dundridge sat down slowly and stared at him.

'She is what?'

Hoskins edged back into the office. 'Opening a Wildlife Park. She's had the whole place wired in and she's got lions and rhinoceroses and . . .'

'But she can't do that. She's had a compulsory purchase order served on her,' said Dundridge stunned by this latest example of opposition.

'She's done it all the same,' said Hoskins. 'There are signs up along the Ottertown Road and there was an advertisement in last night's *Worford Advertiser*. I've got a copy here.' He went through to his office and returned with a full-page advertisement announcing Open Day at Handyman Hall Wildlife Park. 'What are you going to do about that?'

Dundridge reached for the phone. 'I'm going to get on to the legal department and tell them to apply for an injunction to stop her,' he said. 'In the meantime you can see that work resumes in the Gorge immediately.'

'Don't you think we should hold off for a day or two,' said Hoskins, 'and wait for this fuss over the Bullett-Finches' house and Guildstead Carbonell to die down a bit.'

'Certainly not,' said Dundridge. 'If the police choose to regard the whole thing as a trivial matter, I see no reason why we shouldn't. Work will proceed as before. If anything, faster.'

CHAPTER TWENTY-FOUR

At Handyman Hall what was left of the Save the Gorge Committee met in the sitting-room lamenting the passing of Mr Bullett-Finch and seeking to take advantage from his sacrifice.

'The whole thing is an outrage against humanity,' said Colonel Chapman. 'A more inoffensive fellow than poor old Bertie you couldn't imagine. Never a harsh word from him.'

Lady Maud could remember several harsh words from Mr Bullett-Finch when she had taken the liberty of walking across his lawn, but she kept her thoughts to herself. Whatever his faults in life, Mr Bullett-Finch dead had been canonized. General Burnett put her thoughts into words.

'Terrible way to go,' he said, 'having a dashed great iron ball smash you to smithereens like that. Rather like a gigantic cannonball.'

'He probably didn't feel a thing,' said Colonel Chapman. 'It was late at night and he was in bed ...'

'He wasn't you know. They found him in his dressing-gown. Must have heard it coming.'

'In the midst of life we are ...' Miss Percival began but Lady Maud interrupted her.

'There is no point in dwelling on the past,' she said. 'We must concentrate our mind on the future. I have invited Ivy to come and stay here.'

'I rather doubt if she will accept,' said Colonel Chapman looking nervously out of the window. 'Her nerves were never up to much and this latest shock hasn't done them any good and those lions ...'

'Nonsense,' said Lady Maud briskly. 'Perfectly harmless creatures provided you know how to handle them. The main thing is to show you're not afraid of them. The moment they smell fear they become dangerous.'

'I'm sure I'd be no good at all,' said Miss Percival. General Burnett nodded.

'I remember once in the Punjab ...' he began.

'I think we should keep to the matter in hand,' said Lady Maud. 'Much as I regret what has happened to poor Mr Bullett-Finch and indeed to Guildstead Carbonell, there is this to be said for it, it does put us all in a much stronger position vis-à-vis the Ministry of the Environment and this infernal motorway. I think you said, General, that the police were questioning that man Dundridge.'

General Burnett shook his head. 'The Chief Constable has been keeping me abreast of events,' he said. 'I'm afraid they've dropped that line of inquiry. It appears that there was some sort of shindig at the Royal George last night. Seems they're working on the theory that a couple of navvies had a bit too much beer and ...'

'Beer?' said Lady Maud with a strange look on her face. 'Did I hear you say "Beer"?'

'My dear lady,' said the General apologetically, 'I only mentioned beer because I believe that is what these fellows drink. I wasn't for one moment imputing ...'

'As a matter of fact I believe it was vodka,' said Colonel Chapman tactfully. 'In fact I'm sure it was. They found a bottle.'

But the damage had already been done. Lady Maud was looking quite distraught.

In the pinetum Sir Giles was desperately trying to make up his mind. From his tree he had watched General Burnett and Colonel Chapman and Miss Percival arrive. They had come in one car – Miss Percival had left her car outside the main gates and had joined the General in his – and their coming seemed to offer Sir Giles an opportunity to escape if only he could reach the house. Maud could hardly shoot him down in cold blood in front of her neighbours. There might be a nasty scene. She might accuse him of arson, of blackmail and bribery. She might expose him to ridicule but he was prepared to run these risks to get out of the Park alive. On the other hand he wasn't sure that he was prepared to run the gauntlet of the lions who had sauntered away from their last meal and were lying about on the lawn in front of the terrace. Then again he was now extremely hungry and the lions on the contrary weren't. They had just eaten their fill of giraffe.

At least Sir Giles hoped they had. It was a risk he had to take. If he stayed in the tree he would starve to death and sooner or later he would have to come down. Better sooner, he thought, than later. Sir Giles climbed down and got over the railings. Perhaps if he walked confidently ... He didn't feel confident. He hesitated and then moved cautiously forward. If only he could reach the terrace. And as he moved across the grass he was conscious that he was increasing the distance between himself and the safety of the tree while decreasing that between himself and the lions. He reached the point of no return.

In the sitting-room General Burnett was lamenting Sir Giles' absence. 'I've tried ringing his flat in London and his office but nobody seems to know where he's got to,' he said. 'If only we could get in touch with him, I'm convinced we could bring pressure to bear on the Minister to call a halt to the motorway. I'm the last one to complain, but it's at a time like this that a constituency needs its MP.'

'I'm afraid my husband tends to let his business interests get in the way of his Parliamentary duties,' Lady Maud agreed.

'Of course, of course,' said Colonel Chapman. 'He's bound to have a lot of irons in the fire. Wouldn't have got where he has if he hadn't.'

'I think ...' said Miss Percival nervously staring out of the window.

'All I'm saying is that it's about time he made his presence felt,' said the General.

'I really do think you ought to ...' Miss Percival began.

'It's at times like this he ought to raise his voice ... Good God! What the hell was that?'

There was a ghastly scream from the garden.

'I think it was Sir Giles raising his voice,' said Miss Percival, and fainted. The General and Colonel Chapman turned and looked out of the window in horror. Sir Giles was visible for a moment and then he disappeared beneath a lion. Lady Maud seized a poker and opened the french windows.

'How dare you?' she shouted charging across the terrace. 'Shoo, Shoo.'

But it was too late. The General and Colonel Chapman rushed out and dragged her back still waving the poker and shooing.

'Damned plucky little woman,' said the General as they drove home. Colonel Chapman said nothing. He was trying to rid his mind of the memory of those gumboots, and besides, he found the General's description of Lady Maud a little inappropriate even in these distressing circumstances. His left ear was still ringing from the blow she had given him for telling her she mustn't blame herself for what had happened.

'Mind you, I'm afraid it's put an end to the Wildlife Park,' continued the General. 'Pity really.'

'It's also put an end to Sir Giles,' said Colonel Chapman, who felt that General Burnett was taking the whole affair too calmly.

'There is that to be said for it,' said the General. 'Never could stomach the fellow.'

In the back seat Miss Percival fainted for the sixth time.

At Handyman Hall the Superintendent explained to Lady Maud as tactfully as possible that there would have to be a coroner's inquest.

'An inquest? But it's perfectly obvious what happened. General Burnett and Colonel Chapman were here.'

'Just a formality, I assure you,' said the Superintendent. 'And now I'll be getting along.'

He went out to his car with the gumboots and drove off. In the Park the lions were licking their paws and wiping their whiskers. Lady Maud stared out of the window at them. They would have to go of course. Sir Giles might not have been a nice man but Lady Maud's sense of social propriety wouldn't allow her to keep animals that couldn't be trusted not to eat people. And then there was Blott. Blott and the events of the previous evening in Guildstead Carbonell. It was all too obvious what he had wanted Very Special for and it was all her fault. And to think she had invited Ivy Bullett-Finch to come and stay. Well, at least she had a good excuse for cancelling the invitation now. She went through the kitchen and was about to go out when it occurred to her that having tasted human flesh once the lions might not succumb quite so readily to her fearlessness. She ought really to carry some sort of weapon. Lady Maud hesitated and then went on regardless. She owed it to her conscience to take some risks. She went down the path and into the kitchen garden.

'Blott,' she said, 'I want a word with you. Do you realize what you have done?'

Blott shrugged. 'He got what was coming to him,' he said.

'I'm not talking about him,' said Lady Maud, 'I'm talking about Mr Bullett-Finch.'

'What about him?'

'He's dead. He was killed last night when his house was demolished.'

Blott took off his hat and scratched his head. 'That's a pity,' he said thoughtfully.

'A pity? Is that all you've got to say?' said Lady Maud sternly.

'I don't know what else I can say. I didn't know he was in the house any more than you knew he was going to go and get eaten by those lions.' He picked a caterpillar off a cabbage and squashed it absent-mindedly.

'I must say if I had known what you were going to do I would never have given you the day off,' said Lady Maud and went back into the house.

Blott went on with his weeding. Women were odd things, he thought. You did what they wanted and all the thanks you got for it was a telling off. A telling off. That was an odd expression too, come to think of it. But then the world was full of mysteries.

In London Mrs Forthby woke with a vague sense that something was missing. She rolled over in bed, switched on the light and looked at the clock. It said eleven forty-eight and since it was dark it must be nearly midnight. On the other hand it didn't feel like midnight. She felt as though she had been asleep a lot longer than four hours, and where was Giles? She got out of bed and looked in the kitchen, the bathroom, but he wasn't in the flat. Oh well, he had probably gone out. She went back to the kitchen and made herself some tea. She was feeling very hungry too. That was strange because she had had a big dinner. She made some toast and boiled an egg. And all the time she had the nagging feeling that something was wrong. She had gone to bed at eight o'clock and here she was at midnight wide awake and famished. To while away the time she picked up a book but she didn't feel like reading. She turned on the radio and caught the news headlines. '... Lynchwood, Member of Parliament for South Worfordshire, who was killed at his home Handyman Hall near Worford by a lion. In Arizona a freak whirlwind destroyed ...' Mrs Forthby switched off the radio and poured herself another cup of tea before remembering what the announcer had just said. 'Oh dear,' she said, 'this afternoon? But ...' She went through to the sitting-room and looked at the date on the clock. It read Friday the 20th. But yesterday was Wednesday. Giles had said so. She had said it was Tuesday and he had said Wednesday. And now it was Friday morning and Giles had been killed by a lion. What was a lion doing at Handyman Hall? What was Sir Giles doing there, come to that? They had been going to Brighton together for the weekend. It was all too awfully perplexing and horrible. It couldn't be true. Mrs Forthby dialled the nice lady who told the time. 'At the third stroke it will be twelve ten and twenty seconds.'

'But what's the date? What day is it?' Mrs Forthby asked.

'At the third stroke it will be twelve ten and thirty seconds.'

'Oh dear, you really aren't being very helpful,' said Mrs Forthby, and began to cry. Giles hadn't been a very nice man but she had been fond of him and it was all her fault.

'If I hadn't been so forgetful and had remembered to wake up he would still be alive,' she murmured.

At his Mobile HQ Dundridge greeted the news next morning jubilantly.

'That'll teach the stupid bitch to build a bloody Wildlife Park,' he told Hoskins.

'I don't see how you can say that,' said Hoskins. 'All it's done is to create another vacancy in Parliament. There will have to be a bye-election and you know what happened last time.'

'All the more reason for pressing ahead as quickly as possible.'

'What? With Maud Lynchwood in mourning? The poor woman has just lost her husband under the most tragic circumstances and you –'

'Don't give me that bull,' said Dundridge. 'If you ask me she's probably delighted. Wouldn't surprise me to learn she'd arranged the whole thing just to stop us.'

'That's bloody libel, that is,' said Hoskins. 'She may be a bit of a tartar but ...'

'Listen,' said Dundridge, 'she didn't give a tuppenny damn about her husband, I know.'

'You know?'

'Yes I do know as a matter of fact. I'll tell you something. That old cow tried to seduce me one night and when I wouldn't play ball she took a potshot at me with a twelve-bore. So don't come that crap about a sorrowing widow. We're going ahead, and fast.'

'Well all I can say is that you're flying in the face of public opinion,' said Hoskins, stunned by Dundridge's story of his attempted seduction. 'There's Bullett-Finch dead and now Sir Giles. There's bound to be a public outcry. I should have thought now was the time to lie doggo.'

'Now is the time to establish ourselves at the Park itself,' said Dundridge. 'I'm going to move two bulldozers and a base camp up by that arch of hers. If she wants to squawk let her squawk.'

But Lady Maud didn't squawk. She had been more shocked by Sir Giles' death than she would have expected and she felt personally responsible for what had happened to Mr Bullett-Finch. She went about her duties automatically but with an abstracted air, occupied with the moral dilemma in which she found herself. On the one hand she was faced with the destruction of everything she loved, the Hall, the Gorge, the wild landscape, the garden, the world her ancestors had fought for and created. All this would go, to be replaced by a motorway which would be a useless, obsolescent eyesore in fifty years when fossil fuel ran out. It wasn't as if the motorway was needed. It had been concocted by Giles to make himself a paltry sum of money, a mean, cruel gesture to hurt her. Well Giles had got his comeuppance but the legacy of the motorway remained and the methods she had had to use had degraded her. She had fought fire with fire and other people had been burnt, Bertie Bullett-Finch and – quite literally – the poor man who had put the paraffin lamp in front of Mr Dugdale's garage.

It was in this mood of self-recrimination that she attended the coroner's inquest which returned a verdict of accidental death on Sir Giles Lynchwood and commended his widow on her bravery while pointing out the unforeseen dangers of keeping undomesticated animals on domestic premises. It was in the same mood that she superintended the removal of the lions, the last giraffe and the ostriches, before going off to a Memorial Service at Worford Abbey. All this time she avoided Blott, who stuck to the kitchen garden in low dudgeon. It was only when, on her return from the Abbey, she saw the bulldozers parked near the iron suspension bridge opposite the Lodge that she felt a pang of remorse for the way she had upbraided him. She found him sulking among the blackcurrants.

'Blott, I'm sorry,' she said. 'I feel I owe you an apology. We all make mistakes from time to time and I've come to say how grateful I am to you for all the sacrifices you've made on my behalf.'

Blott blushed under his tanned complexion. 'It was nothing,' he mumbled.

'That's just not true,' said Lady Maud graciously, 'I don't know how I would have managed without you.'

'You don't have to thank me,' said Blott.

'I just wanted you to know that I appreciate it,' said Lady Maud. 'By the way as I came in I noticed the bulldozers by the Lodge ...'

'You want them stopped, I suppose?'

'Well, now that you come to mention it ...' Lady Maud began.

'Leave it to me,' said Blott, 'I'll stop them.'

Lady Maud hesitated. This was the moment of decision. She chose her words carefully.

'I wouldn't like to think that you were going to do anything violent.'

'Violent? Me?' said Blott sounding almost convincingly aggrieved at the suggestion.

'Yes, you,' said Lady Maud. 'Now, I don't mind spending money if it's needed. You can have what you want but I won't have anyone else getting hurt. There's been quite enough of that already.'

'Your forefathers fought for ...'

'I think I'm a rather better authority on what my ancestors did than you are,' said Lady Maud. 'I don't need telling. That was quite different. For one thing they were agents of the Crown and acting within the law and for another the only people to get hurt were the Welsh and they were savages. Besides, I'm a Justice of the Peace and I can't condone anything illegal. Whatever you do must be lawful.'

'But ...' began Blott.

Lady Maud interrupted him. 'I don't want to hear any more. What you do is your own affair. I want no part of it.'

She strode away and left Blott to consider her words.

'No violence,' he muttered. It was going to make things a little difficult but he would think of something. Women, even the best of them, were illogical creatures. He walked out of the garden and down the drive to the Lodge. On the far side of the suspension bridge two bulldozers, symbols of Dundridge's task force, stood under the trees. It would have been so easy to disable them with the PIAT or even to put sugar in their fuel tanks but if Maud said he must stay within the law ... Stay within the law? That was another strange expression. As if the law was some sort of fortress. Blott looked up at the great arch towering above him.

He had just had an idea.

CHAPTER TWENTY-FIVE

In spite of his intention to act swiftly the Controller Motorways Midlands found it difficult to act at all. Work on the motorway came to a virtual standstill while the various authorities responsible for the preservation of Guildstead Carbonell and law and order on the one hand wrangled with those responsible for the construction of the motorway and the destruction of the village on the other. To make matters worse there was a walk-out by dumper drivers who claimed they were being victimized by being barred from the Royal George for the damage done to the bar-billiards table by the clog-dancing of the bulldozer men, and a work-to-rule by the demolition experts who asserted that the arrest of Mr Edwards constituted a threat to their basic rights as Trade Unionists. To end the dispute Dundridge paid for the bar-billiards table out of incidental expenses and interceded with the police to release Mr Edwards on bail pending a psychiatrist's report. In the middle of the confusion he was summoned to London to explain remarks he had made in a television interview filmed in front of the ruins of Finch Grove.

'Couldn't you have thought of something better than "That is the way the cookie crumbles"?' Mr Rees demanded. 'And what in God's name did you mean by "There's many a slip twixt cup and lip"?'

'All I meant was that accidents do happen,' Dundridge explained. 'I was being bombarded with –'

'Bombarded? What do you think we've been since then? How many letters have we had?'

Mr Joynson consulted his list. 'Three thousand four hundred and eighty-two to date, not including postcards.'

'And what about "We all have to make sacrifices"? What sort of impression do you think that makes on three million viewers?' shouted Mr Rees. 'A man living peacefully in a quiet corner of rural England minding his own business is battered to death in the middle of the night by some fucking idiot with an iron ball weighing two tons and you talk about making sacrifices!'

'As a matter of fact he wasn't minding his own business,' Dundridge protested, 'he was continually ringing up to –'

'And I suppose you think that justifies ... I give up.'

'I think we have to look at it from the point of view of the potential housebuyer,' said Mr Joynson tactfully. 'It's difficult enough for the average wage-earner to get a mortgage these days. We don't want to give people the idea that they run the risk of having their houses demolished without the slightest warning.'

'But the house wasn't even scheduled for demolition,' Mr Rees pointed out.

'Quite,' said Mr Joynson. 'The point I'm trying to make is that Dundridge here must adopt a more tactful approach. He should use persuasion.'

But Dundridge had had enough. 'Persuasion?' he snarled. 'You don't seem to understand what I'm up against. You seem to think all I've got to do is serve a compulsory purchase order and people simply get out of their houses and everything is hunky-dory. Well let me tell you it isn't that simple. I'm supposed to be in charge of building a motorway through a house and park belonging to a woman whose idea of persuasion is to take potshots at me with a twelve-bore.'

'And evidently missing,' sighed Mr Rees.

'Why didn't you inform the police?' Mr Joynson asked more practically.

'The police? She *is* the police,' said Dundridge. 'They eat out of her hand.'

'Like those lions I suppose,' said Mr Rees.

'And what do you think she built that Wildlife Park for?' Dundridge asked.

'I suppose you're going to tell us next that she wanted to find a way of disposing of her husband,' Mr Rees said wearily.

'To stop the motorway. She intended to whip up public support, gain sympathy and generally cause as much confusion as possible.'

'I should have thought she could have safely left that to you,' said Mr Rees.

Dundridge looked at him balefully. It was obvious that he did not enjoy the confidence of his superiors.

'If that's the way you feel I can only resign my position as Controller Motorways Midlands and return to London,' he said. Mr Rees looked at Mr Joynson. This was the ultimatum they had feared. Mr Joynson shook his head.

'My dear Dundridge, there is absolutely no need for you to do that,' said Mr Rees with forced affability. 'All we ask is that you try to avoid any more unfavourable publicity.'

'In that case I look to you to give me your full support,' said Dundridge. 'I can't be expected to overcome the sort of opposition I'm faced with unless the Ministry is prepared to throw its weight behind my efforts.'

'Anything we can do,' said Mr Rees, 'to help, we will certainly do.'

Dundridge left the office mollified and with the feeling that his authority had been enhanced after all.

'Give the swine enough rope and I daresay he'll hang himself,' said Mr Rees when he had gone. 'And frankly I wish Lady Maud the best of British luck.'

'Must be a terrible thing to lose a husband like that,' said Mr Joynson. 'No wonder the poor woman is upset.'

But it was less the loss of her husband that was upsetting Lady Maud than the bills she was receiving from various shops in Worford.

'One hundred and fifty tins of frankfurters? One thousand candles? Sixty tons of cement? Two hundred yards of barbed-wire? Forty six-foot reinforcing rods?' she muttered as she went through the bills. 'What on earth can Blott be thinking of?' But she paid the bills without question and kept herself to herself. Whatever Blott was up to she wanted to know as little about it as possible. 'Ignorance is bliss,' she thought, demonstrating a lack of understanding of the law which did her little credit as a magistrate.

And Blott was busy. He had spent the lull provided by Dundridge's troubles in preparing his defence. Lady Maud had specified that there must be no violence on his part and as far as he was concerned there would be no necessity for it. The Lodge was practically impregnable to anything short of a full-scale assault by tanks and artillery. He had filled all the rooms on either side of the archway with bits of old iron and cement and had sealed the stairway with concrete. He had covered the roof with sharpened iron rods embedded in concrete and entangled with barbed-wire. To secure an independent water supply he had run a plastic pipe down to the river before the concrete was poured into the rooms below and to ensure that he could withstand a prolonged siege he had laid in enough foodstuffs to last him for two years. If his electricity was cut off he had a thousand candles and several dozen containers of bottled gas and finally, to prevent any attempt to drive him out with tear gas, he had unearthed an old army gas-mask from his cache in the forest. Just in case the mask was no longer proof against the latest gases he had turned his library into an air-tight room to which he could retreat. All in all he had converted the Lodge from a very large ornamental arch into a fortress. The only entrance was through a hatch in the roof under the barbed-wire and spikes, and to enable him to leave when he wanted Blott had constructed a rope ladder which he could let down. Finally and just in case things did get violent he had collected a rifle, a Bren gun, a two-inch mortar, several cases of ammunition and hand-grenades with which to deter boarders. 'Of course, I'll only fire over their heads,' he told himself. But there would be no need. Blott knew the British too well to suppose they would do anything to endanger life. And yet without endangering life, and Blott's life in particular, there was no way of building the motorway on through the Park and Handyman Hall. The Lodge, now Festung Blott, stood directly in the path of the motorway. On either side the cliffs rose steeply. Before anything could be done the Lodge would have to be demolished and since Blott was encased within it, demolishing the arch would mean demolishing him. They couldn't even use dynamite to blast the cliffs on either side without seriously risking his life and threatening the collapse of the arch. Finally to ensure that no one could even drive through the gateway he erected a series of concrete blocks in the middle of the archway. It was this last that forced Lady Maud to ask him what the hell he thought he was doing.

'How do you expect me to do my shopping if I can't drive in and out?' she demanded.

Blott pointed to the Bentley and the Land-Rover parked beside the two bulldozers on the other side of the suspension bridge.

'Good Lord,' said Lady Maud, 'do you mean to say you moved them without my permission?'

'You said you didn't want to know what I was doing so I didn't tell you,' Blott told her. Lady Maud had to admit to the logic of the answer.

'It's going to be very inconvenient,' she said. She looked at the Lodge. Apart from the spikes and the barbed-wire on the roof it looked as it had always looked. 'I just hope you know what you're doing,' she said and made her way through the concrete blocks and across the bridge to her car. She drove into Worford to see Mr Ganglion about Sir Giles' will. From where she had been able to ascertain she had been left a widow of very considerable means, and Lady Maud intended to put those means to good use.

'A fortune, my dear lady,' said Mr Ganglion, 'an absolute fortune even by today's standards. Properly invested, you should be able to live quite royally.' He looked at her appreciatively. Now that he came to think of it she had every right to live royally. There was that business of Edward the Seventh. 'And as a widower myself . . .' He looked at her even more appreciatively. She might not be to every man's taste but then he wasn't up to much himself and he was getting on in years. And ten million pounds in property was an inducement. So too were those photographs of Mr Dundridge.

'I intend to re-marry as soon as possible,' said Lady Maud. 'Sir Giles may have left me well provided for but he did not fulfil his proper functions as a husband.'

'Quite so. Quite so,' said Mr Ganglion, his mind busily considering Dundridge's accusation of blackmail. It might be worth his while to try a little expeditious blackmail himself. He turned to his safe and twiddled the knob.

'Besides, it's not good for you to have to live alone in that great house,' he continued. 'You need company. Someone to look after you.'

'I have already seen to that,' said Lady Maud. 'I have invited Mrs Forthby to come and make it her home.'

'Mrs Forthby? Mrs Forthby? Do I know her?'

'No,' said Lady Maud, 'I don't suppose you do. She was Giles' ... er ... governess in London.'

'Really?' said Mr Ganglion glancing at her over the top of his glasses. 'Now that you come to mention it I did hear something ...'

'Well never mind that,' said Lady Maud, 'there's no point in flogging a dead horse. The thing is that from what I have seen of the will he had made no provision for the poor woman. I intend to make good the deficiency.'

'Very generous of you. Magnanimous,' said Mr Ganglion and took an envelope from the safe. 'And while we're on the subject of human frailties, I wonder if you would mind glancing at these photographs and telling me if you have seen them before.' He opened the envelope and spread them out before her. Lady Maud stared at them intently. It was obvious she had seen them before.

'Where did you get those?' she shouted.

'Ah,' said Mr Ganglion, 'now I'm afraid that would be telling.'

'Of course it would,' snarled Lady Maud, 'what do you think I asked you for?'

'Well,' said Mr Ganglion, putting the photographs back into the envelope, 'a certain person, let us say a prospective client, consulted me ...'

'Dundridge. I knew it. Dundridge,' said Lady Maud.

'Your guess is as good as mine, my dear Lady Maud,' said Mr Ganglion. 'Well this client did suggest that you had been using these ... er ... rather revealing pictures to ... er ... blackmail him.'

'My God,' shouted Lady Maud, 'the filthy little beast!'

'Of course I did my best to assure him that such a thing was out of the question. However he remained unconvinced ...' But Lady Maud had heard enough. She rose to her feet and seized the envelope. 'Now if you feel that we should institute proceedings for slander ...'

'Accused me of blackmail? By God I'll make him regret the day he was born,' Lady Maud snarled and stumped out of the room with the photographs.

Dundridge was in his Mobile HQ drawing up plans for his next move against Handyman Hall when Lady Maud drove up. Now that he was assured that the Ministry would throw their full weight behind his efforts he viewed the future with renewed confidence. He had spoken to the Chief Constable and had demanded full police co-operation should Lady Maud refuse to comply with the order to move out of Handyman Hall and the Chief Constable had reluctantly agreed. He was just giving Hoskins his instructions to move into the Park when Lady Maud stormed through the door.

'You filthy little swine,' she shouted and tossed the photographs on to his desk. 'Take a good look at yourself.' Dundridge did. So did Hoskins.

'Well?' continued Lady Maud. 'And what have you got to say now?'

Dundridge stared up at her and tried to think of words to match his feelings. It was impossible.

'If you think you can get away with this you're mistaken,' bawled Lady Maud.

Dundridge clutched the telephone. The filthy bitch had come back to haunt him with those horrible photographs and this time there was no mistaking who was playing the main role in these obscene contortions and this time too Hoskins was present. The look of horror on Hoskins' face decided him. There was no way of avoiding a scandal. Dundridge dialled the police.

'Don't think you can wriggle out of this by calling a lawyer,' Lady Maud yelled.

'I'm not,' said Dundridge finding his voice at last, 'I am calling the police.'

'The police?' said Lady Maud.

'The police?' whispered Hoskins.

'I intend to have you charged with attempted blackmail,' said Dundridge.

Lady Maud launched herself across the desk at him. 'Why, you filthy little bastard,' she screamed. Dundridge lurched off his chair and ran for the door. Lady Maud turned and raced after him. Behind them Hoskins replaced the telephone and picked up the photographs. He went into the lavatory and shut the door. When he came out Dundridge was cowering behind a bulldozer, Lady Maud was being restrained by six bulldozer drivers and the photographs had been reduced to ashes and flushed down the pan. Hoskins sat down and wiped his face with a handkerchief. It had been a near thing.

'Don't think you're going to get away with this,' Lady Maud shouted as she was escorted back to her car. 'I'll sue you for slander. I'll take every penny you've got.' She drove away and Dundridge staggered back to the caravan.

'You heard her,' he said to Hoskins slumping into his chair. 'You heard her attempt to blackmail me.' He looked around for the photographs.

'I burnt them,' said Hoskins. 'I didn't think you'd want them lying around.'

Dundridge looked at him gratefully. He certainly didn't want them lying around. On the other hand the evidence of an attempted crime had been destroyed. There was no point in calling in the police now.

'Well at least if she does sue me you were a witness,' he said finally.

'Definitely,' said Hoskins. 'But she'll never dare.'

'I wouldn't put anything past that bitch,' said Dundridge recovering his confidence now that both Lady Maud and the photographs were out of the way. 'But I'll tell you one thing. We're going to move into Handyman Hall now. I'll teach her to threaten me.'

'Without the photographs I'm afraid you would have no case,' said Mr Ganglion when Lady Maud returned to his office.

'But he told you that I was blackmailing him. You told me so yourself,' said Lady Maud.

Mr Ganglion shook his head sadly. 'What he said to me, my dear Lady Maud, was by way of being a confidential communication. He was after all consulting me as a solicitor and since I represent you in any case my evidence would never be accepted by a court. Now if we could get Hoskins to testify that he had heard him accuse you of blackmail . . .' He phoned the Regional Planning Board and was put through to Hoskins at the Mobile HQ.

'Certainly not. I never heard anything of the sort,' said Hoskins. 'Photographs? I don't know what you're talking about.' The last thing he wanted to do was to appear in court to testify about those bloody photographs.

'Peculiar,' said Mr Ganglion. 'Most peculiar, but there it is. Hoskins won't testify.'

'That just goes to show you can't trust anyone these days,' said Lady Maud.

She drove home in a filthy temper which wasn't improved by having to park the Bentley outside the Lodge and walk up the drive.

CHAPTER TWENTY-SIX

If her temper was bad when she returned to the Hall that afternoon it was ten times worse the next morning. She woke to the sound of lorries driving down the Gorge road and men shouting outside the Lodge. Lady Maud picked up the phone and called Blott.

'What the devil is going on down there?' she asked.

'It's started,' said Blott.

'Started? What's started?'

'They've come to begin work.'

Lady Maud dressed and hurried down the drive to find Dundridge, Hoskins and the Chief Constable and a group of policemen standing looking at the concrete blocks under the archway.

'What's the meaning of this?' she demanded.

'We have come to begin work here,' said Dundridge keeping close to the Chief Constable. 'You are in receipt of a compulsory purchase order served on you on the 25th of June and ...'

'This is private property,' said Lady Maud. 'Kindly leave.'

'My dear Lady Maud,' said the Chief Constable, 'I'm afraid these gentlemen are within their rights ...'

'They are within my property,' said Lady Maud. 'And I want them off it.'

The Chief Constable shook his head sorrowfully. 'I'm sorry to have to say this ...'

'Then don't,' said Lady Maud.

'But they are fully entitled to act in accordance with their instructions and begin work on the motorway through the Park. I am here to see that they are not hindered in any way. Now if you would be so good as to order your gardener to vacate these ... er ... premises.'

'Order him yourself.'

'We have attempted to serve an eviction order on him but he refuses to come down. He appears to have barricaded the door. Now we don't want to have to use force but unless he is prepared to come out I'm afraid we will have to make a forcible entry.'

'Well, I'm not stopping you,' said Lady Maud. 'If that's what you have to do, go ahead and do it.'

She stood to one side while the policemen went round the side of the Lodge and hammered at the door. Lady Maud sat on a concrete block and watched them.

The police battered at the door for ten minutes and finally broke it down only to find themselves confronted by a wall of concrete. Dundridge sent for a sledgehammer but it was quite clear that something more than a sledgehammer would be required to make an entry.

'The bastard has cemented himself in,' said Dundridge.

'I can see that for myself,' said the Chief Constable. 'What are you going to do now?'

Dundridge considered the problem and consulted Hoskins. Together they walked back to the bridge and looked up at the arch. In the circumstances it had assumed a new and quite daunting stature.

'There's no way round it,' said Hoskins, indicating the cliffs. 'We would have to move thousands of tons of rock.'

'Can't we blast a way round?'

Hoskins looked up at the cliffs and shook his head. 'Could do but we'd probably kill the stupid bugger in that arch in the process.'

'So what?' said Dundridge. 'If he won't come down it's his own fault if he gets hurt.' He didn't say it very convincingly. It was quite clear that killing Blott would come under the heading of very unfavourable publicity at the Ministry of the Environment.

'In any case,' Hoskins pointed out, 'the authorized route runs through the Gorge, not round it.'

'What about the blasting we did back at the entrance?'

'We were authorized to widen the Gorge there because of the river and besides that section doesn't come within the area designated as of natural beauty.'

'Fuck,' said Dundridge. 'I knew that old bitch would come up with something like this.'

They went back to the arch where the Chief Constable was arguing with Lady Maud.

'Are you seriously suggesting that I ordered my gardener to cement himself into the Lodge?'

'Yes,' said the Chief Constable.

'In that case, Percival Henry,' said Lady Maud, 'you're a bigger fool than I took you for.'

The Chief Constable winced. 'Listen, Maud,' he said, 'you know as well as I do he wouldn't have done this without your permission.'

'Nonsense,' said Lady Maud, 'I told him he could do what he wanted with the Lodge. He's been living there for thirty years. It's his home. If he chooses to fill the place with cement that's his business. I refuse to accept any responsibility for his actions.'

'In that case I shall have no option but to arrest you,' said the Chief Constable.

'On what grounds?'

'For obstruction.'

'Codswallop,' said Lady Maud. She got down from the block and walked round to the back of the arch and looked up at the window.

'Blott,' she called. Blott's head appeared at the circular window.

'Yes.'

'Blott, come down this instant and let these men get on with their work.'

'Won't,' said Blott.

'Blott,' shouted Lady Maud, 'I am ordering you to come down.'

'No,' said Blott and shut the window.

Lady Maud turned to the Chief Constable. 'There you are. I have told him to come down and he won't. Now then, are you still going to have me arrested for obstruction?'

The Chief Constable shook his head. He knew when he was beaten. Lady Maud strode back up the drive to the Hall. He turned to Dundridge. 'Well, what do you suggest now?'

'There must be something we can do,' said Dundridge.

'If you've got any bright ideas, just let me know,' said the Chief Constable.

'What happens if we just go ahead and demolish the arch with him in it?'

'The question is,' said the Chief Constable, 'what would happen to him if you did that?'

'That's his problem,' said Dundridge. 'We've got a legal right to remove that arch and if he's in it when we do we're not responsible for what happens to him.'

The Chief Constable shook his head. 'You try telling that to the judge when they try you for manslaughter. I should have thought you'd have learnt your lesson from what happened at Guildstead Carbonell.' He got into his car and drove away.

Dundridge walked back across the bridge and spoke to the foreman of the demolition gang.

'Is there any way of taking that arch down without injuring the man inside?' he asked.

The foreman looked at him doubtfully. 'Not if he doesn't want us to.'

As if to give added weight to his argument Blott appeared on the roof. He was carrying a shotgun.

'You see what I mean,' said the foreman.

Blott looked expectantly over their heads, raised his gun and fired. A wood pigeon plummeted out of the sky. Dundridge could see exactly what he meant.

'There's nothing in our contract to say we've got to take unnecessary risks,' said the foreman, 'and a bloke who cements himself into an arch and shoots pigeons on the wing constitutes more than an unnecessary risk. He's a bloody loony, and a crack shot into the bargain.'

Dundridge thought wistfully of Mr Edwards. He turned to Hoskins.

'I think,' said Hoskins, 'that we ought to contact the Ministry in London. 'This thing's too big for us.'

At the Hall Lady Maud heard the shot and picked up a pair of binoculars. Through them she could see Blott on the roof with the shotgun. She telephoned the Lodge.

'They're not shooting at you, are they?' she asked hopefully.

'No,' said Blott, 'I was just shooting a pigeon. They're still talking.'

'Remember what I said about violence,' Lady Maud told him. 'We must keep public sympathy on our side. I am going to get in touch with the BBC and ITV and all the national newspapers. I think we can make a big song and dance about this business.'

Blott put down the phone. Song and dance. The English language was *most* expressive. Song and dance.

At his Mobile HQ Dundridge was on the phone to London.

'Are you seriously trying to tell me that Lady Lynchwood's gardener has cemented himself into an ornamental arch?' said Mr Rees incredulously. 'It doesn't sound possible.'

'The arch in question happens to be eighty feet high,' Dundridge explained. 'It has rooms inside. He's filled all the bottom ones with concrete. There's barbed-wire on the roof and short of blowing the place up there's no way of getting him out.'

'I should try the local fire brigade,' Mr Rees suggested. 'They use them to get cats out of trees.'

'I have tried the fire brigade,' said Dundridge.

'Well, what do they say?'

'They say their business is putting out fires, not storming fortresses.'

Mr Rees considered the problem. 'I imagine he'll have to come out sometime,' he said finally.

'Why?'

'Well, to eat for one thing.'

'Eat?' shouted Dundridge. 'Eat? He doesn't have to come out to eat. I've got a list here of the things he ordered from the local supermarket. Four hundred tins of baked beans, seven hundred cans of corned beef, one hundred and fifty tins of frankfurters. Need I go on?'

'No,' said Mr Rees hastily, 'the fellow must have a constitution like an ox. You would have thought he would have chosen something a little more appetizing.'

'Is that all you've got to say?' said Dundridge.

'Well I must admit that it does sound as if he intends to make a long stay of it,' Mr Rees agreed.

'And what are we going to do? Cancel the motorway for a couple of years while he munches his way through that little lot?'

Mr Rees tried to think. 'Can't you talk him down?' he asked. 'That's what they usually do with people threatening to commit suicide.'

'But he isn't threatening suicide,' Dundridge pointed out.

'It amounts to the same thing,' said Mr Rees. 'A diet of corned beef, baked beans and frankfurters in the quantities you've mentioned would certainly kill me. Still, I see what you mean. A man who can even contemplate living off that muck obviously means business. Have you any ideas on the subject?'

'As a matter of fact I have,' said Dundridge.

'Not another ball and crane job I hope,' said Mr Rees anxiously. 'We can't have another little episode of that sort so shortly after the last one.'

'I was thinking of using the army,' said Dundridge.

'The army? My dear fellow, this is a free country. We can't possibly ask the army to blast a perfectly innocent Englishman out of his own home with tanks and artillery.'

'To be precise,' said Dundridge, 'he doesn't happen to be an Englishman and I wasn't thinking of blasting him out with tanks and artillery.'

'I should think not. The public would never stand for it,' Mr Rees said. 'But if he's not an Englishman what is he?'

'An Italian.'

'An Italian? Are you sure? It doesn't sound like them to go in for this sort of thing,' said Mr Rees.

'He's naturalized,' said Dundridge.

'That explains it,' said Mr Rees. 'In that case I can't see any objection to using the army. They're used to dealing with foreigners. What precisely did you have in mind?'

Dundridge explained his plan.

'Well I'll see what I can do,' said Mr Rees. 'I'll call you back when I've had a word with the Minister.'

In Whitehall the wires buzzed. Mr Rees spoke to the Minister of the Environment and the Minister spoke to Defence. By five o'clock Army Command had agreed to supply a team of commandos trained in rock climbing on the explicit understanding that they were to be used simply in a police support role and would not use firearms. As the Minister of the Environment explained, the essence of the operation was to occupy the Lodge and hold Blott until the police could evict him in a lawful fashion. 'The great thing is that the media haven't got on to the story yet. If we can get him out of there before the newsmen start nosing around we can hush the whole thing up. The essence of the thing must be speed.'

It was a point that Dundridge made to the commandos when they arrived for briefing that night at his Mobile HQ. 'I have here a number of photographs taken this afternoon of the target,' he said handing them round. 'As you can see it is amply provided with handholds and there are two means of access. The two circular windows on either side and the hatch in the roof. I should have thought the best method of attack would be a diversionary move to the rear and a frontal assault —'

'I think you can leave the tactical details of the exercise to us,' said the Major in charge who didn't like being told his business by a civvy.

'I was only trying to help,' said Dundridge.

'Now then,' said the Major. 'We'll rendezvous at the Gibbet at twenty-four hundred hours and proceed on foot ...' Dundridge left them to it and went into the other office.

'Well, for once we're getting things done,' he told Hoskins. 'That old bitch isn't going to know what's hit her.'

Hoskins nodded doubtfully. He had been in the army himself and he didn't have Dundridge's faith in the efficiency of the military machine.

Blott spent the evening reading Sir Arthur Bryant but his mind was not on the past. He was considering the immediate future. They would either act quickly or try to wear him down psychologically by sending a succession of well-meaning people to talk to him. Blott had seen the sort of visitor he could expect on the television. Social workers, psychiatrists, priests and policemen, all of them imbued with an invincible faith in the possibility of compromise. They would argue and cajole (Blott looked the word up in his dictionary to see if it meant what he thought and found he was right) and do their best to make him see the error of his ways and they would fail, fail hopelessly because their assumptions were all wrong. They would assume he was an Italian whereas he wasn't. They would think he was acting on instructions of that he was simply being loyal, whereas he was in love. They would think a compromise was possible ... With a motorway? Blott smiled to himself at the stupidity of the idea. The motorway would either go through the Park and Handyman Hall or it wouldn't. Nothing they could tell him would alter that fact. But above all the people who came to talk to him would be city-dwellers for whom talk was currency and words were coins. An Englishman's word is his bond, Blott thought, but then he had never had much time for stocks and shares. 'Word merchants' old Lord Handyman had called such people, with contempt in his voice, and Blott agreed with him. Well they could talk themselves blue in the face but they wouldn't shift him. Everything that he cared for and loved and was lay there in the Park and the Garden and the Hall. Handyman Hall. And Blott was the handyman. He would die rather than give up the right to be needed. He undressed and climbed into bed and lay listening to the river tumbling by and the wind in the trees. Through his window he could see the light on in Lady Maud's bedroom. Blott watched it until it went out and then he fell asleep.

He was woken at one o'clock by a noise outside. It was a very slight noise but it awoke in him some instinct, an early-warning system that told him that there were people outside. He got out of bed and went to the window and peered into the darkness below. There was someone at the foot of the left-hand column. Blott went across the room to the other window. There was someone in the Park too. They must have climbed the fence to get in. Blott listened and presently he heard someone moving below. They were climbing up the side of the Lodge. Climbing? In the dark? Interesting.

He crossed to a cupboard and took out the Leica and the flash gun and went back to the window and leant out. The next moment the entire side of the Lodge was a brilliant white. There was a cry and a thud. Blott went to the other window and took another photograph. This time whoever it was who was climbing to the side of the arch shut his eyes and clung on. Blott put the camera down. Something stronger was needed. What would make climbing difficult? Something greasy. He went into his kitchen and came out with a gallon can of cooking oil and climbed the ladder in the corner of the room to the hjatch in the roof. Then he crawled to the edge and began pouring the oil down the wall. There was a curse from below, the sound of slithering and another thud

followed by a cry. Blott emptied the rest of the can down the back wall
and went down the ladder into his room and shone a torch out of the
window. There was no one on the side of the arch now. At the foot a
number of men in army uniforms stared up at him angrily. They had
blackened faces and one of them was lying on the ground.

'Is there anything I can do for you?' Blott asked.

'Wait till we get hold of you, you bastard,' shouted the Major. 'You've
broken his leg.'

'Not me,' said Blott, 'I never touched him. He broke it himself. I didn't
ask him to climb up my wall in the middle of the night.'

He was interrupted by a sound from the other side of the Lodge. The
sods were coming up there too. He went into the kitchen and fetched
two cans of cooking oil and repeated the process. By the time he was
finished the sides of the Lodge were streaked with oil and two more
climbers had fallen.

Down below there was a muttered conference.

'We'll use the grappling irons,' said the Major.

Blott peered out of the window and shone his torch on them. There
was an explosion and a three-pronged hook shot past him on to the roof
and stuck in the barbed-wire. It was followed by another. Blott raced
into the kitchen and grabbed a knife. A moment later he was on the roof
and had cut through one rope. He crawled under the wire and cut
another. There was another thud and a yell. Blott peered over.

'Anyone else coming up?' he asked. But the army was already in
retreat. As they carried their wounded back across the suspension bridge
and up the road Blott watched them wistfully. He rather regretted their
going. A full-scale battle would have been marvellous publicity. A full-
scale battle? Blott went to the cupboard where he kept his armoury. He
would have to act quickly. Then he climbed up on the roof and let down
the rope ladder. Ten minutes later he was standing on the suspension
bridge with the Bren gun.

As the commandos trudged back up the road towards their transport
at the Gibbet they were startled to hear the sound of automatic fire
behind them. It lasted for several seconds and was repeated again and
again. They stood still and listened. It stopped. A few moments later
there was a much larger thump and it was followed by a second. Blott
had tried out the PIAT and it still worked.

At the Hall Lady Maud sat up in bed and struggled to find the light
switch. She was used to the occasional shot in the night but this was

something entirely different. A positive bombardment. She reached for the phone and rang the Lodge. There was no reply.

'Oh my God,' she moaned, 'they've killed him.' She got out of bed and dressed hurriedly. The firing had stopped now. She phoned the Lodge again and still there was no reply. She put the phone down and called the Chief Constable.

'They've murdered him,' she shouted, 'they've attacked the Lodge and killed him!'

'Killed who?' asked the Chief Constable.

'Blott,' yelled Lady Maud.

'No?' said the Chief Constable.

'I tell you they have. They've been using machine-guns and something much bigger.'

'Oh my goodness gracious me,' said the Chief Constable. 'Are you sure? I mean couldn't there be some mistake?'

'Percival Henry,' screamed Lady Maud, 'you know me well enough to know that when I say something I mean it. Remember what happened to Bertie Bullett-Finch.'

The Chief Constable remembered all too well. Midnight assassinations were becoming a commonplace occurrence in South Worfordshire and besides Lady Maud's tone had the ring of sincere hysteria about it. And Lady Maud, whatever else she might be was not a woman who got hysterical for nothing.

'I'll get every available patrol car there as soon as possible,' he promised.

'And an ambulance too,' screamed Lady Maud.

Within minutes every police car in South Worfordshire was converging on the Gorge. At the Gibbet twelve men of the 41st Marine Commando, two of them with broken legs, were detained for questioning as they were about to leave in their transport. They were driven to Worford Police Station loudly protesting that they had been acting under the orders of the Area Commander and that the police had no legal authority to hold them.

'We'll see about that in the morning,' said the Inspector as they were herded into their cells.

At the Lodge Blott climbed up his rope ladder and hauled it up behind him. He was delighted with his experiment. All the weapons had worked splendidly and, while it was impossible in the darkness to tell what damage they had done to the Lodge, the sound of splintering stonework had suggested that there was plenty of evidence to show that the army had carried out its assault with undue force and quite unwarranted violence. It was only when he was back in his room that he could see how effective the Projectiles Infantry Anti-Tank had been. They had blown two substantial holes in the frieze and the room was littered with bits of stone. Both windows had been blown out by the blast and there were holes in the ceiling. He was just wondering what to do next when he heard footsteps running down the drive. Blott switched off his torch and went to the window. It was Lady Maud.

'Don't come any nearer,' he shouted, to lend verisimilitude to his recent ordeal and to tell her that he was unhurt. 'Lie down. They may start firing again.'

Lady Maud stopped in her tracks. 'Oh thank Heavens, you're all right, Blott,' she shouted. 'I thought you'd been killed.'

'Me? Killed?' said Blott. 'It would take more than that to kill me.'

'Who was it? Did you get a good look at them?'

'It was the army,' Blott told her. 'I've got photographs to prove it.'

CHAPTER TWENTY-SEVEN

By next morning Blott was famous. The news of the attack came too late to be carried by the early editions but the later ones all bore his name in their headlines. The BBC broadcast news of the atrocity and its legal implications were discussed on the *Today* programme. At one o'clock there were further developments when it was announced that twelve Marine Commandos were helping the police in their inquiries. During the afternoon questions were asked in the House and the Home Secretary promised a full Inquiry. And all day reporters and cameramen swarmed into the Gorge to interview Blott and Lady Maud and to photograph the damage. It was clearly visible and extensive. Bullet holes pockmarked the entire arch, suggesting that the army's fire had been quite extraordinarily wild. The heads of several figures in the frieze were missing and the PIATs had torn gaping holes in the wall. Even hardened correspondents used to the tactics adopted against the urban guerrillas in Belfast were astonished by the extent of the damage.

'I've never seen anything like this,' the BBC correspondent told his audience from the top of a ladder before interviewing Blott at the window. 'This might be Vietnam or the Lebanon but this is a quiet corner of rural England. I can only say that I am horrified that this could happen.

And now Mr Blott, could you tell us first what you know about this attack?'

Blott looked out of the window into the camera.

'It must have been about one o'clock in the morning. I was asleep and I heard a noise outside. I got up and went to the window and looked out. There appeared to be men climbing up the wall. Well I didn't want that so I poured oil down the wall.'

'You poured oil down the wall to stop them?'

'Yes,' said Blott, 'olive oil. They slipped down and then the firing began.'

'The firing?'

'It sounded like machine-gun fire,' said Blott, 'so I ran into the kitchen and lay on the floor. Then a minute or two later there was an explosion and things flew around the room and a few seconds afterwards there came another explosion. After that there was nothing.'

'I see,' said the interviewer. 'Now at any time during the attack did you fire back? I understand you have a shotgun.'

Blott shook his head. 'It all happened too suddenly,' he said. 'I was all shook up.'

'Quite understandably. It must have been a terrifying experience for you. Just one more question. Was the oil you poured down the wall hot?'

'Hot?' said Blott. 'How could it be hot? I poured it out of the can. I hadn't got time to heat it up.'

'Well thank you very much,' said the interviewer and climbed down the ladder. 'I think we'll cut that last remark out,' he told the sound man. 'It made him sound as if he would have liked to have poured hot oil on them.'

'I can't say I blame him after what he's been through,' said the sound man. 'The buggers deserve boiling oil.'

It was an opinion shared by the Chief Constable.

'What do you mean, a police support role?' he shouted at the Colonel from the Commando Base who came up to explain that he had been ordered by the Ministry of Defence to send a team of rock-climbers to assist the police. 'There weren't any of my men within miles of the place. You send your killers in armed with rockets and machine-guns and blow hell out of . . .'

'My men were without any weapons,' said the Colonel.

The Chief Constable looked at him incredulously. 'Your men were without weapons? You can stand there and tell me to my face that your men were unarmed when I've seen what they did to that building. You'll be telling me next that they had nothing to do with the incident.'

'That's what they say,' said the Colonel. 'They all swear blue they had left and were on their way back to their transport when the firing occurred.'

'I'm not bloody surprised,' said the Chief Constable. 'If I had just bombarded somebody's private house in the middle of the night I'd say I hadn't been near the place. That doesn't mean anyone with any sense is going to believe them.'

'They weren't carrying weapons when you arrested them.'

'Probably ditched the damned things,' said the Chief Constable. 'And in any case for all I know there were others who got away before my men arrived.'

'I can assure you –' the Colonel began.

'Damn your assurances!' shouted the Chief Constable. 'I don't want assurances. I've got the evidence of the attack itself and I have twelve men trained in the use of the weapons needed for that attack who admit that they attempted to force an entry into the Lodge last night. What more do I need? They'll appear before a magistrate in the morning.'

The Colonel had to admit that the circumstantial evidence ...

'Circumstantial evidence, my foot,' snarled the Chief Constable, 'they're as guilty as hell and you know it.'

'I still think you ought to look into the business of the civil servant who gave them their instructions,' said the Colonel despondently as he left. 'I believe his name is Dundridge.'

'I have already attended to that,' the Chief Constable told him. 'He is in London at the moment but I have sent two officers down to bring him back for questioning.'

But Dundridge had already spent five hours being questioned by Mr Rees and Mr Joynson and finally by the Minister himself.

'All I did was tell them to climb into the arch and hold Blott till the police could come and evict him legally,' he explained over and over again. 'I didn't know they were going to use guns and things.'

Neither Mr Rees nor the Minister was impressed.

'Let us just look at your record,' said the Minister as calmly as he could. 'You were appointed Controller Motorways Midlands with specific instructions to insure that the construction of the M101 went through with the minimum of fuss and bother, that local opinion felt that local interests were being looked after and that the environment was being protected. Now can you honestly say that the terms of reference of your appointment have been fulfilled in any single particular?'

'Well ...' said Dundridge.

'No you can't,' snarled the Minister. 'Since you went to Worford there have been a series of appalling disasters. A Rotarian has been beaten to a pulp in his own house by a demented demolition expert who claims he was incited ...'

'I didn't know Mr Bullett-Finch was a Rotarian,' said Dundridge desperately trying to divert the floodwaters of the Minister's mounting fury.

'You didn't know ...' The Minister counted to ten and took a sip of water. 'Next, an entire village has been wrecked ...'

'Not an entire village,' said Dundridge. 'It was only the High Street.'

The Minister stared at him maniacally. 'Mr Dundridge,' he said finally, 'you may be able to make these fine distinctions between Rotarians and human beings and entire villages which consist only of High Streets and the High Streets themselves but I am not prepared to. An entire village was wrecked, a pedestrian was incinerated and twenty persons injured, some of them seriously. And this village, mark you, was over a mile away from the route of the proposed motorway. A Member of Parliament has been devoured by lions ...'

'That had absolutely nothing to do with me,' Dundridge protested. 'I didn't suggest he fill his ruddy garden with lions.'

'I wonder,' said the Minister, 'I wonder. Still, I shall reserve judgement on that question until the full facts have been ascertained. And finally at your instigation the army has been called in to evict an Italian gardener ... No, don't say it ... an Italian gardener from his home by bombarding it with machine-guns and anti-tank weapons.'

'But I didn't tell them —'

'Shut up,' roared the Minister. 'You're fired, you're sacked ...'

'You're under arrest,' said the detective who was waiting outside Mr Rees' office when Dundridge finally staggered out. Dundridge went down in the lift between two police officers.

Mr Rees sat down at his desk with a sigh.

'I told you that stupid bastard would hang himself,' he said with quiet satisfaction.

'What about the motorway?' asked Mr Hoskins.

'What about it?'

'Do you think we can continue with it?'

'God alone knows,' said Mr Rees, 'but frankly I doubt it. You seem to forget there's another bye-election due in South Worfordshire.'

It was not a point that had escaped Lady Maud's attention. While the reporters and cameramen still swarmed about the Lodge, photographing it from all angles and interviewing Blott from the tops of ladders hired for the purpose, she had been applying her mind to the question of a successor to Sir Giles. A meeting of the Save the Gorge Committee was held at General Burnett's house to discuss the next move.

'Stout fellow, Blott,' said the General, 'for an Eyetie. Remarkable, standing up to a bombardment like that. They used to run like rabbits in the desert.'

'I think we all owe him a debt of gratitude for his sense of duty and self-sacrifice,' Colonel Chapman agreed. 'Frankly I think this latest episode has put the kybosh on the motorway. They'll never be able to carry on with it now. I hear there's a proposal for a sit-in of conservationists from all over the country outside the Lodge to see that there's no repetition of this disgraceful action.'

'I must say I was most impressed by Mr Blott's command of the English language on television the other night,' said Miss Percival. 'He handled the interview quite wonderfully. I particularly liked what he had to say about English traditions.'

'That bit about an Englishman's home being his castle. Couldn't agree with him more,' the General said.

'I was thinking rather about what he said about England being the home of freedom and the need for Englishmen to stand up for their traditional values.'

Lady Maud looked at them all contemptuously. 'I must say I think it is a poor show when we have to rely on Italians to look after our interests for us,' she said.

The General shifted in his seat. 'I wouldn't go so far as to say that,' he murmured.

'I would,' said Lady Maud. 'Without him we would have all lost our homes.'

'As it is Miss Percival's lost hers already,' said Colonel Chapman. 'You can hardly blame Blott for that.'

Miss Percival took out a handkerchief and wiped her eyes. 'It was such a pretty cottage,' she sighed.

'The point I am trying to make,' Lady Maud continued, 'is that I think the best way we can demonstrate our gratitude and support for

Blott is by proposing him as the candidate for South Worfordshire in the forthcoming bye-election.'

The Committee stared at her in astonishment.

'An Italian standing for South Worfordshire?' said the General. 'I hardly think ...'

'So I've noticed,' said Lady Maud brusquely. 'And Blott is not an Italian. He is a nationalized Englishman.'

'Surely you mean naturalized,' said Colonel Chapman. 'Nationalized means state-controlled. I would have thought he was the exact opposite.'

'I stand corrected,' said Lady Maud magnanimously. 'Then we are agreed that Blott should represent the party at the bye-election?'

She looked round the table. Miss Percival was the first to agree. 'I second the proposal,' she murmured.

'Motion,' Lady Maud corrected her, 'the motion. The proposal comes later. All those in favour.'

The General and Colonel Chapman raised their hands in surrender, and since the Save the Gorge Committee was the party in South Worfordshire Blott's candidacy was ensured.

Lady Maud announced their decision to the press outside the Lodge. As the newsmen dispersed to their cars she climbed the ladder to the window in the Lodge.

'Blott,' she called through the broken panes, 'I have something to tell you.'

Blott opened the window and leant out. 'Yes,' he said.

'I want you to prepare yourself for a shock,' she told him. Blott looked at her uncertainly. He had been prepared for a shock for some time. The British army didn't use 303 ammunition nowadays and PIATs had been scrapped years ago. It was a point he had overlooked at the time.

'I have decided that you are to succeed Sir Giles,' said Lady Maud gazing into his face.

Blott gaped at her. 'Succeed Sir Giles? Gott in Himmel,' he muttered.

'I very much doubt it,' said Lady Maud.

'You mean ...'

'Yes,' said Lady Maud, 'from now on you will be the master of Handyman Hall. You can come out now.'

'But ...' Blott began.

'If you'll hand me the machine-gun and whatever else it was you used I'll take them down with me and we'll bury them in the pinetum.'

As they walked back up the drive with the PIAT and the Bren gun, Blott's mind was in a state of confusion. 'How did you know?' he asked.

'How did I know? I telephoned you of course as soon as I heard the firing,' said Lady Maud with a smile. 'I'm not as green as I'm cabbage-looking.'

'Meine Liebling,' said Blott and took what he could of her in his arms.

At Worford magistrates court Dundridge was charged with being party to a conspiracy to commit a breach of the peace, attempted murder, malicious damage to property, and obstruction of the police in the course of their duty.

It was the last charge that particularly infuriated him.

'Obstruction?' he shouted at the bench. 'Obstruction? Who's talking about obstruction?'

'Remanded in custody for a week,' said Colonel Chapman. Dundridge was still shouting abuse as he was dragged out to the Black Maria. In the cells he was interviewed by Mr Ganglion, who had been appointed by the court to conduct his defence.

'I should plead guilty to all charges,' he advised him.

'Guilty? I haven't done anything wrong. It's all a pack of lies!' Dundridge shouted.

'I understand how you feel,' Mr Ganglion said, 'but I understand the police are considering additional charges.'

'Additional charges? But they've charged me with everything under the sun already.'

'There's just that little business of blackmail to be attended to. Now I know you wouldn't want those photographs to be produced in court. You could get life for that, you know.'

Dundridge stared at him despairingly. 'For blackmail?' he asked. 'But I was the one being blackmailed.'

'For what you were doing in those photographs.'

Dundridge considered the prospect and shook his head. Life for something that had been done to him. He had been blackmailed, obstructed, shot at and here he was being charged with these offences. If there was any conspiracy it was directed against him.

'I don't know what to say,' he mumbled.

'Just stick to "Guilty",' Mr Ganglion advised. 'It will save a lot of time and the court will appreciate it.'

'Time?' said Dundridge. 'How long do you think I'll get?'

'Difficult to say really. Seven or eight years I should imagine, but you'll probably be out in five.'

He gathered up his papers and left the cell. As he walked back to his chambers he smiled to himself. It was always nice to combine business with pleasure. He found Lady Maud and Blott waiting for him to discuss the marriage settlement.

'My fiancé has decided to change his name,' Lady Maud announced. 'From now on he wants to be known as Handyman. I want you to make the necessary arrangements.'

'I see,' said Mr Ganglion. 'Well there shouldn't be any difficulties. And what Christian name would he like?'

'I think we'll just stick to Blott. I'm used to it and all the men in the family have been Bs.'

'True,' said Mr Ganglion, with the private thought that some of the women had been too. 'And when is the happy day?'

'We are going to wait until after the election. I wouldn't want it to be thought that I was trying to influence the outcome.'

Mr Ganglion went out to lunch with Mr Turnbull.

'Amazing woman, Maud Lynchwood,' he said as they walked across to the Handyman Arms. 'I wouldn't put anything past her. Marrying her damned gardener and putting him up for Parliament.'

They went into the bar.

'What'll you have?' said Mr Turnbull.

'I feel like a large whisky,' said Mr Ganglion. 'I know it's prohibitively expensive but I need it.'

'Have you heard, sir?' said the barman. 'There's fivepence off a tot of whisky and tuppence off a pint of beer. Lady Maud's instructions. Seems she can afford to be generous now.'

'Good Lord,' said Mr Turnbull, 'you don't think it has anything to do with this election, do you?'

But Mr Ganglion wasn't listening. He was thinking how little things had changed since he was a boy. What was it his father had said? Something about Mr Gladstone being swept out of office on a tide of ale. And that was in '74.

CHAPTER TWENTY-EIGHT

It was a white wedding. Lady Maud with her customary frankness had prevailed over the Vicar.

'I can damned well prove it if you insist,' she had told him when he had raised one or two minor objections but the Vicar had surrendered meekly. Wilfrid's Castle Church was packed. Half the county was there as Lady Maud strode through the pinetum with Mrs Forthby as her bridesmaid. Blott, now Blott Handyman, MP, was waiting at the church in top-hat and tails. As the organist broke into 'Rule Britannia', which Blott had chosen, Lady Maud Lynchwood went down the aisle beside General Burnett, emerging half an hour later Lady Maud Handyman. They posed for photographs and then led the way down the path and across the footbridge to the Hall. The place was resplendent. Flags flew from the turrets; there was a striped marquee on the lawn and the conservatory was a blaze of colour. Everything that Sir Giles' fortune afforded had been provided. Champagne, caviar, smoked salmon, jellied eels for those that liked them, cucumber sandwiches, trifle. Mrs Forthby had seen to them all. Only the cake was missing. 'I knew I had forgotten something,' she wept but even that was found eventually in the pantry. It was a perfect replica of the Lodge.

'It seems a pity to spoil it,' said Blott as he and Maud stood poised with Busby Handyman's old sword.

'You should have thought of that before,' Maud whispered in his ear. They cut the cake and the photographs were taken. Even Blott's speech, authentically English in its inarticulacy, went down well. He thanked everyone for coming and Mrs Forthby for her catering and made everyone laugh and Lady Maud blush by saying that it wasn't every man who had either the opportunity or the good fortune to be able to marry his mistress.

'Extraordinary fellow,' General Burnett told Mrs Forthby, who rather appealed to him, 'got a multitude of talents. They say there's talk of him becoming a Whip.'

Mrs Forthby shook her head. 'I do hope not,' she said. 'It's so degrading.'

Mr Ganglion and Mr Turnbull took a bottle of champagne into the garden.

'They say that the occasion produces the man,' said Mr Turnbull philosophically. 'I must admit he's turned out better than I ever expected. Talk about silk purses out of sows' ears.'

'My dear fellow, you've got it quite wrong,' said Mr Ganglion. 'It takes a sow's ear to know a silk purse when she's got one.'

'What on earth do you mean by that?'

Mr Ganglion sat down on a wrought-iron bench. 'I was just considering Sir Giles. Remarkable how conveniently he timed his death. Have you ever thought about that? I have. What do you suppose he was doing in gumboots in August? It hadn't rained for weeks. Driest summer we've had for years and he dies with his gumboots on.'

'You're surely not suggesting ...'

Mr Ganglion chuckled. 'I'm not suggesting anything. Merely cogitating. These old families. They haven't survived by relying on chance. They know their onions.'

'You're just being cynical,' said Mr Turnbull.

'Nonsense, I'm being realistic. They survive, my God, how they survive, and thank Heavens they do. Where would we be without them?' His head nodded. Mr Ganglion fell asleep.

In bed that night the Handymans lay in one another's arms, blissfully happy. Blott was himself at last, the possessor of a new past and a perfect present. There was no railway station waiting-room in Dresden, no orphanage, no youth, no uncertainties or doubts. Above all no motorway. He was an Englishman whose family had lived in the Gorge for five hundred years and if Blott had anything to do with it they would be living there still five hundred years hence. He had said as much in his maiden speech in the House on membership of the Common Market.

'What do we need Europe for?' he had asked. 'Ah, but you say "Europe needs us". And so she does. As an example, as a pole-star, as a haven. I speak from experience ...'

It was a remarkable speech and too reminiscent of Churchill and the younger Pitt and of Burke to give the front bench much comfort.

'We've got to shut him up,' said the Prime Minister and Blott had been offered the Whip.

'You're not going to take it, are you?' Lady Maud had asked anxiously.

'Certainly not,' said Blott. 'There is a tide in the affairs of men ...'

'Oh darling,' said Maud, 'how wonderful you are.'

'Which taken at its flood leads on to families.'

Lady Maud sighed with happiness. It was so good to be married to a man who had his priorities right.

In Ottertown Prison Dundridge began his sentence.

'Behave yourself properly and you'll be transferred to an open prison,' the Governor told him. 'With remission for good behaviour you should be out in nine months.'

'I don't want to go to an open prison,' said Dundridge. 'I like it here.'

And it was true. There was a logic about prison life that appealed to him. Everything was in its place and there were no unforeseen occurrences to upset him. Each day was exactly the same as the day before and each cell identical to its neighbour. Best of all, Dundridge had a number. It was what he had always wanted. He was 58295 and perfectly satisfied with it. Working in the prison library he felt safe. Nature played no part in prison life. Trees, woods, and all the gross aberrations of the landscape lay beyond the prison walls. Dundridge had no time for them. He was too busy cataloguing the prison library. He had discovered a far more numerate system than the Dewey Decimal.

It was called the Dundridge Digit.